Iris Murdoch

THE
PHILOSOPHER'S
PUPIL

PENGUIN BOOKS

Penguin Books Ltd, Harmondsworth, Middlesex, England
Viking Penguin Inc., 40 West 23rd Street, New York, New York 10010, U.S.A.
Penguin Books Australia Ltd, Ringwood, Victoria, Australia
Penguin Books Canada Ltd, 2801 John Street, Markham, Ontario, Canada L3R 1B4
Penguin Books (N.Z.) Ltd, 182–190 Wairau Road, Auckland 10, New Zealand

First published by Chatto & Windus Ltd 1983
Published in Penguin Books 1984
Reprinted 1984

Copyright © Iris Murdoch, 1983
All rights reserved

Printed and bound in Great Britain by
Cox & Wyman Ltd, Reading
Filmset in 9 on 10½ point Monophoto Times by
Northumberland Press Ltd, Gateshead

PENGUIN BOOKS

THE PHILOSOPHER'S PUPIL

Iris Murdoch was born in Dublin of Anglo-Irish parents. She went to Badminton School, Bristol, and read classics at Somerville College, Oxford. During the war she was an Assistant Principal at the Treasury, and then worked with U.N.R.R.A. in London, Belgium and Austria. She held a studentship in philosophy at Newnham College, Cambridge, for a year, and in 1948 returned to Oxford where she became a Fellow of St Anne's College. In 1956 she married John Bayley, teacher and critic. She was made an Honorary Member of the American Academy of Arts and Letters in 1975 and was awarded the C.B.E. in 1976.

Her other novels are *Under the Net* (1954), *The Flight from the Enchanter* (1955), *The Sandcastle* (1957), *The Bell* (1958), *A Severed Head* (1961), *An Unofficial Rose* (1962), *The Unicorn* (1963), *The Italian Girl* (1964), *The Red and the Green* (1965), *The Time of the Angels* (1966), *The Nice and the Good* (1968), *Bruno's Dream* (1969), *A Fairly Honourable Defeat* (1970), *An Accidental Man* (1971), *The Black Prince* (1973), winner of the James Tait Black Memorial Prize, *The Sacred and Profane Love Machine* (1974), winner of the Whitbread Prize, *A Word Child* (1975), *Henry and Cato* (1976), *The Sea, the Sea* (1978), for which she won the Booker Prize, and *Nuns and Soldiers* (1980). She has also written *The Fire and the Sun: Why Plato Banished the Artist* (1977), based on her 1976 Romanes lectures, and *A Year of Birds* (1978), a volume of poetry.

TO
ARNALDO MOMIGLIANO

CONTENTS

PRELUDE

i *An Accident*

A few minutes before his brainstorm, or whatever it was, took place, George McCaffrey was having a quarrel with his wife. It was eleven o'clock on a rainy March evening. They had been visiting George's mother. Now George was driving along the quayside, taking the short-cut along the canal past the iron foot-bridge. It was raining hard. The malignant rain rattled on the car like shot. Propelled in oblique flurries, it assaulted the windscreen, obliterating in a second the frenetic strivings of the windscreen wipers. Little demonic faces composed of racing raindrops appeared and vanished. The intermittent yellow light of the street lamps, illuminating the grey atoms of the storm, fractured in sudden stars upon the rain-swarmed glass. Bumping on cobbles the car hummed and drummed.

Stella was usually silent when George had one of his rages. On this occasion she spoke up.

'George, let me drive.'

'No.'

'Let me drive.'

'I said no!'

'Don't drive so fast.'

'Don't touch me, damn you, leave me alone!'

'I am leaving you alone.'

'You never do, never, never.'

'Change gear, you're straining the engine.'

'It's my car, I can do what I bloody like with it.'

'Don't drive so fast, you can't see.'

'I can see with my own eyes. You can't see with my eyes, can you? So shut up.'

'You're drunk.'

'Fancy that!'

'You make your mother drink too much.'

'Why come then? You like to see us degrade each other, is that it?'

'She shouldn't drink so.'

'I hope she dies of it, the fiend. Oh if only she could get on with dying!'

'She sets you off, she always does.'

'*You* set me off. She hates you.'

'All right, I know.'

'You seem quite pleased.'

'No.'

'You're jealous of her.'

'No.'

'You think you're better than all of us.'

'Only in some respects.'

'Only in some respects! Oh *Christ*!'

'I'm only answering your idiotic remarks. I wish you'd be quiet and drive better.'

'You needle me all the time with your beastly calm superiority, nothing touches you, nothing, you never cry like a real woman.'

'Maybe I don't cry when you're around.'

'You don't cry. You can't. Tears are human. When you're alone you sit with a little self-satisfied smile, like a Buddha.'

'Let's not talk. I'm sorry –!'

'Oh, you *torment* me so –!'

'You torment yourself.'

'People detest you, do you know that?'

'No.'

'All right, they detest me too.'

'I should say you were rather popular.'

'Because they don't know what I'm like.'

'Because they do. Everybody loves a black sheep.'

'Black sheep! What a banality!'

'Do you want me to call you something worse?'

'They don't bloody know what you're like. They think you're a prig. They don't know you're a devil.'

'Oh do be quiet.'

'I can't stand your physical proximity.'

'Stop the car then and I'll get out.'

'Oh no you don't, you stay here. I won't let you get out!'

'Oh how it rains!'

'You provoke me so that you can blame me. I know your tricks. You go on and on about how I lost my job, you keep bringing it up.'

'You bring it up.'

10

'You say you're sorry, but you think that I'm a rotten contemptible failure.'

'That's what you think, not what I think.'

'I could kill you for saying that.'

'You only care about losing face, not about the harm that you do, not about things that matter.'

'Such as you.'

'Such as being kind to me.'

'Are you kind to me?'

'I try to be. I love you.'

'That's the most cruel thing of all, to keep saying that when it isn't true, when I need real love not your bloody power mania, that's your excuse, you think if you just say that it lets you off and you can do anything you like to me. Christ, you even destroy the bloody language, you stand beside me with your pretended love like a nurse waiting for the patient to collapse. You think one day I'd fall helplessly into your arms, but I never will, never never never. I'll kill myself first, or you, you make an absolute nonsense of my life. If I'm mad you made me so –'

'You're not mad.'

'You said I ought to have electric shocks.'

'I didn't.'

'You lie.'

'I said someone else said so.'

'Who?'

'Oh never mind.'

'*Who?*'

'The doctor.'

'Oh, so you've been seeing the doctor about me!'

'No, I just met him at Brian's.'

'You said, my husband has gone mad and I want him locked up.'

'Do stop this farce.'

'Farce, that's what you reduce me to. I'm your puppet, you reduce me to a gibbering puppet and put me in your pocket. You're so hard, so cold, no gentleness, no tenderness, no repose. If I'd married a sweet kind woman I'd be a different man. Oh it's all so *black*, so *black*. Why don't you go away?'

'I don't want to.'

'Someone might blame *you* for once! You hate me, don't you? You are hating me, you are *loathing* me, in this very minute. Why don't you admit it?'

'I won't say so.'

'You mean it's true, only you won't say it, so why do you speak of love, you foul hypocrite?'

'I didn't say that. I said something different.'

'I didn't say that, I said something different! Are you crazy?'

'I might say I hated you but it wouldn't be true. I guard my tongue.'

'You guard your tongue! Our life together is a madhouse. Why did you ever marry me? Everyone was amazed. Your father was stunned. Well, why did you –?'

'Oh – it doesn't matter.'

'It doesn't matter. You always say that. You'll say it when I'm dying. You're a leech, a flea, a blood-sucking parasite. You're quietly pouring all my blood into your body. You'll suck me white and dry and prop me up in a corner and say to people, "There's my husband, poor George!"'

'You don't believe any of this, why do you say it?'

'I do believe it. You imagine that however much I shout I really need you, and as soon as I stop you think it's all right between us.'

'Yes.'

'It's a lie, your lie, your illusion. God, if I could only cram it down your throat and put an end to you. Do you think I could talk like this if I didn't hate you in the deepest part of my soul?'

'Yes. You don't hate me.'

'You've been sent by the devil to torment me. Why don't you go away before I kill you? Can't you be unselfish enough not to get yourself murdered? But oh no, you won't go away, you'll never go away, you want people to admire you and say "There's long-suffering Stella, the virtuous wife!"'

'Don't drive like that, you're hurting the car.'

'You're sorry for the car, what about me?'

'I wish I could help you.'

'You'd better help yourself. You'll be sorry –'

'You know perfectly well that I love you and care about you.'

'What a way to put it, what a tone to use. You ought to take some lessons in being a woman.'

'How can I put it when you're like this?'

'Haven't you any feelings?'

'Not at the moment. I've switched off my feelings. If I had feelings now I'd be screaming.'

'Scream away, I'd like to hear you scream.'

'One scream is enough.'

'Why don't you say that you hate me?'

'If I say I hate you it's the end, there's no more sense in the world, it's all darkness –'

'If you said it you'd make it true? Then it must already be true –'

'No, no –'

'Roll on darkness. It's covered me already. God, how you torture my nerves.'

'Well, don't say so, why can't you be silent. Keep all this filth inside yourself. Other people manage to, why can't you?'

'Yes, you keep your filth inside, but it stinks all right, it rots and it stinks. You're sour and foul and rotten all through.'

'Oh shut up, damn you!'

'What did you say?'

'It doesn't matter.'

'*What did you say?*'

'You're crazy. You're crazy with fear because that man is coming.'

'*What?*'

'You're crazy with fear because Rozanov is coming.'

'You *bitch* – you –'

George struck sideways at her, catching her cheekbone with the back of his hand.

'George – stop – stop the car – *stop* –'

'Hell, hell, *hell* –'

George wrenched at the wheel, turning the car violently round in the direction of the canal. He dragged at the wheel as if it were some evil plant which he was striving to haul up by the roots. The car swerved, lurching and sliding on the uneven stones, and the lights of the nearest lamp post crackled across the windscreen in a starry trail as the rain struck with a difference and jumped about as if the car were shaking itself like a dog. George felt that in another moment he would suffocate; all his blood seemed to have rushed up into his head and to be bursting out there into a blazing bleeding wet red flower. He thought, I'm having a heart attack or something, I must get out into the air or I'll die. Gasping for breath, he fumbled the door open and half fell out, slithering on the cobbles and stumbling against the wet slippery side of the car. The rain drenched his burning face. He saw the dark surface of the canal close below him, covered with tiny mobile rings like grey coins. He saw the high elliptical curve of the iron foot-bridge beyond. The car, its wheels almost at the edge of the quay, was moving away from him in automatic drive. He must have braked instinctively as he swung it round. He cried aloud in a furious despairing wail. Why hadn't it gone away into the water as he had intended it to, why was it all still to do? Let everything pass from him into destruction. His hands were sliding along the wet metal. A vast feeling like sex, like a *sense of duty*, took possession of his body, a thrill of frantic haste and pure absolute fear. Hurry, hurry, hurry, must, must, must. He fell against the back of the car, bracing his feet against the rough stones of the quay and trying to push with open palms upon the back window. He felt the rainy muddy glass and raised his mad enraged face up like a howling dog. He heard screams, his own and another's. At the same moment he looked towards the iron bridge and saw that there was a figure on it, a tall figure in a long black coat. It's the devil, thought George, the devil come at last to –

Then he fell headlong on the stones. Nothing was there, no car, no figure, nothing. He lay with his face in a pool of water. He had heard a great sound, a great hollow explosion like something bursting inside his brain. He lifted up his head.

He lifted up his head. He was in his bed in his room at home, and the daylight was showing through the curtains, present in an insubstantial pattern of yellow flowers. So, he thought, it was only a dream! I dreamt I'd killed Stella. Not for the first time either, by God! And the devil was in the dream too. He was crossing the bridge. I always connect him with water. And Stella was drowned, I drowned her. George often dreamed this, only usually he drowned Stella in a bath, holding her head down below the water and wondering how much longer he needed to do it to be quite sure that she was dead.

He peered at his watch in the dim light. It was seven-thirty. Then he remembered that he had lost his job. In a fit of rage he had destroyed the Museum's small but very precious collection of Roman glass. Only one little bluey-greeny beaker had survived George's fury, bouncing in a miraculous manner upon the tiled floor. George pictured the timidly anguished face of the director as, looking ready to weep, he carefully picked up the survivor. Spite against George followed; things always ended in spite against George. Perhaps he ought to appeal. No one got sacked nowadays.

Oh to hell with them, he thought. Then he thought, why am I such a *bloody fool*, I do such damn stupid things, it's all my own fault, God I am unlucky. He wondered if he should reflect about whether to try to get that job back or whether to get another job and if so what and how, and decided not to reflect.

A stab of pain, a different one, alerted George's drowsy mind to another matter and he sat up abruptly in bed. John Robert Rozanov. George now pictured John Robert's face, a huge spongy moist fleshy face, with a big pitted hooked nose and an avid sensual mouth always partly open. He saw John Robert's red wet lips and his terrible clever cruel blood-shot eyes. At the same time George became fully aware of the frightful headache which had been plaguing him ever since he became conscious. His face felt bruised too. He must have been foully drunk last night. He tried to remember last night but could not. John Robert was coming back. Oh God, oh *God*.

George decided that what he needed now was milk, a nice long drink of creamy cold milk from the fridge. Slowly and gingerly, holding his head with one hand, he pulled back the bedclothes and moved his legs to dangle over the edge of the bed. He put his feet carefully on the floor. A kind of cramp seemed to be curling them into balls, and they refused to uncurl into flat surfaces which could be stood upon; it was like trying to stand on two fists. He managed to stand awkwardly, holding on to the bedpost, then hobbled to the window and drew back the curtains. The sun was shining upon George's small garden and upon a poplar tree which Stella had planted when ... Lord, how full of pain the world was. The tree was tall now, its young buds glowing. The sun also shone upon George's little triangular green view of the Common, and upon the intrusive curious malignant windows of other houses. George turned away. He stumbled over something.

It was the pile of his clothes, lying upon the floor. This was where they usually lay. But what was odd was that they were all soaking wet and black with mud.

George remembered. It was not a dream. *It had all really happened.* The car had fallen into the canal with Stella in it. Was Stella dead then?

He walked unhurriedly out of the bedroom door and across the landing to Stella's room. The room was bright with sun, the curtains pulled back, the bed not slept in. George sat down on a chair. No, Stella was not dead. Was he glad? Christ, what a lot of bloody trouble he had landed himself in, he would lose his driving licence. He recalled painfully, shamefully, remorsefully the way things had happened last night. He could see it all now.

When George had sat up upon the wet rainy cold stones of the quay, and found that the car had *gone*, he was at first confused. Where had it gone to? Some terrible ghastly frightening *noise* had taken place. His arm was hurting, strained somewhere by a violent effort. He jumped up and ran to the edge of the quay. The lamp light showed the canal waters, black with mud, foaming and churning and boiling as if the devil himself were rising up to the surface like a black whale. In the midst of this turmoil was a gleaming pale expanse which it took George a moment to identify as the roof of the car. George executed a sort of dance upon the edge of the quay as if he were about to walk straight out into the air; then he began to run along the edge and to descend a flight of slimy greenish stone steps of whose existence he had somehow known. He even put his hand confidently on to a great iron ring which was hanging from the wall half-way down the steps. The cold water took hold of his trouser legs.

George was a good swimmer. Yelping with fear and horror and the cold he reached the car. Down in the canal everything was confused and dark and terrible. No light seemed to come from above. He felt he was about to lose his senses. He had no conception of the shape of the car or what to do with it. He could not make out how high the water had risen inside. He held on helplessly to the rim of the roof. Even as he touched the car he could feel it sinking, slowly settling down into the mud. His knee touched something. A door was open. With what he remembered as a curious blind slowness George fumbled at the black aperture, holding on to the door with one hand and trying to bring his legs down at the side of the car. The end of the door struck him in the face. Stella came out like a creature sliding from a chrysalis, like a moist dark bat from a cranny, like a dream of a child being born. It seemed to George as if he had then led her back to the steps; he could not recall pulling her through the water. On the steps it was different. She was a heavy inert dripping sack which had to be hauled up step by step; and at that moment it occurred to him that she was dead. Up on the quay it was at once apparent that she was not. She lay on the stones, moving, gasping, writhing like a worm.

George recalled without surprise what he had done next. He had *kicked* her soggy limp body, shouting, 'You bitch! You bitch!'

An ambulance came. The police came. Stella was taken to the hospital. George was taken to the police station where he made a confused statement and sat moaning while it was established how drunk he was. He had not recalled then, but he recalled now the identity of the black-clad figure who had been passing across the bridge. It was the priest, Father Bernard Jacoby. He must have raised the alarm. He must have seen George pushing the car. Did that matter? Christ, what a mess.

'How are we feeling?'
The questioner was Gabriel McCaffrey, Stella's sister-in-law.
Stella continued to cry, saying nothing.
Gabriel herself often cried. Not that she had anything very terrible to cry about, since she was happily married and had a lovely son, but she cried often for the anguish of the world because of its little vulnerable places, or because of the frailty of everything she loved. Stella on the other hand had always plenty to cry about. However, Gabriel had never before seen her crying or even imagined her crying.
The two women were not intimate friends and not allies but they liked each other. Stella might well suppose that Gabriel pitied her because Gabriel was married to nice Brian while Stella was married to awful George. On the other hand, Gabriel might well imagine that Stella thought that George was interesting, whereas Brian was boring. The relations of Stella and George were a mystery to Gabriel and Brian. Of course, Stella had been to a university and was educated and clever. Yet she had made nothing of her cleverness, while Gabriel, who had not been to university, had a more successful 'life'. Gabriel was happier. But was not battle-scarred Stella 'more real'? There were, indeed, further complexities, of which they were both aware and above which, usually, they were able to look at each other calmly enough.
Gabriel did not feel calm now. She had always known and feared George's capacity to introduce absolute disorder into all their lives.

17

George could destroy us all, she sometimes felt, and sometimes, George *wants* to destroy us all. Of course this was irrational, though it was equally irrational to regard George as simply 'accident prone'. How I hate bullies, Gabriel thought, thank heavens I'm not married to one.

Father Bernard Jacoby had telephoned Brian and Gabriel on the previous night to tell them about the accident, the car in the canal, Stella and George safe, Stella in hospital, George gone home. He suggested (to Brian's relief and Gabriel's disappointment) that it was too late for visits, both of the victims would be asleep. It was now nine o'clock in the morning. Stella, in a private room, was propped up in bed. She had a black eye and a cracked rib and what the nurse called 'severe shock'. George had not answered telephone calls. Brian was going round to see him.

'Please stop crying,' said Gabriel, 'you are tiring yourself and upsetting me.' This firm calm manner, unnatural to Gabriel, was how her sister-in-law preferred to be addressed.

Stella had been crying into a handkerchief. She now laid this aside and revealed her wet swollen bruised face, shocking to Gabriel. Stella began rolling her head to and fro upon the pillow, visibly trying to control her respiration. Gabriel touched her arm lightly. Stella did not like hugging and kissing. Gabriel had never kissed her.

'Shall I stay, shall I talk to you?'

'Tell me something.' The stream had abated, though Stella kept blinking tears out of her eyes.

Gabriel, who was good at decoding, knew that this meant: tell me anything. 'It's a sunny day. You can't see from here, but the sun's shining.'

'Did you come by car?'

'Yes.'

'Where did you park?'

'In the hospital car park, there's plenty of room.'

'You've got a new dress.'

'I bought it in Bowcocks sale. Do you know, you can see the High Street from the window, and the Botanic Garden and the Institute –'

'I haven't looked.'

'How are you feeling?'

'Terrible.'

'What happened? Or would you rather –?'

18

'George was drunk. He jumped out. Then he pulled me out.'

'All's well that ends well,' said Gabriel, who hoped that this banality would irritate Stella into saying something more.

'It was my fault,' said Stella.

'I *know* that's not true.'

The family often discussed Stella's situation, how she put up with George's tantrums and his infidelity, how she persistently imagined that her love would cure him. She kept hoping, looking for little signs. Gabriel thought, it's odd how stupid a clever person can be. She feels that not blaming George will somehow make him improve.

'I argued,' said Stella. 'I said a particular thing that annoyed him. Then the car went out of control.'

'He's easily annoyed!'

'George was crazy as a fox last night.'

'Always was, always will be. One day he'll go too far.'

'If he ever does he'll get better.'

'You mean repentant?'

'No.'

'You always make excuses for him, he can get away with anything, he's always forgiven and first of all by you!'

'It's my privilege to be first.'

What a hypocrite she is, thought Gabriel, and yet she's sincere. Can there be sincere hypocrites? Yes, and they're the most maddening of all. There was no doubt that Stella was an odd fish, an alien, a changeling. She was a handsome tall strong woman. She sees him as a challenge, thought Gabriel, she sees it as a fight, and she thinks that's love. George ought to have married a gentle submissive girl, not this noble ridiculous person. And she thought, this is the most intimate conversation I've ever had with Stella.

'You ought to go away for a while, have a holiday from George.'

'Don't be silly.'

'You should, you should go to some foreign city.'

'He'll lose his driving licence.'

'Poor George!'

'He wanted us to walk away.'

'You mean last night? Just walk away, after *that*? Before the police came, I suppose!'

'I would have walked if I could,' said Stella.

'Oh God, here he comes.'

Through the open door of the room Gabriel saw George approaching along the corridor.

'Good-bye, Gabriel, thank you for coming to see me.'

With a little wave to Stella, Gabriel moved out of the room. George advanced, walking with a characteristic self-conscious deliberation as of someone fairly confidently walking on water. He leaned forwards as he walked, setting his feet down noiselessly on the thick, soft, spongy pale grey hospital linoleum. His arms swung in a light poised manner. He looked like an athlete, off duty, aware of being photographed. When he saw Gabriel he narrowed his eyes and smiled a faint amused smile. Gabriel, disturbed by mixed emotions, made an impatient gesture with her hand. She frowned, but her mouth could not help smiling in an involuntary nervous spasm.

George McCaffrey had been spared the visit of his brother Brian by having left the house before Brian arrived. Before leaving, George had telephoned the hospital and learnt that Stella was 'comfortable'. He set off, but went first of all to the canal.

The canal was no longer in use. It ought to have been beautiful, as it curved into the town, with the cobbled road beside it and the huge square granite slabs at the edge of the quay and the great rings upon the walls where the painted barges used to tie up. The elliptical foot-bridge was reproduced (reflected in still water) upon postcards, and the small elegant container (still in use) of the nearby gas works, with its fretted cast-iron coronet was a period piece prized by industrial archaeologists. But somehow the sluggish brown stream looked dirty and melancholy, and attempts to rejuvenate it for purposes of pleasure always failed. The canal remained in mourning for its useful past, expressing the grim puritanical character of local history rather than any desire to be reborn as charming. The area on the far side remained derelict, except for a scattering of poor post-war housing, mostly condemned, and was known as 'the wasteland'. Against the rusty railings which fringed the road only the uglier weeds grew; the grass between the tilting cobbles was flabby and sad, and the glittering points in the square granite slabs looked like symptoms of a post-industrial disease.

It was beginning to rain when George arrived. Several people were standing looking down at the car. (The drama had of course been reported in the *Gazette*.) Aware of being recognized, George joined them. Several of the on-lookers walked hastily away. Those who remained removed themselves to a little distance.

The car was upright, its white roof just breaking the surface. It must have settled down in the mud since last night. The brown rain-pitted canal water, very slowly passing it by, possessed it as if it were a rock or a clump of reeds. It looked peaceful.

George had never had any fantasies about driving cars over quaysides, though he had had plenty about drowning, death by water, his own or another's. He had fantasies, or were they dreams, of drowning someone, as it might be Stella, and burying the corpse in a wood and visiting the quiet grave regularly as the months passed and the years passed and the seasons changed and the wild flowers grew upon the place and no one ever suspected. Sometimes he dreamt that he had killed Stella and then suddenly met her again alive and then realized that it was not her, but a twin sister of whose existence he had never known.

How could I have done that, he thought, looking down. As on similar occasions in the past, he felt a cleavage between himself and the George who did things. Yet he was that person and felt easy with him, chiding him gently. What a damn *stupid* thing to do, he thought, now that he was in the land of consequences. I was fond of that car. What will the insurance people say, I wonder. God, if only we could have got away before the police came.

Stella had started crying again when George arrived. She was very anxious indeed to stop. She regarded crying as a kind of rather shameful and unusual disease. It gave her no relief. She rolled her head about, trying to breathe slowly, but could not stop her lower lip from shuddering convulsively and her heart from racing. She put her hand to her damaged side and panted, turning her wet mouth away from her husband.

'How are you?' said George.

'OK.'

'Are you feeling OK?'

'Yes.'

'You've got a black eye.'

'Yes.'

'So have I, at least it's swollen, can't think how I got it.'

'Oh – yes –'

'The people here seem nice, the nurse was nice to me.'

'Good.'

'You're not in pain?'

'No.'

'That's good.'

'I can't stop crying.'

'Not to worry.'

'I suppose it's hysterical. Not like me.'

'No. Gabriel got here early.'

'Yes.'

'What did she say to you?'

'Nothing.'

'What did you say to her?'

'Nothing.'

'Nothing?'

'I told her nothing.'

'I can't remember much about last night.'

'I'm glad you can't, neither can I.'

'If you can't remember, why are you glad I can't?'

'It was a horrid accident, better to forget it.'

'We do a lot of forgetting. How long will you be in here?'

'I don't know. You could ask matron.'

'Do you want anything, flowers or books or anything?'

'No, thanks.'

'I feel awfully tired.'

'You're suffering from shock.'

'Yes, that's it, I suppose I am.'

'Better go home and rest.'

'No, I think I'll go swimming, that always does me good.'

'Yes, go swimming, that'll do you good.'

Pat-ball, thought George, pat-ball. It's either this or rows. Stella can't talk to me, that's her trouble; she can't make silly jokes or play about like other people, she can't really talk to anyone, she's cut off from the human race. She's grand like royalty, I married a princess. I hate seeing her crying, it's so unnatural, she looks like a wet pig. She hasn't any soft warm being, no haven there, no safety. Oh God, how much fear I feel now, how much help I need, with *him* coming. Why must I always suffer so, this is *hell*. Familiar black resentment rose in his heart, in his gorge. I am *poisoned*, he thought.

'Here's Alex,' said Stella, and checked her weeping.

George rose quickly and made for the door. His mother stood aside to let him pass. They exchanged a quick bright look but no words.

PRELUDE

ii *Our Town*

I am the narrator: a discreet and self-effacing narrator. This book is not about me. I knew, though not in most cases at all well, a number of the *dramatis personae* and I lived (and live) in the town where the events hereinafter recounted took place. For purposes of convenience, for instance so that my 'characters' may be able (very occasionally) to refer to me or address me, I shall call myself 'N'. But as far as this drama is concerned I am a shadow, Nemo, not the masked presence or secret voice of one of the main characters. I am an observer, a student of human nature, a moralist, a man; and will allow myself here and there the discreet luxury of moralizing.

It will be necessary to talk a good deal about our town, and as I would prefer, for obvious reasons, not to use its real name, I shall call it after my own, 'N's Town', or, let us say, 'Ennistone'. Ennistone is situated in the south of England, not exceedingly far from London. A fairly frequent train service increasingly takes 'commuters' daily to their work in the metropolis and brings them home at evening to a green countryside. However, most of our people still work in and around Ennistone, and old-fashioned Ennistonians would certainly resent the idea of being considered a 'dormitory town'. The place has a strong identity and, one may say, a strong social conscience. New housing estates have recently diluted our old community life, but strenuous efforts are made by 'responsible citizens' (it is characteristic of our town to have many of these) to draw the newcomers into our many 'worthwhile activities'. There are church groups, women's groups, drama groups, debates, evening classes, a Historical Society, a Fine Art Society, a Writers' Circle. There is a lively museum and a Botanical Garden. There is plenty of musical activity, including an operatic society, a silver band and the 'Ennistone Orchestra'. We were (and to some extent still are) thus well able to amuse ourselves. I should also mention here a passion for playing bridge, though this is not now so common among the young people and the newcomers.

This account may suggest that Ennistone is a rather self-satisfied little place, and perhaps this is true. It was as if we pulled back our skirts from the sins and vices of London, which from here was seen as an exotic and dangerous playground. At one time even television was frowned upon, and some of the 'responsible citizens' made a point of banning these corrupt machines from their homes. We have a strong and long-standing puritan and non-conformist tradition, one result of which is that there are even now very few public houses in Ennistone. An 'Austrian Wine Bar' recently opened in the High Street occasioned a long controversy in the *Ennistone Gazette* (our worthy local paper edited at the time of this tale by Gavin Oare, an ambitious youth with his eye on Fleet Street). Ennistone was, in a rural way, a manufacturing town (I am speaking of the nineteenth century) and the fine Tweed Mill 'as big as a palace' still remains as an abandoned remnant of commercial glory. Several old Quaker families (the McCaffreys are one of these) founded the fortunes of Ennistone at that time, and still (together with some Methodists) control various less prosperous commercial projects which now provide our main sources of employment. Many Ennistonians, I should add, work on the land, but big landowners have not figured in our recent history.

Ennistone is situated upon an attractive river (which I shall call 'the Enn'). The Romans were here (there is a Roman bridge over the Enn) and some interesting remains attest earlier inhabitants. There are some megaliths upon the common which are known as 'the Ennistone Ring' although there are only nine of them and one a mere stump. Professor Thom visited our stones and made some calculations but could make nothing of them (we were rather proud of that). Of the medieval village little survives except St Olaf's Church, situated in the poorer part of the town. There are some good eighteenth-century buildings, including the Quaker Meeting House, the Crescent, and the Hall, and an eighteenth-century bridge (alas much altered) still called the New Bridge. Although so ancient, we cannot alas claim to have produced any very famous sons. History knows of a bishop who got into trouble in the seventeenth century for being a Cambridge Platonist. And there was a poor non-conforming fellow in the eighteenth century who, after becoming a famous preacher, suddenly declared that he was Christ and occasioned some sort of little revolt. His name was Elias Ossmor, and the Osmore family of today claim descent from him. On these and other matters see *Ennistone, Its History and Antiqui-*

ties (published 1901) by Oscar Bowcock, forebear of our Percy Bowcock. Oscar's younger brother James was the founder of our one big shop, Burdett and Bowcock, usually known as Bowcocks. I think the book is out of print, but a copy survives in the public library. There used to be two copies but one was stolen. At the time of this story I can mention only two Ennistonians who are at all well known outside our gates; the psychiatrist Ivor (now Sir Ivor) Sefton, and the philosopher (about whom more will be heard in these pages) John Robert Rozanov.

I have not yet mentioned the feature for which Ennistone is most famous. Ennistone is a spa. (The town was called Ennistone Spa in the nineteenth century, but the name is no longer in use.) There is a copious hot spring with alleged medical properties, which of course attracted the Romans and their predecessors to the site. Shadowy historical evidence suggests that the worship of a pre-Roman goddess (perhaps Freya) was associated with the spring; a rudimentary stone image in the Museum is supposed to represent this deity. A beautiful Roman inscription, also in the Museum, more solidly suggests a cult of Venus. The Romans honoured the spring with a handsome bathing establishment, of which unfortunately only foundations and a piece of wall remain. The idea that the waters had an aphrodisiac effect was periodically popular. Shakespeare's sonnet 153 is said to refer to Ennistone, wherein the Bard's lively fancy pictures the spring deriving from a prank of one of Diana's nymphs who cooled the fiery penis of sleeping Cupid in a cool spring which thence became hot, and whose waters were said to cure the 'sad distempers' and 'strange maladies' which attend imprudent love. A seventeenth-century medical pamphlet makes an ambiguous reference to the Ennistone waters (see Bowcock's book, the index under 'venereal disease'). Our ancestors in their folly pulled down most of the fine architecture with which (as we see from prints) the spring was surrounded in the eighteenth century, including a Bath House of transcendent beauty. A minor eighteenth-century poet called Gideon Parke wrote a masque called *The Triumph of Aphrodite* which was to take place in the Bath House, and included a scene where the goddess emerges from the steam of the hot spring itself. This work survives and was performed in the nineteen-thirties with music written by the Rector of St Olaf's. (There was some disagreeable fuss about it at the time.) Of the eighteenth-century buildings only the Pump Room remains, now no longer connected with the waters, used for assemblies and concerts and known as the 'Ennistone Hall'. The spring has been the victim of a kind of periodical puritanism, and Ennistonians had, and to some extent still have, oddly mixed feelings about their chief municipal glory. Before the first war a Methodist minister even managed to have the establishment closed for a short period on an allegation, never proved, that it had become a secret centre of heathen worship. A vague feeling persists to this day that the spring is in some way a source of a kind of unholy restlessness which attacks the town at intervals like an epidemic.

Let me try to describe the spa buildings as they are now. The main edifice is Victorian, a long tall lamentable block of glazed yellow brick with a lot of 'Gothic' ornament upon it. At the time of the erection of this pile the establishment was christened 'the Bath Institute' and is still referred to as 'the Institute', though many people more familiarly call it 'the Baths'. The Institute building contains, as I shall explain, together with the 'machine room' of the spa, a refreshment area, changing-rooms, offices, and two indoor pools. Next to the Institute, and divided from it by a garden about which I shall also speak shortly, is the Ennistone Hall (1760), beautifully proportioned and built of the local stone, a powdery golden-yellow, full of fossils and unfortunately rather soft. Ladies representing the virtues, reduced to four for convenience, who adorn the corners of the roof, have weathered to shapeless pillars. A pediment at one end contains a reclining god, said to represent the river Enn, who has been similarly reduced. Beyond the Hall is the park, or Botanic Garden, containing many rare and interesting plants and trees. There is a lake, and a Victorian 'temple' which houses our small but well-arranged Museum with its treasured collection of Roman antiquities. In the same building there is a modest art gallery containing nineteenth-century romantic paintings and some prettyish work by Ned Larkin, an Ennistonian follower of Paul Nash. The open space which separates the Hall from the Institute, and forms part of the premises of the latter, is known as Diana's Garden. This garden contains an excavated area showing foundations of Roman walls and some water pipes. (A mosaic found here is in the Museum.) Also to be seen is the only 'natural' manifestation of the great spring which is visible to the public, a steamy stone basin (perhaps the site of the exploit mentioned in sonnet 153) where scalding water spits up at intervals to a height of three or four feet. The basin is not ornate, it is even rudimentary and of uncertain age, suggestive of the country shrine of some little local god. It is traditionally called 'Lud's Rill' but is more popularly known as the 'Little Teaser'.

At the other end of the Institute and joining it at right angles is a long concrete structure, now a little strained and battered, built in the nineteen-twenties in the Bauhaus style and at that time considered a model of modern architecture. Between the end of this building (called the 'Ennistone Rooms') and the end of the garden runs a wall made of yellow glazed bricks, similar to those of the Institute building, and decorated here and there with mauve and blue tiles made up into pictures of dolphins and such. The large rectangle enclosed by these four sides contains the Outdoor Bath, an expanse of natural warm water (26° to 28° Centigrade at all seasons) over which in winter there hangs a thick pall of steam. The Outdoor Bath is said to be the largest swimming-pool in Europe, but this may be an exaggeration. It certainly meets Olympic standards and is frequented, especially in the colder months, by athletes in training. A large clock with a second hand at one end records the speed of the swimmers. Between the brick wall and the pool at the Diana's Garden end runs a row of sizeable round concrete wells filled with water at a series of temperatures running from 36° to 45° Centigrade. Into each of these wells, which are tiled at the bottom, a stairway descends, and there is a seat round the edge upon which bathers can sit and soak, with their heads a little above the water level. Each well can in this way contain some ten to fifteen people. These hedonistic places of meditation are known as the 'stewpots' or just 'the stews'.

This completes my account of the outside of the Institute. I now move inside. Through a doorway like that of a Renaissance palace, above which in Roman mosaic style is inscribed the Institute motto, *Natando Virtus*, one gains access to the first public area, the Promenade. This is a large rather shabby place, painted a melancholy green, dotted with tables and chairs where simple refreshments may be obtained, such as tea, lemonade, bars of chocolate, sandwiches, and of course (free of charge) the famous water. The healing stream flows from the brass mouth of a marble lion, but the filled glasses stand upon the counter. No alcohol is served in the Institute. This rule is maintained in spite of periodic protests by younger citizens. It is held that a bar would radically alter the atmosphere of the place, and no doubt this is true. At the end of the Promenade opposite the main door there is access to the changing-rooms. There is also a long observation window looking on to the Outdoor

Bath. (Those who want to watch but not to swim pay a reduced entrance fee.) On the right of the Promenade are situated the Indoor Bath and its facilities and beyond it the Infants' Pool and the Institute offices. The Indoor Bath replaces (but unfortunately does not copy) its eighteenth-century predecessor. The latter, built of local stone, felicitously (as we see in pictures) imitated the classical through a natural affinity. Our Bath is built of marble, and its architect, who also thought he was imitating the classical, has produced something resembling an indifferent Victorian picture of a bath in a harem. (Some such idea seems to have haunted a local painter commissioned to paint some frescoes of classical scenes, but whose designs were turned down by the Committee.) However, the place, with its double row of columns and marble steps descending into warm clear water has a certain charm, though spoilt by unsightly masses of potted plants. The Indoor Bath used to be hired out for private parties, but after a gathering which was reported in the national newspapers this custom was discontinued.

On the left of the Promenade a door leads to a large and curious octagonal room known as 'the Baptistry'. This room enshrines the entrance, complete with pseudo-classical pillars and pediment, to the great 'machinery' or 'engine room' to use the traditional terms, of the installation. These machines, now modernized of course, were the pride of a well-known nineteenth-century engineer, and the huge subterranean area which they occupy used to be on show to the public. Now, however, for a variety of reasons (thought by some who canvass the matter regularly in the *Gazette* to be sinister) this area is closed off and the way into the Baptistry is marked PRIVATE. The Baptistry is used as a store-room, and the great hot bronze doors, studded with pseudo-nails, which guard the access to (as we say and imagine) 'the hot spring itself', are locked against all except 'authorized personnel'. Even to glimpse these doors, through which steam eternally seeps, is a rare treat for citizens managing to peer in from the Promenade. A door on the far side of the Baptistry leads to the Ennistone Rooms, but the public entrance to the Rooms is of course on the street, and not through the Institute.

I turn now to the Ennistone Rooms, the modern (well, not so modern) extension of the Institute. The Rooms, as I explained, are a nineteen-twenties building meeting the Institute at right angles. The 'nose' or narrow end of the building, with an austere but handsome public entrance, is on the same street as the Institute, the walls being coterminous. The Rooms stretch back skirting the Outdoor Bath, from which they are separated by a garden and a high beech hedge. (The windows on the Bath side are double-glazed.) Of course a therapeutic use of the waters dates back a long way, perhaps as far as any human occupation of the site. Certainly a 'cure' existed at Ennistone in the seventeenth and eighteenth centuries, and the eighteenth-century buildings included a wing devoted to private baths and treatment. In the nineteenth century these facilities were housed inside the Institute Building, but were considerably curtailed after the construction of the Indoor Bath. After the first war, when 'health crazes' were much in the news, the Town Council decided to invest in a new building and make a greater profit out of science.

The Rooms comprise consulting rooms, offices, massage par-lours, mud baths, a gymnasium, a common room, but mainly the enterprise takes its name from the set of luxurious bedrooms with private baths attached. These large bed-sitting rooms, modelled on similar installations in continental spas, were designed for wealthy invalids. They were adorned in an *art déco* style which contrived to be, at the same time, severe, exotic and insipid. The colour schemes were predominantly black and white, trimmed with beige, orange and light green. There were a lot of triangular mirrors with zigzag edges, and curly tubular steel chairs which swayed alarm-ingly when sat on. The beds were also made of tubular steel, moving on casters to stand against carved light oak headboards attached to the wall.

Beyond the louvred double doors the bathrooms were walled with iridescent coloured glass depicting thin ecstatic ladies on hill-tops, leaping fawns, enormous cocktails, aeroplanes, airships and so on, together with pieces of furniture made of fur, and various alcoves protected by moorish lattices. The baths themselves (black), sunk into the floor and shaped like boats with blunt ends, were large and deep enough for a swimmer to take two or three strokes. Only the big goldeny Edwardian brass taps were remini-scent of a more traditional taste. These were put in by mistake, much to the annoyance of the Swedish architect, but never changed, since by then the cost of the building had exceeded the wildest estimates. (Most of the fittings came from Sweden; there were rows about that too.) I have used the past tense in this description since the Rooms have changed a good deal since the days of their glory. The famous orange and white 'sunrise' crockery has been mostly broken and not replaced, as have the zigzag mirrors and iridescent glass. The tubular snakes have sagged under their burdens and been succeeded by sturdy ugly chairs. The glittering black Swedish tiles are gone from the baths and decent white British tiles reign in their stead, though the shape of the baths and the Edwardian taps remain. The Institute suffered considerably from blast during the war, when it was used as an Air Raid Precautions centre. (The Outdoor Bath remained in use throughout the conflict and was very popular with the Army Camp upon the Common.) In general the *décor* of the Rooms has suffered, in a way which ought to have been better foreseen by the architect, from perpetual steam, since the hot water streams continuously from the great brass taps, maintaining a lowish water level in the baths (which may be raised by putting in the plug). The temperature is kept at 42° Centigrade. (Once the water supply suddenly became scalding hot by mistake and drowned an elderly gentleman who was unable to get out in time, but we do not speak of that.) The deafening noise of the water, together with the thick steamy moist air, gives the Ennistone Rooms a strange atmosphere. More than one woman has admitted to me that she feels a sexual thrill on entering.

The Institute occupies a central place in the social life of Ennistone. Its role has been compared to that of the agora in Athens. It is the main rendezvous of the citizenry where people idle, gossip, relax, show off, hunt for partners, make assignations, make business deals, make plots. Marriages are made, and broken, beside these steamy pools. It is like what going to church used to be, only it happens every day. This aspect of our lives is of course described by responsible citizens in high-minded terms. Swimming is the very best kind of exercise for old and young, and is undoubtedly also good for the soul. This lofty conception of the spiritual utility of swimming battles continuously with the (also recurrent) notion of many citizens that the Baths is a temple of hedonism. The old *thés dansants* (with three-piece orchestra) upon the Promenade have long ceased to be. But the danger always remains that innocent and healthy disciplines may degenerate into pure pleasure.

Be that as it may, the people of our town make the fullest possible use of this natural bounty. Everybody swims. Babies learn at the age of six weeks in the Infants' Pool, where mothers with amazed joy watch the tiny creatures taking boldly to the water, striking out with puny arms, and floating fearlessly with noses just above the surface. The aged swim, unashamed of their bodies, pot-bellied men and ancient wrinkled women in bikinis. Decency is maintained, however. Recent suggestions about nude bathing (a sign of the times) have been quickly extinguished. We swim every day seven days a week. Many of us swim before going to work, or, if the lunch-hour allows, at midday, a popular time. Then there are evening swimmers, many of whom have also been morning swimmers. Persons of leisure or housewives, mothers with children, come at less crowded hours and sit about and talk. We swim all the year round. The Outdoor Bath, floodlit after dusk, has a quite special charm in winter when we run from the changing-rooms, crossing a patch of frost or snow, to plunge into the warm water which is covered by so thick a cloud of steam that visibility may be reduced to a few feet and we swim about in strange insulated bubbles. Most swimmers favour the Outdoor Bath as being suited to the serious swimming which is a matter of pride in our town. The Indoor Bath is usually frequented by certain kinds of women, I do not mean prostitutes, but shy or withdrawn people who shun the more boisterous atmosphere outside; and the place has lately developed, especially at weekends, a curious clientele of its own.

I must say something more about the Ennistone Rooms. Unfortunately for the town, the cult of the Rooms by rich invalids from elsewhere did not last for long, and Ennistone's hopes of becoming an internationally famous spa were soon dashed. A medical report published in *The Lancet*, and reprinted in the national press, to the effect that the Ennistone water, though harmless, had no curative properties whatever, was probably unconnected with the change of fashion which returned Ennistone Spa to comparative obscurity. (It is also doubtless untrue that the then Director of the Institute tried to have the report hushed up.) Various postmortems bemoaned various mistakes, such as not enough advertising, or the wrong kind, bad food, unattractive masseuses, and so on. One trouble with the project was that its original creators never made up their minds whether they were designing a hospital or a hotel, and it was later argued that the Rooms performed neither function. This would perhaps not have mattered had the waters been more widely credited with magical properties. In any case, and for whatever reason, the troop of highly paid doctors and nurses and physiotherapists who had run the Rooms in its early days departed, leaving the town with a much-diminished asset with which, of course, something had to be done. What was done was to let out the Rooms at a more modest cost

31

for short periods, even by the day, to locals and tourists simply as hotel rooms where those who enjoyed such things could soak and sleep, and soak and sleep again. No further 'treatment' was offered but twice a week a doctor was in attendance to discuss medical problems for a fee. (Even about this there were arguments, everything about the Institute provokes arguments.) Sufferers from arthritis, undeterred by the medical report (or more likely not having heard of it) came in small but regular numbers. Some were encouraged to come by local Ennistonian practitioners. No restaurant facilities were offered, but food could be ordered from the snack bar on the Promenade. Some pilgrims continued to travel to the great Ennistonian spring, but the main custom of the Rooms increasingly came, rather to the surprise and dismay of the Committee, from ordinary Ennistonians who thought it fun or even chic to hire a room for a day or two and enjoy the handsome private bath and the luxury of relaxing in a place which still bore some resemblance to an exotic hotel. The cost was not great. Students came with their books. Writers came. Slimmers came. Convalescents came. Some doctors (including Ivor Sefton) recommended this 'cure' to people recovering from nervous breakdowns. I should add that married couples (and *a fortiori* any other kind) are not allowed to reside together. The Rooms are all single rooms and are kept under such supervision as to preclude any improper occurrences. Alcohol is also banned, though the ban is difficult to enforce. The popularity of the Rooms has (perhaps this is to be expected) occasioned criticism from the anti-hedonist lobby, who claim that excessive enjoyment of the waters must be demoralizing and that hot baths and beds give people ideas. It is even alleged that people make a habit of leaving their offices early at four-thirty, bathing and resting until six and then proceeding to the pub. I have met some of these offenders myself.

I have portrayed our citizens as rather sober and strait-laced folk, and this is indeed true of the majority. However, there is also manifest, and not only in the young people, a certain restless sensationalism, something almost superstitious, which seems bound to erupt at periodic intervals. A visiting evangelist made a deep impression some years ago by crying out 'You have dethroned Christ and worship water instead.' Some serious persons went about shaking their heads and speaking of 'grave spiritual hazards'. This sort of unhealthy excitement or 'moral unrest', something vague, almost fanciful, came at fairly rare intervals, yet regularly enough for people to attempt to chart them. Perhaps there was nothing to these 'phases' except a periodic infectious need for people to say 'We're going into one of those things', or 'We're going to have one of our funny times.' It might be as if, morality being tiring, a holiday from it had at certain intervals to be decreed, at least ostensibly, by some covert social complicity. These 'holidays' took various forms, sometimes appearing simply (or initially) in the guise of some prevalent 'craze', which was then taken rightly or wrongly as a symptom of deep psychological or moral disorder. Some years before there had been a sudden passion for interpreting dreams, then for experiments in telepathy, seances, automatic writing, then perfectly rational people began to see ghosts (and so on). At such periods more was always to be heard of the old speculation about the waters having an aphrodisiac effect. (I recall a harmless little Roman Catholic shop called 'Our Lady of the Grotto', which had existed among us for some time, being suddenly made an object of interest, even persecution, by people who went round murmuring *What* lady, of *what* grotto?' It eventually changed its name to 'The Pentecostal Bazaar'. This example suggests the quality, as well as the irrationality, of these seizures.)

At the time of this story some nonsense of this sort was again at large in the community, particularly among the younger people and among the idler older women who liked to have something weird or shocking to gossip about. A large number of letters (so large as to suggest a concocted campaign, though this was never proved) were received by the *Ennistone Gazette* suggesting that the Bath Institute should be thoroughly shaken up and hustled into the contemporary world. The suggestions were various but similar in tone: the Institute should be renamed (this prompted many facetious proposals), it should be open till midnight, alcohol should be served, there should be regular dancing on the Promenade. One letter signed by some 'bright young things', even suggested that a Casino should be established. (One of the signatories was young Gregory Osmore; this caused some distress to his parents.) These letters were not really very shocking, and a number of people, some of them Friends (Quakers), tried to 'take over' the 'outbreak' by saying that it was indeed not absurd to suggest that the Institute should become a big 'money-spinner' for the town and thus help to provide better housing for our poorer citizens. A left-wing group on the Town Council took the occasion to demand changes in the way the Institute was administered. This too was perfectly sensible.

However, various less sensible folk chose to see these discussions as symptoms of some local upheaval, and seemed intent on spreading a sort of self-conscious excitement and anticipation of scandals. A group of the 'bright young things' before mentioned were discovered to be planning a production of Gideon Parke's masque *The Triumph of Aphrodite* in a new and more daring version, which had been unearthed by a solemn scholar, a visitor to the town, who had been delving in the archives. The scholar (called Hector Gaines) was at first dismayed and later flattered at being taken up by our *jeunesse dorée*. He was rumoured to have found a lot of pornographic lines which had been deleted by a nineteenth-century editor.

In February of the year of this tale (not long before George McCaffrey's 'accident') an elderly man called William Eastcote, a most respected citizen and pillar of the Friends' Meeting House, a non-drinking, bridge-playing intimate of Percy Bowcock, saw an unidentified flying object, a large luminous tilted saucer, hanging motionless over the Common, quite low down. No one else witnessed this phenomenon; but a week later several young people, including Greg Osmore and Andrew Blackett, returning from a concert at the Hall, saw something similar rather farther off, and there was one more dubious sighting after that. This was of course a popular topic (with all of us, I must confess) and there were plenty of theorists to link the saucer with the Ennistone Ring by various familiar sorts of wild speculation. Here indeed was a genuine portent, a veridical harbinger of the onset of a 'funny time'. Another portent followed of which I was myself a witness. Lud's Rill, the 'Little Teaser', the modest hot jet in Diana's Garden, suddenly became more animated and began sending up great spurts of boiling water to a height of some twenty (when I saw it) or even thirty feet. Some people who were nearby when the jet suddenly first erupted were quite seriously scalded. The garden was then closed. The spring continued to perform for about three weeks and then stopped of its own accord. The garden remained closed for some time and was then reopened after the introduction below ground of some grand new 'valve' which, we are assured, would preclude any repetition of such exuberance. There was disappointment and general annoyance at what was felt to be an unjustified interference with a marvel of nature. Most of us would gladly have surrendered the garden to the whims of the scalding jet.

An account of all this nonsense is not irrelevant to our story, since it was in the first or anticipatory stage of this unhealthy mood that George McCaffrey's 'exploit' occurred, and at another time it might have attracted less notice. The incident with the Roman glass, which had happened over a year earlier and which had led, though because of bureaucratic delays not at once, to his dismissal, had caused less of a stir at the time, partly of course because few people in Ennistone cared deeply about Roman glass, but also because the psychological climate was then less highly charged. As it was, it came later to be regarded as highly significant, and added a new dimension to George's already considerable reputation or 'myth'. Past happenings, including the Roman glass, were recalled and refurbished. Better read citizens instanced similar times in Ennistone's history, as in the case of the man who thought he was Christ, when some violent action (in that case a murder quite unconnected with the poor fellow's delusion) heralded a period of upheaval. It was interesting that almost everyone, at once and on no evidence, took it for granted that George had driven the car into the canal on purpose, though opinions differed about whether or not he had intended to kill his wife. Serious citizens and prudes who did not care for this kind of irresponsible speculation said that all this showed was how glamorous a thoroughly nasty man can seem to be. Others, however much they disapproved, saw George in a different light. It would be an exaggeration to say that almost every man in Ennistone envied George's liberation from morals and almost every woman believed she could save him from himself, but it is an exaggeration worth recording. However, I anticipate. All I want to add here is that George's 'accident' was, for whatever reason, taken by the serious-minded as an example of how pure disorder at one level can cause a fall of moral barriers at another.

As there are quite a large number of McCaffreys in the story that follows, I might, before concluding these introductory remarks, give a brief account of the family. The McCaffreys, as I have already mentioned, were originally commercially minded Quakers. (The name of course is Scottish, but no connection north of the border remains on record.) George's great-great-grandfather, William McCaffrey, had inherited money and some sort of leather business from his father, who was said to be a saddler. William built up a flourishing leather trade and founded a glove and shoe manu-factory which he passed on to his son Albert, and which Albert passed on, in a less flourishing condition, to his son Gerald who was George's grandfather. George's father, Alan McCaffrey, was not interested in the business and Gerald sold it in due course to the Newbolds, an Anglican family associated with St Paul's Church, Victoria Park. (The glove factory still exists partly under their management.) In his later years Gerald McCaffrey left his wife and went to live with a Danish mistress in Copenhagen where he was said to have 'gambled away the family fortune'. He seems in fact to have left Alan reasonably well off, though there were some who said darkly that Alan had inherited more than money from his father, meaning that he inherited a rather unsatisfactory temperament. (The word usually employed was 'raffish'.) Alan became a doctor, reputed to be a good one, and served in a medical capacity in the Second World War. When still fairly young he married Alexandra Stillowen, whose family, also Ennistonians, were Methodists, formerly involved in trade (connected with the defunct Tweed Mill) but now professional people of various kinds. Alan was clever and handsome, and Alexandra was a high-spirited beauty, and the marriage gave general satisfaction, to which predictions that she would 'rue the day' also contributed. The old McCaffrey house in the Crescent had by now been sold to the Burdett family, and the happy pair moved into Alexandra's father's house, Belmont, which her father, a successful lawyer who had moved to London, had only intermittently occupied. In due course two sons were born, first George, then Brian. It also appeared in due course that the gloomy prophets were right. Alan was restless, said to be interested in other women, though without producing any very palpable scandal. Alexandra was said to be concealing her unhappiness. However, Belmont life went on, and the two boys continued to grow up into and indeed out of their teens before anything decisive occurred. Theories differ about exactly how and when the marriage finally broke down, and how this related in time to the advent of Fiona Gates. In fact, to do Alan and Fiona justice, it was fairly clear that Alan and Alexandra were already alienated from each other by the time Fiona appeared on the scene, and divorce proceedings had been talked of, perhaps instituted. Again, the Fiona Gates story is told in several different versions – of which I give the one which I credit most myself.

Fiona, the child of sensible ordinary parents living in East Anglia (her father worked in a bank), being then eighteen years old, at a pop festival jumped impulsively on to the back of a teenage boy's motor cycle with the intention (which she fulfilled) of running away from home. She ran away with her handbag but without a coat. Her youthful 'abductor' took her on his bike as far as Ennistone where, after an argument, he abandoned her. The first person she then met was Alan McCaffrey. She spent the night with Alan (where is not recorded) and then and there (so the legend has it) conceived a child. This child, after causing its parents some initial dismay and indecision, forged resolutely ahead and was duly born and soon thereafter known as Tom McCaffrey. Alex divorced Alan (I shall start to call her 'Alex' now as this is how she is familiarly known) and Alan married Fiona with whom it appeared he was genuinely in love. 'Feckless Fiona', as she was called, must have been a person of charm. 'A dotty girl', people would say, and as they said so they would smile indulgently. And they said that she had 'a happy temperament'. However, Fiona was not destined to be happy for long, since she died of leukaemia when Tom was three years old. It is not true that when she was dying Alex entered the room and took the child away. What is certain is that Tom went to Belmont to join his brothers, with Alan's consent, soon after his mother's death. Alan, very evidently afflicted, left Ennistone and went into practice in Hong Kong where he died three years later in a mysterious accident in a laboratory without ever seeing his youngest child again.

Tom was of course very much younger than George and Brian, who were by this time grown-up. It was said that Alex doted on her little stepson to the exclusion of her sons, causing the latter to conceive a deep hatred for the child. A variant story has it that although Alex adored Tom she never got over her original passionate attachment to her first-born, George, and that although George may have hated Tom, Brian developed a protective fatherly relationship to the newcomer. Meanwhile it should be recounted that George and Brian were busy getting themselves married. George married Stella Henriques, not an Ennistonian, daughter of an English diplomat of Sephardic Jewish extraction. Stella was said to be 'academic' and 'awfully clever', though she gave up her studies on marriage. Brian married Gabriel Bowcock, a cousin of Percy Bowcock who runs the big shop (the Bowcocks are also Quakers). Two other McCaffreys deserve mention: Adam McCaffrey, son of Brian and Gabriel, and Rufus McCaffrey, son, deceased, of George and Stella. Rufus died as a small child in some sort of mishap at his home. Those who take a tolerant view of George's 'temperament' attribute it to continued shock as a result of this loss. Others, less tolerant, put a more sinister construction upon the child's death. At the time of this story Alex is sixty-six, George is forty-four, Brian is forty-one, Tom is twenty, and Adam is eight.

THE EVENTS IN OUR TOWN

A bird was singing in the cold spring-time afternoon in the garden at Belmont. The sky was radiant on one side, leaden on the other. A rainbow had glowed intensely, then faded quickly.

In the drawing-room a wood fire was burning. Beside the fire stood Alexandra McCaffrey, *née* Stillowen. Near the door stood her old servant, Ruby Doyle. Ruby had just asked Alex about a pension; she had simply said, 'What about my pension?' Alex did not understand. She paid Ruby good wages. Did this mean that she wanted to leave? Ruby had been with her since Alex was sixteen.

'Do you want to leave?'

'No.'

'Do you want to stop working?'

Alex asked this question sometimes as a matter of form, but she did not conceive that Ruby would want to stop working; she was in good health, and whatever could she do if she stopped working?

'No.'

'Or work less? I told you I would arrange a daily woman.'

'No.' Ruby had always jealously resisted the idea of a 'daily'.

'If you stopped work I would give you a pension,' said Alex, 'but wages are more than a pension. Do you understand? You don't need a pension. People don't have pensions and wages too.'

'A pension.'

'Just try and understand what I've said,' said Alex, 'Could you take the tea tray?' She poured the dregs of tea out of her cup into the pot, as she always did, so that Ruby could save washing-up by using the same cup.

Ruby advanced and picked up the tray, holding it easily in one hand.

'I saw that fox again.'

'I told you not to talk about foxes.'

Ruby left the room.

The servant was a tall stout woman, as tall as Alex, with a strong grave face. She had a dark complexion and her eyes stared at the world with unemotional critical curiosity. She had a square face and a straight profile and straight bushy hair, almost black. The brown skin of her powerful arms was rough and resembled fish scales. Someone once said that she 'looked like a Mexican', and although this did not make much sense it was accepted as an expressive description. She was a silent woman and wore her skirts very long. She was at first thought to be half-witted, but later on people took to saying, 'Ruby's no fool, she's deep.' Alex herself declared, 'She's a mystery.' Yet she had not felt this until lately; she had not really believed that Ruby was a substantial alien being with thoughts and passions which she concealed.

Alex could make no sense of Ruby's statement about a pension. It might be just one of Ruby's obstinate ephemeral misunderstandings, her tendency to 'get the wrong end of the stick'. On the other hand, it might have been uttered with a special purpose; it might positively mean something else. In fact, now that Alex reflected, she felt sure that it did mean something else, something which Alex did not like. Alex recalled a world of starched white aprons and caps and extremely long stiff damask tablecloths covered with scarcely visible silvery flowers. She had been little more than a child when her father, Geoffrey Stillowen (so the story runs), 'discovered' Ruby in the gipsy camp beyond the Common, in which he took a philanthropic interest, and engaged her as his daughter's maid. Ruby was two years older than Alex. She had looked then as she looked now, brown and hard and strong, solid with a dark rind. They were joined by an old mutual bond. Was this love? The question seemed out of place. It was more an awesome necessity, as if they lived together in prison. Sometimes Alex felt that she could not stand Ruby's presence in the house, but the feeling passed quickly. Usually there was no feeling, only the bond. What did it consist of? Perhaps simply of orders. They spoke about shopping and household arrangements easily and without constraint. They mentioned the weather or occasionally television but without anything like conversation. 'What makes good servants is working with them,' Alex's mother had said. Alex had never worked with Ruby. It's not my fault, Alex thought. Ruby was perfectly intelligent, she was 'all there', only she was a non-talker. They had never eaten together. They never touched each other. Alex had had a full life of triumphs and disasters and marriage and children and thoughts. She had a copious past and vivid interesting dangerous future. Ruby lived under another law. Alex did not feel that she herself was old, and had only lately come to think that Ruby was. Was Ruby wondering whether she would tend Alex in Alex's old age, or Alex her in hers? But something much less rational than that was now at issue.

Alex had never quite dominated Belmont. She had not lived in the house as a child. Her father often let it, and when, between tenancies, the family occupied it for a while Alex felt that she was a visitor. This feeling persisted after she came home to it as a bride. The children, now departed, had made no mark upon the place, and Alan had always regarded it as her father's house. It was a big white stucco house, one of the finest in Victoria Park, with bow windows and 'Strawberry Hill Gothic' windows and a wide graceful curving staircase and a turret. But in spite of the thick spotless glittering white paint which covered every piece of wood, inside and out, it was a sulky house full of its own moody thoughts. Alex could feel them vibrating. It was a frame within which she and Ruby moved about on their separate paths. The house evaded Alex, a reflex of her loss of grip upon life. It menaced her at night with smells of smoke and fears of fire. She had dreams in which she lost her way in the house and came upon rooms she did not know existed where some other form of life was proceeding, or had proceeded recently and ceased. Not that there were dead people there, but dead things. At these times of evasion it seemed that Ruby was more at home in Belmont than Alex was, and Alex turned to Ruby as to a monumental security. Yet this had an opposite aspect. Ruby's great silent being could seem to be maliciously in league with the house against Alex. There were places where things disappeared, dropped out of the world or into another one. It was absurd how things vanished. Yet Ruby would always find them. Ruby, with her gipsy blood, was popularly credited with having second sight. But was it not more likely that Ruby could find them because Ruby had, perhaps unconsciously, hidden them?

It's being alone together at last, thought Alex; we get on each other's nerves. Ruby had been nurse to the three boys, she had seen them grow up and go. Tom, now a student, had gone last. Ruby had never got on with Brian, but she had been close to George and to Tom. Alex had not felt jealous of Ruby in the past; the idea of jealousy would have seemed absurd. But a little while ago when she had seen Ruby talking to George she had felt her servant as an alien power. And only yesterday she had come into the drawing-room

41

and found Ruby sitting there. Ruby had risen and departed silently. No doubt she had just been dusting and had felt tired. But Alex felt menaced as if she were suddenly diminishing in Ruby's eyes. Alex's mother had worked with the servants; she had been at ease with them because the distance between them was absolute. She could never have been where Alex was now and feared what Alex now feared. Was there then a power with which Alex would have to *treat*? Was she supposed to make some significant move, some concession? If so, the old order was falling and a new law was coming to be. Could there be a sudden failure of obedience, a failure of respect which would bring them face to face in some unimaginably crude and painful encounter? The sulky house echoed and Alex could hear Ruby locking and chaining the doors each night. Did she imagine that Ruby was noisier and rougher and clattered more and banged? Alex told nobody about these irrational insubstantial fears which were perhaps nothing more, though indeed nothing less, than the general shadow of her death.

Leaning at the mantelpiece, her bowed head reflected in the big arched gilt-framed mirror, she gently touched the little encampment of bronze figures which had been there so long, since Alan's day. The fire licked its wood hungrily and subsided, image of her thought. How sweet and clean the grey ash was which Ruby scooped out into her pan and mingled with the dust: light and sweet and clean as death. The bird was still singing its wild skirling lyrical song, the missel-thrush, 'the stormcock' Alan used to call it, and 'Northwest Jack'. He had liked birds.

Alex moved to the window and looked out. There was a slight rain like pelting silver in the cool light. The green tiled roof of the Slipper House gleamed wet through the reddish haze of the budding copper beech tree. The curving lawn was luridly bright. Something brown moved across it. A fox. Alex never admitted to anyone that she saw foxes. Ruby was afraid of them. Alex loved them.

She looked at her watch. At six o'clock Brian and Gabriel were coming. They would want to talk about George.

'How was Stella when you saw her?' said Gabriel to Alex.

'Less tragical.'

Gabriel was silent.

Three days had passed since George's exploit. Stella was still in hospital.

For drinks with Alex, they stood. There was a definite time scheme, a symphonic pattern or temporal parabola, definite places; such things calmed the mind. The bow-windowed drawing-room, on the first floor, looked out on the garden. The lamps were on but the curtains were not drawn.

Brian held his glass of apple juice with both hands, like someone holding a candle in a procession. He sometimes drank alcohol, but more and more rarely. He had many things to worry about; money, his job, his son, his brother George. Just now he was worrying about Ruby. He hated the off-hand way in which Alex behaved to Ruby. Yet when he was markedly polite to her (as had happened this evening) Ruby smiled a quick zany mocking smile as if to indicate that she knew he was being condescending.

Brian was not good-looking, but he had an impressive head. Someone had remarked that George and Brian ought to exchange heads. The hearers understood. Brian was pock-marked. He was red-lipped, with sharp wolfish teeth. When younger, with a blond beard, he had looked piratical. Now he was clean-shaven, with very short greyish hair growing in a neat swirl from his crown. He was not very tall, with an assertive face and long blue eyes. He looked anxious and melancholy, and was often irritable. Of course compared with George he was 'nice', but he was not all that nice.

Gabriel was taller, anxious too, with restless moist brown eyes. She had a rather long nose and floppy fairish limply curling hair which she tossed from in front of her face, where it often found itself, with a quick pretty jerk which annoyed Alex. She had an air of fatigue, read by some as gentleness and repose. She always dressed up for visits to her mother-in-law.

Alex was tallest, still handsome everyone said, though as the years went by this saying had become traditional and worn away a little. She had an oval face and a pretty nose, and she had remained slim. She had long eyes like Brian's, of a darker blue, which narrowed by thought or emotion in a fleeting cat-look. (Whereas Brian used to open his eyes wide and stare.) She painted her eyelids discreetly but never used lipstick. She had a long strong consciously mobile mouth. Her sleek well-cut copious hair was a light greyish blond, still managing to glow and gleam, certainly not dyed. She never bothered much with her clothes for these meetings with the Brian McCaffreys. This evening she was wearing a shabby smart rig, an old well-tailored dark coat and skirt, a careless white blouse.

Adam McCaffrey was in the garden with his dog.

'Did the matron say when she was coming out?' said Brian.

'Soon.'

Alex and Gabriel were drinking gin and tonic. Gabriel was smoking.

'Where do you think she should go then?' said Gabriel, tossing back her hair.

'Where do you think?' said Alex. 'Home.'

Gabriel looked at Brian who would not catch her eye. Gabriel thought Stella should come and stay with them when she came out of hospital. Not uttering this thought, she said vaguely to Alex, 'Oughtn't she to rest, to convalesce?'

'Go to the sea,' said Brian, deliberately confusing matters.

'That makes no sense,' said Alex. 'There isn't anywhere to go to at the sea.' The seaside house had been sold; Alex had sold it without consulting the children.

'I suppose we'll go on our excursion as usual,' said Brian. The annual seaside family picnic was an old custom. They had observed it last year, even though the house was sold, going to the same place, only a little farther along the coast. Brian and Gabriel had loved that house, that place, that precious access to the sea.

'That's the future,' said Alex, narrowing her eyes. 'I never know the future.'

'The doctor says we mustn't swim in the Enn any more,' said Gabriel, 'because of the rat-borne jaundice.'

'I never understood why you bothered with that muddy river when you have the Baths,' said Alex.

'Oh well, Adam likes the river – it's more natural and – sort of private and secret – and there are animals and birds and plants and – things –'

'Did he bring Zed today?' said Alex. Zed was Adam's dog. Adam and Zed had run straight out into the garden.

'Yes. I do hope he won't root anything up like when –'

'I always wonder why Adam wanted such a little pretty-pretty dog,' said Alex. 'Most boys like a big dog.'

'We wonder too,' said Brian, aware that Gabriel was hurt and would be deliberately silent. Gabriel knew Brian knew she was hurt, and tried to think of something to say. Alex understood them both and was sorry for her remark but annoyed with them for being so absurdly sensitive.

Adam's dog was a *papillon*, one of the smallest of all dogs, a little dainty long-haired black and white thing with floppy plumy ears and a jaunty plumy tail, and the very darkest of blue-brown shining amused clever eyes. Adam had named him. Asked why, he had replied, 'Because we are Alpha and Omega.'

Gabriel had thought of something to say, not very felicitous perhaps, but she had determined against Brian's advice to say it this time. 'I wonder if you've thought again about letting Brian and me have the Slipper House? It needs living in, and we'd look after it very carefully.'

Alex said at once with a casual air, 'Oh no, I don't think so, it's too small and not a place for children and dogs, and I do use it, you know, it's my studio.'

Alex had used to mess around with paints and clay and *papier mâché*. Brian and Gabriel doubted whether she still did. It was an excuse.

The Slipper House was a sort of folly in the form of a house built at the farther end of the garden in the nineteen-twenties by Alex's father, Geoffrey Stillowen. It was not all that small.

Alex added, 'You can live there when I'm underground, which will be any day now, I daresay.'

'Nonsense, Alex!' Brian said, and he thought: with George in Belmont? Not bloody likely! The unknown and unmentionable provisions of Alex's will were of course of interest to the brothers.

Gabriel said, 'When's Tom coming?'

'In April.'

'Will he be in the Slipper House?'

'No, here of course.'

'He did stay there once.'

'That was in summer, it's far too cold now and I couldn't afford the heating.'

'Is he bringing a friend?' asked Brian.

'He mumbled something on the phone about "bringing Emma," but you know how vague Tom is.'

'Who's this Emma?'

'I've no idea.'

'Anyway a girl, that's good.'

There was some anxiety in the family about whether Tom mightn't be homosexual. Tom, now a student of London University, was living in digs near King's Cross.

'Have you seen George?' said Brian, coming at last to the topic of the evening.

'No,' said Alex. She awaited George. George would come in his own time.

'Have you –?'

'Heard from him, communicated with him? No,' she added. 'Of course not.'

Brian nodded. He understood Alex's feelings. He had tried to telephone George; no answer. And though urged to by Gabriel, he had not written, or again attempted to call.

'I feel we ought to do something,' said Gabriel.

'What *on earth* can we do?' said Alex. George was an emotional subject for all of them.

'People talk so,' said Brian.

'I don't care a damn about people talking,' said Alex, 'and I'm surprised to hear that you do!'

'It isn't –' said Gabriel.

'Of course,' said Brian, 'I care about him, I care if he's hurt or damaged, by what people –'

'I believe you're thinking of yourself,' said Alex.

'I'm thinking of myself too,' said Brian, staring.

'Some people say he was heroic,' said Gabriel, 'rescuing Stella from –'

'You know that's not what they're saying,' said Brian.

'It's not what they're *enjoying* saying,' said Alex. She had received sympathetic remarks from people at the Institute, but she had seen the gleam in their eyes. At the frivolous level at which such agreements were reached, it seemed now to be generally agreed that George McCaffrey had indeed tried to kill his wife.

'I think George should have himself seen to,' said Brian.

'What a perfectly horrible phrase,' said Alex. 'Why don't *you* have yourself seen to?'

'Maybe I should,' said Brian, 'but George – I sometimes feel now that he might do – almost anything –'

'What rubbish you talk,' said Alex, 'it's just spite.'

'I don't feel like that about him,' said Gabriel.

'What do you want him to do about himself anyway?'

'I don't know,' said Brian, 'see a doctor –'

'You mean Dr Roach? Don't be silly. George drinks too much, that's all. So does Gabriel.'

'She doesn't,' said Brian.

'All George needs –'

46

'It's more than that,' said Brian. 'It's more than just drink, of course it is. Call it a chemical imbalance if you like!'

'George is like everyone else, only in his case it shows.'

'Because he's more honest!'

'Because he's a fool.'

'You know perfectly well that George isn't like everyone else, it's gone on too long, he's violent to Stella –'

'Is he? Who says so?'

'Well, not Stella, naturally. You know he gets into rages and hits people and he lost his job because –'

'All right, but –'

'It's more, it's something deep, it's not just being tipsy and stupid, it's –'

'You mean it's something evil, is that what you mean?'

'No, who am I to judge –'

'You seem to be doing nothing but judge.'

'I think we should try to help him as a family,' said Gabriel. 'I think he feels very isolated.'

'I don't mean evil,' said Brian, 'I mean psychologically deep.'

'George doesn't hate anyone,' said Alex, 'except himself.'

'He might talk to Robin Osmore,' said Gabriel. Robin Osmore was the family solicitor.

'If he hates himself,' said Brian, 'let him act accordingly.'

'Do you want your brother to commit suicide?'

'No, I just mean swallow his own bile, not involve other people.'

'I think –' said Gabriel.

'Get himself some electric shocks.'

'Don't *drivel*,' said Alex.

Gabriel said, 'Oh *no*.'

'All right then, what about our great psychiatrist, Ivor Sefton?'

'Sefton is a booby,' said Alex. 'He never cured anyone, they come out dafter than they go in. And he charges the earth.'

'He can have it free on the National Health.'

'Only in a group, imagine George in a group!'

'No one would join his group anyway,' said Brian. 'At least George has got a good pension, I can't think why. His pension is about the same as my salary!'

'George isn't mad.'

'I didn't say he was.'

'Leave him alone. You know we've got to leave him alone.'

'I wonder if Professor Rozanov could help him,' said Gabriel.

'Who?' said Alex.

'John Robert Rozanov,' said Brian. 'Why should he? Anyway he's old and pretty gaga by now.'

'I wonder what happened to the little girl,' said Gabriel.

'What little girl?'

'Wasn't there a little grandchild, the one Ruby's cousin or something was looking after once?'

'I've no notion,' said Brian. 'I don't think Rozanov ever saw the child at all, he wasn't interested; he only cared about his philosophy.'

'And that's the man you imagine could help George!'

'Well, wasn't he his old teacher?' said Gabriel.

'I can't see George bothering with him,' said Brian.

'Leave George alone,' Alex repeated.

In the silence that followed Gabriel drifted over to the bow window, past chairs and sofas piled with cushions embroidered by Alex. This move was a part of the symphony, the sign that Brian and his mother could now take looks at each other and bring the conversation to a suitable close.

Gabriel saw the reflection of her cigarette grow brighter in the glass pane. Then she could see the familiar burly outline of the trees against a dull darkening sky. The self-contained stillness of that garden always troubled her with emotions – awe, envy, fear. She sighed, thinking of that future of which Alex could say nothing. She looked down. A little white thing sped across the lawn like a ball swiftly bowled, then a boy. They vanished under the dark trees. Such a frail little dog, the very image of her destructible son. Adam was not growing, he was already exceptionally small for his age. She had asked the doctor who told her not to worry.

When Adam arrived in the Belmont garden he went straight to the garage. The garage, which used to be known as the 'motor house', was a building with a little French-looking turret which was exactly like the big turret on the big house. There was a row of last year's martins' nests under the eaves, but this year's martins had not yet come. Inside the garage was the white Rolls-Royce which Alan McCaffrey had driven carefully in on some long ago evening, perhaps, as he pressed down the brake, not even knowing that he was about to leave his wife forever. He never came back for the car; and Alex had not touched it since. It was said to be very valuable.

Adam climbed into the Rolls and sat holding the wheel and turning it cannily to and fro, while Zed (who always had to be helped up however earnestly he tried) sat complacently upon the soft old smelly leather seat beside him, looking in his white feathery fur like a plump roosting bird. Zed had one or two elegant black spots on his back, and long dark plumed black and brown ears which crowned his head like a wig or hat. He had a little domed head and a short slightly retroussé nose and beautiful dark brown eyes with hints of dark blue like shot silk. He could look magisterial and amused and sardonic, or sometimes flirtatious, hurling himself back in graceful abandoned attitudes; but then, suddenly romping and undignified, his entire concentrated person could express the purest of pure joy.

When Adam got tired of driving the Rolls he ran across the lawn to the Slipper House, which was locked of course, and peered in through the windows. He had been inside but not often. He liked being outside looking in, watching the quiet old-style furniture in the silent rooms which were now becoming so dark and lonely. With pleasant dread he imagined seeing some strange motionless person standing inside and looking out. After that he had to visit various trees, the copper beech and the birches and the fir tree whose noble reddish trunk twisted up so high, visible here and there amid its heavy piles of dark foliage. He especially loved the ginkgo, so odd and so old. He gently touched the lower parts of the tree where the little stalkless scrolls of green were just beginning to appear. He lay down under the tree and let Zed jump on his chest and sit with neat front paws resting on his collar-bone. However quickly he raised his head, he could not surprise Zed looking anywhere else than straight into his eyes with his provocative intent mocking stare. When they tired of this game, Adam crept away into the long grass trying to avoid hurting the snails whom the rain had tempted forth, and whose weight bent the blades into arches. He crawled under some brambles and under some ivy into the deepest part of the shrubbery beside the old tennis court overgrown with elder bushes, where the foxes lived. Adam, like his grandmother, knew but kept the fox secret. The great earth, under mounds of finely dug soil, had wide dark entrances into which Adam and Zed gazed with awe, only Adam kept a firm hold on Zed in case he should be tempted to go down. (In fact Zed had no intention of going down, not that he was not a brave dog, but he suffered from claustrophobia and the whole place smelt extremely dangerous.)

Adam's mother called him across the dark garden.

'Coming!' He picked up Zed and put him inside his shirt, warm soaking-wet dog against warm soaking-wet boy.

'Damn, that creepy priest is here,' said Brian.

'How do you know?'

'There's his bike.' A lady's bicycle was propped against the fence.

Brian and Gabriel and Adam and Zed were returning from their visit to Alex. Their house (though it was not in Victoria Park) was not far away. It was dark now and the sweeping headlights showed the bicycle, the fence, the yellow privet hedge, the side of the house, painted pink, as the car turned off the road into the garage.

They tumbled out, Adam and Zed racing first along the side passage toward the kitchen door which was always left open. And into the kitchen indeed, and not for the first time, the creepy priest had penetrated.

When Brian and Gabriel arrived Father Bernard had already established his usual easy relations with Adam and Zed, holding the little dog up aloft in one hand while Adam laughed and tugged at the black robe.

Gabriel, aware of how much Father Bernard annoyed Brian, and of how jealous Brian was of people who got on easily with Adam, quickly, after greeting the priest, put Adam's supper, which was standing ready, on to a tray. 'Here, Adam, take your supper, then quick to bed, no television. Good heavens, you're soaked, find a towel –'

Adam and Zed vanished.

'It's your supper time,' said Father Bernard, 'I won't trouble you, I'm just calling for a little minute, I won't stay –'

There could be no question of his being asked to supper. Gabriel, avoiding Brian's look, said, 'Have a quick sherry.'

The priest accepted the sherry. Turning politely to Brian he said by way of greeting, 'Christ is risen.' It was the week after Easter.

Brian said, 'I know, he rose last Sunday, I suppose he is still risen.'

'Good news is never stale,' said Father Bernard.

Brian thought, he's come to talk to Gabriel about George. This thought, together with the postponement of his supper, caused him extreme irritation. He could not decide whether to stay and spoil the *tête-à-tête* which no doubt they both wanted, or go and leave them to it. He decided to go. Gabriel would feel guilty and he would get his supper sooner. He marched into the sitting-room and turned on the television. He despised television but still craved to see the misfortunes of others.

Gabriel and the priest sat down at the kitchen table. Gabriel took some sherry and a cigarette. She touched his sleeve (Gabriel was a 'toucher'). Of course, being a Quaker, she did not officially belong to his flock, but he took a liberal view of his responsibilities.

Father Bernard Jacoby, a convert of Jewish origin, was the parish priest. He was an Anglican, but so 'high' that it did not occur to anyone to call him 'the Rector' or address him as 'Rector'. He was addressed as 'Father' by those who approved of him. Many viewed him with suspicion, not least his bishop, who had been heard to remark that Jacoby was 'not a priest, but a shaman'. Some opined darkly that the time would come when he would celebrate one Latin Mass too many. His Church reeked of incense. He was a comparative newcomer of whose past not much was known, except that he had been a chemistry student at Birmingham and a champion wrestler (or perhaps boxer). He was thought to be homosexual, and lived permanently under various small clouds.

'Well, Father –' Gabriel knew that he had come to talk about George and some excitement stirred within her.

'Well and well and well indeed. I was refreshed to see Alpha and Omega so happy. We should welcome such glimpses of pure joy and feed upon them like manna.'

'Not everyone is glad to see others happy,' said Gabriel. In talking to Father Bernard she adopted a solemn mode of speech which was not her usual manner.

'True.' The priest did not pursue this evident but pregnant idea. He gazed amiably at Gabriel with an air of cunning attention.

Father Bernard was fairly tall, a handsome man though odd-looking. He wore his dark straight sleek hair parted in the middle and falling in fine order to the level of his chin. He had a large nose with prominent nostrils, and rather shiny or luminous brown eyes whose penetrating directness expressed (perhaps) loving care or (perhaps) bland impertinence. He was thin, with thin mobile hands. He always wore a black cassock, clean, and of material suited to the season, and somehow managed to make his dog-collar look like old lace.

'How is Stella?'

'Wonderful,' said Gabriel.

'Of course, but how is she?'

Gabriel, who had seen her that morning, reflected. 'She only says *accurate* things. I don't know what she feels, but whatever it is she's making some enormous effort to get it right. She cares about her dignity; in her it's a kind of virtue.' She added, 'Why don't you go and see her?'

'I have. I wondered what you thought.'

Stella was not to be numbered among Father Bernard's fans. It was somehow typical of the man to have fans. She did not dislike him, as Brian did, but she was suspicious. She did not believe in God. But then neither did many of the fans.

'What did she say?' said Gabriel. This question was prompted by senseless jealousy. She was full of senseless jealousies.

'We spoke. She said little. I said little. I sat. I went.'

'I'm sure she was glad.'

'I don't know.'

Gabriel wondered if Father Bernard had been disappointed at not having 'got something out of' Stella. Brian said he was always scurrying about trying to charm afflicted people.

Gabriel said, 'About George – if you want me to tell you what really happened I can't, I mean I only know –'

'Oh what really happened – who ever knows what really happened – God knows.'

George was not a fan either, but he was, to Gabriel's mind, a more promising subject for the priestly charm than Stella was. At any rate, she liked the idea of some finally desperate and broken-down George being mastered by Father Bernard.

'What do you think happened?' he said.

'It was an accident, of course.'

It was remarkable how readily people, including Gabriel, thought ill of George. In fact Gabriel thought George had done it on purpose, and kept in fascinated suspense the idea that he had half intended to kill Stella. She had once only, for a moment, seen George in one of his rages, shouting at his wife 'I'll kill you!' It was a terrifying sight, Gabriel had never seen anything like it. Gabriel knew that Stella would never forgive her for having had that glimpse behind the scenes. Stella tried to conceal George's undoubted domestic violence, just as she tried (vainly) to conceal his sexual infidelities. He had also attacked people who annoyed him, a gipsy, a bus conductor, a student, perhaps others: 'losing his temper when drunk' was one way of putting it. A charge of 'grievous bodily harm' was once in view, it was said, only clever Robin Osmore kept George out of court. Alex's professed view that George was just a random forgivable drunk was not generally held. The absence from his life of ordinary norms of politeness was taken as a sign of deeper moral anarchy. It seemed that there were barriers instinctively erected by civilized citizens, which just did not exist for George. People were afraid of him, and Brian was not alone in thinking that George 'might do anything'. People sensed a monster, no doubt they wanted a monster. Yet what did the evidence amount to?

Gabriel said, 'Everyone speaks ill of him.'

'They like a scapegoat, to have someone at hand who is officially more sinful than they are.'

'Exactly. Perhaps he's made worse by our opinions. But I'm sure he is terrible to Stella.'

'You said it was an accident.'

'Of course – but I mean – I think she ought to get away from him.'

'Because he might kill her?'

'No, to be alone and have another life, she's obsessed by George, she's wasting herself, her love doesn't do him good, it just enrages him. Her love is like duty, like something sublime, made of idealism and awful self-confidence. She thinks she'll elevate him. She ought to kneel down beside him.'

'Do you tell her this?'

'Of course not! She's too proud, she's the proudest person I know. I wish you'd talk to George.'

'And do what to him?'

'Batter him, break him down, make him weep.'

'Tears of repentance and relief?'

'You could save him, George could be changed by love, not Stella's, another kind. His awfulness is an appeal for love.'

The priest laughed, heartily and too long, then snapped his fingers, a habitual gesture when he wanted the discussion to change course. He stood up. 'Do you know when Professor Rozanov is coming?'

'No, I don't,' said Gabriel, rising too, annoyed at this brusque treatment of her moving appeal.

'Did you ever meet him?' Father Bernard knew of our distinguished citizen only by hearsay.

'No,' said Gabriel. 'I saw him in the street once. Brian met him, and of course George was his pupil.'

During the last exchange Brian had turned up the sound of the television considerably in order to demonstrate his displeasure.

'What does Brian think of him?' said the priest, raising his voice.

'Better ask him,' said Gabriel, raising hers and opening the door. 'Brian! Father Bernard wants to know what you think about Professor Rozanov.'

Brian came in, walked across to the gas stove and peered into one of the saucepans, pulling its lid off and banging it on again. He stared at the priest who did not, however, at once repeat his question, but said instead, 'Why is Professor Rozanov visiting us?'

'He isn't visiting me. I don't know, arthritis, come to take the waters –'

'Do you know where he'll be staying?'

'No idea, Ennistone Royal Hotel.' (Queen Victoria had visited Ennistone when Victoria Park was building, and went to the Institute where the Prince Consort praised the waters and spoke of Baden-Baden.)

'He hasn't been here since his mother died,' said Gabriel, 'but people say he's coming back now for good, he's going to retire here.'

'What is he like?' The television noise from the next room was almost drowning their voices.

'Rozanov? He's a charlatan. You know what a charlatan is, a fake, a trickster, an impostor, a busybody who pretends to be able –'

'Oh don't *shout*,' cried Gabriel as she ran to turn off the television.

The priest made his adieux.

Later in the evening Gabriel and Brian were still talking about George and Stella and Alex.

'You must drop that Slipper House idea,' said Brian, 'Alex would never let us live there. Besides we'd hate it, right on top of her.'

'We'd use the back gate –'

'Forget it.'

'I *want* that house.'

'You're so acquisitive. And you think Alex is wasting our substance.'

'She's so extravagant –'

'You mustn't think like that, it's mean, it's petty.'

'I know!'

'You shudder if Alex breaks a cup.'

'She's careless, and she will use the best stuff all the time.'

'Why not, it isn't your cup, it probably never will be. She'll leave everything to George. You know we wouldn't lift a finger.'

'She might have consulted us before selling Maryville.'

Maryville was the seaside house.

'It was nothing but trouble, that place; dry rot and then squatters –'

'Going to the sea isn't the same after you've lived there; it's made that lovely piece of coast seem all sad.'

'There you go again, property, property, property!'

'Alex doesn't use the Slipper House. That time last summer I saw her painting stuff, it was just the same as it was years ago.'

'Maybe she meditates there, it isn't our business, try to imagine her life, for heaven's sake. You don't like this house.'

'I do because it's our house, but it's so small.'

'The trouble with you is you've never got used to being a poor Bowcock.' Gabriel's branch of the family had not, for some reason, shared in the ancestral money.

Gabriel laughed. 'Maybe! But we need more room. If we have Stella here –'

'Do we have to have Stella here?'

'I think so.'

'She wouldn't come.'

'I talked to her again, very tactfully. I think she's afraid to go back to George.'

'Husbands and wives often understand each other better than well-meaning outsiders imagine.'

'Anyway she wants an interval.'

'You seem to want her to leave George.'

'She goes on thinking she can cure him, she goes on looking for little signs that things are getting better –'

'That's love.'

'It's an illusion.'

'In a way,' said Brian, 'it can't be an illusion.'

'I think George really hates her.'

'That's something she will never believe.'

'That's the trouble. Think of the misery there must be in that house, and George involved with that other woman. I think Stella should have a quiet time to think it over. She's still in a state of shock, she's sort of prostrate.'

'Stella prostrate? Never!' Brian admired Stella.

'Do you know, George hasn't been to see her since the first day?'

'George is demonic, like Alex,' said Brian. 'He would feel it stylish not to turn up, then it would seem inevitable.'

'You keep saying he's a dull dog.'

'Yes, he's commonplace, a thoroughly vulgar fellow, like Iago.'

'Like – really! But Alex isn't demonic, she's become much quieter, a sort of recluse, I feel quite worried about her.'

'You love worrying about people. Alex just doesn't want to see how old and decrepit her friends are. She sees herself as a priestess, she goes on playing the *femme fatale*, she imagines men falling madly in love with her.'

'I suppose they did. Wasn't Robin Osmore madly in love with her?'

'Dozens of them were. But that was a hundred years ago. And it wasn't Robin Osmore, it was his father. *That*'s how old she is.'

'She doesn't look it.'

'I keep longing for the time when Alex is just a poor old wreck, a pathetic confused old thing wanting to be looked after, but it never comes.'

'You'll hate it when it does.'

'I shall dance.'

'You won't. You're proud of her, you all are. There's a sort of governessy *grande dame* aspect of Alex which supports you.'

'OK, but that's a metaphysical matter and strictly private. Just don't ask me to love her.'

'You should talk to her about George, it's no good with me there. I really do think we should take some sort of collective responsibility for George.'

'Women always want to rescue men, to save them from themselves, or help them to find themselves, or something.'

'I said *collective* responsibility –'

'George needs electric shocks and some of his brain removing.'

'I can't think how he can live with himself.'

'Stella ought to ship him out to Japan. He'd do well in Japan, they are all Georges there.'

'He must be in hell.'

'George in hell? Not a bit of it. He blames us.'

'Well, we are to blame because we speak ill of him, we've turned against him and abandoned him.'

'I mean he blames us, everybody, the world, everything except George. He has chronic hurt vanity, cosmic resentment, metaphysical envy. George has always behaved as if he were being outrageously cheated, something stolen, something lost.'

'I suppose he has guilt feelings.'

'It isn't guilt, it's shame, it's loss of face. He's probably more worried about losing his driving licence than about having nearly killed his wife. Anything wicked or evil in himself he immediately shifts on to the enemy, the others. He's lost all sense of ordinary reality.'

'He feels insecure.'

'I daresay Hitler felt insecure!'

'You're exaggerating wildly. Everyone says how violent George is, but we don't know the circumstances, it all builds up by hearsay. I think people are just against him because he's unconventional and that frightens them. They're afraid of him because he's not polite!'

'He's certainly given up the niceties of human intercourse, but that's just a symptom. George hates everybody. He makes one understand terrorists.'

'Can't you feel pity for him? Do you think a day or an hour passes when he doesn't think about Rufus?'

'Loss of child, loss of face.'

'How can you –'

'He probably pitched the child down the stairs in a fit of rage and then convinced himself it was Stella's fault.'

'Don't say that, Brian, I know other people do, but *you* mustn't, *please* –'

'Sorry, you're right, don't cry, for God's sake what are you crying about?'

Tears, the tears that came so easily, had risen into Gabriel's eyes. Her happiness was so terribly haunted by fears, images of loss, terrible images, mad images. If Rufus had lived he would have been Adam's age. She had developed a fantasy that George would kill Zed. Then that he would kill Adam.

Brian did not know what she was thinking (for of course she did not divulge such insane notions) but he knew the sort of things she was thinking. He patted her wet hand on which tears had fallen. 'There now, there now. It isn't Rufus, you know. George was a little horror when he was a boy.'

'I expect you were too.'

'He *enjoyed* drowning those kittens.'

'Don't tell me that story!'

'Well, they had to be drowned. Don't cry about it.'

'I still think Professor Rozanov might help him,' said Gabriel, drying her tears. 'You didn't really mean what you said about Rozanov to Father Bernard?'

'No, of course not. I meant it for your creepy friend!'

'I don't think he came about George at all, he came about Rozanov.'

'Makes a change.'

'George respects Professor Rozanov, he'd pay attention to him. After all, he went all the way to America to see him that time.'

'Whatever happened on that occasion,' said Brian, 'it was certainly not a success. George may have admired Rozanov at one time, but I doubt if he cares a fig for him now. The trouble with George is he gets away with things. He's popular because people like horrible men. Hitler, Napoleon, Stalin. Who's our most loved king? Henry the Eighth. If only George could get into really serious trouble it might sober him up. Or if everyone ganged up against him and *did* something, not just gratifying their malice by talking, I think George ought to be lynched. And he will be lynched one day if he goes on. There's collective responsibility for you.'

'No,' said Gabriel, 'no.' And 'Oh dear –' She often said that. One of these awful fantasies had taken hold of her. How could George bear to see Adam growing up? To banish it she breathed deeply, breathing in some absolutely quiet air which she knew was really everywhere, but which she only experienced at these moments of refuge. But fear too was in the quiet air. She hoped Adam could not read her mind. He had said to her once, 'You mustn't protect me against the sad things.'

She said now, 'Do you think Adam might be a vet when he grows up, or a naturalist? He cares so much about animals.'

'I don't think so,' said Brian. 'He's not interested in details, he would never do a botanical or anatomical drawing. This animal thing, it's different – it's part of something else – sort of sentimental – well, no, symbolic rather – like a sort of funny little religion –' He could not explain, though he felt and saw what he meant. It was all somehow part of Adam's changeling quality, his strangeness and absoluteness as a boy; and Brian could not imagine Adam grown up and did not want to picture him as a deep-voiced youth with a hairy chest and a sex life. Perhaps he could not imagine the future because the future did not exist. And Adam was not growing. Would his son live on as a dwarf with a child's mind? And here his deep confused thoughts were perhaps reaching out and touching the deep confused thoughts of his wife.

'It'll be good to see Tom again,' said Gabriel. 'He hardly ever comes now. Do you think he's avoiding George – or Alex?'

'Young chaps avoid possessive mothers.'

'I think he sheered off because George was jealous.'

'Because Alex is so attached to Tom? Poor deprived old George. Here we go again. Let's go to bed.' Brian stood up. He said, 'Tom – yes – Tom – he's *happy*.'

And you are not, thought Gabriel sadly.

They went to bed.

Brian and Gabriel McCaffrey had known each other forever; they went to the same Friends' Meeting House, to the same children's parties, then to the same dances. Brian, growing up, was handsome, a young Viking. Gabriel fell in love. Later Brian did too. He disliked forward sexy girls. Gabriel was pretty, quiet, shy, hiding behind her floppy hair. She peered admiringly at Brian. Brian was a sober and serious-minded young man. He wanted a loyal truthful gentle wife and an open peaceful simple mode of existence. Time proved he had chosen well. Gabriel and Brian continued to love each other although in many ways they belonged to different human tribes.

Brian, unlike his father and grandfather whose relation to Quakerism had been merely sentimental, took religion seriously. He may have been influenced in this by his 'godfather', William Eastcote (popularly known as 'Bill the Lizard'), a very devout person and pillar of the Meeting, and a cousin of the well-known philanthropist Milton Eastcote. The Eastcotes were a wealthy family (also originally 'in trade') and William retired early from a career at the bar to devote himself, like his cousin, to good works. Brian, with Gabriel and Adam, went to Meeting every Sunday. He did not believe in God, but the Ennistone Friends were not anxious about this matter. The Mystery of God was one with the Inner Light of the Soul, and the illumined Way was the Good Life, where truthful vision spontaneously prompted virtuous desire. Herein lay the perfect simplicity of duty. Brian pictured himself as austere and pure in heart. He wanted to live the Good Life with his wife and his son, but he found this difficult. He also wanted to do some great thing in the world. (Gabriel had believed in Brian's great thing.) But now it was clear he would not. He worked on the Ennistone Town Council in the education department.

Brian found the Good Life difficult for simple but deep reasons. He was selfish. He did what he wanted and Gabriel did what he wanted too. This had gone on so long that Brian imagined (wrongly, as it happened) that Gabriel had ceased to notice it. Gabriel wanted to travel. Brian hated travel, he wanted to stay at home and read. They stayed at home and read. Gabriel wanted to entertain. Brian thought social life was insincere. They did not entertain. Brian ate fast, Gabriel ate slow. Meals ended when Brian had finished. Brian was often irritable, sometimes angry, and (but this more rarely) if he was very displeased he withdrew himself from Gabriel. This sulky withdrawal, the result simply of his own ill-temper, he felt as a black iron pain, an experience of hell, yet he could not inhibit this form of violence. He did not display anger to Adam, but felt in his relation to his son a terrible vague inadequacy, a sheer awkward embarrassed clumsiness which distorted communication. Sometimes it seemed to him that Adam understood this and came to him with deliberate olive branches, little touching reassuring gestures of affection, which Brian found himself accepting gracelessly as if he were being condescended to. Brian lusted after other women to an extent which would have amazed Gabriel had she known about it, but this aspect of his frailty he was able to keep strictly under control. Some said there was a George inside Brian waiting to be let out, but so far there had been no manifestation of this hypothetical presence.

Gabriel was aware of her grievances without being obsessed by them. Her chief grievance, apart from Brian's selfishness to which she quietly gave in, forgiving though not forgetting, was that she had never studied anything and at the age of thirty-four knew nothing. Brian had studied sociology at the University of Essex. Gabriel, after a year at secretarial college, had begun to think she might after all go to a university when she was overtaken by marriage. Now who and what was she? Brian's wife, Adam's mother. When she compared herself with Stella or Alex she felt unreal. She was a 'poor Bowcock', one of the muddled ones who had no grasp on life. Her father, a municipal engineer in South London, was dead. She had got on well with her mother and her brother but they had gone painlessly to Canada when her brother married and it did not even matter to her now that they detested Brian. Gabriel knew that a certain kind of self-satisfaction was essential to her and she was determined not to become a discontented woman. She made her home her fortress where she was secure and content to be invisible. She was not out in the open, battle-scarred and unhoused like Stella and George whose adventures appalled and fascinated her. She was not like them. When in the early morning she let the cold clear water run and filled the kettle to make tea, she felt innocent and fresh. One of the qualities of her interior castle she had acquired from Adam – a sort of animism whereby everything, not only the flies which had to be caught and let out of windows, the wood lice which had to be tenderly liberated into the garden, the spiders which were to be respected in their corners, but also the knives and forks and spoons and cups and plates and jugs, and shoes, and poor socks that had no partners, and buttons which might become uncherished and lost, had all a life and being of their own, and friendliness and rights. All these became an extension of her existence as they were an extension of his and in this common being, as in a vulnerable extended body, she secretly mingled with her son.

The family at large, though accepted as 'hers', meant less to her. She admired and envied and pitied Stella. She liked and was interested in and annoyed by Alex. She was fond of Tom about whom Brian had such mixed up feelings, but she bridled her fondness in case Adam should sustain any tiniest jealous hurt. On the whole she regarded Tom as a simple fellow, blessedly harmless. Like Brian, she envied Tom's cheerfulness, but on Adam's behalf not her own. When Adam was twenty would he be cheerful? She doubted it. Would Adam ever be twenty? George was another matter. Gabriel had strange thoughts about George. These thoughts had gained a definition for her from an incident which occurred a few years ago. Gabriel had been sitting in Diana's Garden at the Baths with some acquaintances and the talk had turned to George and several people (Mrs Robin Osmore was one, and Anthea Eastcote, then a school girl) had said some mildly disobliging things about her brother-in-law. They fell silent when George appeared nearby, having undoubtedly overheard. As he went away Gabriel felt constrained to leap up and run after him. She caught him up as he was coming out of the Institute building into the street. She touched his arm and said blushing, 'I didn't say anything against you, I don't

61

think anything bad about you.' George smiled, bowed slightly and went on. When she next met him in company, his eyes showed consciousness of the significant occasion. Gabriel was already regretting what now seemed her imprudent impulse, which she had not mentioned to Brian. What she had said was not even true. She did think bad things about him. And now she had made a secret link between them, an invisible bond like a rope the other end of which she could occasionally feel George sardonically, maliciously, ever so gently, twitching. There was some little, very small, piece of Gabriel's heart which harboured the belief, allegedly so common among Ennistonian women, that she and she alone could save George from himself.

Alex put the key into the door of the Slipper House. It was eleven o'clock at night on the evening of Brian and Gabriel's visit. As the door opened a damp woody smell emerged. Suddenly frightened, Alex fumbled for the light, went in and closed and locked the door behind her.

The Slipper House had been built by Alex's eccentric father, Geoffrey Stillowen, in the nineteen-twenties, and was known to the few local persons interested in this matter as a 'gem of *art déco*'. It dated from roughly the same period as the Ennistone Rooms. It was made of concrete, once white, now a stained blotchy grey, with curving corners and curving steel-framed windows and a shallow sloping green-tiled roof. There was a sort of Assyrian (or possibly Egyptian) superstructure, originally painted green and brown, over the front door. The door had an oval stained-glass panel depicting very upright stylized red tulips. There was more floral stained-glass on the upper landing and a large stained-glass screen in the drawing-room representing an aeroplane among clouds. The drawing-room also contained a very slippery window seat with carved ends and the original cushions with green and grey wavy designs, a fine large mirror with a fountain cut into the glass, and a table with a glass top supported on a metal arabesque. The flat fat oatmeal-coloured three-piece suite in the drawing-room was also original, and so was a set of tall mauve vases whose members were dotted here and there. The house was sparsely furnished, partly with oddments made of bamboo which Alex had put in during her 'creative' period. The floors were all of the most exquisite pale parquet, with designs made out of different woods. It was from this that the house had got its name, since Geoffrey Stillowen had insisted that no ordinary shoes, only soft slippers, be worn in the house, and there still stood beside the door a box of various-sized and coloured slippers which he had provided. Our townspeople made their own assessment of the odd name which sounded in their ears vaguely improper, as it might be of some oriental bower or seraglio, a discreet house of ill fame where exotic women pad.

Brian had not been far wrong in thinking that Alex used the Slipper House as a place of meditation. She liked the emptiness, the spaciousness of the house, its lack of clutter after the mass of objects and trophies which filled the big house. Once, she had played at painting there, made figures out of clay and *papier mâché* and painted them like little gaudy Indian gods. She had done watercolours when she was young and had returned, after Alan left her, to what she thought of as her career as a failed painter. The little study room next to the kitchen was still strewn with paints and brushes which she had laid down a long time ago. She looked at them briefly as she went through the house turning on the lights. As she went she shuddered with a superstitious uncanny feeling which was also a kind of pleasure of aloneness.

Alex had long ago lost the Methodist religion of her childhood, but a religious sense subsisted in her, perverted into a kind of animistic obsession. Adam had some such odd sense of the world, only his pantheism was innocent, partook perhaps of that primal positive innocence which has made so many thinkers want to believe in metempsychosis. Alex's quickening of the world about her was neurotic and corrupted, the final distortion of those artistic impulses with which she had so irresolutely played. It was as if things appeared and disappeared, dematerialized with malicious whimsy. Some things were like little animals; or rather, they were live things, with the clumsiness of objects, which fell about, shuffled, jolted and rolled. Perhaps Alex's painted fetishes had been homeopathic attempts to placate these tiny malign deities. There were little thing-creatures that hid things, mouse-like movements in corners which ceased when Alex looked, substantial shadows which she flinched to avoid and which vanished as she moved. Alex had always collected things, but now it was as if they were gradually turning against her. In a way she knew that 'all this was nonsense', and although it frightened her, it did not frighten her very much because of a kind of complicit frisson which these experiences brought with them.

This leak of her unconscious mind into her surroundings, this theft of her vitality by malicious forces, was now becoming connected for Alex with the problem of Ruby, and this upset her much more. She did not really think that Ruby deliberately hid things and found them again, but it was as if Ruby had become the human 'front' of a revolt against Alex of her most familiar world. Alex could not imagine her life without Ruby, if Ruby were simply to go away. Herein Ruby appeared as a defence, not before recognized as such, against gathering forces. On the other hand, if what Ruby wanted was to be welcomed at last, by some revolutionary change, into an equal and quite different relationship with her employer, this Alex felt to be unthinkable, the final breakdown of sense and order. There were no ordinary gestures of affection and recognition between them which could possibly mediate such a change. It could not be done. Alex would resist it to her last breath.

Frightened by the dark shiny windows of the Slipper House through which beings could look from the outside, she went round closing the shutters, on the inside of which in a faraway time the young Ennistonian painter Ned Larkin, a discovery of Geoffrey Stillowen, had painted powdery garden scenes in pastel shades. The pictures vaguely represented the Belmont garden, the ginkgo, the fir tree, the copper beech, the birch trees, now suitably modified into pastness, with distant views of Belmont and the Slipper House. In the drawing-room, members of the family were similarly represented, in period costume, in antique poses, in a faint golden long ago light. Geoffrey Stillowen in white flannels, blond and youthful, was seated, reading a book with a tennis racket leaning against his knee. His wife Rosemary, standing behind, was opening a white parasol. There was also a picture of Alex as a pretty little girl holding some flowers. And a slim beautiful golden-haired youth, Alex's elder brother who had been killed in the war, a shadow now, a shade, scarcely ever entering Alex's thoughts except when she saw his image in this place. She turned from it. The Slipper House lived in the past, Alex's hall of meditation was a time machine; but the past for which she craved was a faintly scented atmosphere, untroubled by the staring ghosts of individual people.

Tonight, however, individual people pressed upon her, and she could not attain the detached nervous vagueness which her aloneness needed. As she walked, for she always prowled all over the house in these late secret visits, she began to think about George. She wondered if George would come to her and speak to her, as he sometimes used to. She felt every day the minute movement of something which separated him from her. Perhaps this was her sense of old age, so inconceivable yet so near. She had lost George and found him again. Would he come to her now? The woman, a prostitute, with whom George was said to be 'involved', was some sort of connection of Ruby's. Ruby had many such connections, and Alex disliked this connecting up of things which ought to be separate; it had begun to fit in too well with her sense of an evil conspiracy. There was a bad network. Perhaps it was to escape that network that Tom had withdrawn from her. Alex loved Tom; not best, George was best. About Brian she felt little. The women were outsiders; Gabriel with her droopy hair and her paper handkerchiefs, Stella so intelligent, so hard, so bad for George. Adam was a disturbing object, kin to her yet inaccessible.

Another individual occupied Alex's restless mind this evening: John Robert Rozanov. (Alex had only pretended not to pick up his name when it was mentioned by Gabriel.) Alex had got to know John Robert slightly when he was young, already a little famous (he was older than Alex) and no longer living in Ennistone but returning from his grand university world to visit his mother who still lived in the town. His parents (his grandfather was a Russian émigré) were not well off and lived in the poorer quarter, in an area called Burkestown, remote from leafy Victoria Park. However, the Rozanovs were Methodists (John Robert's father had married a local girl) and attended the same church (in Druidsdale near the Common) as Alex's family, hence a slight acquaintance. Geoffrey Stillowen, engaged as a church-goer in various charitable enterprises, met John Robert's father. Alex vaguely remembered seeing John Robert as a boy, then as a youth. She had never felt any interest in him, partly (she was not snobbish) because she found him physically repulsive. Then when (after the publication of his first book, *Logic and Consciousness*) he turned out to be 'brilliant' and began to be well-known as one of the 'young philosophers', it became chic for people in Ennistone to boast about him, announcing casually that they had known him all their lives. Alex, then nineteen, indulging in this little falsehood, caught the attention of one of her friends, a girl called Linda Brent with whom she had been at boarding-school. Linda was now at the university and was thrilled to learn that Alex actually knew John Robert Rozanov.

Alex, continuing to show off, asked Linda to come and stay, saying she would exhibit the prodigy. Alex's stranger mother, another alien, had died not long before, and Geoffrey Stillowen was occupying Belmont. Linda came. A little party was arranged and John Robert was invited. ('He won't come,' said Alex's brother Desmond. 'He will, he'll be delighted,' said Geoffrey, who had a high sense of his own importance.) He came, and Alex introduced him to Linda. Linda of course (ignoring handsome Desmond) at once fell in love with him. Alex laughed. She laughed less when she read in a newspaper a remarkably short time afterwards that fabulous young John Robert Rozanov, after whom so many clever young ladies were chasing, was about to marry Miss Linda Brent. Alex never forgave either of them. More than that, she became, as she saw it afterwards, temporarily insane. She fell madly in love with John Robert Rozanov herself. Why on earth had she introduced this wonderful person to Linda? It was sheer stupid vanity. Why had she ingeniously done herself this awful damage? Why had she not had the wit and the creative imagination to cultivate this very unusual man? Surely by rights he belonged to her. *She* ought to have married him!

She did not see Rozanov again until some time later when a slightly apologetic Linda visited Ennistone with her husband, and by then Alex was engaged to charming popular Alan McCaffrey and had recovered from her paranoiac episode. The Rozanovs went to America where Linda later died leaving a daughter with whom, rumour had it, Rozanov never got on. The daughter married an obscure American academic called Meynell; she died and he either died or vanished, leaving behind a child, the little neglected waif before mentioned, about whom, it appeared, Rozanov cared even less. Rozanov came back to England for a time and taught in London, where George McCaffrey became his pupil. Later the philosopher went back to America whither, on the occasion described by Brian as unsuccessful, George followed him. Alex did not see Rozanov during his London period. She had troubles of her own and wanted to hide her unhappiness. (Like George, she hated to 'lose face'.) Alan had left her and was living in Ennistone with Fiona Gates. Then when Fiona became ill Alex developed her obsession about getting hold of Tom, whom she had always coveted. All this while the John Robert whom Alex, during the brief time of her insane remorse, had so intensely imagined, lay dormant within her: an imprint, a little live ghost, an abiding private double

66

of a man who no longer concerned her. This double now stirred and grew in her imagination with the news that John Robert Rozanov was returning to Ennistone. Why was he returning? Was it possible he was returning for *her*?

'What a bloody mess,' said George. He used to chide Diane for her untidiness. Now he viewed the signs of increasing disorder with a certain satisfaction.

'Have you seen Stella?' asked Diane.

'No. I meant to go again. I felt I ought to go. You charmingly told me to go. I didn't go. Then it became difficult to go. Then it became impossible to go. Then it became essential not to go. It became a duty not to go, it became a sexual urge. Do you understand?'

'No. I'm sorry about the mess, I'd have tidied it up if I'd known you were coming, I never know when you're coming, I wish I did.'

'So do I. Like the Messiah I am eternally expected. I expect myself.'

'I miss you. I am starved of love.'

'If that is so then derry down derry it's evident very our tastes are one.'

'I wonder if you'll ever marry me.'

'If I married you I'd murder you.'

'Better dead than unwed.'

'You yearn for respectability.'

'Yes, yes.'

'Most respectable people yearn to shed their respectability but they don't know how; they cannot get out, said the starling. Think how lucky you are. You are out.'

'You mean I have no further to fall.'

'Change the metaphor. You are free.'

'Is that a metaphor?'

'Almost everything we say is a metaphor, that's why nothing is really serious.'

'*You* are never really serious. I think it's how you try to escape being awful.'

'It's how I escape being awful.'

'Was I free before I met you?'

'No, you had illusions.'

'I'm disillusioned now all right.'

'Unillusioned. I liberated your intelligence.'

'I'm not free now. I'm a slave.'

'You love it. You kiss the rod. Don't you?'

'Don't be coarse. I do what you want.'

'Whores are so fastidious.'

'Please don't –'

'A verbal point. My service is perfect freedom.'

'I think I've never been free. Who's free anyway? Is Stella free?'

'No.'

'Then is Stella –?'

'Shut up about Stella. I don't like her name in your mouth.'

'Her pure name in –'

'Shut up.'

'Who's free?'

'I know only one person who is free.'

'Who?'

'In the end you'll be my nurse, that's what you're waiting for, the smash. You think you'll pick up the pieces.'

'I don't want you smashed. I love you.'

'It thrills you to tell me my duty. You'd be sick if I did it.'

'So you think I have no illusions now.'

'How can you have? I tell you the truth. I am a fount of truth in this place.'

'I think you do tell me the truth,' said Diane, 'and I suppose that's something.' She looked at George's calm round face, his clean white shirt sleeves neatly rolled up, his pale arms covered with sleek silky strokable black hairs. She said, 'You're *here*.'

'I'm here, kid. Look after me. I'm as full of rapiers as a doomed bull.'

'You ought to ring up, I might have been out.'

'Out? You mean you go *out*?'

'I go as far as the Baths and the Church. I go to the Food Hall at Bowcocks.'

'One day I'll immure you.'

'We are two people in despair.'

'You flatter yourself.'

'You mean you aren't in despair?'

'I mean *you* are not. Women are incapable of despair.'

'How can you say that!'

'Oh they can cry, that's different. God, this room smells of cigarette smoke.'

'I never smoke when you're here.'

'You'd better not.'

'If you were here more I'd smoke less. Shall I open the window?'

'No, stay put, Miss Nightwork. I like the cosy stench of face powder and cigarette smoke and alcohol. Only I wish you wouldn't put those potted plants in the bath. Potted plants in the bath are an image of hell. Chaos and Old Night. Not like your corset on the floor, which I rather like.'

'It's not a corset.'

'Whatever it is. Chaos and Old Night.'

'Would you like another drink?'

'Hey nonny nonny – no. You have one, dear daughter of the game. I'll walk about.' George rose and began to walk, across the room, out into the hall, into the kitchen, back again to the window. He often did this. Reclining on the sofa with her shoes off, Diane watched him.

Diane Sedleigh was the most genteel prostitute in Ennistone. (The man she had imprudently married once upon a time was called Sedley, but Diane thought that Sedleigh was more elegant.) She was a small slim woman with almost black straight hair which was cut short and clung to her small head, sweeping in a little neat pointed curve round her face on either side. Her dark brown eyes were not large but were ardent and eager, not unlike the eyes of Zed, Adam McCaffrey's dog. She liked to hint that she had gipsy blood. No one believed this romantic hint but it was none the less true. She was a cousin, possibly a half-sister, of Ruby Doyle. (She had been christened, at St Olaf's, her mother being Church of England, 'Diamond', but early decided that she had enough troubles without owning such a bizarre name. The familiar 'Di' easily became the elegant 'Diane'.) There was a third girl too, sister or cousin. The gipsy father or fathers were legendary beings from another era and there had never been any family life. Diane had very small feet and small nicotine-stained hands. She sometimes wore black silky dresses, very short, with black stockings, and thought of herself as a 'flapper'. She was dressed like that today, with a barbarous metal necklace which George had given her. His only gifts, apart from money, were cheap exotic jewellery. Sometimes when she wore trousers she posed differently, legs wide apart and shirt coming loose, showing her small breasts, a tiny defiant female pirate. Of course she pronounced her name Dee-ahn, not Die-ann.

Diane had been beautiful when she was young, and had experienced the claims upon the world which beautiful women feel, especially if they are poor. She was now nearly forty. She came from a poor home in the Burkestown area of Ennistone. Her father left her mother, her mother went away with another man. Diane lived unhappily with a series of vague 'aunties', whose relationship to her and to each other remained conjectural. When she left school she worked as a waitress, then as a shop assistant in Bowcocks, then as a clerk in a betting office. One day she let her boss take some photographs of her in the nude. Was that the beginning of it all, was it fated, could it have been otherwise? It was a long story, the old story, Diane preferred not to remember how it went. She became pregnant twice, each time abandoned, and had to look after her expensive secret abortion herself. She was briefly married to that Sedley somewhere along the way. Men were beasts. She took to prostitution as a temporary, she thought, expedient in a moment of misery, not really for the money but as a kind of suicide because she didn't care. A Mrs Belton whom she met at the Baths told her there was a 'vacancy' in a 'nice house'. She offered it as a kind of privilege. Diane did not stay long in the house, but already she felt it impossible to 'go back'. What was there to go back to? She was by now not indifferent to earning money easily. She saved herself from real suicide by acquiring a more positive image of her trade. She picked up and treasured the word 'courtesan'. Some of her clients told her tales of whores in other lands, exotic women in cages in Calcutta, motherly women knitting in lighted windows in Amsterdam. She set herself up in a flat and affected to be 'merry'. She decorated her flat 'tastefully' and became more 'exclusive'. Respectable men arrived and endowed her with a kind of odd derived respectability. Older men came and discussed their wives, not always unkindly. Young men and adolescents came for initiations and to talk about 'life'. Diane began to feel that she was a wise woman performing an important public service. Her earliest clients had been rough fellows. Then men with fast cars took her out to road houses. Later these were joined by professional men. She had a fantasy about a rich bachelor, no longer young, and despairing of finding a woman to understand him, who would suddenly carry her away into a secure and cherished married life. For a time she even kept a suitcase packed for the advent of this impetuous admirer. But then Diane's respectability had taken a new and strange turn.

George had come her way many years before, but casually. They met at the Baths. He had come to her once or twice unmarried, then once or twice married, aloof and sardonic, as if carrying out some private wager. The polite precise way in which he treated her as an instrument maintained a distance between them, which was also an easy bond. Then he fell in love with her. Well, surely he *did* fall in love? George was rewriting history so fast, it was hard to remember what had really happened. What was now taken for granted between them was that she was in love with him. George had certainly become extremely possessive. He announced that she was to have no other clients. He moved her from her tasteful flat to a smaller flat in Westwold of which he paid the rent. George gave her money and visited her, though he never spent the night. ('If I did I would detest you in the morning.') Diane tried to think that she was no longer a common prostitute, she was George's mistress. Even the phrase 'kept woman' could console her a bit. But she knew in her heart that she was not George's mistress. That was not how it was between them. She was just a reserved prostitute, like a reserved table.

Diane knew that George was supposed to be 'an awful man', though equally she had the fascinated forgiving feeling about him which she shared with other Ennistone ladies. She felt nervous with him at first and awaited the sudden uncontrolled rages for which George was famous. They did not come. George and Diane, it appeared, simply got on well together. George was often moody and irritable and sarcastic, but never seriously angry. Diane, it must be admitted, knew how to keep her head down. She did not contradict. He spoke of how he could rest with her, find repose. They chattered easily. George disliked ordinary expressions of tenderness. Profound or sentimental topics were equally banned. There was a sort of lightness and hardness in their converse. Diane learnt a new language, a new kind of banter, which was their usual mode of communication, and it was in teaching her this that George might reasonably have claimed that he had 'awakened her intelligence'. For a time, and although his visits were entirely irregular and whimsical, their ease together was such that Diane had dreams of a 'real life' somehow to be realized with George. Time would perhaps change their relationship, *redeem* it, and in doing so redeem him. If she had been a shrewder woman, and if she had been less afraid of him, for she remained afraid of him, even though he behaved so quietly with her, she might have tried to prompt the redemptive process and encourage him to leave his wife by threatening a withdrawal of her favours at a time when he was most addicted to them. However, Diane did not do this. Such blackmail would sort ill with the ideal role which she planned for herself in George's life, and anyway she lacked the nerve and the wit. Meanwhile she was gratified to know that George, so outrageous elsewhere, was a lamb to her, and this gave her a comforting sense of superiority. In this she paused and rested. She knew that she was envied by women who would of course never have admitted it. (Though neither of them spoke of their relationship it had become common knowledge.) However, Diane also knew that George's kindness to her depended on her good behaviour. At first she had embraced his monastic 'rule' as one in hopes of heavenly joy. Later the narrowness of her life irked her and although her love for George did not diminish, she had less hope of salvation. She lived in a world of idleness and waiting. She smoked and drank. She watched television. She had once hoped to gain some sort of education from George, but now if she got an 'improving' book from the library he just laughed at it. She experimented with cosmetics and altered her clothes. She went to Bowcocks and to Anne Lapwing's Boutique and bought scarves and cheap 'accessories' to cheer herself up. She went to the Institute, then hurried back. George came less often now and it was some time since he had made love to her, though he remained as possessive as ever. Once, recently, he had said to her in a gentle tone, 'If you ever have anything to do with either of my brothers, I will kill you.' He smiled and Diane laughed.

Would George be able to 'afford her' now that he had lost his job? She was poorer, kept by George, than when she had plied her trade freely. Would she not, for him, face poverty, destitution? For him, with him, yes. But as it was? Would it not have to end, must it not end, yet how could it end? She had made loving George her sole occupation. She had no friends, no social life. There were a few women with whom she talked at the Baths, but these were not the women she would have chosen to talk to. Nun-like, she did not look at men, and they avoided her. She did not envisage running away, it was impossible to vanish, it was too dangerous and too expensive. Besides she did not want to, she had given her life to George, thoughtlessly, stupidly, but just as tenderly and devotedly as if he had been her dear husband. A Women's Lib group in Burkestown had made themselves known and indicated that if ever she needed help they would 'stick by her', hide her, spirit her away, they appeared to suggest. They seemed kind and sincere but Diane did not pursue the acquaintance. They thoroughly disapproved of George and she was afraid he might think she was plotting with them. She began to be afraid of things he might imagine, lies people might tell him. She was aware that people eyed her in the street, stared at her at the Baths, but Diane pretended not to notice, not even caring to know whether the looks were friendly or hostile. In the past Gabriel McCaffrey had smiled at her. So had Tom McCaffrey. They certainly knew of her relation with George, yet they had smiled. Diane could not be glad since she could not respond and these mysterious tokens increased her sense of isolation. She did not from day to day imagine that George intended to leave her. Yet lately she had begun to feel that a time of crisis was at hand. Perhaps this was simply an expression of her own unconscious desire for a crash, a final solution. Did she not sometimes, darkly, fear that in spite of everything George would kill her in the end?

'I'm more popular than ever now that I've killed my wife,' said George.

'I am not amused.'

'Well, I had a good try. Better luck next time.'

'You ought not to speak like that about her,' said Diane. Her mission to 'save' George scarcely now extended beyond such improving remarks, which pathetically hinted at a complicit superiority. Who was she to tell George how to behave, or to indulge in cries of 'poor Stella'? Sometimes it seemed as if George were prompting just such admonitions so as then to crush them with violent sarcasm.

'I hoped she'd drown, but alas it was not to be.'

'Don't talk silly.'

'I've had several more of those letters from women. Bash your wife and get sympathetic letters from women. Shall I read you one?'

'No.'

'"Dear George McCaffrey, I feel I must write to express my sympathy. I have thought a lot about you and feel I know you well. People are so unkind they don't try to understand. I know you are a lonely unhappy man, and I feel sure that I would be able to –"'

'Oh stop!'

74

'"Please feel free to telephone me –"'

'Horrid, stop!'

'Why horrid? It's well meant.'

'Well meant!'

'Maybe a kind word does help. Maybe we don't say enough kind words.'

'You despise kindness.'

'You would like to think so.'

'I don't mean –'

'Lonely women sitting in lonely rooms. You ought to be sorry for them.'

'I am a lonely woman sitting in a lonely room. I am sorry for myself.'

'I think I'll ring her up.'

'Go on then, there's the telephone.'

'God bless women, they never write a man off. Men judge, women don't. What would we do without them? That women's world of quietness and forgiveness to which we return battle-scarred. You soothe and animate our images of ourselves.'

'What about our images of ourselves?'

'You have none. Yours are illusions.'

'You think that women –'

'Oh don't, women's problems are so boring, they even bore women.'

'When you get those letters –'

'Oh damn the letters. It's no fun, I can tell you, being the local *âme damnée*. What's the matter with you, kid? You seem nervy today.'

'Nervy! God!'

Diane wanted to cry, but she knew that George hated tears. Curled into a little black ball like a disturbed spider, she tucked her black-stockinged feet in and fingered the jagged metal necklace which they laughingly called her 'slave's collar'.

When is Stella coming home?' she asked.

'Buzz buzz. Hickory Dickory Dock.'

'I suppose she is coming home?'

'You dream that one day she won't. You dream that she will get fed up and leave me one day. That day will never come. Stella will never leave me. She will cling to me with the little steel claws of her love until violent death ensues for her or for me.'

'Violent death?'

'All death is violent.'

'I've stopped expecting her to leave you.'

'Stella would like me in a wheel chair and her pushing it.'

'Do you really think –'

'Oh shut up about her, I told you to, didn't I? Say something interesting, for Christ's sake.'

'Let's go to France, I've never been out of England, let's go to that hotel in Paris, the one you mentioned, where you used to go as a student, I always remember that hotel, I think of it in the night –'

'Well, don't. You'll never go there. Forget it.'

'Oh do sit down, darling, wild beastie, stop walking like that, stop padding and pacing, you make me want to scream, come and hold my hand. I'm full of darkness today.'

'I'm always full of darkness.'

Westwold, where Diane's flat was situated, is a 'mixed' area of small shops and modest suburban houses and cottages, tucked in between the river Enn and the railway, with Druidsdale on one side and Burkestown on the other. The railway, I should explain, passes beneath the common in a long tunnel, another feat of Victorian engineering. It emerges on the Burkestown side of Ennistone where the railway station is situated, most inconveniently for the inhabitants of Victoria Park, whose ancestors insisted on this remote siting. Westwold, together with the part of Burkestown round St Olaf's Church (fourteenth century, Low Church of England), contains some of the oldest houses in Ennistone, none unfortunately of any size or interest. There is also a pub called the Three Blind Mice. Diane's flat was not far from here in a quiet street of two-storey terraced houses, above a small Irish-linen shop where an elderly man quietly unfolded large white towels for infrequent customers.

The area in which George was now walking was cluttered up not only by Diane's clothes, her 'corsets' and things which he was treading on, but also by her possessions, little things bought to console her, stools, baskets, plants, a leather elephant, a yellow china umbrella-stand full of walking-sticks, a rack for shaggy magazines, objects which filled the interstices between the larger articles of furniture. Among the latter was an upright piano with an inlaid floral pattern and brass candle-holders. Diane, who could not play, had bought it cheap for the use of some hypothetical pianist client. She had pictured a tender scene, candle-lit. (There were occasional tender scenes.) But no piano player had come and the piano was, even to her ear when she idly strummed it, patently in need of tuning. The top of the piano was crowded with small objects, miniature dolls, bits of china, toy animals. 'These are your children,' one of her clients once told her, 'you express your frustrated maternal feelings by taking pity on these bits of junk in shops!' The speaker had a wife and four fine children, Diane saw them at the Baths. After he went away she cried for a long time.

George brought a chair near to the sofa and sat and held her hand, facetiously at first, then seriously. George was wondering whether it mattered that the priest had (had he?) seen him pushing the car. Not that he imagined that the priest would tell the police or say anything which George could not safely deny. What troubled George was the bond which had now come into being between him and the priest. He had sometimes felt that the priest was 'after him', though in just what way was never clear. All sorts of baneful and inauspicious bonds joined George to the people who surrounded him; almost any incident could make a bond, create an enemy. These bonds were the cords with which people tried to tie him down, to net him as a quarry to be killed. He was the doomed maypole round which people danced to truss him as a victim. The priest, as witness, was but one more symptom of the mounting crisis in George's life; of course George's life had always been in crisis, in the sort of crisis where ordinary morality is felt to be abrogated, as it is in wartime. But now he felt at moments that it was the *lutte finale*.

He looked down at Diane's little nicotine-brown hand, like a child's hand with tiny bitten finger-nails. He lifted it and smelt it, then kissed it and continued absently to hold it.

'What is it?' said Diane. 'Is it Professor Rozanov?'

George had briefly mentioned his teacher's return, Diane was guessing.

George did not answer this, but said, 'You spend time gossiping at the Baths, you hear what people say. Who will he come to?'

'What do you mean?'

'Who are his friends here?'

'What about N?'

'He quarrelled with N.'

'William Eastcote?' (This was Bill the Lizard, Brian's godfather and the man who saw the flying saucer.)

'He's about that age, he's the sort of person Rozanov might tolerate –'

'Is Rozanov as old as that?' said Diane.

'That's not old.' George let go of her hand. 'What made you think of Eastcote?'

'Someone said he'd had a letter from Professor Rozanov.'

'Well, keep your ears open, kid, watch and pray.'

George's face in repose had a calm benevolent expression. His ceaseless troubles had not yet made marks upon that bland surface. He had the darker brown hair of the McCaffreys (the Stillowens were blonds) which he wore cut short and sleek in an old-fashioned mode. (It was even rumoured that he used hair oil.) He was taller than Brian but not as tall as Tom. He had been slim but was now heavier. He had fine wide-apart brown eyes, which could suddenly narrow, but his 'cat-look', unlike Alex's, was amused and quizzical. His face was rather round, his nose was rather short, and he had small square separated teeth set on a wide arc, giving his face a boyish frank look when he smiled. He wore light grey check suits with waistcoats, and was often to be seen (as he was now) wearing the shiny-backed waistcoat without the jacket. It was this habit which prompted people to say he looked like a snooker player. A remark made by Brian that 'bar billiards' was George's game manifested more malice than insight and reinforced in Brian's critics the view that Brian was something of a blunt instrument. George was not a frequenter of bars and there was something at least superficially stylish about him. He had been a graceful cricketer when young.

George, more than most people, lived by an idea of himself which was in some ways significantly at odds with reality. To say he was a narcissist was to say little. We are mostly narcissists, and only in a few, not always with felicitous results, is narcissism overcome (broken, crushed, annihilated, nothing less will serve) by religious discipline or psycho-analysis. George was an accomplished narcissist, an expert and dedicated liver of the double life, and this in a way which was not always to his discredit. That is, he was in some respects, though not in others, not as bad as he pretended to be, or as he really believed himself to be. Herein perhaps he intuitively practised that sort of protective coloration which consists in sincerely (or 'sincerely', sincerity being an ambiguous concept) giving one's faults pejorative names which conceal the yet more awful nature of what is named. All of which goes to show that it is difficult to analyse human frailty, and certainly difficult to analyse George's.

When George was younger he used to say, '*Que faire*? I love good food and good wine and pretty women.' This, which George did not regard as a falsehood, was misleading, not only because George was not seriously interested in food and drink, but because he was not (in the crude accepted sense) seriously interested in women. He pictured himself as 'highly sexed', as no doubt a great many men like to do. (When does one ever hear a man announce that he is not highly sexed?) In fact he was a good deal less erotically interested in women than was his brother Brian. He was credited with some brief affairs both before and after marriage, but these were (in my view) probably nervous cravings rather than great passions. His relation with Diane was the only 'illicit' union which had lasted, and in this conventional lust played a minor role.

Stella in some way stunned George, as if she had hit him very hard on the forehead. (They met at London University as fellow students.) Perhaps this initial *coup* was what he could never forgive. She was the cleverest strongest woman that he had ever met. Though later he said that he was never in love with Stella, only obsessed and hypnotized, there is no doubt that he was in love. She was in love too, though for some reason people always wanted to explain this away by saying things like, 'She took him on as a challenge.' George early gained the idea that Stella intended some-how to 'break' him; and there was perhaps such an element in her love. She had begun to feel that she was the stronger, and George could not bear this. Violence was his answer. It was a ménage which lacked the language of tenderness. Yet George admired and, in a way, prized his wife, and Stella's love *was* love, loyal absolute commitment, the love of an intelligent realistic person capable of unselfishness. She was one of the few women who were entirely unsentimental about George. People argued about whether Stella 'knew what he was like' when she married him. I think she did; but she overestimated the influence of her kind of love upon this kind of man. She was without feminine wiles, and could not conceal her strength as a more cunning or intuitively tactful woman might have done. She never soothed or accepted George's manner of being himself. Strength and love were one for Stella, love redeeming strength, power corrupting love. 'I've married a policewoman,'

79

George complained early on, before things became very bad, and before Rufus died. (About the death of the child and its effect opinions differed.) Stella's father, a diplomat, detested George and a coolness arose between Stella and her parents. When Stella's mother died, David Henriques retired and went to live in Japan, whence he sent presents and affectionate letters in which George was not mentioned. Henriques became an expert on netsuke.

Many men are violent (the sealed doors of houses conceal how many). George conformed to a less usual type in that he made violence his trademark. He made a point of his aggressiveness and bad temper to define his *esse*; and this in some quarters actually made people more tolerant and forgiving. As Brian said, George 'got away with things'. Some smilingly described his conduct as 'rudeness à outrance', others pointed out (and this had an element of truth) that he was prudentially violent; or else he was lucky. (That he was lucky was something that George believed too, a belief he managed to combine with seeing himself as a 'doomed bull, full of rapiers'.) The causes of a habit of violence are mysterious and not often lucidly studied, since those who take an intelligent interest in violent cases usually have deep psychological reasons for preferring certain explanations. (This is almost always true in politics, and often in analysis.) Alex said (and half believed) that George simply drank too much. Others said it was because of Rufus, some blamed Stella, some Alex, some Alan. Yet other theories saw George as a repressed homosexual, or an Oedipus victim, or a one-man protest against the bourgeoisie. He figured indeed upon many flags which were flown. And although George never systematically took up the game of explaining himself, he dabbled in it to the extent of tinting his excesses here and there with ameliorating hints of a more interesting ethical background. He felt, or affected to feel, that his chaotic and unbridled personality was in some important sense more real than the decorous natures that surrounded him. George was supposed to be closer to awful aspects of the world which other people preferred to ignore, and was thereby somehow sympathetically joined to the afflicted and the oppressed. I once heard him say of his brother Brian, 'He doesn't realize how terrible and how *serious* life is.' This use of the word 'serious' is idiosyncratic but highly significant. I may add that, on the occasion in question, George then laughed. In such contexts Brian was in turn perhaps quite right to hazard that George helped one to understand terrorists.

Frustrated ambition, or as some more plainly put it George's chagrin at discovering that he was no good, was also mentioned as a cause or an excuse. As a student, George had studied philosophy, then history and archaeology. Later, although he got a first-class degree, he failed to get the academic posts which he coveted. He wrote plays which no one would perform and (it was rumoured) poems which no one would publish. There is no doubt that he was consumed with envy of artists and thinkers. He did some historical research, inclining to call himself an archaeologist although he had done no field work beyond a fortnight's junior grubbing at the Roman Wall. He entered the 'museum and archive' world and held one or two posts, then becoming deputy keeper at our Ennistone Museum, where he also drew a stipend as 'research scholar'. He was said to be compiling some important work. However the fact remained that at the age of more than forty he had published nothing except *A Short History of The Ennistone Museum*. (This little work, which is still in print, is well written but necessarily of limited importance.) George was in fact a clever man, he was the lively gifted promising person whom Stella had loved and married. (She could not have loved a fool.) Only somehow he had never managed to do anything substantial with his talents. Instead he set about destroying himself. No one was very surprised when he ended his museum career by smashing all that Roman glass.

I confess that I cannot offer any illuminating explanation. Every human being is different, more *absolutely* different and peculiar than we can goad ourselves into conceiving; and our persistent desire to depict human lives as dramas leads us to see 'in the same light' events which may have multiple interpretations and causes. Of course a man may be 'cured' (consoled, encouraged, improved, shaken, returned to effective activity, and so forth and so on) by a concocted story of his own life, but that is another matter. (And such stories may be on offer from doctors, priests, teachers, influential friends and relations, or may be self-invented or derived from literature.) We are in fact far more randomly made, more full of rough contingent rubble, than art or vulgar psycho-analysis lead us to imagine. The language of sin may be more appropriate than that of science and as likely to 'cure'. The sin of pride may be a small or a great thing in someone's life, and hurt vanity a passing pinprick or a self-destroying or even murderous obsession. Possibly, more people kill themselves and others out of hurt vanity than out of envy, jealousy, malice or desire for revenge. There was some deep (so deep that one wants to call it 'original', whatever that means) wound in George's soul into which every tiniest slight or setback poured its gall. Pride and vanity and venomous hurt feelings obscured his sun. He saw the world as a conspiracy against him, and himself as a victim of cosmic injustice.

At the time of this story not much was known about George's relations with John Robert Rozanov, so those relations did not figure in the 'George theories' or the 'George legend'. George became John Robert's pupil when he was studying philosophy in London. George was twenty, John Robert in his fifties. The Rozanovs were, as has been related, a poor family living in Burkestown. The grandfather, a Marxian socialist, had fled from Czarist Russia. (He was related, it was said, to the painter of the same name.) He came to England, freedom, poverty, obscurity and disappointment. His son, John Robert's father, married a local girl, a Methodist, became a Christian and lost, indeed had never shown much, interest in politics. He was an electrician, sometimes unemployed. The grandfather lived long enough to be consoled by realizing that his grandson at least was some sort of remarkable creature. John Robert, an only child, proceeded to Ennistone Grammar School (now alas defunct) and then to Oxford. After graduating, he went to study in America, where he taught in California, then in New York. He returned to teach in London, then went back to America, thereafter making regular, sometimes prolonged, visits to the English philosophical scene. As he retained a tender relation with his parents, his face was occasionally, until his mother's death, to be seen in Ennistone, and his fame was kept green among us. He had few friends here, however, and was generally said to be no maker of friends. He kept up with William Eastcote and with an eccentric old watchmaker with whom he had philosophical conversations.

George McCaffrey was deeply affected by his teacher. He 'fell in love' with Rozanov, with philosophy, with Rozanov's philosophy. However, his soul was so shaken that (and this too was no doubt due to Rozanov's influence) he never told his love; and although he spoke admiringly of Rozanov when he went home he never revealed how absolutely this man had taken possession of his soul. Whether George was ever a 'favourite pupil' is open to question. What is certain is that Rozanov advised George to give up philosophy and George took the advice. A brief word is necessary here about Rozanov's philosophical views. (I should mention that I am not a philosopher and cannot offer any commentary or detail.) As a 'brilliant' young man, John Robert was a sceptic, a reductionist, a linguistic analyst, what is (incorrectly I am told in this context) popularly called a 'logical positivist', of the most austerely anti-metaphysical school. His Methodist upbringing had it seemed slipped from him painlessly or been with a certain naturalness transformed into a methodical sort of atheism. He was and remained deeply puritanical. In America he became interested in philosophy of science (he had a considerable knowledge of mathematics) and spent a lot of time arguing with physicists and attempting to clear up their philosophical mistakes. He had already published his two youthful books; one, *Logic and Consciousness*, a demolition of the views of Husserl, the other about Kant's view of time. He now added a long book called *Kant and the Kantians* which established his reputation as something considerably more than a 'clever boy'. His well-known studies of Descartes and Leibniz followed, then *Against the Theory of Games*, and the seminal work, *Nostalgia for the Particular*. He then became, by way of Kant, interested for the first time in moral philosophy, which he had dismissed when young; became for a while an obsessive student of Plato and wrote a book called *Being and Beyond*, considered marvellous but eccentric, about Plato's Theory of Ideas. (He also wrote a short book, difficult to find now, on *Plato's Mathematical Objects*.)

It was at this rather chaotic and eclectic stage of his development that George encountered him, when he was (as William Eastcote later put it) 'letting off fireworks in all directions'. The next news about John Robert was that declaring (as he did from time to time) that philosophy was 'impossible', 'too hard for human beings', and that his own mind had 'gone to pot', he had decided to become a historian. He had been interested in Greek history since his Oxford days, and during a sabbatical year he composed and published a study of the causes of the Peloponnesian War. He also wrote a short book, considered a classic, about Greek ships and sea warfare. (There was arguably an engineer as well as a mathematician hidden inside John Robert.) He then further amazed everyone by writing a book about Luther. After that he went back to philosophy. There is some dispute about this later phase. Some said that he had become a neo-Platonist. He certainly published some fragmentary stuff about Plotinus. Others said he had 'taken up religion'. There was said to be a 'secret doctrine' and a 'great book'.

Some pupil-teacher relationships last a lifetime. George maintained his side of the relationship, though it is doubtful whether Rozanov animated his. George later regretted having taken his master's advice and given up philosophy. As a graduate student he still haunted John Robert's lectures and classes. He tried to 'keep up' and 'keep in touch'. He even submitted to a semi-learned journal an article which purported to 'explain' John Robert's philosophical position. The editor informed the philosopher, who sent George a curt note, and the article was promptly withdrawn. George made no further attempt to 'popularize' Rozanov's work, but he continued to regard him as his teacher and on one occasion followed him to America.

George had kept the tally against fate. He knew what he was owed: something great, little less than salvation. Why was John Robert coming back to Ennistone? Was it for him, the lost sheep, the one just man, the justified sinner? He had always believed in magic, and he knew that John Robert Rozanov was a magician.

'What's on telly, Di? Roll on the San Francisco earthquake. That's what I want to see pictures of.'

'I left my evening bag behind at the Blacketts',' said Gabriel.

'You're *always* doing that!' said Brian.

Jeremy Blackett was a master at the Comprehensive School. He and his wife Sylvia were dedicated bridge players. Gabriel did not play bridge, but Jeremy's sister Sarah and his brother Andrew made up the foursome when Brian and Gabriel went to the Blacketts'. (Gabriel always took a novel.) It was to the powerful widowed mother of these Blacketts, May Blackett, that Alex had so disgracefully sold Maryville, the seaside house.

'Jeremy will be here,' said Gabriel, 'or Sylvia or Sarah.'

'Why can't you bloody remember your stuff?'

'Sorry –'

It was Saturday morning. Everybody went to the Baths on Saturday. (I was there myself on that particular Saturday.) It was a frosty morning and the Outdoor Bath was covered by a thick blanket of steam. The life guard upon his ladder could only glimpse a swimmer here and there as the white cloud rolled about in the brisk easterly breeze.

Brian and Gabriel and Adam were in the Promenade, looking out through the window. They had just arrived. The window was misted, but they had rubbed three round holes at different levels through which they looked at the steamy scene outside. Behind them a few people were sitting at the tables drinking coffee.

Gabriel never failed to feel a curious visceral excitement when she came to the Institute, even though she did so nearly every day. 'It's like a Time Machine,' she said to Brian, and then could not explain what she meant. From behind the studded bronze door which concealed the spring there was often the sound of a beating pulse, and the whole building seemed to tremble. Gabriel had learnt to swim in these waters. Yet it was as if some kind of not unpleasant guilty or expectant emotion attached to them. There was a delicious faint thrilling feeling as one slipped into these warm pools, especially in winter time when the hot spring seemed such a miracle and bathing in it such an exotic rite.

'When are you fetching Stella?' said Gabriel.

'About five.'

Stella, detained in hospital, was today coming to stay with Brian and Gabriel. Gabriel had suggested. Stella had agreed. It was significant that Stella was not going back to her own house. This significance, on which no one had yet commented, frightened Gabriel. George had still not been to see his wife. Although she wanted Stella to come, Gabriel felt afraid with a tremor which vibrated in harmony with the guilty thrill inspired by the steaming water. She wanted now to swim, quickly, quickly, quickly.

'There's Sylvia Blackett,' said Brian.

'Oh yes –' Gabriel waved her little wave to Adam, waggling her fingers. Adam did not like this wave and frowned. Gabriel went out through the door and turned along the edge of the pool toward the changing-rooms.

'Twelve o'clock,' said Brian to Adam, meaning they should meet in the Promenade at twelve. The McCaffreys went their separate ways at the Baths. That was part of the pleasure of the place, as if each one's enjoyment was especially private. It was an aspect of what Gabriel felt as its 'dangerousness'.

Adam inclined his head. He walked a little way away and stopped, to signify that he had withdrawn from society and was now alone.

Brian followed Gabriel out of the door.

Adam was small and compact, a dark McCaffrey, round-headed, round-faced, with dark straight short hair, resembling Alan, indeed slightly resembling George. He had none of his father's wolfish Viking look. He had brown intent eyes and rarely smiled. He went to a private preparatory day school, Leafy Ridge School, in a suburb of that name, not the Comprehensive where Jeremy Blackett taught. His father was uneasy about this, but he wanted Adam to learn at least two foreign languages, and the Comprehensive was not very successful in teaching one. Gabriel wanted him to be protected from rough boys. (In fact there were rough boys at the prep school too, but Adam did not tell his mother this.) She also liked the uniform, brown knee breeches and long sky-blue socks. Adam did not like boys. He did not like girls either, though he rather wanted to be one. The awkwardness which separated him from his parents made him solitary at school, where he was also conspicuously small for his age. His mysterious refusal to grow seemed to signal a quiet hostility to any public role. Of course he loved his parents, and sympathized silently with their attempts to communicate with him. Sometimes they seemed to him almost grotesque in their efforts to behave naturally. He often looked at his mother and when she looked at him he would smile and go quickly away. He rarely looked at his father, but he sometimes touched him encouragingly.

He stood now a while staring at nothing. He was wondering what Zed was doing with himself at home. He often wondered this. Occasionally he had managed to spy on Zed, to see the little animal playing all by himself in the most imaginative way. But Adam was never sure that Zed did not somehow know that he was being watched and had put on a show for his master's benefit. Wittgenstein says that a dog cannot be a hypocrite or sincere either. Adam, who had not yet read Wittgenstein, considered Zed to be quite capable of hypocrisy.

He did not follow his parents through the outside door. Unlike his mother he was in no hurry to swim. He enjoyed the special before-swim tension which made everything look vivid and strange and somehow slow. He went back across the Promenade vaguely aware that there were one or two people whom he knew (or rather who knew him, Mrs Osmore for instance) sitting at the tables, but he did not look that way. He dreaded conversation, even the catching of an eye. He passed through a communicating door into the area of the Indoor Bath. Adam very much wished to bring Zed to the Baths, only dogs were not allowed, except in the Promenade. He kept imagining how it would be, just Zed in the Indoor Bath, breaking the smooth silky surface of the water with his quiet confident rat-like motion. Zed swam well. Adam had often swum him in the river, only now this was not allowed either because of something the doctor said.

The Indoor Bath was a peaceful scene on weekdays, since a notion persisted among the older Ennistonians that it was a rather 'sissy' place, even unhealthy. However it had recently been 'taken over' by the '*jeunesse dorée*' of Ennistone, who used it, at weekends, as a rendezvous. This *jeunesse*, it should be said, tended to be women, at present most notably Valerie Cossom, the Eurocommunist, and Nesta Wiggins, one of the Women's Libbers who had tried to befriend Diane, Olivia Newbold, one of the Glove Factory Newbolds, and Anthea Eastcote, great-niece of William Eastcote. Gavin Oare, editor of the *Ennistone Gazette*, who liked to hang around these ladies, was treated with a certain disdain. On the other hand, Michael Seanu, a cub reporter, a little scamp just out of school, was a current pet, and Maisie Chalmers (daughter of the Institute Director) who did the Women's Page on the *Gazette*, was a valued recent recruit to right ideas. At the moment of Adam's entrance there was a great deal of splashing in the pool which he felt ought to be so quiet and water-ratty, as Valerie was racing lengths with Peter Blackett. Peter was Jeremy Blackett's son, not very much older than Adam, but as tall as Jeremy. Valerie's father, Howard Cossom, was a dentist who lived in Leafy Ridge and was famous for being unable to swim. Valerie and Nesta were studying sociology at the Ennistone Polytechnic. On the steps, their feet in the surging water, sat and stood a group of young women in very scanty swim-wear, their long wet hair streaked in darkened tresses over their necks and shoulders. Their slim soft bodies were faintly tanned by a winter of daily outdoor swimming. They were as tall and lithe and pleased with themselves as young Spartans. Above them upon the slippery wet marble, his shoes splashed, his glasses misted, stood Hector Gaines. They were discussing *The Triumph of Aphrodite* which was to be played, with Hector's shocking new material, at the Ennistone Midsummer Festival. Hector and Anthea were to direct it. Valerie Cossom was to be Aphrodite. The set and costumes were to be designed by Cora Clun who was studying dress design at the Poly. Hector was confused and excited, partly because he was in love with Anthea, and partly because, among so many delightful naked figures, he still had all his clothes on. This *déjeuner sur l'herbe* effect positively made his head swim.

The central part of the Indoor Bath, the pool itself and its surround and the double row of Corinthian columns, were made of white black-webbed marble, but the outer area, covered with potted plants, was merely tiled. The place had its own peculiar smell, thrilling to devotees, compounded of warmth and water and chemicals and healthy wet green foliage. Adam loved this smell. He did not approach the pool but went in among the plants. He touched their strong shiny powerful leaves. The girls noticed him, and Anthea and Nesta waved. Adam waved back. He did not mind the *jeunesse dorée* as he knew that, with the tact or indifference of youth, they would not want to talk to him. He stood a while, smelling the plants and looking with satisfaction at the wet marble and hugging the private thrill of his own soon-to-be-swimming sensations. Then he turned slightly and looked across the pool and saw George McCaffrey, who had just entered on the other side.

George gazed at the pool and the scene. He was not especially interested in the almost-naked young women, the sight of whom did not produce in him the mechanical excitement which it would have aroused in his brother Brian. It was the place and the smell which he liked. He paused and sniffed. Anthea Eastcote, who had known George all her life, called out 'Hello!' Valerie Cossom, who was secretly in love with him, stopped swimming and rose silently in the shallow end, revealing her beautiful body.

George smiled vaguely, not looking at Anthea, turning his head and narrowing his eyes, and was about to pass on in the direction of the Promenade when he saw Adam. As soon as their eyes met, Adam sat down. He did not hide, but sat down among the plants, holding his knees, his head emerging from among the leaves. With intent unsmiling eyes, he stared at George. George (who was fully clothed) stared back. Once, some time ago in Adam's short life, when he had been looking thus at his uncle (it was in the garden at Belmont), George, turning towards him, had suddenly, silently, winked. This episode had made, for the boy at least, a curious bond, intimate yet menacing. The ambiguous signal was never repeated, and yet, Adam sometimes felt, it still flashed, magically, frightfully, in any exchange of looks between them.

George stopped in his tracks at the sight of Adam as abruptly as a Japanese might be stopped by a badger. He did not want to pass his nephew, nor did he want to impede his progress should Adam want to proceed to the changing-rooms by the interior route. George receded into the corridor and turned off it into the clinical chamber of the Infants' Pool. This room, which seemed small by contrast with the Indoor Bath, was by other standards quite large. It was a remnant of the Institute arrangements which predated the Ennistone Rooms. The Infants' Room, as it was also called, was early Victorian hospital style, unadorned, with plain tiles and dark linoleum. Its only charm was the pool itself, white-tiled, round and breast-deep, sunk into the floor and filling most of the room. It had been intended for the genteel dipping of rheumatic patients or of persons recovering from injured limbs, sufferers who were later accommodated in the Rooms. Now the famous waters, tinted blue, contained, as George entered, a number of cooing smiling mothers and as many swimming, splashing or floating infants. The aquatic infants were indeed an amazing sight. Tiny children, some less than six months old, who on land crawled with awkward sprawling arms and legs, took to the water in the most uncanny way, like funny little animals of some quite other species. Ivor Sefton was extremely interested in the whole phenomenon and had published an article about it in *The Lancet*. This practice, pioneered in Ennistone, and now occasionally to be met with elsewhere, has had to make its way against prejudice and misunderstanding. Adam longed to 'swim' Zed and was joyful to see a walking running dog become a swimming dog. (Adam and Rufus had both swum in the Infants' Pool when scarcely larger than Zed.) Most dog-owners share this instinctive urge, which is discussed in Sefton's article. But the Ennistone mothers had not felt any instinctive desire to swim their infants, and had to be taught, and to see many successful demonstrations, before they believed it desirable or even possible. Many outsiders still regard this aspect of 'growing up in Ennistone' as dangerous or slightly scandalous. (Special attention must be paid to the chemicals in the water.) It was originally proposed that the Infants' Room should be 'Mothers only', but the reasonable wishes of fathers had to be met too, and the Room was eventually opened to all. An attendant controls the numbers of spectators, and only women are allowed in the water.

Standing in the middle of the pool, offering quite unnecessary help and encouragement, amid the tiny naked swimming forms and wet protective arms, was Nesta Wiggins. She was drawn to the place because it was a rendezvous of women. The sound of excited exclamatory voices, rebounding from the domed tiled roof, made a shrill cacophony, pleasant as bird-song to Nesta's ears. Nesta hoped to indoctrinate some of the cooing mammas. But, in spite of her disapproval of matrimony and child-bearing, she could not help being delighted with the scene, to which she often returned.

There was a slight lull in the chatter when George appeared. Ennistone had few tourists in March, and the mothers had had the place to themselves that morning. Indeed fully clothed males always seemed out of place, and were duly shy. Most of the women knew who George was; but even those who normally felt a secret indulgent sympathy for him were here affronted. Some deep female solidarity drew them together against George as he lounged, staring. Nesta, who really hated George, sensed this communal emotion with satisfaction. George sensed it too, also with satisfaction. Nesta, tall and large-breasted in the midst of the bubbling cauldron of wet ample female flesh and slithery babies, glared at George. George, who knew her by sight and found her physique vaguely pleasing, did not meet the glare. He looked instead, with an amused thoughtful face, at the splashing infants and thought, How I'd like to drown the little beggars! He imagined pressing a large firm hand down upon those little pink faces.

Alex had arrived with Ruby. Ruby could not swim, never had swum, never would swim, she hated water. However, she attended Alex to the Baths, and had done so ever since they were girls together, when (so remote were those days) she had come as a chaperone. Now she came because she always had, to see people and hear the gossip (she rarely uttered any herself) and to look after Alex's clothes. The changing-rooms, strange wet slippery smelly places where people padded nervously, consisted of four areas: in the first one disrobed in a cubicle, in the second one placed one's clothes in a locker, in the third one placed the key of the locker in a numbered cubby-hole, in the fourth one took a shower; then one emerged to swim. Alex, who never trusted the security of the system, preferred to put her clothes in a bag which she handed to Ruby waiting outside. This she did now as she came out, slim, handsome, wearing her green-skirted costume (she deplored bikinis) and no cap (caps were not worn at the Institute). The chill air coated her warm body and made her gasp. She tiptoed cautiously across the sparkling frosty pavement and dived gracefully into the cloud of steam which hid the pool. She swam beautifully in the warm kind water under the merciful white cloud.

Diane had swum earlier and now, wearing a smart woollen jersey, a smart woollen cap, matching gloves, woollen socks pulled up over her trousers, an overcoat, scarf and boots, was sitting in Diana's Garden. On the side farthest from the pool and separated by a fence were the Roman excavations, a few low walls and some holes, very significant no doubt but not picturesque. At one end of the garden was the little spurting hot spring known as Lud's Rill, or 'the Little Teaser' which had caused such a scandal some time ago by suddenly hurling its jet of water high up into the air. The water of the Rill was extremely hot, at boiling point as it emerged, but its normal intermittent spittings were not dangerous since they only reached a height of about three feet, and the basin into which they fell was now surrounded by an unsightly railing which excluded the darting youngsters whom the Little Teaser used chiefly to tease. The basin was rugged and massive and unadorned, made of the brownish-yellowish local stone. It was about five feet in diameter and three feet deep, with a hole or crack in the middle where the scalding spitting water jetted up and ran away. The general belief was that the water came up 'on its own' from deep in the earth and was not 'laid on' from the main system. The official guide-book is, perhaps deliberately, unclear on this point.

Beside the basin there were some wooden seats, and on one of these, having flicked the frost away with her copy of the *Ennistone Gazette*, Diane was sitting with Father Bernard and Mrs Belton. Mrs Belton was the 'Madam', now very old, who had inducted Diane many years ago into her present profession. Diane usually avoided her because she was a reminder of horrible things and because she affected a grand and irritating 'knowingness'. She, like Diane herself, had risen in the trade. Mrs Belton, who had been good-looking and no fool, had indeed realized one of Diane's former ambitions, and acquired a fine house where (so it was said) artists and intellectuals resorted for drink and talk. It was at one time the height of chic to go to Mrs Belton's not for sex but for conversation. (However this may have been a myth; I never myself went along to see.) Mrs Belton's glory was past, however, and even Diane could now feel sorry for her. After a police raid (there was talk of drugs) she had sold the fine house, and had now the air of a shaggy neglected old woman. Diane had sat in the garden hoping to catch a glimpse of George whom she was at that moment very anxious to see. George's rule was that at the Baths they never spoke or gave any recognition sign; but he might now, she felt, break the rule if he saw her alone. However, Mrs Belton had promptly arrived, and then the priest.

Sitting beside Diane and leaning across her to Mrs Belton, Father Bernard was trying to persuade the old woman to come to his church.

'Come to service, Mrs Belton, it's beautiful, you'll see.'

'I've never been in your church, well, I been in. It's like a bazaar.' Mrs Belton was a non-conformist.

'You don't go to your own church, come to mine. Come to the warmth and light. You are cold and your soul is dark.'

'Who says my soul is dark?' said Mrs Belton.

'I do. Come where love is.'

'It's like a shop at Christmas time, all scarlet, not my idea of Church.'

'Such precious goods, and all for free! Ask and you shall be given, knock and it shall be opened. Come to the bazaar! Scarlet for sin, and scarlet for redeeming blood. Wash in the blood of the Lamb, immerse yourself and swim unto salvation. You knew all these things once, recall them now, be as a little child, be born again, be justified, be saved.'

'There's nothing beyond the grave,' said Mrs Belton.

'The Kingdom of God is now,' said the priest. 'The mystery of our salvation is not in time. You need a magician in your life. You have one. His name is Jesus. Stand before him and say simply – help – help –'

While he was speaking, leaning ardently forward, Father Bernard, unseen by Mrs Belton, was holding Diane's hand. He had got his own hand inside her woollen glove and was kneading her palm. Diane, though used to some of her pastor's eccentricities, still did not know what to make of him.

Mrs Belton got up. She said, 'You got no right to think things about me, I know what you think, and set yourself up so. Leave meddling with others, get some help yourself, you'll need it one of these days, from what I hear.' To Diane, 'Good-bye, dear. I'm going to swim.'

As she moved away, stiff with the dignity of arthritis, George, in swimming-trunks, suddenly appeared at the edge of the pool. Diane wrenched her hand away, losing her glove to the priest. She wondered if George had seen. George dived into the pool and disappeared under the steam.

'Silly old bitch,' said Father Bernard, 'I hope she drowns.' He absently returned Diane's glove. 'I preach the good news. No one listens. Automatic salvation. No time, no trouble. Turn a switch and flood your soul with light.'

'You don't say that to me,' said Diane.

'You haven't got simple faith. She has.'

'Have you?'

'I am old, old –'

'You're not –'

'Salvation is not in time. Did you see that apparition of George?'

'Yes. Why apparition?'

'Unreal. Made of ectoplasm.'

'I wish you'd help George.'

'Everyone wants me to help George. I can't. If I laid my hands upon him, took him by the throat, I would hold only melting yielding stuff like toasted marshmallow. That is my damnation, not his.'

'Don't talk of damnation. Tell him about Jesus. Tell him *something*.'

'If God brings him to me, God will give me words. Meanwhile he bores me. Come and see me, child. Come to the old scarlet bazaar. I'm going to swim now. It is the solution to all problems in this blessed town.'

Diane thought, George is so alone, he has made himself alone. Perhaps that's what Father Bernard means by saying he's unreal. And she shuddered at the thought of her return now into her own solitude.

In the vast expanse of the Outdoor Pool some people splashed quickly, privately, others swam about purposefully, looking for their friends, others systematically, obsessively, swam length after length, seeing nothing, their heads deep in the warm water. Alex, idling across the centre, ran into Adam. They seized each other, laughing. On land, their bodies could not communicate. Alex never kissed her grandson, never touched him. In the water it was different; they had new bodies, beautiful and free, warm and full of grace. Suspended, they dandled each other. They sometimes met like that, as it were in secret. 'Isn't it lovely?' 'Yes.' This simple praise of the waters was always exchanged as if this daily blessing always came as a surprise. 'How's Zed?' said Alex. 'Fine. How are you, are you all right?' Adam always asked Alex if she was all right when he met her in the water. 'Yes, fine. Lovely to see you.' 'Lovely.' They parted and swam away.

George, leaving the nauseating sight of the swimming babies behind him, and having instantly forgotten about Adam, had proceeded to the changing-rooms and was soon in the pool. He had walked along the side, looking for a space among the swimmers, before diving in, but he had not noticed Diane nor was he thinking of her. He was now, with his perfect effortless Ennistonian crawl, doing lengths, his head well down, his hand extended at each end to touch the wall lightly as he turned. His dark hair swirled about the crown of his head, looking like Brian's hair. He breathed unobtrusively, mysteriously, deep in the water, as if he had indeed become a fish and the healing stream were flowing through his gills.

Gabriel, who had had her swim and was now dressed, standing upon the edge of the pool, noticed George as he approached along his strong self-chosen line. ('Doing lengths' was a priority activity, and other swimmers kept out of the way of these blind fanatics.) She moved so that she was directly above him as, without raising his head, he curled and turned. She saw (as of course she had seen before) the way George's hair grew, that it was like Brian's, only this was obscured by George's hair being combed from a side parting over the crown. This observation always gave Gabriel pleasure. She was pleased too by being able to watch him unobserved and by the way that George's hand, touching the wall of the pool as he turned, was just below her feet. He disappeared almost instantly under the hanging cloud of steam. Gabriel waited for him to return. Brian, also now clothed, standing nearby, watched Gabriel watching George. He came forward.

Gabriel said, 'I just saw George. Don't you think we should write to him to say that Stella is coming to us?'

'Hasn't she told him?'

'She says not.'

'Let the bugger find out.'

'I think we should write to him. It seems so unkind not to.'

'No.'

For George the day had begun early with a sound of pigeons speaking in human voices. He had heard this before: the soft murmur of people speaking close to him, frightening intruders, people near him where no people should be. Burglars, police, intruders of some more terrible nameless kind. Perhaps it was just the pigeons.

He was surprised, as he was every morning now, to find himself not upstairs in his own bed, but downstairs on the large drawing-room sofa where he had been sleeping ever since Stella left, or went to hospital, or whatever she had done. There was a downstairs lavatory and wash-place. He did not need to go upstairs any more. He and Stella occupied separate bedrooms, but her presence somehow lingered upstairs, not in smells (she used no scented cosmetics) but in other signs, clothes, the always disturbing sight of her bed. Downstairs was more open and anonymous and public. He had stowed away various objects, including ornaments and a picture. The kitchen was already chaotic, that of a bachelor. George could feel that he was camping or back in 'digs'. He woke to this strange sensation of being in a new place. He also woke to the being of Stella, Stella's world, her existence, her consciousness, her thoughts, still continuing. God, how alive she was.

As he lay, listening for the voices which had now ceased, he became aware that his mouth was open. He closed it quickly. Several times lately, on waking with his mouth open, he had had a strange conviction. First, he had felt that in the night he had been dead. The mouths of dead people fall open. Then, as something connected with this, he had become aware (or imagined or remembered) that during the night something had crawled out of his mouth and rambled round the room and over the ceiling and had then returned into his mouth again: something like a large crab-like insect or claw-footed worm. This persuasion was extremely vivid and accompanied, as he now quickly closed his mouth, by the rising of a bitter gall in his throat. He wondered, sitting up, whether he had actually swallowed a large spider.

He rose and put on the rest of his clothes (he now slept in his underwear), shaved and drank some coffee standing up in the kitchen. He considered and rejected the idea that today he should 'do something about Stella'. It was not that he wanted to, or felt that he ought to, do something about Stella. It was just that doing something (anything) would remove a certain discomfort. If he (for instance) sent her a postcard. He wanted to perform some kind of holding or postponing movement, something that would put Stella, for the moment, in cold storage, out of play. He did not want to see her, but neither did he like to think of her as active elsewhere. However, he could not think of anything to do and he dismissed the matter from his mind. He was, indeed, absolved from solving this problem. He himself was in cold storage; he was separated, waiting, as pure and as solitary as an anointed king awaiting coronation or a sacred victim awaiting the knife. This was the loneliness which Diane had sensed round about him, and which he himself felt rather as a frightful agonizing state of grace. It was as if now, in this interim, he *could not sin*.

He washed up his cup and his plate and made his way by a roundabout route to the Baths, where he went first, as has been recounted, to the Indoor Pool. As he emerged later, ready to swim, from the changing-rooms, he noticed something disturbing. The number 44, which was the number of the cubby-hole where he left his key, was the same as the number of his house and was also the last two figures in the number of his car. It was also his age. Little things were significant. It was a portent and all portents now were frightening.

Swimming, George did not see Diane, he did not see Brian and Gabriel, nor did he see Alex or Adam, all of whom saw him. He swam and swam, tiring himself, passing the healthful healing water through his gills, emptying himself in his solitude of the bitterness of living.

At last, exhausted, he crawled out, hauling himself up the iron steps and moving away from the pool. The pavement beside the pool edge was wet and slightly warm, but a step away the stone was dry and still sparkling with frost. George set penitential feet upon the frost and walked a little, shivering inside his quickly cooling body and turning to look at the footprints made in the frost by his warm feet. He felt slightly giddy and dazed by the emergence not only into the cold air but into the bright light. While he had been swimming in the semi-dark of the merciful steam cloud the sun had come out. The sky was blue. He walked along beside the high beech hedge which protected the Ennistone Rooms garden, and then turned along the other edge of the pool, by the yellow glazed wall, in the direction of the stews. He saw ahead of him, standing at the water's edge, the tall gaunt near-naked figure of William Eastcote. Eastcote was combing back and checking over with his fingers his thinning but persistent strands of wet hair. He was talking to a fat man whose swimming-trunks clung on almost invisibly beneath his paunch. The fat man had a big bony puckered face and stiff flat brush of grey hair which was evidently still dry. As he now turned his head George recognized John Robert Rozanov. Reaching the pool in three paces, George dived back again into the steam.

Alex had also seen Rozanov. Walking along beside Diana's Garden toward the stews, she stopped abruptly, then turned back. She did not notice Diane, who was still in the garden bursting to tell George that Rozanov, whom she recognized, was there. Alex's heart swelled and contracted, warming her whole body with a rush of consciousness. It did not occur to her to walk straight on and greet him. With the first glimpse came the need to hide, to wait, not to know – to know what, what was there to know? Besides, trim and handsome as Alex looked in her green skirted costume, she did not want to meet Rozanov with her hair dripping and her make-up washed away. She hurried along the warm verge of the pool until she came to where Ruby was waiting outside the changing-rooms, holding the bag with Alex's clothes. She grabbed the bag and whisked inside and pattered over the wet wooden duck-boards which gave out such an old melancholy exciting smell. She found a cubicle and sat down and peeled off her costume and sat there panting and holding her breasts until her face was calm and her heart was quiet. It was a great many years, she hated to think how many, since she had glimpsed Rozanov in the street, perhaps at the time when his mother died. But now, passing over all intermediate time, she recalled so intensely his monstrous handsome youthful face, how he looked when she might have reached out her hand to take him.

Ruby, who had noticed John Robert some time earlier, as he emerged from the changing-rooms with William Eastcote, had no such coy misgivings. She waited dog-like for Alex to come back for her clothes, then, released, she went along the side of the pool looking for him. She noticed Diane in the garden but as usual they exchanged no sign. She found Rozanov standing talking with East-cote at the place where, coming from the other direction, George had seen him, and she stood quite near, her feet apart, her hands clasped, staring at him. Several other people who had recognized the philosopher were also standing nearby, but not daring to come so close. John Robert did not see her, however, but still talking went with Eastcote down the steps into one of the stews.

The 'stews', as I explained earlier, are round holes about twelve feet deep and fifteen feet across, with a seat around the edge at the bottom. An iron staircase winds down into the water, which is just deep enough to allow the head and shoulders of the seated hedonist to emerge. The temperatures, at different graded levels in the different stews, are considerably higher than that of the pool, and in cold weather the atmosphere below is thickly and breathlessly steamy. Ruby peered over the side, but could see nothing of her hero.

John Robert was saying in his rather hard decisive voice to William (Bill the Lizard) Eastcote, as they stewed at 45°C., 'Thank God there's still no piped music here.'

'Yes, some people wanted it, but it would make the whole scene quite unreal, and the great thing about the Baths is it's such a *real* place, if you see what I mean.'

'I see very well.'

The only other inhabitant of the stew, recognizing Rozanov, moved away at once and climbed the steps in shy confusion. (He was in fact Nesta Wiggins's father, a ladies' tailor in a small way in Burkestown.)

'So the Rooms have been done up again,' said John Robert, 'and you can book in like a hotel.'

'Yes.' Eastcote added, 'You could be peaceful there, you could work undisturbed.'

John Robert was silent.

At that moment Adam came down the iron steps into the steamy hole. He stood on the steps with the very hot water up to his knees and looked to see who was there. He hoped the stew would be empty. He recognized Eastcote, but not Rozanov whom he had never seen.

William said, 'Hello,' but Adam had already turned and skipped back up the steps.

Rozanov said, 'How very like his father Rufus has become. That was Rufus, wasn't it?'

'No. Don't you remember. I told you ages ago, Rufus died as a child. That is the other boy, Brian McCaffrey's son, Adam.'

'Oh yes – you told me in London.'

The old friends had met occasionally over the years in the metropolis when Rozanov made philosophical visits.

'He does resemble George, or rather Alan.'

'I'm sorry Alan's not still around; an interesting man, though I scarcely knew him. You tell me Hugo's gone too.'

'Yes, Belfounder died several years ago.'

'What about all those valuable clocks?'

'He left them to that writer, I forget his name.'

'I'd have liked another talk with Hugo.'

'There must be someone here for your purposes.'

'For me to make use of!'

'I don't mean it like that.'

'Of course not, Bill. Damn it, there's you!'

'I still play bridge, but that's not your scene! What about N?'

'No.'

'George McCaffrey, you said –'

'No.'

'Well, there's the priest. I told you –'

'A Jew?'

'Yes.'

'That's good.'

'Shall I –?'

'Don't do anything. I want everything to happen slowly.'

'Are things going to happen then?'

'Perhaps only in my mind.'

'Will you come to Meeting with me on Sunday?'

'I love your Quakerish Meeting and your Quakerish ways, but it would be false.'

'You mean it would seem false.'

'You should have been a philosopher. How is your cousin Milton, still busy saving people?'

'Yes, he's very well.'

'How are you, Bill? You've got very thin.'

'I'm fine.' But Eastcote had just had some disturbing news from his doctor.

'I wish I was thin, I feel lean and hawk-like. May I have lunch with you? What a pity Rose has gone, I loved to see her at your table, it was like visiting some wholesome past.'

'Well, she has gone too.'

'Don't say "soon it will be our turn".'

'I wouldn't say that to you!'

'You can say anything to me! Come, let's go, I'm boiled.'

They clambered up the steps, holding hard on to the iron rail, and emerged into the cold air, coming out of the steam into the sunshine.

'There's the priest,' said Eastcote.

Not far away Father Bernard, not yet immersed, stood looking down at the water. He sported a certain peculiarity, not wearing swimming-trunks but a full-length black costume, rather loose and rumoured to be made of wool, as if it might be a bathing-cassock.

'He looks a clown,' said Rozanov.

'He is not that,' said Eastcote, 'but he is an odd man.'

'Why does he wear that costume? Is he scarred?'

'I don't know.'

At that moment Father Bernard sat down on the edge of the pool and let himself slide down gingerly into the water, then swam away with an awkward breast-stroke. He was not a good swimmer.

'Can't he dive?'

'I don't think so,' said Eastcote.

'He doesn't look as if he can swim either. He'll be in difficulties directly.'

'Some non-swimmers are not fools.'

'Do you tell me so? I live so out of the world! Where did I leave my glasses?'

As John Robert turned he came face to face with Ruby, who was still standing near the railed top of the stew. He recognized her.

'Why, Miss Doyle. It is Miss Doyle, isn't it?'

The recognition, without his glasses, was something of a feat, since John Robert had not seen Ruby for some years.

Ruby smiled her wide rare huge smile. She was overjoyed at being recognized by Rozanov. She hoped that one or two people whom she knew who had been standing nearby were still there to witness the scene. She nodded her head. She stared rapturously up at the philosopher. It did not occur to her to speak.

At this moment Ruby heard, from across the steam-covered expanse of the Bath, the voice of Alex calling her. 'Coo-ee, coo-ee.' This, very high-pitched, was Alex's special call for Ruby, which she used, regardless of surroundings, in all sorts of situations, in shopping centres, swimming-pools, parks, as well as in the garden at Belmont. Ruby ignored the call.

'Now wait a moment please, Miss Doyle,' said John Robert. 'Bill, where are my glasses?'

'Here.' William Eastcote fetched the glasses, in their case, from a seat.

John Robert opened the case and drew out a sealed envelope folded in two.

'Coo-ee, coo-ee!'

'Now would you give this – is she still in service with Mrs McCaffrey?' He did not seem to expect her to speak.

'Yes,' said Eastcote.

'Would you give this to your mistress, please? I thought I would probably run into one or other of you at the Baths.'

'*Coo-ee!*'

Ruby nodded and took the letter.

John Robert said, 'It's quite like old times, isn't it?'

He smiled, and Ruby, smiling again, turned quickly away. Ruby, unknown to Alex, had carried the correspondence of lovers between John Robert and Linda Brent.

'Wherever did you get to?' said Alex as they left the Institute. It was not a long way to Belmont and they always walked. Ruby carried the bag with the swimming-things, now wet and heavy.

Ruby did not respond to these words which were not intended as a question. The two women walked along together in the bleak spring sunshine, dressed in their winter overcoats. They did not walk fast.

Ruby touched John Robert's letter in her pocket. She drew out the seconds and the minutes. It was like waiting for a natural function, like waiting for a sneeze, pleasurable. At last she produced the envelope.

'He gave me this for you.'

Alex did not know Rozanov's writing, which she had not seen since he wrote to thank her for the expensive wedding present which she had sent to him and Linda. But of course she did not need to be told who 'he' was. She said nothing and put the letter into her handbag. She and Ruby walked on together, stony-faced, like two marching goddesses. Robin Osmore, raising his hat unnoticed on the other side of the road, turned and stared after them.

Stella McCaffrey, *née* Henriques, was lying on the sofa in the sitting-room at Brian and Gabriel's house. Brian and Gabriel lived in the sober and not very new housing estate called Leafy Ridge. Their house had been called 'Como' by its previous owner, and although (since Brian despised such pretensions) the name was not used as an address (the address being simply number 27), it lingered on as a family nickname.

Stella was lying back propped up on cushions. Her legs were extended and covered with a blue-and-white chequered rug. Adam had just placed Zed on top of her, positioning him carefully just below her throat. The little dog had stretched his front paws forward in a gesture which seemed protective. She could feel his blunt claws against her neck. He looked into Stella's face with a mixture of curiosity and affection which she found quite unbearably touching. Afraid that tears might come, she coughed and lifted the little creature up, feeling the frailty of the skeleton which she could almost have crushed between her hands. Adam came forward and took Zed back. He stared at Stella unsmilingly but with concern. Then he went out through the glass doors into the garden.

At the foot of the sofa stood Brian. He also, with an expression resembling his son's, looked at his sister-in-law with grave concern. He admired and valued Stella. He could not put a name to his feelings for her; of course he loved her, but 'love' denotes many things. There was a mutual shyness between them. Sometimes when he kissed her, as he did rarely, for instance at Christmas, he squeezed her hand. He would have liked to be sure that she understood his esteem. His hostility to George was partly compounded of his sense of how unappreciated Stella was. He wished he could have an easy family comradeship with her. He imagined a happy family life in which he would effortlessly enjoy Stella's company, chat with her, make jokes with her, work with her, have supper with her, play bridge with her (Stella was a good player). None of this happened. Now that Stella was suddenly away from George, in Brian's house, he did not know what to do with her, he did not know what it meant or what it would bring about.

Gabriel, also gazing at the phenomenon of Stella lying on the sofa, was also at a loss. It had been her idea to bring Stella here; she had wanted it very much, she could not now remember exactly why. She too loved Stella. She wanted to help her and protect her and *spoil* her, to tend her and cherish her. She wanted to touch that proud head with a sympathetic hand. She wanted to rescue Stella, at least for a while (or perhaps, why not, forever) from her dangerous life. She wanted to give Stella a holiday from being bullied, a holiday from fighting. She wanted to get Stella right away from George. She wanted George to be isolated and accursed. She wanted Stella to be vindicated and rescued. She wanted to condemn George to loneliness, she wanted to think of George as being alone, she wanted to think of him as absolutely shut away in that tragic solitude which she had so much felt when she last looked down at his dark unconscious wet swimming head which scarcely broke the surface as he turned. Such thoughts and feelings, half-conscious and thoroughly mixed up together, conflicted in Gabriel's bosom as she gazed at her handsome clever afflicted sister-in-law. Gabriel was of course aware of Brian's admiration for Stella, and it caused her a very small local pain, but there was nothing dark or ill in her sense of this connection, and she too would have liked an ordinary happy family life wherein Stella would come to supper and talk and play bridge while Gabriel made sandwiches in the kitchen and listened to them all laughing.

Standing watching Stella from near the door was Ruby Doyle. Ruby had been 'sent over' by Alex to 'help out' in 'settling Stella in'. Alex might have been expected to come herself, but she did not want to and did not. Instead (as on other comparable occasions) she sent Ruby, as a monarch might send a diplomat or a valued craftsman. In fact Ruby, at Como, was rarely of any use at all and Gabriel did not know what to do with her. Gabriel had no servant, no maid, no char; she was temperamentally incapable of having an employee, she did everything herself. She did not want help. Brian sometimes vaguely and insincerely exhorted her to improve her mind: 'Take up some study,' 'Do a degree or something.' Nothing came of this, and to persuade herself of its impossibility Gabriel liked to be fully occupied. She enjoyed housework. She had enjoyed preparing and arranging Stella's room and putting in daffodils.

There were three bedrooms at Como, two middling-sized ones and one little one. Adam occupied the little one so as to leave a decent 'guest room', and because he preferred it. Although they hardly ever had guests, since Brian detested them, Gabriel had taken pleasure in making the guest room attractive, choosing 'guest books', arranging reading-lamps, writing-paper. When Ruby arrived, there was nothing relevant to Stella which Gabriel could think of for Ruby to do. Gabriel had already washed up breakfast and cleaned the bathroom. She could not ask Ruby to weed the garden. She made Ruby a cup of coffee.

Ruby liked Gabriel, though mutual shyness made them speechless with each other. She did not like Brian, since she regarded him as hostile to George, and she had 'taken over' Alex's view of Brian as somehow not quite a member of the family. Ruby liked Adam, with whom she had a silent semi-secret friendship. As a small child he had held on to her skirts, and sometimes still touched or twitched her dress as a remembrance of old times. She did not like Zed, a tiresome yappy little rat-like thing upon which she was always in danger of treading (she was short-sighted); but she inhibited her irritation for Adam's sake. She did not like Stella, whom she regarded as the sole cause of George's misfortunes.

Stella, lying on the sofa and looking at the way her upturned feet made a bump in the chequered rug, felt altogether alienated from her customary reality, or was perhaps realizing that she had not, and for some time now had not had, any customary reality. She looked past Brian at the tiny garden, the overlapping slats of the fence, some horrible yellow daffodils jerking about in the wind. She very much wanted to cry. She lifted up her head and hardened her eyes and wondered what on earth she, *she*, was doing in this place among these people.

Vanity, she thought, not even pride, vanity. I am stiffened by it, it is my last shred of virtue not to be seen to break down. I married George out of vanity, and I have stayed with him out of vanity. Yet she loved George. She had often wished George dead, painlessly removed, blotted out, made never to have been. Her father was right, George was a vast mistake, but he was *her* mistake, and in that *her* was all her vanity and all her love, jumbled together into something mysterious and valuable. If she could have done so she would have taken him away, would even now take him away, to some other place where no one knew the old George, where he was not surrounded by people who licked their lips and thought they

105

understood him better than his wife did. Stella would like to have been alone, shipwrecked on a desert island with George, amid dangers.

Stella felt her particular Jewishness as an alienation from English society, as a kind of empty secret freedom, as if she were less densely made than ordinary people. She had perceived, but had never understood, George's alienation, which she had seen first as a virtue, later as a charm. He had charmed her, he charmed her still. But what an ugly graceless mess it all was, and what a doom was upon her. She lifted up her handsome Jewish head and smoothed down her strong dark hair which grew up like a crown or turban above her brow. Her father had made her feel like a queen. Why on earth had she *talked* to dear well-meaning Gabriel and allowed herself to be brought to this house?

For the first time in her life Stella was feeling really ill and tired. She must be unusually weak to be, as she now was, afraid of George, afraid that he might actually kill her, of course by accident. He might, on seeing her, become, for an instant, mad with rage because of the car accident, which had been her fault, because she had needled him into a frenzy, because she had survived. Disgust at what had happened might work in George as a sudden irresistible urge to 'finish it off', and by this well-known method to destroy himself. Stella felt too weak and too confused to go back, too weak to fight George physically as she had sometimes done in the past, to hold him off until the impulse of rage should fall back into dull self-hatred. People who thought that Stella lived in hell were not wrong; but like all those who do not, they failed to understand that hell is a large place wherein there are familiar refuges and corners.

Lately a new and poisonous growth had developed in Stella's mind: jealousy. Of course she had known for years that George 'frequented' Diane Sedleigh, and some 'well-wisher' had made it her business to inform Stella that George had 'set up' the little prostitute in a flat for his own exclusive use. Something of Stella's own original respect for George had made her virtually ignore these tidings. She knew how low George could sink, but there were ways and ways of sinking, there were styles of it. She saw George as proud, even in his own manner fastidious, and with this she connected her own conception of how high, in spite of everything, he placed his wife. (Some of those who intuited these thoughts of Stella's considered them completely daft.) He and she remained, Stella felt, above and apart from anything which George might do with a whore. Now, perhaps as a result of physical shock and debility, this agnostic magnanimity was shaken. Stella began, like any crude ordinary person, to imagine George with another woman. That way real madness lay, and a kind of ignoble detestation of her husband which she had never yet allowed herself to feel. When she felt this poisonous pain she became weak, with the weakness which had made her come to Gabriel to be safe and looked after: the weakness which made her sometimes yearn to take a taxi to Heathrow and a ticket to Tokyo. She pictured her father's wise clever gentle loving face, and she felt the accursed wild tears again trying to flood her eyes out.

'I've made your room so nice', said Gabriel, 'and we'll get you any books, won't we, Brian, and you must just *feel free* and on your own and not mind us at all. You know you must rest, I think you should play the invalid for a while, stay in bed and be waited on. Don't you think, darling, that she should stay in bed?'

'Certainly not,' said Brian, smiling.

Stella, who longed to stay in bed, to lie quiet and sleep for a week, echoed, 'Certainly not.'

There was a tap at the door of the room and Father Bernard, who had come in through the kitchen, put his head round. 'Hello, can I come in?'

'Why, here's Father to see you!' said Gabriel.

Brian said 'Oh God!' just audibly, grimacing to Stella who, he thought, shared his view of the 'creepy priest'.

'I heard you were here,' said Father Bernard to Stella. 'Hello, Ruby.'

'Oh,' said Stella, 'does everyone know then? Is it a topic of conversation at the Baths?'

'Mrs Osmore told me,' said Father Bernard, smiling his charming smile. In fact Gabriel had told him by telephone, but he thought it more tactful not to mention this.

'How does she know?' said Brian crossly. 'We don't want Stella bothered with bloody people dropping in.'

'I just thought a little offering,' said Father Bernard, and handed over a long thin package wrapped in newspaper which turned out to contain half-a-dozen daffodils, still in earliest bud, entirely straight and green and cold, like six little rods.

Stella thanked him, adding, 'I'm not an invalid, you know.'

'I'll just put them in water,' said Gabriel. 'What darlings, they'll soon come out.' She bustled off with the flowers.

Stella did not in fact dislike the priest, she might have enjoyed an intellectual conversation with him, but she mistrusted his role and avoided him. She was a little bothered by his being a converted Jew. She discerned in him a desire to see the strong made weak and the lofty made low, and to make those thus afflicted his spiritual prey. This was what Brian saw as the vampirish aspect of the priest's character. Stella was sickened by the idea that Father Bernard might want to 'help her' and that Gabriel had perhaps asked him to come along with this in view.

Father Bernard looked at Stella with his gentle inquisitive light brown eyes and stroked back his fine girlish dark locks. He understood her attitude to him perfectly. His visit, motivated by curiosity, was at least partly pastoral as well. He did not think it impossible that he might somehow at some time be of assistance to this interesting woman. He did not mind running the risk of seeming an intrusive fool. In his view, people in such matters erred more by not trying than by trying too much.

He said in answer to Stella's remark, 'I know,' and 'I just came by to look at you, and to be looked at, like in the hospital. I too exist. A cat may look at a queen.'

'What's that supposed to mean?' said Brian, thereby playing into the priest's hands.

Stella laughed and returned Father Bernard's smile.

The priest did not press his advantage. He snapped his fingers noiselessly and said to Brian, 'I hear Professor Rozanov has arrived.'

'Has he?' said Brian. 'Hip hooray.'

'George will be pleased,' said Gabriel, who had just come back. 'Won't he.'

'Delighted,' said Stella.

'I've put the flowers in your room,' Gabriel told Stella.

'Will he stay long?'

'Oh, I don't imagine so,' said Gabriel quickly, as Brian was opening his mouth.

'Someone said he was going to stay –'

Somewhere elsewhere Zed could be heard barking. Then the door flew open and Tom McCaffrey came in. Zed ran in, Adam ran in.

Gabriel cried, 'Oh Tom!' Tom, knocking into Ruby as he entered, shouted 'Ruby' and kissed her. Gabriel kissed Tom. Brian slapped his shoulder. Adam hung on to his jacket. Tom said, 'Hello,

Father,' and then scooped up Zed and tried to stuff him inside his jacket pocket. Stella watched the family scene with loathing and sick despair.

'How super, all of you here, well, lots of you. Where have you hidden George? It's so nice to be back. Is this a conference? What's up with Stella, why isn't she booted and spurred? Are you all right? Have you got the 'flu? I had it, there's an awful variety going round London.'

'Stella had an accident,' said Brian.

'Oh I am sorry, are you OK?'

'Yes, yes, yes.'

'I mean really OK, please nothing awful?'

'Nothing awful, really not.'

Tom, even more than Adam, made Stella think of Rufus. She wanted to escape to her room, but wondered if she could climb the stairs unaided.

'Oh good, poor Stella, I'm so sorry. Let me kiss you. Here, I'll give you Zed, he'll cure anything.' Tom came and kissed Stella on the brow, stroked her hair lightly, then put Zed down carefully on the chequered rug in the warm depression between Stella's legs and the edge of the sofa, where the little dog settled down quietly as at a post of duty.

Tom McCaffrey, then twenty years old, was certainly the tallest and arguably the best-looking of the three brothers. He was neither sleek like George nor wolfish like Brian. He was slim but not skinny, with a soft almost girlish complexion. He had a great deal of curly brown hair tinted with gold which fell down on to his shoulders. His upper lip was long and smooth, his sensuous mouth glowed like a child's. He had the bold blue innocent eyes of Feckless Fiona.

'Oh good, what luck to find you all! How is old George, by the way? I'm quite out of the picture. How's Ma?'

'Ma's fine,' said Brian refusing to catch Gabriel's warning look. Tom evidently knew nothing of 'George's latest'.

'I think I'll go upstairs,' said Stella. She wondered if she would be able to rise. She rose. The rug and Zed descended to the floor. Stella made for the door. Gabriel followed her out.

'What's wrong with Stella?' said Tom.

'George tried to drown her,' said Brian.

'I must be off,' said Father Bernard. He moved and his blackness faded from the room. Adam and Zed ran after him.

Brian said to Ruby, 'Can't you find something to do, Ruby? Go and polish something. There must be something to clean somewhere.'

Ruby gravely set herself in motion. Tom touched her as she went out. He looked at the angry pock-marked face of his brother but did not speak. Gabriel came back. She knew from Tom's look that Brian had 'said something'.

Gabriel said brightly to Tom, 'What about the girl? Have you brought her?'

'The girl –?'

'Yes,' said Brian, 'Emma.'

'Oh good heavens,' said Tom, 'Emma – I *forgot* – how stupid.'

He ran from the room.

'You told him –' said Gabriel.

'Oh hang it, what does it matter?' said Brian. 'Someone is bound to tell him. What does it matter, what does anything matter? We're too fastidious, we're too particular, we're too fine, in a world reeling with violence and starvation and filth of every sort. What does it *matter* what George does? I'm sick of George, Stella is sick of George, I'm going out for a walk.'

But before he could leave, Tom came back accompanied by a tall thin youth with pale blond hair and narrow rimless spectacles.

'This is my friend Emmanuel Scarlett-Taylor.'

Brian said, 'Oh dear,' then covered it with a cough. There were friendly exclamations and hand-shakes, during which Scarlett-Taylor gave one abrupt smile but said nothing.

Gabriel said, 'Have you been to Belmont yet, shouldn't you ring Alex and say you're coming?'

'Oh we won't be at Belmont,' said Tom. 'We're house-sitting.'

'What?'

'Greg and Judy Osmore are away. They said we could look after their house. Here's the key.' He flourished the key.

Gregory Osmore was the younger son of Robin Osmore the solicitor.

'I think Alex is expecting you,' said Gabriel, 'so you'd better ring up and say you're *not* coming.'

'But we've come!'

'Not coming to stay, I mean.'

'I said as much,' said Scarlett-Taylor to Tom.

'Oh well, I *will* ring Alex,' said Tom, 'only not now, Gabriel, *please* –'

Scarlett-Taylor's brief remark had betrayed that he was Irish. Brian with his usual quick tact said, 'You're Irish.'

'Yes.'

'How nice,' said Gabriel. 'The Emerald Isle. A hundred thousand welcomes, isn't it? We had such a lovely holiday in Killarney once.'

'It rained all the time,' Brian said, smiling wolfishly.

Scarlett-Taylor looked at Tom.

'We must be going,' said Tom. 'We've got this house to sit.'

Adam and Zed came in.

Tom said, 'This is Adam.'

'Dog,' said Scarlett-Taylor. '*Papillon.*' He picked Zed up.

'Zed,' said Adam.

Scarlett-Taylor then smiled his real smile, which was rather logical and intellectual, the smile of an older man. He handed Zed to Adam with a graceful formal gesture.

Adam did not smile, but looked approving.

'What are you going to *do* here?' said Brian.

'Do?' The question puzzled Tom. 'Oh – have fun.'

They all reached the front door. 'Come and see us.'

'Yes, sure.'

Brian, as the door closed, said, 'Fun? What's that? Ah, youth, youth. Oh God, Ruby's still here, can't you get rid of her? And Stella's upstairs! I'd forgotten that too!'

Tom pressed the key, which he had proudly waved before his brother, into the lock and turned it. It functioned. The door opened. Tom had not quite believed beforehand that this would happen. It was like something in a fairy-tale which was too good to be true. Some demon or wicked godmother would put a binding spell upon the door, or else it would open upon some weird alien scene, empty or else full of silent hostile people, then closing again, quietly and irrevocably, behind the hapless hero. None of this happened. The door opened. The rather dark interior of the house was recognizably that of Greg and Judy Osmore. It was also immediately clear that the house was empty. It smelt empty, already a little musty and full of echoes. Another less far-fetched of Tom's fears had been that it would turn out that Greg and Judy were still there and had not gone away at all.

'Whoopee,' said Tom, softly and appreciatively, standing in the hall.

Emma followed him in.

Tom did not in fact know Gregory Osmore very well, but he had known him all his life, and in Ennistone that counted for a lot. Meeting Greg recently at a party in London, he had heard him lamenting about having to leave his house empty while he spent a month in America, with Judy, on a business course. Burglary and vandalism, once unknown in the town, were on the increase. Tom saw, quick as a flash, that sublime concatenation of duty and interest for which we so often wait in vain. He offered his services. He would spend the vacation working in Greg's house and keeping it safe and happy. Greg and Ju agreed. For Tom, the plan had everything. Apart from anything else, it provided a very good excuse for not staying at Belmont. Alex would probably have put up with Scarlett-Taylor, but would Scarlett-Taylor have put up with Alex? Tom wanted to show his native town to his new friend. On the Belmont basis he had envisaged only a brief visit. Now, however, given this glorious independence, they could spend the whole vacation there, see a bit of the countryside, be amused by the dear silly old town, and get away from their cramped dingy London digs and their censorious landlady.

Tom and (to use his nickname) Emma were at the same college in London. Emma was a little older, now in his third year of studying History. Tom was in his first year of studying English. They had known each other vaguely for a while, then lately much better after Emma had taken lodgings in the same house as Tom. Emma wanted to see the Ennistone antiquities and to visit the Museum. He did not imagine he would be very interested in the Ennistonians whom Tom promised him as the chief entertainment. Emma looked a little critically upon Tom's tendency to like everything and everybody.

'Our house,' said Tom. 'Our very own for now. Oh good!'

He had never in his life been the proprietor of so much domestic space. He began to run about, opening doors, peering into cupboards, racing up and down stairs.

Emma glanced into the sitting-room, then found Greg's study and began to look at the books. He noted with pleasure a number of historical works. (Greg had studied History at York.) Emma went over the shelves systematically. He pulled out Pirenne's *History of Europe* and sat down, and was instantly absorbed in reading.

Meanwhile Tom was in a state of rapture. He investigated the

kitchen. No crouching in grates or cooking on gas rings here. Tom
liked cooking, in a random eccentric sort of way. He investigated
the larder and the fridge. He went into the sitting-room and studied
all the pictures and ornaments. He had been in the house before,
of course, but only on social occasions, and he had never seen the
sitting-room empty. Tom liked pictures, he liked things, he ap-
preciated the visual world. He would have liked to be a rich man
and be able to collect. However, he had no plans for becoming a
rich man; he had as yet no plans.

Greg and Judy, who were still childless, lived in a pleasant part
of Ennistone, on the far side of the town from the Common on the
way towards the Tweed Mill. This area was called, for some reason,
Biggins, and consisted largely of Victorian terrace houses, lately
gentrified, their brick façades painted different colours. Of course
the place to live in Ennistone was the Crescent, near the eighteenth-
century bridge, the abode of Eastcotes and Newbolds and Burdetts.
However, there were parts of Biggins which were regarded as very
desirable residential areas, quite the equal of Victoria Park. The
'best road', called Travancore Avenue in memory of some Ennistonian who had served the Raj in that city, started in some splendour near the Crescent and ended more humbly but agreeably
enough on the edge of the countryside, with views of the Tweed
Mill. House agents described the residences, all sought after, as
being 'at the Crescent end' (or 'adjoining the fashionable Crescent')
or 'at the Tweed Mill end'. Ivor Sefton occupied a late eighteenth-
century villa at the Crescent end. The Gregory Osmores lived in a
pretty little detached house behind plane trees at the Tweed Mill
end. Greg had purchased this house when, after working in London
as an accountant, he had (quite recently) become an all-purpose
businessman in the management of the Glove Factory, where, it
was said, he was certain to become quite a 'big cheese'. His elder
brother, equally successful, was a barrister in London.

Tom inspected the bedrooms. There were four, all good rooms.
All the beds were made up with clean sheets. Excluding Greg and
Ju's room, Tom liked best the one with the view over the garden,
though the front ones were nice too, whence the minaret chimney
of the Tweed Mill was visible between the planes. He decided to let
Emma choose. Biggins occupied a 'healthy eminence', and standing
at the back window Tom could see most of the principal monuments of Ennistone: the Institute, the gilded cupola of the Hall, the
blunt grey tower of St Olaf's, the striated spire of St Paul's (Father

113

Bernard's 'shop'), the thin spire of the Catholic 'tin church' in Burkestown, the bulky Methodist church in Druidsdale, the Friends' Meeting House, Bowcocks department store, the gasworks, the Glove Factory (a castellated nineteenth-century brick building) and the new controversial Polytechnic building beyond the Common.

Tom inspected the bathroom. The bathroom at his London digs (near Kings Cross) was a squalid penitential room, not clean and probably not cleanable, shared by a number of male lodgers. The Greg and Ju bathroom was a bower of luxury (Judy had a thing about baths) with the king-size bath set low in the tiled floor, and a matching basin *and* bidet all made of curiously fat and sensuously rounded red porcelain. The tiles were black. The taps and towel-rails were made of (presumably imitation) gold. Fat fluffy black towels trimmed with red hung from the rails. Upon a gleaming black shelf was a row of jars and bottles containing (Tom had no doubt and he soon checked) celestial unguents. A tiled curtained archway concealed a shower, another such archway the loo. Tom decided that he must have a bath *at once*. He began to run the water, pouring in the oil and wine of the unguent shelf. A heavenly smell arose.

While this was making he went into Greg and Ju's bedroom and opened the sliding door of the huge wall cupboard which ran the length of the room. A glittering array of garments met his eye. Both Greg and Judy were vain about their appearance; they were a handsome pair and loved clothes. Tom feasted his gaze upon Greg's numerous well-tailored suits (he *never* wore jeans), sleek evening dress, fancy shirts, some with *lace*. A thousand silk ties. Ju's clothes were nice, too, and smelt nice. She wore very feminine stuff with flounces, tucks, ruffs, gathers, nonsense, which she wore long and pulled in with little belts, to her slim waist. In winter she wore fine light tweed dresses over brilliantly coloured blouses with smart scarves even silkier than Greg's ties. Her summer dresses were made of that sort of feather-weight polyester which is what cotton is like when it goes to heaven. Tom fingered some of these dresses and sighed. He reflected that these yummy clothes must represent Greg and Judy's *second* team. The first team was even now gladdening the eyes of Americans in Florida.

As the clothes slid silently and easily along the rail upon their sleek hangers, Tom's hand fastened on something which looked as if it was made of feathers and felt as if it was made of gauze. He

114

drew it out: a very pale blue *négligé* with multiple cufflets and collarettes. He thrust his hands into the sleeves and pulled it on and gazed at himself in the long swinging mahogany-framed mirror which must so often have reflected that beautiful and fortunate pair. With his tumbling curly locks and his smooth fresh complexion Tom looked, well, quite extraordinary. He looked at himself for a moment with surprise and admiration, then decided to go and show himself to Emma. He skipped daintily down the stairs and flounced into the study.

'Aren't I lovely?'

Emma was still reading. He read: 'Luther was merely advancing still further upon the path which had been trodden before his time by Wycliffe and John Huss. His theology was a continuation of the dissident theology of the Middle Ages; his ancestors were the great heretics of the fourteenth century; he was absolutely untouched by the spirit of the Renaissance. His doctrine of justification by faith was related to the doctrines of the mystics, and although, like the humanists, though for very different reasons, he condemned celibacy and the ascetic life, he was in absolute opposition to them in his complete sacrifice of free will and reason to faith. However, the humanists did not fail to applaud his sensational debut.' He looked up. He was not pleased to see Tom in drag. Emma himself suffered from secret transvestite fantasies; Tom's caprice struck him as the idle profanation of a mystery. He said coldly, 'You ought to telephone your mother.'

'Not now,' said Tom.

'Yes, now.'

'Oh, all right.'

The telephone was in the hall.

As Tom dialled the number his heart sank. It also beat faster. He hated the telephone. He particularly hated talking to Alex on it. He felt guilty at not being at Belmont, at not having told her, at a hundred matters arising from his imperfect conduct.

'Yes?' said Alex at the other end. She always said 'Yes?' in that disconcerting way.

'Hello, it's me, Tom.'

'Where are you, when are you coming?'

'Look, I'm sorry, I should have told you.'

'What?'

'I should have said, I met Gregory Osmore in London –'

'Who?'

'Gregory Osmore, and he absolutely begged me to look after his house –'

'To what?'

'To look after his house.'

Emma rose and closed the study door. He did not think it proper to overhear Tom's conversation with his mother. He regretted that he had already heard Tom tell a lie. He had been present at the party where Tom met Gregory Osmore, and the boot had rather been on the other foot. It was Tom who had (discreetly) insisted to Greg that the house-sitting idea was such a good one. Emma did not approve of lying, and it caused him pain that his friend occasionally indulged in *suppressio veri* and *suggestio falsi*.

'You know Greg and Judy have gone to Florida?' said Tom.

'Where?'

'To Florida.'

'Have they?'

'Yes, and they asked me if I would occupy their house while they were away, to keep it safe, you know. So I won't be – I won't be able to stay with you – but I'll come round and –'

'You aren't going to stay at Belmont?'

'No.'

'Where are you now?'

Tom thought of saying 'in London', but he did, after all, possess some sense of truth. He said, 'I'm at their place, at Travancore Avenue.'

'Are you alone?'

'Am I –?'

'Are you alone there?'

'No, I've got a friend with me, a chap.'

'A man?'

'Yes.'

'When are you coming to see me?'

'Oh, soon – tomorrow, I – I've got to fetch some stuff –'

'Telephone first, would you?'

'Yes, sure.'

They were both silent. Alex hated the telephone too. Neither of them was good at ending a conversation.

'Good-bye then,' said Alex, and put the 'phone down.

Tom replaced the receiver. He felt curiously uneasy, as if disappointed. He had hoped that Alex would not make a fuss about his not staying with her. Well, she had seemed not to mind too much.

116

Of course on the telephone one couldn't tell. He hated fuss. Yet he wanted her to mind.

He opened the study door.

'All right?' said Emma.

'All right. I say, let's go out, let's go shopping.'

'Shopping? Why?'

'To buy something for lunch.'

'I don't want any lunch.'

'Well, I do, I'm starving.'

'You go, I'm reading.'

'I wish I could read like you.'

'You can read.'

'Not like you. Put you down anywhere and you start reading. And you remember what you read, it goes into a slot in your mind. My mind has no slots. Let's have a drink. I found a cupboard absolutely crammed with bottles.'

'We can't drink their stuff.'

'We can replace it.'

'Do take that thing off.'

'Sorry, I forgot I had it on. My God, I left the bath running!'

Tom raced upstairs. He thought, the sitting-room ceiling will come down and we've only been here half an hour!

But all was well. An interesting funnel at one end of the bath conveyed the overflowing water into a depression in the tiled floor where it ran away harmlessly through a grating. Tom took off his shoes and socks and danced on top of the grating, feeling the steamy exuberant water running away between his toes. He tucked up his trouser ends, but the hem of Ju's *négligé* got a little wet.

Tom McCaffrey was an object of interest in Ennistone 'society'. 'Society' in Ennistone was, by this time, classlessly elitist; it was also plural. This was particularly evident of the Institute. Indeed the existence and peculiar nature of the Institute helped this process. History too assisted. Ennistone had lost its 'landed gentry' early on, and had become democratic and non-conformist well before the nineteenth century. Some notion of 'the best families' persisted, well mixed up with high ideals and moral leadership, but even this, by the time of our story, had virtually disappeared. To take an instance, the mind of William Eastcote, an exceptionally good man, probably contained some grain of irrational superiority, while I

117

believe that absolutely no blemish of this sort existed in the mind of Anthea. Snobbery was with us intellectual and moralistic rather than social in the old sense. Groups of people freely 'set themselves up' as arbiters and judges with pretensions to cultural or moral superiority. There was, in so far as such initiatives were concerned, an atmosphere of 'free enterprise'. There were of course members of the Victoria Park 'old school' who simply disliked change, there were those who 'kept themselves to themselves', and those who hated everybody. There were differences of opinion and differences of style. My point is simply that those who thought well of themselves tended to think they were right rather than that they were grand. Our old Quakerish Methodistic priggishness promoted this advance, if it was an advance; I think it was.

Our 'society' looked tolerantly on Tom McCaffrey. Perhaps this was likely to happen since Alex, George and Brian were in their different ways looked at askance: George for obvious reasons, Alex because she was 'stuck up', and Brian because he was brusque and sardonic, and in his own way rather priggish. Tom was seen, by contrast, as young, unspoilt, and 'rather sweet'. He was also pictured somewhat as setting out on life's journey with a plume in his helmet and a sword at his knee. He was good-tempered and had as yet been guilty of no outrages, in Ennistone at any rate. Mothers sometimes held him up as an example to their sons. 'There's Tom McCaffrey, he's not on drugs or chasing girls all day, he's got himself into the University, he'll make something of his life.' 'He chases girls in London,' the sons sometimes darkly muttered. 'Well, he does it discreetly,' the mothers would reply, thus further confusing the moral sense of their offspring. It was true that Tom was not seen to chase Ennistone girls. Many of the potential chasees were sorry about this, but were at least spared the chagrin of seeing a rival preferred. Match-makers had long ago decided that Tom and Anthea Eastcote were made for each other. What these two young people thought was still obscure. Tom was also noteworthy and even popular because of the legend of 'Feckless Fiona', and folk memories of her charm, her 'dottiness', her cheerful happy ways, and her sad early death.

Tom had indeed, after a worthy career at Ennistone Comprehensive School, got himself into a distinguished London college, where he was supposed to be 'doing well', though some said he was 'talented but lazy'. Darker critics predicted a nervous breakdown: after all, the boy had lost both his parents very early and had been brought up by an eccentric emotional step-mother, with two strong-willed mutually hostile half-brothers playing the role of father. However, of this breakdown there was admitted to be no sign.

Tom had, unlike his introspective friend Scarlett-Taylor, little conception of himself; at any rate he did not reflect much about himself, about his character, abilities and prospects. He was not ambitious and had no plans. It is true that he wrote verses, and was even spoken of in Ennistone as a 'poet', which Tom knew perfectly well that, as yet, he was not. His future remained enormously far away, separated from him by a vast cornucopious present. He enjoyed his studies and intermittently tried to do well. He was perhaps lazy, at any rate easily deflected to other pleasures, of which he had a great many. Among those pleasures sex was not obsessively primary. Tom was credited, by some of his ex-school-fellows, with many sexual conquests in London. This supposition was needed to explain his apparent lack of interest in Ennistone girls. Of course some said that he was homosexual, but this was not the general view. In fact, although Tom did not trouble to deny the supposition, he had had fewer adventures than was supposed. He *had* had adventures but was ruefully aware that he had rarely initiated or controlled these. 'Knowing girls' had on occasion decoyed Tom into bed, and Tom had not complained; moreover his vanity was flattered. But whether he had ever been in love was a subject which he often discussed with Scarlett-Taylor.

He often thought about his parents but with a carefully bounded vagueness. He imagined Fiona arriving on that motor bike and at once meeting Alan, as the legend ran; the absolute *chance* that had initiated his existence. These thoughts were very private. Other people tactfully avoided the subject. There was felt to be something both touching and awful in the circumstances in which Tom had been born and orphaned. Tom felt this too and was gentle with himself. Fiona Gates's family had not figured in Tom's life, he was never entirely sure why. Robin Osmore, 'feeling it his duty', had said something about the matter when Tom was a schoolboy. It seemed that Fiona, living unmarried with Alan, had written to assure her parents that she was well, but probably without revealing her whereabouts. When she wrote later to announce Tom's existence and her marriage plans, her parents were shocked and upset. Whatever it was (and Tom had no idea) that had induced Fiona to leave home had certainly not been mended by time and her antics. Heated letters passed between Alan and the father. Alan took the pretext to be angry, and relations were, it was then assumed temporarily, broken off. In fact it seemed that Fiona's parents were mild inoffensive people, bullied by Fiona, intimidated by Alan, and after Fiona's death by the McCaffrey phalanx in the form of Alex, George and Brian momentarily united. Stunned by their daughter's death (they had lost her brother as a child), they went to join cousins in New Zealand. From here, later on, they wrote occasional sad inarticulate letters to Tom, to which he never replied since (he never knew this) Alex in her wisdom destroyed them on arrival. Once she had made Tom her property, Alex never tolerated even the most shadowy hint of any other claim upon him. Alex never spoke of these obscure grandparents, and it was Robin Osmore who told Tom of their decease. Later Tom wished that he had 'done something' about them. Later still he felt it was a mystery better left alone. He felt the same, with much more intensity, about his father's death. Alan had died in some 'medical experiment' in a laboratory in Hong Kong. No details ever emerged. When he was a schoolboy Tom thought he might go there one day and find out. He even wondered whether his father had been murdered. He vaguely pictured him as someone who might have been murdered. But more recently he had decided to leave Alan in peace. He was afraid of some awful hurt, some awful pain, which might result from probing. He knew there were demons in his life. He thought he could remember Alan. He could not remember Fiona. He possessed some photographs of his parents: his handsome dark-haired father, a figure of authority, his mother, so curly-haired and pretty, so childish-looking, always laughing. If she were still alive she would not yet be forty years old. He also had, and kept in a little wooden box, her wedding ring. (Robin Osmore had given it to him.) On what appalling evening, in what quiet room, had Alan McCaffrey drawn that ring from the thin white finger of his dead wife?

Tom had loved and accepted Alex, from his earliest childhood, with the whole of his heart, but he had never thought of her as his mother. Some simple person, Ruby perhaps, had told him early on that his mother was an angel, and thus he had pictured her, a curly-haired and rather boyish angel, recognizing her image in the hermaphrodite winged figures in the Victorian stained-glass windows of St Paul's Church, which he occasionally visited out on walks with Ruby. Alex was something else, something wonderful and very

120

powerful which he adored. Ruby was the dear animal being in whose smell he took refuge from power. George and Brian figured as dual fathers vying for his affection, then suddenly and incomprehensibly punishing. It was Brian who particularly set up as his moral mentor, correcting and admonishing, and leading him every Sunday to the Friends' Meeting House. Meanwhile Alex watched these fraternal influences jealously, particularly irritated by signs of mutual affection between Tom and George. Tom early learnt to be tactful, even circumspect. This combination of rivalry and possessiveness and authoritarian love, the lack of stability between the rulers of his life, often made up, for the child, a difficult regime. Under these strains Tom could have been forgiven for being a sad crazy mixed-up boy, but he simply was not. His guardian-angel mother, always so young, had somehow preserved in him intact her own unquestioning faith in life, her capacity for joy, her vast indomitable self-satisfaction.

Tom did not reflect upon the dynamics of these various relationships which would have been (and indeed were) of such interest to (for instance) Ivor Sefton. He loved Alex, Ruby, Brian and George thoughtlessly and in differing ways which he apprehended but did not analyse. He did not want to *bother his head* about such matters, and if they ever started to puzzle him he would *shake* his head as if to send away a swarm of bees which seemed to wish to settle in his brain. They were easily dispelled. He hated rows and walked away from them and found (such was his felicity) that his nearest and dearest did not in fact want to involve him, had already instinctively invested him with a kind of blessed neutrality, a status of someone not to be enlisted or dragged into taking sides. His easiest relations were with Ruby and Brian. With Ruby his ordinary natural selfishness simply ran riot in the space which the servant opened to him. He never found himself wondering what she thought or whether she judged. Brian was an alien whom he loved and respected and who had quite convincingly played the role of father. (In a sense, Brian had been more resolute as Tom's father than he was being as Adam's.) He was not 'close' to Brian, but he knew that in a shipwreck he and Brian would know how to stand shoulder to shoulder. Alex and George were the 'funny ones'. When Alex annexed Tom (*not* walking into Fiona's room and seizing him from the cradle), Brian, in early independence, was beginning his long revenge upon his mother for having always so patently preferred George. George, meanwhile, especially unhappy at this period of his life, was taking *his* revenge on Alex for her possessive and undisguised affections. Alex, who pictured herself as a fighter, felt alone, menaced and rejected. Tom was the key, the godsend, the new love object. (Alan brought Tom to Belmont in his arms, the child clinging to the lapels of his coat like an animal; Alex had difficulty in detaching the fierce little claw-like hands.) Of course she loved and wanted the little boy for himself; love was always Alex's game. She had coveted the child from the moment he existed, and no doubt her jealousy was salved by the triumphant possession of Fiona's son. But she needed him too, instinctively, as a weapon against his two brothers, especially against George.

How far this plan of establishing a rival worked in practice was never clear; perhaps in a way it worked only too well. Brian was certainly annoyed, but his sense of duty consoled him here, as it had always done in his other trials. Brian, the owner no doubt of a difficult temperament, was actually capable of being cheered up by the exercise of rational activity. Tom was in danger from Alex's emotions, from George's 'frightfulness'. Brian waded in, as if he had seen the child struggling in a river. He must be hauled out, shaken, dried, stood up, told what was what; and Brian could not help loving what he thus served and protected. George, in so far as he exerted himself *in loco patris*, did so with motives more obscure. Tom, as a child, was sometimes afraid of George, but only in a rather immediate sense. He was, on a few memorable occasions, at the receiving end of George's violence. He felt no resentment, however. The strange thing was that while Brian, who was certainly more like George than Tom was, simply did not understand George at all, Tom did somehow understand him. Tom had not in his being one iota of that which made George what he was, but Tom saw and apprehended *that*, not intellectually or theoretically, but with (for of course he loved George) a loving intuition. This led the now adult, or almost adult, Tom to fear George in a new way and to fear *for* him. Something in this understanding led Tom to make the only conscious move he had so far made in relation to his family. In the obscure machinery of the familial stars and planets it was time for George to move back towards his mother. They were two of a kind, Alex and George, and Tom's special task was in a sense done. The old pact between George and Alex had never really been broken. Tom began to move aside, to move away; and as he retired, George came quietly, loping on dark paws, into the space near Alex which Tom was leaving. As they thus passed each other, did they exchange a glance? Perhaps. If so, it was a very ambiguous one.

Emmanuel Scarlett-Taylor was a comparatively new phenomenon in Tom's young life. In general, Tom liked everybody and was friends with everybody, and in so far as there had been closer ties, these had tended to be contextual. His love affairs, which he thought of as 'romances', had been comparatively uncomplicated and unhurtful, largely because of the witty good sense of the girls concerned. (This was pure luck.) Tom did not yet possess the concept of a *deep* relationship except in the unconscious form of his connection with his family. The Irish boy was something of a novelty. He was two years older than Tom, at an age when two years counted for much. Tom had been vaguely aware of him as being a bit of an intellectual 'grandee', tipped to get a 'first', a gloomy proud solitary sort of fellow. He had a reputation for being arrogant and rude. He had never been rude to Tom, but then on the other hand he had never paid any attention to Tom whatsoever. When Scarlett-Taylor moved into the shabby and cheap lodging-house where Tom was living, Tom had felt dismay, even annoyance. However, his view of his fellow student soon began to change.

The first and most dramatic change had occurred on a drunken evening in December. Tom was setting out with some friends for a 'pub crawl' in central London. As they were leaving Tom's lodgings they ran into Scarlett-Taylor. Out of an impulse of politeness and curiosity, since he still scarcely knew the Irishman, Tom asked him to join them. Rather to his surprise Scarlett-Taylor agreed, and accompanied them though with a silent and preoccupied air. The 'crawl' was to begin at the Black Horse in north Soho, to proceed through the more riotous pubs of south Soho, through Leicester Square, and down Whitehall to the river. The pubs were decorated for Christmas, noisy and rather full. Scarlett-Taylor said little but drank, Tom noticed, a great deal. First beer then whisky. The final objective was the Red Lion at the far end of Whitehall, but by the time they got as far as the Old Shades most of the others had disappeared, leaving Tom, finally, in charge of his rather drunken fellow lodger. When they arrived at the Red Lion it was closed. Tom and Scarlett-Taylor went on to the river, on to the bridge, then along the embankment. The tide was in and, leaning over, they could almost touch the water which was being whipped into wavelets by the east wind. Scarlett-Taylor's spectacles actually fell off and were caught in mid-air. They began to walk back along

Whitehall with their coat collars turned up. Tom, feeling the airy liberated bonhomie of the happily drunk man, took Scarlett-Taylor's arm, but was not put out when his friend, as he now thought of him, quickly detached himself. Then Tom began, rather loudly, to sing. He had a pleasant modest baritone from which he derived considerable pleasure and which, when it did not seem too much like showing off, he liked to exhibit. He began to sing an Elizabethan song: *If she forsake me I must die. Shall I tell her so?* In the second verse Scarlett-Taylor joined in. Tom checked his own voice abruptly, stopped in his tracks and held on to a lamp post. Scarlett-Taylor possessed a marvellous counter-tenor voice.

When we suddenly learn that some unobtrusive fellow is a chess champion or great tennis player, the man is physically transformed for us. So it was with Tom. In the instant, Scarlett-Taylor was a different being. And in the instant too, deep in his mind, Tom made an important and necessary decision. He was interested enough in singing to recognize an exceptional voice and to covet it. There was a quick tiny fierce impulse of pure envy, a sense of passionate rivalry for the world. But almost in the same moment of recognition, making one of those moves of genuine sympathy by which we defend our egoism, Tom embraced his rival and drew him in to himself, making that superb voice his own possession. He would be endlessly proud of Scarlett-Taylor and take what he later called 'Emma's secret weapon' as a credit to himself. Ownership would preclude envy; this remarkable sound and its owner were now his. Thus Tom easily enlarged his ego or (according to one's point of view) broke its barriers so as to unite himself with another in joint proprietorship of the world: a movement of salvation which for him was easy, for others (George, for instance) very hard.

The immediate problem, however, was to stop Emma from singing. Tom's untrained voice had been loud. Emma's trained voice was resonant, piercing and so extremely *strange*, almost an uncanny sound. Windows opened in the Horse Guards Hotel. Several people crossed the road from the Old Admiralty Building. Others, leaving the Whitehall Theatre, stopped amazed, gazed about bewildered. Roisterers in Trafalgar Square approached like rats after a piper. A policeman appeared. Tom bundled Emma, still singing, into a taxi, where the Irish boy promptly fell asleep. Tom laughed quietly, profoundly, with tears of pure pleasure in his eyes, all the way back to the digs.

*

Emmanuel Scarlett-Taylor as he was 'in himself' was not soon known to Tom, though they became friends, and doubtless never entirely known (but then who is ever entirely known?). Some general account must, however, be briefly given of him who is Horatio to our Hamlet, or (for they often exchanged roles) Hamlet to our Horatio.

Scarlett-Taylor was born in County Wicklow, between the mountains and the sea. His father's ancestors had been land-owners in the west of Ireland, but his father and grandfather, proceeding from English public schools to Trinity College, Dublin, were Dublin lawyers. His mother (*née* Gordon) came from Ulster, the County Down, where her ancestors had been sheep farmers, her father a doctor. She had been sent to a 'finishing school' in Switzer-land and then to Trinity, where she met Emma's father. Both sides of the family were Protestants and horsemen. Emma was an only child. His father died when he was twelve, and his mother went to live in Brussels, near her sister who had married a Belgian architect. Emma began his growing-up in Dublin in a Georgian house near Merrion Square with a semi-circular fanlight and a shiny black door with a brass dolphin knocker, and continued it in Brussels in a big dark flat in a gloomy respectable street not far from the Avenue Louise, with pollarded plane trees and tall thin peaky houses made of pale yellow brick. His handsome sweet witty mother grew older. The Belgian architect and his wife were no more. Emma, vaguely destined for Trinity, declined to return to his native land. He liked Brussels, not the old grand parts, not the shiny new parts, but the melancholy bourgeois streets, still so quiet and full of a not inaccessible past, where suddenly on a corner there would be found a little bar with red check table-cloths and aspidis-tras and a black cat. He liked London too, and foresaw his future as a Londoner. He hated, with all his heart and soul, Ireland, the Irish, and himself.

Dr Johnson said that when a man says his heart bleeds for his country he experiences no uncomfortable sensation. With Emma it was otherwise. It had mattered little to him as a child that his great-grandfather's house had been burnt by 'the rebels'. He had admired the men of 1916 and the fight for Ireland's freedom. Ireland, indeed, had made him a historian. His father never talked politics, lived in a narrow company of old friends, seemed more at home with his books. Sometimes it seemed as if his father had had a piece of his past removed; like losing a lung or a kidney, one had to 'take things quietly'. He easily forgave Emma's indifference to horses, he wished he had been a scholar, he wanted Emma to be one. He died before the resumption of the 'troubles'.

Emma had been brought up as a vague Anglican. Both his parents were vague Anglicans, occasional church-goers, whose sacred text was Cranmer's Prayer Book. Emma's mother taught him to pray, then left him alone with God. Emma and God parted company, but he felt an attachment to the Church. He went to an English public school where he sang in the choir and obtained his nickname. He had never been anti-Catholic. He envied the ritual, he loved the Latin mass, he approved of the full churches. Religion was history, and history taught tolerance. Then the shooting started. Emma watched the slaughter taking place in the gratuitous untimely cause of a 'United Ireland'. He saw with unutterable grief the emergence of Protestant murderers, as vile as their foes. He felt guilt and misery and rage. The little town near his mother's family house was blown apart by a bomb placed in the sad little main street with its white houses and its six pubs. Protestants and Catholics died together. He visited Belfast and saw the handsome city wrecked, its public buildings destroyed, its abandoned streets turned into bricked-up tombs. As it seemed to him nobody cared much, not even the decent English taxpayers who paid the bill, not even the Protestants in the South. So long as the bombs stayed in Ulster, there was even a mild satisfaction in hearing about them. For the first occasion in his own lifetime Emma had a close-up view of human wickedness; and in his very private confused self-rage he rejected his Irishness, he tore it to shreds in sick futile anger, sometimes scarcely knowing what it was he detested most in the stew of hatred for which he so despised himself. He never mentioned Irish matters to his mother, and she never spoke of Ireland either. When their native land was named by others he saw on her face the same frozen look which he felt on his own. He had no country. He envied Tom who had no sense of nationality and did not seem to need one. (That, presumably, was the essence of being English.) Yet when in his mind Emma tried to resolve himself into being English, it was impossible, he was utterly utterly not English. When people said (for his voice, damnably, betrayed him), 'You're Irish?', and he replied, 'Anglo-Irish', and they said, 'Oh, so you're not real Irish,' Emma Scarlett-Taylor smiled faintly and said nothing. He felt equally bitter and even more taciturn over another problem to do with his sense of identity. He was not sure whether or not he was homosexual. Perhaps this did not matter too much, however, since after a few unpleasant little adventures he had decided to give up sex.

Scarlett-Taylor's given name had a double meaning, so that he had even entered the world with a dual nationality, under two flags. His father was thinking of the great philosopher, his mother of the Redeemer. His father had regarded Anglicanism as a religion of the Enlightenment, at any rate as a rational protest against the foul superstition with which, in Dublin, he was surrounded. His mother was romantically pious and still attended the English Church in Brussels and sang the old hymns in her sweet fading voice. (She had a pretty soprano and used to do amusing imitations of Richard Tauber.) Emma resembled his father, whom he loved very much: the shock waves of that loss still stirred him. He was, like his father, tall, with straight straw-coloured hair and delicate pale lips and narrow light-blue eyes. He dressed, like his father, in smart old-fashioned suits with waistcoats. (Only, whereas his father had had the best tailor in Dublin, Emma bought his clothes second-hand.) He wore butterfly collars and cravats, and possessed (his father's) a watch with a chain. He wore narrow rimless glasses in imitation of his father's pince-nez. He looked like a scholar and a gentleman. He was also athletic. His father had been a good tennis player and had organized 'the cricket game' in Dublin. (For Emma's father cricket, like Anglicanism, was a protest activity.) Emma was also good at tennis, and at school had been able to hit a cricket ball harder and further than anyone else. By now, however, he had given up athletic games, partly because he had become increasingly short-sighted. He had also, more lately, given up chess.

The next thing to give up was singing. Emma was not timidly modest about his accomplishments. He knew that he was, in the academic sense, very clever. He did not need to be told by his tutor that he would get a good first-class degree. Then some time after that he would *become a historian*. He also knew that he had an exceptionally good voice. Various people had urged him to become a professional singer. Emma regarded the exercise of his gift rather in the light of a temptation. He knew, and part of him clearly loved, the remarkable unique personal sense of *power* which a good singer experiences, something more psychosomatically *personal*, perhaps, than the exercise of any other talent. His pleasure in his vocal triumph at school seemed to him sinister, quite unlike the clean satisfaction of academic work. In any case, he now simply had no time for singing. Whenever possible he kept his talent a secret, and was angry with himself for having got drunk (which he rarely, but then extremely, did) and given himself away to Tom McCaffrey, whom he had thereafter sworn to secrecy. However, he had not yet broken off relations with his dangerous and charming gift. He still went to see his singing teacher, a gloomy man, a failed composer, once an opera singer, who lived near Harrods, and from whom he continued to take lessons, and conceal how little he practised. Emma had learnt some harmony from the music master at school; this represented another and different temptation into which also Tom tiresomely entered. Emma had first met Tom when Emma's piano, being lugged up to his room by some cross removal men, had stuck on the stairs. Tom had never yet heard a sound out of the piano, but invented by himself the idea that Emma could compose music. Tom's next idea was a pop group, music by Emma, lyrics by Tom, to be called 'the Shaxbirds'. Emma certainly did not, even momentarily, hate music the way he hated Ireland; but he could not come to terms with it any more than he could with his sex life.

Emma's first view of Tom was that he was a tactless nuisance. How had it come about that he had let Tom seem to 'acquire' him? Tom was indiscreetly anxious to show off his friendship with some-one whom he regarded as so superior and *difficile*. Tom's thought-less assumption of the possibility of affection between them alarmed Emma, Tom's capacity for happiness amazed him. At Christmas Tom had unexpectedly given Emma a book (Marvell's Poems). To reciprocate, Emma had hastily given Tom a cherished knife. How had that come about? Tom positively wanted to look after him. The trip to Ennistone, awfully unwise perhaps, was part of this process. Emma could not help being moved by the sheer confidence of Tom's friendliness to him, but he was not at all sure that he wanted to be looked after, or that Tom had the faintest idea what his new friend was really like.

When Alex had returned with Ruby from the Institute, with John Robert Rozanov's letter burning away in her pocket, she had gone straight upstairs to the drawing-room but had not at once opened the letter. Standing in the bow window, looking out at the cold startled trees and the wet green roof of the Slipper House, she had given herself up to a tide of emotion. Or perhaps it was more like being on a slow dreamy switchback, flying down, then flying up, a sort of giddiness, a moment of anticipation felt in the entrails. There was slight nausea and a sense of being moved suddenly about as in some state of drunkenness. Alex was surprised at her sensations, yet she apprehended too that she had been in an emotional state for some time now, as if expecting something to happen. This was not just the melancholia of the ageing woman; there was something more positive, more like an exasperation with the world expressing itself as a desire for violent change. She recalled that she had dreamed of her nanny last night; that was a portent, not always a happy one.

She took out the letter, fingered it and at last hurriedly opened it. It read as follows:

16 Hare Lane
Ennistone

Dear Mrs McCaffrey,

    I wonder if you could be so good as to come and see me? There is something I would like to ask you. Any morning would be suitable. Could you let me know when? I am afraid that I am not on the telephone.

    With kind regards,

Yours sincerely,
J. R. Rozanov

Alex stared at this text for a long time. It remained opaque, as disturbing and impenetrable as a message in a foreign tongue suddenly flashed upon a wall. Its immediate effect upon her was of disappointment. What had she crazily expected? 'Alex, you have always been in my heart. I feel I must ... etc.' This formal note 'with kind regards' was cold indeed. 'There is something I would like to ask you.' No passionate proposal would be heralded by such language. Alex felt, for a moment, intensely childishly let down. She crumpled the letter in her hands. Then she uncrumpled it again.

It was cool but was it not nevertheless sufficiently mysterious? After all, if John Robert did want to approach her in sentimental mood he would be far too proud to show his hand at once. In fact such a letter would be exactly the kind which he would write, suggesting a meeting, giving nothing away. He would want to look at her, converse perhaps with a show of indifference, make some estimate of *her* feelings. At the Baths he had seemed to be looking around in search of someone. Why had he come back to Ennistone? It could not just be to try the effect of the waters on his arthritis.

Alex had met John Robert at a period of youth when deep and lasting impressions are made. Had John Robert, attracted by Linda, really loved Alex? He might well have thought that Geoffrey Stillowen's daughter was beyond his reach. Had he vividly and regretfully remembered her all these years? And in a moment Alex was saying to herself: how could he *not*!

She checked these speculations, however. A self-protective cunning made her deliberately calmer. She set herself to think more simply about the mechanics of the visit. He did not suggest visiting her, that was understandable. Alex had already devoted some imagination to the scene of her meeting with the philosopher. She had certainly not wanted to confront him at the Baths. She had pictured meeting him here, in her own drawing-room. Ruby would let him in. She would hear his heavy step upon the stair. She had even considered pretexts upon which she could invite him. She was fortunate to have the problem of the first move so promptly solved, though a walk through Ennistone in this weather would not improve her appearance. He too wanted the advantage of his home ground.

Hare Lane. She did not recognize the address. She rang the bell for Ruby. Ruby, with a tread as heavy as Rozanov's, mounted the stairs and presented her stony face and monumental incarnation.

'Ruby, Professor Rozanov has written to me from an address in Hare Lane. Where is Hare Lane?'

Ruby replied, 'It's in Burkestown, near the level crossing.' She added, 'It's the old house.'

'What?'

'It's his old house, his mum's place, where he was born.'

Alex considered this. 'How do you know?'

'Number sixteen,' said Ruby. 'Everyone knows that!'

'Thank you, Ruby.'

Ruby departed.

Alex felt annoyed that Ruby had known so much. Too much.

Should she reply to the letter at once? It might be a mistake to seem too eager. Suppose she waited a few days, then wrote casually as if his letter had slipped her mind? But she could not feign this. The idea of setting pen to paper was already too attractive. Her reply must catch today's post. Having decided this, she prolonged her reflections, luxuriated in them up to the neck as in the hot water of the 'stew'. At last, with slow movements, she went to her desk and set out pen and paper and wrote as follows:

Dear Professor Rozanov,

Thank you for your letter. I could call on you about eleven a.m. on Wednesday (the day after tomorrow). I will assume that suits you unless I hear otherwise.

With kind regards,

Yours sincerely,

Alexandra McCaffrey

The tone of the letter presented no problem; her reply must be at least as cool as his request. She was only unsure about 'kind regards'. Could it sound like a sarcastic parody? 'Affectionate greetings'? Certainly not. 'I look forward to seeing you'? No. She sealed up the letter and went out and posted it.

Now it was Tuesday; and tomorrow she would see John Robert Rozanov. She wished now that she could delay the meeting which her ridiculous mind was making so fateful. She was alone. When Tom had telephoned to say that he was not coming to stay at Belmont, Alex had felt a stab of black distress, as if it were a nudge from her own personal private death. Now, with this new thing to think of, she realized that it was better so. She wanted, in whatever battle (as she envisaged it) she might engage in with John Robert, to be alone in the house: visitable, available, unwitnessed. For this action, decks must be cleared. As for the incidental information that Tom's companion at Travancore Avenue was a male, Alex welcomed it. She affected to share the family anxiety about Tom's tendencies, but secretly she hoped that he was homosexual. Alex did not care for daughters-in-law.

As she stared once again out of the window at the wind-ravaged daffodils, a fox appeared. Alex saw at once that it was the vixen. The dog fox was larger and had a strong dark diabolical mark. The vixen was graceful, dainty, very feminine, with black stockings. She moved fastidiously, skipping a little sideways, then sat down among the daffodils. She lifted her head and gazed fixedly up at Alex with her pale blue eyes.

John Robert Rozanov was tired of his mind. He was tired of his strong personality and his face and the effect he had upon people. He often thought about death. But something still remained which bound him to the world. It was not philosophy.

He was sitting in the house in which he had been born, in the room in which he had been born. He had a persistent illusion that as he emerged from his mother's womb he had heard his father and grandfather talking Russian. John Robert did not know Russian. He wished now that he had learnt it, but it was too late. It was too late for other things he wished he had done.

Now every morning as he assumed the burden of consciousness he reflected upon its strangeness: the mystery of mind, so general and so particular. Why do thoughts not lose their owners? How does the individual stay together and not stray away like racing water-drops? How does consciousness continue, how can it? Could the curse of memory not end, and why did it not end? Did not the instant, of its nature, annihilate the past? Was not remorse a fiction, an effect of a prime delusion? How could a feeling be evidence of anything? All those days and nights he had spent with the many and the one, how little wisdom they had brought him, now when thoughts were changing into living sensa, and appearance and reality contended inside his frame which seemed at times as huge as the universe, and racked with as large a pain. The point of solipsism, often missed, was that it abolished morality. So if the pain he felt seemed like a spiritual pain, must he not be the victim of a mistake? How little it all helped him now when he was pitch-forked back into this mess of tormented being. The Other, whose hard fine edge he had aspired to trace, and in whose very absence he had sometimes gloried, was no more than an amoebic jelly, an unsavoury ectoplasm of wandering ideation. Truth was just a concept which had attracted him once.

Who could fathom Plato's mind? Unless one is a genius, philosophy is a mug's game. There were not even any books any more. All the books were inside him now. Even the familiar act of reading had been taken from him. It had been his fate not to be interested in anything except everything. If he could live another hundred years, could time reverse its sense and lead him gently into a precious clarity? As it was, he saw through every notion that he had ever had, the 'insights' won by a sustained asceticism appeared to him now as so much vacuous rather nasty stuff which he had made up out of nothing. Artists have beauty and nature at their side, but a philosopher must contain his world inside his head until . . . it be unified, clarified . . . until he can become a god . . . or else perceive that his all is nothing. Once long ago John Robert had believed in *that* which lies beyond. He had felt himself confronted by a thin thin film, something paper thin, through which, if he would, he could pass his hand; and which, in his precious philosophical faith and his precious philosophical patience, he did not yet presume to touch. Now he could see through it all as through some substance which had rotted away into scraggy fibres; and beyond was chaos, the uncategorized manifold, the ultimate jumble of the world, before which the metaphysician covers his eyes. Even some last lingering belief that someone, somewhere, at some time had had a pure unlying thought was, in *his* mind, a festering sore.

Speculation about Rozanov's return had not limited itself to conjecture about his arthritis. John Robert did indeed retain an old childish faith in the efficacy of the waters. In America he had gained much benefit from the hot baths at Saratoga Springs. He had already reserved himself one of the Ennistone Rooms for a pro-longed treatment. But many Ennistonians preferred the more touching view that the philosopher had 'come home to write his great book'. ('Returned like a priest-king to his people', as Nesta Wiggins's father, who belonged to the Writers' Circle, was heard to say.) It was held to be deeply significant that Rozanov had never sold the family house in Burkestown which he had inherited from his parents. In fact, the 'great book' (containing the 'secret doctrine' if any) was already in existence. Of course no philosophy book is ever finished, it is only abandoned. John Robert could well have settled down in the little terrace house to rewrite his book. But to this he had not made up his mind. Looking at his early childish writings, he could see how much he had learnt in fifty years. Oh for another fifty! If human life were longer, art and science might be much the same, but philosophy would be *an entirely different matter*. Why had he not written *this* book when he was younger, and able to go on past it, into the light? But, younger, he could not have. He had formed no intention of publishing it; but there it was, and he knew that if he left it behind it would be published after his death. Half of him, the more authoritative half, hated it. It was extremely long, his final philosophy. Sometimes he told himself he would condense it all into a hundred exquisitely lucid pages. *To write down nothing but the truth*; had that ever seemed a simple, even an intelligible, project? The crystalline truth, not a turgid flood of mucky half-truths; not even half-truths, but desecrating obfuscations, harryings, muddyings, taunting vilifications of the truth. But here the book itself lay in his way as a major obstruction. He knew how bad it was. Unfortunately he also knew how good it was, how superior to what was being done by others, by lesser men. John Robert was sometimes puzzled, almost childishly puzzled, by the extent to which his life was still ruled by vanity, even though he had recognized this fault long ago, and had passionately wanted and passionately attempted to overcome it. He had long since stopped resisting the obvious view, to which he was driven by experience, that he was superior to his contemporaries. But his vanity far outpaced such comparisons.

When John Robert Rozanov surveyed his big flabby handsomely-ugly face in the mirror and when, as he often did now, he considered his life retrospectively as if he were already dead, he concluded that what he had mainly lacked was courage. He left it to others to charge him with 'solipsistic dottiness' or 'ruthless selfishness'. Courage was the name he chose for that virtue which should have cured his quite particular lack of nerve, his crucial compromises and shilly-shallyings, the imperfection of work which could have been far far better. He ought never to have got married. No philosopher ought to marry. He had loved Linda Brent, he still loved her and could quake for her. But that was just something personal which he ought to have had the strength to toy with and then pass by, as he had done in later fleeting relations with women. The self-inflicted pain of her loss *then* would have strengthened him. The pain of her loss later, inflicted by fate, weakened him, wasted his time, and impaired his work over a long period. He had not been a good father. He had resented the little burdensome girl who was left behind, and had never made terms with her. He was widely quoted as saying 'I detest children,' an observation which George McCaffrey used to quote with relish.

John Robert had lived for so many years in the foggy space of his own thoughts, never pausing, never resting, the prey of incessant anxiety, carrying innumerable abstract interconnections inside his bursting head. He could *feel* the billion electric circuits of his frenzied brain, and how his mind strained and slipped like a poor overloaded horse. And was he *now* to work as he had never worked before? Sometimes he seemed to traverse vast heavens, sometimes to be enclosed in an iron ring, tied to one place, rooted in one spot. Sometimes it seemed to him that in all those strenuous metamorphoses he had hold of only *one* idea. He descended into primeval chaos and rose grasping some encrusted treasure which instantly crumbled. He pursued quarries into thickets, into corners, into nets, and at the end found nothing there. Such were his own images of his terrible addictive trade. If only he could get down deep enough, grasp the difficulties deep deep down and learn to think in an *entirely new way*. He perceived amazing similarities, startling light-bringing connections, problems which seemed utterly disparate merged into one, suddenly and with dream-like ease, then when the great synthesis seemed at last at hand, fell apart into strings of shallow aphorisms. He gazed and gazed with amazement at what was most ordinary, most close, until the light of wonder faded, leaving him unenlightened, without clue and without key. Philosophy may be called a sublime ability to say the obvious, to exhibit what is closest. But what is closest is what is farthest. He longed to live with ordinariness and see it simply with clear calm eyes. A *simple* lucidity seemed always close at hand, never achieved. He longed for thoughts which were quiet and at rest.

He had lived for so long among the problems with which the greatest minds of the past had fumbled like children. He had contemplated, almost indeed become, the images of the great metaphysicians, spawning his own imagery with a foaming spontaneity worthy of any madhouse. He had fled from these warm shades to the clean company of non-sensible things, numbers, mathematical forms; and had returned refreshed and hungry. He had created a moral system based on the *Timaeus*, and wondered in the silent night why great Plotinus spoke at last of touching, and not seeing, the One. Long did he live with the Ontological Proof, and try to frame a language wherein to speak about the Form of the Good. He indulged, then denied, then indulged again his heady image-making power, and sometimes, holding his head, cursed the luck which had so authoritatively made of him a philosopher and not an artist. Sometimes his life seemed to him to have been, not a progression of pictures, but noise, continuous noise, not music yet containing ever-elusive hints of musical form. And now, when there might perhaps burst forth some great symphonic finale, the crown of his laborious trial, at the crucial point demanding the purest most refined thinking of all, he was old, losing the clarity of his mind, losing his words and mislaying his thoughts. Could he *stop* thinking? What could he *do* but think?

Contrary to what many believed, John Robert's metaphysical strivings had nothing to do with religion. *That* distinction had always been for him a clear one. His interest in the Ontological Proof was purely philosophical. What lay behind all *that* was certainly not God. John Robert was sometimes described as a metaphysical moralist, but if the tag was just, it did not imply that his morality was to turn out (perhaps in the alleged 'secret doctrine') to be religion after all. He was concerned with 'the real' and thus by his own confident implication with 'the good'. He regarded religion, as he understood it, as a phenomenon of a different kind, something on which philosophy could not pronounce. Dogmatic belief he had none, nor was he troubled by its absence; and his own personal morality had a simplicity (some might say a naivety) which his philosophy certainly lacked. He had of course been indelibly marked by his Methodist childhood. As his would-be biographers, already hanging around like hyenas waiting for him to die, liked to remark in their 'perceptive' articles, Methodism had made of him a puritan with an obsessive guilt-ridden sense of truth which some saw as a motive for philosophy. If he had any convenient traditional label (he gave himself none) he was perhaps a stoic; and this too might be connected with the rigorous and bracing moral atmosphere in which he had lived as a child. His Eros was *Amor Fati*. He had been practising dying all his life, but had never, and certainly not now, been emotionally interested in death. He would have considered any quasi-religious collection of his soul as deluded sentimentality. He was aware of death as the imminent cessation of his labours. As a thinker, he was content to regard it as inconceivable.

And now his purposes had brought him back to Burkestown, to the house and the room where he was born, where the old shabby graceless furniture was much as it had been when he had leapt into the world as his ancestors were conversing in Russian. He did not look at those old patient shabby things, nor did they touch his heart. He had never cared for the external world. He was sitting on the bed and thinking, but not about conceptual matters. He needed, like a drug, someone to talk to, preferably another philosopher. He wanted to talk philosophy even if he could not (at present) write it. All his life he had talked with pupils and colleagues. He felt ill now with the deprivation.

He looked at his watch. It was still early, not yet ten. It was Wednesday morning. At eleven o'clock he was expecting Alexandra Stillowen.

Suddenly the bell rang. He had not heard the bell with its old funny familiar voice (it was an electric bell which made a conspiratorial hissing sound) since his return to 16 Hare Lane, and he shuddered. It was too early for his expected visitor. He rose and peered down through the lace curtains. The person at the door was George McCaffrey. John Robert moved abruptly back.

He never swore, his Methodist upbringing had made such vulgarity impossible. He frowned slightly and shook his head to and fro. It did not occur to him not to answer the bell. That would have been a lie or subterfuge. He thought, I shall have to see George sooner or later. I had better see him now. He went down and opened the door.

George McCaffrey had, like his mother, meditated carefully upon exactly how soon and how he was to present himself to John Robert Rozanov. He had fled promptly from his teacher's apparition at the Institute: a meeting *then* would have been a miserable botched affair. Though, on the other hand, George felt later, it would have been, now, a relief to his mind if he could simply have got over the 'first sighting', for instance by passing by and giving and receiving a friendly nod. He observed, with calculating detachment, his mounting frenzy. He *could not* absent himself too long. He had to be in Rozanov's presence, with all the danger which that represented.

One thing encouraged him. He knew that, wherever he was in the world, Rozanov had to have someone with whom he could talk philosophy: a colleague, or failing that a pupil. George was the only person in Ennistone who fitted this role. (It was often said that Rozanov did not make or need friends: he only needed people to

137

argue with.) At moments now George saw (or heartily attempted to see) the philosopher as lonely, abandoned, awaiting rescue. In the very early days George had aspired to be a favourite pupil, imagined himself the beloved disciple. He had even thought himself destined to be the prime interpreter of John Robert's thought to the world. There was a kind of helplessness about the philosopher, some absolutely monumental lack of common sense, which seemed to demand the assistance of a more worldly *chela*. Now that George appeared to be without competitors, might he not be, without comment, simply 'resumed' into John Robert's life? It was possible. Yet George also knew how terribly wrong, through no fault of his own as he so often agonizingly thought, his relations with Rozanov had gone. It was not just that John Robert had 'ruined George's life' by discouraging him from philosophy and thus somehow in effect from an academic career. John Robert had also mortally wounded George's soul, setting at the same time therein the eternal need to be justified, to be healed, to be saved by the executioner himself. He and only he who had dealt the wound could heal it. *What* it was, and how and even when it had happened, was now unclear to George. He knew that his attempts to return to philosophy after he had, with such stupid obedience, left it, his pretentious letters (unanswered), his hauntings of John Robert's classes, had annoyed the philosopher. He recalled (he tried deliberately to forget, stirred and muddied his memories in vain) one or two awful occasions when John Robert had been positively angry with him. No, it was not anger, it was cold as if the philosopher, while crumpling George up and casting him aside, had been thinking about something else. There had been psychological analysis, moral summary, spiritual devastation, inward wreck. He was not accused or savaged, simply annihilated. Nonetheless at a later time he had had to, *had to*, follow Rozanov to America and once more haunt him, waiting around under palm trees on hot dusty roads in California. It was almost as if anything, a gesture of the hand which recognized his existence, could cure him, so great was his need, so humble his expectation. Rozanov had been casual, but somehow *awful*. He had made it clear that he did not want to see anything more of George. George had become more persistent, then crazy, furious. Was he not ruining his life to spite a charlatan? He had been suddenly possessed by wild destructive hatred; only it was not really hatred, he *could not* hate John Robert, it was madness. Rozanov had responded with a ferocity suited to the occasion. George tried to see him again, tried to apologize. He returned to England and from there wrote a number of extremely long letters, some indignant, some abject, which received no answer. Of course he told nobody about this nightmarish pilgrimage. However, the idea somehow got around in Ennistone that George McCaffrey had pursued Professor Rozanov to America and been rebuffed. George felt he could murder the people who sent these rumours about, no doubt repeating them with satisfaction.

Sometimes it was the very vagueness of the situation which tortured George most. If he had committed some definite crime for which he had been punished by exile, this period might intelligibly be expected to come to an end. If he had offended he might be forgiven. Yet what *was* his crime, was there one, in Rozanov's eyes? In Rozanov's eyes, where his reality subsisted. He had been, very often, a damn nuisance, and once, very rude. But had Rozanov really noticed? He could not even put it to himself that he had failed John Robert, let him down, disappointed some cherished expectation. There had been no such expectation. One day I'll commit a real crime, George thought, since I'm being tortured for non-existent ones. Why should I be made *invisible* in this way? And yet, how could he not hope, in spite of everything, that John Robert would undertake his salvation after all? Was it not *significant* that the philosopher had returned to Ennistone? Why had he returned? There were meanings in the world. He had seen his own double in the Botanic Gardens. Perhaps it was just someone very like him, but that had meaning too. Twice now he had seen this double, capable of anything, walking about and at large. Once, talking to someone in his office, he had seen through the window a man fall from a high scaffolding. He had immediately apprehended that man as himself. He said nothing about this at the time or later. There were meanings in the world. He had seen the number forty-four chalked on a wall.

That morning he had woken early with the clear conviction that today was the day. He could wait no longer. Had he expected a summons, a letter, had he even hoped for one? In his mind he had composed letters himself, suppliant letters, proud letters, asking for a meeting, but he had not written them. Receiving no reply would be too terrible an experience, and he must cherish himself. He must simply go and knock on John Robert's door. The resolution filled him with a strange fierce exciting emotion, as he got up from the crumpled sofa and wandered with energetic restlessness from the dining-room to the sitting-room to the kitchen and back. He felt anxious to do something, as if there were something to be done in the house, some task which he had left unfulfilled; and he found himself again in the kitchen, opening a drawer and taking out a hammer. He looked at the hammer, swinging it, weighing it in his hands; then he ran quickly up the stairs and into Stella's bedroom.

Stella had, some time ago, moved into her own room the little collection of Japanese netsuke, gifts from her father, which had once stood upon the sitting-room mantelpiece. She had ranged them upon the white window-sill facing the end of her bed. George burst in with this hammer, eagerly anticipating the work of destruction. But the window-sill was bare. He looked about the room, opened the drawers: gone. The little gaggle of ivory men and animals had disappeared. Stella must have come, foreseeing his rage, and taken them away. She treasured them as tokens of her father's love. George felt a pang of jealous misery and frustration. He went to the dressing-table and swept off it on to the floor the few oddments, some little silver boxes, make-up, a hand mirror, which had lain there untouched since the evening when he and Stella had set off to see Alex, a hundred years ago. He kicked the delicate legs of the dressing-table, cracking one. Then it suddenly seemed to him strange and rather amusing that Stella should actually have come to the house, secretly, fearfully turning her key in the door, and put the little netsuke into her pocket. Or perhaps she had sent someone else to fetch them. George did not proceed to wonder where his wife was now. Wherever she was, she would be being well looked after. *She* was all right. He went downstairs and put on his overcoat. It was a cold dull windy day. He had not breakfasted, of course; breakfast was out of the question.

George and Stella lived in a modest pretty house, an old cottage long modernized and painted blue, which backed on to the Common. There was a view of the monoliths, the Ennistone Ring, from the upper windows. The area was called Druidsdale in homage to the legendary creators of the Ring; it was not very far from Victoria Park and counted marginally as one of the 'nicer parts' of the town. The quickest way from Druidsdale to Burkestown was by taking the path along the edge of the Common as far as the level crossing. However, George avoided the Common since a contentious encounter with a white-heather-selling gipsy. (There is, and has long been, a gipsy camp, persistently persecuted by Ennistonians, on the far side of the Common.) Passing through the town, it would be possible to cross the River Enn by the Roman bridge and go past the Glove Factory, or else to cross by the New Bridge and go past the Ennistone Royal Hotel (whose sumptuous grounds coted the river). For Hare Lane, the way by the hotel was slightly shorter, but George wanted to avoid the vicinity of Travancore Avenue. Bill the Lizard, from whom he had learnt of Rozanov's whereabouts, had also told George of Tom's advent. Eastcote cared about George and thought about him a lot. It was by now general knowledge at the Baths that Tom McCaffrey was in town and living in Greg and Ju Osmore's house with a mysterious male friend. (Tom himself had not yet turned up to swim because he could not persuade Emma to come with him.)

As George was crossing the Roman bridge he became aware, in the cloudy daze in which he was walking, of an awkwardness. He had put the hammer into the pocket of his coat and it was knocking regularly against his knee. He took it out and went onward holding it in his hand, passing a row of little modern houses called Blanch Cottages, built after a bomb had devastated this piece of Ennistone during the war. Some of the front gardens had bushy evergreen shrubs which leaned out over the pavement. George dropped the hammer over a low fence into the branches of a yellow privet bush. He was beginning to wish that the walk could last forever. He knew the house in Hare Lane since he had been long ago, in his very earliest Rozanov days, *invited to tea* there when John Robert, teaching in London, had come to Ennistone to visit his mother. Mrs Rozanov, a sturdy bonny Ennistonian Methodist, not at all in awe of her famous son, had been kind to George. George did not want to remember that occasion. He must have been very happy.

Now at last, sick with apprehension and horrible frightened joy, he had reached the door and rang the bell.

Opinions differed about whether John Robert Rozanov was 'in his own way' rather handsome, or whether he was one of the ugliest creatures ever seen. He was tall, he had always been burly and was now stout. He had an extremely large flat-topped head and a low brow, with hair which had always been very short and grizzled, curly, almost frizzy, and was now grey with no sign of balding. His eyes, large and with an odd fierce rectangular appearance, were an unnerving shade of light yellowish-brown and gleamed brightly. His face was broad and high-cheek-boned, and when one knew about his Russian ancestry could look Slavonic. He had a big strong aquiline nose and a big wet sensuous flabby mouth which pouted out above his chin. He dressed carelessly and was voted by women, some of whom found him attractive, some repulsive, to look a 'perfect wreck'.

The door opened and Rozanov confronted his pupil. There was no pretence on either side that this was a social call, supposed to be a surprise or uncertain in its purpose. George said nothing. Rozanov said, 'Come in,' and George followed him into the little dark parlour at the back of the house. Rozanov turned on the lamp.

Apart from the shock glimpse at the Baths, it was some years since George had seen his old teacher and (as he later observed, at first he was too stunned) Rozanov had changed a good deal. He had become fatter, slower in his movements and stiffened by arthritis. The shabbiness and shagginess was now clearly that of old age. A little saliva foamed at the corners of his protruding lips as he talked. His once-smooth brow had grown soft pitted flesh, humped between deep lines of wrinkles. Coarse hairs were growing from his nose and ears. Grey braces, visible under his gaping jacket, supported his uncertain trousers half-way up his paunch. He had always looked rather dirty and now looked dirtier. He filled the little room with his bear-like presence and his smell. He stared gloomily at George.

George did not attempt to conceal his emotion. He found a sweet aggressive little pleasure in giving in to it. He leaned back against the wall and put a hand to his throat. He rubbed his hand across his eyes, and said, 'Well, hello.' His voice shook.

Rozanov said, 'Hello, how are you?' He had a curious stilted voice which mingled English academic with American and traces of his mother's Ennistonian.

George said, 'God.'

Rozanov, scratching and poking his large fleshy ear, moved across to the window and looked out at the scrap of back garden with the Cox's Orange Pippin tree which his father had planted. Other thoughts, momentarily dispelled, pressed obsessively back into his mind.

George took hold of his wits and shook himself like a dog. He advanced a little. There was not far to move. The room was very small and there was a desk and a sideboard and two armchairs in it. He said, 'I'm glad to see you.'

John Robert said, 'Oh yes,' still looking out of the window.

'We hope you're going to stay in Ennistone.'

'Yes –'

'You *are* going to stay with us?'

John Robert turned round from the window and stood awkwardly with his back to it. He said, 'I don't know.'

'Anyway we can have some talks,' said George. As the philosopher did not reply he added, 'That's good.'

There was a silence. He could hear the philosopher's noisy breathing and the little tearing sound as he began to pick at the top of one of the chairs.

'Are you writing your great book, I mean the final one?'

'No.'

'Well, I don't mean the final one, you're not all that old, I suppose. I hope you're writing philosophy?'

'No.'

'What a pity! Why not, are you tired of it at last? I often wondered if you'd ever get tired of it and give it up.'

'No.'

'Look, there's an awful lot I'd like to talk to you about, an awful lot I'd like to ask. You know I always felt there was something *behind* everything that you said.'

'I don't think there was,' said John Robert. He was now regarding George with his pale fierce eyes.

'I mean a sort of secret doctrine, something you only revealed to the initiated.'

'No.'

'Well, I hope you won't mind if I ask you lots of questions, about philosophy I mean, not personal ones of course, and not today, I just came today to say hello, to look at you sort of, we can fix times later, I expect you'll be glad of someone to talk philosophy to, I've been reading philosophy, you know, I've kept it up. I'll tell you what I've been reading, not now, I don't want to bother you now. I expect lots of people will want to see you and bother you, I expect the *Ennistone Gazette* has been after you.'

'No, it hasn't.'

'Maybe they're afraid of you, people seem to be, I was I remember, yes, I was you know. Perhaps you've mellowed, as they say! I wonder if you're writing your memoirs?'

'No.'

'You ought to write your memoirs, you've had an interesting life, after all. I wonder what you think about your philosophy now, what it amounts to? How would you classify it?'

'How would I *what*?' said John Robert.

'Sorry, that's a silly word, I wondered what you felt your contribution had been, along what line? I used to think it was my destiny to explain your philosophy to the world. That was stupid of me, I daresay. But I'd still like to! There's so much for us to talk about, so much you could explain. We'd need time. You used to say, in philosophy, if you aren't moving at a snail's pace you aren't moving at all!'

'I'm afraid I won't have time,' said John Robert.

'We could just talk a bit every week, I'd value it so much, there aren't any other philosophers in Ennistone so far as I know.'

'*I won't have time*,' John Robert repeated. He looked at his watch. 'I'm expecting someone, I hope you don't mind –'

'When are they coming?'

'Eleven,' said John Robert who was incapable of inventing a social fib or telling a direct lie.

'Then we've a bit of time yet, perhaps I'm talking stupidly, it's shyness, I'm shy and nervous –'

'If you've got anything *definite* to say –' said John Robert.

'I suppose you've heard that I lost my job?'

'No.'

'I've got a pension, so it's all right. You'll never guess how I lost it.'

'Perfectly true.'

'I broke all the Roman glass in the Museum.'

'All the Roman glass?' This idea roused a faint interest in John Robert.

'Yes, on purpose, I hurled it on the floor and it smashed in pieces, all of it.'

'Have they glued it together again?' the sage asked.

'I've no idea. They started picking it up very carefully. One of the girls was crying. Then I left.'

There was a silence.

'Do you want to know why I –?'

John Robert said abruptly, 'How's your wife?'

George, who had been blushing and wearing, he now realized, a perfectly ridiculous expression, hardened his face. He moved out from behind one of the armchairs. He said, 'I tried to kill her.'

John Robert raised his eyebrows.

144

'I drove our car into the canal, on purpose of course like the glass, I jumped out and she went in with the car. Only she got out somehow. Too bad. Better luck next time.'

John Robert said, 'You haven't changed much.'

The remark pleased George. He relaxed a little. He said, 'I wonder if I did really intend to kill her? I've asked myself that. It's something I'd like to discuss with you, it's like things we used to talk about. What is consciousness, after all, what is it, does it exist?'

'What else is there?' said John Robert gloomily.

'What are motives, is one responsible? You said once we all have contemptible motives. But some thinkers say that crime is a form of grace. Sometimes I've felt a crime is like a duty. Isn't that a kind of transcendental proof? If crime is a duty then evil be thou my good has sense. You once said it hadn't.'

'Did I?'

'You denied it had any content, I think it has. I wonder why you put me off philosophy? Well, you haven't, I've continued on my own. I'd like to tell you what I've been thinking. I'm very interested in things you said about time. Sometimes I feel I lose the present moment, like losing the centre of one's field of vision, my sense of my individuality goes, I can't feel my present being –'

'I suggest you see a doctor.'

'I'm making a philosophical point! Why did you stop me from doing philosophy?'

'I thought you weren't good enough,' said John Robert looking at his watch again. '*Vous pensiez trop pour votre intelligence, c'est tout.*'

'Christ, can't you even *tutoie* me after all these years? You said "always attempt what is too hard for you". Didn't you? That's just what you prevented me from doing. I was a coward anyway. But now perhaps if you'll help me –'

'I don't think –'

'You ruined my life, you know. Do you know? If you hadn't discouraged me just at that crucial moment I might have made something of my life. I never recovered from your high standards. So you owe me something!'

'I owe you nothing,' said John Robert, but he said it without animosity, indeed without animation.

'Kant cared about his pupils. Not like Schlick. Kant looked after his pupils years later –'

'You know nothing about Schlick.'

'You destroyed my belief in good and evil, you were Mephistopheles to my Faust.'

'You flatter yourself.'

'You think I don't have Faustian temptations? You have stolen me from myself. You used to say philosophy was like the Grand National, or else it's nothing. Maybe I've broken my neck. If I've broken my neck, I wish to God you'd shoot me.'

'Your head seems to be full of things I used to say. Please don't get so excited.'

'I've read a lot of things about you, I read an article saying you believed Plato's Form of the Good was a large marble ball preserved somewhere on top of a column. Did you read that?'

'No.'

'It wasn't very polite. So you've given up philosophy?'

'No.'

'I thought you said you had.'

'No.'

'You look much older. How old are you? You've got false teeth, you didn't have when I saw you in California. I hope I'm dead when I'm your age. I suppose you're waiting for me to apologize?'

'What for?'

'Being bloody rude to you in California.'

'It doesn't matter.'

'It does. I do apologize. And for being rude today. I prostrate myself. Caliban must be saved too.'

'What?'

'Caliban must be saved too. You said that in a lecture. Have you forgotten?'

'Yes.'

'I haven't. I knew you were talking about me. God, how much more real I feel now that I'm with you at last, more bloody real than I've felt for years, for *years*. I've *craved* for your presence. John Robert, you must help me. You stole my reality, you stole my consciousness, you're the only person who can give them back to me. Salvation is by magic, you said that once. I beg you, I beseech you. It's a matter of salvation, it's a matter of living or dying. Christ, can't you even *look* at me, can't you concentrate on me for a moment? Please let me see you, let me be with you, it doesn't matter what we talk about.'

'George,' said John Robert, looking at him at last, 'you are suffering from an *illusion*. There is no structure here to make sense of the language you are using, there is no context for any conversation between us. If I was kind to you now and encouraged you to come and see me I would be lying to you. I don't want to discuss your soul and your imagined sins. I am not interested, I haven't any wisdom or any help to give you. You have an entirely illusory view of our relationship. And do stop worrying about philosophy – in your case philosophy is just a nervous craving.'

'You reject me!'

'No. I'm sorry. I haven't got that much concern about you. I haven't any concern about you. I just don't want to see you.'

'That *can't* be true! Why are you taking up this attitude? Why are you so angry with me? What have you been thinking about me?'

'I am not angry with you. I have not been thinking about you. You are simply making a *mistake*. Just *go away*.'

At that moment the front door bell rang.

John Robert, looking exasperated at last, moved past George to get out into the hall. George stood in the doorway, conscious now of the violent beating of his heart, and gazed at his teacher's bulky form in the dim illumination that came through the little fanlight above the door. The next moment the grey but clear light of the street revealed the apparition of Alex, in her best fur coat, with her long eyes aglow, and her long pale mouth smiling. As John Robert, saying nothing, stepped aside, and she stepped forward, she saw George. The expressions of mother and son were suddenly similar, brilliantly cat-like. Alex stopped smiling, then smiled again, a quite different smile. George intensified the frown he had been wearing for John Robert, adding an accompanying smile or sneer.

John Robert, turning, said to George, 'Good-bye.'

Alex moved forward again, past John Robert, who was holding the door open, and stood at the foot of the staircase to get out of George's way. George passed her with averted head. His hand touched the soft grey fur of the long coat which she wore pulled well in to her slim waist with a steel chain belt. He smelt her face powder. He passed John Robert with a shudder and the door closed.

Once outside George was consumed by hate, jealousy, misery, remorse, fear and rage. Emotions blackened the sky and tore his entrails like vultures. He imagined taking his shoe off and breaking the window. However, his face was impassive; even the frown had left it. He walked quietly away from the house, walked on about twenty yards, and then stopped and stood perfectly still for several minutes. Two students from Ennistone Polytechnic who were going to drop a notice about a political meeting in on Nesta Wiggins, recognized him and promptly crossed the road.

George knew himself. He knew what a terrible piece of work had been accomplished that morning, what a mass of material for his grief and chagrin he had heaped up during that short visit. Everything he had said to Rozanov had been wrong. He had behaved like a petulant child, not like his real self at all. He now saw clearly what he ought to have said, what tone he ought to have adopted. He had deliberately not decided on any policy beforehand, had prepared no speech. That was folly. He should have said ... or else have written a letter explaining ... He began to walk along, recalling with nausea the pleading accents with which he had begged for what he wanted. And then Alex arriving. *What* on *earth* did that mean, what unholy alliance, what threat to *him*? He had never connected Alex with John Robert; she had never spoken of him except for vaguely mentioning that she had met him. How *sickening*. Was Alex to be friends with John Robert excluding George? Would John Robert turn Alex against him? What were they talking about *now*, those dreadful two, *they must be talking about him*.

As he came up toward the Roman bridge he remembered the hammer. An elderly lady, a Miss Dunbury, retired from doing very fine work at the Glove Factory, who lived at number three Blanch Cottages, saw with excitement a man pause to pick a blunt instrument (as she perceived it, being a great reader of detective stories) out of her privet bush. She began to search for her glasses in order to scan the *Ennistone Gazette* for murders. Being short-sighted, she had not recognized George. If she had, she would have been even more excited.

Alex, who had arrived by taxi and combed her hair on the doorstep, recovered quickly from the shock of seeing George, upon which she had no time to speculate. For some reason, George had not figured at all in her imaginings, as if she had perfectly forgotten that he had been Rozanov's pupil. She felt a quick physical tremor as he passed, which blended quickly into her general nervous agitation.

John Robert went past her into the back room and she followed him. The glimpse at the Baths had prepared her to see him older. Now, dressed in a big loose shabby corduroy jacket falling off one shoulder and wearing a grey pullover under his braces, he looked less old. Unbid, Alex pulled off her coat and threw it on a chair. She took in the room, so small, with a thin little black grate and a narrow little grimy mantelpiece and a couple of miserable sloppy armchairs and a shiny little sideboard with a crumpled lace cover on it. There was a small school desk, the top open, stuffed with papers and a general dotting of china ornaments, puppy dogs and ballet dancers and such, placed there long ago by John Robert's mother. There was a hole in the carpet and dust everywhere and a damp smell.

John Robert seemed momentarily tongue-tied, which set Alex more at her ease. She smiled at him.

'How kind of you to come.'

'Not at all. I'm very glad to see you.'

'Would you like some – some tea?'

Alex would have liked a whisky and soda but she remembered that John Robert had been a teetotaller. She said, 'No, thank you.'

'Or coffee – I think there's some?'

'No thanks.'

He said, 'I'm sorry, I'm a non-drinker, there isn't anything else in the house. Would you please sit down?'

Alex sat on the arm of one of the armchairs, raising a little puff of dust.

'What a pretty garden, so small and – and easy to manage.' As there was a little silence she added, 'I'm sure George was very glad to see you.'

The mention of George was just a nervous urge, she did not want to talk about George.

'Oh yes, yes.'

John Robert sat heavily into the other armchair, then finding himself almost on the floor pulled himself up again, grunting, with some difficulty and sat on a creaky upright chair which swayed alarmingly.

Alex said, 'Are you glad to be back?'

John Robert considered the question seriously. 'Yes, I am. I remember a lot of faces of people round here, in the shops and so on, changed of course. My parents liked living here, it was always a friendly neighbourhood.'

'After America, Ennistone must seem so quiet and small.'

'Nice and quiet, nice and small.'

Alex stared at John Robert who was not looking at her, and her heart moved within her. His big head sunk inside the collar of his jacket, he looked almost like a hunchback. She saw the coarse pitted texture of his skin and the strength of his nose of a bird of prey and the way his large wet mouth pouted and drooped. She felt an impulse to reach out and touch, not his knee but the shiny dirty material of his trouser leg.

'Mrs McCaffrey –'

'I wish you'd call me Alex. We have known each other a long time.'

'Indeed, I wanted to ask you something.'

'Yes –?' Alex's eyes stared as if she would flatten him with them and pin him to the wall.

'You must say frankly if you feel you don't want to, or that you'd like to think it over –'

'Yes –?'

'In any case it may be impossible After all –'

'*Yes, yes* –?'

'I was wondering,' said John Robert, 'if you would be so kind as to let me rent the Slipper House.'

This was so much what Alex was not expecting (and yet what was she expecting?) that she could not answer at once, could not even immediately understand the words or collect her wits to consider whether or how she was displeased or *disappointed* or – yet what right had she? But what did it *mean*?

'I'm sorry, I can see that this is not something you want to do.'

'Oh, I do,' said Alex decisively, 'I do want to, I should be absolutely delighted to rent the Slipper House – to you –'

'You should perhaps reflect a little.'

'I've reflected. I should be very pleased indeed.'

'I thought perhaps it might be occupied by someone else.'

'No, no, it's empty. I have no one – it may be a bit damp – I'll put all the heating on – and it needs more furniture – it's got beds and chairs of course but –'

'I beg you not to go to any trouble. I can provide anything extra that is necessary.'

'What a wonderful idea!' said Alex, whose imagination had been in motion. The whole picture now seemed perfectly charming and full of possibilities. 'Would you like to come round now and we can look at the place together?'

'No, no thank you. I don't need it just yet. I just wanted to know if it was available.'

'Oh it is, oh yes, *available*.'

'Thank you –'

'I expect you're going to write your great book there?' said Alex. 'It's very peaceful. I'll see no one bothers you. I could cook for you –'

'I'll let you know, if I may, when – And you'll tell me about rent, and conditions –?'

Alex resisted a desire to cry out that no rent was required. She said, 'Mr Osmore will fix all that, I'll ask him to write to you.'

John Robert rose to his feet. The interview was evidently over. Alex wished she had accepted the cup of tea. She rose too and pulled on her big soft coat and drew in her metal belt by an extra link.

'Well, we'll be in touch.'

'Yes, thank you for coming.'

In a moment Alex was out in the windy street, careless now of her tossing hair. She walked along briskly with her hands in her pockets, smiling to herself, then laughing.

'Almighty God, Father of our Lord Jesus Christ, Maker of all things, Judge of all men, we acknowledge and bewail our manifold sins and wickedness, which we from time to time most grievously have committed, by thought word and deed, against thy Divine Majesty, provoking most justly thy wrath and indignation against us. We do earnestly repent and are heartily sorry for these our misdoings, the remembrance of them is grievous unto us, the burden of them is intolerable . . .'

Diane uttered these solemn and terrible words meekly kneeling upon her knees in the darkness of St Paul's Church, Victoria Park, at chilly draughty 8 a.m. early service (poorly attended on weekdays). She had uttered those words innumerable times since her earliest childhood, had chumbled them with her tongue and her lips until they were very smooth but not quite weightless. She did not bother her head about God's wrath and indignation, she knew unreflectively that there was no such thing. The burden of sin was another matter: there was a burden and a grievous remembrance, hurt and damage and remorse.

George had not been to see her for a week. She felt powerless as in dreams when the muscles will not tense and the limbs will not move. She felt as if she were in public view in a pillory, stared at, laughed at, whispered about. She needed to nerve herself to go to the Baths, to the shops, to the Church, her contacts with life, her last innocent occupations, swimming, shopping and praying. Yesterday in Bowcocks all the lights had gone out because of a power-cut. The big internal areas of the shop, scarcely penetrated by the afternoon light, were suddenly dim as if foggy. Diane, who had been fingering some cheap jewellery, which she had no intention of buying, put it down abruptly. As she stood in the middle of one of the aisles, watching the ghostly figures move, a gale of fear came up out of her soul as if she had been transported to hell. She loved Bowcocks, where she had worked once; it was a safe warm not a sin) but did include scanning the newspapers for murders and feeling disappointed when there were none.

Saint Paul's Church, Victoria Park, built in 1860 by an admirer of William Butterfield, was a huge barn-like structure, without side aisles, dominated by the towering gilded reredos. (The rood screen, by Ninian Comper, has been added later.) The dwindling worshippers sat in some stocky modern pews near the east end, leaving the large space behind to be occupied by Victorian ghosts. There were four suitably bedizened side chapels, mere recesses however, not the encrusted caves which Father Bernard would have preferred. The walls of the church were decorated by a large solemn play of reddish and yellowish bricks and tiles, now revealed almost in its entirety since many of the Victorian funeral monuments had been shaken down by the wartime bomb which destroyed the tower and the Rectory. Post-war austerity had not restored these relics which languished in the crypt, ignored by Father Bernard who found the walls quite glorious enough as they were, assuming that they could not be covered by oriental hangings. The floor was paved by matching tiles, bearing many ingenious geometric devices and stylized flowers, from which Father Bernard had stripped away the senseless modern carpets installed by his predecessor. Persian rugs would have been acceptable, but the days of rich patrons were over. There was, one of the last donations, one lonely tapestry hanging under the west window, designed by Ned Larkin, representing Christ as a very pale clean-shaven young working man, holding with evident anxiety the tools of a carpenter. (The same donor had contributed a John the Baptist by a pupil of Eric Gill.) The exquisite rood screen had been miraculously undamaged by the bomb, as had the Victorian glass which a zealous rector had taken down and stored. It was without special merit but ensured darkness.

Father Bernard loved his church and its high Anglican tradition which he did not let down but rather quietly elevated as far as he was able. (Mr Elsworthy at St Olaf's catered for the lower brethren.) He had however suffered various defeats at the hands of his bishop. He no longer heard confessions, although there was a beautiful confessional, gaudy as a sedan chair, which a devotee had brought over from Germany. His plain-song choir had ceased to be, and he now only said one Latin mass a month. He still otherwise made exclusive use of Cranmer's Prayer Book although he had been expressly told not to. In return for being allowed to muffle the crucifixes during Lent, he had surrendered no less than three plaster madonnas. He did this, however, with feigned reluctance, since he was not interested in the cult of the Virgin, and it did no harm to have a grievance. Someone, he did not know who, appeared to be informing on him to the bishop. He did not yearn for the big Victorian rectory but lived modestly in a small 'clergy house' where he looked after himself, could reasonably dispense with pretentious 'entertaining', and was able to practise his private cults unmolested. He had no curate: better so, any curate now would be an episcopal spy. He was well aware of his reputation for being 'not a priest but a shaman'. He did not mind. Salvation itself was magic: total redemption by cosmic act of the whole visible world. His own cruder spells, material symbols of a spiritual grace, were surely acceptable. Acceptable to whom? Father Bernard had ceased to believe in God. As he paced often alone in his large handsome church he felt increasingly conscious of the absence of God, the presence of Christ. But his Christ was a mystical figure, the blond beardless youth of the early Church, not the tormented crucified one of flesh and blood.

Some of his parishioners once complained that Father Bernard's sermon on 'prayer' consisted of advice about breathing exercises. Yet Father Bernard had once chattered freely to the Almighty; not to the stern Jewish God of his childhood, but to a milder and less manly deity. He had been a student at Birmingham where he studied chemistry and gained a black belt at judo. The hated chemistry was the last thing he did to please his earthly father, whose heart he broke soon afterwards by his conversion to Christianity. Father Bernard carried that unhealed wound (that crime) secretly within him. His father, never reconciled, was dead now. Father Bernard could no longer commend him to God since that channel of communication was also closed. He often thought about his father, and about his darling mother who had been so dreadfully taken from him before he collapsed into the arms of Christ. He sat and breathed. He knelt and breathed. And every day, by the magic power which had been entrusted to him, he changed bread and wine into flesh and blood. He continued to revere this mystery and to find it endlessly and thrillingly arcane.

Father Bernard had long ago decreed solitude for himself: that included celibacy. He did not disapprove of homosexual love, and would have made the same decision if he had been heterosexual, which he was not. After messing about with human sexual adventures he decided to devote his love, that is his sexuality, to God.

156

When God passed out of his life he loved Christ. When Christ began, so strangely, to withdraw and change he just sat, or knelt, and breathed in the presence of something or in the presence of nothing. He was never now seriously tempted to break his vow of chastity, but he remained, in the common abject sense, a sinner. He had considerably disturbed the equanimity of a young chorister whose hand he had sometimes held in the dark empty church after choir practice. (This was in the days of the plain-song choir, conducted by a Jonathan Treece, sadly gone from Ennistone. The musical art now depended on the simpler skills of lady organists.) Worse still, alarmed by his own feelings, Father Bernard had hurt the boy by suddenly 'sheering off' without an explanation. This child, now a youth and no churchgoer, worked in London but occasionally, on visits to Ennistone, met Father Bernard in the street and cut him. This caused the priest much pain and obsessive sessions of planning how to 'retrieve' a situation which was, he always had to conclude, better left alone. He could but hope that the main damage was to his own vanity. There were of course young men whom he simply could not get out of his head. Tom McCaffrey was one. Father Bernard had seen Tom grow from a schoolboy into a student. They met frequently. He would very much have liked to take Tom in his arms. Instead he lowered his eyes. Did Tom know? Perhaps.

Father Bernard was well and fairly calmly aware that in many ways he was a perfectly rotten priest. He celebrated, to his own personal satisfaction, the rites that pleased him, often with no one present but himself. He did not go round visiting, as his predecessor had done, and as he had done himself in his early days in the parish in Birmingham. He was uninterested in politics. He did not run debates, or discussion groups, or encounter groups, or a youth club, or a mothers' union, or a Sunday school. He liked to have his evenings to himself, after evensong, which he celebrated every day, usually alone. He wanted plenty of time to meditate and to read theological books which he perused with a kind of unholy excitement as if they were pornography. Occasionally he spent the evenings having long emotional talks with special penitents. He enjoyed that. He did not go out seeking sinners, but remained comfortably at the receipt of custom in case they should come seeking him. He had steady vaguely sentimental relationships with a small number of women (Diane was one, Gabriel would have been one too if it had not been for Brian) wherein he allowed himself a little bit of hand-holding. He knew how confoundedly lazy and selfish he was. But although this troubled him a little more than his heresy did, it did not trouble him very much. He knew the things which he absolutely must not do. He did not seriously consider that he ought to leave the priesthood. Only very lately had he begun to feel sometimes insecure. Was scandal possible, disgrace, banishment, after all?

Mass being over, he processed himself off the scene, took off his glittering vestments, and reappeared in his black cassock at the west door of the church in case anyone wanted to talk to him. Three of his communicants were there, Hector Gaines, Benning (whose first name was Robert) and Diane. Father Bernard made a bee-line for Benning, who was thin and large-eyed and looked touchingly starved, and shook him by the hand. 'Glad to see you again, Bob. Do we call you Bob?'

'Bobbie,' said the youth, blushing a little and holding on to the priest's hand.

'That's good,' said Father Bernard, briskly releasing him. 'Come again, won't you, Bobbie. Church is home.'

He turned to Diane, giving a friendly wave to Hector, which indicated to that intelligent fellow, with whom the priest was on close and amicable terms, that he did not want to talk to him just now.

Hector and Benning turned away together into the cold morning wind which was blowing a little rain.

'Rum jerk,' said Bobbie.

'Who?'

'The parson.'

'He's a *very nice* jerk,' said Hector, 'and he knows *a lot of things*.'

They continued to walk together, Hector thinking about Anthea Eastcote (to banish whose image he had been hoping to enlist clerical assistance), and Bobbie Benning wondering gloomily how on earth he was to go on teaching a subject which he had lately realized was far too difficult for him.

Father Bernard turned a switch at the door, darkening the altar lights, leaving only the red sanctuary light, and led Diane back down the aisle. They sat side by side, the priest holding her hand, kneading it gently. 'Well, little one?'

Diane squeezed his hand, holding it for a little longer, then letting it go and drawing back. She found the priest attractive but utterly strange; he was so unlike other men, so devoid of the coarseness which men had. She liked touching him but was always nervous in case George, whose absent presence always haunted her, should suddenly appear from behind a pillar. She valued her friendship with Father Bernard, especially since George tolerated her church-going.

In reply to the priest's question. Diane, still overwrought by the emotions attendant upon receiving the sacrament, began to cry.

'Now, now, stop it, you can, have a bit of courage.'

'Courage! I'm nothing, I'm a jelly. A jelly can't have courage.'

'A jelly can pray.'

'I can't.'

'Be quiet and breathe God. Seek help. Ask and it shall be given. Knock and it shall be opened.'

'Ask what, ask who?'

'If you really ask, you are certain to be answered. You must fight your own demon with your own Lord. He knows. Lo, thou tellest my flittings, put thou my tears in thy bottle.'

'I'm so worried about George,' said Diane. 'I'm so *miserable* for him. He isn't really so bad, it's just a myth people keep going. All right, he did push that man out of the window –'

'I hadn't heard that one.'

'It was an accident, he didn't mean to, and I don't believe he tried to kill his wife like they say –'

The priest had heard various recitals of George's misdeeds. They varied considerably. It was true that people *wanted* to think ill of him. Of course Father Bernard was interested in George, in what Brian called his 'predatory' way, but he found this lost sheep very difficult to think about, as if what he thought was constantly falsified at the start. His heart, usually a trusted guide, did not guide him here. He would never have said so to Diane, but he was afraid of George. He sensed something unusual in him, a sort of liberated malice. Yet this too could be an illusion.

'If only he'd stop drinking,' she said, 'he'd get better. Oh I do wish you'd do something for George.'

The priest stared at her with his light luminous shining eyes. He was feeling tired and hungry. He had been in the church fasting since five-thirty. He said, 'I can't.'

'You can. Summon him. *Order* him to come and see you.'

'He wouldn't come.'

'He would. It's just the sort of thing that would amuse him.'

'Amuse him! You think he'd come to scoff and remain to pray?'

'Once you started talking to him –'

'George is beyond me,' said the priest. 'I'd better not meddle.' He snapped his fingers softly.

There was a familiar scraping sound, then a loud creaking, then a metallic clang. It was the west door opening and shutting. Father Bernard moved a little away from his penitent. His eyes, accustomed to the dim light, were dazzled for a moment by the gleaming reds and blues of the tall judging Christ, who, leaning upon his sword, was represented in the west window. A heavy tread, a bulky form was coming down the aisle. Father Bernard rose to his feet.

John Robert, his vision even more affected by the sudden change from light to dark, made his way towards the risen figure which was slightly illuminated by the sanctuary light, and in spite of the different garments which it was now wearing, recognized it as the man who had been pointed out to him at the Baths by Bill the Lizard. He approached the priest and said, 'Rozanov.'

This sound, muttered in John Robert's odd voice, might have conveyed nothing were it not that Father Bernard had, on the same occasion, had the philosopher pointed out to him by several people.

'How do you do,' said Father Bernard, 'I am Father Bernard, the Rector, I am glad to see you.' His heart made itself felt, large and warm. 'This is Mrs Sedleigh – perhaps you already –'

Diane had now also risen. She had of course never met John Robert, though she had occasionally seen him. She stood in breathless trembling panic like a doe which has suddenly smelt the close proximity of a lion. (There was actually a musty animal odour coming from the philosopher which Father Bernard's fastidious nostrils had also detected.) This big man, who had come so alarmingly near to her, held George's fate in his hands, the power of life or death. As Diane shuddered with this sudden intuition she wondered, does he know who I am? (In fact he did not.)

John Robert nodded. Diane murmured that she must go and went, her light swift feet tapping almost noiselessly upon the tiles as she ran toward the west door.

Father Bernard waved vaguely after her. He was feeling rather dismayed himself. He felt surprised, embarrassed, anxious, shy, and obscurely frightened.

'I should like to ask you something,' said Rozanov, his voice coming through clearly now.

'Surely, wait a moment, let's have some more light.'

The priest moved softly, with a rustle of his gown, to the nearest

160

switchboard, and illuminated a side chapel containing a Victorian picture of Christ at Emmaus.

He combed out his girlish hair with his fingers and returned to John Robert who had sat down. Father Bernard settled in the pew in front of him, curled himself up with a swirl of skirts, and turned to face the philosopher.

'I'd like to say "welcome back", but then you have scarcely been away. Is it for me to say "welcome back"? At any rate, welcome to my church.'

This slightly complex speech seemed to interest Rozanov. He thought about it for a moment and seemed pleased.

'Thank you.'

'You never worshipped here, I think?'

'No, I was brought up as a Methodist.'

'Are you still a believer?'

'No.'

There was silence for a moment. Father Bernard began to feel a burning anxiety. What did this strange creature want, and how could he, somehow, *keep* him? This was an odd thought. Odder still was the image which next came to the priest of Rozanov, large and quietly captive, sitting in a cage. He smiled and said, 'If I can assist you in any way I shall be very glad to. You have only to speak.' Father Bernard found himself adopting this rather stilted style in addressing Rozanov, as if he were talking in a foreign language.

The philosopher seemed in no hurry to do as he was bidden. He looked about the church with curiosity, chewing his large lower lip.

'May I show you round the church? Would you like that? There are points of interest.'

'No, thank you. Another time perhaps.'

After another silence Rozanov, still gazing about him, said, 'I want to talk to you.'

'Yes – what about?'

'About anything.'

'About – anything?'

'Yes,' said Rozanov. 'You see, I have only lately ceased to teach, returned from America, and for the first time I have no one to talk to.'

Father Bernard felt a little giddy. He said, 'But surely there are plenty of people –'

'No.'

'You mean – just talk?'

161

'I should explain. I have always, over very many years, had pupils and colleagues with whom I could talk philosophy.'

'I am not a philosopher,' said Father Bernard.

'Yes, and that is certainly a pity,' said Rozanov. He sighed. 'You don't happen to know of any philosophers in Ennistone? Not of course that any philosopher would do –'

Father Bernard hesitated. 'Well, there's George McCaffrey, but of course you know him.'

'Not McCaffrey. Do you know of any –?'

'I'm afraid not.'

'Then you will have to do.' The words had an authoritative finality.

'I shall certainly do my best,' said Father Bernard humbly, rather dazed, 'but I'm still not quite clear about what you want.'

'Simply someone to talk to. Someone entirely *serious*. I am accustomed to clarifying my thoughts in the medium of conversation.'

'Suppose I don't understand?' said Father Bernard.

John Robert suddenly smiled, turning towards the priest.

'Oh *that* doesn't matter. So long as you say what you think.'

'But I –' Father Bernard felt it would be graceless to protest. Besides he was now in a fever lest his preposterous vistor should change his mind.

He said, 'You want someone to, sort of, hit the ball back?'

'Yes. An image which – yes.'

'Not that I am in any way a match for you, to pursue the metaphor.'

'That is unimportant.'

'I'll try.'

'Good for you!' said John Robert. 'When can we start? Tomorrow?'

'Tomorrow's Sunday,' said Father Bernard faintly.

'Well then Monday, Tuesday?'

'Tuesday – but look, what sort of – how often –?'

'Could you manage every two or three days? As it suits you of course, I don't want to interfere with your parish work.'

'No, that's all right – would you like to come to the Clergy House?'

'No, I like to talk when I'm walking.'

Father Bernard detested walking, but he was already himself captured and caged.

162

'Yes, fine.'

'Could you call for me at my place, you know, 16 Hare Lane in Burkestown, about ten?'

'Yes, yes.'

'Thank you, I'm most obliged.'

Rozanov got up and marched off. Father Bernard rose too. The church door scraped and creaked and clanked shut again. Father Bernard sat down. He felt amazed, flattered, appalled, alarmed, touched. He sat still with his luminous eyes shinier than ever. Then he began, like Alex, quietly helplessly to laugh.

Hattie Meynell was sitting on her bed in the dormitory at school. Girls were not supposed to be in their dormitories during the day except to change before and after games. Games were over and Hattie had changed and had tea and ought to have been at prep. However, since she was so senior and this was her last term she felt, although she had always had a great respect for the school rules which were ever so rational, that she might, just now for a bit, do as she pleased. Younger at school, when she had yearned for oblivion even more than she did now, she had regarded her bed as her home, and something of this sense of refuge still remained. There were two other beds in the room, with white coverlets like the one which Hattie was rumpling by sitting on (which ought never to be happening). The big Victorian windows showed outside, in a clear soft evening light, a lawn with coniferous trees, then tennis courts whose wire cages made a silvery geometrical fuzz, then the mild green hills of the English countryside. Two girls were playing tennis, but not 'officially' since this was not a tennis term (they were allowed to play of course, but there was no coach). Hattie was wearing her changed-for-supper uniform, a silky light brown blouse with an embroidered collar and a round-necked dark brown pinafore dress of very fine corduroy. She had kicked off her shoes and was holding, lifted up on to her knee, one of her brown-stockinged feet. The girls were not allowed to wear tights, which were deemed bad for their health. Hattie was the 'little waif' referred to earlier, John Robert Rozanov's grand-daughter. She was seventeen.

The school was a very expensive rather progressive rather old-fashioned boarding school. It was progressive in its political and social ideas, old-fashioned in its discipline and academic standards. Hattie had been a pupil there for five years, during which time her American accent had been overlaid by a very different English one. She had crossed the Atlantic more times than she could remember.

She had wanted a pony, then ceased to want one. She had worn a gold band on her teeth, then ceased to wear it. She had plaited her hair in a pigtail, then put it up. She had passed a number of exams. At night she slept curled up with her hands crossed over her breasts. She was very unhappy but she did not recognize what ailed her as unhappiness.

Tomorrow she would have her hair washed by Miss Adkin, who came on Saturdays to wash the girls' hair. This hair-washing was a 'funny time', which Hattie could not decide about; many things at school were like that. Miss Adkin established herself in one of the bathrooms, and the girls, dressed in their pretty dressing-gowns, queued, always laughing a lot; for some reason hair-washing was ridiculous and somehow thrilling. Miss Adkin was a rather jokey lady but looked like a priestess, as if she might suddenly have produced a pair of shears and cut off all the girls' hair instead of washing it. Her customers sat in turn with their heads over the bath, and Miss Adkin sprayed on hot water, soaped, sprayed, soaped and sprayed and soaped again, while the semi-inaudible client complained that the water was too hot and the soap was getting in her eyes. Most of the girls had long hair, and there was something strange and shocking in the sudden transformation of dry fluffy tresses into long dark snakes swirling about in the water that kept rising in the bath, while Miss Adkin's strong claw-like fingers searched each bowed and suppliant scalp. Then a warm white furry towel was wrapped around each damp head and the turbaned victim ran red-faced and giggling away. Hattie disliked having her hair washed, but it excited her.

Beside each bed there was a chest of drawers, and on these the junior girls were allowed to place only three personal objects. Senior girls could please themselves so long as decorum was observed. Make-up was of course forbidden, as was jewellery and anything suggestive of display. Hattie had few possessions. On her chest there was a brown china rabbit scratching its ear, which had come up with her through the school, and which she could not bear to put away though other girls derided it; there was a long sleek Eskimo seal made of black soapstone, and a little pink-and-white Japanese vase (into which she never put flowers as that was not allowed). The dormitory was a weird place, though not terrible like the big dormitories in which, as a younger girl, she had cried herself to sleep every night. The stairs and landings, which were blurred by her little weeping ghost, stained by her tears, had always been strange haunted spaces to her, as if already removed into the brown haze of the past. Was it her *future* sadness which made the place so dim and foggy? It was hard to believe that soon she would be leaving it *forever*.

Hattie, though thin and pale, was very healthy and hardy, good at games and gymnastics. She was a pale straight girl, neither tall nor small, with long straight white-blond hair and blue eyes of a disconcerting pallor, as if they had great blobs of creamy whiteness mixed into the blue. Her father, Whit Meynell, had had an Icelandic mother. Hattie had never met her father's parents. Her mother had died when she was a small child. After that she travelled with her father during his academic peregrinations. Whit Meynell was a sociologist; he had got into an intellectual muddle early on in life and never managed to get out. No one would publish his book, however many times he rewrote it. He was a loving though extremely fretful and anxious and inefficient father. He set up his tents in various different universities, from all of which he was soon tactfully evicted. He never achieved 'tenure'. His frightful anxieties about the future were mercifully ended by a fatal (entirely accidental) motor crash. Hattie was ten.

After that, Hattie went to live for a time with her aunt, Whit Meynell's younger sister, who lived in a small town called Westfield, original home of the Meynells, situated in a woody desolation beside a muddy lake not far from Austin, Texas. Hattie missed her father agonizingly and wept longer than anyone thought at all proper. She got on quite well with Whit's sister Margot, but the arrangement only lasted a couple of years because Margot, who was unmarried, driven by a sudden and interesting desperation, decided to go and seek her fortune in New York, and could not see how to include Hattie in this enterprise. Margot wrote to this effect to Hattie's only other visible relative, John Robert Rozanov. John Robert had of course 'turned up' in Hattie's life at intervals. He had never got on well with Hattie's mother, Amy, though he maintained the forms of communication. Whit he could not stand and was at pains not to see. (There were kinds of intellectual muddle so degrading that John Robert preferred not to be reminded of their existence.) If he was 'giving a paper' anywhere near where Hattie's house happened to be, he would occasionally come and take the child out to tea. These 'treats' were rather glum, since Hattie, who heard no good of her grandfather at home, was frightened of him, and both of them were thoroughly awkward. Here too, however, the proprieties were observed, and John Robert replied promptly to Margot's letter. His idea was that the best way now to dispose of Hattie was to put her in an English boarding school. (He had made himself financially responsible for the child since Whit's death.) He expressed the wish that Margot might 'have' her in the holidays. Hattie was by now twelve. The holidays were at first a jumbled business, with Hattie dispatched to France or Germany to stay with strange families, on arrangements made by the school in accordance with John Robert's wishes, then whisked across the Atlantic to live in rooms near Margot's flat, since Margot's way of life could not just then be shared with an innocent young girl. Margot had by this time got as far towards New York as Denver, Colorado, where she finally married a Jewish lawyer called Albert Markowitz, and was able to establish a respectable home to which Hattie could come, but that was a little later.

Meanwhile something unusual, even odd, had happened in Hattie's life. An idea had germinated in the brilliant, but (in worldly matters) rather naïve and confused mind of John Robert. Perhaps he felt a bit guilty about having been inattentive, and wished to defend himself against a charge of wilful neglect. Perhaps he wanted simply to save himself the trouble of organizing and supervising Hattie's movements round the world. Whatever the reason, he decided that Hattie must have a permanent female companion, a person who in the old days could have been called her 'maid'. And in order to find such a person John Robert came back to Ennistone. He wanted an English girl, he needed advice, he did not want to waste time on the operation. He arrived and established himself (at the Ennistone Royal Hotel, 16 Hare Lane being let at the time). He had written beforehand to William Eastcote (Rose Eastcote was already dead) but Eastcote happened to be away at a Friends' conference in Geneva. The only other person in Ennistone whom he cared to trust in this matter was Ruby Doyle. John Robert had conceived, not exactly an affection, but a kind of respect for Ruby in the old Linda Brent days when Ruby, then young but looking much the same, had been so discreetly helpful. There was a kind of monumental thing-in-itselfness about Ruby which pleased the philosopher. Ruby, scarcely capable of speech, was incapable of lies. He felt that Ruby would do the few things that she could do without fuss and without the interference of any messy general ideas. She also knew how to keep her mouth shut. John Robert, by nature secretive, did not want his project discussed in Ennistone.

He wrote to Ruby and summoned her to the hotel. Ruby could not read or write but, so I am told, she took the letter to the gipsy camp. She certainly said nothing to Alex. When John Robert had explained what he wanted, Ruby responded promptly and without emotion that she had a connection, a cousin, who was now unemployed and who might suit the professor. How exactly the young woman in question (Pearl Scotney, she was called) was related to Ruby, and to Diane, was a matter of speculation. Some said they were all half-sisters, probably none of them knew for certain. Ruby bore, she said, her father's surname, Pearl bore her unmarried, abandoned, mother's name, and Diane had borne her unmarried, abandoned, mother's name (Davis) until her marriage with the disastrous Sedley. It might even have been that the connection between them had been originally suggested by their being called Pearl, Ruby and Diamond. John Robert interviewed Pearl in London and decided that she would do. He gave her an airline ticket to Denver and instructions about where to find Hattie. He also wrote to Margot, who was surprised, annoyed and relieved. Pearl arrived ánd found Hattie spending her first summer holidays in a dim flatlet in the large complex where Margot lived, and trying to do her holiday tasks while suffering from agonizing loneliness and chronic tears. Hattie was thirteen, Pearl was twenty-one.

John Robert had not, in conceiving his project, worked it out in any detail; he had not for instance wondered what Pearl was to do when Hattie was at school, and had to have this problem brought to his attention by Pearl. Pearl had no home in Ennistone, and in any case John Robert had made it clear that he did not want her to sojourn, perhaps talk, in his native town. It was decided that Pearl should continue to live where she had been living in north London and, when not in attendance upon Hattie, to continue if she wished her part-time secretarial work, without any diminution of the generous salary which John Robert paid her. Hattie's boarding school was in Hertfordshire, and here it was also Pearl's duty to visit her, and see she was contented and supplied with all that she needed.

This idea of John Robert's, which might, for all the care or common sense that he exercised in setting it up, have proved disastrous, in fact turned out well. Hattie vividly recalled, and she and Pearl often talked it over later, Pearl's first arrival in Denver. John Robert had sent Hattie a short note to tell her that he had engaged a 'companion' for her. Hattie tearfully anticipated the arrival of some gorgon. Pearl on her side was already beginning to regret what had at first seemed a miraculous adventure. What horrid neurotic little brat perhaps awaited her? Pearl went first to Margot's flat, then to the nearby cubby-hole where Margot had stored Hattie. Hattie's first sighting of Pearl was not reassuring. It could not exactly be said that Pearl resembled Ruby, yet there was something of Ruby's 'Mexican' look in Pearl's hard strong face. Pearl was lean with very dark brown straight hair and a sallow complexion and a thin nose which came straight down from her forehead and thin fierce lips. Her eyes were of the greenish light-brown colour known as hazel. She glared nervously at Hattie, and Hattie vanished into the dim haze of her frightened childish face. Then Pearl smiled, and then Hattie smiled. They both said later that they knew at once that it would be 'all right', although perhaps all that happened was that Hattie saw that Pearl was considerably younger than the person she expected (John Robert had failed to specify Pearl's age) and Pearl saw that Hattie was timid and harmless.

Pearl Scotney, born in Ennistone, had grown up in London whither her unhappy mother had transferred her. Pearl could not remember her father. Her mother had followed Diane's profession, only Pearl never told anyone this. She always said her mother was a dress-maker. The mother drank, then died. Pearl went to a foster home. Up to this time Pearl's connection with her 'family' in Ennistone had consisted of 'keeping in touch at Christmas', at least Ruby and Diane sent Christmas cards; giving evidence that they knew Pearl existed and where she was. Pearl sent nothing. Her mother had wanted no family ties, no remembrances, no connection with her nightmarish past. Pearl's foster-mother rather randomly initiated a *rapprochement* by writing to Ruby and Diane asking for money. Diane sent some. Ruby came to see the child and manifested some gruff affection. Ruby in fact would have liked to bring Pearl to Ennistone and install her at Belmont, only she could not think out how to suggest this to Alex. As soon as Pearl left school, her main aim in life was to get away from her foster-mother (the feeling was mutual) and Ruby found her a temporary job in Ennistone as a maid and child-minder with some visiting Americans. During this period Pearl taught herself typing (and spelling) and then became a secretary. She had some small messy love affairs and felt very confused and unhappy. However, she was able to earn her living and to begin to be, which she never thought as a child that she ever would be, a real person. She had an uneasy sort of relation with Ruby and Diane. Ruby was moodily affectionate, sometimes suddenly possessive, prompt in detecting rebuffs. Diane was (so Pearl thought) resentful, even envious of a sort of irresponsible independence which she attributed to the younger girl. So things had been going along when John Robert Rozanov interfered in the course of Pearl's life. John Robert judged that Pearl Scotney 'had her head screwed on'; and it appeared that John Robert was right.

Arrived in Denver, and after her relief at finding Hattie so harmless, Pearl was suddenly filled with power. Challenged by a rather peculiar situation, she took charge of it. She felt all of a sudden free, competent, and (she noticed one morning) very nearly happy. Being a very long way from London, and from Ennistone, helped too. She was in a germless void, and she loved every minute, though also telling herself that it would not last. The first thing was to tackle Margot Meynell. Hattie could wait, and *did* wait, silent with admiration. Margot, whose love life was in a delicate and complex state, viewed the newcomer with dismay. Margot had not told John Robert that Hattie was not living in her flat. She feared Pearl as a hostile informer and agent of a superior power. However, Pearl had a frank conference with Margot which made the latter feel much better. It was clear, said Pearl, that she and Hattie must find a considerably larger, considerably better flat. John Robert had said nothing about flats. Perhaps he had assumed that Margot would house both the girls. Perhaps he thought Pearl would arrange things as she thought best. Perhaps he had not reflected on the matter at all. Pearl, in her new role, wrote John Robert a 'business letter' over which she laboured long, saying that she thought that Hattie and herself should move into a flat near to Miss Meynell's, as quarters were a bit cramped. This, without lying, implied that Hattie had been living with Margot (not that Pearl minded lying half as much as, for instance, Emmanuel Scarlett-Taylor did). John Robert, who was certainly not short of money, replied that he had opened an account for Pearl in a Denver bank and she was to do as she thought fit. After this Pearl took complete charge and Margot gratefully retired, though without forfeiting the allowance which John Robert continued to pay her.

After Pearl came, Hattie stopped hating Denver. The girls learnt to ski. (Pearl persuaded Margot to ski too, only she promptly broke her leg.) However there was now less of Denver and more of

Europe. Pearl delivered Hattie to the 'families' or accompanied her to some of the better-known monuments and museums. Hattie could now speak French, German and Italian. Pearl had learnt no language at school and been taught no grammar. For a time she tried secretly, and in vain, to teach herself French. Then regretfully gave up. When they went sightseeing, Pearl had a simpler cause of unease; she was afraid that something might happen to Hattie. She did once lose her in Rome and had a terrible half-hour. Back in the USA there was travelling too. Sometimes John Robert came to Denver, sometimes the girls flew to see him in California, once to Boston where he was spending a semester, once to St Louis, more than once to New York. On these occasions they saw little of the philosopher, meetings being still rather in the 'having tea' style. John Robert would then question Hattie about her school studies and about where she had been and what she had done, but he would soon start looking at his watch. Once he asked her to read a passage of Racine. On these occasions John Robert was polite and grateful to Pearl but managed somehow (perhaps unconsciously) to mark the difference between the girls, who by now regarded each other as sisters. Hattie was 'the mistress', Pearl 'the maid'. Pearl put this away in a package of resentment which however remained fairly small. Hattie and Pearl were both rather afraid of John Robert. But during his absences Hattie, at least when she was younger, did not trouble her head about him, whereas Pearl did.

Pearl was an employee, one whose employment could be terminated. This fact which had not at first occupied Pearl's attention much, or Hattie's at all, now began to disturb them both. New feelings and understandings were bodying themselves forth in Hattie's mind. Pearl had been a mother, then a sister. This had never seemed odd before. Why should it feel so now? Once at school Hattie overheard one of the mistresses, talking about her and Pearl, say, 'It's an unhealthy relationship.' Hattie, in secret tears, had been hurt and puzzled. Pearl was an employee, a servant. John Robert had established her by fiat. He could remove her by fiat. And now Hattie was leaving school, that too had been decreed. She supposed there would be more travel, more museums, more and different teachers, the university. Soon she would be eighteen. She felt unready for this or indeed any other future. Had she a future? Or was the problem rather that she had nothing else, an excess of future, white and unmarked and blank? *Her* future. Could she own such a thing? One of the teachers talked about a crisis of identity. Hattie had no identity and nothing as creative as a crisis. She thought, I am nothing, I am a floating seed which a bird will soon eat. 'Lives of great men all remind us we must make our lives sublime, and departing leave behind us footprints in the sands of time.' So they sometimes sang in chapel, where Hattie had acquired some vague Anglicanism. The unprinted sand stretched ahead, making Hattie feel weary, weary, as if her life were already over. Her only positive feeling was a sense of her own innocence. She had not yet 'become bad' as so many people, as she knew, became. Evil, that too was part of the white blankness of the future.

Such thoughts flitted in her head as she sat now on her white school bed, and held her warm brown-stockinged foot in her hand. They flitted around with lots of other thoughts, memories of snowy slopes mauve with aspens, of that melancholy lake in Texas, of her dear father frowning with anxiety as he prepared his lectures, of the awful little flatlet where she had cried so much before Pearl came, of the kindly nervous guilty face of Margot Meynell, now Mrs Albert Markowitz, and distantly distantly dimly of Hattie's mother, the unhappy dead lady who had once been Miss Rozanov.

A distant bell rang. Hattie thrust a clean handkerchief into her knickers, and emerged substanceless as a seed into the brown spaces of the landing and the stairs which she was destined to dream about for the rest of her life.

John Robert Rozanov was floating like an enormous baby in the hot flowing waters of his private bath in the Ennistone Rooms. His bath was a large boat-shaped affair made of white tiles with blunt ends. At each end there was a seat which was under water when the bath was full. There was a fan which expelled the steam, but John Robert had not put it on; he liked steam. The hot curative waters flowed in, indeed roared in, from the fat glistening brass taps which were never turned off by day or night, so that the Rooms were full of a ceaseless roaring to which the inmates were quickly accustomed and said to deafened visitors 'I don't hear it!' 'They may not hear it, but it affects them,' someone said darkly to the Director of the Institute, Vernon Chalmers, who quickly prepared and kept in reserve a little monograph on the therapeutic powers of sound. Dazed, almost drowsy, with unheard noise John Robert floated, his white-skinned whale-belly huge before him. His big flipper-like hands kept him buoyant, moving slowly to and fro in the space of the bath, while the steaming water fell from the taps at a controlled temperature of forty-two degrees Centigrade. The bath could be filled by turning a brass handle to close the plug at the bottom, after which the water rose to an outlet vent near the top. When the plug was lifted, the water subsided to a uniform level of about a foot, spitting and gurgling under the violence of the jets from above.

Last night John Robert had dreamt that he was being pursued by a lot of squealing piglets who turned out to be human infants running very fast on all fours. Later he saw the same creatures lying on the ground as if asleep, only now they were dolls, and he thought, 'they were dolls after all.' Some of them lay quiet, and these he took to be dead; others were moving and twitching slightly, and these he took to be dying. He thought, but surely dolls *must* be dead. He picked up one of the dead ones and put it in his pocket. His mother came and asked to see it. When he brought it out he saw with horror that it was alive and in pain. In the morning he

173

woke up early and went out for a walk. He looked into the big
bright clean Methodist church where he had worshipped as a child.
He had not been there for a long time and felt a weird shock when
he recognized the numbers of the hymns. He then visited the little
corrugated-iron Roman Catholic chapel where his mother had
once told him that they worshipped a goddess. Why had she frightened him by saying that, was it meant to be a joke? He looked
inside into the dark which was full of images. An aged priest
appeared who said that he remembered his grandfather. People in
Burkestown all knew John Robert, smiled at him and said, 'Good
morning, Professor.'

John Robert propelled himself to one end of the bath and adopted
a sitting position, his head and shoulders now above the water. He
mopped his red swollen steamy face with an adjacent towel, and
began to go through the exercises which his Japanese doctor in
California had recommended for his arthritis. When John Robert
went to Texas and Arizona his arthritic symptoms disappeared.
Since his return into the English spring he had felt old familiar pains
together with new strange ones. As he rotated his head and twitched
his shoulders and turned his arms into snakes he sighed, then
groaned into the hurly-burly of the roaring stream. The warmth
was kind to his bulky pain-ridden body. As he swayed himself
gently in the waters he could not but believe in their therapeutic
power. But for the weary diminishing cells of the mind there was
no alleviation, unless it might be a strong electric shock to shake
them all up again like counters in a game. He was so tired and so
old, and he had so much to decide and such terrible things to do.

Meanwhile outside at that very moment the sun was shining on
the Outdoor Bath, which was less steamy today because the air
temperature was higher. The sky was blue, clothes and bodies
looked bright and hard-edged and clear, and the cries which people
always utter in swimming-pools echoed in the sunny northern light.
In Diana's Garden Ruby, Diane and Pearl were standing together,
a rare conjunction, not marked since few people in Ennistone knew
Pearl by sight. Pearl had been to visit her foster-mother who lived
in Kilburn and who had written to her asking for money. Pearl
could have sent the money by post, but decided to visit the old lady
at least partly so as to exhibit her own affluence and sophistication.
The foster-mother, visited, made a point of not being interested in

174

Pearl's life. Then she wept self-pityingly. Pearl left, upset and cross. Unhappy stirred up memories then made her suddenly want to go to Ennistone, where there was no particular reason for her to be and where she rarely went, since she knew that it was out of bounds under John Robert's rules. She came to the Baths looking for Ruby.

Diane was wearing a dark blue tweed coat which she had bought at the second-hand shop. She ought not to have bought it. She had savings, but George's non-appearance was reducing her spending money. It can't go on, she told herself. She was not sure what this meant, but at least it suggested that her troubles would end somehow. Everything was disorderly and menacing. A lot of things had been stolen on the day when the lights went out at Bowcocks. Supposing someone were to accuse her of thieving? Everyone would be thrilled to believe it, she was vulnerable to any accusation. Suppose her money ran out, could she ask Ruby or Pearl for a loan? Impossible. Ruby regarded Diane as a fallen woman, someone who had ruined herself and was finished. Diane could not forgive this. Nor could she forgive Pearl for being young and free, and for looking so horribly healthy and independent in a corduroy jacket and trousers. Diane felt close to tears. How pleased everyone would be to see her crying in public. Everyone, that is, except George, who would be furiously angry. Fortunately George was absent. I had better go, thought Diane, I've been away for long enough, perhaps he'll come – Oh, if only I could *go to the cinema* like ordinary people do. Where will I be a year from now? Will I be *somewhere else, could I be*? Will I be dead? Will he be dead? The idea that George was going to commit suicide had now lodged in her mind. This did not appal her, it gave her a kind of relief, not because she felt she would survive George, but because she apprehended it as her own death.

Ruby was brown and monumental and self-absorbed, not even showing the little signs of pleasure, like tiny droplets glistening upon a rock, which she usually exhibited when Pearl was present. Ruby was totally fascinated by her new relationship with Alex. At least Ruby's side of it was new. Alex did not really *know*. Ruby had not yet moved. Ruby was actually far more alarmed by her new state of mind than her employer was. Some old unquestioned thing had quietly gone out of her life. Was it good that it had gone? Ruby sensed her power and was appalled by it. It was almost as if she could, if she wished, *destroy* Alex. Did she want to? No. But the pension, that meant independence, equality. Equality? She had only to stretch out her hand and decree it. She had only to go and sit in the drawing-room with Alex and say, we must eat together henceforth, we are two old women living together from now on. Could she do that? Ruby could picture doing it, but could not picture what might follow. It did not occur to her that Alex might tell her to go. The idea of being 'dismissed' did not exist for Ruby. How could it? She had brushed Alex's hair when Alex was sixteen.

'How's the little madam?' said Diane.

'All right. I haven't seen her lately.'

'Aren't you paid to keep an eye on her?'

'No.'

'Don't you call at the school?'

'She doesn't like it.'

'Why, is she ashamed of you?'

'No.'

'Off to USA soon, I suppose?'

'Yes.'

'Don't do it,' said Ruby suddenly.

'Do what?'

'Be like me.'

'It's not like that,' said Pearl, 'I'm not her –' She could not find the word.

'Who's that girl?' said Emmanuel Scarlett-Taylor.

'My brother's mistress.'

'Good heavens.'

'Which girl do you mean? The girl in the tweed coat is George's mistress. The big old brown thing is my mother's servant. I don't know who the girl in trousers is.'

'Servant,' murmured Emma. 'What a strange old-fashioned word.'

Tom was garbed for swimming, his wig of long curly hair still dry. Emma was dressed, complete with coat and waistcoat and high collar and bow tie and watch chain.

'Why don't you talk to her?'

'Which?'

'Either.'

'I can't talk to the mistress, so I can't talk to the servant.'

'Why not? You smiled at the mistress.'

'Yes, but she didn't smile back.'

176

'So I saw. Why?'

'Why what?'

'Why these prohibitions?'

'Because of George.'

'George is a reason?'

'Yes.'

'Is George here?'

'I don't know.'

'I want to meet him.'

'I don't advise it.'

'You seem to live under a reign of terror. What's that?'

'What?'

'That thing with the railing round it.'

'That's the Little Teaser.'

'The what?'

'That's what we call it. Lud's Rill. It's a hot spring. It jumps up a little. It's very hot.'

'I don't think much of it. Where's the real hot spring?'

'You can't see it. It's somewhere down below.'

'Have you seen it?'

'No.'

'Who's *that* girl?'

'Anthea Eastcote.'

'She didn't smile either. You smiled at her.'

'She didn't see me.'

'She did. She cut you.'

'Oh never mind. Perhaps she wants to make me jealous.'

'You're upset.'

'I'm not!'

'The trouble with you is you want everybody to love you.'

'Stop *nagging*, Emma.'

'All right, I won't say another word.'

'And don't sulk either.'

'Who's the chap with her?'

'Hector Gaines. He's a historian. You'd like him.'

'Introduce me.'

'Not now.'

'You drag me here and you won't introduce me to anyone.'

'There's Alex!'

'Where?'

'There.'

'You mean the girl in the green costume who's kicking up the water and twirling round and round like a corkscrew?'

'Yes. She likes doing that.'

'She reminds me of something I saw once in a pool in the west of Ireland.'

'Well, I'm going swimming now. Be good.'

Tom dived in and swam toward Alex. Like Adam, he felt easier with her in the water. She had stopped her whirligig and waved to him. Tom passed her, touching her wet smooth shoulder, squeezing it slightly. She put her hand to his head, tugging the wet curls. He passed on with a lighter heart. It was true that he wanted everyone to love him, *everyone*.

Alex looked after him. She was well aware that Tom's not staying was an important gesture, a declaration of independence. On the other hand she knew that Tom wished to have it both ways, to stand away and yet to be absolutely wanted. He had come to see her yesterday. She had not play-acted preoccupation, distraction. She had been really unable to attend to him and to fuss over him as she usually did. He had found her in the Slipper House with Ruby, cleaning, moving furniture, installing new things which she had ordered. Tom and Ruby carried some of the heavier objects up the stairs. Alex did not explain these changes to Tom. She had not explained them to Ruby. Robin Osmore had written to Rozanov with details of the let. Alex felt uneasy, happy. Life was, again, vivid and unpredictable at last.

'Don't drip all over me.'

'Sorry, Emma.'

'I want to meet George.'

'He isn't here!'

'Isn't that your other brother coming, with the boy?'

'Hello, Brian. You remember Scarlett-Taylor.'

'Hello. I hear you went to see Alex yesterday.'

'How did you know?'

'Gabriel telephoned. We've stopped seeing her.'

'Really?'

'A wishful thought.'

'Do you know Alex's latest? She wants to keep bees!'

'She must be stopped *at all costs*.'

'How's dog, *papillon*?' said Emma to Adam.

'Zed's fine,' said Adam, with distant but friendly dignity.

'Isn't he here?'

'He's not allowed. I want him to swim. He swims well. He loves it.'

'Are we going to the sea?' said Tom to Brian.

'The family seaside jaunt is on, I believe, come the summer.'

'Staying in a hotel?'

'No, just the day.'

'Not near Maryville, I couldn't bear it.'

'There's the moon,' said Adam to Emma. And there indeed it was, quite full and as pale as a cream cheese in the brilliant blue sky.

'Why doesn't it shine?'

'The sun doesn't let it.'

'Have you got a dog?'

'No,' said Emma. Then something caught him in the throat. He had had a dog when he was Adam's age, a darling spaniel with a spotty nose. It had been run over and killed before his eyes. He said, 'I did have one – once –'

Adam understood and looked away.

'Look out,' said Tom, 'Percy Bowcock with Mrs Osmore.'

'Too late, hello, Percy. Good morning, Mrs Osmore.'

'May I introduce my friend, Emmanuel Scarlett-Taylor? Mr Bowcock, Mrs Osmore.'

Percy (a rich Bowcock, Gabriel's cousin) said to Brian, 'Do you think Professor Rozanov could be persuaded to give a lecture in the Ennistone Hall?'

'How should I know, I'm not in charge of the old fool,' said Brian. Brian's rudeness sometimes made people say that he was simply George by other means, but that was only a *façon de parler*.

Tom said to Adam, 'Give me an idea for a pop song.'

'Why?'

'Because Scarlett-Taylor and I are going to write a pop song and make our fortunes.'

'We are not,' said Emma.

'I shall write the words and he will write the music. Think of something, a pop song only needs one line.'

'What about – what about – "It's only me." '

'It's only me?'

'Yes. There's two snails on a leaf, one on each side. Then one comes round the leaf and says to the other one, "It's only me." '

'Must they be snails?' said Tom after a moment's thought.

'I see them as snails,' Adam said firmly.

'I think it's *brilliant*,' said Tom.

Mrs Osmore asked Emma how he was enjoying Ennistone. Emma said it was a very interesting place.

'You're Irish, Mr Taylor?'

'Yes.'

'Oh I know. The sorrows of Ireland! You must feel such resentment against us for still occupying your country.'

Emma smiled sweetly.

'Is that Tom McCaffrey?' said Pearl.

'Yes.'

'He's grown up.'

'He's not as pretty as he used to be,' said Diane, who had funny feelings about Tom.

'How are things at Belmont?' Pearl asked Ruby.

'Bad.'

'Why?'

'It's the fox. The fox does it.' This was a piece of old gipsy folklore.

'Don't be silly,' said Diane.

'It will come to bad things.'

'I suppose you're going to see Professor Rozanov?' Diane said to Pearl. 'Will he give you your severance pay?'

'Not that I know of.'

'Jobs are hard to get these days.'

'Luckily I don't need one.'

'Don't be touchy.'

'Are you going to see him now?' asked Ruby.

'Not *now*.'

'Tomorrow? Isn't it funny that he's back at the old house at Hare Lane?' said Diane. 'Where are you spending the night? The Royal Hotel, I suppose?'

Pearl blushed scarlet. Rozanov had not told her or Hattie that he was coming to Ennistone. She had supposed him safely far away in California. If he were to see her. . . . Aflame with guilt, she looked round the clear brilliantly coloured scene. She said, 'I must go, I've got to telephone, nice to have seen you.' And she turned and ran for the exit.

'What do you suppose –' began Diane.

'Here's Madam,' said Ruby.

She still sometimes referred to Alex in this way.

It had begun to rain.

'Put your umbrella up, you're getting wet,' said Tom to Emma.

'You go and get dressed, you're shivering with cold.'

'I'm not.'

'Well, I am, looking at you.'

'I say, there's George.'

Emma, who had put his umbrella up, put it down again.

George, dressed in black swimming-trunks, was standing absolutely still on the edge of the pool. He was looking into the distance and thinking. He had woken up this morning and once again heard the birds uttering human speech. Then he had thought it was Stella, speaking outside on the stairs, only there was no one there. He went into the garden and saw a fish swimming in a tree, only it was a memory of a dream which had somehow got loose. He rang up the Ennistone Rooms and found out that John Robert had engaged a room. He went to the library to find out exactly what had happened to Schlick, but he could find no book about Schlick.

As he came out to the pool he had seen Diane, seen her see him, and seen her turn away slowly and go. He wanted, in a way, very much to go to Diane, to be in that familiar room, to smell her cigarettes and hold her hand, just that. But he was afraid to go to her. He must not, now, make himself weak, gentle, consoled. He almost felt he could have wept in that room holding her hand. There was in George something that was not himself, something puny, even pathetic, a little miserable bedraggled animal which disturbed him with its whimpering. He would, if he could, *kill* that mean frightened little animal. Against it now he summoned up his world-resentment, his sense of cosmic injustice, his hatred of his enemies, and his old valuable contempt for women. The rain beat down upon his hair, making it even darker and flattening it in to his head. The rain rolled over his brown body, brown as all the heliotropic Ennistonian swimmers were. The rain studded his body with bright points.

Valerie Cossom, looking at him from across the grey pitted

water, constrained her heart with her hand, and stiffened her mind by trying to think about the party line. She had never spoken to George. She wondered if she ever would.

'Introduce me to George.'
'No.'
'You're afraid.'
'Oh *Emma* –'
'I shall introduce myself, now.'
'You don't know – stop – oh all right.'

Tom, nearly naked, and Emma, fully clothed and getting very wet since he had not reopened his umbrella, advanced along one side of the pool, then set off along the next toward George, who was standing by himself, the rain, now sharp and biting, having driven most of the swimmers back into the water.

George became aware of an approach, then of Tom, and very slightly turned his head.

'George – hello –'

George kept his head slightly turned, his wide-apart eyes slewed round toward his brother but not looking at him. Tom had an odd impression, rather like a memory, of a madman in a cupboard. He felt intensely, what he had in the past more vaguely felt, George's uncanny quality, unpleasant like the smell of a ghost.

Tom went on, 'George, I'd like you to meet my friend, Emmanuel Scarlett-Taylor.'

George said nothing. He moved his body. Tom flinched. Then George, still without looking directly at Tom, took hold of Tom's adjacent arm, squeezed it for a moment extremely hard, then pushed him away with the palm of his hand, turning as he did so to his previous posture of contemplation.

Tom moved back, cannoned into Emma, turned smartly and led Emma away.

'Damn you.'
'Sorry –'
'You see what he's like. Or rather you don't.'
'Well, what is he like?'
'Oh fuck him. I'm getting bloody cold. I'm going in to dress.'

Tom, hurrying to the changing-rooms and now shuddering with cold, could feel his arm burning from George's vicious grip. He could also feel the flat sensation of the palm of George's hand upon his shoulder. As he turned into the door he saw farther down, just entering the Promenade, the back views of Anthea Eastcote and Hector Gaines. He found the key which would release his clothes from the locker, and felt, for a moment, a storm of emotion inside his peace-loving breast.

On the Promenade Anthea Eastcote and Hector Gaines were drinking coffee. Anthea had put on her round tinted glasses. She was really rather short-sighted, and skilfully concealed the fact. She had however seen Tom smile and had pretended not to. She felt upset about this now. She was very fond of Tom, whom she had known since they were tiny children, not of course in love; it was just that sometimes he seemed a little too cheerfully at home with the prospect of never possessing her.

Hector Gaines, agonizingly aware of Anthea's breasts, now safe and snug inside her tight mauve sweater, was telling himself that he was thirty-four and she was twenty-one, and that he had finished his work on Gideon Parke and ought to go to Aberdeen to see his mother, whose loving letters never complained about his infrequent visits.

Brian McCaffrey, also vividly aware of Anthea Eastcote's breasts, came up to the counter to order his coffee and Adam's special of pineapple juice and Coca-Cola. He greeted Anthea, whom of course he knew well since she too was a Friend, and Hector, whom he knew slightly.

He said to Anthea, 'How's your uncle Bill? Someone said he was a bit off colour.'

'Oh he's fine. Hello, Adam, what are you doing, being a tree?'

Adam, who was standing with his arms spread out, said, 'No, I'm drying my wings.'

Brian and Adam retired a little way with their drinks, Adam, who never called Brian 'Daddy' or anything of that sort, said, 'Why is the moon sometimes there at night and sometimes there during the day?'

'Because it's going round the earth while we're going round the sun.'

'But how exactly?'

'Oh heavens – it's – I'll look it up.'

Brian sat down and banged his coffee cup on to the table. He had just heard that economies at the Town Hall were likely to bring his job to an end.

Hector said timidly to Anthea, 'Shall we go and see the sculpture exhibition in the Botanic Gardens or the Ennistone Art Society in the Hall?'

Anthea said, 'You go, I'll join you there.' She wanted to go and make her peace with Tom.

'But which?'

'Which what?'

'Which exhibition?'

'Oh, the Art Society, it's still raining.'

Gabriel had arrived. She swept in, in dripping mac and black sou'wester, and plumped down at Brian's table.

'You're late,' said Brian.

'She's gone.'

'Who's gone?'

'Stella. She disappeared while I was out shopping. She left a note just saying she felt she should go and not to worry.'

'Well, she's been with us long enough and we weren't doing her any good.'

'But where's she gone to?'

'If you don't know I certainly don't.'

'She *can't* have gone back to George!'

'I don't see why not. Anyway it's none of our business.'

'Suppose she kills herself?'

'She won't.'

Gabriel burst into tears.

'Oh stop that! Come on, we're going home.'

Vernon Chalmers, Director of the Institute, sitting in his office in the Annexe, was startled by a sudden uproar which seemed to come from the direction of Diana's Garden. He thought at first that some sort of fight or riot must have broken out. Then he realized it was a sound of laughter. He got up from his desk and went to the window.

Tom McCaffrey, emerging clothed into the abating rain, heard the same sound. Anthea caught him up. 'Hello.'

'Hello, Anthea, what's up?'

'Let's go and see.'

Tom took her hand for a moment and they ran along the edge of the pool.

A small crowd had gathered near Lud's Rill. Tom, racing ahead, saw the following strange sight, Emmanuel Scarlett-Taylor, his clothes soaked and dripping, dancing about in helpless frustration inside the railing which surrounded the spring.

What had happened was simple. Emma, disturbed by the memory of his dog, was filled with a sudden desire to approach the little fount and feel how hot the water really was. It was easy enough, stepping upon a nearby stone, to vault in. Getting out was another matter. There was nothing inside to step on, and the railings, breast high, had spiked tops curving inwards. Enraged at his own folly, and now provoked by the laughter of spectators, he ran from place to place, peering through his rain-spotted glasses, trying to find somewhere to put his foot, then attempting to draw himself up by placing his hands on top of the curving rails. They were too high, he was not strong enough. The encouragement of the spectators became more ribald. An authoritative figure strode forward: it was Nesta Wiggins in her bikini. She shouted, 'Stop laughing, help him!', which prompted more laughter. But there was nothing that Nesta could do. Emma refused her proffered hand. She ran off crying, 'Get a ladder!'

Tom roared with laughter. Then he hurried on and, reaching the enclosures, knelt down, thrusting one sturdy knee through the railings. Emma ran to him, put one foot on his knee, gripped one of the rails at the top, and leapt to freedom. Clapping and cheers greeted his escape. Crimson with chagrin, Emma had already set off for the exit.

Tom ran after him. 'You've left your umbrella behind. Shall I get it?'

Emma walked on in grim silence, and Tom followed him out, laughing again.

'Do you believe in God?'

'No.'

'Come, anything counts as belief these days.'

'No.'

'So you're an odd sort of priest.'

'Yes.'

'You reject God?'

'Yes.'

'It is not enough to reject him, you must hate him.'

'Do you hate him?'

'I abominate the concept.'

Father Bernard said, 'So do I,' but in a whisper.

'Why do you whisper, do you think he's listening?'

'I don't believe in a personal God.'

'You mean "God" isn't a name?'

'But I believe in a spiritual reality.'

'What does "reality" mean here, what is "spiritual", could you give examples?'

It was Tuesday and Father Bernard had called at Hare Lane at ten o'clock as instructed. He had avoided the Institute in the interim so as not to 'spoil' the meeting, to which he looked forward with a ridiculous excitement and alarm. (He never swam on Sundays as an act of abstinence. He once gave up swimming for Lent and suggested to his appalled congregation that they should do likewise.) On arrival at the philosopher's house he had been dismayed to find John Robert all ready to *go for a long walk*. Father Bernard, who had lost the athletic tastes and talents of his youth, disliked long walks and could scarcely envisage having any sort of difficult conversation while in motion (he was slightly deaf). Now Rozanov was talking of going across the Common and out into the country. The priest marked his displeasure by asking for some safety pins and fussily pinning up the hem of his cassock. He was determined *not* to go out into the country, and hoped (rightly as it turned out) that once they were talking he could lead John Robert along an easier route. He therefore suggested that since he had to pay a brief pastoral visit at Blanch Cottages (a lie), they should go by West-wold and the Glove Factory and the Roman bridge and through Victoria Park and Druidsdale and thus to the Common and thus (as far as Father Bernard was concerned) back to Burkestown. John Robert agreed and they set off at first in silence, with John Robert walking uncomfortably fast, and had crossed the bridge when John Robert kindly remembered that the priest had forgotten to call at Blanch Cottages. Father Bernard, rather ashamed, went back to pay a pointless call on Miss Dunbury, leaving that blame-less lady puzzled and scrutinizing her conscience. By now they had entered the outskirts of Victoria Park, walking at the slower pace which Father Bernard had resolutely imposed upon the philoso-pher.

'For instance, are you saved?'

'What does that mean?' countered the priest.

'Answer first.'

'No, of course not!'

'When I was young,' said John Robert, 'people used to ask me that, as if it were a simple question. I even thought I understood it.'

'Did you think you were saved?'

'No, but I thought my mother was. People meant salvation by magic, being totally changed.'

'In virtue of a cosmic event, as explained by St Paul.'

'The cosmos would have to shudder and shake to change a single man.'

'So you think we can't change?'

'Paul, what a genius, to see that the crucifixion was the thing that mattered, what courage, to make the cross *popular*! The Gospels are so self-important and pompous –'

'Pompous!'

'"And he passed over into Galilee." No! In Paul we hear the voice of a thinking man, an individual.'

'A demon, I think.'

'He had to invent Christ, that required demonic energy. I *envy* Paul. But don't you believe in salvation without God? What do you offer to your flock? Or do you tell them lies?'

'What indeed?'

187

'Enlightenment and so on?'

'When I think of such matters I feel humble and afraid.'

'I don't believe you. What do you do about it?'

'I pray.'

'How can you?'

'I reach out to Christ.'

'To Christ? He died long ago.'

'Not mine. We know nobody as well as we know Jesus. A mystical being.'

'Of your own invention.'

'No – not invented – not like other inventions – really – just somehow there. That's *it* in a way.'

'It?'

'Our problem now, the problem of our age, our interregnum, our interim, our time of the angels –'

'Why angels?'

'Spirit without God.'

'So you expect a new revelation?'

'No, just to hang on.'

'Until?'

'Until religion can change itself into something we can believe in.'

'Surely you don't credit these historical dramas?' said John Robert. 'History is fictitious. To want, however modestly, salvation by history is to live a lie. All prophets are devils, vile peddlers of illusions.'

'I was only hoping –'

'Anyway, when it comes to it, what do you want to save?'

'Oh – I don't know – certain images – certain rites – certain spiritual situations – the conception of sacraments – certain words even.'

'Why call it religion?'

'It certainly isn't morality.'

'True. But this mystical Christ of yours, do you talk to him, ask him things?'

'I come to him. I live him and breathe him.'

'Are you a mystic?'

'No, that would be to claim merit.'

'Never mind merit, are you a mystic?'

'I believe in a spiritual world as if it were very close to this world, as if it were – well, I believe that it is – this world – exactly the same and yet absolutely different.'

'You have an experience?'

'Not like a vision. More like a vibration.'

'Isn't that sex?'

'Well, isn't sex everywhere? Is it not an image of spirit, is it not spirit itself? Can spirit, our spirit and there is no other, ever rise so high that it leaves sex behind?'

'Death excludes sex. Its proximity kills desire. Wisdom is the practice of dying.'

'Surely sex as spirit embraces death too.'

'That old romantic stuff! I am surprised at you. Your spiritual sex is about suffering. Christianity is a cult of suffering.'

'Not if Christ didn't rise it isn't. And it is essential that he did not rise. If he be risen then is our faith vain.'

'That is good. Only don't deny that it is the suffering that attracts you. If there is any absolute it condemns our evil to death, not to purgation.'

'What about redemptive suffering?'

'Is there such a thing?'

'Of course there is, we are surrounded by it – when someone loves another person and suffers for him, with him – this releases spiritual energy – like an electric charge.'

John Robert reflected. 'Well – silent fruitless love there's plenty of, and we would need a God to give any point to *that*. I don't believe in your redemptive suffering. A delightful idea, like your mystic Christ – a lie. It's self-flattery, illusion, like almost anything that pleases. Are you a homosexual?'

'Yes, but I live chastely. I don't mind what other people do.'

'So you are a narcissist?'

'Certainly, narcissists can look after others because they are content with themselves. They are creative, imaginative, humorous, sympathetic. Those who lack narcissism are resentful envious husks. It is they who try to give it a bad name.'

John Robert laughed, then frowned.

At that moment they were walking, at the modest pace imposed by the priest, along the road called Forum Way which bordered the end of the Belmont garden. Behind the wall could be seen the tall dramatic gawky form of the ginkgo tree, and the shallow green roof of the Slipper House shining from the recent rain. There was a glossy black-painted wooden gate in the wall. John Robert cast a glance towards the Slipper House, then at the gate.

'You're a Jew?'

'Yes.'

'Does that worry you?'

'Should it?'

'Being a Christian, isn't that treason, doesn't it feel like a betrayal?'

'No! I am a religious man. That at least my religion does for me.'

'Frees you from guilt.'

'From irrational guilt.'

'But does it change you at all, does your Christ *do* anything for you?'

'He stops me from doing things.'

'That was what Socrates's daemon did.'

'But – it's not difficult –'

'You mean you don't make sacrifices?'

'No.'

'So there's not much at stake for you then, with your Christ.'

'At stake? Everything's at stake.'

'If you don't really have to raise a finger, everything is not at stake.'

'I mean – it's a totally different world.'

'The world of faith, of your faith?'

'I know ... that there is always ... more quietness, more silence ... more space ... into which I can move ... on ... and be made ... better, somehow ... It's not a drama, not sort of exciting, or violent, like things being at stake.'

'I like your picture. Morality makes mincemeat of metaphysics by the simplicity of its claims. And that fool Ivor Sefton thinks that metaphysical imagery is paranoiac! We are all image-makers. So a quiet life and no guilt? What do you do in your parish work?'

'I enact rites. I wait for people to summon me.'

'A fireman priest! Not a fisher of men.'

'I am a fish not a fisher, a fish in search of a net.'

'I will make you fishers of men if you follow me. There was a little sect who used to sing that, in Burkestown, when I was a child.'

'They're still there, down beside the railway.'

'Simple faith. *They* think they are saved.'

'Faith means – at least, not having to count your sins.'

'But if there is no God you must count your sins, since no one else will, or do you believe that virtue is a harmony of good and evil?'

Father Bernard was horrified. 'I am not a Gnostic! A most detestable heresy! That really is magic!'

'Heresy! Are you not up to your neck in it? But why magic?'

'The desire to know can degenerate into mere trickery. Our natural love for evil makes us think we understand it. Then we read good into it, like turning lead into gold. But it's not like that – the difference between good and evil is absolute – the two poles are not in view – we are not gods.'

'You believe in this absolute difference, this – distance?'

'I think we experience it at every moment. Yes, I believe in it – don't you?'

Rozanov said after a moment, 'Why are we so sure about this? Is it the sort of thing we can be sure about? What would be a test? What does seem clear is that the spiritual world is full of ambiguities, full of these "readings", full of the magic you are so afraid of. If you appeal to experience, well we experience that all right. What about your mystic Christ. Isn't he an ambiguous magical figure? For instance, you are in love with him, aren't you?'

Father Bernard had begun to feel upset, annoyed with Rozanov, and even more with himself for having so crudely spoken about things which were, when unspoken, so clear and pure. He said, 'I shouldn't have spoken of him.'

'Ah, I understand, I understand. We'll leave him alone. But isn't religion bound to descend into consolation? You don't want to change, or to sacrifice anything, but because of some vague experience you regard yourself as excused, as innocent, *simul iustus et peccator*?'

They were now quite close to the Common, walking through Druidsdale, and the priest noticed that Rozanov, who had hitherto allowed his companion to determine the route, had taken a sharp right-hand turn in order to avoid going along the road where George McCaffrey lived.

Father Bernard did not answer directly, but said, 'You were right to mention love. Isn't that somehow the *proof* that good and evil exclude each other?'

'Plato might have thought that, Plotinus might have felt it, but I doubt if *you* can make sense of it.'

'Perhaps I can't – but – when we love people – and things – and our work and – we somehow get the *assurance* that good is there – it's absolutely pure and absolutely *there* – it's in the fabric – it *must* be.'

'We like to make much of this word "love", to pat it and stroke it – but does love as we know it ever appear except as a mask of self? Ask your own soul. Who was that?'

191

At that moment they had been passed by Nesta Wiggins's father, who raised his hat respectfully to the philosopher.

'Dominic Wiggins, a tailor, he lives in Burkestown, a nice man.'

'I remember the Wigginses,' said John Robert, 'they were Catholics.'

They were now walking on the Common where the ground was damp and muddy. Father Bernard hated getting mud on his shoes. Part of his cassock had become unpinned and was trailing on the wet grass verges. He was beginning to want a drink. If they stayed on the shorter path back into Burkestown by the old railway cutting they could reach the Green Man in twenty minutes. Or had someone told him that the confounded philosopher was a teetotaller?

Father Bernard said, 'We like to say that everyone is selfish, but that's just a hypothesis.'

John Robert said, 'Good, good!' He added, 'Your mind interests me. But you haven't answered my question.'

'When we love pure things we experience pure love.'

'People? Wretched crooks, thugs to a man?'

'Loving others as Christ – I mean loving Christ in them.'

'That really is sentimental twaddle. Kant thought we should respect Universal Reason in other people. Bunkum. If *ex hypothesi* I wanted you to love me, I should want you to love *me*, not my reason or my Christ nature.'

'Well – yes – of course you are right.'

'And things – I believe you mentioned loving things – how's that done?'

'Anything can be a sacrament – transformed – like the bread and wine.'

'What for instance? Trees?'

'Oh trees, *yes – that* tree –'

They were just passing a hawthorn bush, it could scarcely be called a tree, which was putting out, amid its healthy shining thorns, sharp little vivid green buds.

'The beauty of the world,' said John Robert. 'Unfortunately I am insensitive to it. Though it might have point as a contrast to art. Art is certainly the devil's work, the magic that joins good and evil together, the magic place where they joyfully *run* together. Plato was right about art.'

'You enjoy no art form?'

'No.'

'Surely metaphysics is art.'

192

'That is – yes – a terrible thought.' The philosopher was silent as if appalled by some dreadful vision which these words had conjured up. He said, 'You see – the suspicion that one is not only not telling the truth, but *cannot* tell it – that is – damnation. A case for the millstone.'

As Father Bernard could think of nothing to say to this the philosopher went on:

'Your idea of loving pure things is trickery, and I doubt if the notion of loving Christ in rotten swine like you and me even makes sense. It's sentimentality. It's all done with mirrors like the Ontological Proof. You imagine a perfect love which emanates from a pure source in response to your imperfect love, in response to your frenetic desire for love – then because this gives you a warm feeling you say you're certain.'

'I *know* that my Redeemer liveth.'

'*Mutatis mutandis*! I suppose that's what's called faith. You feel it all coming beaming back. But you would need the God you don't believe in to make it real. It's all the same imperfect stuff churning to and fro. You want a response. You can't have a real one so you fake one, like sending a letter to yourself.'

Father Bernard said, 'It's true – we *do* hunger for love – *that's* deep all right. You too – you long to be loved – don't you?'

After a moment Rozanov said, 'Yes, but it's a weakness – that's the thing that *I* say in a whisper. Ah – well. Do you love your parishioners, the chap you visited? You see, after all you *do* visit them.'

'A woman – well – not exactly.' The image of Miss Dunbury accused Father Bernard and he laughed. 'No – but I'm glad she exists.'

'You laugh? She makes you feel happy, pleased?'

'Yes, she's funny. She's virtuous and absurd.'

'Isn't happiness your good then?'

'No, no, no. Good is my good.'

'What does this tautology do for us? Good is a Cheshire cat.'

'But don't you think then that we can – do – anything?'

'Morally? We can be quiet and sensible and feel contempt for ourselves. And there is the idea of duty, an excellent conception. I mean, these things go on. But chiefly – we can see ourselves as petty and ridiculous and – and base.'

'That is *your* happiness.'

John Robert laughed. 'There isn't any deep structure in the

world. At the bottom, which isn't very far down, it's all rubble, jumble. Not even muck, but jumble.'

'Isn't this stoicism, protecting yourself from being surprised by anything? *Nil admirari*.'

'Protecting yourself from being surprised, or disgusted, or horrified, or appalled into madness – by anything – especially by yourself.'

'Is morality a mistake then?'

'A phenomenon.'

'I think you are being – shall we say – insincere.'

'Insincere. Good. Go on.'

'You seem to me to be a very *moralistic* person. For instance, you seem to set some absolute value on truth.'

'Moralistic is not moral. And as for truth – well, it's like brown – it's not in the spectrum.'

'What do you mean?'

'It's not a part of morality, not like you mean morality. Truth is impersonal. Like death. It's a doom.'

'Cold?'

'Oh, these metaphors!'

'But you can't just recognize one value.'

'Why not?'

'I mean if you recognize one value won't you find all the others hidden inside it? *Must* one not be able to?'

'What sort of "must" is this? Are all values to come tumbling out of one like goodies out of a stocking? Truth is *sui generis*. And as for the rest – there is no spectrum, that was a bad image, a slip.'

'A significant slip, I think.'

'The idea of the internal connection of virtues is pure superstition, a comforting illusion, the sort of thing that I believed when I was twenty. *That* doesn't bear close examination.'

'Oh *no* –' said Father Bernard, or rather he murmured it. 'Oh *no, no.*'

They were now in sight of the Ennistone Ring, the point at which the sage must at all costs be prevented from setting off diagonally across the Common and out into the countryside. Father Bernard was glad to see that he was flagging a little. The path had been uphill and they were both short of breath.

'Bill the Lizard saw a flying saucer up here,' said Rozanov.

'But you don't believe in such things?'

'Why not? Think what *we* can do, and add a million years.'

194

'But they don't – appear – interfere.'

'Why should they? They're studying us. I should like to think that there were intelligences *absolutely* unlike my own. It would somehow be such a *relief*. Perhaps they live longer and have – oh – wonderful – *real* – philosophers.'

'I find the whole idea uncanny,' said Father Bernard, 'and somehow – horrid.'

'Bill didn't feel this. He felt it was something good – a wholly good visitation. But then – he would be likely to see – something good.'

'Even if it wasn't there? I imagine you don't class Mr Eastcote as one of us rotten swine?' This casual characterization had been festering in Father Bernard's mind.

'No,' said Rozanov with discouraging curtness. Then, 'Why, whatever have they done to the Ring?'

The priest and the philosopher gazed at the megaliths which were arranged in a broken circle some sixty yards in diameter. There were nine stones. The earliest reference to them is eighteenth-century, when four of them were standing. The others were un-covered and collected and erected in their present still-disputed positions by a nineteenth-century archaeologist. Six of them are tall and narrow, three (one of these fragmentary) roughly diamond-shaped, suggesting the two sexes. Here even speculation ended. It was hard to believe that mortal men had placed them there at some time for some purpose. There they stood in the pale sad damp light, occupying a temporal moment, wet with rain, transcending history, oblivious of art, resisting understanding, monstrous with unfathomable thought, and dense with mysterious authoritative impacted being. The wind blew the long grasses at their feet, while beyond and between them could be seen rounded hills and woods where here and there grey church towers were successfully illumined by the shifting cloudy light.

'They've *spoilt* them!'

'There was a lot of argument,' said the priest.

'They've taken off all the moss and those yellow rings.'

'They cleaned them with electric wire brushes. It shows the grain of the stone, but of course all that spotty lichen has gone.'

'They *cleaned* them, they *scratched* them with vile brushes, they dared to *touch* them, these, the nearest things to *gods* that our contemptible citizens will ever *see*.' Rozanov stood there, his coat blowing, his mouth open, his face crinkled up with pain.

The priest watched him, then ventured to pull at his sleeve so as to urge him back in the direction of the town. Then as they started down the hill it began a little to rain, while they saw before them the sunlight momentarily touching the gilded cupola of the Hall and the golden weathercock of St Olaf's Church.

'What do you regret most in your life?' said the philosopher.

'What kind of regret? Not to have established unselfish habits. Not to be destined to be alone. Well, no, not that. And you?'

'Lies. The sin of silence. What do you fear most?'

'Death.'

'Death is nothing, you will not know it, you mean pain, you see you still confuse the two.'

'Oh all right – and you?'

'To find out that morality is unreal.'

'But isn't that just what you think – that it is a phenomenon?'

'A phenomenon is something. Duty is something, a barrier. But to find out that it is not just an ambiguity with which one lives – but that it is nothing, a fake, absolutely unreal.'

'To find that there are no barriers?'

'That there could come a place, a point, where morality simply gave way, did not exist.'

'There can be no such place.'

'God would be needed to guarantee that, and any existent God is a demon. If even one thing is permitted it is enough. A prison with one way out is not a prison.'

Father Bernard thought for a moment.

'Aren't you just doing what you wouldn't let me do? I wanted to draw all good out of one good. You want to discredit all good because there is one evil which good can't get at.'

'A good image. If in the pilgrimage of life there is any place beyond good and evil, it is our duty to go there.'

'Our duty?'

'That is the final paradox. When one reaches a certain point, morality becomes a riddle to which one *must* find the answer. The holy inevitably moves toward the demonic. Fra Angelico loved Signorelli.'

'Perhaps he did. But then didn't Signorelli love Fra Angelico? The demonic moves toward the holy.'

'No. That is my point. If the holy even knows of the demonic it is lost. The flow is in that direction, the tide runs that way, water flows down hill. That is what "no God" means, which is still a secret even from those who babble it. Everything in the cosmos is reversed, as in some theories in physics. Philosophy teaches us that, in the event, all the greatest minds of our race were not only in error, but childishly so. The holy must try to know the demonic, must at some point frame the riddle and thirst for the answer, and that longing is the perfect contradiction of the love of God.'

'This sounds like – that awful – doctrine –'

'No, not your puerile heresy.'

'I don't follow you. Nothing in heaven or earth can alter my duty to my neighbour.'

'It can put it ever so little out of focus. Have you not felt just that, you who are tainted by the holy?'

The priest considered silently. He said, 'It's nonsense. But what is the way out of what you call the prison? Do you mean suicide?'

'The proof. It could be. There are many gates. But for one man perhaps one gate.'

'One thing he is tempted to do which would make everything else permissible? Why not murder then?'

'Why not?'

'And you become the demon who is God.'

'We are being carried away by a metaphor, it is my fault, I have lived too long with images. One thinks one is on a high place, at an edge, where the air is purer and clearer.'

'You had better stop thinking,' said Father Bernard.

'I can't. But don't worry –'

'You're not tempted to commit suicide or murder?'

'Certainly not.'

'But you are – tempted – to do something awful – the – as you said – the proof?'

'No,' said Rozanov, 'no, no.'

They were descending a grassy slope into the abandoned railway cutting, sometimes known as Lovers' Lane, a place of leafy resort for courting couples, which served as a path from the Common into Burkestown. The cutting ended, on the Common side, in the abrupt bricked-up mouth of a tunnel, and became gradually shallower on the Ennistone side where it ended at a level crossing near to the station. A few drops of rain still fell, and Father Bernard noticed shining drops poised upon the primroses and pendant grasses and raggedy hawthorns, and celandine and fretty chervil and brambles and briar bushes which now rose up above their heads. Suddenly there was a rushing tearing sound as if a ghostly train had emerged

197

from the tunnel, or one of John Robert's demons were charging in the form of a large animal through the foliage. Something big and heavy and extremely agitated came rolling and bundling down the bank and out on to the level grass in front of the walkers' feet. This, a moment later, turned out to be Tom McCaffrey and Emmanuel Scarlett-Taylor still engaged in a scuffle which had started at the top of the slope. They sat up laughing still clutching each other, then became aware of witnesses and leapt up, making way.

'Hello,' said the priest raising his hand, as he and Rozanov now continued their journey, passing between the two boys who had stood back, one on each side.

'Hello, Father.'

The walkers heard behind them an outbreak of giggles and *fou rire*.

'There's a happy man,' said Father Bernard. 'Happy because innocent, innocent because happy.'

'Who?'

'Tom McCaffrey, the one with the long hair, didn't you recognize him? I don't know who the other boy is.'

They walked on in silence. The level crossing was in sight. Father Bernard felt a strange pang, a contraction of the heart like an onset of disease. He felt there was something he ought to do while there was still time. He wondered if he would ever talk to the philosopher again. He said, 'I wish you would do something to help George McCaffrey.'

'I want to ask you one thing,' said Rozanov. 'I will make it a condition of our having any further conversations that you do not mention the name of that young man.'

'Oh, as you will.'

As they walked on into the town Father Bernard wondered to himself, do I like him, do I love him, do I hate him, *is he mad*?

It was Sunday morning again. In St Paul's Church Father Bernard was leading the faithful in telling God that they had erred and strayed from His ways like lost sheep, had followed too much the devices and desires of their own hearts, had offended against His holy laws, had left undone those things which they ought to have done, and done those things which they ought not to have done, and generally had no health in them.

In the Quaker Meeting House a profound silence reigned. Gabriel McCaffrey loved that silence, whose healing waves lapped in a slow solemn rhythm against her scratched and smarting soul. The sun was shining through wind-handled trees outside, making a shifting decoration of yellow spear-heads upon the white wall. The room was otherwise bare of adornment, a big handsome high-ceilinged eighteenth-century room, with tall round-headed windows. The benches were arranged in three tiers, forming three sides of a square, of which a plain oak table occupied the fourth side. The party who wanted flowers on the table were regularly defeated by those who felt that God's spirit was embarrassed by corporeal charms.

Present were Brian, Gabriel and Adam, William Eastcote and Anthea, Mr and Mrs Robin Osmore, Mrs Percy Bowcock, Nesta Wiggins, Peter Blackett, Mrs Roach the doctor's wife, Nicky Roach the doctor's son, now studying at Guy's Hospital, Rita Chalmers, wife of the Institute Director, Miss Landon who was a teacher at Adam's school, Mr and Mrs Romage who kept a grocer's shop in Burkestown, and a Mrs Bradstreet, a visiting friend who was staying at the Ennistone Royal Hotel and taking the cure for a condition in her back. The attendance varied, being today rather sparse. A week ago Milton Eastcote the philanthropist, William's cousin, had been present and had given an address about his work in London. Dr Roach was often kept away by professional duties, too often said those who thought that the doctor was more attached to the natural light of science than to the illumination from above. Nesta Wiggins was a recruit of several years standing, having abandoned the paternal Catholic fold for the douce blank Quaker rites. She esteemed the Friends, who were active in good works in Ennistone, and was particularly attached to William Eastcote. Peter Blackett, whose parents were 'humanists', came out of curiosity and admiration for Nesta. Nesta was sorry she could never persuade her friend Valerie Cossom to come along, but Valerie regarded all religious observances as superstitious opiates. Percy Bowcock, who had used often to accompany his wife, now came no more, and Gabriel had heard someone say that he had become a *Freemason*. Gabriel knew little of Freemasonry, and whether it was compatible with the ideals of the Society of Friends, but she was sorry not to see her cousin (to whose house she was rarely invited). She was fond of him and admired him very much and only coveted his wealth a little, and could not help feeling a bit censorious about the Freemasons, since they were secretive, and Friends did not approve of secrets.

But what about her own secrets? She stole a glance at Brian (she was sitting as always between her husband and her son) and saw the usual look of strained brooding anxiety. She looked across at the calm pale face of William Eastcote who was sitting opposite to her. Eastcote smiled. The silence breathed with long slow soundless exhalations, with slower deeper rhythms, seeming ever more unbreakable and profound, as if everyone in the room would soon come to some absolute stop, perhaps quickly peacefully serenely die. Sometimes during the whole meeting no one spoke. Gabriel liked that best. Human speech sounded so petty, so unforgivably stupid, after that great void. Some people spoke with piercing exalted voices. Today, however, her own trivial thoughts were bubbling in her ear. She was thinking about a cracked jug which she had seen in a junk shop in Biggins. She had said to Adam, who was with her, 'What a pretty jug, but it's cracked.' Adam had immediately taken the side of the jug. 'He wants someone to love him and look after him, we'll love him and look after him, we'll take him home and wash him and dry him and find him a place to sit.' Sometimes Adam's determination to personify his surroundings upset Gabriel to the point of wild annoyance. Adam seemed to be deliberately playing upon her tortured sensibilities. 'That jug, he's saying to himself, will that nice lady buy me.' Gabriel said, 'Don't be silly, it's all cracked, it's no use,' and hustled him on. Now it had become clear to her that nothing in the world was more important than going back to that shop and buying that jug. She would go early tomorrow morning. But, oh, suppose it had gone! Tears rose up behind Gabriel's eyes. All these things were somehow images of death. Adam had such awful dreams sometimes. She encouraged him to tell his dreams. Gabriel had once heard Ivor Sefton lecture at the Ennistone Hall. He said that children should tell their dreams and join the symbolic dream material to their waking life. But Adam's dreams frightened Adam and Gabriel, and surely telling them would make him remember them. Adam dreamed so much about drowning. I am a silly woman, thought Gabriel, and Brian blames me for losing Stella, as if I had made a *mistake*, as if I had opened the door and let her run out! I couldn't comfort Stella, she is so hard and silent and superior. She is an *opposite* woman to me. But I should have done better, I didn't look after her properly; and where is she now, has she killed herself? Is she with George? Brian

200

had telephoned and called round but got no answer. At the thought of Stella comforting George, forgiving him, holding him in her saving arms, Gabriel felt nothing but pain, and she knew that it was a wicked pain. Her feelings about George were part of her silliness, part of the stupid feeble sensibility which made her encourage Adam's funny soft porous attitude to the world, and be hurt by it at the same time. Brian thought she was making Adam weak and dreamy. But it was all to do with feeling so sorry for everything. Her feeling for George was like that, feeling very very sorry for him, feeling oh so much protective possessive pity-love, a sort of desperate sorry-for affection. It's so private, she thought. But then all my love is private, as if it were a secret.

Adam was conscious of a ball of slightly mobile blazing warmth up against his side which was Zed curled up in the pocket of his duffle coat. Zed was not allowed in the Institute but he was allowed to come to Meeting. Why should not dogs be present, since the waves and particles of the Inner Light flowed through them too? Besides, there were precedents. Mrs Bowcock's mother's corgi had attended for years. Zed's little delicate head with its black-and-white domed brow peered from the top of the pocket. After looking about for some time with an alert critical air, he had fixed upon Robin Osmore, staring intently at the legal man with an expression of amazed quizzical curiosity. Osmore, aware of the scrutiny, became uneasy, disconcerted, fidgeted, looked elsewhere, then looked back to find the little beast still staring, its clever humorous gaze giving an extraordinary impression of a judging intelligence, a strange little spirit, not really a dog at all. Adam touched the silky fringy end of Zed's long ear with his finger tips. He was thinking about Rufus. When he thought about Rufus it was as if a kind of lurid gap appeared in the world through which something red and black kept flashing out at him. He knew instinctively that these thoughts were dangerous, perhaps bad. He never told his mother the very strange weird things he dreamed about Rufus, and about Zed. Sometimes in dreams he *was* Rufus. Adam never mentioned Rufus, and his parents imagined that Adam had forgotten that Rufus ever existed. Sometimes Adam wondered whether he himself were not really George's son, and had been exchanged for Rufus when he was in the cradle. They were almost exactly the same age. It was as if Rufus by dying had laid a kind of debt upon him. He had to grow up for Rufus, to carry him along like an invisible twin. Yes, he thought, I'm growing up for Rufus, in a way I am Rufus.

And this thought led him back to George and to the way George had winked, and the way George had stared at him when they saw each other that day at the Institute, when Adam had sat down among the potted plants.

Anthea Eastcote was sitting next to her great-uncle. There was a bond of love between these two, though they were shy with each other. William was childless and awkward with children. Anthea, who turned so many heads and always looked so radiantly pleased with herself, had had her troubles. Her father, a talented mathematician, had run away to Australia with one of his students, her brother had emigrated to Canada and was no more seen, her beautiful mother had died of a wasting illness three years ago. Now, supported by a lifetime of such Sunday mornings, she sat quiet with folded hands, gazing with large wide-open pensive eyes above the heads of the McCaffreys opposite. Her smooth sweet face, luminous like a pale lighted lantern, glowed with health, her soft lips were pursed in a little bud of reflection, and her brown-golden curly rumply hair arched on her head, electric as silk. Used to employing such times for self-scrutiny, she was ruefully examining the way in which she was leading poor Hector on, while all the time she was vainly in love with a fellow student, one Joey Tanner, at York University where she was studying History.

Brian McCaffrey was thinking to himself, when I consider how much rage and spite and malice and jealousy and envy and lust I carry around inside myself, how can I blame anybody for anything? He inspected a tiny almost invisible dot-like insect which was walking slowly across the back of his hand, crushed it with a fingertip, then cast an anxious guilty look in Adam's direction. He raised his gaze once more, focusing on a point between William Eastcote's chin and Anthea Eastcote's mouth. He thought to himself, *Christ*, Tom could have that girl if he wanted to. He's only got to try, he could have that handsome clever sweet girl just by stretching out his hand. Well-off too. He must be *mad*. Why is he so bloody lazy and careless and stupid? If he exerted himself the least little bit he could get her, he could *marry* her. Oh *God*! She's so beautiful, she's so intelligent, she's so angelic, she's got everything, oh if only I were young again, if only I were free and young, as now I shall never be. I wonder if I should say anything to Tom? No, certainly not, I should go *crazy* if Anthea were my sister-in-law. Let her go away, since I can't have her, let her go away, I don't want to know she exists. Curse her, curse everything. My bloody job is

202

on the rocks and I haven't even told Gabriel yet. Oh damn, damn, damn, he said to himself, as Alex used to say when he was a child, bending down awkwardly with her dustpan and brush. Anyway I'm getting old. Thank God I shall be out of the future of this rotten old planet. As everything is going to be blown up, what does it matter what I do? One gets bloody tired of morality. I would do what I want at last, except that I can't. Oh *hell*. Roll on nuclear war.

At this moment there was a commotion at the back, behind where Mrs Roach and Nicky were sitting, and Tom McCaffrey and Emmanuel Scarlett-Taylor came in rather out of breath. They sat down noisily, audibly panting, then quickly composed themselves and put on solemn expressions. Several people smiled at Tom. Silence reigned again. After a suitable interval of glazed contemplation, Emma began to look about him with surreptitious curiosity. He had never been to a Quaker meeting before, and his historian's instincts were aroused. He adjusted his glasses and gazed about, impressed by the dense atmosphere of repose and feeling suddenly rather happy. Then Tom felt a little tickling and shuddering sensation beside him and heard a slight noise as the bench began to vibrate. Emma was silently laughing. He had noticed Zed peering out of Adam's pocket. He pointed, nudging Tom. Zed transferred his stare from Mr Osmore to Emma, gazing with an air of amused and rather impertinent attention. Tom began to laugh too. He stuffed his handkerchief into his mouth and closed his eyes upon happy tears. The next moment he was praying, as if he were lifted up and carrying others with him. Love flowed in his soul. He would love them all, save them all: Alex and Brian and Gabriel and Stella and Emma and George and ... oh especially George.

Nesta Wiggins was blushing scarlet as she always did when it occurred to her that it was her duty to rise and speak. She was a nervous public speaker, but, driven by conscience, a frequent one. She had realized that she ought to get up and suggest that the money voted for the repainting of the Meeting House ought instead to be donated to the recently opened appeal for the new community centre on the wasteland beyond the canal. (The treasurer, Nathaniel Romage, who loved the fabric of the House, was secretly hustling on the painting since he feared exactly this conscience-searching for worthier objectives on the part of some members of the Meeting.) However, as Nesta's breath came quick and she leaned forward to get up, William Eastcote rose to his feet. Nesta relaxed, satisfied. No one at Meeting ever spoke after William Eastcote had spoken.

Bill the Lizard had been thinking about his wife Rose, and how Rozanov had remembered her as presiding over their 'wholesome feasts' of long ago. He had been thinking too about something which Dr Roach had lately said to him. He had given himself a dispensation to lie to John Robert about his health. Something was wrong, but perhaps not cancer. He was to go to the hospital tomorrow. He thought about his father, who had used the Quaker 'thou' and who now seemed to belong to an infinitely remote past, as if William's own life were itself being quickly transformed into history, and as if those who had formed him and taught him and given him their precious stainless examples, his parents, his teachers, his friends, were already gathering round.

When he felt the urge to rise, his heart, like Nesta's, beat hard. He was always a diffident speaker. He said, 'My dear friends, we live in an age of marvels. Men among us can send machines far out into space. Our homes are full of devices which would amaze our forebears. At the same time our beloved planet is ravaged by suffering and threatened by dooms. Experts and wise men give us vast counsels suited to vast ills. I want only to say something about simple good things which are as it were close to us, within our reach, part still of our world. Let us love the close things, the close clear good things, and hope that in their light other goods may be added. Let us prize innocence. The child is innocent, the man is not. Let us prolong and cherish the innocence of childhood, as we find it in the child and as we rediscover it later within ourselves. Repentance, renewal of life, such as is the task and possibility of every man, is a recovery of innocence. Let us see it thus, a return to a certain simplicity, something which is not hard to understand, not a remote good but very near. And let us not hesitate to preach to our young people and to impart to them an idealism which may later serve them as a shield. A deep cynicism in our society too soon touches old and young, forbidding us to speak and them to hear, and making us by an awful reversal ashamed of what is best. A habit of mockery destroys the intelligence and sensibility which is reverence. Let us prize chastity, not as a censorious or rigid code, but as fastidious respect and gentleness, a rejection of promiscuity, a sense of the delicate mystery of human relations. Let us do and praise those things which make for a simple orderly open and truthful life. Herein let us make it a practice to banish evil thoughts. When such thoughts come, envious, covetous, cynical thoughts, let us positively drive them off, like people in the olden days who felt they were defeating Satan. Let us then seek aid in pure things, turning our minds to good people, to our best work, to beautiful and noble art, to the pure words of Christ in the Gospel, and to the works of God obedient to Him in nature. Help is always near if we will only turn. Conversion is turning about, and it can happen not only every day but every moment. Shun the cynicism which says that our world is so terrible that we may as well cease to care and cease to strive, the notion of a cosmic crisis where ordinary duties cease to be and moral fastidiousness is out of place. At any time, there are many many small things we can do for other people which will refresh us and them with new hope. Shun too the common malice which finds consolation in the suffering and sin of others, blackening them to make our grey seem white, rejoicing in our neighbours' downfall and disgrace, while excusing our own failures and cherishing our own undiscovered secret sins. Above all, do not despair, either for the planet or in the deep inwardness of the heart. Recognize one's own evil, mend what can be mended, and for what cannot be undone, place it in love and faith in the clear light of the healing goodness of God.'

William sat down and found his heart still beating hard. He bowed his head and folded his hands, which were trembling. He wondered to himself, whatever possessed me to utter all those high-flown words, wherever did they come from? Then the memory piercingly returned to him of what the doctor had said, and he shuddered with weakness and fear.

The silence continued, ringing now with the echoes of what William had said, and each person present promised himself some amendment of life. Brian thought, what a skunk I am, and how *lucky* I am to have such a dear good sweet wife and such a marvellous son, I must go and see Alex *soon*, and bloody stop hating everything and everyone. Gabriel thought, dear, dear William, how much I love him, yes, I must stop being so feeble and silly, and I must not think those mean spiteful thoughts about Stella, and I must think differently about George, but how? Adam thought, I must stop imagining those funny things about Rufus and I must be kinder to my father and talk to him and not tease him. Anthea Eastcote thought, I must be frank with Hector Gaines and I must *give up* Joey Tanner. Nicky Roach thought, I must work harder and not go to bed with girls all the time (but he felt rather sad about this). Mrs Roach thought, I must stop spending these crazy amounts on clothes. I must be mad! Nathaniel Romage thought, perhaps I ought to reconvene the committee before I have the house painted? Mrs Romage thought, I had better stop cooking the books. Ought I to confess to Nat that I've been cooking the books? No. Miss Landon thought, I must prepare my lessons better and, quite simply, stop *loathing* the children. Nesta Wiggins thought, I ought to go to Mass now and then to please my father and stop being so ridiculously pleased with myself. I'm just a stinking sinner. Well, I am, aren't I? Mrs Bradstreet had a very serious sin, not unconnected with her late husband, upon her conscience. Sometimes she felt she was damned, sometimes she felt she should tell everything to the police (how much did they know?). She decided that for the present she would follow William Eastcote's advice and lay it all before God. However, she had done this before to no avail. Emma thought, I must go and see my mother, I must go and see my singing teacher, and I must ... just somehow ... try to become .. less *awful*. Tom thought, I'm innocent, I'm good, I love everybody. I shall go on being innocent and good and loving everybody, oh I feel so happy! What Zed thought is not known, but as his nature was composed almost entirely of love, he may be imagined to have felt an increase of being.

'A chair does a lot for a picture' was one of Alex's sayings. At this moment she was trying out this guidance in the Slipper House, as she moved a bamboo chair with a pink cushion on it and placed it underneath a contemporary print of the eighteenth-century 'bath house of transcendent beauty' which had been pulled down to make way for the Institute building. The effect was good. It was Sunday evening. The bells of St Olaf's, distinctly audible in damp weather with a west wind blowing, were decorating the muzzy soft brown twilight. All the lights were on in the Slipper House, the central heating was on, the shutters were closed. Every window had inside shutters, all of which had been decorated by the young painter, Ned Larkin, Geoffrey Stillowen's discovery. The most ambitious scene, representing the family in Belmont garden, was in the sitting-room downstairs, but each room had its window into the fantasy world of Mr Larkin. The main bedroom, where Alex now stood, revealed in the space of the shuttered window above the window seat, a blue sky traversed by a silver airship, and down below looking up a dog, a black-and-white terrier whom Alex dimly remembered, but not his name. The upstairs shutters and curtains had not been touched for some time and turned out to be full of dust and moths and spiders. With Ruby, she had cleaned the whole house thoroughly, and could now enjoy it by herself. Working silently with Ruby had been a strain. How easily her mother would have chatted all the time, encouraging the servant, cheering her on.

Alex looked at the bed, a plain strong single bed with handsome plain ball-headed posts at each corner made of a grainy gleaming nut-brown wood, a fine piece, a relic of its time. In the centre of the headboard an incised oval design was carved, representing perhaps a seed or the cosmos. This carving had excited Alex when she was a girl. Here John Robert Rozanov would sleep. In the little room next door, in a plain handsome nut-brown matching wardrobe, he would keep his clothes. In the sitting-room downstairs, or perhaps in the second bedroom which Alex had prepared as a study, with a light oak desk and a lamp with a leaded-glass shade, he would write his great book. In the evenings when he was tired he would talk to Alex, first of old times, then of other things. Further than this Alex did not allow her thoughts to wander, at least with any clarity. Indeed much was unclear. The kitchen was scrubbed and accoutred, but who would cook his meals? Ruby and Alex had worked hard. A few pieces of furniture had been brought in from Belmont, but the house still had the airy, empty, rather pale, faintly provisional look which somehow suited it. It had never really been occupied. It had been a place for summer parties and populous fêtes of Stillowens long gone and scattered. Had her father, after her mother's death, ever slept in this room, with the silver airship and the little dog and another woman? Alex could not believe it. The house, which the Ennistonians believed to be such a strange ambiguous place, was somehow innocent and unstained and unused, like her golden-haired brother who had died in the war, blown to pieces by a shell near Monte Cassino. She had seen his neat clean white little gravestone among hundreds of others in a beautiful Italian cemetery.

Alex padded down the slippery shallow wooden stairs and stood in the sitting-room, near to the picture of her childish self holding the little bouquet of flowers upon the shutter. There was a smell of wood smoke from a fire which she had experimentally lit in the big open grate in the kitchen. She had brought in an oval folding table from Belmont in case John Robert should elect to work downstairs. The beautiful parquet floor, upon which Alex's slippers now skated softly, was dotted with rugs, geometrical Persian rugs from

Belmont, and curious woollen rugs and rugs made out of rags which the architect had inspired Alex's mother to buy especially for the Slipper House. Upon the walls, painted egg-shell blue, some wood engravings of curvaceous willow trees were hanging. There was an intense silence, outside of which a motor car was passing on the road at the bottom of the garden along which Father Bernard and John Robert had walked on their way to the Common. With a discreet sidelong glance she observed her reflection in the cut-glass fountain mirror. She felt ageless, poised and young, ready to begin the world anew.

At that moment a fox barked with a sharp hoarse anguished sound very near to the house, and the front door opened abruptly and someone came in. Alex put a hand on her heart. It was Ruby. Ruby looked through the open door of the sitting-room, saw Alex and came quickly towards her with an arm outstretched. Alex shuddered and stepped back, then accepted the letter which Ruby was holding out. For a moment she had felt as if her old servant were about to strike her. The impression was so strong that she was not able to bring out the dismissive 'thank you'. She said nothing. The big brown creature stared at her, then turned and marched out. She had failed to take her shoes off at the door. Alex, who had already recognized John Robert's handwriting, sat down on the window seat below the painted shutter. The letter had evidently been delivered by hand. She tore it open.

Dear Mrs McCaffrey,

   I have received the details from Mr Osmore and am in agreement with the conditions of the tenancy of the Slipper House. I will pay the rent quarterly by banker's order as suggested. I should perhaps have explained to you that I do not propose to occupy the Slipper House myself, but require it as a temporary residence for my granddaughter Harriet Meynell and her maid. The young women will of course look after themselves and not disturb you, and can come and go by the back gate. I am grateful to you for this convenience. I will give due notice of closure of tenancy in accordance with the agreement. I am shortly returning to the USA and take this opportunity to thank you and to bid you good-bye.

Yours sincerely,

J. R. Rozanov

Alex crumpled up the letter and stuffed it into her pocket. She stared across the room at one of the wood engravings and noticed how the willow branches had made a face, a rounded head, something like her son George. She felt instant ravening hatred for the 'young women' who would spoil and desecrate the beautiful innocent house. She wondered if she could now refuse the tenancy. No, it was too late. George's head tangled into the willows looked as if it were drowning. She went out into the hall and shook off her slippers into the slipper box and put on her shoes. All the lights could be turned out by switches at the door, and she turned them out. She went out of the house and closed the door and locked it. The church bells were silent, the wet grass was soaking her shoes, she felt an old anguish which had perhaps been hanging somewhere in the garden in a thought-cloud from the past, her sudden piercing obsessive jealous remorse when she had heard that Linda Brent was going to marry John Robert Rozanov. Love she could give to no one expanded painfully in her heart.

'Sing to me.'
'No.'
'Oh come, oh come, Emmanuel!'
'No.'
'Are you going to see your singing teacher?'
'I put him off.'
'Again?'
'Again. Are you going to see your mother?'
'Don't nag me!'
'What's the stuff in that bottle?'
'Ennistone water.'
'Christ, I put it in my whisky. What's that noise?'
'Owls. The wind. The night mail approaching Ennistone station. Did you sing at evensong?'
'Don't be silly.'
'What was it like?'
'High. I saw the "servant" in church.'
'Who?'
'Your mother's servant.'
'Oh Ruby – did anyone talk to you?'
'The priest followed me, he said good evening.'
'He's an odd bird. He meditates to jazz music. He used to be a wrestler.'
'Why didn't you come?'

'It would create a sensation. Did you like St Paul's as well as Meeting?'

'Yes.'

'Better?'

'No.'

'Good. What was it Adam said to you after Meeting?'

'He told me that a hoverfly has thirty thousand brain cells and we have billions.'

'Got to keep our spirits up somehow. What did you like about Meeting?'

'The silence. The little dog. What Mr Eastcote said.'

'Yes – he makes one feel purified, washed clean, whiter than snow.'

'Does he?'

'Don't you feel like that after communion?'

'I haven't taken communion for years. I haven't been to church for years.'

'Why did you go this evening?'

'Because of Mr Eastcote.'

'There you are!'

'How long does your feeling go on?'

'What feeling?'

'Whiter than snow.'

'Oh most of the time. I feel unfallen. How does wickedness start? And don't pretend *you* know!'

'Of course I know. Your ignorance is exceptional.'

'Well, I always knew I was exceptional. I've nearly finished our song.'

'Our song?'

'The one you're going to write music for and make our fortune.'

'I can't write music.'

'You said you could.'

'You misunderstood me.'

'Will you swim tomorrow?'

'No.'

'But you'll come?'

'I want to stare at the philosopher.'

'Wasn't it delightful the way we rolled at his feet.'

'It doesn't delight me to appear a perfect fool to someone I respect.'

'Of course you've read some of his books.'

'If I'd had a hat I would have taken it off with a conspicuous gesture.'

'Well, you certainly fell at his feet.'

'My glasses got bent.'

'We'll hang around and have a retake.'

'And I want to stare at your brother.'

'George? I've still got a bruise where he savaged me.'

'You think it was hate. Why shouldn't it be love?'

'I take a simpler view of love.'

'If I had a brother like George I'd do something about him.'

'If you had a brother like George you'd know you couldn't.'

'I'd bloody try.'

'He fascinates you. He fascinates a lot of people. The unfascinated ones throw up their hands.'

'And what do you do?'

'Oh I care for George, but he's impossible, he systematically destroys all the little links with life that most people depend on.'

'Did he try to drown his wife?'

'No, that was just something that Brian said! Brian hates him.'

'Where is she?'

'No one knows, probably gone to Japan.'

'Japan?'

'Her father lives there. He hates George too.'

'Why don't you drink? You annoy me sitting there with nothing to do.'

'Why don't you sing? Sing Phil the Fluter's Ball.'

'Yah.'

'Where's all that wild gaiety and smiling eyes and warm humorous charm?'

'Shut up.'

'You're just pretend Irish.'

'All Irish are pretend Irish.'

> You don't know what to say, I know,
> In a way you want to stay,
> In a way you want to go.
> You can't make up your mind.
> You want to go away
> But not leave me behind.
> Let's sit together and see,
> In the same room just quietly,
> Don't be in pain, don't talk of doom,

211

Don't catch that train just yet.
While you play out your game
I'll always be the same,
Let's wait and see. Just don't forget,
It's only me.

I want you but only forever,
I can't settle for less you.
I want you but only forever,
I won't press you,
I won't distress you
If I can't possess you.
Don't feel it a sin
You can pack it in at any time,
It's not a crime,
I'll bear it and I'll grin!
I'll be a hero most of all in this,
I'll let you go with a loving kiss,
My heart is full of fear,
But you are free,
Don't go away, my dear –
But if you do, I'll smile and say
Good-bye, don't cry, for you are you,
And I am only me.

Don't tear yourself apart, darling,
How much I love you, you know, that's not in doubt,
I don't want to bruise your heart, darling,
You're always free to go – out.
I won't scream and shout.
Why should you love me after all,
There's no good reason.
Any time can be the fall,
You can leave in any season.
I want you for my wife,
I want you all my life,
But if you fly away, and we can't be together,
I won't die, I'll say
Good-bye, good flying weather, from only me.

I want you but only forever
Nothing else will do,
I want you but only forever,
That is my only you.
If you take flight
I won't die out of spite,

212

I won't cry out of spite,
I won't be unkind
If you change your mind,
I won't torment you,
Hide the pain in my heart,
Make it easy to part,
I won't prevent you.
I want your happiness,
I won't be bad,
I'll say good-bye, God bless you,
And don't be sad, darling –
It's only me.

Tom was pleased with his pop song which had developed so quickly out of Adam's germinal idea about the two snails. Later in the evening, after the conversation recorded above, he and Emma had got rather drunk together, and Tom had then retired to his bedroom to polish up his ode. Now it was after midnight. Tom occupied the back room with the view over the garden, and beyond over the town where the floodlight upon the cupola of Ennistone Hall had just been switched off. The town, beneath dark night clouds, composed a pattern of yellow dotted lines, a few pale window squares still visible here and there. The Ennistonians went early to bed. Tom had given himself over to the song, imagining in touching detail the situation which it portrayed: he, the hero, in love, but restraining his fierce possessive desire, the girl shy, gentle, timid, (a virgin?) unable to decide. He respects her indecision, even loves the vagueness which torments him, the fuzzy shadowy helpless non-logical uncertainty and lack of definition which Tom somehow associated with the girl whom he would one day love. (That very evening he and Emma had decided that neither of them had ever really been in love.) Tom, the hero, stands back, gives to the girl freedom, space and time, pressing down in his heart the fear of failure together with the painful need which would attempt to cage her. He wants her, but only forever, and must therefore envisage her loss, though this now seems like death. Tranquillizing his anguish of suspense, he is gentle with her, making her feel how simple, how friendly and kind, how very undangerous he is, just her old familiar admirer. But do girls *like* that sort of chap, Tom wondered suddenly. Well, in this song they do. Perhaps he would now write another song with a different sort of hero, not a gentleman. But in fact Tom did himself aspire to be a gentleman and believed that he was one. He could, he felt, never descend to the base level where sex is coarsely spoken of and women are deemed to be cattle. Of course Tom's imagination occupied itself with women. He imagined protected girls who snuggle down in virgin cots at night. He thought too about rather wicked wild girls, who had run away from home, but he did not associate them with his mother. Perhaps Tom's thoughts about women were influenced more than he ever realized by the shade of Feckless Fiona, eternally young Fiona, waif and victim, whom it was somehow his task to save and keep unmarked by the world. And for her perhaps he had remained a little childish, and still thought of himself as innocent. As he had said to Emma, he felt unfallen and did not yet understand how wickedness began.

Emma was in bed in the larger front bedroom where the budding green plane trees filled the window, their speckled branches swaying in the wind, visible in the light of the street lamps of Travancore Avenue until Emma had drawn the curtains. He had spent some time earlier on trying to straighten out the frame of his glasses which had become twisted in the tumble down the slope in the railway cutting. He fiddled for a while, screwing up his eyes and occasionally rubbing the red mark which the wire bridge made upon his nose. Desisting at last, he had got into bed and resumed his reading of *The Origins of Military Power in Spain 1800–1854*.

Now he had closed his book and was thinking about his singing teacher, Mr Hanway. Emma and Mr Hanway had been together for several years, but their relations had remained formal. Emma called Mr Hanway 'Sir', never by his first name which was Neil, and Mr Hanway called Emma 'Scarlett-Taylor'. The formal pattern of their dealings did not however prevent Emma from suspecting, it went no further than suspicion, that Mr Hanway felt for him a love which exceeded the natural affection of a teacher for a gifted pupil. Sometimes, as it seemed, through the conventional gauze of their converse, Mr Hanway's eyes blazed momentarily at Emma with some involuntary signal of emotional need.

Emma was not unduly disturbed by this suspicion. His moral temperament was fastidiously reticent and agnostic, devoid of the eager curiosity which often masquerades as benevolence. In any case, music made a holy world within which Emma and Mr Hanway could lead safe intelligible lives, making sense of each

214

other through the bond of a transcendent necessity. When Emma
sang to his teacher, or when they sang together, they were joined
in a communion which was not only more spiritual than any
alternative but more satisfying. Sometimes when Mr Hanway criticized his pupil or chided him for carelessness or laziness or forget-
fulness of precept, Emma felt an emotion which resonated far away
at the back of Mr Hanway's calm pedantic tones. But Emma felt
sure that Mr Hanway did not want to change anything, suspecting
as he must that no change could better him, and finding perhaps
a satisfaction, which went beyond anything which Emma could
imagine, in the state of affairs as it was. Thus their relationship
could have gone on and on, as such relationships between singers
often do; only now Emma had come, in a terrible way, to question
the value and doubt the future of his own talent.

It was not that he was tired of singing. The physical joy of that
strange exercise still transported him, and the sense of absolute
power with which it filled him was undiminished. Singing, the
creation of sound by a disciplined exercise of mind and body, is
perhaps the point at which flesh and spirit most joyfully meet.
There is a travail and a bringing forth as a purified sound enters
the world. The perfected cry of an individual soul. Somewhat of this
did Emma think and feel. Nor did he undervalue his endowment
and what he had made of it. But it was just beginning to seem, since
he could not give his whole life to it, pointless to go on. His
discouragements were in part his own, personal and metaphysical,
and in part those which he shared with other counter-tenors. (Mr
Hanway had, of course, other pupils, but arranged the timetable
so that Emma, at least, never met any of his fellows. When he was
with his teacher it always seemed that Mr Hanway had endless time
to spare for Emma alone. Of course this impression may simply
have arisen from his being a good teacher.) The counter-tenor voice
is a highly developed falsetto, not a boy's voice nor a castrato's.
(Purcell was a counter-tenor.) It has a narrow range, and the
counter-tenor repertoire is small and perceptibly finite. Emma had
pretty well been its rounds. He had sung many English lute songs;
the gloomy sadness of Elizabethan and Jacobean poetry and music
suited him well. He sang Purcell and Handel. He and Mr Hanway
had combed the 'early music' offerings, and the formal love-banter
of the eighteenth century had been for them a natural tongue. Now
Mr Hanway was taking Emma through the part of Oberon in
Britten's *Midsummer Night's Dream*, singing the other parts himself

with his remarkable voice which was able to become so many 'other voices', as his piano was able to become an orchestra. Mr Hanway (a tenor) had been an opera singer once; but he never spoke of those days.

Of course Mr Hanway wanted Emma to become a professional singer. Emma did not now talk about his work at the university. On the subject of the further future they had both become cowards. Mr Hanway was always suggesting occasions, urging the necessity of public singing as part of Emma's ascesis. During his first year in college Emma had sung with a consort, and also contributed a solo, at a student musical evening. The amazed congratulations of his fellow students embarrassed rather than pleased him. His unusual talent was by now becoming a guilty secret. He had sworn Tom to secrecy as far as Ennistone was concerned. He continued to practise, but gradually less. At Ennistone he had got up early on two mornings and crossed the common, beyond the gipsy camp, to practise; but had simply felt ridiculous as if he had lost confidence in the whole operation. What was the *point*? He could not be a historian and a singer, and he wanted to be a historian. Why go on and on training an instrument which he could not use? The sad thing that Emma had lately realized was that if he ceased to keep his voice at its very best he would not want to use it at all. Since that was the future, had he not better embrace it at once? To become a professional singer was out of the question. So he must make up his mind to *stop taking lessons*. Normally he went every week to Mr Hanway. Now he had cancelled two weeks. He would have to go to Mr Hanway ... and tell him ... that he would not ever be coming ... for another lesson. Which would mean that they would never meet again, since they had no other bond.

He could not do it. He knew that he would go on as usual and say nothing and lie and avoid seeing the anxiety in his teacher's eyes. Nor could he indeed, for himself, make such a terrible choice, surrender such a joy, such a gift. Not to sing again? It was unthinkable. So there was perhaps no decision to be made after all.

Tom McCaffrey had laid aside his verses and had stood for some time at the window. He could see, not far away, a street lamp making lurid greens among some pine trees in Victoria Park. Beyond was the darkness of the Common on one side and the Wasteland on the other. The feeling of universal love which had so uplifted his heart in the Meeting that morning was still with him. He felt, as he looked out over the sleeping city, the tautness and strength of his youth being as it were dedicated, transformed into a kind of wisdom. He felt like a healer, one who has perhaps only lately become aware of a divine gift, and holds it in reverent secrecy among a people in need. Soon his mission would begin. Some unconquerable feeling, expressing itself as joy, wrought in his body and made him tremble. He remembered Emma's words, 'If I had a brother like George I would do something about him.'

Tom pulled the curtains upon the remaining lights of Ennistone and took off his shirt. Looking in the mirror he saw the bruise upon his arm which plainly showed the marks of George's fingers. He thought, George is drowning, and he held on to *me*. And Tom felt that the very next day he would go to George and just sit in his presence and utter some good thing, some simple thing which he would be inspired to say; and George would suddenly see that there was one place in the world where there was and could be no enemy. Of course he may curse and chuck me out, thought Tom, but later he'll reflect and he'll *understand*. It must be so. He thought, I'll see George and I'll see Alex and I'll tell them – what – oh it's like conversion, being changed, being saved, what's the matter with me? I'll do them good, I must do, it will simply *flow* out of me like electricity, a life ray, I'm changed like after an atomic explosion, only it's all good. Is it something that Mr Eastcote did to me? Not just that, it can't be. Mr Eastcote was just a sign, it's God existing, ought I to kneel down?

Tom took off his shoes and socks. He did not kneel down but stood slightly swaying as if yielding to a shaft or stream of force which was coming up from below like bubbles rising blithely through water. He took off his vest and put on his pyjama jacket. He took off his trousers and pants and put on his pyjama trousers. Was he, after this revelation, this showing, this transformation of his flesh into some pure transcendent substance, going simply to bed, to sleep? Looking at his bed, he felt all of a sudden very tired as if he had been walking, working, travailing for a long time, and he knew that if he went to bed he would be asleep in a second. He thought, I won't sleep, I'll prolong it. I'll go and tell it all to Emma.

When Tom got to the door of his room he felt his energy taking the form of an agonizing sense of urgency. He flew across the landing and burst into Emma's room. Emma, with his bedside light

217

on, had returned to his reading. As soon as he saw Tom's face he took off his glasses.

Tom said, 'Emma – oh – Emma.'

Emma said nothing, but he drew the bedclothes aside. Tom, still in the swift impetus of his wafting, came to his friend, and for a moment they lay breast to breast, holding each other in a fierce bruising clasp, their hearts beating with a terrible violence; and so they lay in silence for a long time.

George had once witnessed a brawl in a pub in London. A thug
had attacked a man and knocked him down. Now the thug was
kicking the head of his victim who was lying on the floor. No
one intervened. Everyone stood spellbound, including George who
watched fascinated. (He could still recall the sound of the kicking.)
Then a girl ran forward and shouted, 'Stop, stop, oh stop.' The
thug said to the girl, 'Give me a kiss then, and I'll stop.' The girl
went to him and he kissed her, dragging brutally at her hair. Then
he said, 'Undress!' The girl began to cry. 'Undress, or I'll kick
him again.' The girl pulled herself away and ran out of the door,
and the thug kicked the fallen man again. George, who was near
the door, followed the girl out. She was walking along the street
audibly crying, wailing. Was she a prostitute who knew the thug,
or a friend of the victim, or else a brave bystander? George didn't
want to know, he didn't want to speak to the girl, he just
followed her for a while, excited by the scene, then slowed down
and lost her. About a year later he saw her again, in another
part of London, and the coincidence gave him a curious kind of
fright. He did not follow her on this occasion. Now, yesterday,
here in Ennistone, he had seen the girl for the third time. It was
near twilight, and George was walking from the library towards
Druidsdale, when the girl turned out of a side road and began
to walk on ahead of him. George followed her and fear came upon
him in the form of a compulsion to run to catch her up and speak
to her, although this also seemed impossible. When she turned
a corner ahead of him he slowed down. When he reached the
corner he saw her walking on the other side of the road. Only
now, between him and her, there was another man, a familiar-
looking man wearing a black mackintosh. George realized with
a coldness which made him almost faint that this other man
was himself, and that if he ever saw the face of that man he
would fall down and die. George turned and ran back in the other

219

direction, running and running through the darkening streets of the town.

Now in the morning this seemed all like an evil dream, something he desired to dismiss absolutely from his mind without even wondering whether it was fantasy or 'real', whatever these terms might mean. He thought he had heard a continued screaming in the silence of the night, composing the silence. He had heard the pigeons saying 'Rozanov, Rozanov' in the early dawn. A kind of beastliness possessed George now, a wanton slovenliness, which was necessary to his way of life. The place where he slept downstairs, on a sofa in the sitting-room, had become dirty and smelt like an animal's lair. He no longer undressed to sleep, simply took his shoes off. He shaved occasionally, not often enough to prevent his face becoming bluish and dark. He rose each day as to a mysterious programme, which misery and bitterness made it impossible to execute. He wanted to see Diane, yet felt that her sentimental pity and her sheer stupidity would make him want to kill her. Sometimes, for a second, he thought about Stella as of something remarkable but unreal: clean, shining, made of metal. He walked round to Hare Lane and knocked on John Robert's door and, receiving no answer, sat down on the pavement.

After a while a number of people came to look at him from a distance. At last someone (it was Dominic Wiggins) approached him to say that Rozanov was not now at Hare Lane, but had gone to live in the Ennistone Rooms. George got up and set off slowly toward the Institute. As he walked, it began to rain. He did not go into the Baths, but entered the Rooms by the street door where there was a porter in a glass box. There was also a board listing the names of the occupants and the numbers of their rooms and also whether they were in or out. George saw with a tremor but without surprise that Rozanov's room was number *forty-four*. Rozanov was said to be in. George went on into the furry-carpeted corridor. Here the sound of the waters was considerable and their smell sulphurous. George knocked on Rozanov's door, but could hear no answering call. He opened the door.

Rozanov, fully clothed, was sitting at a table by the window writing. There were books on the table. Rozanov frowned when he saw George, and drew one of the books over the paper he had been writing on.

John Robert's room retained some remnants of past splendour, surviving in the form of a meaningless gloomy pretentiousness, suggestive of an abandoned night club. Three walls were covered with sheets of a brittle black material, cracked in places. The wall opposite the door was papered with a zigzag pattern of silver and light green. A tall thin chest of drawers of a black shininess which declared itself neither as wood nor as metal, and a tall thin matching wardrobe with a tall thin elliptical mirror stood about with the awkwardness of huge ornaments. The carpet continued the silver and light green pattern, varied with wavy black lines. A low light green sofa with fat flat arms embraced a lot of small black cushions. A chintz armchair and an office-furniture-style plastic-covered table and chair had entered as aliens to represent in their humble way utility and comfort. A little steam crept through the wooden louvred doors of the bathroom. The room was warm, and full of the water noise which so soon became inaudible.

George said, 'Nice place you have here,' and sat down on the chintz armchair, but rose again, finding it too low. He stood near the tall thin wardrobe and saw himself in the tall thin silver ellipse of the mirror. He thought, *that*'s the man I was following. (He looked dirty and unhappy.)

John Robert said, 'I'm busy now.'

'Writing your great book?'

'No.'

'I remember you used to talk about seeing thoughts like Melville's whale far below. What's in the sea now? Monsters?'

'I am busy, please go away.'

'Will you talk to me?'

'No.'

'Why not? I was your favourite pupil once.'

'No.'

'You lie, I was. Why should it worry you anyway if I say I was your favourite pupil? Are you so vain that you feel ashamed of me?'

'Please –'

'Everything I said to you last time was wrong. I demeaned myself, I crawled, that was a mistake. You know what I want. I want to be justified, you can justify me, I want to be saved, you can

221

save me. I am just stating facts. Other minds, other minds, how we used to worry over *that* one! I want to know what you think of me.'

'I don't think anything about you.'

'You do, you *must*.'

'You keep imagining I think about you, I don't.'

'You thought enough about me to destroy me. Or did you do it by accident, without even noticing?'

'I didn't destroy you, George,' said John Robert with a sigh.

'You mean I am destroying myself?'

'I don't think so. You are just disappointed.'

'What about you? Aren't you disappointed? Everything went wrong since Aristotle, you used to say. That's a long time. And big you were going to sort it all out! Have you? Of course not. No one reads your books now. What are you worth? Have I wrecked my life for a charlatan?'

'That's enough.'

'You flayed me, you took away my life-illusions, you killed my self-love.'

'I doubt that,' said John Robert, 'but if I *did* kill your self-love I am very much to be congratulated and so are you.'

'You know what I mean. Without self-love there is nothing but evil. I wish I'd never met you.'

'What you call evil is simply vanity. You have lost your self-esteem for some reason which does not interest me, and you are suffering from withdrawal symptoms. Go and scratch your sores somewhere else.'

'You suggest I go home and pull myself together?'

'No, I suggest you go to Ivor Sefton and he will tell you a story about yourself which will cheer you up.'

'You don't know what these hurts are like.'

'You mean loss of face.'

'Loss of face, loss of soul, loss of child. You know nothing of real pain. But I don't want to talk to you about *that*, you wouldn't understand. You've never loved anybody in your life, not a single being. You only married Linda Brent to spite my mother, because she wasn't interested in you.'

'George,' said John Robert, 'I know quite well that you are only saying these wild things to annoy me so that –'

'You were mad with spite because you weren't invited to the grand houses!'

222

'To annoy me so that I shall become angry and my anger will make a bond between us, but you will not succeed. You simply don't interest me enough.'

'We're alike, you know. We're both demons, you're a big one and I'm a little one, the big ones make the little ones scream. You hate me because I'm a caricature of you. Isn't that so?'

'I don't hate you.'

'How can you treat another human being with such contempt? And I *was* your pupil, and does that not mean anything to you? Can't you even *react*? You've lost all your fire!'

'I wish –'

'Did I push the car? Doesn't that interest you?'

'What car?'

'The car with my wife in. If I pushed the car does that mean I intended to kill her? What was I *thinking* at just that moment? Did I *intend* to drive the car into the canal? Now I've killed my wife, all is permitted. Someone in Dostoyevski thought that if he killed himself he could become God.'

'Well, go and kill yourself somewhere else.'

'But wouldn't it be a better way to become God to kill someone else? That's harder than killing yourself.'

'You are as restless and peevish as ever. It's a sign of stupidity.'

'Peevish! Now you really are trying to provoke me.'

'I assure you I am not – I just want you to go away.'

'You told me long ago to draw in my horns. But I can't. My horns are permanently out and my eyes are staring forward into the dark.'

'It's hard to stare into the dark. Very few people do it.'

'Do you think so poorly of my mind?'

'No.'

'So you *do* encourage me?'

'No, I mean I don't care a fig about your mind.'

'My mind is full of such strange trash. Jingles and – spells – I can't explain. Do you think I'm mad?'

'No.'

'You said it's not philosophy unless it makes you tremble. You are an incurable teacher. I am trembling now. Teach me.'

'Why do you go on worrying about philosophy? It doesn't matter.'

'So you admit that at last, after all those dull years!'

223

'I mean, think your own thoughts. Why do you want to think mine?'

'You know why. The guards in the concentration camps realized with joy that they *didn't care*. They had been afraid that they would care. But they found they didn't, they were free! Isn't that worth thinking about?'

'You are not thinking,' said John Robert. 'You are simply suffering from a nervous craving of the will. Now let us close this ridiculous conversation.'

'You don't want it to end. You want to go on tormenting me. I am approaching the limit. It's strange out there. Something terrible could happen.'

'Go and buy yourself some Nazi badges.'

'You think I'm playing at it?'

'Yes. You're a fake, a *faux mauvais*, pretending to be wicked because you're unhappy. You're not mad or satanic, you're just a fool suffering from hurt vanity. You lack imagination. What made you bad at philosophy makes you bad at being bad. It's a game. You're a dull dog, George, an ordinary dull mediocre egoist, you will never be anything else.'

'Don't try me too much.'

'You never tried to kill your wife, you dropped the Roman glass because you were drunk, you're just a clown. Now go away unless you want me to start feeling sorry for you.'

George moved in the room. He opened the wardrobe door and looked inside and touched John Robert's overcoat which was hanging up. He opened the door of the bathroom and looked into the steamy pit of the bath. He closed the door again. He said:

'What's the matter with you? Where's all the power you used to have? You care for no one, you are alone. I doubt if you've ever had a woman. You had a daughter, but who was her father? You hated her and she hated you. Who's supposed to feel sorry for whom, I wonder? You're old and toothless and you smell. It's the end, you're losing your mind, it's vanishing day by day and you haven't anything else. You've seen through philosophy, you're vindictive and drained dry, and you are alone. No one loves you, you love no one. Isn't all that true?'

'Just shut up, please, and go.'

'Don't you care what I think about you?'

'As far as I'm concerned you don't exist.'

'I existed for you once. When did I cease to exist and why? Tell me, I've got to know.'

'This is a pseudo question. You remember enough philosophy to know what that is. Ask, why is the question posed? Only ask yourself, not me.'

'Have you no advice for me?'

'Yes, stop drinking.'

'John Robert, I know I was very rude to you in California, and I've been rude to you today, I know I haven't been what I ought to be – Christ, now I'm crawling again – but you've banished me long enough and punished me long enough, let it be over now.'

'These emotive words imply a state of affairs which simply does not exist between us. Nothing exists between us.'

'You say you think I'm –'

'Oh never mind what I said! I don't think anything about you. There isn't any structure here for communication.'

'There *is* structure! How can you deny it? There *is*! we are human beings! You taught me philosophy and I love you.'

'George, listen, you want me to be angry with you and even to hate you, but I *can't*. Take this as a kind word and *please go*.'

'Oh damn you, damn you, damn you!'

'*Get out!*' said John Robert. He stood up.

The loud hum of the sealed-off water had covered the sound of Father Bernard knocking timidly on the door. He knocked twice and then entered. He saw, and at once partly understood, the end of George's battle with Rozanov.

Rozanov said again, but quietly, 'Get out, go.'

George was wearing a black mackintosh, like his *alter ego*. The collar was still turned up as it had been when, coming in out of the slight rain, he had arrived. His uncombed hair was standing jaggedly up on end, his untidy open shirt collar and dirty vest were visible at the neck of his mackintosh. He stood, his hands in his pockets, looking with burning eyes towards the philosopher who had risen, hunched and glaring, like a huge cruel-beaked bird behind the desk.

Father Bernard had been peacefully meditating to the sound of Scott Joplin when Rozanov's letter had arrived that morning, simply summoning him to the Rooms. None too soon for the priest had the letter come, for he had heard nothing from Rozanov since their conversational walk upon the Common. A yearning had come upon Father Bernard, a need, an obsessive desire to be with the philosopher again, to be in his presence; and with this a fear that Rozanov had, after their conversation, found him wanting in the qualities necessary for a chosen companion. Father Bernard 'had thought of writing to Rozanov, but after being told to wait till he was summoned, did not yet dare to. He had composed many letters in his mind, some of them polemical.

Now, seeing George in defeat, so evidently rejected, and intuiting the appeal which must have been made to so ambiguous a power, Father Bernard felt himself in danger. But he recognized too a 'high moment', a moment of grace such as sometimes came upon him quite suddenly, and he felt elation. He hesitated only a moment before going forward and kissing George upon the cheek. It was an odd action. It was some time since the priest had kissed anybody. Hand-holding was different.

George was evidently startled, as if unaware whether he had received a kiss or a light slap. He stepped back. Then with vague eyes and without looking the priest in the face, he circled round him and went out of the door, leaving it open. Father Bernard closed the door.

John Robert was annoyed. He was annoyed with himself, with George, and now with Father Bernard. He took the kiss as an affront to himself, even a criticism, certainly an intrusion, the striking of a deliberate false note. The incident filled him with disgust. He was cross with himself for having at the end, and possibly in a muted way earlier in the conversation, exhibited emotion. He was not as indifferent as he had feigned to be to some of George's taunts. He found hurt feelings of that kind extremely unbecoming. He was annoyed now because he thought that Father Bernard, who stood with downcast gaze, had already intuited his whole complex of feelings.

John Robert sat down noisily, fiddling with his books and papers, and motioned the priest to a seat. The priest put two of the sofa cushions on the chintz chair and sat down, looking now at John Robert with his glowing brown eyes which could not help admitting understanding and asking for pardon.

'I'm sorry,' Father Bernard actually said.

'What for?'

'Oh – interrupting.'

'It doesn't matter,' said John Robert. He seemed to be at a loss.

Father Bernard, his high moment still upon him, said, 'You could help George so much. Just a little gentleness. You have so much power.'

'Are you telling me what to do?'

'Yes.'

'I asked you not to speak of him.'

'Forgive me. I would not have done so without –'

'Without the impression you have just received.'

'Precisely.'

'And what is that impression?'

Father Bernard was silent a moment, and then said, 'You ought to be kind to him. Just – quietly. It wouldn't take up much of your time. Anything would do, any signal of kindness. Then he would be docile, he might even leave you alone!'

'You know nothing about it.' John Robert felt immediate contempt for himself for saying anything so banal and so patently untrue. He had so many and so pressing things to think about which had nothing whatsoever to do with George. To be put in the wrong by the priest and urged to examine himself in this matter was really too much. For a moment he felt such intense loathing for his visitor, he was tempted to tell him to go. He glared at Father Bernard. 'Are you familiar with Dante?'

'Yes.'

'*Guarda e passa.*'

'No,' said the priest, '*no*.'

Father Bernard tossed his finely combed hair (he had combed it down in the corridor before entering), his nostrils dilated and his cheeks burned. He raised a defensive hand and made as if to snap his fingers, but he said nothing and continued to stare at the philosopher.

Rozanov said, 'Let us not talk of that. I called you here because I want to ask you a favour. I won't keep you long.'

'Oh?' Father Bernard felt disappointment. He had assumed that another philosophical conversation would ensue, and had already planned to tell Rozanov that he disliked having to think when he was walking. He had enjoyed playing the young man to John Robert's Socrates. He had hoped that a routine was being established.

'I shall be going back to America rather sooner than I expected.'

'Oh, I'm sorry –'

'You perhaps know, or perhaps you do not, that my grand-daughter Harriet Meynell is coming to live in Ennistone.'

'Yes?' This was the first that Father Bernard had heard of the existence of a grandchild.

'I would like you to keep a helpful eye upon her.'

Father Bernard felt instant alarm. He pictured a toddler. In any case, tasks, trouble, danger. 'How old is she?'

'Seventeen, I think. Perhaps eighteen. She has been at boarding school.'

'What do you want me to do?' Father Bernard now pictured a noisy American teenager. He must keep his head and say no quickly.

'Just see her, know what she's doing.'

'Just that?'

'I should say that she will have her chaperone with her.'

'Her chaperone?'

'A maidservant. They will be living in the Slipper House. That is the folly, or whatever one may call it, in the garden at Belmont, Mrs McCaffrey's house.'

Father Bernard nodded. Everyone knew about the Slipper House. He was still alarmed. 'What will she be doing?'

'How do you mean?'

'How will she be employing her time? Will she be working, finding a job, studying or –?'

'I want her to proceed to an English university but she may need a – supervisor, a sort of tutor – could you do that?'

'No!' said Father Bernard wildly. 'I mean what is her subject?'

'I don't know exactly. Some arts subject. Perhaps you could discuss it with her?'

'But shouldn't *you* discuss it with her?' said the priest.

'Oh, I shall talk to her, but I imagine – probably nothing will be decided. She is still young. There would be things to be found out – I mean about her capacities and wishes – and about – entrance requirements and – could you do that?'

'No, I don't think so,' said the priest. 'Well, I suppose I could.'

'Just see that she's reading something, and not wasting her time. I would pay you of course.'

Father Bernard stared at the big bony face of the philosopher

228

and his large power-hungry nose and his moist pendant mouth and yellow bloodshot eyes. With his shock of stout stiff slightly curly grey hair and flat head he looked like a very old general, a *Russian* general. It was impossible to suspect him of impertinence. These ideas emerged with a kind of mad solipsism, a massive lack of connection with the world. Father Bernard said, 'I don't want to be paid. I have a salary and I have duties which I may or may not perform. I am prepared to add this child to my list of duties, that's all. I will talk to her and see what she can do and if necessary find someone to coach her, I suppose – but don't expect too much of me, I can't be responsible – if I write you letters, will you answer them?'

'About the girl, yes.'

Here Father Bernard almost stamped with exasperation. 'But will you –?'

'In emergency you can telephone me collect, that means reversing the charges.'

'But –'

'I shall feel better if someone here is keeping an eye on her. I saw you as that – as a sort of pedagogue – but if you can just – I leave it to you. I'm most grateful. I will let you know when she arrives.'

Father Bernard fell back helplessly in his chair. It had by now occurred to him that the young girl might constitute a permanent link between him and the philosopher. Did he really want such a link? Evidently he did. But what a responsibility, what a time-consuming possibly irritating burden, and ... a girl of seventeen ... suppose something went awfully wrong ...

'Yes, all right,' he said.

'That's settled then.' Rozanov began to rearrange his desk, a clear indication that the interview was over. He added, 'If you ever do have to telephone me, which I hope won't be necessary, do remember to check the American time first.'

Father Bernard stood up. He said, 'I'd like to talk to you again.'

'What about?'

'About anything. Like we did up on the Common. Or were you just testing me for the post of tutor?'

'I – no – that had nothing to do with it.'

There was a silence during which Father Bernard felt an almost overwhelming impulse to say something more about George.

Rozanov said, 'I feel sure you should consider leaving the priest-hood.'

'Oh. Why?'

'Wouldn't it be more honest? With your beliefs you must feel you are in a false position, living a lie. You must have taken vows. Aren't you breaking them?'

'Well, nowadays people are fairly relaxed about –'

'But didn't you swear something or other?'

'I swore that I assented to the Thirty-nine Articles of Religion.'

'But that's old-fashioned realistic theism! You don't believe that?'

'No.'

'What else did you swear?'

'To obey the bishop.'

'And do you?'

'No.'

'What then does it mean to you to be in Holy Orders?' The phrase came oddly and pompously and impressively out of John Robert's mouth. 'How can you go on?'

Father Bernard felt suddenly sick, he was going to be sick with rage, a black vomit of sudden positive hatred of Rozanov was going to spill out of his mouth on to the carpet. He swallowed and said, 'I just can, that's all. Well, good day.'

He marched to the door and jerked it open. Vast clouds of smoke and heat rolled out at him together with a sudden roaring noise, and for a moment he thought the place was on fire. Then he realized that the element was water not fire. He had opened the door of the bathroom by mistake.

He banged the door shut and made for the other door and got out into the carpeted corridor which belonged neither to a hospital nor to a hotel. Here he was again aware of the sound of water. He wondered, should I go back and apologize. Then he thought, am I mad? Apologize to that maniac? Whatever for? And he realized with horror that now and henceforth John Robert Rozanov was there *inside his mind*, like a virus, something that could not be cured. He had a new disease. Rozanovism.

Hattie and Pearl were in the Slipper House. They were as happy as two little mice in a doll's house. They had never had a house before.

The effect upon them both was extraordinary, far beyond anything which they could have expected, even though they had looked forward to their unexpected new habitat with considerable excitement. They laughed and ran about like mad things. They were drunk with pleasure, although they could not at all coherently have said what it was that pleased and amused them so much.

Perhaps the poor neglected misunderstood Slipper House had stored up a lot of vague sweet innocent ownerless happiness from its past, the past when Alex and her brother Desmond were young, and when Geoffrey and Rosemary Stillowen invented games and parties for scores of beautiful young people, Quakers and Methodists, for whom sex was a future mystery and a present romance, and whose lives were still unshadowed in a world where nobody believed that there would ever be another war.

That may have been so. But also of course the two girls, at a moment when both of them were anxiously and silently feeling the cold turning band of time entering a new phase, had received a curious reprieve. Suddenly everything was fun, everything flowered into a kind of dotty youthfulness together which they had never really had before. Now suddenly Hattie was older and suddenly Pearl was younger. The strict old-fashioned upbringing which John Robert had distantly decreed for Hattie had not at all prepared her for this shock of gleeful joy. She and Pearl were 'gay young things', imprisoned perhaps and perhaps doomed (there were ideas which they sometimes glimpsed, as it were, over their shoulders) but for the moment compelled to have no other occupation but to inhabit the present, and carry on, in that exquisitely artificial little house, what felt like a delightful charade.

Pearl had arrived first with suitcases. The taxi had deposited her

231

in the twilit evening at the back gate where she had found Ruby waiting. Before that, letters had been flying to and fro, letters which were more like army instructions than works of epistolary art. John Robert had written to Pearl to say that he wanted her and Hattie to 'abide' (his use of the word 'abide' was the only point of stylistic interest in his letter) during the summer at the Garden House ('Slipper House' was a nickname of course), Belmont, Tasker Road, Ennistone, by courtesy of Mrs McCaffrey, whom they were not to bother, but to use the back gate in Forum Way. He wrote in similar terms to Hattie. His letter to Pearl began 'Dear Pearl!' and ended 'Yours sincerely, J. R. Rozanov.' His letter to Hattie began 'My dear Hattie' and ended 'Yours J R R' (scrawled). He had never established himself as 'granddad' or 'grandpapa' or any such. Hattie had no name for him and called him by no name. Alex had written to John Robert with marked coldness that she 'noted his arrangement'. He had not replied. Pearl had written to Ruby saying when she would arrive. (Ruby did not show the letter to Alex but took it to the gipsies to be read.) Neither Pearl nor Hattie had written to Alex since Pearl did not feel it was their place to do so. Alex did not write to Hattie because she did not know her address and felt affronted. Ruby casually informed Alex of Pearl's arrival date.

Ruby, strong as a horse, had helped Pearl carry the numerous suitcases to the house. These contained Pearl's own clothes and Hattie's English summer clothes which were stored at Pearl's flat. Hattie's school trunk and book box was to come by rail. Pearl and Ruby got the stuff inside and closed the door. They went into the sitting-room and turned on the light and sat down.

Pearl closed her eyes and said, 'Oh!' Some extraordinary painful excitement caught hold of her like a sudden cramp, mixed with very private fear. She wished Ruby would go away. She wanted to explore the house by herself.

'It's all nice here, we did it,' said Ruby, wide-legged, staring at Pearl with her brooding predatory stare.

'We –?'

'Me and her.'

'Good – thanks –'

'I'm to clean.'

'No – don't – I can.'

'You don't want me here.'

'It's not that.'

232

'You don't. Will you come up to the house and see her?'

'I don't see that I need to. Do I?'

'Please yourself. Well, there you are. When's Missie coming?'

'Tomorrow.'

'Everyone here's mad to see her.'

'How do they know?'

'They know. They're mad to see his grand-daughter. They want a good laugh.'

'Why should they laugh?'

'People always laugh. What'll you do with your two selves?'

'I don't know,' said Pearl. 'Enjoy them, I hope!'

Ruby said, 'It's well for some. She's not pleased.'

'Mrs McCaffrey?'

'You'd better see her and curtsey, tomorrow.'

'Oh all right. Only I won't curtsey. I suppose that's a joke.'

'Please yourself.'

'Ruby, dear, don't be cross.'

'I'm not cross.'

'What's that strange noise?'

'The horrible fox animal. It lives here, in this garden.'

Pearl heard the strange noise again later that night as she went up to bed alone. Next morning she went to Belmont and showed herself to Mrs McCaffrey who was aloof and gracious and vague. That evening Hattie arrived.

'What fun this is.'

'But it won't last.'

'Don't keep saying that, Pearl darling. Aren't you happy?'

'Yes. That doesn't stop me from being happy.'

'I'm happy.'

'I've never heard you say that before.'

'Don't sound sad about it, it isn't your fault.'

'I know.'

'Our life is so odd.'

'Yes. How you've grown up.'

'You mean because I say our life is odd?'

'It *is*. But a year ago you wouldn't have said so.'

'There are many things we say now which we wouldn't have said a year ago.'

'How awfully far off Denver seems.'

'Like a dream.'

'Does *this* seem real?'

'No, but it's so *present*. In Denver we were always looking *up*.'

'You mean up at the snow?'

'And sort of far away.'

'Perhaps into the future.'

'Oh, the future –! This is all so much more hereness and nowness.'

'That's what you mean by happy.'

'The snow was like the sea and yet it wasn't. I do wish we lived by the sea. I wish this house would fly away to the sea. I can imagine this house flying, I'm sure it can.'

'I wish it would fly away somewhere.'

'Away from here? Away from what?'

Pearl was silent. It was ten o'clock at night and they had been talking since their picnic supper. Everything had been, since Hattie's arrival two days ago, a picnic. Continual rain had served as an excuse for staying in the house. They had gone out to shop and Pearl had taken Hattie on a rainy walk round the centre of Ennistone. Not only had Hattie of course never visited Ennistone, where John Robert had never resided during her lifetime so far, she had scarcely until lately heard of the place. John Robert never talked about his past, and Pearl's life history made no reference to the now so momentous town. Moreover the girls had previously, in their of course fairly frequent talk about Hattie's grandfather, avoided any deep or searching discussion of him. The *mystery* of John Robert remained unplumbed and indeed unreferred to. Pearl had felt, when Hattie was younger, that it would be improper to discuss the great man in any way which was in danger of bordering on the disrespectful. Pearl had, also, thoughts of her own about John Robert which she would not have risked revealing. Hattie, in a curious childish way which was peculiar to her own situation, simply did not think much about him at all. He had figured, when she was younger, in the light of a rather burdensome duty. The occasions of 'having tea' and answering perfunctory questions about her welfare had been ordeals to be got through without making mistakes. The atmosphere of these meetings was, in Hattie's memory, heavy, soggy, airless, infinitely depressing, and faintly menacing. She was always a bit, though not exceedingly, frightened of John Robert. Pearl was also, and more, frightened of him. Now, for the first time, they were both, it appeared, settled in a place where he too, for the moment at any rate, was living. It so 'appeared' simply from the fact that the address given on his letters was 16 Hare Lane, Ennistone. No doubt John Robert would manifest himself. Both the girls tried not to worry about that.

With the house to play with, it was not too hard not to worry. After Hattie had had her glimpse of the town they settled down to arrange and inhabit. Hattie's trunk and box of books had come. They set out books and hung up clothes. They moved the furniture about. Hattie placed on her chest of drawers the brown china rabbit scratching his ear, the sleek black slug-like Eskimo seal, and the little pink-and-white Japanese vase, into which she put some primroses which she had intrepidly picked down at the Forum Way end of the garden. They had run about everywhere and opened every drawer and every cupboard and swung out every painted shutter. In a room downstairs they had been startled to open a cupboard door and be confronted by a staring bevy of little gods, made out of clay and *papier mâché* and painted in gaudy colours. These were Alex's old 'fetishes' which she had meant to remove, but had forgotten when she 'gave up' the Slipper House after learning that it was not destined to contain John Robert. She had removed the paint and brushes, sad picturesque reminders of her old life as a failed painter, but she had left the little gods behind. Hattie had carried one of them, a red dog-headed thing with staring eyes, up to her bedroom to join the rabbit and the seal and the Japanese vase, but some superstitious scruple soon made her return him to his cupboard. On her first night alone Pearl had elected to sleep in the smaller bedroom which faced Belmont (which Alex had destined for John Robert's study) rather than the larger room (with the dog and the airship) which looked down the rest of the garden toward the back gate. But Hattie, when she came, had preferred the view towards Belmont because it contained a birch tree and the copper beech and the ginkgo.

'I suppose I really ought to go and see Mrs McCaffrey tomorrow.'

'The professor said not to bother her. I told her we'd come. We'll meet her in the garden.'

'I suppose we can go in the garden.'

'He didn't say anything about the garden.'

'How near the trains sound in the night air. Did you lock the door?'

'Yes.'

They were sitting in Hattie's bedroom, Hattie in her mauve-and-white long-sleeved school nightdress, Pearl in a dark blue petticoat and dark blue stockings. Hattie sat on the bed, Pearl in one of the oriental bamboo chairs. They sat up straight, intent, alert, as at a meeting. Hattie's almost silver hair was in a long thick plait down her back; it had a strange sleek vegetable look, like something which might be found growing in an exotic tree. Her marble-pale eyes roved anxiously as if she might suddenly see, in what surrounded her, some unexpected fault or void. One hand was at her lips, while the other touched her brow as if settling or adjusting some dim turban-like aura which hung about her head. Her childish complexion was smooth and translucent, unmarked by any line. Tonight Pearl did not look her stern age. She had just washed her dark brown hair, bringing out reddish lights in it, as it hovered for a brief time buoyant and frizzy about her face. Even tomorrow it would be darker and straighter and stiff once more. Sometimes Pearl's sallow brow and the thin nose which ran from it so unwaveringly straight, like a line drawn down to point to her thin straight mouth, had a brownish puckered look which could almost be described as 'weather-beaten'. Today, Pearl's brownness was waxen, handsome, slightly burnished, touched as by a southern sun, and her brown-green eyes were pensive and not fierce.

'I must mend this nightie. Look, it's tearing at the shoulder.'

'I'll mend it,' said Pearl, 'just leave it around tomorrow.'

'No, why should you mend my clothes?'

Pearl did not answer this question. A kind of unnerving background to such questions had been assembling itself for some time. She said instead, 'It's time you bought some more clothes. You are a funny girl, most girls are mad about clothes.'

'I'm not,' said Hattie. Then she said, 'We must save money.'

This gave another of those unnerving vistas.

'We?' In fact Pearl was saving money, she saved a lot of her own salary, and she had also saved Hattie's money in that it had so far proved difficult to persuade Hattie, who was still remarkably indifferent to clothes and 'good living' generally, to spend much of it. 'The professor' (as Pearl always called him) did not inquire, and Pearl did not feel it her duty to tell him that Hattie's allowance was piling up in the bank. One day Hattie might need that money. Pearl, with her straight thin nose and her straight thin mouth, kept her head, and this 'keeping' included not speculating too much about the giddy-making openness of the future. She was glad that the money, hers and Hattie's, was there; and this, her relief, and

236

Hattie's, in all the circumstances so puzzling and question-raising 'we', brought up for them something which was distressing. Although they never said so, neither of them altogether trusted Rozanov, so powerful, so unpredictable, so extremely peculiar.

'Wouldn't you like to go to London to buy some clothes? We could make a sensible list. There are things you need.'

'No, Pearl, no. I want to stay here.'

'Then we could go to Bowcocks, that's the big shop in Ennistone.'

'No. When I say here I mean *here*. I want to stay in this house and *hide*. I'm so happy here with *you*. Let's not get involved with other people and going about.'

'Hattie, dear heart, you mustn't hide, it's bad for you. Now you've left school.'

'Oh I know, *I know* –'

Tears were suddenly in Hattie's eyes.

Pearl ignored them. 'You must come into the town, you must come swimming, you know you *love* swimming.'

Hattie had heard about the Baths. The idea of the hot spring tempted her.

'But people would see me. Well, I suppose they wouldn't bother because they wouldn't know who I was, and why should they bother even then? But I don't want to be looked at. I couldn't wear a bikini.'

'Why not? People do here!'

'I'll get a proper costume, I don't want to wear a bikini any more anyway.'

'So we'll have to go to the shops!'

'I think I won't go to the Baths, it must be so public.'

Pearl recalled Ruby's remarks about 'people laughing'. Of course the news about Rozanov's granddaughter must be all round Ennistone. The curiosity about Hattie would be intense, and not altogether benevolent. Hattie's fear at being looked at was prophetically just. Pearl said, 'Oh don't be so *silly*.'

'Pearl.'

'Yes, darling?'

'About sex.'

'Oh!'

'I know we've talked about it and I didn't want to ask you what you didn't want to say.'

Pearl did not help Hattie out with her questions.

'Pearl, whatever is it *like*?'

Pearl laughed. 'You mean –'

'Oh, you know I know *everything* – but – don't laugh – I know – and I've read – but what is it *really like*?'

'You mean, is it nice?'

'I just don't see how it can be. Am I very odd? I find the whole idea *absolutely disgusting*.'

Pearl did not say, as she was suddenly tempted to, that that was exactly how she had found it. She said, 'You're not odd, just childish, like a girl from the past. Most girls of your age – Hattie, don't worry about it. It all depends on people. If the man is nice sex is nice, I daresay.'

'So you didn't like it! Sorry, I know once before you wouldn't talk about it –'

'I didn't like the men, those particular ones – I was a fool.'

'I don't think I shall *ever* like *any* men,' said Hattie. She began slowly to unplait her hair. Pearl got up to help her.

'Pearl dear –'

'Yes.'

'About my grandfather.'

'Yes.'

'You do like him?'

'Yes, of course.' Pearl's quick fingers undid the thick cold pale rope of hair at the nape of the warm neck.

'Do you think he thinks much about us?'

'Not much. But enough.'

'Pearl – oh how I wish – no matter – I was thinking about my father.'

'Yes.'

'He was such a good dear man, so quiet and sort of – lost –'

'Yes.'

'Pearl, you won't ever leave me, will you? I couldn't be parted from you now, we've grown together, like – not like sisters exactly, just like *us*. You're my only *person*, and I don't want anyone else ever. I'm so all right with you.'

'I'll be around,' said Pearl.

She hated this conversation, which stirred up her own fear with an exact and accurate touch, like a finger far outstretched to disturb a wound.

'I don't think I'll ever grow up. I'll crawl into a crack and go to sleep forever.'

'Hattie, stop, don't be so *feeble*, think how lucky you are, you're going to the university –'

'Am I?'

'And you'll meet lots of nice men there, gentlemen, not like the ones I knew.'

'Gentlemen!' Hattie began to laugh, a sort of wild groaning laugh, tossing her silky hair all round her face.

There was a sudden screeching sound down below, then another. The telephone. The girls looked at each other in amazement and alarm.

'Who can it be, so late? You go, Pearlie.'

Pearl darted down the stairs on her slippered feet. Hattie followed barefoot, her warm feet leaving sticky prints on the gleaming parquet which Ruby had polished so carefully.

Pearl in the hall was saying, 'Yes. Yes.' Then, 'Hattie, it's for you.'

'Who –?'

'I don't know, a man.'

Hattie took the telephone. 'Hello.'

'Miss Meynell? This is Father Bernard Jacoby.'

'Oh.'

'I'm the – did your grandfather tell you –?'

'No.'

'I'm the – the clergyman – your grandfather asked me to – to –'

'Yes?'

I should have worked this out beforehand, thought Father Bernard at the other end, and I ought not to have had that last glass of port, and dear me, it's so late, and I do think he might have told the girl.

'He asked me to have a talk with you about your work.'

'My work – you mean – like a tutor?'

'Sort of, not quite – don't worry, we'll invent something. I mean we'll work something out – just a talk really. Could I come round tomorrow morning, about eleven say?'

'Yes. Do you know where –?'

'Oh yes, I know the Slipper House, we all know the Slipper House!'

'Oh – yes – thank you.'

'Goodnight, my child.'

Good heavens, what a bungler I am, thought Father Bernard. He had even managed to chuckle in a suggestive way when talking about the Slipper House. The girl had sounded quiet and civil, but you never knew with Americans. He poured out another glass of port.

'He said he was a tutor, a clergyman,' said Hattie. 'He's coming round tomorrow.'

'Well, never mind tomorrow, let's go to bed.'

'Oh, Pearl, what's that noise?'

'That's the fox barking. It lives here in the garden.'

Pearl opened the front door. A wave of silent moist warm fragrant spring air came with a great slow stride into the house. Pearl turned off the hall light and they looked out into the darkness.

'Foxie,' said Hattie softly, 'dear foxie – he lives right here in our garden –'

'Would you like to go out, dear? I'll get your coat and shoes. We could walk on the lawn.'

'Oh no, no, no. Foxie, oh foxie –' Tears began to stream down Hattie's face and she gave a little sob.

'Hattie, *stop*. You're not ten years old now! Go to bed, you silly idiotic baby.'

'Yes, I will. Don't come. I'm going to turn out my light. Stay here a little. I'd like to think you were outside – only don't go far – and don't forget to lock the door.'

Hattie fled up the stairs.

Pearl walked out on to the grass. The shutters were closed upstairs, only a little light came dimly through the stained-glass landing window. A lighted upstairs window at Belmont could be seen through the trees.

Pearl breathed the soft fuzzy moist surprising spring air with its message of new life and pain and change. She stroked her hand down her straight brow and her thin nose. She thought, I have got everything wrong, I have played every card wrong, I've had luck, oh such luck, but I didn't understand, I didn't *think well enough* of myself – I had such mean small expectations, I wanted too little, and now it's too late.

She looked at the Belmont lights. A curtain was blowing out below a sash window, frighteningly, like a ghost leaning out. Ruby was going to bed, watching television perhaps. Of course she was not going to be like Ruby. Hattie was a girl from the past. Ruby too belonged to the past. A life like Ruby's could not be lived now. Ruby was an anachronism, an old brown dinosaur. But had not Pearl made a similar mistake, missed a turning, taken a road that led not higher up, but into a low mean small life? It was the money, thought Pearl, I spent those precious years just being pleased that I had money! And even the other day I got *pleasure* out of going to see that poor old wreck my foster-mother and showing off in front of her! As if I *had* anything to show off really! I've just been lucky, and I enjoyed the luck in a stupid selfish way and didn't *use* it. I'm like someone in a story who is given a fairy wish, and wastes it asking for a pretty dress or a cake. I didn't use my luck when I could to *get up*, to *get out*. I could have learnt the things Hattie was learning, or some of them. I could have learnt French at any rate, or *something*. I let her do all the talking and the looking while I just packed the cases and mended her clothes. Well, I did *look*, but I didn't know enough and now I can't remember. It isn't that I'm lazy, but I have the soul of a servant and it didn't occur to me. I was so glad just to be travelling and using money and feeling like someone in an advertisement. I didn't see that the *door was open*. Why didn't I feel more resentment? That might have helped me. If only I had hated Hattie, as I thought I might. But loving Hattie – that's terrible – and now –

Pearl thought how in a very little while Hattie would change. Hattie was at the precious crystalline end point of her childhood, of her innocence. The sense of this was in Hattie's own confused pain, her tears, her cry of 'Foxie – oh foxie'. And her wish that she and Pearl might stay forever in the never-never land of her own arrested youth, which time was sweeping on toward the rapids of absolute change. Hattie would remember with blushes the sweet silly words she had uttered tonight. She would *show* Pearl how much she had changed, she would have to.

But she won't show me, thought Pearl, because I won't be here. I shall be far away. We shall be separated. *He* told me to come, to be what I am, and for years I have obeyed him. Now, soon, he will simply tell me to go and be no more seen.

Loving Hattie. Ah, that was bad enough. But Pearl's predicament was even worse than that. She loved John Robert.

'Let me have a look,' said George. He took the field glasses from Alex.

They were installed at the drawing-room at Belmont. Beyond the birch tree (whose droopy pose always reminded Alex of Gabriel) one of the upper windows of the Slipper House was clearly visible.

241

The hazy budding April branches of the tree just brushed the lower right-hand corner of the image. The window was one of the windows of Hattie's bedroom. George was lucky. He saw what Alex had failed to see, Hattie in a white petticoat suddenly skipping across the room. It was the middle of the morning, and Hattie was an early riser, but she had suddenly decided that she wanted to change her dress. The clergyman was due to call in half an hour, and the subtle voice that tells a woman, even a careless girl, how to dress for a man had told her she must change. Hattie came back into view carrying the dress over her arm, and paused. Her hair was undone and was streaming about everywhere until, with her free hand, she slowly gathered it away behind her bare shoulders. Then she passed out of sight again.

George pressed his lips together and lowered his glasses.

'See anything?'

'No.' He turned away from the window.

Alex followed.

'A maiden bower,' said George.

'I doubt if they're maidens.'

'Oh surely the little young one is.'

'She hasn't had the courtesy to come and see me.'

'Two sequestered girls. The town will be in quite a tizzy.'

'The little cat will get out.'

George had arrived unannounced. Alex came down to find him standing in the hall. George had a way of standing, with his head slightly tilted, which suggested, simply by the way in which he occupied the space, that he had just been *slinking along* and was now *only partly visible*. So he stood, looking up under his eyebrows, at his mother. God, how *conceited* he is, she thought as she looked down on him. But, also, her heart turned over for him, it shifted and burned.

Now, in the drawing-room, he had wandered, touching things, moving the little encampment of bronze figures which had stood more or less in that same place on the mantelpiece since he had been a child.

Alex's unease about George's arrival blended with a baneful memory of a dream which she had had last night. She dreamed she was in Belmont, but the house had become enormous like a palace, and rather dark and twilit as if pervaded by a yellowish fog. Alex was walking through the house, sometimes accompanied by a woman who seemed to know it better than she did. In the course of this walking, Alex found herself alone in a gallery from which she looked down into a large dim room, almost like a hall, which was full of all sorts of lumber. The room was obviously abandoned and, Alex felt, had not been entered for a long time. Tables and chairs and boxes and piles of things like lamp-stands and old clocks lay about in disorder, and near the middle of the room there was an old-fashioned gramophone with a huge horn. Alex, looking down into the silent abandoned foggy room, felt terrible fear. She thought, but there is *no such room* in Belmont. Where could such a large secret derelict room *be* in my house? She hurried away and told her discovery to the woman who seemed to know the house so well. The woman said, 'Oh, that's just the old downstairs sitting-room, remember?' and threw open a door to reveal a shabby disordered room which Alex recalled as a former housekeeper's room. Alex thought with relief, oh yes, that's all it is! Then, looking, she realized that this ordinary room was not the room that she had seen.

George had taken off his black mackintosh. He was wearing one of his light grey check suits with a waistcoat and, today, had put on a tie and combed his hair. His head had its sleek hair-oil look. He took off his jacket and stood before Alex in his shiny-backed waistcoat, staring at her and showing his little square separated teeth. It was not exactly a smile.

Alex thought, he's different, he's the same yet different. He *smells* different, sort of sour. And then she thought of the room in her dream. And she thought, he's the same, yet he is *mad*.

Alex looked at George with her cat-look, while with clever quick fingers she adjusted the collar of her blouse. She was wearing an old coat and skirt. If she had known George was coming she would have changed. She noted the little instinctive movement of her vanity.

'How are you, George?'

'Fine. How are you, Alex?'

'All right. Would you like some coffee?'

'No, thanks.'

'A drink?'

'No.'

'Any news of Stella?' Alex said this, and indeed at that moment felt it, as if it were the most ordinary sort of inquiry after someone's wife.

'No,' said George after a moment, almost thoughtfully, in a kind

243

of dreamy pensive manner, as if seeing a truthful vision, '*Stella* is all right.'

'You've heard something?'

'No. But you may be sure . . . that *she* is *all right* . . .'

'Good,' said Alex. Sometimes she and George quarrelled in such an odd painful senseless way because their conversation *went astray* at some point, *took a wrong turn*. It was as if George, from a position high above, had decided how the conversation ought to go if it were not to break some law. When the hidden law was broken Alex, punished by pain and confusion, always felt it was her fault. Was their talk, this time too, going to become something awful? She must try hard, she must *keep in touch* with George. She wanted to place her hand upon his arm, just above the shirt cuff, but of course that was impossible.

'*We* may be dead, and indeed perhaps are . . .'

'Are you coming with us to the seaside?' said Alex.

There was something crude, almost pointless in this appeal to a family tradition, just a substitute for touching George's arm.

'Lordie, are we going?' said George, and smiled. He had stopped moving about and sat down near the fire-place, looking up at his mother with his wide-apart eyes and wrinkling his small nose.

'Yes, I don't care, but Brian and Gabriel insist.'

'It isn't yet anyway. Why do you bring it up? Isn't it time we stopped going there? You know, we shall never forgive you for selling Maryville.' George was still smiling.

'Well –'

'How's your friend Professor Rozanov?'

So that's it, thought Alex. He has come to *find out* . . . And of course I too want to find out . . . A dull stale sadness came over her.

'I don't know. He asked me to come to talk about letting the Slipper House, that was all.'

'You haven't seen him since?'

'No.'

George seemed relieved. He now leaned back in his chair, letting his attention wander.

It was Alex's turn to walk about the room.

'How are *you* getting on with Rozanov?'

'Me?' said George. 'He loves me, he hates me, he pushes me, he pulls me. It's the old story. How will it end? He'll be dead soon anyhow. The *old people* are being cleared away.' He cast a malévolent look at Alex. 'We who remain will have other troubles. Hey nonny nonny – *no*.'

Alex, who had wandered to the window, turned her back on him. 'Good heavens!'

'What?' George got up and joined her at the window.

There were people in the garden.

Alex had lived her life with the view from the window, the drooping birch tree, the copper beech, the fir tree whose noble reddish shaft on which the sunlight glowed soared up so high, the furry lithe awkward ginkgo, and down below the perfect lawn, mown to a shaven sleekness by the gardener, more often now (since he was grown so old) by herself. She had been a child, looked at, in that garden, where she had later looked at her own children. But after, for years and years, there had been no one in the garden, it had remained as the Slipper House. No one, that is, except, when Brian and Gabriel came visiting, Adam and Zed whose presence there she so intensely resented.

Now in fact the first person whom she saw was Zed, right in the middle of the lawn, quite near to the house. She thought, what is that white thing, has someone left a bag there? Then, as she recognized the dog, Adam walked across the grass in the direction of the garage, touching the birch tree and the fir tree on his way. Never before had Adam entered the garden except under licence from Belmont. The back gate had always been kept locked. Now beyond there were figures under the trees near the Slipper House, even a sound of voices. Alex recognized Brian, Gabriel, Pearl Scotney, and coming into view the ill-omened priest in his cassock.

'The damned impertinence,' said Alex.

'Well, you let the place,' said George. 'Why did you let it if you hate it all so?'

'I thought Professor Rozanov would be there.' Alex immediately regretted this entirely unnecessary revelation.

George said, 'Oh,' and then, but without intensity, 'Don't mess with Rozanov, he's dynamite.'

'Of course they came in through the back gate,' said Alex. 'Anyone can come in now. They'll wear a path across the grass. Oh damn, damn, damn.'

George laughed. He said, 'The defences are breached. Everything is deep but nothing is hidden. There are meanings in the world.'

The door behind them opened and Ruby came in.

Ruby stood there mute. She was wearing a long white apron, not

245

spotless, over her long brown dress. She stared, not at Alex, but at George.

George said, 'Hello, old Ruby thing!' He went forward and touched her shoulder.

'Ruby, could you get some coffee?' said Alex.

Ruby vanished.

'Why should she come in?'

'She came to look at me,' said George.

'Who invited her? She just comes into rooms now, she just *walks in*.'

'Maybe she reckons she lives here.'

'She takes things. I think she takes and hides them and then finds them again. She's becoming very peculiar. I had to ask for the coffee to get rid of her.'

'You ought to pet her a little. She wants to be touched.'

'Really –!'

'Plato said that everything you say to a slave should be an order. You carry out that advice pretty well. Now I come to think of it, I've never heard you say *anything* to Ruby which wasn't an order, not even something like "It's raining." '

Alex felt suddenly that she might burst into tears, weep bitterly like a child in front of her eldest son. Everyone was against her, everyone criticized her and attacked her. She said, 'Why don't you go and join them at the Slipper House.'

'And spoil the fun?'

'You want to see the girl. Go and see her.'

'And seduce her? What about my coffee?'

Alex was silent, calling up old allies, rage and hate, to blunt her grief and dry her tears.

'All right,' said George, well aware of those mounting emotions. 'I'll go. And when Ruby comes with the coffee ask her to sit down. I'd like to think of you having coffee together.'

He picked up his coat and jacket and faded from the room.

George went downstairs and into the garden by the back door, but he did not go to join the 'intruders' who were standing outside the Slipper House. There had been, at this juncture, no glimpse of 'the little one'. He stood near the garage looking down the garden. Adam, who had been sitting in the Rolls, heard the sound of the opening and shutting door. Standing up on the seat of the car he could watch George through the dusty window of the 'motor house'. He had never observed George like this before, at such close quarters, unobserved himself. It was exciting. George's face at that moment was worth observing, being like that of a tragic actor registering indecision together with some deep emotion, then clearing and becoming round and benign. He was carrying his mackintosh and his jacket over his arm. He dropped the mac on the grass, put on the jacket, then slowly put on the mac, still gazing down the garden. Something like what Alex saw as his 'conceited' look had returned. Then he turned and went away along the path which led to the street in front of the house (Tasker Road). Adam sat down again and took hold of the steering wheel of the car. Somewhere, he heard Zed utter a bark.

George, though he was indeed curious about 'the little girl', decided not to join the group at the Slipper House. Something almost like shyness deterred him, a sudden sense of how it was becoming harder and harder to communicate with *anyone*. He had visited Alex partly to find out the meaning of her visit to John Robert (of which he believed her account) and partly to reassure himself that, confronted with his mother, he could actually talk to her. Alex would have been surprised to know that in some way his talk with her had fortified him. George was also deterred from going to the Slipper House by a very special feeling of fear which came to him quite suddenly, a sense of taboo. The image of Hattie in her petticoat came back to him with intense vividness. He had thought: that girl, *his* grand-daughter, is dangerous, she's the most dangerous thing in the world. It was as that thought came to him that his face had cleared; for he had not at all liked the sense of being, almost, too *embarrassed* to walk up naturally to those *strangers*. As he neared the front gate some movement caught the corner of his eye and he saw that he was accompanied by Zed. The little dog, as George's head turned, barked at him, then retreated and posed, front feet down, back up, the rump and plumy tail aloft. Then he sprang up, stamped his tiny paw, whined eloquently, then barked again. George lifted a threatening fist and Zed snarled, showing white pointed teeth. George thought with satisfaction, even the dogs bark at me now. He went out into the road, banging the front gate after him. He thought, shall I go to the cinema? No, I'll go and see Diane. She'd better be in.

*

Zed ran past a viburnum bush and came face to face with a fox.

Zed had not meant anything in particular by barking at George. He had followed George from the garage, sniffing at his heels. George always smelt different from other humans; but today there was a new smell, stronger and more exciting, but also rather nasty. It was an animally smell, yet also it offended Zed in some fastidiousness of his soul, which was clothed in white plumage and burning with ecstasy and love. Zed was endlessly interested in George. He smelt him, when he could get near enough (which was not often) with a special nose-wrinkling fascination. If he had seen George buried he would have dug him up. When Zed saw the front gate he began to run on toward it, but was startled by George's sudden turning and his threatening gesture. This gesture wakened an old feeling in Zed that George was dangerous to Adam. So he had snarled (which he very rarely did) and then, satisfied with his performance, scampered back toward his master. As it happened, Adam, who was still in the garage, had shut the door, so Zed ran on down the garden; and it was then that he came face to face with the fox. It was the big dog fox.

Zed had never seen a fox but he had smelt the strong frightening odour and he knew what the apparition was. He recognized, as he had never done before, an absolute enemy. Cross humans and snappy dogs were hazards. But this was different. Zed, as he came to an abrupt stop, felt suddenly his solitude and with it the completeness of his doghood, only in which lay now his salvation. It did not occur to him to bark for help. Indeed as his black eyes stared at the fox's blue eyes he felt incapable of barking.

The big fox looked down at Zed with its cold pale eyes, which were sombre and ruthless and sad, awful eyes which knew not of the human world. The fox's face, with its heavy black marking, looked macabre and wild, a face that devoured other faces. Zed knew that he must stand. If he turned and ran the fox would pursue him and in a few steps those jaws would crack his back. Zed could see the fox's teeth, wrinkling a little the soft black lip of the muzzle. And still they stared, the fox's black paw still raised in the attitude in which Zed had surprised him. They were so close that Zed could feel the warm current of his enemy's breath. He stared up. There was no movement he could make to assert his doghood. At any movement the fox might think he was about to flee, and leap. Zed measured the terrible strength and the more terrible will that con-

248

fronted him. He stared, calling up his own will and the strange
authority which his species derived, alone among other animals,
from the society of the human race.

Then a strange thing happened. The fox turned his head a little
and lowered it right down until his muzzle almost touched the grass,
still keeping his blue pale wild eyes fixed upon Zed. Then he
dropped his black paw and sidled a little, as in a slow dance, moving
round the dog. Zed moved slightly keeping his face resolutely
toward the fox and staring with his blue-black eyes in which there
was reflected so much of the expression of man. The fox continued
to move round Zed with his head lowered and his eyes gazing,
moving as in a very slow rhythmic dance, and Zed continued, upon
the same spot, to turn. Then, quite suddenly, there was a noise
nearby, human voices. The fox turned and in a second vanished.
Zed sat down where he was. He felt so strange, as if he pitied the
fox, or almost envied him, and did not want to return to the world
of happiness. After a moment or two, avoiding Brian and Gabriel
(for it was they), he ran back toward the garage, where the door
was still shut. Outside on the gravel he began playing with the
stones, tapping them with his little white paw as if they were his ball,
and he forgot about the fox.

'He's *sweet*,' said Hattie, holding Zed in her arms.

On entering the garden from the back gate, Adam and Zed had
run straight on toward the garage, passing the Slipper House
toward which the grown-ups wended their slower way. Adam had
sat in the Rolls, turning the wheel this way and that, stood up to
observe George, sat again, then emerged to find Zed waiting and
had inspected the colony of martins underneath the eaves who were
busy renovating last year's nests. Later in the summer the baby
birds would be closely visible, propped up in the nests like little dolls
with white faces. Then Brian and Gabriel had come to find him,
and he had run back with Zed to find Hattie and Pearl standing
outside on the grass with Father Bernard. Zed had run straight to
Hattie, who had picked him up and was pressing her nose into his
furry shoulder while he licked her forehead. The combination of the
dry coolish tickly fur and the warm round small body agitated with
slightly struggling but trustful doggy affection and the smooth wet
tongue caressing her brow quite overcame poor Hattie. She could
feel Zed's heart beating fast and her own heart beat fast too. She

wanted to hug the dog and cry. She put him down hastily. 'What's his name?'

'Zed,' said Adam. He touched the skirt of Hattie's dress. Hattie had put on a flowery summer dress earlier in the morning, but had changed into a straight many-buttoned navy blue shift over a blue-and-white striped shirt blouse when she decided to put her hair up.

'They are alpha and omega,' said Father Bernard smiling.

The cool April sun was shining out of a cool blue sky, making the green tiles of the Slipper House glisten as if they were wet. Dew upon the grass, newly come into the moving sunlight, flashed like diamonds; and a trail of dewy footprints across the lawn from the little copse which occupied the bottom of the garden presaged the footpath dreaded by Alex.

Pearl, who had persuaded Hattie to emerge, now stood behind her in the doorway of the house. She was wearing over her brown dress an apron which she had deliberately failed to remove when she saw from the window the advancing 'company'. She had folded her arms in front of her and stood at attention, wearing her calm dour Mexican look, brown as her dress. She was aware of the priest casting curious glances at her and trying in vain to catch her eye with his nervous girlish smile.

The Brian McCaffreys returning from a shopping expedition (it was Saturday) had met Father Bernard who had proudly announced his destination. Gabriel was at once anxious, with this excuse, to 'drop in' and catch a glimpse of the famous girl. The news that John Robert Rozanov's grand-daughter was installed at the Slipper House was the talk of the Institute. Her appearance there was eagerly awaited. In a sudden gust of possessive emotion, about which she felt secretive and almost guilty, Gabriel felt that she must see the waif and establish a special relation with her before she became the property of everybody. She tried to conceal the quality of her interest from Brian and Adam. She also wanted to find out whether John Robert had committed Hattie to Alex's care. She had suggested a subsequent visit to Alex, but Brian was in no mood to see his mother. Although he complained he was, however, not unwilling to demonstrate his independence of her by visiting the Slipper House, and he too wanted to look at the girl.

Gabriel had impulsively handed over a cake (purchased for Leafy Ridge tea-time) which Hattie had handed to Pearl who had put it inside the front door on the floor. Gabriel's earnest wet eyes were fixed with diffident sympathy upon Hattie. Gabriel had today

250

had the infelicitous idea of tying her floppy hair back with a ribbon. Her face looked strained and shiny, her nose red in the April wind. Arrived, she felt embarrassed and apologetic, having awkwardly refused Hattie's suggestion that they should come in. She now regretted this refusal, but could think of no way of retrieving the blunder which kept Hattie out on the grass shivering slightly in the cold wind. Gabriel was also upset because she had seen for a moment, just as she arrived at the Slipper House, the figure of George standing near the back door of Belmont and looking down the garden.

Hattie's simple pinafore dress made her look schoolgirlish, although her white-blond hair had been assembled, without Pearl's aid, into a large woven bun which climbed up the back of her head. She looked thin, almost ill (which she was not), untouched by sun, her pallid unmarked complexion damp like the stem of a winter plant. Her face, timid again, now after she had set Zed down, so lacked emphasis and colour that she seemed like a study in white by a painter whose whim it was to make a girl's face scarcely appear from the faint hues of a uniformly milky canvas. Only her lips, poised and pouting a little with some persisting question, showed a faint natural pink. And her eyes, marbled with whiteness, were a faint but very clear pale blue.

Brian, standing behind Gabriel and smiling, showing his wolf teeth, thought, what a funny little drowned rat of a thing. And yet in two or three years that could be a beautiful woman.

Gabriel was saying, 'If you need anything, please just let us know. Our telephone number, I'll write it down, sorry I haven't got a – Brian, could you write down our telephone number for –'

'It's in the book,' said Brian.

'Oh, of course, anyway I expect Mrs McCaffrey is looking after you?' Even after years of marriage it did not really occur to Gabriel that there was any Mrs McCaffrey except Alex. She cast a glance toward Belmont. The figure of George had disappeared.

'Oh no,' said Hattie, 'we're on our own. I haven't even met Mrs McCaffrey. I suppose I ought to have done?' She turned for a moment to Pearl, who remained rigid with folded arms.

'I expect your grandfather drops in to see you have everything –'

'No, I haven't seen him either – we don't know, do we, Pearl – whether he's – where he is exactly –'

'Oh dear!' said Gabriel. 'I mean –'

'What are you doing here?' said Brian.

251

'I don't know,' said Hattie, not comically but awkwardly, making Brian's brusque question seem even ruder. Realizing this she added, 'I expect I shall be studying.'

'*We* shall be studying,' said Father Bernard smiling.

'What will you study?' said Gabriel.

'I don't know – I don't really know anything much –'

'Can you swim?' said Brian.

'Oh yes –'

'Then I expect we'll see you at the Baths. Everyone in Ennistone comes to the Baths. Eh?'

There was a pause. Adam had withdrawn with Zed and was standing behind Brian on the side toward the back gate, looking as if he wanted to go away. He stood with his feet wide apart, wearing the corduroy knee breeches and brown jersey which was the uniform of his school. His round brown eyes scanned Hattie with the puzzlement of a young savage.

Hattie looked at him and said, 'I like your togs.'

The word 'togs' emerged from Hattie's lips betokening, in a way which all present obscurely understood, her curious unbelongingness, her statelessness, her lack of a native tongue and a native land.

Adam bowed.

'It's his school uniform,' said Gabriel.

'How nice –'

'Well, we must go,' said Brian. 'We must leave you two to your studies! Come on, Gabriel.'

'You will, won't you –'

'Yes, of course –'

'Good-bye, then –'

'So kind –'

Brian and Gabriel emerged from the back gate into Forum Way. Adam and Zed had run out before them.

'Well, what did you think?' said Gabriel.

'Was that *her* school uniform?'

'Of course not! It was rather smart, I thought –'

'She's an infant. She ought to be in white frills.'

'What did you think of her?'

'Nothing. She's a skinny little American.'

'She hadn't much of an American accent, more English public school.'

'Yuk!'

'I thought she was sweet.'

'Of course you did. She thought Zed was sweet.'

'Why are you so cross?'

'I'm always cross.'

'You were quite rude.'

'So were you, you were salivating with curiosity.'

'Oh dear –'

'And what on earth possessed you to give her our cake?'

'We can get another.'

'They'll all be gone.'

'Did you see George?'

'*George*? Has he got himself inside that house already?'

'He was standing up near Belmont – I think –'

'You imagined it. I didn't see him. You've got George on the brain.'

'We ought to have said something nice to the maid,' said Gabriel. 'No one spoke to her.'

'I suppose she's American.'

'No, someone at the Baths said she was some sort of relation of Ruby's.'

'Of Ruby's? How perfectly horrible.'

'Why?'

'Because it makes things connect. I don't want things to connect.'

'But why?'

'All connections are sinister. I don't want *anything* to connect with *anything*.'

'Did you like her, the little girl, Miss Meynell?' Gabriel asked Adam whom they had just caught up with.

'No.'

'No?'

'No.'

Gabriel thought, Oh *dear*, he's *jealous*! And he wasn't really pleased because I'd bought the cracked jug, well, he was pleased but not *enough*. And Brian thinks I think about George. And I *do* think about George. I suppose that *was* George I saw and I didn't imagine it? I do wish I had more children. I'd love a little girl like Hattie. I wish George was my child too. Oh what *nonsense* my poor head is full of. She said, 'Let's invite her round.'

'Who?'

'Miss Meynell of course. She must be lonely –'

'She won't be lonely for long,' said Brian. 'Mark my words, that girl will be a troublemaker.'

'I can't think why you –'

'And we will *not* invite her round. For heaven's sake, don't let us mess about with anything to do with Rozanov. Everything about that man brings bad luck. And do take that bloody ribbon off your hair, do you want to look sixteen too?'

After the Brian McCaffreys had disappeared out of the back gate and Hattie and her 'tutor' had gone into the sitting-room, Pearl Scotney was left alone. She put Gabriel's impulsive cake away in a tin and put on her coat and went out into the garden. Near the Slipper House the lawn, broad and tree-dotted near the house, began to narrow to a meander of green, coming to an end in the thicker maze of trees and shrubs at the end of the garden. Here there was a garden shed, a space for a bonfire, and an area which had once been a grass tennis court. There was also the remains of a small vegetable garden. (The old gardener no longer came regularly.) Pearl walked this way, away from Belmont, and threaded between lilac and viburnum and buddleia and azalea and rhus and small Japanese maples which were putting out vivid curly red buds which looked like decorations made out of coral. Here and there were some taller trees, fir and chestnut and an old ilex. This region, which mixed higher and lower vegetation, was sometimes called 'the shrubbery', sometimes 'the copse'. The paths were grassy, or else of sad dark earth grown over with green moss.

Pearl, who liked plants and trees, noticed her surroundings and, as human beings can, took a little pleasure in them in the middle of her general large unhappiness. She felt as she walked, giddy, suffering one of those fits of non-identity which probably attack most souls at some time. As she had stood at attention behind her 'young mistress' at the door of the house she had felt, in her apron uniform, invisible. Well, the priest had noticed her; but she had not liked his notice. That young Mrs McCaffrey had thrown her one or two of her vague over-sweet smiles, but that meant nothing. Hattie's 'we' meant nothing too. Well, it meant something just now in Hattie's heart; but Hattie's heart was entering a danger zone, vulnerable to the world, soon to be public property. Her heart which now hugged its little world in a small space, curled up as in a womb, would soon be enlarged to welcome many, perhaps very many, new loves. New desires, new attractions, new knowledge must come now. Hattie was at the end, the very last soft inaudible breath, of her childhood. It was the time, the *logical* time, for Pearl to let go, indeed to be forced to let go. A mother might feel like this, she thought. But after all a mother is forever. I am not Hattie's mother or her sister or even her second cousin. Hattie has no conception of my relationship to her, and will easily begin to feel it to be unreal and to belong to the past.

Pearl had thought these thoughts many times before, prophetically. Now that the time had come to think them for real, she was so tired of them that she could not regard them as posing any problem she could possibly solve. She had wondered whether, in putting Hattie and herself into the Slipper House, like two dolls put away in a doll's house, John Robert had had any particular end in view. Pearl had imagined, continuing her unremitting guesswork about John Robert's mind, that he had intended Mrs McCaffrey to 'keep an eye' on Hattie, perhaps to take her over. But this peril, which Pearl had been determined to resist, had not so far materialized. Meanwhile she discouraged Hattie from seeing Alex. It seemed that they were really 'on their own'. After all, had they not always been so? Only when Hattie was a child 'on their own' had had a different sense. Hattie had survived marvellously, they had both done, without a social world. They knew a few of Margot's (new very respectable) friends. They had made, in their tramping about Europe, no permanent acquaintances, and this had been partly, Pearl now recognized, because of Pearl's possessiveness as well as because of Hattie's shyness. Hattie had school friends (Verity Smaldon, for instance) to whom Pearl had surrendered her for brief visits. But these were fragile attachments, mere contextual connections. Hattie, so infinitely and emptily ready for the world, was still, unless Pearl possessed her, unpossessed.

But what about John Robert? Throughout the years of Pearl's regime the philosopher had manifested an extraordinary combination of absolute correctness and absolute indifference. Money and plans and instructions materialized with prompt effective clarity. Go here, go there, do this, do that. But mainly the great man had remained invisible, and when he did appear his attentions to Hattie were vague, distracted, absent-minded and reluctant. He was always 'elsewhere'. He notoriously 'did not like children', and had never made any serious attempt to 'get on' with his grand-daughter, whose wordless diffidence matched his own monumental awkwardness and lack of tact. His relations with Pearl had been even more, though correct, without substance. John Robert had taken one look at Pearl and had decided to trust her absolutely. It seemed to her that he had never looked at her since. How much he must have understood in the first look. Or more likely, how carelessly he had gambled with Hattie's welfare and her happiness. If Hattie had detested Pearl she would never have told John Robert. Did he realize this, did he care? The absoluteness of the trust, the large sums of money involved, the larger sums of more important matters, sometimes stunned Pearl and *touched* her with a terrible deep touch. At the same time, once the trust was given, she became invisible, she received only *instructions*, never encouragement or praise. These she would more cheerfully have done without if she had felt that John Robert thought of her even sometimes as something other than an efficient instrument of his will.

Pearl had, at the start, been frightened of John Robert and of the whole situation, though also, of course, excited and elated by it. It was later, when Pearl felt calm and secure enough to *observe* Rozanov, herself unobserved (and since she was 'invisible' she had many such chances) that the terrible ailment began. How charmless that big, awkward man was, careless about Hattie, egotistically absent-minded, consulting always his convenience and oblivious of theirs. How ugly he was too, fat and flabby and wet-mouthed with jagged yellow teeth. (This was before he had acquired the false ones commented on by George.) His big head and big hooked nose made him look like a vast puppet in a carnival. His movements were graceless and clumsy. His stare was startled and disconcerting as if, when he looked at someone, he simultaneously recalled something awful which had nothing to do with the person looked at. With all this there went a certain decisive precision which Pearl, reciprocating his trust, relied upon. Where the girls' arrangements were concerned, he meant and did what he said. But what he said to *her* were only orders. They never had a conversation.

How differently, two years later, did Pearl feel about the impossible being in whose hand their fates rested. She mistook, at first, her warmer feelings for protectiveness, even pity. She ran to fetch his coat, though she did not presume to help him on with it, an operation which his arthritis had rendered difficult. His stick was not only in view, but polished. She also cleaned his shoes. (He never commented.) Sometimes he told her to make telephone calls to hotels. Once he asked her to go out and buy him a hat. ('What kind?' 'Any kind.') That had caused Pearl a lot of joy and pain. She used to say to herself, though never to Hattie, 'the poor old chap'. He was a shambling eccentric who needed to be looked after. Too late she realized that her heart was involved.

If he had really just been a 'poor old chap' she would probably have loved him too, but differently. As it was, there was an extra spice of fear and admiration. Not that either Pearl or Hattie had ever read any of his books, but they took it for granted that he was 'awfully distinguished'. Pearl actually got one of his books out of a library once, but could not understand it and hurriedly took it back for fear he should suddenly arrive and find her reading it: which she knew would displease him very much indeed. Also, she wanted to disguise her obsession from Hattie, and had so far succeeded. It was not Pearl's 'place' to love John Robert. Meanwhile he walked in her dreams, surrounded by the joy and fear which had been dimly presaged in the adventure with the hat. She must do *everything right*, she must be perfect and *not fail*. Above all, she must not be discovered. It did not occur to her to console herself by taking a heroic stance; her situation was without choice, her course the only possible one. She lived inside a love so improper and so hopeless that she felt sometimes almost *free* to enjoy herself therein. Love, even without hope, was a joyful energy. When John Robert wrote to her she blushed under her dark complexion. Before he came she imagined his coming a hundred times. When he came she was scarlet, faint, but invisible, always efficient. As she stood at attention and awaited his instructions she longed to seize his hand and cover it with kisses. She loved his orders. That was all that he gave her, and it was much. She trembled and he looked through her with his preoccupied and distant eyes.

I must give them up, thought Pearl, as she stood on the green mossy path and looked through the trees at the April sun on the lawn beyond. I must give them *both* up. I must cut off, cut away, and become *another person*.

Quelconque une solitude
Sans le cygne ni le quai
Mire sa désuétude
Au regard que j'abdiquai

Ici de la gloriole
Haute à ne le pas toucher
Dont maint ciel se bariole
Avec les ors de coucher

Mais langoureusement longe
Comme de blanc linge ôté
Tel fugace oiseau si plonge
Exultatrice à côté

Dans l'onde toi devenue
Ta jubilation nue.

'What is the subject of *longe*?' asked Father Bernard. By this time he was becoming rather confused himself.

Hattie suggested '*solitude*'. This had not occurred to Father Bernard. He said, 'Oh, not *oiseau*?'

'Could be *oiseau*,' Hattie said politely.

He had reflected with interest, even with a little excitement, upon the prospect of meeting Miss Meynell and examining her to see what stuff she was made of, since thus he interpreted John Robert's vague idea. He thought, the great man has no conception of the girl, doesn't know what on earth to do with her. He can't go on hiding her away in a boarding school, he has to make a decision but doesn't know how to. All right, I'll have a look at her at least. But I shall leave him in no doubt about his responsibilities! I'm not going to be saddled with her!

Having accepted the idea that he was to 'examine' Miss Meynell, Father Bernard felt at a loss how to proceed. He decided to be frank, to explain that he was not in any sense her 'tutor', and that he simply wanted to explore with her, if he could, the subjects which she had found interesting at school, testing her in a friendly way so as to give a helpful report to her grandfather. 'Not mathematics,' he added, laughing, at which he had been a perfect dunce. Miss Meynell, not admitting to having been a dunce, agreed it was unnecessary to discuss this subject. She received him nervously and, when the 'visitors' had gone, ushered him into the sitting-room. The maid, a girl with an interesting head, looked in to ask if they wanted coffee, which they did not. When Father Bernard had explained his plan, Miss Meynell became quiet and business-like. He had already had a surprise. He had expected a big loutish 'grown-up' girl, 'all over the place', but this small, quiet creature was both more childish and more composed than his picture of an 'American teenager'.

He began by asking her to make a *précis* of the leading article in *The Times*, which, together with some books, he had brought with him. This she did creditably, saying that they often did *précis* at school. He then inquired whether she knew any foreign languages, and when she admitted to German asked if she could speak it at all, at which she uttered a fluent outburst of remarks which he could not altogether follow. Hastily leaving German, he inquired about her Italian. Yes, Miss Meynell knew some Italian. Father Bernard, leaving Clergy House in a hurry, had picked up his copy of Dante, and now turned, with new-found caution, to a passage which he knew well in the third Canto of the *Inferno*. '*Per me si va nella città dolente, per me si va nell'eterno dolore, per me si va tra la perduta gente . . .*' It was only when he had the book open that he realized with a curious pang, even with a sort of fright, that the passage he had chosen contained the terrible words which John Robert had uttered in condemnation of George McCaffrey: a condemnation now seen to be of such resonance and such finality, and against which, as Father Bernard had known at the time, and knew now with an added poignancy, he ought instantly to have protested. He asked Hattie to read the first fifty lines of the canto in Italian, which she did readily and with an expression which declared her understanding. She then proceeded to an occasionally hesitant but accurate translation. Dante and Virgil have passed the gate to hell but have not yet crossed Acheron. In this no man's land, rejected both by heaven and hell, Dante gets his first glimpse of tormented people, and is duly horrified. (He was to see worse. Did he get used to it?) 'Who are these people so overcome by pain?' Virgil replies that 'this is the miserable condition of wretched souls who lived without disgrace and without praise. Mixed with them are the vile angels who are neither rebels nor loyal to God, but were for themselves.' 'Master, what makes them cry out so terribly?' 'They have no hope of death, and their blind life is so abject that they envy every other lot. Mercy and justice alike despise them. *Non ragioniam di lor, ma guarda e passa.* Do not let us speak of them; just look and pass by.' How terrible, Father Bernard thought, that this ferocious judgement and those words should have come spontaneously into John Robert's mind when Father Bernard wanted to talk about George; and the priest felt a sudden rage, almost a hatred, rising in him against the philosopher, and mingling with the lurid and exalted emotions aroused by the fierce words of the great poet.

'Do you believe in hell, Miss Meynell?'

'Please call me Hattie. I'm Harriet – but that's what they call me – Hattie.'

'Do you believe in hell, Hattie?'

'No. I don't believe in God and the after life. I'm sorry.'

Father Bernard did not think it consistent with his tutelary role to say that he did not either. He said, 'We are subject to time. We cannot conceive of eternity. All we can know of hell is what happens to us in the present. If there is hell it is now.'

'You mean people live now in hell? You mean like – hungry people?'

'I mean like evil people.'

'But the people here weren't evil, were they?'

'No, but then they weren't quite in hell, were they?'

'It seemed awful enough,' said Hattie. She added, 'I feel so sorry for poor Virgil being drawn into that *terrible* world.'

'You mean the Christian world?'

'Well – yes –'

Father Bernard laughed and patted her hand as he took the book from her. They left the theological discussion at that point and proceeded to the French language, and it was here that Father Bernard found himself in really deep water. He had brought a few books of French poetry with him including Mallarmé, whom he now picked up and opened more or less at random. He had intended to choose a less difficult poem, but the book had opened automatically at one of his favourites, and he had laid it on the table between them. Looking at it now, he realized that although he could 'sort of' understand the poem, and liked it very much, he could not construe it.

Neither, of course, could Hattie, who had never seen the poem before.

Hattie's attempt at a literal translation began: 'A sort of solitude without a, or the, swan or quay reflects its disuse in the look which I abdicated, or removed, from the glorious – no, the vanity – so high it can't be touched, with which many skies streak themselves with the golds of sunset, but languidly wanders like white linen taken off a sort of fugitive bird if it plunges –' By the time Hattie had broken down here they were both laughing.

'It's impossible!'

'You read it aloud as if you understood!'

'Well it's beautiful – but whatever does it mean?'

260

'What do you think it's about, what sort of scene is the poet evoking?'

Hattie looked silently at the text, while Father Bernard admired her smooth boyish neck over which tendrils of pale-fair hair from the complex bun were distractedly straying.

'I don't know,' she said. 'Since he says there is *no* swan and *no* quay, I suppose it might be a river?'

'Good deduction. After all it's a poem!'

'And there's a wave at the end.'

'And – *nue*?'

'Someone naked, perhaps someone swimming naked.'

'Yes. It's like a puzzle picture, isn't it.'

'He's turning away from the *gloriole* that means sort of false showy something, doesn't it, which is too high to touch compared with – no, well – and the bird can't be the subject because then *longe* wouldn't be right – I think – so I suppose *regard* is the subject – but –'

'Oh never mind about the subject –'

'But I *do* mind! The solitude, the *uninteresting* solitude, reflects its swanless desolation in the look which he had turned away from the false glory, too high to touch, with which many skies dapple themselves in sunset golds – perhaps he thinks sunsets are vulgar – then, or *but* why but? – something or other, either his look on a fugitive bird, no I see, his gaze coasts languidly, no, languorously, along like white linen taken off – that can't be right – has *longe* got an object, could it be the bird? – perhaps the bird is like the linen, maybe it's a white bird that plunges – like the – the clothes which – no, no, surely the jubilation plunges – and the languorous gaze coasts along the jubilation – I mean – then "but" would have sense – it's all rather dull until my gaze languorously – no – if a (but why if?), if a bird plunges like white linen taken off, my gaze languorously follows, exulting beside me, or it, in the wave that you have become, your naked jubilation – oh *dear*! that can't be right –'

Hattie had become quite excited. With one hand she absently pulled the hairpins out of her hair, gathered the mass of silky silver-yellow stuff together, and pushed it all down the back of her dress.

Father Bernard was excited too, but not by the grammatical quest. He had never, he now realized, subjected the poem to the sort of scrutiny which even Hattie's jumbled commentary comprised. What was the subject of what? Who cared? The general sense of the poem was perfectly clear to him, or rather he had made his own sense and hallowed it long ago.

He said, 'Let's get the general picture. You said there was a river and someone swimming naked. How many people are there in the poem?'

Hattie replied, 'Two. The speaker and the swimmer.'

'Good. And who are they?'

'Who are they? Oh, well, I suppose the poet and some friend –'

Father Bernard's imagination had, in taking charge of the poem, taken advantage of the fact that the sex of the swimmer was not specified. In the blessed free-for-all of fantasy he had pictured the charming companion, whose underwear slides off with the languid ease of a bird's flight, as a boy. The final image was particularly precious to him of the young thing diving in and rising into the wave of his plunge, tossing back his wet hair and laughing. And all about, the green river bank, the sunshine, the warmth, the solitude . . .

'Do you think it's a love poem?' he asked her.

'Well, it could be.'

'How can it not be?' he almost cried. He thought, she is unawakened. 'The poet is with his –' he checked himself.

'Girl friend, I suppose,' said Hattie stiffly. She was feeling shocked at Father Bernard's evident indifference to the pleasure of finding out main verbs and what agrees with what; and she had not failed to notice his dismay at her outburst of German.

'Girl friend! What a phrase. He is with his mistress.'

'Why not his wife?' said Hattie. 'Was he married?'

'Yes, but that doesn't matter. This is a poem. We don't want wives in poems. He is with a lovely young woman –'

'How do you know she's lovely?'

'I know. Just *see* the picture.'

Hattie said more kindly, 'Yes, I think I can – it's like that picture by Renoir – *La baigneuse au griffon* – only there – well, there are two girls, not a man and a girl.'

This did not interest Father Bernard, at any rate he did not pursue it, but the evocation of the lush greenery and the Impressionist painter accorded with his racing mood. 'Yes, yes, it's sunny and green and the river is glittering and the sunshine is coming through the leaves and dappling, that was a good word you used, the naked form of the –'

'The sun doesn't dapple the girl, it's the *gloriole*, no it's the sky or skies that dapple themselves with –'

'Never mind, you must get the sense of the whole – the linen, white like the bird, slips away –' The image which had now, with magisterial charm, risen up in the priest's mind, lily-pale and glowing with youth, was that of Tom McCaffrey.

At about the same time that Father Bernard was taking liberties (and they went rather far) with the shade of Tom McCaffrey, the real Tom, standing in Greg and Ju's sitting-room in the house in Travancore Avenue, was gazing with puzzlement and alarm at a letter which he had just found lying upon the door mat. It had been sent by post to Belmont, whence it had evidently been redelivered by hand. It read as follows:

>   16 Hare Lane
>   Burkestown
>   Ennistone
>
> Dear Mr McCaffrey,
>   I wonder if you would be so good as to come round and see me, as soon as is convenient, at this address? There is something which I want to ask you. During the next few days, I shall be at home until midday.
>   Yours sincerely
>   J. R. Rozanov
>
> P.S. I would be grateful if you would treat this request as a matter of confidence.

Tom's first thought, when he saw the startling signature, was that, of course, the letter was intended for George. He inspected the envelope again, where John Robert had certainly and clearly written 'Thomas McCaffrey', to which he had ridiculously added 'Esquire'.

Scarlett-Taylor came in. Tom handed him the letter. 'What do you think of this?'

Emma read the letter, frowned, and returned it to Tom. 'You've let him down already.'

'What do you mean?'

'He asked you to treat it as a matter of confidence. Now you've shown it to me.'

'Oh well – yes – but –'

'Fortunately for you, I shall observe perfect discretion about your lapse.'

'He asked me to treat it as a matter of confidence, but I didn't say I would –'

'Any gentleman would respond –'

'Damn it, I only got it a minute ago.'

'I fail to see what difference that makes.'

'I didn't have time to think!'

'That shows that you are instinctively irresponsible, you cannot even be trusted for a minute.'

'You're romantic about him, you wish he wanted to see you.'

'Don't be a perfect fool.'

'You're jealous!'

'You're childish!'

'You're sulky.'

'Do you want a punch?'

'You wouldn't punch anybody.'

'Couldn't I –'

'I said you wouldn't, not couldn't. Emma, don't be cross with me – you aren't cross, are you? We can't quarrel, we *can't* quarrel, *we* can't –'

Since the occasion of Tom's momentous visit to Emma's room, an uneasy odd relationship had existed between them. That, the visit, had been something noumenal, as if they had slipped out of time, out of ordinary individual being. They had not made love in any of the rather *mechanical* senses in which Tom had hitherto understood a *making* of love. It was rather that, instantly, they had become love. For Tom it was like being embraced by an angel, being inescapably held between the wings of an angel who was and was not Emma. This enfolding was perfect happiness, perfect bliss, perfect unproblematic, undramatic sexual joy. Tom could not remember having, after Emma took him in his arms, moved *at all*. As he recalled it, they had both lain, gripped together, absolutely motionless, in a spellbound ecstatic trance, perfectly relaxed yet also in extreme tension, in a holdingness of immense urgent power. In this entranced state Tom had fallen asleep. He had awakened near dawn and was at once aware of where he was and that Emma, still utterly close to him but no longer holding, was awake too. As soon as Emma felt Tom awakening he murmured to him, 'Go, Tom, go.'

Tom instantly and obediently left Emma's bed and returned to his own where he fell at once into a blissful deep happy sleep from which he did not emerge until after eight o'clock.

He dressed quickly and ran out to the kitchen where he could already hear breakfast sounds. Emma, frying sausages, gave him a glance and a curt good morning. Emma, dressed in his suit, complete with waistcoat and watch chain, with his narrow rimless spectacles, looked alien, almost forbidding.

Tom said hello and sat down at the kitchen table. Then he got up and laid the table and fetched fruit juice from the fridge. He was given two sausages, said thank you, and ate them. Emma drank some fruit juice but did not eat or say anything or look at Tom.

At last Tom had said, 'Thank you very very much for last night. But you're angry with me.'

Emma said, 'Last night was *unique*.' After this he got up and went away into his room.

When he had gone Tom felt a dark, dense anguish curiously shot with joy. Later Emma emerged from his room and made some quite ordinary remarks and generally signalled the resumption of ordinary life, which Tom, rather to his surprise, found himself able to join in resuming. Since then they had carried on as before and yet not as before. There were no strange looks or new and unusual touches or contacts. It was rather as if they both moved more gracefully in an enlarged space. There was a new consciousness in the air; but this remained vague, and Emma's occasional 'sulks' did not seem different in quantity or quality. At bedtime on the next day it had been somehow clear that Tom was to occupy his own bed and not Emma's. Tom was not upset. He lay in his bed and laughed quietly. And in the days that followed, during which 'that night' was not referred to, he was not unhappy. He felt a diffused excitement, a sort of secretive tenderness, which increased his bodily well-being and his natural cheerfulness. Today (the day of the arrival of John Robert Rozanov's letter) Emma had been especially testy and touchy, but still without making any allusion to their 'happening'. Would it now, Tom wondered, disappear undiscussed into the past, and become like a dream, gradually unhappening into oblivion?

'Are you going?' said Emma.

'To see Professor Rozanov? Certainly I am. Wouldn't you? I'm dying with curiosity.'

'You could go now, this morning. It's not eleven yet. How long would it take you to get there?'

'Twenty minutes. Whatever can it be? Could it be something *awful*?'

'You mean like his having secretly married your mother?'

Tom began to laugh, then abruptly stopped. Good heavens! That he could not *endure*; but of course it was only a joke –

Emma went on. 'Don't worry, if he had he would say "I have something to tell you", not "I have something to ask you".'

'But what can he want to ask?'

'Something about George?'

Tom felt suddenly disappointed, then frightened. 'God. I hope not. I don't want to muck around with George's emotions. I mean – Christ, I hope George doesn't find out I've been visiting his guru – that *would* be trouble.'

'You haven't visited him yet. Maybe it would be wise not to go.'

'Oh I'm going! I'm going now!'

'You ought to shave.'

Tom ran to the bathroom and shaved carefully and combed his hair.

'*And* put on a tie.'

Emma was looking round the bathroom door and Tom could now see Emma's face wearing its old familiar quizzical mocking look. He turned and went to his friend and put his arms around his neck.

'Emma, all right, I'm not going to talk about it if you don't want, but something or other did occur, heavens knows what, and I just want you to know that I'm not worrying about it at all and that the most important aspect of the matter as far as I'm concerned is that I love you.'

'I love you too, you dope, but nothing follows from that except that.'

'Well, isn't that rather a lot? And that night –'

'A *hapax legomenon*.'

'What's that?'

'Something that only occurs once.'

'You mean like the birth of Jesus Christ?'

'Don't be damn silly about this –'

'Well, the world can be changed –'

'Oh just shut up, will you. Put a tie on.'

Tom found a tie. 'Do you think I should clean my shoes?'

'No. You aren't visiting God.'

'Oh. Aren't I? Will you walk with me?'

'No. Clear off.'

*

266

By the time Tom McCaffrey had reached John Robert Rozanov's door he had worked himself up into a fair fever. He had pictured every sort of embarrassing, maddening, painful, disastrous business involving George, Rozanov, and himself. Rozanov wanted him to tell George never to communicate with him again. Rozanov wanted him to console George and ask him not to be too upset because Rozanov was too busy to see him any more. (Tom could imagine how George would greet such an embassy.) Rozanov wanted him to instruct George to print some public amendment of some article in which George had misrepresented or plagiarized Rozanov. Trying in desperation to think of something that Rozanov might want which was *not* connected with George, his disturbed fantasy put forward the idea that perhaps John Robert was about to reveal that he was really Tom's father! Tom had never entertained this speculation before and did not now entertain it for long. It was promptly driven from his head by the indignant shade of Alan McCaffrey, assisted by that of Fiona Gates. Love for his parents suddenly filled Tom's soul, disturbing him even more. And these two, as they had always been, comforting and benign ghosts, gave Tom a heightened sense of the vulnerability of happiness and of how dangerous and unpredictable and just bloody tiresomely powerful this eccentric philosopher might prove to be.

Arrived at the door of 16 Hare Lane, he dabbed nervously at the bell, which made a tiny grunt. He pushed it again harder and longer and produced a loud impertinent hiss. The door opened instantly and was filled by the stout burly form of the philosopher.

John Robert said nothing, but stepped awkwardly backward into the dark hall to make way for Tom who stepped awkwardly forward into the space. John Robert then moved backwards, followed by Tom, to the door of the sitting-room, then turned his back on the boy and blundered forward into the room.

Outside, a brilliant April light dazzlingly displayed blue sky, fast white cloudlets, the Cox's Orange tormented by wind, a disconsolate fence with slats missing, unkempt ruffled damp grass. The room by contrast was dark, low-ceilinged and narrow, the tiny grate and mantelpiece like a slit.

John Robert said, 'Please sit down. Please – sit – down –'

Tom took in two hopeless slumping low-slung armchairs, and since he had to obey the command rapidly, reached out and seized from beside John Robert an extremely rickety upright chair which he placed on a black lumpy rug beside the fireplace and sat down.

John Robert looked at the armchairs, made as if to sit on the arm of one and decided not to. Tom leapt up.

'No – you sit – I'll – there's another chair – in the hall –'

John Robert pushed past Tom who was still standing, and returned with another upright chair which he put with its back to the window. He then closed the door into the hall. They both sat down.

Tom felt he should say something, so said 'Good morning', which sounded rather stilted. He had not only never spoken to Rozanov before, he had never been at close quarters with him or had an opportunity to inspect his face. This in fact was difficult to do now with the dazzling light behind, and the moving clouds making the room seem to tilt like a ship laid over.

'Mr McCaffrey,' said the philosopher. 'I hope very much that you will excuse the liberty – if it is a liberty – of my asking you to hear – what I want to say –'

Tom felt a pang of fear which he had recognized as a pang of *guilt*. It had not occurred to him in his imaginings as he walked along that John Robert might want to *accuse* him of something. What had he done? What *could* he have done, to harm, hurt, annoy, incense this great man – or to make the great man imagine that he had been harmed or hurt and could justly be annoyed or incensed? Tom searched his conscience, at once a prey to vague huge remorse. Where in his imperfect conduct could this fault lie? Did John Robert think that Tom had encouraged George to – or told George that –? But almost at once, as he confusedly accused himself of he knew not what, he was aware that John Robert was himself upset, perhaps even nervous.

'Please –' said Tom, 'there's nothing you could – I mean if there's anything – I could do – or –'

'There is,' said Rozanov, 'something that you could do –' He stared at Tom, wrinkling up his pitted brow, his big moist prehensile lips thrust forward.

Tom thought: Oh God. It *is* about George.

'Before I explain – or at any rate – before I – introduce – what I want to – I hope you will not mind if I ask you a few simple questions.'

'No.'

'And may I say, as I said in my letter, that I desire – indeed I require – that you should regard everything that is said in this room as strictly confidential, or to use a simpler and stronger word, as a *secret*. You understand what that means?'

'Yes.'

'You will not speak of this conversation with *anybody*?'

'Yes. I mean no, I won't –' It did not occur to Tom to query this requirement, which after all, since nothing had yet been revealed, might have seemed unreasonable, so much was he already under the spell of the philosopher. In any case, he would have promised as much and more at that moment, so great was his curiosity.

'I want to ask you, then, these questions, which I believe you will answer truthfully.'

'Yes – yes –'

'How old are you?'

'Twenty.'

'And in good health? Well, obviously you are.'

'Yes.' Tom thought, he wants me to go on an expedition to find something, buried treasure in California, for instance.

'You are at the university in London?'

'Yes.'

'What are you studying?'

'English.'

'Do you enjoy your work?'

'Yes, on the whole.'

'What sort of degree will you get?'

'Second-class.'

'How will you earn your living?'

'I don't know yet.'

'What would you like to do?'

'I'd like to be a writer.'

'A writer?'

Tom thought, he wants me to write his biography! What perfect fun, trips to America –

'What have you written so far?'

'Oh, just poems and one or two stories –'

'Have you published anything?'

'Just one poem in the *Ennistone Gazette*. But of course, I think I could write *anything* – I'm interested in biography –'

'You don't want to be a philosopher, do you?'

'No – no, I don't.'

'Good. Would you say that you were a cheerful person?'

'Oh yes. I think I'd be a good travelling companion.'

'A good travelling companion.' John Robert was interested in this point.

'Oh yes, I'm awfully good-tempered and practical –' John Robert and Tom, his biographer, secretary, his privileged aide, travelling about America, but the world, together ... George would be furious. Oh God, George. But could it all be somehow about George after all? Perhaps he wants me to be George's *keeper*? Tom gazed fascinated at John Robert's huge face and fierce yellow-brown eyes and red lips pouting with will.

'Your family are Quakers. Do you practise your religion?'

'I go to Meeting – to the Quaker Meeting – sometimes. It means something to me.'

'Did you go last Sunday?'

'Yes.'

'Good. Are you engaged to be married?'

'No. Certainly not.'

'Are you – please excuse these questions – but – well – are you living with a young lady?'

'No.'

Tom's mind switched back to buried treasure. An adventure, a quest. Good. A dangerous one? Not so good. Suddenly he thought, he wants to recruit me for the Secret Service! That's what all this 'confidential' business is about! I'll say no. I couldn't stand *that*. But it's exciting all the same, and jolly flattering really!

'But you have done – I mean – you have had – sexual experience?'

'Yes, but not much, and not now.' Unless what happened last Sunday night counted?

'Are you heterosexual?'

'Yes.' Tom thought, that settles it, it must be the Secret Service. It's true I'm heterosexual. But suppose he asks if I'm homosexual too?

This question did not occur to John Robert. He pondered. Tom had begun to feel, staring at the philosopher and distinguishing his face from the light behind, slightly giddy. The dazzling white clouds were driving the narrow tilting ship-room swiftly along. John Robert's face, huge with command and troubled concentration, was difficult to keep in focus. Tom thought, he is coming to the point, whatever in heaven and earth the point may be. He could hear his own fast breathing and Rozanov's.

'I imagine you know that I have a grand-daughter, Harriet Meynell.'

This took Tom completely by surprise. He had not heard the local gossip. He was vaguely aware that such a person existed, but

270

he had never seen her or thought about her and felt extremely vague about her age. He thought, does he want me to take her on visits to the Natural History Museum? Jesus, how can I get out of this?

'Yes.'

'She is seventeen.'

This put a slightly different complexion on the matter. Was he to show her round London, take her to *Hamlet*? Where was she anyway? He said, 'Is she in America?'

'No, she is in Ennistone, at the Slipper House. Didn't you know that I have rented the Slipper House from your mother?'

'No.' Tom did not feel bound to go into his relationship, incomprehensible to himself, with Alex.

'She is there with her maid,' said John Robert with a ridiculous solemnity.

'Oh – good –'

'She has never been in Ennistone before.'

'I could show her the town, if that's what you want –' Or was the weird old codger merely chatting?

'I want you to meet her, to get to know her.'

'And introduce her to some young people? I could do that. I could give a party for her.' Already Tom was planning whom he would invite.

'I don't want her to meet anybody else. Only you.'

'But why – why only me?'

'Only you.' John Robert was breathing audibly through his mouth which he had opened wide, and was gazing at Tom with a look which seemed like hatred but was no doubt only the result of concentration. Being so concentrated upon was beginning to give Tom a panicky feeling of being trapped. He wanted to get up and lean on the mantelpiece, or open the door into the hall. But he could not move. He was fixed by John Robert's glare and John Robert's purpose.

'Perhaps you could *explain*,' said Tom, trying to sound forceful but sounding timid.

'She needs a protector.'

'Oh, I'll protect her – I mean when I'm here – I'm usually not here. I can protect her for a fortnight.'

'I shall require more than that.'

Tom thought, he is mad, he is totally unhinged. He is mad, and yet he is not mad. As he underwent the philosopher's gaze Tom felt

271

rather mad himself as if he might suddenly have to get up and go to John Robert and *touch* him.

'I've got to go back to London and – and work –' said Tom. 'I can't sort of – do you mean a sort of chaperone? I'm not the person you want.' As he said this he felt a sudden pain, as if to be separated from John Robert forever, after this conversation, would be terrible anguish! Is he hypnotizing me? Tom wondered.

'You *are* the person I want.'

'But what to do, what for –'

'I don't want a lot of people, a lot of men –'

'A lot of men?'

'Vying – for my grand-daughter.'

The word 'vying' sounded so odd and foreign to Tom as John Robert said it that Tom could hardly for a moment understand it.

Tom said, 'She's only seventeen! And anyway, why not? Am I supposed to keep them off?'

'She is nearly eighteen.'

'Then can't she look after herself? Girls can these days. If you want a chaperone, can't her maid do it?'

'You ask if you are supposed to keep them off. Yes. I want that to be – clear.'

'But how can it be! I can't devote the rest of my life to her!'

John Robert was silent, leaning back now and staring.

What *is* this that I'm being turned into, this *task* that is being *forced* on me, Tom thought. Shall I go, shall I *run*? Shall I suddenly be *bloody rude*? He could not. He said, leaning forward and speaking gently as to a child, 'Do you want me to sleep in front of her door?'

'No.'

'Do you want me to be her brother?'

'No. I do *not* want you to sleep in front of her door, I do *not* want you to be her brother.'

Tom took in the emphasis. 'Whatever do you want then?'

'I want you to marry her.'

John Robert rose to his feet, and Tom, as the philosopher's huge form blocked the light, sprang up too and retreated to lean against the flimsy shiny little sideboard. They remained so, John Robert staring open-mouthed and Tom gazing at the blurred image of the philosopher's head, beyond which the cold brilliant sun was shining on the agitated branches of the apple tree. Then, as if there was nothing else to do, they both sat down again. Tom found that his heart was racing and that he was blushing violently. He thought, I didn't know that one could blush from *fear*.

John Robert, as if what he had just said was something perfectly ordinary, went on, 'I shall settle some money upon her, not a great sum. I hope, of course, that she will go on to the university if she proves able to. Marriage should not interfere with that.'

'But I don't want to marry her! I don't want to marry anybody!'

'You haven't even met her yet.' John Robert said 'even' in a tone which suggested that he had understood Tom to say the exact opposite of what he had said.

'But I don't want to meet her, I have to go back to London tomorrow –'

'Surely that is not so.'

'All right, it isn't, but –'

'I would be glad if we could arrange now –'

'But *why*, what is this, why me, what about her, she's a child, she won't want to marry, and if she does she won't want to marry me. I mean things aren't like that –'

'Oftener than we think,' said the philosopher, 'we can make things be the way we desire.'

'But why – why *marry* her?'

'Do you suppose that I am simply inviting you to seduce her?'

Tom felt positively guilty before John Robert's indignant look. Was he then already so far entangled that he could be accused of some sort of levity? It had occurred to his confused mind that John Robert was some sort of crazy *voyeur*. He seemed to be *offering* Tom his grand-daughter, but with what motive? He was a madman from California, a dangerous *crazy* man. But Tom was, at that moment, too dominated by John Robert, too much under the spell of his high serious tone, to be able to see his proposal in any crudely sinister light. He did, however, very much wish that he was somewhere else, that he was *free* again as he had been.

'Look,' said Tom, 'let's take this slowly. I mean, what's this idea for?'

'I should have thought,' said the philosopher, 'that it was clear what I wanted. In many parts of the world marriages are arranged. I am attempting to arrange this one.'

'But –'

'It is often said that an arranged marriage gives the best hope of happiness.'

'Not for liberated people. I mean she hasn't grown up in purdah!'

'She has had a very sheltered upbringing,' John Robert said primly.

'Yes, but that's not a reason – really I – *why* try to arrange this –?'

'I want to see her settled.'

Tom thought, he wants to *get rid* of the child, he wants to *palm her off* on someone he thinks he can intimidate! He said, 'But why choose me? I told you I was going to get a second class degree.'

'A middling talent makes a more serene life.'

Tom, incensed, said, 'But I might become a great writer, and you know how selfish writers are.'

John Robert replied gloomily, 'Some risks must be taken.'

'But the world is full of young men – what about your pupils – there must be someone –?'

'I do not think a philosopher would be suitable.'

'Why, are philosophers under a curse?'

John Robert took this exclamation seriously. 'Yes.'

'All right, but there are plenty of men around who are not philosophers! You must have had some positive idea in your head when you selected me. Or have you already tried dozens –?'

'No! Only you.'

'But why –?'

John Robert hesitated. Then he said, 'There are, it is true, accidental features involved. No doubt I could have made a more – a more brilliant choice, if I may put it so. But if I had made a contest of all the world I would have consumed time and probably bred confusion. I want it all to be simple.'

'Simple! I was available and you thought I'd agree!'

'I thought,' said John Robert, 'that you – I have the impression that you – I have been told that you have a happy temperament. I wonder if you realize how rare that is?'

'No – yes – but –'

'I want my grand-daughter to be happy.'

'Yes, of course, but –'

'You seem to be a clean-living young man.' Echoes of John Robert's Methodist childhood, and some American campuses, were in the tone of this utterance, which sounded to Tom, although it had some echoes for him too, utterly ridiculous in the context.

'But I said I'd had girls!'

'Some experience is desirable. I assume you are not promiscuous.'

'No, I'm not,' said Tom, though he was not sure just what standard of clean-living he was thereby claiming.

'There you are then,' said John Robert, as if this finally proved Tom's suitability for and acceptance of his plan. 'I do not want her,' he went on, 'to enter a world of vulgar sexuality. I want her innocence to be respected. I want a simple clear arrangement, without – confused situations or – false melodrama.'

'I appreciate,' said Tom, picking up John Robert's measured tone, 'that you do not want to *waste your time* on this matter. I am sure you have a great many *more important things* to do. You want to get all this fixed up and *finished with*!'

John Robert ignored or perhaps did not notice the sarcasm. He said, 'Finished with, yes. Some money will, of course, come with her, as I told you.' The 'of course' was uttered as to an established suitor. He added, 'I need hardly mention that *she* has had no experience – she is – a virgin.'

Tom felt that he was being steadily entangled simply by forms of words. He looked away from the philosopher's face and gazed, blinking, out of the window. He saw, two or three gardens away in the middle distance, a man in a tree. The man was sitting astride a branch and holding something, perhaps a saw. Tom immediately thought about Christ entering Jerusalem. There must be some picture, he thought, where there is a man up a tree watching Christ passing by. How ludicrous and weird it is that I am sitting here and watching a man up a tree while I try to think what to say to this perfect lunatic. How can I get *out*? Of course it was all crazy, but he must be polite to the old eccentric. And of course it was, in a way, flattering . . . and awfully interesting . . .

He closed his eyes, then looked down at the threadbare red-and-blue Axminster carpet which at once began dancing and jumping before his gaze. Now the blue was the background, now the red was. The carpet was flashing at him like a lighthouse.

'Well?' said John Robert.

'Have you told *her* –?' Tom was endeavouring to focus once more upon the big face which now seemed to overhang the room like a pendent rock. John Robert seemed to be getting larger. Soon he would resemble Polyphemus.

'No, of course not,' said John Robert, as if this were obvious.

'Why not?'

'When and if you agree, I shall inform her.'

'But I can't agree, it isn't possible –'

'In that case I will ask you to go. I am sorry I have taken up your time.'

275

'Wait a minute –' I can't go now, thought Tom in anguish, I *can't*! He said, 'She won't like me, why should she? And perhaps I won't like her – and anyway it's daft.'

'Naturally,' said John Robert, 'I do not expect you to promise to succeed. I doubt if, except in certain simple cases, it is conceptually possible to promise to succeed.' He paused for a moment to consider this, then went on, 'I want you to promise to try.' He added, 'I should *require* you to promise to try.'

Tom plunged his hands into his curly hair and pulled. 'But you can't control people like this –'

'I can attempt to. You are perfectly free to say no, and if you do meet her you are both perfectly free to decide against the plan. In which case I shall try again.'

'With another man.'

'Yes.'

'Oh God!'

'I do not see,' said John Robert, 'that I am proposing anything particularly unreasonable. Nobody is being forced to do anything.'

I am, thought Tom. It must be hypnosis. He said, scarcely crediting his own words, 'May I think it over?'

'No. Either you agree now to meet her with a view to marriage –'

'How can I meet her with a view to marriage? I've never seen her, she's seventeen, I'm twenty, it's not – it's not the picture, it's not the scene –'

'All right, then I bid you farewell. I am grateful to you for having come.'

'No, *no*, this is most unfair, how can I say – it's all so extraordinary –'

'I should have thought the situation was fairly clear. You don't have to do anything except be serious.'

'But I can't just make myself be your sort of serious, I mean taking this as serious –'

'Come, Mr McCaffrey, you do not think that I am jesting.'

'No, of course not, I just mean –'

'As I say, you can try. You can keep the end in view. I should add that if you decide at this stage to proceed no further then I must request you to make another promise.'

'Another promise?'

'You have already promised not to reveal to anyone what has passed between us today.'

'Have I? Well, yes –'

'I must also ask you to promise, should you decide not to proceed in this matter, not ever to meet or become acquainted with Miss Meynell.'

'But how can –'

'And, should you try and fail, you must engage never to see or approach her again.'

'I don't see –'

'You are not a fool. You must understand the point of these requests.'

'Oh – yes – I suppose so –'

'Well, will you make the attempt?'

The phrase 'make the attempt' rang in Tom's ears like the rattle of a chain – or was it more like a bugle call? He thought, is this madman carefully and by magical words, by little planned psychological movements, making me his prisoner? Or is it all random and crazy? Will what I say have consequences? Should he, he wondered, see it as a trap, or as an ordeal, a quest? Why should he accept such a ridiculous *uncanny* sort of plan? Except that ... he could not by now perhaps bear not to ... *could* he, in leaving the room, just leave it all behind? All sorts of emotions which he could not understand were already engaged.

Tom said desperately, just to gain a few seconds more time, 'But do you really mean it – everything that you've said?'

'Don't ask idle questions. Concentrate your mind.'

Tom thought, *am* I being hypnotized? Am I going to undertake this insane business just to oblige him, just to obey him, just, oh heavens, *not to be separated from him*? He said, 'All right, I'll try.'

John Roberts gave a long sigh. He said, 'Good – good – that's settled then.'

'But,' Tom gabbled, 'it'll be no use, it's certain not to work, she won't like me, we're bound to dislike each other, it's all impossible, we won't get on, she'll hate the idea –'

'You have agreed to try, further speculation is pointless. You will of course speak of this conversation to no one. And when you approach her, use every discretion. This is not an escapade. There must be nothing noisy, nothing public.'

'But people will know I've met her –'

'There is no need for this to become a subject of gossip. I desire that it should not. The Slipper House is secluded.'

The phrase sent Tom's imagination reeling. 'All right, but –'

'Am I to infer from the fact that you seemed unaware of Miss Meynell's arrival that you are not staying at Belmont?'

'No. I'm at 41 Travancore Avenue. Down the Tweed Mill end.'

John Robert wrote the address down in a notebook. 'And now,' he said, 'it is time for me to go to the Institute. We will not walk together.'

'But, wait, what am I to do, what do you want me to do, will you take me to her?' Like mating dogs, he thought.

'I shall have nothing more to do with the matter.'

'Nothing more to –?'

'You will make your own arrangements about meeting her.'

'But you'll tell her?'

'Yes –'

'But how am I to do it?'

'I leave that to your – experience.'

John Robert had risen and Tom stumbled up. He watched the philosopher put on his overcoat and gloves and a brown woollen cap which he pulled down over his ears.

Tom realized there was something that he had not asked and which in so dangerous a situation it would be as well to have clarified. 'Can we – suppose we – well – make love – people do now when they're not sure – and then she decides not –'

The question seemed to annoy, even dismay, John Robert. This possibility was evidently new to his imagination. He frowned. 'We need not look so far ahead.'

'But I'd like to know –'

'I have not enjoyed discussing this matter and I do not want to discuss it any further. We have said enough.' He spoke as if the whole disagreeable problem had been forced upon him by Tom.

Tom stood aside to let Rozanov sidle past him. They went into the hall where they stood awkwardly face to face for a moment. Rozanov was as tall as Tom. Tom smelt the philosopher's garments, a philosophical smell of sweat and thought. Rozanov fumbled behind him, undid the front door and backed out of it. Tom followed him out and closed the door.

'Now I go to the right and you go to the left. Remember your promises.'

The bulky man began to recede down the street until he came to Burkestown High Road and disappeared from view. Tom watched him go, then turned and walked in the other direction as far as the Green Man. The Green Man was open, but Tom did not go in. He was already like a drunken person, his head whirling and his heart dilated with a very queer mixture of pain and fear and joy. *Joy*? Why on earth joy? Was it simply that he was *flattered* by this amazing *attention*? He kept saying to himself, he's mad, it doesn't matter, it's not real, I'm not involved in *anything*! He walked beyond the pub, as far as the level crossing and watched a train go by. Then he turned back.

When Tom, on his way back to Travancore Avenue, had crossed the eighteenth-century bridge and got as far as the Crescent and reached the middle of the curve, he saw Scarlett-Taylor waiting for him at the other end. As he passed number 29, the home of the senior Osmores, Robin Osmore and his wife happened to be looking out of one of the tall windows of their handsome drawing-room on the first floor. Robin said, 'Why there's Tom McCaffrey. What a handsome boy he has grown up to be.'

Mrs Osmore said nothing. She resented the way in which everyone, even her husband, praised Tom as if, by common consent, he had been elected to be a sort of *hero*. He was no better-looking than Gregory and not half as clever. She mourned Gregory's absence and was permanently wounded by his imprudent marriage to that pert Judith Craxton child. Oh why had Greg not married Anthea Eastcote, as Mrs Osmore had a thousand times urged him to do, ever since they were children together at the Crescent play school? She was also annoyed that Gregory had lent his house to Tom without telling her (she learnt it at the Baths). She felt sure that Tom, who was so careless and thoughtless, would do the house some serious damage, perhaps burn it down. He might even wear Greg's clothes. It would all end in tears.

Meanwhile as, filled with foreboding and curiosity, Emma left the house and walked toward the Crescent whence Tom was likely to return, he had been reflecting on the mysterious nature of physical love. What after all does it consist in? What makes it *absolutely unlike* anything else at all? Suddenly the reorientation of the world round one illumined point, all else in shadow. The total alteration of corporeal being, the minute electric sensibility of the nerves, the tender expectancy of the skin. The omnipresence of a ghostly sense of touch. The awareness of organs. The absolute demand for the presence of the beloved, the categorical imperative, the haunting. The fire that burns, the sun that expands, the beauty

279

of all things. The certainty; and with it the great sad cool knowledge of change and decay. Emma was never on good terms with his own strong feelings, and with half of himself was determined not to love Tom, not to love him at all, since he was not yet *in* love. Even as he lay, he too, in the angelic clutch and felt Tom, with such wonderful trust, falling asleep in his arms, as he lay and held Tom feeling as protective as God and as all-powerful, while desire was blessedly diffused in a cloud of anguish, he was even then coldly planning how he would minimize, belittle and liquidate this happening as a part of his life, making it small and without consequence. He gloomily observed some utterly new happiness, something created *ex nihilo*, which had come to him and put its finger upon him. And when, this very morning, Tom had put his arms round his neck and cried 'I love you,' Emma had felt the joyful 'whiff of eternity' which accompanies any real love. But it would *not do*. He knew how impulsive and affectionate Tom was, how little perhaps it meant. Tom was a lover of all the world, constantly reaching out his warm hands to touch things and people. In any case, Tom was framed to delight in and be the delight of women. Maybe I'd better go to Brussels and see my mother, Emma thought. But he knew he would not.

'What happened?' said Emma. 'What did he want?'

'He wants me to marry his grand-daughter.'

'*What?* No. You're joking.'

'Honest! He wants to dispose of her, he wants to marry her off, and he's chosen ME! Isn't that crazy, isn't it a laugh?' And Tom laughed and continued to laugh as he took hold of his friend's arm and began to lead him back in the direction of Travancore Avenue.

Emma pulled away. 'But how – so you know this girl?'

'No! Never set eyes on her! I think she's never been here, she's been living in America.'

'He must be mad.'

'Mad as a hatter, crazy as a coot, nutty as a fruitcake! And fancy his wanting ME!'

'You told him politely to get lost.'

'No. I've agreed! The marriage is arranged! All I've got to do now is make her acquaintance! She's in Ennistone –'

'*Tom –*'

'He guaranteed she's a virgin, she's seventeen, he's going to settle some money on us, we shall buy a house in the Crescent –'

'Stop talking like that, damn you.'

'Don't be cross. Why, I believe you're jealous!'

This charge, whether seriously made or not, enraged Scarlett-Taylor. 'You're talking in a vile vulgar way which I resent!'

'Well, don't froth at the mouth, it's not my idea!'

'But of course you told him it was crazy, impossible –'

'I tried to, but he wouldn't listen. He said marriages were sometimes arranged and he was trying to arrange one. He said I was to go and see her and he'd tell her I was coming. He thinks he can make people do things. He can make people do things.'

'He can't make you marry his grand-daughter!'

'Can't he? Time will show. I've agreed to try.'

'You *agreed*? You agreed to something so absurd – so – so improper – so immoral?'

'I don't see what's immoral about it –'

'He's playing with you.'

'Oh, I assure you he was serious!'

'I mean one can't proceed like that, one can't do such things, a gentleman can't –'

'Why not, what are you getting at? I'm not sure I'm a gentleman anyway.'

'If you aren't I don't want anything more to do with you. And you oughtn't to have told me about it.'

'You oughtn't to have asked me!'

'You're right. I oughtn't to have asked you.'

'Don't be so bloody censorious then! Look, I just said I'd see her. He may be serious, but I'm not.'

'You're not *serious*?'

'You got so bothered when I said I'd agreed – now you're bothered because I say I haven't really!'

'You're deceiving him, you lied to him!'

'Are you on his side now?'

'I'm going back to London!' Emma stopped and actually stamped his foot, red in the face.

'Oh come now – stop it, Emma, we mustn't quarrel about this. I said I'd have a look at her. Why not? It seemed to me rather a lark.'

'A *lark*?'

'Well, why not? Come on, walk along with me, don't stand there in a rage.' They walked on.

'You ought to have said *no*, clearly and simply.'

'Why?'

'Because you can't *intend* to marry a seventeen-year-old girl you've never seen before. Think about her –'

'I can't, I don't know what she's like –'

'How will *she* feel about this? You'll simply upset her, you'll upset yourself, and make a horrible painful muddle, a horrible *moral* muddle, something disgusting and *vile*. How can you have been such a crazy irresponsible fool!'

'I can always say I've changed my mind. After all, I haven't *done* anything yet.'

'Thank heavens you haven't. You'll write and tell him it's off?'

'No, I don't think I will. Not yet anyway. I want to meet her. Why ever not?'

'I've told you why not.'

'I'm curious. Wouldn't you be? Let's go and look at her together. Only do stop being angry. You distress me when you're angry, you frighten me, and I don't like being distressed and frightened.'

'Leave me out. And don't expect me to help you later when you're wishing like hell you'd followed my advice!'

'Of course I shall expect you to help me! Calm down. Why are you so excited?'

But Tom was shaken by Emma's attack, not least because he saw the good sense in it. There *could* indeed be some sort of nasty mess: he preferred not to imagine the details. But he knew that he was caught; his curiosity, his vanity, a dotty sense of adventure, a sense of fate, urged him on. It was as if his *value* had been changed, and John Robert had made him a new person. How could he, having in his thought, even for this short time, *touched* this seventeen-year-old girl, *promise* as John Robert required (and he would have had to promise) not ever to come to know her? This prohibition alone was enough to 'set him on'. And if he refused, he could never now be as he was. Some uncanny magic was already at work. He might indeed regret having tried, but he would even more, and bitterly, regret having funked the challenge. If he refused he would 'lose' Rozanov: Rozanov whom even this morning he had cared nothing about, had lived contentedly without, and who now represented some sort of necessity. He was no longer free, he was even perhaps no longer innocent: no longer happy.

Emma said, 'And he told you not to tell anyone.'

'Yes.'

'You scoundrel.'

'You won't tell. It's like talking to myself or God. Come, let's make up, let's sing, let's sing that German round you taught me. I'll begin.'

Tom began to sing softly,

> 'Alles schweiget. Nachtigallen
> Locken mit süssen Melodien
> Tränen ins Auge
> Sehnsucht ins Herz.'

When he had sung the round through and started again Emma joined in, not using his full voice but with a high clear pure whispering sound. And by the time they turned into Travancore Avenue, although there were not positively tears in their eyes, there was a great deal of mournful yearning in their hearts.

'My God, it *is* snowing!'

An awful iron grey silence had possessed the town since early morning. The sky, appearing like a dull solid dome low over the roofs, had been grey, then yellowish, then almost white. Now scarcely visible very small snowflakes were dancing up and down like midges. As Brian and Gabriel watched them (it was lunch time) they (the snowflakes) were to be seen, not as it seemed falling, but jigging about just above the pall of steam which (as the temperature fell in the direction of zero) once again covered the surface of the open-air pool.

'Snow in April!'

'It can snow any time in this bloody country.'

Brian and Gabriel returned to the little white cast-iron table, covered with circular brown stains, at which they had been sitting and drinking tea out of plastic cups. The white snowy light revealed in terrible detail the pale stained flaky green walls of the Promenade and the cold, wet brasswork of the lion disgorging Ennistone water into a kind of sink. Zed, established upon one of the chairs, was with them today. Dogs were allowed, in the Promenade only, upon leads. Gabriel had brought him with her, from her shopping and his run in the Botanic Garden, and had given up her swim so as to sit with him over coffee, waiting for Brian and Adam to arrive. Adam was still out there swimming, somewhere underneath the roly-poly blanket of the steam. Gabriel banished from her mind rapid mental movies of Adam drowned, his limp body lifted from the water, et cetera. She returned to the topic of the seaside visit. Brian detested this topic and refused to help her to think about it. He sat scratching his pockmarked face with blunt, audible fingernails, and glaring unseeingly in the direction of Gavin Oare and Maisie Chalmers who were giggling at a corner table, and of Mrs Bradstreet who was drinking some of the sulphurous water and brooding over her terrible secret.

'If we want to go to a hotel we ought to book now.'

'One day's enough, isn't it?'

'I think it would be fun to go to a hotel –'

'I don't. Why go at all?'

'Well, it's a family tradition. Alex sets store by it.'

'I don't think Alex "sets store by it", whatever that means. With Maryville gone it's pointless anyway.'

'We did it last year without Maryville.'

'And what a frost it was.'

'I don't think so –'

'I know why you want it.'

'Why?'

'Because you want George to come.'

'Don't be silly!' It's true, thought Gabriel, but not in a bad way. It was so important to let George know that they cared.

'I've never seen such a dog for playing.'

'Yes, remember when we watched him through the kitchen window playing there all by himself –'

Zed, fluffed up on top of Gabriel's shopping bag, had his roosting bird look. He had what Gabriel called his 'winsome look', his black lip a little curled to show a flash of teeth, his blue-black shot-silk eyes staring flirtatiously at his admirers. He touched the handle of the bag with one tentative white paw, stared at Gabriel, then patted it twice as if inviting co-operation in a game or ritual.

'Zed! Where's ballie?'

'Don't excite him, Gabriel.'

'Zed, you darling, kiss hands!'

'Soppy little blighter. There are small dogs, but this is ridiculous. A miserable sissie little object that couldn't defend itself –'

'Dogs in Ennistone don't have to fight for their lives!' She added, 'Oh dear.' Such a tiny defenceless *crushable* animal. Oh *dear*.

'He's not a dog, he's a cuddly toy. Adam treats him like a toy.'

'Adam treats everything like a toy.'

'How does such a ridiculous little animal know that it's a dog at all? Put him down, he's sitting on the cheese.'

Gabriel put Zed on the ground where he immediately began to frisk and dance at her feet, moving his round black and white rump voluptuously, as a preparation for attempting to jump up. She lifted him on to her knee where he settled himself, staring with intense insolent private amusement at Brian.

'We could stay at that little hotel –'

285

'I'm not paying out money for hotels.'

'Then if we go for the day –'

'What's the use of a day? We'd spend half the time getting there and getting back.'

'No we wouldn't. It's very quick now by the motorway. And a day by the sea is – so special – if we're all together. Brian, please don't say no. It's our *only* family thing except Christmas, and you know how much I enjoy Christmas.'

'And you know how much I hate it! Alex hates it too, remember how she wrecked the last one.'

'Don't be cross, I have to organize this because nobody else will, like I have to organize Christmas because nobody else will. You're all glad enough when I've done it!'

'You deceive yourself.'

'Tom suggested we should take tents and camp.'

'Oh *did* he!'

'I'll make the sandwiches, Ruby will help, you know how she enjoys it –'

'You're always *imagining* that other people *enjoy* things, but they are *not* like *you*!'

'Well, they're not like you either, you don't enjoy anything!'

'I used to enjoy things, but they've all gone, the nice things, like waltzing with you at the *thé dansants* we used to have in this room before everything got so awful.'

Gabriel was touched by this memory. She too had enjoyed the sentimental old *thé dansants* with the three-piece orchestra. 'Darling! And the tangos and the sambas and the rumbas and the slow fox-trot –'

'No. Only the waltzes. But they've gone. We shall never waltz again. Oh *God*, must you *cry* about it?'

I'm not just crying about that, thought Gabriel, though I am crying about that. Why am I always so near to tears? It annoys Brian so. Are other people's lives like mine – always so near to the edge of something infinitely touching, awfully moving and significant and sort of deep – Can it be God? No, it is too small.

Adam had been upset this morning because Gabriel had destroyed his 'bear'. This 'bear' was a smudge upon the kitchen wall which resembled a bear, which had somehow become Adam's property. Busily cleaning, Gabriel had accidentally mopped his bear away. He's like me, she thought, and yet with him it's different. He loves all sorts of funny little things which are almost non-things.

For him the world is full of such things. He owns the world – it's always *his* blackbird that's singing, *his* spider that has made a web in the corner. The thought about the lost bear reminded her somehow that last night she had dreamed about Rufus, and in the dream he was her son. She often had this dream, which she told to no one.

There was something else too, something which had just happened as she sat at the table in the Promenade waiting for Brian to join her. An Indian man, perhaps a Pakistani, a thin, youngish man with a beard, had sat down opposite to her, as she sat reading the *Ennistone Gazette*, and asked her one or two trivial questions. Gabriel had answered his questions briefly and gone on reading. She did not easily talk to strange men. After a short while the 'intruder' went away. A few minutes later, after he had disappeared, and just before Brian came, Gabriel put down her paper, penetrated by a terrible pang of conscience. The man had been lonely, perhaps he had only lately arrived in England, a new immigrant, living alone, made to feel unwanted, looked askance at, victimized. His trivial questions were an appeal, for conversation, for human contact, for a smile, for a *look*. Perhaps he had thought she had a kind face. And she had utterly failed, she had been curt, almost rude. And now he was gone, and that precious moment would never come to her again. This too was what made tears come into her eyes when Brian recalled the *thé dansants*.

Father Bernard was standing at the long window of the Promenade looking at the fascinating play of the tiny snowflakes which, in the very cold windless air, seemed unable to decide whether to go up or down. Some however must be reaching the ground since the edge of the pool was white, blotched and criss-crossed with the dark prints of bare feet. As he watched, Tom McCaffrey, stripped for swimming, passed him close upon the other side of the glass. Tom stood a moment on the edge of the pool, tense, erect, enjoying the cold beneath his feet, the chill touch of the air, the tiny feathery caresses of the snowflakes upon his warm skin. Then lifting his head and tossing back his hair, he breathed in luxuriously air and snow, flexed his body, dived into the plump rounded cloud-cover of the steam and disappeared. Father Bernard, who had been holding his breath, let out a sigh. *Dans l'onde toi devenue ta jubilation nue.*

The priest, who had had his swim, was feeling exceptionally full of spiritual well-being. After mass that morning he had composed a suitably pompous letter to John Robert to the effect that he had examined Miss Meynell's capacities and found her, though immature, proficient in modern languages. He especially commended her careful attention to grammar. After that he had put on his longest tape of Scott Joplin and sat down opposite his long-eared Gandhara Buddha, whose austere calm stern visage, with pursed lips and downcast musing eyes (the creature was *thinking*) seemed to him so much more spiritual than the tormented face of the crucified one. He sat in an upright chair, his spine straight, his eyelids drooping, his hands relaxed upon his knees. While his paltry mind chatters on he breathes, aware of air moving, gently pulsating airy movement which becomes slower ... and slower ... Darkness wherein a joy which has no owner quietly evaporates like a disintegrating rocket. Is he changed? No. Is this enlightenment? No. What is it then? A harmless semi-miraculous private diversion costing strictly nothing.

Now on his way from the window to the tea counter he paused at the table where Brian and Gabriel were sitting.

'Good morning. Why there's Omega. What a proof of God's love that little animal brings us, how humble we should feel –'

'Why?' said Brian.

'What an upspring of spirit in that tiny beast, such good humour, such inexhaustible good temper, what selfless affection burns in those eyes –'

'Tosh,' said Brian. 'He's a completely egoistic, self-centred animal.'

'God is everywhere visible in his creation.'

'In this tea cup also?'

'Yes.'

'Then we don't have to be sentimental about dogs.'

'Isn't the snow delightful?'

'Bloody awful.'

'What did you think of Miss Meynell?' said Gabriel.

'A childish, simple girl, but –'

'Simple, you mean mentally deficient?'

'Of course he doesn't, Brian.'

'Simplicity is a divine attribute.'

'Yes, just look at the world.'

'May I ask if you have had any news from Stella?'

'No,' said Gabriel, 'I'm very worried, she hasn't written, she's just vanished. It isn't like her.'

'Don't worry,' said the priest, 'the Institute is always filled with nonsensical rumours. People love crimes and disasters.' He moved on to the counter.

'What are these rumours?' said Gabriel to Brian. 'I haven't heard anything.'

'Oh fascinating, I even saw Mrs Osmore talking to Mrs Belton about it.'

'But *what*?'

'The latest idea is that George has done away with Stella, the only question being what he's done with the body.'

Another witness of Tom McCaffrey's elegant dive was William Eastcote. William, also stripped, was standing on the edge of the pool. He had been swimming and was now experiencing the familiar feeling of his warmed body cooling. (The water temperature was 28° Centigrade, the air temperature 2° Centigrade.) He thought instinctively, scarcely framing the thought but mixing it up with his sensations: I *would* have enjoyed this warm and cold feeling, the ice-cream-pudding feeling Rose used to call it. I *would* have enjoyed the snow and seeing Tom stand there and dive. Only now I can't. And I am envious of Tom, I am envious because he is young and strong and will live, and I am not, and will not. It seemed so paradoxical and so awful to William that today his own lean brown near-naked body stood up as sturdily as ever and looked as solid and felt as strong, while all the time, as he now knew, it carried inside it the inevitable engine of his own imminent death. He thought, shall I tell Rozanov? The disclosure would be *embarrassing* to them both. John Robert did not like failure; and what greater failure could there ever be than that one?

Something touched William's hand and he looked down to find Adam McCaffrey looking up at him. 'Hello, Adam.'

'Hello.'

'Isn't the snow nice?'

'Yes, I heard the birds singing in the snow.'

'Even in the snow they know it's spring.'

'A wren can sing a hundred and six notes in eight seconds.'

'Can it really?'

'Yes. Did you know?'

'No, but I can imagine.'

'I was up on the common with Zed. We saw a white horse all by itself.'

'Perhaps it belongs to the gipsies.'

'It was rolling on its back. Then when it saw Zed it jumped

up. When it saw a dog near it was frightened. It went away then.'

'A big horse frightened by a little dog!'

'It was a pony more than a horse. I saw Uncle George coming out of the library, but he didn't see me. Once I saw Uncle George being in two different places at the same time.'

'He can't have been, unless you were too.'

'I was on top of a bus, you see.'

'Does that make it different?'

'Yes.'

'Perhaps there's someone else who looks like him.'

'Perhaps. I will just rescue that fly.'

William saw a bright-winged fly lying on top of the glossy restless water which was moving quietly about at their feet. Adam slid into the pool easily, noiselessly, like a water rat, not disturbing the glossy surface. He carefully floated the fly on to the back of his hand and reached up to tilt it on to the concrete near to William's bare feet. The fly shook itself, drew its legs briskly over its wings, and flew away. Adam waved a little polite farewell wave and swam off into the crowding steam. William, who had forgotten about his death during his conversation with Adam, remembered it again. He thought, when that boy is twenty I shall have been dead for twelve years.

Soon after his dive which had aroused such strong but different feelings in the breasts of two observers, Tom McCaffrey ran into Diane Sedleigh. Before this encounter Tom had swum along, exercising his quiet effortless Ennistonian crawl, with a lot of unhappy muddled thoughts buzzing around inside his handsome head about which his wet darkened hair flopped or swirled. It was now two days since his extraordinary interview with John Robert. During this time Tom had done nothing, had, almost, *hidden*. He had made no plan. He had stayed at home, unable to read *Paradise Lost*, unable to work on his pop song, unable even to watch Greg's colour television. He felt physically sick with anxiety and foreboding, alienated from himself as in a bad attack of 'flu. The curious excitement he had felt just after the interview had faded, or been changed into some lurid less pleasing sense of being captive. He still felt it was impossible to 'get out of it'; certainly he could not now (though, as Emma pointed out, in a way nothing was easier) simply write a letter to Rozanov saying that he had decided not to proceed.

This letter would have to contain (he had not told Emma of John Robert's terrible proviso) his promise never to attempt to come near Harriet Meynell. Never? At *his* age? How could he be in such a far-fetched predicament? He *had* to go on, he *had* to see the girl, although the prospect held no attraction except that of acting out a dream-like destiny. He felt now no 'romantic curiosity', no ardour for some challenging 'quest'. What he did feel as he swam along so privately, so wretched, inside the steamy roly-poly, was a kind of restless, nasty erotic adventurism. He had been perfectly happy as he was. Now he was being *forced* to think about girls! All right! He thought to himself, yes, John Robert has changed my value. He has made me worse! At that moment he ran straight into Diane who was swimming equally strongly in the opposite direction. Emerging at close quarters into visibility, their outstretched arms entwined, then they heeled over knocking each other away.

'Sorry.'

'Diane!' Tom had of course had his brother's mistress pointed out to him long ago by someone, perhaps Valerie Cossom, who took such an interest in George's activities. Tom had never learnt Diane's surname and had, in so far as he ever thought of her, used her first name, which now instinctively came out.

Diane, with her dark little cap of short hair, looked much the same whether her head was wet or dry, which was not the case with Tom. With wet hair his face looked gaunter, fiercer, older. Diane did not know who he was.

'It's Tom, Tom McCaffrey. Don't be afraid.' Tom was not sure why he said this. He took hold of the strap of her blue bathing costume.

'Oh – please let go –' Diane's wet hand scrabbled helplessly at Tom's hand. She gulped water. 'Let go, you're pushing me under.'

Tom let go, but barred her way, treading water and touching her arms with his finger tips. At close quarters her wet face looked childish, red, the make-up a little smudged.

'How's George?' said Tom.

'I haven't seen him.'

'May I come and talk to you, just talk, you know? I'd like that. George wouldn't mind, would he?'

'No.'

'So I can come?'

'I mean don't come, *please* don't come.'

'I just want to talk to an older woman, I need advice.'

291

'No.'

'Be a sport, Diane. I say, is it true that George has murdered Stella? That's what they're all saying!' Tom uttered these idiotic words as a sort of joke. He now saw Diane's small face crumple into a grimacing animal's mask, and in a second, she shot away from him as swiftly as an otter, her departing kick jabbing his leg. Tom did not try to follow. He felt degraded and rotten. He thought, I *will* go and see her, I don't care!

'Hello, Tom!' It was Alex. They danced round each other in the warm water, touching each other like ballet dancers pretending to be boxers.

'Shall we go home, then?' said Pearl a bit crossly to Hattie.

Pearl and Hattie were still in happy ignorance of John Robert's plan, since the sage had not yet managed to compose the letter which was to explain it. In fact he had now decided to overcome his nervous reluctance and to visit the Slipper House in person on the following day.

Pearl had at last persuaded Hattie to come to the Institute. Hattie had bought a sober black one-piece bathing suit with a skirt at Bowcocks. She had also visited Anne Lapwing's Boutique with Pearl, and had bought a summer dress, which Pearl chose. Now today it was snowing.

Hattie and Pearl were standing in Diana's Garden beside the railings which surrounded the pitiful jumpings of Lud's Rill. Pearl wore a hooded anorak and trousers, Hattie an overcoat and a woollen cap and woollen stockings. They had got as far as the changing-room when Hattie suddenly funked it.

'What was the matter anyway?'

'It was just like Denver.'

'What on earth do you mean?'

'And it's all so public, I don't want all those women looking at me.'

'But people have looked at you all over the place, and not only women!'

'Yes, but it's different here, it's *awful*. And everyone swims so frightfully well –'

'So do you.'

'No, not – I'm sorry.'

'Well, shall we go or stay?'

Hattie had been appalled by the crowded and so public scene in the women's changing-rooms, with so many women of all shapes and sizes with practically nothing (sometimes nothing) on, taking showers and standing about and chattering to each other. The place was so full and animated and noisy, and you couldn't keep your cubicle, you had to carry your clothes to a locker and have a key to look after and so on. Hattie had pictured something much more dignified and discreet and private, and how, in her black costume, she would issue quietly to the water and slip noiselessly in. Pearl had said to her, 'No one will bother you, no one will *notice* you, why do you think you're so important!'

Hattie said, 'I don't, I just want to be quiet.' There was little quietness in the changing-room, indeed it was difficult to find anywhere to stand without being jostled by wet fleshy women. And although she did not explain it properly to Pearl, the *dérèglement* of Hattie's senses was increased by something quite unexpected which filled her with a terrible sick nostalgia before she could even make out what it was. The combination of the warmth, the smell of wet wood, and the snowy light outside brought back so intensely the atmosphere of skiing in the Rockies, at Aspen, the return from snow into the warm wooden interior with dripping skis and wet boots. Hattie had never been very happy at Denver, but this piercing reminder came with a whiff of a far-off home, a lost home, a lost childhood.

'Let's go back. We'll light a fire in the kitchen like you said. Don't be cross with me, Pearlie.'

When Tom, now dressed, approached them, Emma and Hector Gaines, having discovered each other as historians, had been talking for some time. Emma was muffled up in a long fur-collared coat and a Trinity scarf, both of which had belonged to his father. The smell of the coat had mingled disturbingly with the smell of his mother's face powder on her letter which, just arrived, he had thrust into the coat pocket as he was leaving the house. Now, out of doors, it was too cold to smell anything. Hector had abandoned his *déjeuner sur l'herbe* act, and was in swimming-trunks desperately resolved to display his not inconsiderable physique to Anthea: he had been a rugger blue at Cambridge, and had a lot of red curly hair on his chest. (Anthea had not turned up, however.) He had boiled himself scarlet in the stews, but was careful not to exhibit his mediocre swimming. Now, as he glanced anxiously around, he was shivering with cold. Emma had steered him off the emotive topic, on which Emma's accent had started him, of nineteenth-century Irish history. They had been discussing *The Triumph of Aphrodite*.

'Hello you two, you've found each other, good.'

'He's told me a lot I didn't know about the relation between Purcell and Gay,' said Hector to Tom.

'How's the masque going, Hector?'

'Terrible. We're having trouble with the chorus of animals. And we need a counter-tenor.'

Emma's leg kicking Tom met Tom's leg kicking Emma.

'Oh,' said Tom, 'but surely there aren't any any more? Besides, who likes that funny noise? It's like what Shylock said about the bagpipes.'

'I don't care for that weird falsetto myself,' said Hector, 'but the music needs it. Jonathan Treece says we can make do with a tenor.'

'You're freezing,' said Emma. 'Go and dress or go back in one of those holes.'

'Yes, well – have you seen Anthea, Tom? No? Well, I'll stay a bit. Good-bye. We'll settle the Irish question another day.' Blue, he shuddered off.

'We bloody won't!'

Tom said, 'Here comes my mother.'

Alex, also dressed, came brightly up.

'Alex, this is my friend Emmanuel Scarlett-Taylor. Emma, my mother.'

'I'm glad to meet you,' said Alex, 'I've heard such wonderful things about you, I hope you'll come and see me, Tom will bring you. Oh hello, Gabriel. This is my daughter-in-law Gabriel. What's the matter?'

Gabriel, distraught, her wind-chapped face rawly framed in a tight cotton scarf knotted under her chin, had found a pretext to run out to look for her Indian. It had occurred to her that she had despaired too soon. The man might not have left the Institute. He might have gone to swim. The text (a favourite of Bill the Lizard) occurred to her, 'in so far as you do it unto the least of these you do it unto me'. The bearded Indian even looked a little like Jesus Christ. She had been tried and found wanting.

'Yes, I know Mr Taylor, hello. I'm looking for an Indian man with a beard, have you seen one?'

No, they had not.

'Well, I'll run on – sorry to – well, good-bye –' Gabriel ran on, her medium-high heels slipping on the thin pale-greyish layer of snow on to which the small papery flakes were still uncertainly descending. She began to peer down into the stews.

'My daughter-in-law is so quaint,' said Alex, 'we all love her. Well, *auf Wiedersehen*.' In black boots and fur coat she strode away.

'I wish you would tell your family that my surname is Scarlett-Taylor.'

'What did you think of my ma?'

'Very good-looking. What wonderful things have you told her about me?'

'None. She seems to have taken a fancy to you.'

'She doesn't want you to marry,' said Emma, whose quick suspicious mind had grasped this idea in a flash.

'My marriage seems to be on everybody's mind.'

'Coo-ee, coo-ee!'

'That's my mother calling Ruby.'

'You mean her servant? Why there's that girl again.'

Hattie and Pearl, red-nosed and very much the worse for the weather, were passing by in the direction of the exit. The temperature, which had just fallen another degree, had opposite effects upon their appearance, making Pearl look about forty, and Hattie about fourteen.

'*Coo-ee, coo-ee!*'

Ruby appeared, carrying Alex's bag.

'Hello, Ruby,' said Tom, 'who are those two girls who have just gone by?'

'That's little Miss Harriet Meynell and her lady's maid. I must fly.'

Emma began to laugh. 'Oh God!' He thrust his hand into his pocket and felt his mother's letter. He drew it forth and held its fragrance against his face while he continued to laugh.

George McCaffrey entered the Ennistone Rooms through the little octagonal 'Baptistry' which enclosed the big glowing bronze doors from which one descended to the source, and which also constituted the quickest direct route from the Promenade to the Rooms. The Rotunda, or 'Baptistry' as it was more popularly called, had two doors, one on each side, which were normally kept locked. Sometimes, however, because of maintenance work, one or the other might be found open. For George on this day (the afternoon of the day recorded above) both doors stood open so that he was able to pass from the Promenade to the Rooms without having to pass the 'Porter's Lodge' or Reception at the front entrance of the Rooms. He paused in the Baptistry to inspect the big studded doors, a silvery gold in colour, from behind which steam was continually seeping. (This steam was whisked away by a fan situated above.) George felt the doors. They were hot. He turned the large brass handle and pulled. They were locked. He went on, padding quietly, into the Rooms, entering by a door marked PRIVATE into the main downstairs corridor.

It was quiet in the corridor, or so it seemed to George as he stood there listening to his heart beat. In fact there was a steady background drumming sound which was the noise of the hot water eternally discharging itself into the boat-shaped baths in the bathrooms of the individual rooms. However, if the doors of the rooms were kept shut, this sound was diffused into a deep vibration which soon ceased to be consciously audible. George stood a while experiencing this vibration which seemed so much in tune with his own heart-beats and the vibration of his whole taut being.

He walked on a bit, his feet softly printing the deep furry carpet. When he reached the door of number forty-four he stood and listened. There was only water noise within. He knocked softly. Nothing. Could his knock be heard? Should he knock more loudly? Should he enter? He turned the handle very gently and pushed the

296

door a little. Nothing, except that the water noise was louder and the sulphur smell stronger. He pushed the door a little more and peered in. The room was lighter than the dim corridor, obliquely touched by the sun, and almost dazzling for a moment by contrast, even though a curtain had been half pulled across the window. George saw first a table piled with books and papers, then the bed and the great form of the philosopher lying upon it. He was asleep.

George released his breath and quickly, after a glance behind him along the empty corridor, slid into the room. The noise inside the room was considerable since Rozanov had left his bathroom door open. George closed the outside door. He was not unduly surprised either to find Rozanov in, or to find him asleep. John Robert lived by a rigid timetable which involved early work and late work and a deep sleep of about an hour's duration in the afternoon. (This sleep, he maintained, enabled him to live two days in the space of one.) He was lying, now, upon his back and snoring. George stood, his hand upon his heart, gazing. Then he moved quietly forward.

No young swain of twenty, as it might be Tom McCaffrey, as he approached the half-naked slumbering body, carelessly relaxed, of the young girl (figured perhaps as a shepherdess) whom he adored, could have felt a greater excitement than did George in thus surprising John Robert Rozanov asleep. John Robert was clothed, but with his shirt open and the waist of his trousers undone. He was not inside the bedclothes, but lay on top of them with the crumpled white bed cover pulled up roughly as far as his knees. One shoeless foot, clad in a thick blue woollen sock, protruded. One hand lay upon his chest, the other was extended, palm upward, over the edge of the bed, extended toward George in what looked like an amicable gesture. George studied the open hand. Then he looked at the sleeping face. John Robert's face did not look calm in repose. The open moist lips, through which the slightly bubbling snore emerged, were still urgently thrust forward in the dominating *moue* which was their customary expression. The closed eyes, in their stained hollows, were slightly screwed up. The cheek-bones still protruded upon the flabby face, and the furrows on either side of the large hooked nose were like violent scourings. Upon the forehead, above which the frizzy grey hair had not yet started to recede, the flesh rose soft and pink in little regular pipings between the deep lines. A dirty grey stubble covered the chin and the thick much-folded saurian neck. Only the chin seemed weaker, less formidably decisive. George realized with a little shock the reason for this. John

Robert had taken out his false teeth, which were to be seen glinting upwards in a shallow white cup upon the bedside table.

George gazed, conscious of his own breathing and of the strained heavings of his chest. Then he backed away and, glancing often at the bed, inspected the room. The windows of the lower rooms (which on this side of the building looked across a private lawn to the trees of the Botanic Garden) had, after much controversy, been fitted with frosted glass. George felt in no danger of being seen, other than by the terrible sleeper, as he poked about. He went to close the double doors of the bathroom in order to decrease the insistent noise, then feared that a sudden change in vibration might awaken his teacher. He sidled into the bathroom and gazed on the exotic little scene, familiar to him since he had, in younger and more carefree days, treated himself to the enjoyment of the waters in this particularly intense privacy. The taps disgorged their thick noisy jets with fast aggressive violence, and the foot or so of water which constantly surged and frothed in the bottom of the curving blunt-ended bath was covered in tumbling puff-balls of steam. The tiles gleamed and moistly ran, and the place was filled with a faint warm fog which seemed to put a film over George's eyes as he looked with fascination upon the hot violence.

He stood again at the foot of the sage's bed, and his heart moved within him, twisting and turning like a hooked fish. He saw now, not the familiar features, but, even more familiar, the perpetual lowering frown of purpose and dominating insight which seemed, even in sleep, to be hovering on guard above them; and he felt in the crammed blackness of his soul remorse, regret, resentment, loss, anger and terrible longing, that composition of love and hate which can be the most painful and degrading sensation in the world.

George turned at last to look at the table. Here, it seemed, John Robert had been at work. There were books: George noticed Plato, Kant, Heidegger; minds inside which John Robert had expended, perhaps wasted, his whole life. Hume's *Treatise* was there too, and Schopenhauer's *Welt als Wille und Vorstellung*. There was also a number of thick notebooks, one of which was open at a page which was written in John Robert's inky hand which looked so much like looking-glass writing. George thought, it's the great book, it's all here! He peered at the page, knowing well how to read John Robert's scrawl.

If at a certain point it becomes impossible, for the sort of reasons suggested above, to maintain the conception of personal ownership of inner presentations, it is admittedly difficult to continue to attribute to these anything recognizable as 'value'. The notion of the *possibility* of placing every perception (even) upon a moral scale was argued to be inseparable from the concept itself. But in what sense can value be asserted in the absence of the person? I must refer back at this point to my discussion of Husserl's reduction, and to the peculiar sense in which his method denies transcendence.

George heard a faint sound behind him and swung round in fright; but all was well. John Robert had turned slightly on his side and was snoring less loudly. George stood a moment, while his senses whirled in a wild kaleidoscope, unable to focus upon the room after looking so intently at the white page. Then he tiptoed swiftly to the door and, without looking back, let himself quietly out into the corridor, where again he was blinded by the dimness after the subdued sunlight of the bedroom. He blinked and looked both ways. There was no one there. Yes, there was someone, a woman, standing against the wall down near the door marked PRIVATE through which he had come in. It was Diane.

Ever since the moment when she had started away 'like an otter' from the watery presence, and the so-forbidden *touch*, of Tom McCaffrey, Diane had been in a state near to madness. She could no longer sit patiently at home, taking modest trips abroad and returning like a soldier to her post, waiting for George to come. She had to go now and *search* for him, however fatally displeased he might be when she found him. The desire to see him, to be with him, made a dark sick pain which gradually assumed the aspect of fate. Within this great pain there was a tiny sparklet of joy, which joy was presumably hope. George was unhappy, outcast, alone. *Only she* really loved him and could save him from himself. Diane had, of course, heard (Mrs Belton had seen to that) the Institute rumour that George had killed Stella and hidden her body (some said in his back garden or on the Common, some said in the canal, some in the deep intestines of the Institute itself, where the old workings which went down to the source contained many abandoned chambers and old shafts, some going back perhaps as far as Roman times). The people who eagerly passed this rumour around less than half believed it, and Diane did not believe it at all. But what had made her leap away in anguish from Tom's stupid, thoughtless jest was a deep and wretched desire that something like that might be true, that Stella might somehow be dead, *even if* this meant that George would go to prison for life. Then their parts would be reversed, *he* in prison and wanting to be visited, while she roamed mysterious and free. Out of this poisonous seed had grown the agony which drove her out to look for him.

Diane was so desperate that she set off at first for Druidsdale. She got no further however than the Roman bridge. *Suppose Stella were at George's house*; suppose she had been there all the time, not in a shallow grave in the garden, but living there as part of some *conspiracy*, laughing with George at what the town might think? That this made no sense did not prevent Diane from supposing it. With George, anything was possible. She turned back and made her way up Burkestown High Road to 16 Hare Lane, where she knew Rozanov lived, because at least that was somewhere to go. She walked up and down a bit on the other side of the street watching the door and trying to believe that George might at any moment emerge. She had to cling to one hope after another, each bringing with it a delusive fading gleam, succeeded by the unmitigated pain. When it became as clear to her that George was not there as it had previously been that he might be, she *ran* to the Institute, arriving moaning with breathlessness and fatigue, and installed herself on the Promenade, close to the long window, whence, pacing about, she kept a restless watch, not caring whether people saw her and stared. At last she purchased a cup of tea and sat down in a daze of misery. She awoke from this to see quite plainly the figure of George passing quite close to her (he did not see her) and disappearing through the door into the Baptistry. It was now a slack time of the afternoon and no one saw George, silent as a fox, slink in through that partly open door, and no one saw Diane with equally wary little padding steps follow in after him. She passed the hot bronze doors of the source and came out into the long carpeted corridor which vibrated with water sound and smelt of water. She arrived in time to see George disappearing into one of the rooms. She tiptoed down a little, but did not dare to try to listen outside. She had never been inside the Ennistone Rooms and the mystery of them appalled her, together with the fear of George's finding her, and the impossibility now of going away without seeing him. She retreated toward the door through which she had entered and stood there in aching indecision. She gazed and gazed until her eyes ached and flashed and she could almost believe that he could have gone away without her seeing him.

Suddenly George erupted from the room, stood a moment, then began to *run* towards her. This dreadful *running* made Diane utter a little bird-cry of helpless terror. She flattened herself against the wall. George approached her like a terrible huge deadly animal, not like a lion so much as a towering gorilla, a huge ape with immense swinging arms. As he approached her he raised an arm as if with one blow he would sweep her from his way. Diane sank to her knees and closed her eyes.

'Kid, kid, get up, don't be frightened.'

In a moment he had lifted her and held her sobbing against him.

'Stop it, don't make a noise, let's see if that door's still open, yes it is, good, go now, go home –'

'I'll go – I'm sorry – I'll go.'

'Look, you go on first – I'll come after – I'll be with you in half an hour – go, go, stop crying, you silly baby!'

Sobbing now with joy, Diane made her way home.

Clothed again, Diane lay upon her sofa in the elegant (though not entirely comfortable) pose which George liked. She had put on her black silky dress and her glittering metallic necklace with the long teeth which George called her 'slave's collar'. George in his light-grey check trousers and his pale blue (finely striped with dark blue) shirt, which he still wore unbuttoned and untucked, walked about the room, picking his way, kicking the stuff on the floor out of his path. He walked fast in the small area as a man might walk in a large area, or as a strong wild animal might move in a small cage, walking with unnecessary energy, turning round abruptly, jerkily, at the end of every few steps. Diane looked up at him anxiously, her brief joy still smouldering, fear and panic again at hand. His movements made her feel tired and full of foreboding.

George, having reached the piano, picked up a little black metal monkey, very small, which Diane had had with her in her wanderings since before she could remember. The little things, her substitute children as the man had unkindly said, were, like magical charms which survive into another scene to *prove* that one did not dream the previous one, proofs to Diane's unconscious mind that innocence existed, her innocence and no one else's. George too responded unconsciously in much the same way to the presence of the little things, old and new, which were a visible extension of Diane's soul. He respected them. Now, however, he frowned at the

301

little monkey because it reminded him of one of Stella's netsuke.

He put the monkey down and opened the piano and struck two notes. (He could not play the piano any more than Diane could.) 'The call of destiny'. He turned and looked at her and smiled showing his little square teeth. His eyes, so wide apart, looked rather mad. It had never occurred to Diane that wide apart eyes looked mad. His eyes glowed and gleamed with imminent laughter, but the laughter did not come. He seemed to be in extremely high spirits.

'Hello, kid.'

'Hello, darling. Long time no see.'

'Hey nonny nonny. No? O K?'

'OK.'

'Thank God you're here.'

'I'm always here. I wish you were always here.'

'Oh me – the plough has passed over my back and I have survived. But it is no matter.'

'What isn't?'

'Anything, everything. However, it's going to be *all right*.'

'What is?'

'Anything. Everything.'

'I wish I thought so. Do sit down and hold my hand.'

'I see my way through, I see the light shining beyond, Eternity's sunrise.'

'Am I there – in the light?'

'You? Why are you so self-centred?'

'Aren't you?'

'Yes. But it's your job not to be. What are you for but to be the eternal forgiver? You are God in my life.'

'A powerless God.'

'God must be powerless. Christ was powerless. He didn't save himself.'

'You don't believe in religion, you're making fun of it.'

'I believe in something, but I've forgotten its name. Pure cognition. What happens when you unlock the subject from the object? Then there's no more subject. That's when all is permitted, and why it is.'

'Oh what nonsense – come and sit beside me and hold my hand.'

'I can't, I'm too restless, tiger, tiger, burning bright –'

'George, I do want to be with you in the sunlight one day, in the open, not secret and sort of shameful. I'm prepared to wait, I could

302

wait and wait and be happy so long as I could really hope that one day we could be properly together ...'

'Aren't you prepared to wait anyway?'

'Without hope? Oh – but do say –'

'Say what?'

'Oh – George – you know –'

'The clock struck one, the mouse ran down. It's nearly one.'

'George, I know I'm not supposed to – but now we're together again – you must let me talk and say what's in my heart –'

'Talk, talk, talk, it's a free country.'

'George, you're not going back to Stella, are you?'

'Have I been away? She has.'

'George, where is she?'

'How do I know?'

'You haven't done anything to her, have you, I mean you haven't hurt her –?'

'Why ever should I?'

'Oh – I don't know – because of – well, maybe because of me – or –'

'Hurt *Stella*, because of *you*?' George paused, making his brown eyes round in his round face and opening his mouth in an O.

'Sorry, I didn't mean that, I just wondered about Stella, everybody's wondering –'

'Fuck everybody.'

'Do stop moving about like that, you're manic. I mean, you might want a change, anybody might, you might want someone else.'

'I saw that girl, Harriet Meynell, Hattie they call her.'

'Professor's Rozanov's grand-daughter?'

'I saw her in her petticoat with her hair streaming.'

'Where, how –?'

'I saw her through binoculars at Belmont. You know she's at the Slipper House. She looked – oh –'

'What?'

'Pale. Undamaged.'

'Ah – not like me. You're not falling in love with *her*?'

George paused beside Diane. 'No. But I'd like to –'

'You leave her alone –'

'I have my duties.'

'You mean to Stella?'

'There are duties in the world. Kinds you don't dream of.'

'You've got me. I suit you. I *love* you. No one else does.'

303

'Every woman in Ennistone loves me, I could have any woman I wanted. I could have Gabriel McCaffrey, tomorrow, this evening, I'd just have to wink, she'd come running.'

'She wouldn't!'

'She would. Oh never mind, as if I cared. Sometimes I feel so tired. But it *will* be all right, kid.'

'For us two?'

'You don't know what it's like to think of one person, one thing, day and night.'

'I do know! I think of you day and night.'

'That's just subjective. I mean something – metaphysical.'

'Between us it's not metaphysical, is it?'

'You are a rest from metaphysics. But you aren't real either.'

'Why am I not real? Oh George, I want to be real. Is Stella real?'

'Leave Stella. I told you.'

'I wish you would.'

'Shut up. Don't talk to me like that.'

'Don't let me be utterly cast away and lost, I don't want to be *lost* –'

'Lost, stolen or strayed, a girl no longer a maid, I had her and I paid, I bought her and she stayed, so goes it in the trade.'

'Oh George, be serious, be *quiet* with me –'

'Don't forget you're my slave. Aren't you, kid, dear?' He sat down at last beside the sofa and took hold of her little brown hand.

'Yes, George. I sometimes wonder whether you won't kill *me* in the end.'

'Just look at your hand. You're like a Pakistani girl. When will you give up smoking?'

'When you marry me.'

'This place stinks, your hand stinks, your hand is stained, your hand is brown and dry, my heart is brown and dry, it's like an old dry smelly leather bag. And yet – all will be well – I must go –'

'When will you come again?'

'I don't know. In a hundred years. Watch and pray.'

'Where are you going?'

'To the cinema.'

'Good morning, Pearl.'

'Good morning, Sir.'

Pearl, who had opened the Slipper House door to John Robert's ring, curtseyed. Only for him did she curtsey. It was part of the play-acting which was not play-acting which she put on for John Robert.

'How are you?'

'Very well, thank you. Why, you're all wet!'

The philosopher was indeed all wet and did not need to be re-minded of it. He frowned.

He had dressed with some care for his visit, putting on a clean shirt and a dark suit which he kept for best. He had shaved care-fully, sliding his razor (not electric) into all the folds of his jowl and of his dry saurian neck and removing the old man's grey stubble which had so fascinated George. He had combed his crisp frizzy hair making it stand up on end, and he had put on his overcoat. It was not until he had proceeded a little way along Ennistone High Street, and passed Bowcocks, that he perceived that it was raining, and he then deemed it too late to return to fetch his umbrella, hat and scarf. The rain was not much. However, it increased, and he arrived at Forum Way with his head and neck thoroughly soaked and, in spite of having put up his coat collar, water running down his chest and back. He felt uncomfortable and undignified and chilly. He disliked getting his hair wet.

Of course the girls, alerted by his telephone call earlier that morning, had been expecting him for some time (it was now almost noon), peering out of the window to see him come along the muddy path between the trees. Before that they had been busy, rushing about the house to put it to tiptop rights. (Pearl jealously prevented Ruby from cleaning. She did it herself with help from Hattie.) They also had to decide how to array themselves, whether Hattie should wear her new pretty summer dress and put her hair up. Hattie decided against the new dress which would look out of place on such a dismal wet morning, but she allowed Pearl to help her to stack up her hair. She wore a cinnamon-brown light woollen dress with dark brown stripes and a high collar which made her look older, and, after consultation, knotted a silk scarf round her neck in a way they thought to be sophisticated. Pearl had got herself up to look like a servant in an opera, with a navy blue dress and a rather smart striped pinafore.

When Pearl opened the door, Hattie remained standing in the sitting-room where they had turned on the gas fire. She did not run to the door to welcome her grandfather. She waited and smoothed her dress and fluffed up her scarf and patted her hair and breathed fast. Pearl had taken John Robert's coat away to the kitchen to dry.

She had omitted to indicate where Hattie was. John Robert, who had not entered the Slipper House since he kissed Linda Brent in an upper room during a Methodist fête at Belmont over fifty years ago, looked about, then peered in through the sitting-room door to see Hattie standing there. At that moment Pearl ran back holding a towel.

'What's this?'

'To dry your hair.'

'Oh.' Standing in the doorway he vigorously rubbed his hair and face and neck, then threw the towel back to Pearl without looking at her, entered the room and closed the door behind him.

Of the three persons involved in this little arrival scene or ceremony, John Robert Rozanov was not the one least moved. His heart beat as fiercely as Hattie's as they faced each other.

John Robert had never managed to get on with his daughter Amy. He loved his wife who had died so soon after the child's birth. He mourned Linda, he resented Amy, he did not like children, he had wanted a son anyway. Amy was an awkward suspicious hostile child, he had made her so. She showed no spark of any intelligence which might have interested him. He engaged nurses and housekeepers, then dispatched Amy to a boarding school. Just when he was arranging for her to go to college she ran off with that fool Whit Meynell. Then there was another little girl.

John Robert was never sure later on exactly when he had begun to *notice* Hattie; perhaps not until she was about eight or nine, and her mother, whom she had been so drearily 'part of', was already dead. She was a solemn child, aloof and shy, but, unlike Amy, not patently intimidated. She had Whit's Icelandic mother's stone-blue eyes and silver-gilt hair. But in the totality of her face and tenure she resembled Linda. John Robert's heart had long ago been walled up and frozen; or rather his heart had become an intellectual organ and it was as such that it could beat strongly and warmly. He was at the height of his philosophical powers and in the grip of intense and continual mental turmoil. He had never deeply desired any woman except Linda. As a young widower he had been pursued, especially by powerful American women intellectuals, but any brief involvements had been much regretted by him, and even more by them. This period was short. His relations with his pupils were sometimes intense, but for John Robert these relations were strictly a function of intellectual excitement. When they ceased to be able to interest him philosophically he forgot them. He enjoyed talking with his colleagues on intellectual academic topics, where his interests and his knowledge ranged beyond the field of philosophy (he could have been a historian). But his pleasure in these encounters was concerned with ideas not with people, although there were not a few clever men and women who would dearly have liked to become his intimates. The last thing in the world that he expected was that he should suddenly find himself moved by a child.

John Robert was indeed surprised to find himself, confronted with the young person, experiencing a new emotion. What was it? Interest, tenderness, affection? Whatever it was, he kept it strictly to himself. He had long ago decided upon his 'way of life', and his experience, especially his dismal relation with his daughter, had amply confirmed the decision, also of course confirmed by the world-consuming satisfaction which he found in philosophy. There was no room for anything else *now*. Yet there *was* something else, Hattie. She appeared to him like an awkward unnerving *extra*, a kind of contingent excrescence upon the perfect circle of his life, something *outside*. John Robert reflected deeply upon this, and found that the phenomenon persisted. He began to think about his grand-daughter with certain obscure flutters of the heart. But, to her, he exhibited no emotion whatsoever. Later on, much later on, he had times of the most bitter remorse, that biting 'Oh if only –' which can gnaw its way into the very centre of the soul and there set up a pain which mixes itself with every experience. Remorse, at times, even distracted Rozanov from philosophy. If only he had, earlier on, established some direct affectionate relation, some ordinary *modus vivendi* with Hattie. Other grandfathers, as he could see from looking at his colleagues, were friends with their granddaughters, held their hands, hugged them, set them on their knees, *kissed them*. Except for occasions when he sat next to her in the car or on an aeroplane, he never touched Hattie. He did not pat her head or shake her hand. And, as he sometimes reflected, when he did (rarely) happen to sit next to her, not only did he discreetly shrink from her, she also shrank from him. How could he, he wondered as the years went by, go on and on so thoroughly doing what he did not feel? If only he had been braver and *more intelligent*, he could have had an ordinary affectionate relationship with Hattie ever since she was a small child. This might not have been anything wonderful but it would have been a door to open wider at need. Had he at the beginning *so* hardened his heart that change could not any more happen? But it was exactly his heart which was no longer hard. If only he had, years ago, seized the child in his arms. Would she have shrunk from him? Was it simply the fear of that which had made this long misunderstanding between them? There remained this thing which other people found so simple which he had never in all the years learnt how to do. And now it was too late.

When had it become too late? Had it always seemed too late? As time went on John Robert, in the restless painful working out of his remorse, kept moving the moment at which it *became* too late further and further onward in time toward the present, with which it never caught up. But if 'too late' kept moving on in this way, was it not still in his power, looking at the present from the future, to assert that, after all, *now* was not *yet* too late? The idea of just this freedom was perhaps what tormented the philosopher most. He could still 'do something about Hattie'. Or could he? What could he, after all these years, do? What move could he make now which would not mystify, even appal her? Such speculations were being endlessly examined, metamorphosed and refined in his secret thought, while at the same time he struggled with the most crucial problems of his philosophy, his ability thus to brood and suffer matching but not diminishing his giant ability to work.

He thought often of writing Hattie a letter, explaining that he hoped that she realized how much he loved her. But, as in imagination he perused it, this letter seemed to be so stiffly conventional as to be insignificant or even embarrassing, or else to be something extremely melodramatic and startling. Other people solved such problems without even noticing them, or else lived thoughtlessly without their ever arising; he could not. *Was* it that he loved her? Was this *love*? Did he after all know so little of the world as not to have thoroughly understood this concept? Was it the same thing now as what he had felt when she was eight (or was it nine)? Perhaps the thing he felt, and thought he could identify, was always changing. Had it, in especial, changed lately, as Hattie grew – older? To say that John Robert was 'in love' with his grand-daughter was to employ too vague and dubious a concept. What was certain was that he was obsessed by her.

During years when John Robert thought continually about Hattie he saw her only at rare intervals. He deliberately rationed his visits to her, which had the effect of intensifying her mystery. Of course this was unwise, he later saw; he should have kept the child close to him. But would familiarity have dispelled her charm? He could not see the whole situation or see the situation whole.

Certain necessary hypotheses excluded certain other necessary hypotheses, it was like some situations in philosophy. She would have interrupted his work. Would she have made him 'happy'? Another problematic concept. Inevitably, and in spite of the changes in her life, she seemed complete without him. When he had first 'noticed' her, her father had been still alive; but the philosopher's contempt for Whit Meynell effectively obliterated this figure from the picture in a way in which it had not been possible to obliterate Amy. Amy had been a blot, a thorn, a dismal even sinister growth. Whit Meynell was nothing. In the picture of Hattie which had begun to glow there was not even a shadow. Yet this nothingness, though it made Hattie more visible, did not make her more accessible. She always seemed to be 'getting on' in a sort of life of her own in which John Robert must figure as an otiose outsider, one whose arrival was a bit of a trial. Poor Whit, of course, could make no secret of his ardent desire for his father-in-law's absence, and in this Hattie seemed naturally to share. Later, with Margot, it was much the same. Of course John Robert was aware how scrappy and unsatisfactory, how problematic and provisional, how very *unhappy* Hattie's mode of life must be. But this awareness could not help him to any sensible decision. Sometimes vaguely he dreamed of taking Hattie right away with him, *capturing* her, keeping her with him in some Spanish-style palazzo in some isolated part of southern California and overwhelming her with luxuries and treats. But what would that really be like? Might she not be embarrassed, annoyed, irritated, bored, frustrated, longing to get away? The mere idea of finding her so caused him such anguish as to make the experiment impossible. Was it not better simply to stand by and take such satisfaction as he could in simply watching her grow? His present aloof relation to her at least precluded problems, situations, consequences. Had he not his work to do and must he not protect himself? But ... watching her grow ... As Hattie became fourteen, fifteen, sixteen, John Robert began to feel his 'too late' with an added intensity. If the disclosure of his 'love', or whatever it was, was likely to 'appal' Hattie, was this not because the 'love' was, or was becoming, something 'appalling'? John Robert, who was not accustomed to *stop* himself from thinking, here endeavoured to *stop*.

It is in the context of this secret life of Rozanov that his extraordinary proposal to Tom McCaffrey may become intelligible. But before Tom there was Pearl. John Robert had never liked or trusted

309

Margot Meynell, but for a time he could think of no alternative policy. Pearl was a sudden inspiration, and with amazing luck when he reached out his hand blindly he immediately took hold of exactly the right person. He needed an absolutely reliable watchdog, someone (when she was not imprisoned in her school) who would be with Hattie *all the time*; for control of Hattie's *time* had gradually become a part of John Robert's obsession. He needed positively to seclude her innocence, he wanted to be able to know where she was and what she was doing, to have, in fact, an effective spy in her life; and this role Pearl, without fully realizing it, performed very adequately. John Robert was aware of Pearl as a strong and able person; he respected strong and able people. (His awareness of her, however, had not revealed her much more intense awareness of him.) Lately, however, he had found himself beginning to feel *jealous* of Pearl, and resenting her existence as a barrier between him and Hattie; that was how the thing, poisonously, was growing and how mad it had all become.

The notion of Tom was in a sense a notion of the same sort, though also of course completely different. John Robert had for some time been well aware that the period of her life during which he could keep Hattie *in a cage* was coming to an end. Hitherto, even if he could not imprison her in a Californian palazzo with himself as a gaoler, he had been able to supervise the limitations of her life elsewhere. Pearl was good, the strict old-fashioned boarding school was good, the 'families' were very carefully chosen. John Robert did not want Hattie to live free with bands of disorderly young people; this idea sickened him. He was beginning to realize, with another turn of the screw, how crazy his secret possessiveness was destined to become now that Hattie was seventeen.

Was he now to be the helpless spectator of Hattie becoming a woman? Only yesterday she had been a little slim thing with pigtails and a doll and pale solemn eyes, the *child* who lived in his mind, as she might have lived in his house. He had established his picture of her as an innocent child. He had prepared no picture of her as a young woman. There would be lovers, affairs, scrapes, pregnancies, abortions, all the coarse horror of the world of indiscriminate sex, the degraded sex-mad modern world from which John Robert shrank away with profound moral revulsion. Then there would be no Pearl any more, Hattie would *escape* from her watchdog and dance about free. Could he bear it, and if not what could he do? Sometimes, walking at night in half-

310

nightmares, it seemed to him that the only solution was to kill her.

John Robert could recall, in permanently available cinematograph, many of the occasions, not immensely large in total number, when he had been with Hattie. He saw her in the senseless baked garden of Whit Meynell's bungalow in Texas, a *little* child, not as tall as the flowers. Could he not have made friends with her then, when she reached up her hand and expected him to take it (which he did not), when she had not yet fenced him away with her nervous thoughts? How he perceived it later, that fence: not that he imagined she thought immensely *about* him, but she had a *view* of him, a view which paralysed them both at terrible little tea parties at terrible motels. Later in Denver they had gone on some short expeditions to see lakes and waterfalls, to look at a ghost town (Hattie liked ghost towns), to drive to a high place from which, surrounded by scores of other motor cars, they could look at immense empty flanks of snow mountains behind snow mountains into white distances where the eyes failed. (John Robert hated cars but, being a Californian by adoption, had to drive one.) Margot, later Pearl, had come on these jaunts. Occasionally he was alone with Hattie. Of course, it was possible that he felt as he did about the pure child because she was only available as a set of pictures and not as a continuous active imperfect person. But what difference did such speculations make now? He recalled her too, faintly, perceptibly adolescent, in California beside the ocean, walking on the lawns of campuses in the east, in the west, in a desert somewhere standing with Pearl beside his car and drawing cats in the dust upon it with her finger. Had they not, on those occasions, had 'ordinary talk', 'got to know each other'? No. The occasions had been too rare, and they had both, too early, set up their formal self-protective attitudes. These 'impressions', these 'stills' from her childhood came to him with a piercing sense of her particular odd dim whitish charm and her secluded innocence, her blessed loneliness and awkwardness in anything which showed any danger of being a 'sophisticated' or 'merry' scene. Of course John Robert had always endeavoured to steer her clear of 'merry scenes'. He had done his best to preserve her from any touch or even knowledge of the abysses which surrounded her. He could not, short of total captivity, keep her out of the world. Often it seemed that it *could* not touch her, she was not only too well-protected, she was too naturally fastidious and, perhaps, profoundly naïve. At least it could not

311

touch her yet. Still, still, she was preserved from the abominable vulgarity of *growing up*.

The idea of Hattie simply *walking away* into a secret world of sexual adventure increasingly tortured the philosopher. It was as if he felt, with a crazed passion: she must not sin. This torment, visiting earlier with premonitory pains, now, as if by destiny, raged in full possession exactly at the time when John Robert began to feel, or imagine, that his philosophical powers were waning. That was one way to put it. It was, too, like a loss of religious faith. He began to mistrust not only what he was doing now, and everything he had ever done, but everything *they* had ever done, his philosophers, the great immortal ones, in fact to doubt the whole goddamned enterprise. His pen weakened in his hand, his hand which would soon in any case be stiff and monstrous with arthritis. (He had never learnt to use a typewriter, a machine which he found totally inimical to thought.) He felt world-weary, as if the journey was done, his era was over, John Robert Rozanov was finished. There only and so terribly remained alive the future, which was Hattie.

In this desolation the characteristically dotty idea of marrying Hattie off quickly came to him as a salve. Why should he not at least attempt to arrange her marriage, to meddle thus far in her life and her future? It had been one of his most secret and peculiar miseries, one which he continually revived for his discomfort, that he would never be able to know *when* and *with whom* Hattie lost her virginity, and moved definitely out of the magic circle in which he had installed her. He would have to wait and guess and never be certain, and could he bear that? Hence there arose the idea of hastening the event and controlling it himself. It remained to find a bridegroom. Again, as in the case of Pearl and, as he hoped, with equal luck, he had at once hit upon a candidate. It might have been expected that the world of possibilities would at once have seemed so giddily large as to defeat reflection. Tom McCaffrey's amazement at the choice lighting upon him is easily understood. But in fact the area of selection, once essential requirements were met, turned out to be reasonably small; and here Rozanov's calculations were a strange mixture of extreme self-protective worldly wisdom, and a naïvety as great as Hattie's.

John Robert did not want an American. Americans knew too much. He considered, not seriously but as a clear instance of an impossibility, one of his cleverest younger pupils, Steve Glatz. Steve was a noble youth, but he was already hand-in-glove with life; he lacked that certain awkwardness which characterizes English boys and which, somehow or other, was upon John Robert's list of requirements. Besides, Steve was too old, being now at least twenty-five. Men of other races were out of the question. (Jews were, of course, not excluded, but the only Jews known to John Robert were American ones.) The chosen one must be English and must *not* be a philosopher, that too was clear. Philosophical chat with his grandson-in-law was not part of John Robert's picture of the future. Indeed any chat with this person was rather hard to imagine. The boy must be educated, a university student or graduate. Hattie herself, he supposed, would be proceeding to the university. She would need an educated person, able to earn his living (perhaps as a school teacher) but not too brilliantly clever (nothing like Glatz). Very clever people tended to be, in John Robert's experience, neurotic, unstable and obsessively ambitious. The chosen one must be English, and must, in practical terms, be an Ennistonian. John Robert still, in that large part of himself which remained untouched by sophistication, regarded Ennistone as the centre of the world. Besides, there was nowhere else in England where he knew so many people. He had quickly passed his academic London friends in review, scrutinizing their families in vain. As soon as it was Enni-stone, the light shone upon Tom McCaffrey.

In the wilds of California and Massachusetts and Illinois John Robert had regularly received and studied the *Ennistone Gazette*. This gossipy sheet mentioned Tom on a few occasions as having acted in a review, been a runner-up in the tennis tournament, played well in the cricket team, obtained a university place: modest achievements, but McCaffreys were news. (The *Gazette* had also featured Tom's only publication so far, an extremely bad poem, but this fortunately John Robert had not seen.) McCaffreys were news, and not only to ordinary home-keeping Ennistone, but also to John Robert himself in exile. In an odd way John Robert, bereft of home ties and relations, felt himself connected with the McCaffreys and the Stillowens, the old Victoria Park people, as if *they* were his family. This connectedness, which did not need to include any real friendship or even acquaintance, passed of course through Linda who had been, at the crucial time, so much at home with these folk. Perhaps indeed something even more primitive had been touched within the philosopher's soul. George had, without for a second believing it, hazarded, to insult his teacher, the idea that John Robert, when he was young, had resented not being invited to 'the grand houses'. In fact this was true. John Robert, at a time when he was already well known and admired, was annoyed to find himself ignored, or patronized, by people like Geoffrey Stillowen and Gerald McCaffrey. From this too he retained a deep and mixed feeling about these self-appointed 'grandees'. From this source came his whim to establish Hattie in the Slipper House, an edifice which amid much social fuss and *éclat*, he could remember being built, and which had figured in his youth as a symbol of affluence and social power. Perhaps even the very idea of 'choosing' Tom arose from some scarcely formulated desire to see his grandchild *stoop* to marry a McCaffrey. John Robert did not purposefully intend to dominate and *trap* Tom, yet this he instinctively did and with a perceptible satisfaction.

There was, of course, a sufficiency of simpler motives. The philosopher had been well aware of Tom's developing existence not only through ancestral memories and regular perusal of the *Gazette*, but also through his very occasional 'secret' visits to Ennistone, when he stayed briefly at the Royal Hotel to arrange the letting or repair of 16 Hare Lane. People talked about Tom, he was popular, he was *happy*. John Robert had already made his great decision when he had been struck by Father Bernard's remarks that Tom McCaffrey was 'innocent and happy, happy because innocent, innocent because happy'. Could such a condition perhaps last? And was not this exactly what he wanted for Hattie?

Yet, when he paused, what strange strange fancies crowded inside his mind! Tom fled or dead, John Robert comforting a Hattie now *safe* in secluded widowhood. Could he bear to see her in her husband's house? What sort of old clown's part would there be his? Could he conceive himself welcome ever? If he were capable of being jealous of Pearl, would he not go mad with jealousy of Tom? Did it come to this, that he had finally given up any hope of a relationship between himself and Hattie? Why was he in such a hurry to give her away? Surely he had not imagined the details? *From what horror in himself* was he so precipitately fleeing? His giddy and affrightened thought, shying away from this dark question, even at certain moments wildly imagined that having failed with Amy and Hattie he might be able at last to establish some perfect love relation with *Hattie's daughter*! Prone as he was to melancholia, there were times when John Robert Rozanov forgot that he was old.

*

314

John Robert blinked in the soft dim rainy light of the room where no lamps had been put on and where the pink gas fire quietly purred and fluttered. He was aware at once that Hattie had *grown*. It was nearly a year since he had seen her. He thought, so she can still grow? He glowered at her from under his hairy eyebrows. He thought, my God, she is like Linda, she is more and more like Linda, how is it possible? Hattie was taller, older, with her hair done in such a sophisticated way.

'Do sit down,' said Hattie. She had never before felt like a lady in a house receiving a guest, and such a special guest. It had never been like this in Denver.

John Robert sat in one of the low-slung bamboo chairs which uttered a warning crack. He moved to the window seat. Hattie found an upright chair and sat down.

'How are you?'

'Very well, thank you,' said Hattie. They never managed names or titles.

'You like the house?'

'Oh it's lovely, lovely!' said Hattie with a fervour which warmed the conversation a little. 'It's the nicest, sweetest house I've ever been in!'

'I wish I could buy it for you, I mean I wish I could buy it, only I know Mrs McCaffrey would never sell it. You have met her?'

'Yes, we met, she's very nice.'

'Is she?' said John Robert absently. Hattie was facing the window and with his eyes now accustomed to the greenish light he scanned her milky-blue eyes, her palest-gold interwoven hair, and the un-blemished smoothness of her face and neck. She wore no make-up and her nose shone a little pinkly. Her lips were pale as if simply drawn in with a light pencil outline. These were not Linda's colours, but the structure of her face was very like Linda's.

'Yes,' said Hattie, continuing by an answer to his question.

'Well, well. Are you glad to have left school?'

'Yes –'

'You're quite – almost – grown-up now.'

'Yes, what am I to do next, please?'

This blunt question rather hustled the philosopher who was prepared to come to this, but not immediately. 'We'll have to think about an English university. You've got those A level exams, haven't you? They sent me your marks. How did you get on with Father Bernard?'

Hattie smiled. Her smile was more of a grin than a young lady's smile, and expressed the amusement she felt at the thought of Father Bernard whom she found rather droll. 'Very well.'

'What did he tell you to do?'

'To do?'

'To study, to work at.'

'Oh, nothing. He just told me to read.'

'To read what?'

'Anything.'

'And what are you reading?'

'*Les Liaisons Dangereuses*.' Hattie had, of course, investigated the lines of faded books which had been in the Slipper House since before the war. This copy of Laclos's masterpiece still showed the shadowy inky schoolgirl signature of Alexandra Stillowen.

'Oh yes.' John Robert, who had not read a novel since he left school, had not heard of this one, which sounded rather improper, but he did not pursue the matter. He thought, what *does* she know? He hated to imagine. 'What do you want to study at the university?'

'Oh, languages I guess, that's all I know. I like reading poetry – and stories – and things –'

There was a silence.

Then Hattie said, 'Would you like a drink?'

'A *drink*?' John Robert now noticed on a glass-topped bamboo table toward which Hattie waved her hand, a bottle of gin, a bottle of vermouth, a bottle of tonic water, a container for ice and a glass.

John Robert was a habitual abstainer, having never felt the need to reject the sober habits of his family. However, he was not a fanatic and occasionally at parties, to please his host, took a glass of tonic or soda with a tinge of vermouth in it. John Robert looked with displeasure at this worldly little scenario. '*You* don't drink, do you?'

'Good heavens no!' said Hattie with a laugh. 'I've never had an alcoholic drink in my life!'

Rozanov thought, she's never had one. But she will. And I won't be there. Then he thought, but I *could* be there. Why not now? I can witness her first alcoholic drink, even if I can't witness ... He said, 'Tell Pearl to bring another glass.'

Hattie darted up. In the hall she cannoned into Pearl who was continuing her opera-maid act by listening outside the door and even stopping to peer through the keyhole. 'He wants another glass,' said Hattie breathlessly. Pearl fled to the kitchen and returned. Nothing in the nature of a wink or a nod or a smile or a glance passed between the two girls. It had always been a rule between them, equally willed by both, that they never made jokes about John Robert or spoke of him other than with the most solemn respect.

Hattie returned with the glass and stood beside the bottles holding it in her hand. She said, 'Shall I mix you a Martini? I know how it's done!'

'*How* do you know?'

'Margot showed me once. She thought it might be useful.'

John Robert did not like the idea of Margot teaching Hattie things, yet he found himself smiling. There was something so infinitely touching and moving in the spectacle of Hattie so eagerly holding the glass, and for once, for a moment, his feeling for her expressed itself simply as pleasure. He heaved himself off the window seat. 'I'll mix the drinks.' He went to the table and took the glass from Hattie. He put ice into the glass, then a very small measure of vermouth and a lot of tonic water. It was the mildest drink which could possibly be called a drink, but it *was* a drink. He handed it to Hattie and made a similar mixture for himself. They continued to stand, and this was significant.

John Robert took a sip of the mixture. It seemed to go instantly to his head. Hattie still stood, rather wide-eyed, holding her glass. 'Drink,' he said; and as he said it he felt like some old enchanter.

Hattie sipped the drink. It went straight to her head too. 'Oh!'

John Robert rambled back to his place and they both sat down. Hattie said, 'It's nice.'

'Do you miss America?' he asked her. He did not often ask such direct, even such interesting questions. He felt as if he had never *really* questioned her before.

Hattie considered. She took another sip of her exciting drink. 'I don't think I believe in America. I think it's a fiction. I mean it is for me. I imagined it.'

This was the most thought-provoking observation John Robert had ever elicited from her, it seemed to him very meaningful. 'Yes. I feel that too in a way, though I've lived there much longer than you, of course, I grew up in England. Why is it, do you think?'

'I don't know – I've only just thought of this idea,' said Hattie. 'Perhaps it's just a sort of transferred image of the largeness of it and the empty spaces – as if a human being couldn't survey anything so huge. It's as if one has to make a special effort on its behalf for

317

it to be there at all. One would never feel like that about Europe. And then there's the lack of past. I suppose all this is obvious really.'

The notion that Hattie was very intelligent had never figured in John Robert's obsession about her. Of course she was not a fool. But she patently did not regard herself as particularly clever, and John Robert had never speculated on the point. Perhaps she *was* clever, perhaps (the terrible thought came to him) Hattie might one day *become a philosopher*. Was philosophical talent inherited? He could think of no examples. Keeping his head he said, 'The physical being of the country has always seemed to me unconvincing, as if for real landscape we had to go elsewhere. That may be a matter of scale or because the country hasn't been worked for so long. We recognize ourselves in our work.'

'But it applies to the wild places too. I mean the Alps are more real than the Rockies. I've always felt the Rockies are a kind of hallucination. I wonder if it's to do with the sort of paintings we've looked at.'

John Robert never looked at paintings but he was prepared to pick up the point. 'Artists offer us shapes. European art had a good start. Is it the apparent shapelessness of America that strikes us here? That could affect us as a transferred image, to use your good phrase. What is shapeless is unreal.'

'Some people like that,' said Hattie. 'I mean they think what's shapeless is more real, more sort of informal and spontaneous, like a wild garden or dropping in for lunch.'

'Good,' said John Robert appreciatively, 'but perhaps we should put the problem the other way round. Isn't the trouble with us too that we don't quite feel American. Do you feel American?'

'No. But I *am* half American, and I value that. I've got an American passport.'

'Perhaps what we're feeling short of isn't the landscape at all, it's feeling American, and that makes us feel unreal. And then if there are two things, one real and one unreal, we have to take it that we are the real one, so we transfer the unreality to the other.'

'Feeling American is terribly special. It's such an achievement. It's so miraculously solid, like something demonstrated and proved.'

'Whereas being English isn't. So *we* are the ones who are turning out to be unreal!'

'No, no,' said Hattie. 'I won't let you turn it round like that! America *is* something imaginary. California is imaginary.'

'Oh California –'

'Of course I love the Rockies, I love Colorado, the lovely feeling of the snow at night and the aspens red and then mauve, you know, and the light – but I think I like the ghost towns best –'

'Not the wild country or the big cities but the ruins.'

'Yes – somehow those derelict places – the old empty broken houses and the old mine workings and the wrecked wagons and the wheels lying in the grass – because it's all so sort of recent and yet so absolutely gone and over, it seems somehow more touching and more past and more intense and more – real –'

'So you'll believe in America when it's all over!'

'It's ridiculous,' said Hattie. 'After all I've been – happy – in America.' She paused here as if about to add wistfully: haven't I?

'Do you feel English?'

'Oh no, how could I? I don't feel I'm anything; that is to say, I suppose *I'm* unreal, whatever I am!'

John Robert saw for a moment, as in an insipid wedding photo, the strained anxious faces of Whit and Amy. Perhaps they had actually given him such a photo once. I could have made things different, he thought, and yet could I; it always seemed, for everything I ever thought of, too late. I left her in an empty desert of a childhood, that is her unreal America. And must she not now be recompensed? But not by me. Pain which had been mercifully and briefly absent returned. Then he remembered Tom McCaffrey. He had forgotten his mission, his plan, his final solution. Should he now hesitate, wait, reconsider? He had not rehearsed any speech and everything came out vaguely and casually. Later on he thought that this was probably the best way.

'I must be off. By the way, you've got an admirer.' He rose to his feet as he spoke.

Hattie, who was not expecting him to go, jumped up too, putting down her glass which was now almost empty. 'Oh really, what sort of admirer?'

'What sort do you think? A young man. Tom McCaffrey. He'll probably ring you up. That's what young men do these days.'

'McCaffrey! He must be related to Mrs McCaffrey.'

'Her son, well, step-son, the youngest one. Anyway I thought I'd warn you! I'd like that. He'd make you a nice husband!' The last bit was intended to sound jocular but could not help seeming a bit portentous.

However, Hattie did not take it in, she was trying to imagine how he knew she existed. 'But he can't even have seen me!'

'A lot of people have seen you, a lot of people are *interested* in you.'

'How horrid.'

'Anyway, I thought I'd mention his name in confidence, you know, as an introduction, so that you won't just send him away.'

'But I don't want an admirer! It must be a joke!'

'*You* are not a joke,' said John Robert, and all his awkwardness returned. He said, 'Well, if you don't want an admirer, what do you want?'

'I want a black cat with white paws!' Hattie said this in a jesting tone, but now she was maladroit and awkward too. She added, 'But of course, that's not serious, I couldn't have one, I mean unless I lived somewhere like here, and I don't, and even here – there are foxes in the garden – did you know? – I wonder if a fox would attack a cat?'

'Better no cat,' said John Robert.

'Better no cat.' Suddenly for a moment it looked as if Hattie was going to cry, there was a kind of little gauzy hazy cloud in front of her eyes. She said, 'You asked me what I missed. I miss my father. But that's different. The cat made me think of him.'

Promptly banishing the inconvenient ghost of Whit, John Robert thought how important it was that they had talked about America as if they had between them placed and disposed of that great continent, thereby clearing the decks. Then he thought, if Hattie married Tom they could live right here in the Slipper House.

Pearl was standing in the hall holding his overcoat which was now warm and dry after its proximity to the central heating boiler. Pearl clicked her heels and helped him on with the coat; at any rate standing on tiptoe she held it up while he fought with it, blindly waving his arms behind him and staring at Hattie. Pearl opened the front door, but John Robert suddenly made for the sitting-room again. Hattie, who had followed him, hopped out of the way. He emerged carrying the gin and vermouth bottles. He said, 'I don't want you girls to drink. Please don't keep any liquor in the house. Good-bye then –' He blundered out into the rain.

With a sudden energy of exasperation Pearl spoke after him. 'I hope we will see you again soon, Professor Rozanov.' Pearl could have a strong penetrating voice when she chose to put it on.

John Robert stopped, amazed, but did not turn round. He said,

'Yes, yes,' but went on, not taking the path to the back gate into Forum Way, but going across the wet grass in the direction of Belmont. Pearl shut the door sharply.

Hattie said, 'Ouf!' Then, 'I liked talking to him. It wasn't as difficult as usual.'

'That's because you were both tipsy!' said Pearl.

'He was nice.' Hattie thought, I held my own, I had a real conversation with him!

Pearl had other thoughts. She had seen, in the sharp cameo of her keyhole, John Robert staring at Hattie, and she had not liked what she saw.

They separated, Hattie returning into the sitting-room where she wanted to be alone for a few moments and think about John Robert. Pearl stood in the hall with her hand still upon the door. Then, without a hat or coat, she ran out into the rain. She ran among the trees of the copse where foxie lived, and laid her head against the smooth trunk of a young beech tree.

John Robert meanwhile had walked past the garage and along the path beside the house and into the front porch of Belmont. The porch was a large structure rather like a little chapel with Victorian stained-glass windows. There was a seat in the porch which he remembered and on this he put down the two bottles which he intended to leave there. As the rain just then came on in a fiercer flurry he sat for a moment beside the bottles. Dressed in a mackintosh and head scarf, Alex came out.

'Oh – John Robert –'

'Mrs McCaffrey – I'm sorry – I brought these bottles –'

'How *very* kind! Won't you come in and drink them now? And please call me Alex.' Her blue eyes narrowed as she breathed her shock, standing in the shadow of the big man who had leapt up. She could smell the warm cooked smell, not yet banished in the rain, of John Robert's overcoat. 'Come in, come in, please.' She retreated to the door, pushing it open.

At that moment Ruby appeared from round the corner of the house and stood there, wide herself as a door, and stared at the philosopher.

John Robert, saying 'I must go, sorry,' shot out of the porch and down the path to the road. He thought to himself, I'm drunk! and made his way back to Hare Lane as quickly as he could.

Alex said to Ruby, 'Why did you have to come and stand there like that, like a great toad. Where have you been anyway? You've got the evil eye. Take these bottles in.' She went out into the front garden holding on to her secateurs in her pocket. Two warm tears mingled with the cold rain.

The next day there was a power cut (the electricians' strike was on again) and the shoplifters joyously made their way to Bowcocks. (It was in the evening but it was Thursday and Bowcocks was open till nine.) Diane, who was inside the shop this time as she had been last time, hurried out for fear someone should accuse her of stealing. After George's visit her heart was all scratched and scarred and vibrating all over with a mixture of joy and pain and fear.

Valerie Cossom and Nesta Wiggins, who had been writing a Women's Lib manifesto, shouted down the stairs for lights, for it was already darkish outside, having been another yellow overcast rainy day. Dominic Wiggins, leaving his work, which he could not now continue, came up to the girls bearing a pair of candles. He adored his daughter, but wished she would marry a nice Catholic boy and have six children. He liked Valerie. He lingered, and after a while they all went downstairs and made tea on a primus stove.

Father Bernard was with Miss Dunbury. Miss Dunbury had had a heart attack, and had been told by Dr Burdett, Dr Roach's junior partner (and brother of the St Paul's Church organist) who believed in being absolutely truthful, that another such attack might possibly carry her right off. Miss Dunbury was afraid. Father Bernard was doing the best he could. He had prayed over her a solemn prayer. 'O Almighty God, with whom do live the spirits of just men made perfect, after they are delivered from their earthly prisons, we humbly commend the soul of this our sister into thy hands, most humbly beseeching thee that it may be precious in thy sight. Wash it, we pray thee, in the blood of that immaculate Lamb that was slain to take away the sins of the world ...' After this prayer had ended with ardent hopes of life everlasting and a loud 'Amen' from Miss Dunbury, the lights went out. At this point Father Bernard made a discovery about his parishioner: Miss Dunbury was almost entirely deaf and relied upon lip-reading, at which she had become extremely adept. Miss Dunbury was ashamed of her deafness and had kept it a secret, but now the revelation was unavoidable. Candles were somewhere, but where? Miss Dunbury produced an electric torch and shone it upon the priest's face. They could then

proceed. Father Bernard had an extraordinary deep touched un-
nerved unworthy feeling as he moved his illuminated lips to go on
lying to the sick woman. Her fears, the solemn words, the glimpse of
finality, disturbed him with a sense of his own ending.

'God is there, isn't He? He is a person, isn't He? People sometimes say now He isn't a person.'

'Of course God is a person, we are persons, that is the highest
mode of being that we know, how can God be less than a person?'

'But there *is* eternal life like we pray for? And will I really go on
living and see my loved ones?'

'We cannot understand how this can be, but this is what in our
faith we firmly believe.'

'But will I go on being me? I wouldn't want to live on as somebody else, would I?'

'Eternal life would have no meaning for us if the individual does
not survive. God would not cheat us with a different kind of
survival.'

'I don't know. He can do anything.'

'Not cheat.'

'And you're sure I won't go to hell?'

'I think you can be confident of that, my dear. I doubt if anybody
goes to hell.'

'Not even Hitler? I'd like to think he was there.'

'Come now, you must put away such revengeful thoughts!'

'Will you pray for me?'

'Of course.'

At number 34 The Crescent, William Eastcote, who had been
sitting at his desk and looking at his will, was suddenly plunged into
a twilit darkness. He had made a careful rational will, leaving a
large part of his property to Anthea, and dividing the rest among
various good causes: the Meeting House, famine relief, cancer
research, Amnesty, St Olaf's alms houses, the Asian Centre in
Burkestown, the community centre in the wasteland, the Boys'
Club, the Salvation Army Hostel, the National Art Collections
Fund (this was for Rose who had cared about pictures). Now as
he sat motionless in the increasing dark he felt a strong irrational
impulse to leave the lot to Anthea. Why? Was this a last confused
desire for some kind of survival? (William did not share Miss
Dunbury's hopes.) There was a lot of money, the fine house in the
Crescent, some valuable building land beyond the Tweed Mill.
William realized now how much his wealth had fattened him, made

him feel solid and real. How thin and wraith-like he was beginning to feel now.

A little earlier, Tom McCaffrey had been making his way through the livid rainy evening in the direction of the Slipper House, holding an umbrella carefully up over his head and a bunch of yellow tulips which he was carrying. He felt singularly ridiculous and quite venomously angry with himself. He had yesterday sent a picture postcard (representing the Botanic Garden) to Miss Harriet Meynell which read as follows:

> I shall be at Belmont tomorrow evening and I wonder if I could drop in for a moment to introduce myself? I believe you know my stepmother, and your grandfather wants us to be acquainted since you are a newcomer to Ennistone. I will telephone later to see if a time shortly before nine would be suitable. With best wishes,
>
> Tom McCaffrey

A telephone call in the morning (Pearl answered) had established that that hour would be convenient. Now he was going along, as he put it to himself, to get the thing over with. He had decided against inviting Hattie to Travancore Avenue because of Emma, and also because of the awful possibility that the young lady, once there, would not soon depart. Besides, how could he 'entertain' her? It was only natural in a way for him (pretending to visit Belmont) to 'pass by' the Slipper House, where, after making a token appearance, he could inform Rozanov that he had tried and given up. The glimpse of Hattie at the Baths which had set Emma laughing had been enough for Tom also. He had seen a bedraggled red-nosed rat-child, a *child* about whom, with the best will in the world, no romantic fantasy could weave.

When the lights went out, Tom had entered the garden by the back gate from Forum Way. One moment he could see the street lights revealing the young green branches of trees, the lights of the Slipper House, and beyond the lights of Belmont. The next moment all was dark against the dim rainy twilight of the sky. In the sudden obscurity Tom laid his open umbrella down on the grass and tried to work out the outline of the Slipper House roof. As he peered and blinked, the wind took the umbrella hopping lightly away across the lawn. He dropped the flowers and pursued the umbrella, then could not find the flowers and stepped on them. Suddenly a light flared in the murk ahead. He stood and watched as dim flickering lights appeared in several windows of the house where the girls had not yet closed the shutters. Figures moved carrying candles. He waited a while, watching the pale rectangles of the windows emerging; and as he watched he revived in his heart an old fantasy, that he had been conceived in the Slipper House, when Fiona and Alan lay together on that first night. Then he went forward and knocked.

Pearl opened the door. She had not put on her maidservant rig for Tom. She was dressed in jeans and an old jersey. This evening her part was to look shaggy, sluttish and of uncertain age. She did not regard Tom, bearer of John Robert's bright idea, as a happy portent. If John Robert wanted to marry Hattie off so soon, what was to become of Pearl? Also, Pearl had imbibed, perhaps from Ruby, on her odd visits to Ennistone, the notion of Tom as a little local star, and she felt a very private kind of annoyance at seeing this special young man being offered to Hattie on a plate. Of course Hattie, who declined to regard the introduction as a serious matter, would not take him. But Pearl had divined, as Hattie had not, John Robert's weird seriousness: a curious, in respect to Hattie, intensity which Pearl now felt she was not observing for the first time and which troubled her much. She felt alarmed and apprehensive and jealous. And now there were to be handsome young men to whom she would open the door and for whom she would be invisible and old. That was why she dressed, on that evening, invisible and old. In America she had never felt like a servant.

'Let me take your umbrella. Miss Meynell is in the sitting-room.'

Tom, who had no overcoat, handed over his dripping umbrella. A candle on the window ledge showed half their faces and cast their swaying shadows as Pearl closed the front door.

Tom went into the sitting-room carrying the tulips. Pearl, outside, said, 'I'll bring more light.' Two candles, one on the mantelpiece and one on the glass-topped bamboo table, made a soft dim dome of illumination in the room.

Hattie had aggressively refused to put her hair up. She wore it strained back from her face and hanging in a single thick heavy pigtail down her back. She was wearing a scrappy tee shirt and tight jeans which showed how long and skinny her legs were. Her skin looked little-girlish, not youthful. Her collar-bones but not her breasts were prominent under the shirt. She looked almost as childish to Tom as in his first glimpse of her, though less bedraggled.

'I've brought you some flowers,' said Tom. He held them out and

Hattie took them. 'Oh dear, they're all muddy!' The yellow tulips were dabbled with mud. 'I'm afraid I dropped them.'

Pearl came in with two more candles. 'Where shall I put these?'

'Oh anywhere. Could you wash the flowers?' said Hattie. (These were the first words Tom heard her utter.) She gave the tulips to Pearl who had put the candles down on the window seat. 'Would you like a drink? Is Coke OK?'

'Lovely,' said Tom, who hated Coke. Tom drew his fingers back through his long, now rather damp, curly hair, combing it. Pearl returned with the drinks and with the scrubbed and now rather battered tulips in a mauve vase.

'How beautiful candlelight is,' said Tom.

'We said we'd have the fire,' said Hattie to Pearl, 'and could you close the shutters?'

Hattie and Tom watched Pearl light the gas fire, and close the shutters, revealing Ned Larkin's picture.

Hattie handed Tom a glass of Coca-Cola, taking one herself, and said, 'Oh please sit down.' They sat down on slightly swaying bamboo chairs with fitted cushions.

'Have you any oil-lamps?' said Tom. 'They're useful for these occasions.'

'I don't think so,' said Hattie, and then, after a pause, 'I think you know my grandfather?'

'Yes, I met him once.'

'*Once?*'

'Well, yes –'

'I supposed that he knew you quite well.'

'I hadn't met him before last week, when he asked me to come and see him.'

'Oh,' said Hattie. 'What about?'

'About you.'

'About *me*?'

'Yes, but – he must have told you –'

'Told me what?'

'His idea.'

'What idea?'

'About us.'

'*Us?*'

'You and me. Sorry, I'm not putting it very well –'

'So it was his idea that you should come and see me?' said Hattie.

'In a way, yes. I mean, yes.'

'But why?'

'He wants us to know each other.'

'Why?'

'Well, why not!' said Tom. He was aware of having made a number of blunders already and was acutely conscious of the perfectly horrid falsity of his position, but he was exasperated too by Hattie's hard aggressive tone, as if it was all his fault. He thought, has she no sense of humour, no sense of *fun*? Why is she so cross with *me*? 'I mean,' he said, 'you're a newcomer here –'

'And so –?'

'I could show you round and introduce you and – that's strictly all, I – there's no need to think –'

'Oh I don't!' said Hattie. She seemed to be stiff with anger.

'I wasn't suggesting –'

'Naturally not,' said Hattie with extreme coldness. 'We haven't met anywhere, have we, that I can recall?'

'No, I saw you for about three seconds at the Baths on that awfully cold day when it snowed. Two seconds actually. I can't say that I –'

'No indeed. I see. Well, I'm sorry you've been put to this trouble.'

'No trouble, I assure you – I do hope –'

'My maid knows Ennistone well and will be perfectly able to show me round, so there is no need for you to be inconvenienced.'

'But –'

'Anyway, I am going home soon.'

'Home –?'

'Back to Colorado where I live.'

The American name entered the conversation with a kind of fierce chopping movement, and Tom felt brought up short as if he had been suddenly confronted by an icy cliff of Rockies. 'Oh well – in that case –' he murmured.

There was a silence, during which Hattie picked up her glass from the floor and reached out to replace it with a click upon the glass-topped bamboo table. Then she stood up.

Tom began to say, 'I'm afraid I –' Then he stood up too.

Pearl, who had of course been listening outside, smartly opened the sitting-room door. Tom (this had now somehow become inevitable) marched out into the hall. He turned and faced the two girls, the thin pale young one, the sturdy brown older one, their faces knit up into expressions of extreme hostile anxiety. He thought, this is *absurd*, it is all a *mistake*, I can *explain*. But he could not explain.

327

He said, 'I'm awfully sorry – I'm sorry I bothered you – I'm afraid I didn't manage to say –'

'Not at all,' said Hattie.

Pearl opened the front door.

Tom went out into the rain and began to blunder his way through the now totally dark garden in the direction of the back gate. The rain, soaking his hair and running down his neck, reminded him that he had left his umbrella behind. He turned back and was approaching the house again when the front door flew open. Something was hurled violently out and scattered on the lawn. It was his ill-fated bunch of tulips. As the door slammed shut he stood still, shocked, for a moment, looking at the candle in the hall window wavering wildly in the sudden draught. Then he turned and ran away down the garden.

'But what *is* it?' said Pearl, as Hattie's tears ran through her fingers.

'Didn't you hear?'

'Yes, but –'

'He isn't an admirer, he's a *liar* – and he brought those horrible lying flowers –'

'It wasn't the poor flowers' fault! And why is he a liar?'

'He just came because he was told to.'

'All right then, but he thought you'd understand.'

'Understand what? Something *horrible* –'

'But you're complaining because he's not an admirer.'

'I'm not complaining!'

'You said you didn't want one!'

'I *don't*. I just want to be left *alone*. And then this horrible *spoiling* thing happens. Oh why did he have to *come*? He's a horrible person, so *rude* – and it's *all* spoilt now – oh Pearlie, Pearlie, I want to go home, I want to go home!'

Oh dear, thought Pearl, as she took Hattie in her arms, what a mess, whatever is it all about – and what a handsome boy he is too – well, I suppose that's part of the trouble. Awful things are just starting. And soon poor Pearl was finding tears of her own to shed.

'Are you going for your usual walk?' said Gabriel to Brian.

The notorious McCaffrey summer expedition to the seaside was in full swing. The sun was shining, the east wind was blowing, it was now May. The jaunt had, after discussion, settled down to being for one day only, which was generally agreed to offer the worst of all worlds. Brian usually demonstrated his dislike of this intensive family gathering by turning his back on the famous element and walking inland, thus avoiding any participation in junketings on the beach.

'No,' said Brian.

'Why? Are you too tired?'

'No. I'm not in the least tired. Why should I be?'

'Will you sit here then? Or would you like to go on the rocks?'

'Why do you want to make it all out into a programme? Just don't *bother* me!'

Gabriel gave a little (maddening to Brian) frown at being hurt, and went on silently unpacking the various ritual objects which always made up the Brian McCaffreys' home base on the beach.

Brian asked himself, why don't I want to go for a walk like I usually do? The answer was terrible. He was afraid that Gabriel might find herself alone with George. She might actually *attempt* to be alone with George. Am I going mad? Brian wondered. Why did George come anyway? It was shameless of him to come to the seaside just as if he were an ordinary person.

Of course there were other expeditions to the sea but this was the one which was supposed to assemble all the clan, and which Gabriel had (not felicitously for her husband) compared to Christmas. It continued a tradition of annual family summer gatherings at Maryville and could be seen as a kind of remembrance of, or mourning for, that house which was less than a mile distant from where the clan was now encamped. This was an aspect of it which Brian particularly detested. He had never liked the McCaffrey seaside house, since he so much preferred his own. He had however resented (as they all did) Alex's disgraceful act of selling it without consultation. Now he felt the whole thing was better forgotten. Gabriel always came back in tears, lamenting for the lost house. And if the visit was supposed to show the usurping Blacketts that the McCaffreys didn't care it was clearly misconceived. Of course, that particular bit of coastline, as well as being the nearest unspoilt sea to Ennistone, was exceptionally delightful; but it would have showed more spirit to abandon the place altogether. In a more general sense of course the pilgrimage survived because it had somehow become a family custom, animated and maintained by the sentimentality of the women (that is Gabriel, Alex and Ruby) and the expectations of the children (that is Adam and Zed). Alex pretended indifference, but in fact valued the event as an exhibition of her matriarchal power.

'If only Stella were here,' said Gabriel, as she spread out a large tartan rug, 'it would be –' she was going to say 'perfect', only honesty compelled her to realize that no such picture with Brian in it could be perfect – 'so nice.'

Stella, who had not reappeared, was now said, in terms of a rumour which probably had no sounder foundation than the one that pronounced her dead, to be staying with friends in London.

'Stella hated this jamboree as much as I do,' said Brian, kicking a stone. 'And if we must come I fail to see why we have to have those bloody outsiders.'

The persons gathered, now scattered, upon the windy sunny beach were as follows: Brian, Gabriel, Adam and Zed, Alex and Ruby, George, Tom and Emma, and Hattie and Pearl. Alex had prompted Tom to bring Emma. Tom, who loved the occasion, would have come anyway, and the two 'idle louts' as Brian called them, had evidently found no difficulty in escaping from their university work in London. Gabriel had also, to Brian's disgust, invited Hattie and Pearl, encountering them one day at the Baths. She did this partly out of benevolence to one generally agreed to be a waif, partly out of a sort of motherly possessiveness which she had enouraged herself to develop about Hattie and which had so far found no other expression, and partly out of an obsessive irritated envy and curiosity which she felt about the fortunate tenant of the coveted Slipper House. Anyway, there they all were.

The Brian McCaffreys had driven themselves, together with Tom and Emma, in Brian's old Austin. Pearl had driven Hattie in a hired

330

Volkswagen. (The girls had never been allowed to have a car of their own, but Pearl had learnt to drive in America where they were occasionally permitted to hire a car.) Alex had driven George and Ruby in William Eastcote's Rover, which William always pressed her to borrow whenever she needed it. (It had never for some reason been 'the thing' to invite the Eastcotes, William, Anthea, and when she was alive, Rose, to join this family occasion.) The cars were parked on a track at the upper end of the long sheep-dotted yellow field of wiry wind-combed grass down which they had walked to the sea. The grass ended in a wire fence through which one crawled on to the dark rocks, easy to descend, which fringed the beach all along. The beach itself was gritty, the coarse sand mingling with small pebbles, and the dark raggedy rocks began again seawards, covered with golden brown seaweed and extensively visible at low tide.

Various 'camps' had been established and sheltered spots for undressing 'bagged'. Gabriel had undone her corded bales well out in the middle of the sand, as she never bothered about hiding to undress. Alex and Ruby occupied a little cave-like recess in the landward rocks which was traditionally theirs. Hattie and Pearl had walked away shyly along the beach and evidently found a similar retreat, since they were no longer to be seen. Tom and Emma had carried their kit to a summit of the landward rocks where the serrated tops surrounding a hollow composed a citadel. Adam and Zed had of course run down to the sea whose distant wavelets they were approaching by slithering over the seaweedy rocks, with many pauses to inspect the exciting pools. George, isolated upon a low rock which reared itself some distance away in the midst of the sand, was sitting and gazing at the sea. Further away along the coast, one topmost corner of Maryville could just be seen above the rocks which rose at that point almost to the dignity of cliffs.

A prompt start had been made and it was still early in the day. The usual procedure ('usual procedures' are sacred upon such family occasions) was that there should first be swimming, organized from the separate camps, then sunbathing, should that be feasible, and strolling about, then *drinks* (a ceremony especially sacred to Gabriel and Alex) with the company gathered together to form a 'party', then lunch, also taken more or less together as far as was convenient in terms of using rocks for seats and tables, then more strolling and wandering including sometimes a special short walk (not Brian's walk) inland to a ruined manor house with a wild garden, then a second bathe for those who felt strong enough, then tea, then more drinks, then time to go home. It made a long day. Ruby and Gabriel 'did' all the food (Gabriel loved doing this) and Gabriel and Alex provided all the drinks. On this occasion Gabriel had packed the extra rations for the visitors (outsiders), Emma, Hattie and Pearl.

Since a little time has passed, some explanation is necessary concerning the present state of the parties. The university term had started and Tom and Emma had officially removed themselves to their digs in King's Cross. However, the young Osmores were prolonging their stay in America, and Tom McCaffrey was to be seen at Travancore Avenue oftener, it was said, than was consistent with strict attention to his studies. Of course many Ennistonians now, with the improved rail link, commuted daily to work in London, but it was agreed to be a tiring and time-consuming journey. However that might be, Tom, and sometimes Emma, tended to appear at weekends. Tom had a reason for these sojourns in his native town since he had become involved in the production of *The Triumph of Aphrodite* which was to be performed in June, with assistance from the Arts Council. Tom now, in fact, figured as co-author with Gideon Parke, having learnt to imitate the style of the eighteenth-century poet, providing yards of handy additional stuff which was rumoured to be 'better than the original'. This included a charming extra song for the boy (Olivia Newbold's younger brother Simon) who was, on the advice of Jonathan Treece (formerly choir master at St Paul's, now organist at an Oxford College), to sing the jester's part designed for the undiscoverable countertenor. During rehearsals Tom inevitably saw a good deal of Anthea Eastcote and was to be seen walking with her about the town, thereby reviving old speculations and driving Hector Gaines more often than before to the contemplation of suicide.

Of course Tom had, even in the company of the agreeable Anthea, very odd secret thoughts in his head. In fact he was worrying and annoying himself into a frenzy. He thought he could actually see lines appearing on his forehead. The ridiculous misbegotten interview with Hattie had left a painful throbbing scar upon Tom's soul. Tom was accustomed to an unscarred soul; an aspect of his cheerful temperament was indeed a calm modest sunny little self-satisfaction of which he allowed himself to be aware as harmless. He had had a poem accepted by a periodical, a real literary magazine, not a senseless rag like the *Ennistone Gazette*; but he noticed with horror that this success gave him less than the expected amount of pleasure. His pleasure was being stolen. He felt that he had done badly, he even suspected that he had behaved like a cad, a role in which he had never dreamt to see himself. At the same time the whole thing was hideously obscure and he couldn't clearly make out *how* he had done what he ought not to have done, and even *what* it was that he had done. When he had discussed the matter with Emma, he had hung his head at his friend's strictures without however receiving any enlightenment from him. Yes, perhaps he ought not to have agreed to Rozanov's dotty idea, which he had seen in the light of an innocent lark. It had then seemed reasonable to go and see the girl, so as to satisfy the philosopher if for nothing else. The trouble (was that it?) was that the philosopher had not properly warned the girl, had perhaps even misled her, which was certainly not Tom's fault. And she had been so cold and hostile from the start that he had been unable to get any grasp upon the situation. ('You're annoyed because you failed to charm her,' said Emma.) Now there was a blot upon the world which Tom heartily wished to remove but could not; indeed it paralysed him. He considered writing a letter of apology to Hattie, but any letter he envisaged could be seen as a continuation of some unpardonable rudeness. He told himself that he ought to write to Rozanov and tell him that he had failed. But he hated the idea of writing this letter too. Would he really then have to affirm that he would never speak to the girl again? And now here she was, invited by tactless Gabriel to spoil the family picnic.

'How soon can we go home?' said Scarlett-Taylor, sitting beside Tom on their citadel rock.

'Don't be silly, you've got to enjoy yourself first.'

'Swimming in this wind, in that choppy dark-green sea?'

'It'll make you feel wonderful. Look, there's Maryville. You can just see the top window and the edge of the roof. I suppose you'll say, no wonder Alex sold the place.'

'No, I think this is all marvellous.'

'Well then –'

'I just don't want to swim. But I love this sort of coast. I love the rocks and the seaweed and that black-and-white-striped lighthouse and the gulls crying like that. It reminds me of Donegal. Only,' he added, 'Donegal is far far more beautiful.' And Emma thought to himself how terribly sad it was that he could not love his native land or return to it with pleasure any more. And he thought how sad it was that he loved Tom, and yet that love could not go out and reach its object. It seemed to vaporize, to dissolve as at some invisible barrier. And he thought about his mother, to whom he had paid a guilty, scrappy two-day visit just before term began. And he thought about his singing teacher, Mr Hanway, and how he had not yet managed to tell him that he had decided to give up singing. And shall I really *never sing again*? he thought.

'Look at old George sitting there and brooding. Whatever is he thinking, I wonder!'

'Why has he come?'

'To act lonely and misunderstood. Look at that pose.'

'I want to talk to George,' said Emma. 'I want to have a long talk with him.'

'You want to help him, everyone does, isn't he lucky!'

'Don't you want to help him, don't you love him?'

'Oh, I suppose so, but what can love do if it can't get in, wander round wailing?'

What indeed. 'How I wish I hadn't missed seeing Stella that day at Brian's place.'

'Yes, you just missed her. Stella's strong, she's stronger than any of us. And so beautiful – she's like an Egyptian queen.'

'But where is she?'

'In London. Or gone back to her father in Tokyo is my guess.'

'Isn't it odd?'

'Yes, but George and Stella have always been odd.'

'Why, there's Miss Meynell and Miss Scotney.'

'How do you know the maid's name?'

'I heard it at the Baths.'

'Good heavens, they're starting to undress, they don't know we're up here and can see them, quick!'

Tom and Emma slithered down the side of the rock and ran away across the beach towards the water.

The drinks before lunch had been as follows: Gabriel had brought a gin and fresh orange juice mixture all cold in thermos flasks. Alex had brought two bottles of whisky and two soda syphons. Pearl had brought Coca-Cola. Yugoslav Riesling had been served with lunch. The food at lunch had been as follows: Gabriel's 'spread' consisted of pâté with oatmeal biscuits, Danish salami, slices of tongue, lettuce salad, tomato salad, watercress, new potatoes, rye bread with caraway seeds, cottage cheese, summer pudding and grapes. While Ruby provided ham sandwiches, egg sandwiches, cucumber sandwiches, sausages, veal-and-ham pie, water biscuits, Cheddar cheese, Double Gloucester cheese, custard tarts and bananas. As Ruby and Gabriel never consulted each other about how much to bring, both made sure of feeding everybody, so there was plenty to eat. Emma achieved his ambition of having a conversation with George. He made a point of sitting near him and questioned him about the Ennistone Ring and the Museum. There was a general embarrassment (enjoyed by George) when Emma (who did not know of George's exploit) expressed regret that the Museum's unique collection of Roman glass, about which he had read, was not on display. Coughing by Brian and a kick from Tom then terminated the brief conversation. However, it had *been* a conversation and there had been a little perhaps absurd surprise at the spectacle of George behaving in a perfectly ordinary way. (Yet how did they expect him to behave?) George displayed no eccentricity except that, while answering Emma's questions, he stared fixedly at Hattie. He had taken off his jacket and waistcoat, displaying a new plumpness. His round face looked pleased and calm, and his stare was benevolent though intense. Hattie, aware of it, averted her head. Before lunch Tom had politely asked Hattie if she did not find the sea cold, and she had politely answered that it was no colder than Maine. At lunch he had endeavoured to sit next to Hattie, but had been prevented, intentionally or not, by Pearl who, in the awkwardness of their sitting down on rocks and rugs, took the vacant place. Alex, looking slim and youthful in trousers and a brilliant blue beach shirt, her bushy peppery-salty hair gleaming in the sun, made herself agreeable to the girls, while being acutely conscious of George. Gabriel, also acutely conscious of George, could not help looking at him with a little smile which expressed, look how *good* he's being. She even turned to Brian, indicating George's splendidly normal behaviour with an approving nod. This annoyed both Brian and Tom.

'Where have you been?' said Alex to Ruby. 'I've had to do all the clearing-up myself, everyone's gone away.'

'I went for a walk.'

'A *walk*? You don't walk.'

335

'I went to look at the house.'

'Maryville? We don't want them to think we're spying! Please finish all this now. I've done most of it anyway.'

Alex walked away. She was quite suddenly feeling the most intense regret about having sold Maryville. She thought, I could have invited *him* there, a sort of house party, it would have made sense, he would have come. She had been so near to getting him in through the door of Belmont that time when he appeared with the bottles. What did *they* mean? She felt lonely and resentful on the empty beach and the sound of the sea made her think about death. She wanted to find George, but he had gone; everyone had gone. Looking to see the time, she found that her watch was no longer on her wrist; she must have dropped it somewhere. Moaning with vexation, she began to search the sand.

'Where's George?' said Brian to Tom.

'I don't know.'

'Did Gabriel come with you?'

'No, I haven't seen her.'

Brian had walked along beside the rocks, the lighthouse way, not the Maryville way, with Adam and Zed. He thought Gabriel had set off that way, but she was not to be seen. He hurried back, leaving Adam and Zed on the beach near their camp, 'Don't swim until I come back,' and then ran all the way to the ruined manor house. There was laughter in the garden, Tom, Hattie, Pearl and Emma, but no Gabriel. Brian thought, she's somewhere with George. Puffing, he began to run back to the beach.

'I want to sort of apologize,' said Tom to Hattie. They were for a moment alone together in the wild garden, where the box hedges had grown into ragged monsters twelve feet high. Fragments of old paving, of statues and urns and balustrades, lay about half-buried under grass and moss, and great prickly arches of roses run wild. A distant cuckoo chanted. Invisible larks were singing high above in the blinding blue air.

'Why, there's a hand!' said Hattie. She detached a life-size stone hand from a tangle of brambles.

'How beautiful, how strange.'

'Would you like it?'

'No, it's yours.'

'Is it marble?'

'Limestone, I think.'

'Why sort of?'

'What?'

'Why just "sort of" apologize?'

'Why indeed. I want to apologize.'

'Go on then.'

'I don't know how to do it –'

'Don't then.'

'I mean – I thought your grandfather had told you –'

'Told me what?'

'That he wanted – well, that he wanted us to get married.'

Hattie was silent for a moment looking at the hand. Her hair, fuzzy from immersion in the sea, held at the back of her neck by a ribbon, swarmed down her back. She put the hand in the pocket of her dress (she was wearing her new summer dress from Anne Lapwing's Boutique), but the hand was too heavy and the dress sagged. She took it out again.

'All right. I regard you as having apologized.'

'But –'

'It doesn't matter, it doesn't *matter*.'

'It sounds crazy, doesn't it –'

'What does?'

'What he wanted.'

'Yes.'

'I mean – he is a bit eccentric – things don't happen like that, do they –'

'No.'

'Will you tell him?'

'Tell him what?'

'That I visited you – that I – that I tried –'

'No. It's nothing to do with me. It's nothing *whatever* to do with me.'

'Oh – all right –' said Tom unhappily. 'I'll write to him.' He had hoped that his 'apology' would free him from guilt and the feeling, which Tom hated, that someone thought ill of him. But now it all seemed even worse. What a muddle.

'I've wanted to talk to you for some time,' said Emma. He and Pearl were alone together in another part of the garden where there was an overgrown lily-pond at the bottom of a broken flight of steps. The lilies had covered almost all the surface of the water. Just here and there, in dark-green windows, there was the quick golden flash of a huge orfe.

'How can that be?' said Pearl. 'We've only met today.' Pearl was

337

wearing a summer dress too, not a flowy flowery one like Hattie's, but a straight yellow shift, like a sort of science fiction uniform, roped in at the waist to an increased narrowness. Her head too, with her straight profile, looked narrow as if it were trying to be two-dimensional. The sun had made her dark complexion a shade darker, raising a reddish-brown glow in her cheeks, and finding reddish lights in her dark hair, which she had had expertly cut much shorter.

'I saw you several times at the Baths, at the Institute as they call it.'

'Oh –?' Pearl found Emma very odd. He was perspiring in his coat and waistcoat, and his pale face was burnt to an uncomfortable shiny pink. He peered at her sternly through his narrow oval glasses.

'Yes. You interest me.'

'It's kind of you to be interested! You know I'm Miss Meynell's maid?'

'Yes, that's picturesque but not important. It's quaint for anybody to be anybody's maid these days.'

'You're Irish, aren't you?'

'That too is picturesque but not important.'

'Well, what is important?'

'You are.' Emma threw a stone into the pool but it did not sink, it rested upon a thick water-lily leaf. He threw another to hit the first but missed.

'What can I do for you?' said Pearl, rather curtly.

'Ah, I don't know that yet,' said Emma. 'Possibly nothing.' He added, 'I wanted to meet you before I knew who you were.'

'But why did you want to meet me? I'm sorry, this is becoming a rather silly conversation.'

'I don't think so. A little laboured, but we make progress. Again, I don't know. Why is one impressed by some people and not by others? That's not a matter of logic.'

'I think we should go back –'

'I don't usually talk to girls like this. I don't usually talk to girls at all.'

'It may be better not to talk. You'll find me very dull.'

'Why do you think that?'

'I know nothing.'

'That's all right, I know everything. If you want to know anything, I can tell you.'

'You're a historian –?'

'Yes. Of course all I know is facts and a few tattered ideas I find adhering to them.'

'We'd better go and join Miss Meynell and Mr McCaffrey.'

'My friend is called Tom, your friend is called Hattie. Can't you drop the Misses and Misters?'

'No.'

'As you please. I've thought of a reason why I wanted to meet you.'

'Why?'

'You look dry.'

'Dry?'

'Yes. Girls are seldom dry.'

'What does it mean?'

'Dry as in hard and dry. The opposite to soft and mushy.'

'I thought men liked softness. Perhaps you think I'm like a boy.'

'Tell me something about yourself.'

'What?'

'Anything.'

'My mother was a prostitute.'

'Am I supposed to be impressed?'

Meanwhile Gabriel was having a terrible experience. She had set off walking along the beach (as Brian had seen her do) but had soon climbed up on to the rocks on the landward side and begun to clamber along them. Was she looking for George? No. The idea of being alone with George in this intense wild region filled her with fear. Did she enjoy the fear? She went on and came at last to a place she knew, not far from the lighthouse, where the rocks became steep and the strip of sand between the seaward rocks and the landward rocks disappeared, and the rocks fell sheer into deep water. Here, lifting her head from a difficult scramble, she suddenly saw a man ahead of her, outlined against the sky. For a second she thought it was George. Then she saw that in fact it was not a man, but a tall teenage boy. As she advanced, she saw another boy. They were standing looking down into a shallow pool in the rocks where, above the high-tide mark, the winter storms had tossed some flying water. Gabriel knew the pool. As she came forward the boys saw her. 'Hello.' 'Hello.' Gabriel paused beside the pool and looked down too. Then she felt an instant spasm of pain and premonitory fear. There was a fish swimming to and fro in the pool, a large fish about eighteen inches long. Gabriel thought, that fish has no

339

business in that pool, he must have been put there by the boys. Her identification with the fish was instantaneous. She thought, he will very soon suffocate if he is left here. The pool is foul anyway, the sea never reaches it at this time of year.

She said, 'What a lovely fish. Did you catch him?'

'Yes.'

'Are you going to put him back in the sea?'

'No. Not likely!'

'You can't leave him here –'

'Why not?'

'He'll suffocate in that small pool.'

'We're going to take him home,' said the other boy. 'We've got a bucket.'

'To eat?'

'Maybe. Or maybe just to keep.'

'You wouldn't be able to keep that fish alive.'

'Why not?'

'Won't you please put him back in the sea? We could catch him and just drop him over the edge here into the deep water, and see him swim away. Wouldn't that be a nice thing to do?'

The taller boy laughed. 'I'm not going to put it back. It's my fish!'

The boys were about fifteen, dressed in black leather jackets and jeans, their hair cut close to their heads. The spectacle of Gabriel's distress clearly amused them.

'Please,' said Gabriel, '*please.*' She squatted down beside the pool.

'Hey, leave it alone!'

'He's so lovely, he's so alive, and he may die –'

'I bet you eat fish and chips!' said the other boy.

Gabriel said, with a sudden inspiration, 'I'll buy it from you!'

They laughed again. 'Would you, how much?'

'I'll give you a pound.'

'Two pounds.'

'All right, two pounds.'

'Ten pounds, twenty pounds, a hundred pounds.'

'I'll give you two pounds for the fish.'

'Let's see the two pounds.'

'Oh dear –' Gabriel had no money with her. Her handbag was lying on the sand under a rug with the remains of lunch. 'I haven't got it here. I'll get it from the beach. But can we let the fish go first, please let's, and I promise I'll give you the two pounds. You can come with me –'

'No,' said the taller boy. 'You bring the two pounds and we might, I just say *might*, let you have the fish.'

Tears came into Gabriel's eyes. She stood up. 'You *will* stay here, you won't take the fish away?'

'We won't stay forever!'

Gabriel turned and began to scramble back across the rocks. She slipped and tore her stocking and grazed her leg and scarcely noticed and bundled on.

'Oh *there* you are!' It was Brian who had returned to the beach.

'Oh Brian, darling!' Gabriel slithered down to the sand, wrenching her skirt. 'Could you give me two pounds, quick, please –'

'Two pounds?' said Brian, whose relief had instantly evaporated as soon as it appeared. He was exhausted with running to and fro, and annoyed with Gabriel for vanishing. 'What for?'

'Some boys have got a fish, a live fish, I want to buy it to save it –'

'Two pounds, for a fish?'

'I want to put it back in the sea.'

'Oh don't be silly,' said Brian. 'We're not made of money. Certainly not.'

Gabriel turned from him and ran on laboriously, her feet sinking in the sand, her face red with tears.

> 'And did those feet in ancient time
> Walk upon England's mountains green?
> And was the holy Lamb of God
> On England's pleasant pastures seen?
>
> And did the Countenance Divine
> Shine forth upon our clouded hills?'

The four young people were together again in the wild garden. Tom, after his second defeat, as he felt it to be, at the hands of Hattie, had hastened, with her, to seek for Emma and Pearl. Then they had walked on together and climbed into the ruined shell of the manor house which was filled with grass and buttercups and daisies and white-flowering nettles. Inside the irregular remains of the walls, which contained two fine Elizabethan windows, it felt odd and ghostly, as if, in spite of the bright sun, the place were twilit. In the grassy space which had been the great hall there was a curious echo, and Tom had persuaded Emma to sing, and Emma had sung Blake's beautiful anthem. Emma had drunk as much whisky and Riesling as he could lay hands on at lunch, and this explained his readiness to sing, as well as the temerity of his conversation with Pearl. The sheer sudden force of the singing and the high sweet slightly rough piercing quality of the sound amazed and fascinated the two girls as Tom had intended. Looking at their rapt faces, he felt a sharp pang of envy. He was not always able to feel his friend's gifts as his own.

'I don't understand the poem,' said Hattie, after they had congratulated Emma. 'Why is he *asking* "did those feet"?'

'It's a poem,' said Tom. 'It doesn't have to mean anything exact. It's a sort of rhetorical question. He's just imagining Christ here.'

'But perhaps he was here,' said Emma. 'Miss Meynell is right to notice the question. After all there is that legend –'

'What legend?' said Tom.

'That Christ was here.'

'*Where?*'

'Yes, in England, as a child. He came here as a child with his Uncle Joseph of Arimathea who was a tin merchant.'

'*Did* he? *Christ*? *Here*?'

'It's a legend. Haven't you ever heard it?'

'No. But it's *wonderful*!' said Tom, suddenly transported. 'And it could be true. Fancy Christ here, walking on our fields. It's so – oh it's so *beautiful* – and it's *great*! He came with his Uncle Joseph of Arimathea as a child. Oh that makes me so *happy*!'

Emma laughed at him. 'You're easily excited by what every schoolboy knows!'

'I didn't know it,' said Hattie.

'I must go – I must run –'

'What for?'

'I must tell somebody else, I must pass the news on! Oh I'm so *pleased*! I must run and run!' With these words Tom vaulted over one of the low parts of the wall and ran across the ruined terrace littered with broken stone, leapt to the grass, and began to run away as fast as he could towards the sea down a long avenue of vast ragged yew trees which had once been yew hedges.

Left above with the girls, Emma felt annoyed, annoyed with Tom for deserting him, annoyed with himself for singing, annoyed with Pearl for having been the occasion of that silly conversation, and annoyed with Hattie for being, as he had got it into his head, a touchy stuck-up little miss. He said rather curtly, 'We'd better get back now.' They set off after Tom, walking in silence.

Tom ran fast, then becoming breathless ran more slowly. He ran along a footpath bordered by misty white cow-parsley which was just coming into flower. The footpath ended at a little tarmac road, and across the road was the field and the descending track where they had parked the cars, and the vast semi-circular rim of the sea framed on one side by the old black-and-white lighthouse, and on the other by the promontory and the house set upon it, Maryville, which was fully visible from the top of the field. A man was walking along the road, it was George.

Tom ran up and seized his brother's arm, 'Oh George, George, did you know? Christ was here. Oh, it's a legend but it could be true. He was here in England like in Blake's poem. I never understood it before. He came as a child with his Uncle Joseph of Arimathea who was a tin merchant! It could be true, couldn't it? Fancy Christ here in England! Did you know?'

'I knew of the legend,' said George, detaching Tom's arm, but gently.

'Everybody knew but me. But now I know and it's – like a revelation – it changes things. Oh George, I do want you to be all right, I'd do anything for you, I'll pray for you, I do pray for you when I pray, I sort of pray, I suppose that's what it is, I care for you so much. Stella will come home, everything will be all right again. I think I see that now. I hate to think of you wandering about alone and thinking. Don't be alone and think terrible thoughts, will you, please. Something good will happen to you, something very good will come to you, I feel sure, I feel so sure –'

'Do you really pray for me?' said George, smiling with his little blunt teeth. 'I think that's rather impertinent.'

'Oh come and swim, come and swim with me now, like we used to. You know that would be good.'

'We go different ways. Go on. And as for your friend, he was never here, you may be certain of that. Go on, go on.'

Adam had gone along the beach with Zed and discovered a place where a sort of river or gully of sand ran between the rocks right to the sea itself. Adam and Zed ran down to where the small waves were breaking. Adam took off his shoes and paddled. He knew that he was not supposed to go swimming by himself but it was so nice to be able to walk into the sea on gently shelving sand, instead of hobbling over stones and rocks. He was wearing his bathing trunks,

343

and when the water was deep enough he sat down, then turned over and swam a stroke or two. The water was very cold, but Adam was used to that. He loved the taste of the salt. Zed stood on the sand well back from the foam. He disliked and feared the sea and did not want to get his fur splashed. He wished that Adam would come back. To cheer himself up he pawed a pebble, pushing it a little, but his heart was not in the game. Adam came back and picked Zed up. He thought Zed might like a little swim, he swam so well, and Adam was always strangely and deeply excited to see him swim. He took the dog out beyond the surf and let him down gently into the water, watching the dry white fur become wet and clinging, feeling the warm dog in the cold sea. He let Zed go and watched with joy as the little dog paddled along keeping his fastidious nose and high forehead well above the water. Zed could have let Adam know how much he hated it, but he felt he had to be brave because that is a dog's duty, and had to pretend in order to please his master. Adam swam on a little bit and Zed followed, paddling with his strong little white paws, through the smooth glossy water which so quietly rose and fell. Adam played with Zed, encouraging him to ride on his shoulder. The sea felt warm now, and the blue sky blazed radiantly at them over the close horizon of the rhythmic waves.

Tom ran down on to the beach. Brian and Alex were searching for Alex's watch. He ran up to them. 'Did you know that Christ was in England?'

'What?' said Alex.

'Christ was in England. It's a legend. He came as a child with his Uncle Joseph of Arimathea who was a tin merchant.'

'I've lost my watch,' said Alex. 'It dropped off somewhere here. Or was it here? We've moved.'

'You search over there near that rock,' said Brian. He was upset because he had been nasty to Gabriel, he had not tried to take in what she was saying, and when he followed her to the beach Alex had collared him and Gabriel had disappeared.

'But did you know about Christ?' said Tom. 'It seems to me so extraordinary and so moving. Like in Blake's poem. "And did those feet in ancient time ..." I never understood it before.'

'It's impossible,' said Brian.

'But had you heard?'

'The legend, yes, but it's impossible, as your historical chum will tell you. Does he always drink so much? He reeled off positively sozzled.'

'Please help us to look!' said Alex, red-faced and stooping in an awkward position as she used to when she cried 'Damn, damn, damn!' with the dustpan and brush.

'We ought to get Zed. You remember he found that pack of sandwiches once.'

'Alex's watch doesn't smell,' said Brian.

'For a dog, anything smells.'

'Ruby's gone off again, blast her,' said Alex. 'She went to stare at Maryville. Sometimes I think she's mental.'

'Ruby will find it,' said Tom. 'She's got second sight. It's the gipsy blood.'

'Just search over there, will you? We haven't done that bit. I've got to go and find Gabriel. Have you seen Adam?'

'No. All right, all right!' Tom went over to the rock and looked about vaguely, thrusting at the coarse gritty sand with his foot. Then he sat on the rock and looked at the sea which was dark blue with a glittering crusty look like broken enamel. The tops of the waves were white with crisp creamy foam whipped up by the wind which had become stronger and colder. The sunny sky, where a few white puffy gilded clouds now sailed, was gleaming with a cold northern blue which Tom loved. He felt so happy all of a sudden. He thought, I'll write a pop song about that. 'Jesus was here, he was here, he was *here*, didn't you know, oh, didn't you know.' The combination of the child Christ in England, the familiar poem, Emma's beautiful strange high voice, and the blue-enamel sea made a huge complete perfect present moment.

It had been a wearisome run for Gabriel on the loose sand to reach her handbag and she had been sweating and panting. She took out the two pounds and threw off her cardigan. She ignored Alex who called to her, and ran back, climbing up again on to the higher rocks. The boys were still there. Then it proved very difficult to catch the fish, and Gabriel kept crying 'Let me, let me!' because she was afraid the boys would hurt its fins or pick it up roughly and drop it on the hard rock. At last one of them got hold of the slippery darting fish and somehow (Gabriel closed her eyes) stepped to the rock edge and dropped the fish into the deep water. Gabriel saw it enter the water and swim away and a great burden slipped from her heart. The boys laughed and said, 'If we catch another, will you buy it?' Gabriel began to walk back, happy, but feeling cold without her cardigan.

Adam was swimming round and round in circles and calling and

345

calling. He had lost Zed. In the end he had swum out quite a long way from the shore, it was such fun playing with the dog in the water, he had never done this before, watching him swim, then carrying him on his shoulder, then swimming ahead and calling to him. Zed swam so well, it was a joy to watch him. The waves were becoming a little higher and more rough and developing sharp ridgy crests. They showed darker against the sky, a cloud was crossing the sun, the wind was blowing a stinging white spray off the crests of the waves, Adam swallowed a lot of water; then suddenly Zed was nowhere to be seen. Adam cried out, screamed with fear, called and called, swam and swam. The little dog was nowhere. A moment ago he had been swimming near. Now he was gone. The waves rose now like high hills, cutting off any view. Adam could only try, as he swam over the crests, to survey the empty hollows beyond, hideous and dark and without dog, while the spray blinded his eyes. Exhaustion gripped him in the form of misery, remorse, terror, agony of longing for the precious lost being. Hope deceived him with white curly patches of foam between the waves. He began to scream hysterically. He thought, I must get help, I must get them to come, and he began with hideous hideous slowness to swim back toward the distant shore.

Emma let the girls go on ahead. Without Tom, their company embarrassed him and his clearly embarrassed them. As if let out of school, they ran on ahead laughing, probably at him. He wished he hadn't come. The place didn't really remind him of Donegal, the sea here was a dull navy blue, the land a pallid yellow and grey, Donegal was full of all sorts of colours. But he would never see Donegal again. He had noticed Brian noticing how much he drank. He thought, I scarcely drink at all for ages, then suddenly I drink like mad. Perhaps it's being Irish. Curse it, why do I have to think about being Irish, as if I hadn't enough troubles. And what possessed me to talk to that girl in that familiar way. I don't know anything about her; she must have thought me a complete oaf. And among all those McCaffreys did he not cut, thought Emma, an absurd figure; even worse, a pathetic one? No doubt he figured in their eyes, as he did for the moment in his own, as a lonely man, with no connections, no relations, no friends, who had attached himself forlornly to a family group. It was true that the whole group, with all their bonds and problems, interested him, not only as an extension of Tom. He had never before seen a family at close quarters, and their oddities and quarrels and misunderstandings and loves and hates and imperfect sympathies and impossible yet inevitable togetherness fascinated him very much. George fascinated him. But it was all a sort of hoax. He couldn't ever belong to the McCaffreys. He wouldn't ever, even if his friendship with Tom were to endure. He recalled how Tom had said 'I love you.' That scene seemed like play-acting now. How weak love is; it cannot push aside the big ordinary structures of life which divide different private individuals from each other. Then he thought of his mother, and how disappointed she had been because he had only stayed two days. However, as Emma began to walk down the yellow field he realized that something was very wrong on the beach. Someone was shouting, they were all running. He began to run too.

'What is it?'

Tom passed Emma running along the sand and tearing his jacket off as he ran. 'Zed's lost. Adam took him out into the sea and lost him.'

Pearl and Hattie ran hitching up their skirts, Alex ran bare foot, stumbling, Brian and Adam were ahead, Ruby, who had turned up, ran too. Emma ran after Tom. When they reached the long sandy gully which led down to where Adam had entered the sea they all began tearing off their clothes.

'Won't Zed swim to the shore?' said Emma.

'He wouldn't see the shore. Anyway look at those waves and those rocks. He'd never get in.'

Emma had not gone swimming with the others in the morning. He felt no wish to enter that cold sea. But he began to undress, putting his coat and his waistcoat and his watch and his trousers on to a ledge of rocks. No one bothered with bathing costumes which were all left somewhere behind at the base camps. Tom was rushing into the sea in his underpants. Emma followed him. The two girls, showing no hesitation, pulled off their dresses and kicked off their shoes and ran into the sea in their petticoats. Ruby, who could not swim, watched monumental with folded arms. Adam stood near where the waves were breaking and wept with an absolute abandonment of wailing and gushing tears, his mouth open, his hands raised up.

'What's happened?' shouted Gabriel running over the sand. And when she saw Adam crying so terribly, she began to wail herself.

'Zed's lost in the sea,' Alex cried. She had jumped out of her slacks and was unbuttoning her blue shirt. 'Stay with Adam.' She scuttled down the sandy shore and into the breaking waves. Weeping Gabriel ran to Adam and fell on her knees and clasped him in her arms, but he resisted her, flailing his arms and screaming with terrible woe.

Time passed, and they came back one by one. Alex returned first. She was used to long swims in the warm pool, but only to a brief dip in the sea. Clouds now covered the sun and the wind was sharper. Ruby had sensibly fetched the rugs, clothes, towels and other gear from the various camps. Alex, her teeth chattering, pulled off her wet underwear, dried and put on her slacks and shirt and woollen sweater belonging to Brian and wrapped herself in a rug. She had left her warmer clothes in the car. She did not approach the weeping pair. Hattie and Pearl came in next and seized their bundles and dressed fast. Emma felt it his duty to swim and search for a long time. He was very upset about Zed and so much wanted to be the one to find him and kept seeing little white phantom dogs in the sides of the sullen green waves. At last he gave up. Brian came in next and Tom last. There was no longed-for cry of 'There he is!' Ignoring each other and shivering with cold, the would-be rescuers searched for dry towels and dry clothes. Brian looked for his big jersey and took some time to realize that Alex had it. He put on Gabriel's mackintosh. Ruby had started to distribute mugs of hot tea out of the picnic thermos flasks, and everyone stood or sat about in silence. Hattie was crying quietly. Gabriel was weary of crying and sat with her wet mouth open and her face disfigured, staring out to sea. She refused her mug of tea. Beside her Adam sat hunched up, his face invisible, as if he had become himself a little diminished animal. Someone had to think of something to say. Tom thought of a number of possible things but rejected them.

Alex said at last, 'There's that current that goes round the point.'

Tom said, 'Maybe we should have looked on the other side.'

'It's impossible to get into the sea there.'

'I suppose it's no use going up to Maryville and borrowing some glasses?'

'No.'

'Have they got a boat?'

'If it's at the house we couldn't launch it here, if it's in the sea it'll be down the coast.'

'It's too late anyway,' said Brian.

There was a little silence.

Brian went on, 'He'll have got cold and tired and just drowned quietly. He won't have known what was happening to him.'

'No, he won't have known,' said Tom, 'like going to sleep.'

'Well, let's get ourselves home,' said Brian. 'Come on. It isn't as if one of us had drowned. We've got something to be thankful for.'

After lunch George had kept clear of the party. He walked along the little tarmac road, first away from Maryville, where the road turned inland into a wood (this was 'Brian's walk') and then back again toward Maryville (when he met Tom), passing the house and the promontory on his right, and descending toward the cliff where it was 'impossible to get into the sea'.

George felt so blackly unhappy that he wondered how anyone so unhappy could go on living. Could one not *die* of resentment and remorse and hate? How too could a man feel so stupid and dull, when his soul was so full of frightful fantasies? How would it all end, how could it all end? George thought to himself, I'm like a rabid dog which has rushed growling into a dark cupboard. The best thing that can happen is that my owner will have the nerve to pull me out by the collar and shoot me. Who is my owner? The answer was obvious. But *that* could not happen, nor did George yet seriously consider killing himself. His misery was present to him as an occupation, as a part of the weird 'duty' which increasingly and horribly presented itself. Gentler influences, in so far as they touched him, seemed like frivolity, a waste of time. He had lain as gentle as a lamb in Diane's arms. He had joined the family picnic. He came of course 'to annoy' and because he was expected not to, and to prove who he was through the exercise of old irritations and pains. Seeing Adam always reminded him of Rufus, and this particular grief was even not unwelcome, since it absolutely licensed him to hate the world. Yet he was fond of Alex and he was fond of Tom, and he wanted to see the sea, which had always 'done something' for him, a curative influence which Tom indeed had indicated when he had cried out to him that they should swim together. He would never have got himself to the sea alone. There was a kind of compulsory sanity in being with people he had known so long. Even the curious and interesting distress and excitement, upon which he looked forward to reflecting later, at finding Hattie Meynell of the party, was mingled with his resentment of her as an alien. Beyond, lay insanity. That morning he had looked at his body, at his hands and feet and what he could see of his trunk, and

349

felt his grasp of his being waver. What was this pallid crawling object? He had stared at his face in the mirror and felt mad, as if he might have to rush whimpering and slobbering into the street and ask to be arrested and looked after. The pigeons in the early morning softly said *Rozanov, Rozanov*.

He had dreamt of Stella, he saw her handsome royal Egyptian head in his dreams. He was touched by Diane and she gave him a little peace, but he despised her. He admired Stella but he could not get on with her, she was an enemy. He felt a vague relief that she was somewhere else and no anxiety or curiosity about where she was. Wherever she was she was strong and sane and eating up the reality all round her to increase her own. He reflected, even in an odd way valued, that terrible strength which also made her so dangerous, so hateful. He kept on recalling the incident with the car. He remembered the huge sickening sound of the car entering the water, and the extraordinary way in which Stella came out of the door like a fish. But he could not clearly see what had happened just before. Had he actually *pushed* the car, *could* he have done that? Was he simply imagining that he had put his hands on the back window and braced his feet on the cobbled quay and made the car move forward? Surely that was a fantasy, he had so many violent fantasies and dreams. He was a weak crawling creature and his violence was purely fantastic. He thought, I can't go on like this. I must *finish* my relation with Rozanov. I'll see him again. If he would only say one kind word to me, just *one*, it would change the world. After one kind word I could go away in peace. How can he be so cruel as not to speak that word? And how can I be so abject as to need it?

George had reached the cliff and the other view over the sea which he knew so well. Here the yellowish grass ended abruptly at a steep edge. The dark blackish-brown rocks with red streaks in them did not descend neatly to the water but went down in a jagged graceless mess of cracks and slides and overhanging ledges. In the sea, not very far below but seemingly inaccessible, a mass of brown herring gulls were crowding and crying over some trophy. George looked at the birds' soft spotty backs and their fierce eyes and they gave him some satisfaction. They reminded him, through old sea memories, of holidays and of his father, blessedly so dead. George had disliked his father and early turned him not into a monster but prophetically into a ghost. Twice ghosted, some association with the herring gulls passed like a harmless chill. It seemed impossible to get down to the water; but George had explored the favourite area thoroughly on visits as a child, before Alex bought Maryville, when the coveted house still belonged to a Colonel Atheling who was famous for objecting to the McCaffrey children (big George and little Brian) crossing his land. There was a way down (which George had never revealed to his brothers) where one descended through an elder tree into a round hole in the rock through which one could slither, holding on to a branch, on to a shelf from which one could jump to some 'steps', and so to the water. He undressed on the cliff top, he was out of sight of the house, removing all his clothes and folding them as if for a ritual. He stepped down into the tree and, bracing himself against the rock, felt with his foot for the hole which was invisible from above. He could now only just get through the hole, and the rock chafed his naked body. On the shelf he sat down to lever himself to a flat rock below, then went cautiously down the 'steps'. He thought, I'm getting old. He dived into the deep lifting and falling water and gasped at the coldness.

George was a good swimmer and made his way otter-like out to sea. He thought, as the water laved his head and shoulders, that's *good*, that's *good*. At the same time the cold sea was menacing; one could soon drown in such a sea, one could die of exposure. He thought, I would like to die like that. If I just swim on and on and on I shall die and then I shall really have finished with Rozanov. Well, in that case he will have *won*. But does that matter? He went on, cutting through the tops of the frothy crests, on and on toward realms of sea where land was never seen or heard of. Suddenly, in the green swinging hollow of a wave, he saw below him and nearby something which he took at first for a plastic bag floating. Then he took it for a dead fish, then when it seemed to move for a strange crab or big jelly fish. He turned, halting his course, to look at it. It seemed to be some horrid kind of thing. Then he saw that it was a little four-legged mammal, a *dog*. It was *Zed*.

George cried out with surprise and distress. He saw clearly now the little white muzzle held high, the eyes staring, the paws weakly moving. The next moment the dog was gone, lifted with swift force over the crest of the wave. George followed quickly, his eyes desperately fearfully straining to see the little helpless thing. He was suddenly distracted, aware of the huge sky above, the huge ocean round about, full of fast-moving heights and hollows and dazzling flashes of foam. He perceived Zed again and caught him up, then treading water lifted him. The bedraggled creature hung limply in his hands, but Zed's blue-black eyes gazed with conscious intelligence, at close quarters, into George's eyes. George thought, I can't climb the cliff carrying Zed. Besides *they* must be in a fair state by now. However did the poor little beggar get here? I'll swim on round the point; if I get in close to the rocks I'll be out of the current. It was not easy, cold and now tired, in a strong-running sea, to swim with one hand while holding Zed clear of the sea with the other. But as George paused to rest and tread water, Zed slid as if on purpose on to his shoulder and clung on against his neck (as Adam had just this day taught him to do). George understood, and now holding one strand of the dog's coat and keeping one arm against his chest he could more vigorously make way. Tom was the first who, when George had reached the rocks on the other side and felt shingle beneath his feet and lifted his head up, heard the triumphant shout.

The unhappy group had struggled away slowly over the sand. Alex had looked once more perfunctorily for her watch but had not mentioned it to anyone. Gabriel packed the last few scattered things, Adam's socks, Zed's lead, dropping her tears over them, into a bag. Brian, who was leading, had just reached the inland rocks that led up to the field when Tom cried, 'There's George.' They had forgotten George. At first Tom did not understand George's signals. Then he heard him shouting, 'I've got him! He's all right!'

Tom shouted too. They all turned round and began running back. 'What is it?' shouted Brian, also running.

Tom reached George and took the dog from him. 'Oh George, you hero! But he's cold, quick, find a towel, poor Zed!' For a terrible moment holding the dog Tom thought the little thing was dead, so limp and cold and motionless it felt. Then a pink tongue licked the back of his hand.

Gabriel ran up and seized Zed and wrapped him in a dry towel and sat on the sand and rubbed him. Adam, transfigured, leaned against her shoulder wailing with joy. Brian stood behind them holding out his hands in an incoherent gesture and thankful helpfulness. (Tom said later they looked like the Holy Family with John the Baptist.)

'I'm bloody cold too,' said George.

George, rather plump, stark naked and pink with cold, stood there like some weird manatee. They all ran at him armed with towels, rugs, garments. George sat on a rock, his back hunched, like a big wet sea animal, and they surrounded him and stroked him and patted him as if he were indeed a beneficent monster. Tom tore off his shirt and hopped out of his trousers. Alex handed over Brian's jersey. Brian found an extra pair of socks in Gabriel's bag; Gabriel always packed extra socks. Ruby handed over a mug of whisky. George told the story of the rescue among many exclamations of amazement and praise. Then everyone had hot tea and whisky and felt extremely hungry and ate up all the remaining sandwiches and cheese and veal-and-ham pie. Tom ran in record time in his under-clothes all the way to fetch George's clothes, which he put on himself to run back in, looking very comical. It was some time, however, before poor Zed was quite himself again, and Brian felt an anxiety which he did not impart. The little dog, though he wagged his tail, continued to shiver and tremble, though Gabriel opened her blouse and held him against her warm breasts. At last when he seemed to be warm and dry and lively she gave him into Adam's arms. Then Gabriel went to George and kissed him, and Alex kissed him and Tom kissed him too, and Emma and Brian clapped him on the back, and Hattie and Pearl, who had been standing a little in the background of the family scene, waved him a very special wave. Then Tom and George exchanged clothes and they all decided to go home.

The last act was less edifying. As they went along, Alex paused again (in vain) to look for her watch. George and Ruby led the way up the field. Brian ascended more slowly carrying Zed and holding Adam by the hand. He squeezed Adam's hand at intervals, but Adam would not look up at him. Gabriel followed. She suddenly felt mortally tired as if she might fall on her face, and kept stumbling on the slippery yellow grass. Hattie and Pearl, who had somehow become very separate and alien, climbed by a different route, often pausing to look back at the sea and point things out to each other. Tom and Emma came last, having waited for Alex who was complaining that no one would help her to find her watch.

As Brian neared the top of the field he heard a car start. The others were catching up. Ruby stood waiting, surrounded by bags. Bill the Lizard's big Rover began to bump up the track, reached the tarmac, roared round the corner and disappeared. George had disappeared too.

'My God, the Rover's gone. Where's George?'

Ruby pointed toward the now empty road.

'Alex, George has taken the Rover!'

353

Gabriel said, 'I can understand his not wanting to go back with us after all that.'

'Oh you can, can you! Alex, did you leave the key in the car?'

'I always leave keys in cars.'

'Typical you, typical George!'

Pearl drove Ruby and Alex with Hattie in the Volkswagen. As soon as the car started, Ruby handed Alex her watch. In the Austin, Gabriel sat in the front beside Brian, holding both Adam and Zed in her arms. She and Adam cried quietly all the way home. Brian kept gritting his teeth and murmuring, 'Typical George!' In the back, Emma fell asleep with his head on Tom's shoulder.

'Have they all gone?' said Stella.

'Yes,' said May Blackett, 'I watched the cars go.'

'When is N arriving?'

'He should be here in half an hour or so.'

Stella had moved downstairs to the big first-floor drawing-room at Maryville, with its wide bow windows overlooking the sea. One casement was open and a white curtain blew in and out. The sea was pale grey now, sheened over by a dimming pearly light. From the upstairs corner room, which was her bedroom, Stella had at intervals watched through long-distance glasses the various antics of the McCaffreys on the beach. Hidden, she had seen Ruby come and stand like a totem portent gazing at the house. And she had watched George coming walking along the road and pass by. After George disappeared she stopped looking out and came downstairs. May Blackett checked at intervals to see if the cars were still there.

'He can't have known?'

'George? No.'

'Ruby stared so at the house.'

'Just curiosity.'

'She has second sight.'

I should explain that I, N, the narrator, am about to intrude (though not for long) into the narrative, not to exhibit myself, but simply to offer an unavoidable explanation. People in Ennistone had been wondering whither Stella had fled, where she had so mysteriously gone to. Well, she had gone to me.

On the day, so much lamented by Gabriel, when Stella disappeared from Leafy Ridge, she had not set off for London or for Tokyo. She had taken one of Gabriel's umbrellas (it was raining on that day), and thus concealing her conspicuous dark head 'like that of an Egyptian queen', had walked the distance, not great, to my house, not far from the Crescent, and there, one might say, gave herself up. When I use this phrase I simply mean that she came as one at the end of her tether and (let me emphasize) with no special thought in her head except to get safely away from the McCaffreys. I have had, and have, no 'sentimental' association with Stella, nothing of that sort is involved. I am considerably her senior. I am, as I said at the beginning, an Ennistonian, and I have known the McCaffreys, though not intimately, all my life, and Stella since her marriage. I think I may say that we are friends, and I do not use the word lightly. And we are both Jewish. Stella came to me as to the nearest 'safe house', a place 'out of the world', out of the pressure of time, where she could rest and think and decide. She fled from the kindness of Gabriel, and the smallness of her bedroom at 'Como', and from Adam, who made her think of Rufus, and from a place where George could find her. She came to me, not seeking for advice, or support in some 'policy', but just because she trusted me and knew I would hide her. (She is not the first person I have hidden.) Whether this particular flight was a good idea was something upon which doubt could be cast, and we did, in later discussions, cast it. At any rate, once the door of my house had closed upon Stella, a course of action was set and had to be followed. As Stella put it once, she was 'in blood so stepped, returning were as tedious as go o'er'.

Stella's removal from my house, Bath Lodge, to Maryville was my idea. I removed her simply because we had, for the moment, talked enough. Of course I gave her advice; it was impossible in conversations of such intensity not to. She did not take it; but indeed any view which I could form of the matter was tentative. And Stella was no sickly waif, she was a strong rational self-assertive woman who had, as she realized as time went on, put herself in an impossible position. She was paralysed between different courses of action and, with her pride at stake, unable to decide to move; and the longer the silence and the secrecy went on, the harder it was to see how it could be ended. Stella seemed to me in danger of settling down into an idea of being trapped, which the minute discussions she enjoyed with me tended to reinforce. I suggested an abrupt change of scene, and she agreed to go to Maryville, consigned to the care of a much longer-established friend of mine, May Blackett, the mother of Jeremy and Andrew. Stella was fond of May and respected her. The situation as it then was may best be clarified, at any rate exhibited, by a transcription of the conversation which took place that evening after dinner between Stella and me.

'I see you've set out the netsuke, my old friends.'

'Yes –'

'I especially like that demon hatching out of his egg.'

'You would. You were the only person who really *looked* at them. I'm glad I rescued them from George, he would have enjoyed smashing them. The idea was certain to occur to him some time.'

'Have you written to your father?'

'Not like you said. I just sent a note to say I'd be away in France for a while.'

'It must have been odd to see the McCaffreys at play.'

'A shock, yes. It made me feel such a traitor to them all.'

'Because you've taken refuge with the enemy.'

'Yes. Well, for George everyone is the enemy. But where have I been all this time, what on earth can I ever tell them?'

'Lies. I'll think of some.'

'Don't be facetious. How loathsome it all is. And I've involved you.'

'Don't worry about me, I'm stormproof.'

'I've put myself in the wrong, and that paralyses my willpower. I feel I'm in a steel box or something.'

'People get out of boxes, it's often easier than they think.'

'I can't see how to get out of this one. Have you any new idea? God, as if you hadn't other things to think of.'

'What did you instantly feel when you saw George pass by this afternoon?'

'So close, so *close*. Frightful fear, like an electric shock. Then when I saw he wasn't coming here, an intense desire to run out after him, and that was like fear too. He looked so lonely.'

'You don't feel you could just go back to Druidsdale, just turn up?'

'No.'

'Or write to him, simply to say you're O K?'

'No. I'm not O K. And he doesn't care.'

'Just to have written the letter would be a step. Move one piece and you alter the board.'

'Yes, yes, like you said.'

'Any act might change the scene in ways you can't now foresee, and I don't see that this one would do harm. I'd post the letter in London. It would make for a kind of vagueness, less intensity, more space.'

'I know what you mean. But anything I do would commit me and I'm terrified of making a mistake. I can't do anything until I've cleared my mind. That makes sense, doesn't it?'

'Not necessarily.'

'At least now I'm free –'

'I thought you were in a steel box.'

'I mean I can *think* about it. I feel I'm poised – like a rocket that might go off different ways. Better to wait.'

'You regard George as a problem to be solved. Maybe you should relax and give up.'

'You mean go bobbing back to him like a piece of flotsam, like an *ordinary person*? All right, laugh!'

'Why not go to Tokyo?'

'And tell my father he was right?'

'Or invite him here. You know how much I've always wanted to meet him.'

'Oh, you two would get on terrifyingly well. Invite him into this shambles? No.'

'You want to get everything right all at once. Why not fiddle around with the bits? What does May think now?'

'She thinks I ought to plan carefully how to be happy for the rest of my life! You know, sometimes the thought of happiness torments me. This house reeks of happiness, it drives me mad. Sometimes I'm happy in my dreams. Then it's as if George was blotted out, as if he's never been.'

'Well, why not blot George out?'

'You said go on a journey, only the journey must be a pilgrimage. There isn't any holy place for me to go to.'

'Jerusalem?'

'Don't be silly. That means something to you. It means nothing to me. I used to think that if I went to Delphi I'd receive some sort of illumination, but I know now that Delphi is empty too. My holy place is George. And it is an abomination.'

'I meant to blot him out effectively, write saying you want a divorce, and *imagine* how he'd curse, and then he'd smile and then he'd cheer. *Conceive* that he might be better off without you. That would be one way of taking the weight off yourself!'

'All right, I am self-obsessed. But I couldn't divorce George. It's not possible. All that unfinished business.'

'You want power over him. You want to save him your way. One can't always finish business, put that picture out of your head. If you can't decide to leave him, then go back, without waiting for the right time, without knowing what it's all about and without the intention of fixing or finishing or clarifying anything. You *can* talk to George, *that* remains –'

'Yes, in a way, but –'

'He envies you, he fears you, give up your power.'

'As if that was easy. *You* should know.'

'You're the particular principle of order he rejects. That's as important as the particular religion one doesn't believe in.'

'You flatter me. That sounds like a rational link. There are links, but they are deep and awful.'

'Yes, I knòw. Do you mind if we go over one or two things again?'

'No. All right, you ask the questions.'

'And you forgive me?'

'One has to forgive the executioner. Not to would be fearfully bad form. You told me to keep off tranquillizers and endure it all, I am enduring it all, it hasn't made me wise.'

'About Rufus –'

'It isn't Rufus, it isn't Alan or Alex or Fiona or Tom – not those old theories – not really – it's something aboriginal.'

'I'm talking about you, not George.'

'Oh, I know you've got a theory there too. All right. Rufus's death was my fault, it happened in a second, due to my carelessness and stupidity – and then I couldn't get in touch with George, he wasn't at the Museum, I had to wait until he came home to tell him, I sometimes think I died during that wait and everything since has been a dream of life. Of course I feel the loss of Rufus every second, that death is the air I breathe, I relive that accident ... But that it has got mixed up with ... George and ... that's extra ...'

'Yes.'

'It was impossible to talk about it afterwards, we didn't talk about it to each other or to anyone else. George never asked for the details and I never told them, except for saying it was my fault and saying, oh – very vaguely – what happened. He never *said* anything. I've never looked, even glanced, into the depths of – how George felt, how he blamed me in his heart –'

'Perhaps less than you imagine.'

'How he accused me, what a *process* he set up – these words don't fit – it's ineffable. And then later on people began to say it was his fault, they even hinted it was deliberate, they believed terrible things – and I didn't say a word. And now if I shouted "I did it" they would still think it was him. How can I leave him after that?'

'Because he took the blame.'

'No, no, those words are too feeble, I tell you it's ineffable, it's absolute, it's like being damned together, tied together and thrown into the flames.'

'Isn't this what must be undone?'

'Theories, theories, you keep looking for a key, even this isn't fundamental. Yes, he "took the blame". It has made him worse.'

'I think it has made you worse.'

'You think I should forgive myself.'

'And him in the same movement. Guilt and resentment often get mixed up together. You deeply resent – whatever it was he did – to protect himself – from that terrible thing. You said the other day that he "lapped it up like a cat lapping cream". I remember that curious phrase.'

'Did I say that? Of course that doesn't describe it. His heart was utterly smashed – Rufus was – well, you know – for both of us –'

'Yes.'

'What I meant was that *at once* George began to make it all into something else, something awful, against me – oh, to protect himself, as you just said. But to mix up that awful pain with vile spite and malice and absolute misrepresentation and lies – that sort of deep *determination* to change what really is into a horrible machine to hurt somebody else – that's the activity of the devil – it corrupts everything, everything.'

'But you see it both ways round.'

'Exactly. It *was* my fault and I kept silent about it – I kept silent first because it was too terrible to speak of, and later because – because it wasn't anybody else's business and I couldn't –'

'You couldn't stoop to counter the vile things people were casually saying about George –'

'Yes. It would simply have made them talk more, they would have said I was shielding him, they would have *loved* it. But because of – the thing itself – and the silence – I am to blame. So in a way George is right and can tell himself so. But the way he has made it into a weapon against me – sort of silently, malevolently – is so awful – it's a caricature of any real condemnation, it's the *opposite*, it's the exact opposite of the response which love and pity would have made.'

'So objectively you are guilty and George is right, only as he *works* it he's absolutely wrong.'

'Yes. And what you call seeing it both ways round is part of the torment. It's warfare, it's hell, hell is this sort of warfare.'

'You spoke of George's "determination", but what about yours?

360

You see him as acting silently and malevolently. This is the picture which *you* have worked upon. No doubt George moves instinctively, as we all do, to save himself. So he *makes* something of the matter. But so do you. He can't afford love and pity. But it seems you can't either.'

Stella was silent for a moment, reflecting. 'If I believed that such springs could flow – but all my strength goes into not being destroyed. I don't want to become a machine of misery and hate. I want to stay rational. Just trying to think clearly about George is the best I can do by way of love and pity and such. You don't think he's likely to kill himself?'

'No.'

'Suicide has always seemed to me so abstract. No one could wholeheartedly do it.'

'We are abstract beings and rarely wholehearted.'

'I know you respect suicide because of Masada.'

'Oh don't speak of that. Suicides are often acts of revenge, or proofs of omnipotence.'

'That sounds like George. But no, I don't see him as a suicide either. A lynch mob might kill him one day. Yet inner violence is a power, like magic, people fear it.'

'He'd be protected, hedged!'

'Yes. Like a king.'

'Like a king, which he has to be since you're a queen. You once said you felt like a princess who had married a commoner. "It tells in the end", you said.'

'Did I? The things I say, and you remember them all!'

'Don't be too busy with those pictures. It is good to declare a blankness now and then. We are not anything very much, not even machines. You imagine that your thoughts are rays of power. Simple actions may be a better way to just views.'

'Simple actions –'

'Undertaken in a light shed from outside, some ordinary faith or hope, nothing clever.'

'You are preaching humility again! Like going home. If I could see that as a duty – but I can't. I can't walk into the dark. I've got to have a picture, I've got to have a plan. You still don't think Diane Sedleigh is important?'

'A toy, a *divertissement*. You aren't worried about *her*?'

'Yes. But I understand what I feel about her, it's plain and wholesome compared with the rest. I used to think he might kill her.

I believe he was with her when Rufus died. You don't think George is simply mad?'

'No.'

'Or epileptic?'

'No.'

'Electric shocks, all that?'

'No.'

'But you think it's dangerous, this waiting, this letting time pass? I've become obsessed with "letting time pass", I can't arrest it, I can't use it. I used to classify it all as "an unhappy marriage", but it isn't, it's vast. Of course his having no job makes it worse, he can sit and have fantasies. He imagines awful things. He used to tell me, centuries ago.'

'Were you together in *that*?'

'You mean, was I fascinated? Yes, before I started to –'

'Fear him.'

'Hate him, or whatever it is.'

'And you are still fascinated.'

'It's closer than fascination. I am George. Suppose I went back, would I be safe?'

'He is fully occupied with John Robert Rozanov.'

'So he mightn't notice me? I hope it's a harmless occupation. Does that mean I can wait or that I needn't wait?'

'You don't think George ever realized how friendly you were with Rozanov when you were a student?'

'I wasn't friendly with him. He just thought I was good at philosophy. And I –'

'And you –?'

'Well, you know John Robert, or you did.'

'You think you aren't part of the Rozanov problem?'

'I hope not. When I saw how besotted George was, I gave Rozanov up.'

'And you gave up philosophy, in case George realized you could do it and he couldn't!'

'Don't! That was ages ago, before we were married. I was studying George even then.'

'I recall your saying once that George interested you more than anything in the world.'

'Anyway I don't want to be involved with George while he's involved with John Robert, that would be one Chinese box too many. There is something, if I could only *work it out*, while I'm

362

waiting. You can't explain George by the old theories. You might just as well say he's possessed by a devil. It's more something to pity, like an illness, or an urge, like sex, like a nervous obsessive guilty angry *craving*. He knows now he'll never *do* anything with his life. He's a pathetic figure really. If George was in a novel he would be a comic character.'

'We would all be comic characters if we were in novels. I wish you had gone on studying, philosophy or economics, not George.'

'Yes. It's part of that dream.'

'Of happiness?'

'I dream I'm back at the university. And don't say "why not", don't say "you're still young", don't say –'

'All right. Nothing ever came of those plays George was writing?'

'Of course not. Didn't he show you one?'

'Yes. I'm sorry I lost George. I hate to lose anybody.'

'If you could have kept him – but it's impossible. If you had kept George he would have begun to detest you as he detests Rozanov. I think he tore up all the plays. He tore up my novel anyway.'

'I didn't know you'd written a novel.'

'I might have let you see it. You're lucky.'

'I hope you'll write another?'

'It's not being able to *do* anything, to *impress* anybody – I know you see George as a sort of "hero of our time".'

'The powerless man who becomes apathetic and then nasty.'

'George as a nasty man. That sounds quite soothing. You know George lives in a sort of odd time scheme, as if he were a criminal who had already been punished and set free, although his crimes still lie ahead. He has already paid, and this sanctions his resentment.'

'The justified sinner going on sinning. You said George felt like a Nazi war criminal at the end of a long sentence, purged by suffering, yet unrepentant!'

'Yes. He was fascinated by those people. He read a lot of books about them. He'll never achieve anything now, like studying or writing or anything, but he might achieve some awful *act*. I'm sure he dreams about it – all his little outrages –'

'Like trying to kill you?'

'Well – he tried in a sense – but –'

'He pushed the car.'

'Yes. I can still see so clearly his hands pressed on the back window, all pale like – like some animal's –'

363

'And he kicked you after he'd got you out.'

'I think I resent that more. I did provoke him. I taunted him about Rozanov. If he ever did kill me it would be accidental.'

'Never mind. Go on. All his little outrages, or "pranks" as his admirers call them –'

'Are like – imagery, symbols – like a rehearsal for something he'll do one day that will satisfy him at last – and then he'll stop – he'll be satisfied, or perhaps he'll be disgusted, he'll have destroyed something in himself, he'll be exhausted, weak and pale like a grub in an apple, and the craving will go away.'

'What stage in this process are we at now?'

'That's what I want to *work out*. The Rozanov thing is an interruption. It's serious, but in a way that could be *divertissement* too. It's fortuitous and can pass. Rozanov will go back to America and George will recover. Then we'll know.'

'Whether the *thing* he's waiting for – the act that will cure him – has already happened?'

'*Yes*. I thought the Roman glass was it.'

'Yes?'

'Then I thought that murdering me was it.'

'Except that you're still alive.'

'Yes, but it could be good enough.'

'And if it isn't?'

'He might feel he had to finish me off so as to finish *it* off. He might see it as a fiasco, as a loss of face, as something that went wrong.'

'Is *that* why you wait?'

'No, it isn't, that doesn't make any difference, if I go back to George I take the risk. I just don't want to go back in a muddle, in an undignified scramble, without a clear head and a policy.'

'A policy –!'

'And now I've delayed so long I may as well wait until Rozanov has gone back to America.'

'And if George were cured, "exhausted" as you said, if he were weak and pale like a grub in an apple, docile, would he still *interest* you? Don't you rather *like* the waiting?'

'Sometimes I feel as if George were a fish I'd hooked ... on a long long line ... and I let him run ... and run ... and run ... What a terrible image.'

'What's that strange music?'

'There's a fair on the Common.'

The distant sound of fair music, distilled and sweetened in the warm evening air, faintly and intermittently drifted in the garden at Belmont. Nearer at hand a blackbird, lyrical as a nightingale, was rapturously singing. The ginkgo had on its summer plumage. Its plump drooping branches were like the rounded limbs of a great animal. The garden smelt of privet flowers. In fact the whole of Ennistone smelt sourly-sweet of privet where that valuable shrub was a popular feature.

'Pearl, I feel frightened.'

'What of, my darling?'

'Let's close the shutters.'

'It's too early.'

'I wrote to Margot.'

'That's a good girl.'

'What a nice paperweight my stone hand makes, look.'

Hattie had placed the limestone hand which she had found in the wild garden on top of her neat pile of letters. She had written to her Aunt Margot, to her school friend Verity Smaldon, and to Christine with whose family she had stayed in France.

'Did you reply to that impertinent journalist?'

'Yes, I did that yesterday. Fancy that newspaper knowing that I exist!' The editor of the *Ennistone Gazette* had written to Hattie asking for an interview.

'I hope you said no firmly.'

'Of course.'

Hattie had had a nasty dream last night which still lingered in her head. In an empty twilit shop she had seen on an upper shelf a small semi-transparent red thing which she took to be a big horrible insect. Then the thing began to flutter and she saw it was a very small very beautiful owl. The little owl began to fly about

just above her head causing her a piercing mixture of pleasure and
distress. She reached up her hands to try to catch the owl, but was
afraid of hurting it. A voice said, 'Let it out of the window,' but
Hattie knew that this sort of owl always lived in rooms, and would
die outside. Then she looked at another shelf and saw with horror
a cat sitting there about to spring upon the owl.

'You're so restless today.'

'I can't breathe for the smell of flowers. Father Bernard said he
might come.'

'He won't now.'

'He might, he's always late. You don't like him, Pearlie.'

'I feel he's false somehow.'

'That's unfair.'

'OK, it's unfair.'

'Don't be cross with me.'

'Do stop saying that, I'm not cross!'

'Please don't sew. What are you sewing?'

'Your nightdress.'

'You did enjoy being in London?'

'Yes, of course.'

'I wish you liked picture galleries.'

'I do like picture galleries.'

'You pretend to.'

'Hattie –'

'I'm sorry, I'm awful. It's such an odd light, the sun's shining yet
it's as if it were dark. I feel so peculiar. I hope I'm not wasting my
time.'

'If you read those big books you can't waste your time.' By the
'big books' Pearl meant the major European classics which Father
Bernard had indicated with a flourish of his hand that Hattie 'might
as well get on with' pending John Robert's views on her studies. She
was now reading *Tod in Venedig*.

'Pearl, my dear, now that Hattie is safely at the university I can
at last reveal how deeply I care for you. You have been a great
support and a great comfort and I have come to believe that I
cannot do without you. May I dare to hope that you care for me
a little?' These words, uttered by John Robert, were part of a
fantasy which Pearl was having as she talked to Hattie. *In the end*
(this obscure conception had become important to Pearl of late)
John Robert would *turn to her*, perhaps as a *last resort*.

These visions, which unfurled themselves automatically, co-existed with Pearl's uneasy notion, which had lately grown stronger, that John Robert had a more intense interest in his granddaughter than he affected to have. Of course Pearl said nothing of this to Hattie.

Alex had a recurring dream in which she looked out of the window of Belmont in the early dawn and found the garden, which had become immense, with a lake and a view of distant trees, full of strange people moving about purposively. A sense of impotent outrage and fear and anguish came in the dream.

Now listening to the blackbird and gazing out from the drawing-room where she had not yet turned on the lamps, she felt a stab of this fear as she saw a motionless figure standing on the lawn. She recognized it almost at once as Ruby, but it remained sinister. What was Ruby doing, what was she thinking, standing out there alone? Earlier in the day Alex had seen the vixen lying warily, elegantly, upon the grass while four cubs played round her and climbed over her back. The sight had pleased her, but also caused her some obscure pain, as if she identified with the vixen and felt a fear which was always there in the vixen's heart.

'I can't pray,' said Diane.

'Of course you can, silly,' said Father Bernard looking at his watch.

Diane had come to evensong for once, but on that evening Ruby had not come. Father Bernard had asked Diane into the Clergy House afterwards and held her hand and given her a small glass of brandy, and after that it somehow happened that they went on drinking brandy together.

'You can try to pray. If you say you can't pray you must know what trying to pray is. And trying to pray is praying.'

'That's like saying if you can't speak Chinese you must know what trying to speak Chinese is.'

'The cases are different. God knows our necessities before we ask, and our ignorance in asking.'

'That depends on believing in God, but I don't. If only he'd give up drinking.'

'Anything counts now as believing in God, feeling depressed does, feeling violent does, committing suicide does –'

'Then he believes in God.'

'Just kneel and drop the burden.'

'That sounds like a pop song. Does he believe in God?'

'I don't know. But you do. Wake up. Invent something. Perform a new action. Go and visit Miss Dunbury.'

'How is she, poor old thing.'

'Ill. Lonely.'

'She wouldn't want to see me, she disapproves of me. I wish you'd see George.'

'Devil take George. The sooner he commits some decent crime and gets put away the better.'

'How *can* you say that!'

'I think you should cut and run.'

'Oh, you upset me so.'

'Get out of this dump. Get a train; any train, going anywhere.'

'Have you seen Stella?'

'No.'

'He can't have killed her. Where's she gone?'

'To Tokyo, go to Tokyo, go anywhere, do anything.'

'I bought a new scarf.'

'A new scarf can be a vehicle of grace.'

'I'm drunk.'

'So am I.'

'I heard someone say you don't believe in God.'

'There is God beyond God, and beyond that God there is God. It doesn't matter what you call it, it doesn't matter what you do, just relax.'

'I think George would do anything Professor Rozanov said.'

'I've got to go to the Slipper House, I'm terribly late.'

'You can't go now.'

'I can and will.'

'Are you going to see that girl, Professor Rozanov's niece?'

'Grand-daughter.'

'Funny little girl, little prissy white-faced thing. Couldn't you ask Professor Rozanov to be nice to George?'

'No. Come on. I'm off.'

'I'll walk with you as far as Forum Way.'

It was nearly closing time at the Green Man. As I think I said earlier, centuries of non-conformism has left Ennistone rather short of pubs. There is the Albert Tavern in Victoria Park and a new pub called the Porpoise in Leafy Ridge. There is a rather posh establishment, the Running Dog, which is also a restaurant, in Biggins, near the Crescent, and a pub called the Silent Woman (with a sign portraying a headless female) in the High Street near Bowcocks. In Druidsdale there is the Rat Man, and in Westwold the Three Blind Mice. There are also a few tiny shabby houses of less note in the St Olaf's area, and the ill-reputed Ferret in the 'wasteland' beyond the canal. The Little Wild Rose on the Enn beyond the Tweed Mill hardly counts as being in Ennistone, but makes a pleasant walk in summer. However, Ennistone is not a town for an easy drink, and a surprisingly large number of Ennistonians have never entered a pub in their lives. The resistance to serving alcohol at the Institute remains firm, though this may change in time with the altering *mores* of the younger generation. This younger generation in the form of the classless *jeunesse dorée*, who had 'taken over' the Indoor Pool at the Baths, had lately 'moved in' in a similar manner upon the Green Man, to the annoyance of Burkestown regulars like Mrs Belton.

Tonight the cast of *The Triumph of Aphrodite*, many of them still wearing their costumes, were gathered there, after a rehearsal in the Ennistone Hall. The over-excited cast and their camp-followers had made a noisy procession from the Hall to the pub, and were now standing in a large chattering group spread along the counter. (The pub had lately been redecorated, abolishing the old distinctions between public bar, saloon and snug.) Tom and Anthea were there, and Hector Gaines and Nesta and Valerie and Olivia, with their pet Mike Seanu, and Olivia's brother Simon who was to sing the counter-tenor part, and Cora Clun, daughter of 'Anne Lapwing', and Cora's young brother Derek, star of St Olaf's choir, who had the charming role of Aphrodite's page, and Maisie Chalmers and Jean Burdett, tuneful sister of the St Paul's organist and of Miss Dunbury's truthful doctor, and Jeremy and Andrew and Peter Blackett and Bobbie Benning and other young persons who have perhaps not yet been mentioned such as Jenny Hirsch and Mark Lauder who were both animals, and young Mrs Miriam Fox (divorced) who worked in Anne Lapwing's Boutique and was helping Cora with the costumes. Derek and Peter were both under age but plausibly tall. The masque was in that stage of penultimate disarray when (in any production) it becomes clear to the director that it will never be fit to be seen. The cast, however, remained carefree, filled with absolute irrational faith in Hector (who was now a popular figure, his vain love for Anthea being common knowledge) and in Tom, who had some vague reassuring authority as co-author. Scarlett-Taylor, after making some valuable historical pronouncements which it was too late to do anything about, had distanced himself from the operation; he was in Ennistone that weekend, but not in the pub, having declared himself for a quiet evening of work at Travancore Avenue.

Tom and Anthea were together, with Peter Blackett who was in love with Nesta and half in love with Tom. Beside them Valerie and Nesta, both worrying about their college exams, were discussing Keynes. Valerie (Aphrodite) was still wearing the long white robe which was her under-dress. Hector came up.

'The situation is hopeless.'

'No, Hector, it went very well.'

Andrew Blackett said to Jeremy, 'Is she still there?'

'Yes. Not a word to Peter.'

'Of course not.'

Andrew was wondering whether he should drive straight to Maryville that night and offer his life, his love, his honour and his name to Stella, whose dark beauty he had loved in total secrecy for many years. They would have to emigrate, of course. He pictured himself living with Stella in Australia, and for a second his head swam and he felt quite faint with joy.

Heads of stags and dogs and great crested birds appeared here and there among the drinkers. A shaggy bear came lumbering up to Tom, and revealed Bobbie Benning.

'Isn't that thing terribly hot?'

'Yes, and I've got a bloody cold. It's no joke having a cold inside a bear's head, I can tell you. Is Scarlett-Taylor here?'

'No, he's working.'

Bobbie Benning, still tormented by his inability to teach engineering, and unable to bring himself to confide in Tom or Hector, had elected Emma, obviously a serious scholar, as his confidant but had not yet had a chance to unburden himself.

Hector had been upset earlier in the evening by a difference of opinion with Jonathan Treece whom Hector had, unwisely he now saw, asked to help with the music. Treece had gone back to Oxford in a huff. However, this now seemed a minor matter. Hector was beginning to feel that he would go mad, consigned to his lonely lodgings at 10 p.m. and leaving Tom and Anthea together. 'Let's buy some drink and go on boozing somewhere else. Come to my place.'

'Or let's go up to the Common,' said Bobbie. 'The fair will still be on, won't it?'

'Some people were dancing round the stones at the Ennistone Ring.'

'Some people dancing! Who are they?'

'I don't know, someone said all dressed in white.'

'Druids obviously!'

'Let's go up to the Common.'

'Everyone bring a bottle!'

Tom, laughing, trying on Bobbie's bearhead, was also in torment. He had not yet written to Rozanov, though he had tried several times to compose a letter. How could he tell *that* man that he was not attracted to *that* girl? Of course there were hundreds of ways of putting it: we've talked, and though we like each other awfully ... we both think we're too young ... She doesn't feel I'm quite right ... we're just not interested enough ... But the awful thing was that Tom *was* interested, only not in the right way. He thought almost with rage, that bloody autocrat has tied me to her, I don't want to be but now it's so hard to undo, I've changed. He's made me *think* about her so much. I can't just write a letter and *forget it all*. It's inside me, growing like a nasty poisonous plant. It's degrading to be afflicted like this. She probably hates me. And she frightens me, she seems like an evil maid, a sort of magic doll, bringing ill fortune, a curse, blighting my happiness and my freedom. He's *tied* me, and it's so damnably unfair. But if I get furious with *him* and write him some awful letter, if I write him *any* letter, because any letter is bound to be wrong, I shall go mad with remorse. I *care* about him, I *care* what he's thinking, that's what it's come to!

Tom was experiencing for the first time in his life (and no doubt he was lucky to have escaped it so long) that blackening and poisoning of the imagination which is one of the worst, as well as one of the commonest, forms of human misery. His world had become uncanny, full of terrible crimes and ordeals, and punishments. He felt frightened and guilty, anticipating some catastrophe which was entirely his own fault, yet also brought about by vile enemies whom he detested. It was no good appealing to reason and common sense, telling himself it was all just a dotty episode which he could put behind him and soon laugh about. Oh if only he had just *said no* at the start; it was right, it was easy then. Where was his happiness now, his *luck*, he whom everybody liked so much, and who, once, had liked everybody?

Tom had thought, and there was something childish in the thought, that the day at the sea would somehow 'cure' him. The old idea of the family holiday at the sea was replete with innocence and calm joy. He needed to see Hattie again in some sort of ordinary way so as to wash off, as it were, the painful unclean impression of their previous meeting when he had behaved like a *cad*. But the meeting in the wild garden had been, as it seemed in retrospect, equally horrid. Was it that he wanted to *impress* her more? He had cut a poor figure. She had held the advantage, she had been cold, superior, almost cutting. There had been no exorcism. And after that he had got into that funny exalted emotional state, which he scarcely understood later, about Christ having been in England. He had tried to write a pop song about it afterwards: Jesus was here, he was here, man, do you hear, he came as a child with his uncle the tin merchant, Joseph of Arimathea, don't fear, man, do you hear, and *did* those feet, they did, man, did they those feet, those feet did walk, when he came as a child (and so on). But the spiritual exaltation was gone and he could not get the song right. Then, on that seaside day, there had been the nightmare of losing Zed and Adam's awful crying which the rescue could not efface. And now, later on, what Tom horribly, and with a sense of degradation, remembered most clearly was what he had seen from the top of the rock and not instantly reported to his companion: Hattie undressing, her mauve stockings which matched her dress, the tops of the stockings which were a dark purple colour, and her thigh above.

'Time, gentlemen, please.'

'Have we got enough drink?'

'Where are you going?'

'To the Common.'

'The fair's still on and people are dancing at the Ring.'

'Can I come?'

'Wait, I'll get another bottle too.'

'I've got my transistor set.'

'So have I.'

'What about glasses?'

'Pick them up at Hector's.'

'I'll carry that,' said Tom to Anthea.

'No, I'll carry it, you've got your own.'

They came out together into the warm night where there was still light in the sky. Some drunks gathered on the pavement were softly singing, *I will make you fishers of men, fishers of men, fishers of men, I will make you fishers of men if you follow me*. Tom felt immediately giddy, rather drunk. Anthea took his hand and tears came into her eyes. She passionately loved Joey Tanner who did not love her, and she dearly loved Tom McCaffrey, but as a friend, as a brother.

The road from the Green Man which led down to the level crossing and then through the railway cutting to the Common went past Hector's digs, where Hector and Valerie and Nesta stopped to collect glasses in a basket. The chorus of animals, with whom Hector was having so much trouble, had not yet been ejected from the pub. A bright light from the signal-box shone down on the red-and-white bars of the level crossing, and Tom and Anthea approached it hand in hand, bottles swinging in their other hands.

As they reached the crossing they paused at the little narrow wicket-gate which allowed people to walk across the track. Someone was coming over the rails, and the gate was only wide enough for one. The person who emerged into the light close beside them was Rozanov.

Tom let go of Anthea's hand and dropped his bottle, which shattered on the tarmac. He stopped instinctively as if ducking, as if hiding his face; then when he recovered himself the philosopher was gone.

'Oh bad luck,' said Anthea.

'Damn, all that drink gone west.'

'Wasn't that Professor Rozanov?'

'I think so.'

There was no doubt that Rozanov had seen him and had seen his hand holding Anthea's. Tom turned and made a step as if to run after him, then stopped. Anthea was kicking the broken glass into the gutter.

Someone else came through the wicket-gate. It was Dominic Wiggins.

'Hello, Dominic.'

'Hello Anthea, hello Tom. If you're going to the fair I'm afraid it's over.'

'Someone said there was dancing at the Ring.'

'That's over too. There were some funny people there but they've gone. Still, it's a lovely evening for seeing flying saucers.'

Hector and Nesta and Valerie were coming up the road, with the rout of actors just behind them.

Anthea said, 'The fair's over, and the dancing too.'

'Back to my place then,' said Hector.

'I'm going to the Slipper House,' said Tom.

'To the Slipper House?'

'Yes, there's a party there. I've just remembered. Must be off. Cheerio.'

'What's that? What's Tom saying?'

'A party at the Slipper House.'

'A party! Let's all go!'

'Come on, Tom says there's a party at the Slipper House!'

'Hooray, to the Slipper House!'

'Hooray!'

Exactly how what was later known as the 'Slipper House riot' began was wrapped in confusion for some time, and a lot of wild charges and counter-charges were made afterwards. That it was really quite an innocuous and accidental business, at first at any rate, and in no sense a conspiracy, is made clear by the foregoing account which I had from Tom himself much later on. Many of the more outrageous things which people said and believed were quite untrue; though it must also be added that a number of those involved had good reason to feel ashamed about what happened on that notorious night.

However that may be, shortly after the departure of the rout from Burkestown, Alex's dream came true. She was drinking by herself. (She had taken to solitary drinking lately, and had been twice seen alone in the bar of the Ennistone Royal Hotel.) She looked out of the bow window of the drawing-room and saw the Belmont garden full of strange people and moving lights.

'Whatever's happening?' said Diane to Father Bernard as they reached the back gate to the Belmont garden in Forum Way.

There was a sort of murmurous buzzing noise from within, a subdued sound of voices, occasional loud laughter, faint confused music.

The priest pushed the door open. 'There's some sort of fête or party or something or else they're acting a play.' He went in through the gate.

Diane said, 'I can't come, I haven't been invited,' but she followed him in.

The little damp path led through the shrubs and trees at the end of the garden, and as they followed it they saw the Slipper House with all its lights on throwing an illumination upon the grass. Mostly outside this patch of light, though intermittently in it, there moved or surged a number of people, some in medieval costume, some dressed as animals, some carrying lighted lanterns (these were props from the play). Transistor sets were droning, not loudly, mingling classical music with pop, and a member of the Music Consort was playing a treble recorder. A few people were practising a minuet, while others were absorbedly dancing by themselves. On the darker parts of the lawn groups had settled down and were opening bottles and sloshing beer and wine into glasses. As Diane and the priest advanced, someone with a huge stag's head and antlers came up and put drinks into their hands. Someone else said, 'Hello, Father, I'm not quite sure what's happening here,' and reeled off.

'Who was that?'

'Bobbie Benning.'

Meanwhile on the lighted part of the lawn Tom was having some sort of quarrel or explanation.

'No, you can't go into the Slipper House, there isn't a party, I just said that, it was a joke!'

'Well, there's a party now.'

'Why can't we go in? You said there was a party.'

'Yes, but there isn't – I was upset. It was just an excuse –'

'You brought us here.'

'I didn't, you followed me!'

'I want to go inside, I've always wanted to see inside this house.'

'No, stop, you can't.'

'Let's knock anyway.'

'Let's ask *them* out!'

'I want to go *in*.'

'What's going on, why can't we go in?'

'I wish you'd all *go away*!'

'But it was your idea to come here.'

'It *wasn't*, don't make such a *noise*.'

'Shall we bang on the windows?'

'Let's give the girls a song!'

'*Please* stop, *please* go away from here!'

'There's someone in the garden,' said Hattie. 'There are people in the garden.'

'Don't worry, the doors are locked.'

'Oh Pearl, do you think we should phone the police?'

'Of course not, they're probably guests of Mrs McCaffrey's.'

'I think they're awful people. Pearl, let's turn on all the lights. I feel so frightened in this house. I wish we were living in London. I *hate* this place. I feel someone will break in.'

'All right.' The girls ran all over the house turning on the lights.

'Wait, don't light up my bedroom, we'll look out of the window. They're making a *noise*.'

'Perhaps it's something to do with the fair.'

'They can't be having a fair here. They're all dressed up as animals. Pearl, this is some sort of *attack* –'

'Don't be silly.'

'It is, they're making a mock of us, it's an insult, listen to the people laughing –'

'I think they're drunk.'

'Shall I ring up John Robert?'

'No, for God's sake, he'll think we're perfectly stupid! Anyway he isn't on the telephone!'

'Isn't that Tom McCaffrey there?'

'Yes, I think so.'

'Oh Pearl how awful, how *horrid*, he's brought all these horrible people here to annoy us, I can't bear it –'

'I'm sure he hasn't, it must be a party at Belmont that's just come out.'

'Then why are they all down this end, and more people coming from the back gate –'

'Hattie, don't panic –'

'I think it's *scandalous*. Let's close all the shutters.'

Alex turned away from the window, frightened and angry. A lamp was alight on the other side of the drawing-room, but much of the room was rather shadowy. Something rolled or ran across the carpet in front of her and she gave a little yelp of alarm. She made for the door and turned on all the drawing-room and landing lights. The fine wide curving staircase was revealed with its fretted banisters thickly covered with reassuring white paint. The soft tufty brown stair-carpet glowed with good-as-new fibrous cleanliness. Alex stood at the top of the stairs and called 'Ruby! Ruby!' There was no answer. She shouted once more, frightened by the tone of her own voice. No answer.

She went downstairs and turned on more lights. Ruby was not in the kitchen or in her own room. Alex went to the back door, which stood open, and looked down the garden. Some distance away lights and figures were moving and voices speaking. Alex did not dare to call again. She stepped out on to the pavement behind the house. Then she gasped and mouthed a cry as she saw the figure of a man standing near her.

'Alex –' It was George.

'Oh thank God! What is this awful business in the garden, what's happening?'

'I don't know.'

'Of course, those horrible girls are giving a party, how *dare* they, in *my* garden, they never asked me, I shall go and tell them to stop, there are hundreds of people trampling everything, oh *damn* them, *damn* them –'

'No, don't, there's something odd about it all, I don't think it's that.'

'What is it then?'

'I don't know. Devil's work.'

'Ruby's gone.'

'Go inside, Alex, and give yourself a drink and lock the door.'

'Don't go – you were coming to see me –'

'No, I heard the noise just as I was passing.'

'Where are you going?'

'Just walking about the town, walking to the canal.'

'To the canal? Why? To *that place*? Don't go there, stay with me, please –'

'I'll just go and see what all this business is.'

'Come back, won't you, please –'

George had already disappeared.

*

The shutters of the Slipper House were now closing one by one, quenching the light which had been illuminating the patch of lawn. Outside there was a groan of disapproval followed by laughter. Tom ran forward.

Hattie, spreading out her arms to take hold of the shutters of the sitting-room, cried out when a figure appeared suddenly outside the window, like Peter Pan, close up against the glass.

Tom tapped. 'It's only me! Can I come in?'

Hattie stared, then violently swung one of the shutters across.

Tom, dancing outside the still unshuttered half of the window, shouted, 'It's not my fault! I didn't bring them!'

Hattie swung the other half of the shutter across with a bang and fixed it with a bar. She stood looking into the painted eyes of Alex's eternally young brother. Then she began to cry.

The shutters closed and the lights went out on the lawn just as George was making his way down the garden. Someone rose up from the grass and gave him a glass of wine.

Pearl said to Hattie, 'Look, if you're so upset I'll go out and ask him in.'

'No!'

'Then I'll go and talk to him and find out what's happening, I'm sure he didn't mean to –'

'No, don't go away!'

Nesta said to Diane, 'Come back to my place tonight. Just as a beginning, just to show you can –'

Sitting on a seat embowered in bushes Bobbie Benning, who had had a great deal to drink, was starting to feel sick. He thought, I'm no good, I must resign my job. I'll never get another, I'll be on the dole, whatever will my mother think, it'll kill her.

Peter Blackett was saying to anyone who could hear, 'I gave him a drink, then I saw he was George McCaffrey, did I have a turn!'

Jeremy Blackett said, 'Peter, it's time for you to go home.'

'I think we'd all better go home,' said Olivia Newbold.

'Are things going to turn nasty?'

Valerie Cossom, portentously beautiful in her long white robe, had heard that George was in the garden and was looking for him. Hector Gaines was looking for Anthea. The middle of the garden was dark, but lights from Belmont could be seen at one end, and the street lights in Forum Way at the other illuminated the trees.

Tom was at his wits' end. The noise and the laughter was louder than before and he had the impression that a number of complete strangers had come in through the back gate. He wanted to *explain* to Hattie, but couldn't see how to do this and couldn't bear to go away either. He had thought of something else which distressed him: Dominic Wiggins must have assumed, and would tell Nesta, that he was taking Anthea to 'Lovers' Lane' to lie down under a hawthorn bush.

Father Bernard had lost Diane but found Bobbie Benning. He sat beside the distraught youngster with his arm around him. 'My dear boy, tell me *all*.'

Pearl said to Hattie, 'I'll go out and find him, don't grieve, I won't be long. I'll go the back way, you lock up, and I'll call when I'm back.'

Valerie said, 'Hello, Nesta, have you seen George? Oh hello, Diane, have you seen George?'

'Is he here?' said Diane, and scuttled away among the shrubs.

'She's like a terrified little mouse,' said Nesta. 'It makes me sick to see a woman so frightened of a man.'

Valerie, searching, grieving, had passed on.

Tom thought, I can't go and knock on the door, I'd look a complete fool there not being let in, it's all shameful, I really must go home. I'll write a letter of apology tomorrow. Oh *God*. As he began to walk unsteadily up the garden towards Belmont he became aware that he was being followed by a girl, a strange girl. Heaven knew who was in the garden by now, but there was nothing he could do about it. He felt reckless and remorseful and angry. He said, 'Hello, what are you doing here?' He added, 'What am I doing here, if it comes to that.'

The curtains were drawn in the Belmont drawing-room, but the big uncurtained landing window, which showed the white sweep of the stairs, gave a diffused light. Tom looked at the girl who was giggling, perhaps a bit tipsy, and throwing her longish fair hair about. She was rather tall and wearing a smart silky multi-coloured dress. Now she came on, sidling boldly up against him. Tom, recoiling, looked at her again, more closely.

'*Emma*! You *wretch*! This is *too bloody* much! *And* you're drunk, you *reek* of whisky!'

'Have some, I've brought it with me, let's sit down somewhere.'

'You're horribly drunk. How did you know we were here?'

'I met some drunks near the pub who said there was a party at the Slipper House. Where are the girls?'

'If you mean Hattie Meynell, she's in the house with the shutters closed!'

'I thought you'd come to serenade her, after all Rozanov is forcing you to marry her!'

'Oh *shut* up!'

Emma caught Tom round the waist.

Pearl had been gone for some time and Hattie was very upset. She was standing in the sitting-room, but with the door ajar so that she could hear Pearl's knock and call. She was scared and affronted by the extraordinary mob outside whose noise showed no sign of abating, and deeply hurt and angered by Tom's extraordinary and spiteful treachery. Now everything had gone so wrong and so sour. She regretted having let Pearl go out to look for him, which might seem like a capitulation, as if she were pursuing him.

At that moment Hattie heard a curious sound at the back of the house as of a door opening and a footstep. It could not be Pearl, after whom she had firmly locked the back door, indeed all the doors were locked and the windows fastened. As she held her hands to her face in horror, the door of the sitting-room began to move and a man came in. It was George McCaffrey.

Hattie and Pearl had of course discussed George, casually before, and in more detail after, their meeting with him on the family picnic. Here Hattie had been as ready as the others to appreciate his heroic rescue of Zed, but had resented the insolent and, she felt, mocking way in which he had stared at her. She had also been annoyed by his misappropriation of the Rover, which had meant that she and Pearl had had to convey Alex and Ruby back to Belmont. (Alex had not concealed her dissatisfaction at this arrangement.) Hattie thought people should behave properly and was unamused by George's waywardness which the family seemed too much to condone. Pearl had said, though in vague terms since she knew little about it, that George had once been John Robert's pupil, and this information also, for some reason, displeased Hattie who began to manifest nervous irritation when his name came up. Pearl had earlier imparted to her the usual legend about George's awfulness, together with her own view that he was simply mad.

George certainly, as he entered the room, looked rather mad. His gaze had the squinting intensity of Alex's 'cat look'. His round face was shining, as if covered with sweat, his wide-apart brown eyes were big and moist with emotion, and he was smiling inanely displaying his little square teeth. His head looked weird, like a flickering pumpkin face illuminated from within. He had entered the Slipper House through the coal house, which had an interior window into the back passage which had originally given on to the outside before the annexe was added just before the war. This window, which was covered by a curtain, was inconspicuous and had a faulty catch, promptly highlighted by George's memory as he walked down the garden. He was excited by the sudden strange night scene and by what he overheard someone say about the girls being 'barricaded inside the house'. He began to feel that deep nervous urge which he had described to Rozanov as a 'sense of duty'. He was constrained to, he had to go to the Slipper House and get inside and look again at the girl whose image still chiefly lived in his mind as a flying-haired thing in a white petticoat glimpsed through a window. He had had a good stare at her on the picnic, but this eyeful had on the whole defused the intensity of his interest and fortified his view of her as simply 'taboo'. He could not afford to be fascinated by Hattie, and was relieved to find that after all he was not. But now, as if he had made a *mistake* which was being corrected by the gods, everything had switched round again, and he was being drawn towards her by the constraint of an exquisite and agonizing obligation.

Tom had been called away by Hector Gaines, who was asking him how they could end the awful carnival and persuade everybody to go. Anthea Eastcote had gone home disgusted with it all, so someone told Hector who was now chastened and miserable. A crashing among the magnolias suggested that the garden was suffering damage. Emma was waltzing by himself under the ginkgo tree when he encountered Pearl. He recognized her at once although, for her sortie, Pearl had disguised herself. She had on a long dark coat and a scarf round her head.

Emma said, 'Hello, dear.'

Pearl said, 'Have you seen Tom McCaffrey?'

'No, dear. Don't go, dear.'

'Excuse me –'

'Pearl –'

Pearl recognized him. 'Oh – Mr Scarlett-Taylor –'

'Don't be silly, my name is – let me see, what is my name –'

'You're drunk.'

'I've got a whisky bottle here, have some.'

'It's horrible, dressing up like that, it's vulgar, you look awful, it's all awful, all those people coming and shouting outside our

381

windows, it's hateful, I can't understand it. We're going to call the police. Take off that wig!'

Emma took off the wig. He had found it in Judy's cupboard as he rooted about when Tom was away and it had given him the idea. He had enjoyed deciding which of Ju's various garments to put on. He threw the wig up into the branches of the ginkgo tree. 'Someone said there was a party here.'

'It's a disgrace. Go home.'

'Pearl, do you mind, I'm going to kiss you.'

Emma was only a little taller than Pearl. He dropped his whisky bottle on the ground and put his two arms carefully round her waist, gathering in the black coat and drawing her to him. He raised one hand to thrust back the scarf from her face, then returned the hand to her waist, locking her firmly. Breathing deeply he felt about, feeling her face with his face, seeking her lips with his lips. He found her lips and gently but resolutely pressed his own dry mouth against them. It was a dry kiss between sealed lips. He stood maintaining the pressure, shifting slightly to keep his balance, and closing his eyes. Pearl's hands, which had been against his shoulders, to push him away, relaxed and then moved a little to hold him. They stood perfectly still together.

George stared at Hattie. Hattie had her hair in two plaits which were drawn forward over her shoulders. She had on the mauve dress from Anne Lapwing's, for it had been a warm day, and over it for the cool evening a long loose grey cardigan with its sleeves pushed up. She wore short white socks inside her embroidered slippers. She looked like a thin frail schoolgirl, and yet she had a dignified startled embattled look, her head thrown back, her face, milky brown from the sun but still pale, pouting in a kind of intensity which answered the challenge of George's squinting cat stare. Her lips were thrust forward in an expression of anger, suddenly like that of her grandfather.

George said, 'Good evening.'

Hattie said, 'How did you get in?'

'I hope I don't intrude.'

'You do intrude, you simply walked in, I didn't invite you, this isn't your house, just because you're one of those McCaffreys you seem to think –'

'Why are you so cross with us McCaffreys?'

'You and your brother have organized this monstrous imper-

382

tinence. This is what it's for, that you should come like this, I see now what it's all about –'

'Well, I don't,' said George. 'Don't be so excited.'

'I'm not excited, I'm furiously angry –'

'All right, you're furiously angry, but don't be angry with me, I didn't do this, I'm blameless –'

'You're – you're horrible – just like people said – go away – you frighten me –'

This was an unwise thing for Hattie to say. George's emotions as he had climbed in through the coal house window and tiptoed to the sitting-room had been confused, not excluding fear: a piercing exciting amalgam of apprehension and weird joy and a special old urgent feeling of guilt which was indistinguishable from his special feeling of obligation. The sudden shock of Hattie's presence, and her defiant stance, sobered him a little and stirred him to think. Thought, evidently, had been absent. He had made beforehand no plan or picture of this encounter. So, there was to be a conversation, perhaps an argument, a battle of wits? This prospect changed the tempo, prompting reflection, intellectual strategy. But Hattie's words, 'You frighten me', were a signal which set off a new stream of emotion, now more clearly defined, a sudden desire not to embrace the girl but to crush her as a large animal crushes a small animal, to feel her fragile bones crack between his teeth.

Hattie saw his inane smile and his lighted eyes and she picked up the limestone hand from the table.

'What do you think you're doing?' said Ruby to Diane.

Ruby had been wandering about among the revellers, sometimes standing with arms folded and looking. The scene seemed to afford her satisfaction. Prowling like a dog, sniffing for the hated foxes, round the perimeter of the stone wall which enclosed the Belmont garden she had come across Diane, crouched, balanced awkwardly against the low branch of a yew tree, half-hidden in the thick blackish foliage.

'Are you hiding?' said Ruby. 'What are you hiding for?'

With a little 'Ach!' of misery and irritation, Diane pulled herself up out of the yew. She had come to church without a coat and was now feeling extremely cold. Her dress had become clammy from damp earth and dew as she scuttled like a trapped mouse round the edges of the garden in the dark spongy mossy 'corridor' between the trees and shrubs and the wall, trying to catch a glimpse of

George from whose rumoured proximity she could not bring herself to depart.

Upstairs in the warm brightly lit space of the Belmont drawing-room, behind drawn curtains, Alex opened another bottle of whisky. She was no longer frightened, she no longer cared about what was happening in the garden or who invaded it. She rather hoped there might be some catastrophe, a murder, or the Slipper House catching fire. As she returned across the room she caught sight of herself in the gilt arch of the big mirror over the mantelpiece. Her face was flushed and puffy, her eyes framed by discoloured wrinkles, her hair hanging down in dull witchy strings. She thought, can it really and truly be that I am no longer beautiful? Tears came into her eyes.

'Well, should we just go home?' said Hector.

'We can't go home and leave this mob here,' said Tom.

'Some people have gone.'

'Yes, but others have come, I saw someone coming through the gate with beer bottles just now. I have an unpleasant feeling they're all waiting for something to happen!'

They were standing on the grass just outside the Slipper House.

Valerie Cossom appeared, her white robe now smudged with green from sitting on the grass. 'George is here, have you seen him?'

'*George?* Oh no!'

At that moment the shutters of the Slipper House sitting-room were suddenly thrown open from within, and the bright lights of the room flooded out making a brilliant rectangle upon the lawn. There were exclamations, a little cheer, people appeared out of the dark and crowded forward.

The scene within was clearly visible. Facing the window was George. At the window, in profile to the spectators, was Hattie, who had just opened the shutters. As the jostling, giggling spectators watched, George advanced upon the girl. It was evident that he wanted to close the shutters again. But Hattie, with a gesture of defiant authority, stretched out her arm, half-bare with the cardigan sleeve tucked up, across the unshuttered window. George paused.

Tom, who was standing in front of the others, close up against the window, as he had stood earlier in the evening, thought his head would burst. Then he cried out in a loud voice, 'George, go home – oh George, go home!' In the next second someone (it was Emma) took up Tom's cry, intoning it softly as a chant to the tune of 'Onward Christian soldiers', better known to some as 'Lloyd

George knows my father'. This latter song (as is well known to college deans) is irresistible to drunks and can be guaranteed to charm the savage breasts of troublesome students in their cups. In a moment all the revellers assembled in front of the Slipper House were singing at the tops of their voices, 'George go home, oh George go home, George go home, oh George . . .' The considerable noise of united voices, penetrating through Victoria Park, drew a number of late home-comers including myself (N, your narrator). I had been attending a learned meeting at a house nearby, was coming down Tasker Road just as the song rang out, and was able to witness some at least of its sequel. A little crowd soon collected in front of Belmont. The police arrived when it was all over.

The effect upon George was clearly visible in the utmost detail. He stepped back and a look of embarrassment and irritation, then of extreme dismay, appeared on his face. Those who do not fear disapproval may be abjectly terrified of ridicule. The combination of Hattie's outstretched arm and the loud derisive singing was too much. He turned and vanished from the room. He plunged through the hall to the back door, unlocked it and shouldered his way past Pearl who was desperately knocking on the outside. Pearl skipped in and locked the door. Hattie closed the shutters.

George ran through the garden in the direction of Belmont, then down past the garage to the road, followed by the scornful hooting of those who had spotted his escape. (This ludicrous episode was the nearest which George came at this time to being lynched.) The song continued for a while, then raggedly died away in laughter. George ran away down the road, turning in the direction of the canal. In the confusion not everyone noticed (but I did) that he was followed by two women, first Valerie Cossom, and then Diane. Following the two women padded the priest, Father Bernard, and after Father Bernard padded I.

Tom held his head, which was still bursting. The revellers, pleased with their exploit, were laughing and dancing about. Some had reached the stage of drunkenness where more drink and the continuation of the party had become absolute necessities. Rupert Chalmers, Maisie's brother, son of Vernon Chalmers whose house was close by, was heard asking for volunteers to raid his father's cellar. Hector, in despair, had started drinking again. He was gazing in a confused manner at Emma, who, with his glasses on and without his wig, had evidently forgotten that he was wearing one of Judy Osmore's cocktail dresses.

'Good evening, Scarlett-Taylor,' said Hector, swaying slightly to and fro.

'Emma,' said Tom, 'how on earth are we going to get rid of this lot? Someone will call the police, and I'm scared cold that Rozanov will find out. Oh God, if only you weren't drunk –'

'Well, I got rid of George, didn't I?'

'Yes, yes, marvellous – but now – think of something –'

Emma stepped back with a movement like that of an athlete or dancer about to perform, with perfect confidence, a very difficult feat. He half turned, spread out his arms, and began to sing. He sang now with his full voice, with all its high weird slightly husky penetrating force, he sang as a fox might sing if foxes could sing. The sound of his voice filled the garden and made it resonate like a drum; waves of sound gathered the garden together into a great vibrating bubble of thrilling sound. And beyond the garden, Emma's voice was heard in the night in streets and houses far around, where people awoke from sleep as if touched by an electric ray, and china in distant kitchens shuddered and rang in sympathy. It was claimed later that his singing could be heard as far away as Blanch Cottages and Druidsdale, though this no doubt was an exaggeration. What he sang was,

> Music for a while
> Shall your cares beguile ...
> Come away, do not stay,
> But obey, while we play,
> For hell's broke up and ghosts have holiday.

The effect upon the revellers was indeed that of an enchantment. They became, of course, instantly silent. It would have been impossible to utter speech against the authority of that voice. And they stood where they were, as still as statues, some even in the attitudes in which the music had surprised them, kneeling on one knee or holding up a hand. It was as if they had all drawn a deep breath and were holding it. Their faces, dimly seen beneath the lamp-lit trees, were rapt and grave as the song continued.

Tom whispered to Hector, 'Quick, see them off, quietly.'

Tom and Hector, as if they were the last men left alive, began to move among the throng, touching people on the shoulder and whispering, 'Go now, please, it's time to go,' 'Time to go home, please go now.' Sometimes a little push was necessary. More often the grave-faced listener, as if he were reverently leaving a ceremony in church, turned and tiptoed off. One after the other, the touch of Tom and Hector animated the petrified guests and sent them on their way. Some even bowed their heads and folded their hands as they set off, now trooping in a long line, toward the back gate. At last they were all gone, even Bobbie Benning who had been found asleep on the seat where he had sat and confided in Father Bernard. Even Hector had gone and the song had died away. Tom and Emma stood alone in the garden. They put their arms round each other and silently laughed or perhaps cried.

Did I push the car or did I just imagine that I pushed it? George had reached the canal, the place beside the iron foot-bridge. He had already forgotten (though he would remember later) his humiliation at the Slipper House. Clouds of emotion which had hung about this place were there waiting for him; undiminished, they engulfed him in their stupefying fumes. He had been away, he had had to come back, it was all as before. What on earth happened, thought George, what did I do, what *am* I? It had been raining on that night; he remembered the rain surging to and fro on the windscreen and the way the yellow lights on the quay got mixed up with the rain. He remembered the cruel bumping of the fast-driven car upon the cobbles. He had turned the steering wheel and the car had plunged into the canal. He saw again the wet white top of the car looking so odd just above the dark disturbed waters whose waves were breaking against it. Somewhere in the sequence of events or dream events were his hands, slipping a little, spread out upon the rainy back window of the car and the slithering of his braced feet upon the stones. He seemed to recall now that he had moved his hands lower down to get a better leverage. Then he had fallen. If he fell, did that prove that he had pushed the car? He looked down at the square unevenly tilting granite cobbles and at the edge of the canal, all glittering with tiny sparks in the lamplight. He felt the cobbles springily with his feet, shifting back and forth and trying to remember.

The warm summer night was soft and quiet, and the three-quarter moon rising over the dark countryside beyond the wasteland made a private silver brilliance in the sky which seemed, as George stood under the yellow lamps, very remote from the earth. Beyond the iron bridge the fretty outline of the gas works rose in moon-illumined silhouette. The lamplight showed a lurid green haze upon the quayside where tufts of grass were growing between the stones. Here Ennistone was asleep. There were no lights showing across the canal beyond the empty ragged rubbishy vegetation, which could not be called a field, which separated the canal from the houses. On this side, behind railings, a maze of partly derelict 'light industry' yards and sheds and one-storey brick buildings divided the canal from the road (known as 'the Commercial Road') which led toward Victoria Park. A dog was barking.

George closed his eyes and tried to breathe slowly and deeply. That awful giddiness was coming upon him, that physically announced loss of identity, a most intense sense of his body, of its bulky heavy solidity and of his various views of it, combined with the absolute disappearance of its inhabitant. This suddenly painful body-presence produced a kind of seasickness and a heavy metaphysical ache. He thought, hold on, it will pass. Then somewhere inside the sick weight where he no longer was came the thought, where is Stella, where *is* she? He thought, I know, but I've forgotten. She isn't dead, that's certain. Surely I know where she is? But she's there in the form of a black hole, like not finding a word. I can't remember anything about her, what happened to her after *this*, where she was, where she went. Fancy not knowing. I must find out, I must ask somebody. Perhaps it's drink, I'm drinking more than I used to.

Did I push the car, he wondered as the giddiness receded. If I could only start up some sort of memory. He began weaving about on the cobbles, moving his hands, moving his feet, miming turning the car, stopping the car (did he stop it?), getting out of the car, coming round behind the car and pushing it with his hands spread out like stars. If he now imagined them 'like stars', did that mean that he had actually seen them like that as they slipped and strained upon the window? Or had he in a *fantasy* seen them 'like stars'? Could he not hang on to something here as a *clue*? But the clue slipped away and returned him to a futile empty helpless feeling of blankness. If only someone else could tell him. If only there had been a witness. But surely there had been a witness, and he had even recognized the witness? But this idea too dissolved in his mind and disappeared.

He thought, I'm in a bad way, I must ask people, seek for help. I'll go to John Robert. He *must* receive me *in the end*. This formulation gave comfort. He thought, I'll write him a letter, I'll explain everything. That's what I'll do, a letter will explain it all. He can't really be so cruel, he hasn't understood, it's a *mistake*. I'll write him a *good* letter, a clear honest letter, he'll respect that. Then he'll see

389

me and be kind to me and oh how my heart will be relieved. Hope came back to George like a genial light of an opening door, quietly dispelling the dark and giving him back himself. Now there was a future. He felt gentle, intelligible, whole. He breathed calmly. He thought, that is how it will be. It will be all right. And I will be all right, I will be better. I'll go home now and sleep. He began to walk along the quay in the direction of Druidsdale.

Stationed in different hiding-places, four persons were watching George. Valerie had gone through a gate into a factory yard and was watching him through the railings. Diane was on the quay behind a big elder bush which was growing between the stones. Father Bernard was a little way behind Diane, relying on a curve in the quay for shelter, and peeping and peering so as to keep both Diane and beyond her George in view. I had made a circuit, since I knew what George's objective was, by the Commercial Road and had come out on the quay beyond the iron bridge, where I had mounted on top of a pile of household junk which someone had illicitly dumped. From here I could see George clearly and also command a view of my fellow watchers.

The evening had no dramatic climax, it faded away rather into a kind of melancholy elegiac peace. From my vantage point, lying concealed behind a crest of old mattresses, I could see, for she was close to me, Valerie Cossom's grave beautiful face, looking with such sadness and such anxiety toward George as he performed on the quayside what must have seemed to her mad unintelligible antics. (I had of course realized at once that George was re-enacting his drama.) And I thought how fortunate George was to be loved by this beautiful intelligent girl, and how little his 'fortune' was worth to him. More distantly I could discern poor Diane uncomfortably crouched between her bushy tree and the railings and beyond the dark shape of Father Bernard, his long skirt swinging as he bobbed to and fro, looking, then hiding. There was something ridiculous in the scene, and yet something moving too. We had all presumably come to 'look after' George, though Father Bernard had also doubtless come to protect Diane. The idea that George might suddenly hurl himself into the canal, simply as a crazy act of violence, was certainly in my mind. I did not see him as about to commit suicide. (In any case no Ennistonian would choose to attempt death by drowning.) I was relieved when George turned away from the fatal place and began to tramp off home. The crisis appeared to be over. (I may say that I discussed this scene much later with two of the participants.) As George passed her, Diane crouched down into a little dark ball behind her tree. It is just possible that George saw her and ignored her. Father Bernard, in absurd haste, squeezed himself back through a gap in the railings. Valerie, safe where she was, did not move. I could not help wanting to laugh as I saw the scene dissolve.

Father Bernard emerged and helped Diane out from behind the tree. He put his arm round her and led her away. Valerie, coming through the gate on to the quay, now saw the other two and watched them depart. Then she turned the other way and walked past my place of concealment. I saw her face as she passed. She wore a strange expression, very sad, weary, grave, even stern, and yet with a twist in the mouth which was almost like a smile, though it might have presaged tears. It struck me at the time that this expression very well expressed what, at the end, the very end, if that can be imagined, someone, perhaps God, might feel about George.

At a distance, for I knew where she lived, I followed Valerie to see her home safely. As she walked she seemed to lose a certain tragic exaltation which had possessed her. Her head drooped, she stumbled over her long besmirched white dress and picked up the skirt impatiently in one hand, drawing it upwards with a graceless movement. Now the comfortless tears would be coming. She began to hurry. I followed her until I saw her put her key into the door of her father's house, one of the 'better' detached houses in Leafy Ridge, and disappear inside. The most beautiful girl in Ennistone.

'Well, how are the old sinuses?' said Mr Hanway.

'All right, sir,' said Emma.

'I trust you have been practising as much as you should?'

'No. Not as much. Some.'

'Why? You can use the college music rooms? And I've told you you can come here.'

'Yes, well, I do use the college music rooms and I sing in my digs when there's no one else there, but somehow –'

'I sometimes feel,' said Mr Hanway, 'that you are ashamed of your great gift and want to keep it a secret.'

'No, no –'

'Perhaps you feel that you counter-tenors have still to make your way in the world and fight to be accepted?'

'Not particularly.'

'You're not troubled by *foolish* worries?' Mr Hanway had a prudish delicacy which Emma greatly liked.

'No, of course not.'

'You seem so timid about it all.'

Emma, not used to regarding himself as 'timid', engaged indeed in the not less than heroic operation of sacrificing one of his gifts to the other, flushed with annoyance. 'I'm not timid, I'm just embarrassed. One can't always be forcing people to hear a loud resonant piercing rather unusual noise!'

'My dear Scarlett-Taylor, what a way to describe your exceptionally beautiful voice!'

Emma thought, I ought to tell him *now* that I'm going to give up singing. I'm going to give up serious singing, and that is for him, *and* for me, the same as giving up singing. But looking into Mr Hanway's gentle diffident grey eyes it seemed impossible to utter. Also, in a yet more terrible way, even the touch of Mr Hanway's fingers on the piano (he was an excellent pianist) struck a resonance deep in Emma's soul which made him wonder: am I not irrevocably bound to music?

'I think it is time for you to come out.'

'I'm not ready.'

'Have you heard of Joshua Bayfield?'

'Vaguely. He plays the guitar.'

'He plays the lute, also the guitar. He asked me if you would perform with him. The BBC are interested and there is a possibility of making a record. And there is that flautist I told you of – you know how well your voice accords with the flute –'

'Oh I don't think anything like that yet – I do occasionally perform after all. I've been asked to sing in the college *Messiah* –' Emma did not add that he had refused.

'You sound quite panic-stricken! You mustn't be so modest. Shall I ask Bayfield to write to you?'

'Please, no.'

Emma, who had just arrived, was sitting beside the piano which his teacher was idly touching as an accompaniment to his admonitions. Mr Hanway, once a moderately well-known operatic tenor, was a corpulent man of over fifty, with coarse straight grey hair and grey eyes. He looked like a teacher, more like an economics don than a musical man, but without self-assertion. His face, not wrinkled, had a greyish sad used look, drooping under the eyes and chin. Something vastly poetic and romantic seemed to stray lost and grieving within him. He had been married, but his wife had left him childless and long ago, and his once promising career as a singer was over. He lived in a dark little flat high up in a red brick mansion block in Knightsbridge. Emma liked the flat which reminded him (perhaps partly because of the particular sound of the piano) of his mother's flat in Brussels, though her flat was large and full of big Belgian furniture which Emma's 'I like it!' when they first arrived there many years ago had kept unchanged.

Emma felt no retrospective satisfaction about his two musical triumphs at the Slipper House. He was ashamed at having got so drunk. He had not wanted to go out with Tom and Tom's old friends, of whom he felt jealous. He had seriously proposed to himself an evening of study. But after Tom had gone he felt so depressed that he decided to have a shot of whisky. After that it was necessary to continue drinking. Then he had gone to look at Judy's clothes, and had found the long-haired wig in her cupboard and tried it on. Then it seemed a shame not to try on a dress or two. The effect was so funny and so charming, the transformation so complete, that he felt bound to share the joke and, emboldened by whisky, set off for the Green Man where Tom had said he would be after the rehearsal. In Burkestown he had been told about the 'Slipper House party'. He could not clearly remember the whole of the evening, particularly the later part which seemed to be full of black patches; but once back at Travancore Avenue he had realized that Ju's pretty dress was torn completely apart at the shoulders and irrevocably stained with red wine.

He did remember putting his arms around Tom, and then, not at all long afterwards, around Pearl. This was the effect of drink. It was not how he usually behaved. Yet it was not false or unreal. Had he just transferred the kiss he could not give to Tom to Pearl, who looked so bisexually angelic with her hard straight profile and her thin upright grace? No, that was Pearl's kiss, not Tom's; and he recalled with a kind of guilty gloomy pleasure her quiet acceptance, at least tolerance, of the kiss. He recalled how positively he had *noticed* Pearl on the first occasion when he saw her. But how stupid and pointless it all was. Tom appeared to be half in love with Anthea Eastcote, and was in any case framed by God for women's joy. And this ambiguous 'maidservant' figure, what did he know about her? He had only had one conversation with her in his life. In any case, what was this about except his capacity to get drunk? It would end, if it had not already ended, in muddle, and he hated muddle, and in rejection, and he hated and feared rejection. He was frightened too by his inability to remember the evening, and ashamed to ask Tom about it. Supposing something disgraceful and absurd had happened? Supposing he were to become an alcoholic? He had seen terrible alcoholics in Dublin. His father, a moderate drinker, had always warned him against alcohol. Had his father, for himself, feared this fate? Had Emma's grandfather, whom Emma could scarcely remember, been an alcoholic? Was it not hereditary?

And now he had to tell Mr Hanway that he was going to give up singing and would come no more. The end of singing would be the end of Mr Hanway. They were only close in this place, in these roles, in the benign and sacred presence of music. He would never see Mr Hanway again. Could that be, was it needful? Yes. He could not divide his life, he could not divide his *time*. He was between two absolutes and he knew which one he loved best. His history tutor, Mr Winstock, who cared little about music, and to whom Emma had once vaguely spoken about 'giving up the singing', could not understand his hesitation; and when he was with Mr Winstock Emma could not understand it either. But now he was with Mr Hanway.

The sun never shone into Mr Hanway's flat, but it sometimes slanted across the window illuminating the white window sills and reflecting on to the gauze curtains which, never drawn back, concealed Mr Hanway's life from windows opposite. It shone so now, reminding Emma of sunrise in Brussels illuminating lace. He thought, and will I sing no more for my mother, who so loves to hear me sing? Could I *get used* to singing less than very well? That would be impossible.

'It's not that I want to tempt you with visions of fame,' Mr Hanway went on, 'I know I can't and wouldn't anyway! Fame will undoubtedly come to you, but that does not concern us now. It is time for you to move to another shelf, to face new challenges. As a teacher I have always encouraged your natural modesty. But it is time for you to realize, to acknowledge to yourself, what a remarkable instrument you possess. You must not neglect what God has been pleased to give you, the voice for which Purcell wrote. Your counter-tenor must be heard, the music must be heard that was written especially for you!'

'There isn't much of it,' said Emma gloomily. He was sitting on an upright chair beside the piano. There had been no singing yet. Perhaps there would not be any.

'Bach, Monteverdi, Vivaldi, Scarlatti, Cavalli, to say nothing of Handel and Purcell and some of the divinest songsters who ever wrote, and you say that isn't much! In any case a little of what is perfect should suffice a purist! You have the most austerely beautiful, most purely musical of all voices, like no other sound in music, to honour which the most beautiful words were wedded to the most perfect music by a century of geniuses. Besides, you owe it to music now to let your talent speak. More composers will write for the counter-tenor voice. A contrived voice they may call it, but art itself is a contrivance. We are already witnessing a musical revolution. An old voice, a new voice, wherewith to sing unto the Lord a new song!' (Here Mr Hanway raised his arms.) 'You must give *more time*, Scarlett-Taylor, *more time*, time is the fuel. Of course you will soon have finished your university studies and be able to concentrate on music, but you should now be singing with a group, and having experience of working with old instruments – you must stop playing the lone wolf. Well, we will talk of these things – now let us sing. What shall we limber-up with, something playful? A folk song, a love song, some Shakespeare?'

Automatically Emma stood up. He blew his nose (an essential preliminary to singing). Mr Hanway touched the piano, suggesting several songs. He sang three of Mr Hanway's favourites, *Take, oh take those Lips Away*, *Woeful Heart with Grief Oppressed* and *Sing Willow*. ('What a gloomy unsuccessful lot they were, to be sure!' said Mr Hanway.) After that they sang together. Mr Hanway's famous Glee Club, flourishing when Emma first made his acquaintance, had, like many pleasant things in the teacher's life, ceased to be, but Mr Hanway retained, together with all his musicological pedantry, a strong sense of music as fun. They sang *Fie, nay, prithee John* in round, then *The Silver Swan* with Mr Hanway producing a remarkable soprano, then *Lure, Falconers, Lure*, then the *Agincourt Song*, then *The Ash Grove* in improvised parts. And as soon as Emma began to sing he could not prevent himself from feeling very happy.

'Good, good, but don't feel you have to stand so still, I've told you before, you're a singer not a soldier, all right, some singers jig about too much, but you're *too* afraid of making faces and moving your hands, don't be so *dignified*, too great a sense of dignity can hinder an artist, it's an aspect of selfishness, *give* yourself, *relax*, let *it* sing through you as the Japanese would say! And keep the sound well up, well up, don't think of your vocal cords, put yourself right up in your brow, feel it as a vast area full of empty caverns where free spiralling columns of air vibrate! Vibrate! You still haven't got that *absolute* high *pianissimo* which moves away into the distance into a thin whisper of pure sound like a thin thin tongue of faintly trembling steel. Ah, you have much to do – sometimes I think you are just coasting along.' Mr Hanway's exhortations, often highly metaphorical, were always accompanied with elaborate mime. 'Now, dear boy, let us have special exercises and then on to the Bach *Magnificat*, I shall hear your beautiful *Esurientes* ...'

As Emma came out into the bright sunshine after his lesson, having failed once more to 'say anything' to Mr Hanway, he felt that dazed giddiness again as he shielded his eyes, the vertigo of an abomination of loneliness and loss, where silent endless streaming snowflakes blinded him and obliterated all meaning. He remembered a dream where he had wandered in vast vibrating caverns, realizing with despair that they were caves of ice deep underneath a glacier where he was destined soon to fall to his knees and die.

'Must we have all the light shut out by those bloody plants?' said Brian.

'I like to have a living thing near me,' said Gabriel.

'Aren't I a living thing? Do you want me to squat on the window ledge while you wash up?'

'Sorry, I'll move them.'

'And I wish you wouldn't smoke in the kitchen, you smoke over the sink, it gets everywhere –'

It was two days since the events at the Slipper House (which had occurred on Saturday, it being now Monday). Gabriel and Brian were having breakfast in the kitchen at Como. Brian was cross this morning because it was Monday and because Gabriel, reaching out in the night for the glass of water she always kept beside her, had tapped her wedding-ring upon the glass top of the dressing-table and woken him up, after which he was unable to go to sleep again.

Sitting on a chair in the corner, Adam was holding Zed on his knee and murmuring to him almost inaudibly. This ritual occurred every morning. Gabriel knew without being told that Adam was explaining that he was only going away to school and would very soon be back and that Zed was to be a good dog and not to worry. Zed listened to these comforting admonitions on each occasion with an air of alert bright-eyed interest, occasionally thrusting forward to lick Adam's nose. This scene filled Gabriel with the old familiar mixture of intense love and intense fear, each emotion as it were jacking the other up.

Adam was dressed in his prep school uniform, the 'togs' which had pleased Hattie, blue jersey, brown corduroy knee-breeches, and blue socks. Last night Brian and Gabriel had been arguing again about where Adam was to go to school next. Gabriel did not want him to go away from home, but she thought the Comprehensive School was 'too rough'. There was a small private secondary school with quite a good reputation not far away on the road to London, and could he not go as a day boy, there was a school bus which ran in and out of Ennistone. Brian said this was out of the question, it would be far too expensive, especially as he would soon be out of a job. Gabriel said, good heavens, this is the first I've heard. Brian said he just meant everyone would soon be out of a job. Anyway what was wrong with the Comprehensive, it was a good school, the maths were excellent under Jeremy Blackett. Gabriel said what about his French and Latin which he was doing well at, the Comprehensive didn't start French till fourteen and had never heard of Latin. Brian said he was exhausted and was going to bed.

Looking at Adam and Zed, Gabriel thought about the awful scene at the seaside, and about her adventure with the fish. She had not talked to anybody about the fish. This connected in her mind with something weird which had happened last week. By herself in the house in the afternoon, washing some saucepans at the kitchen sink, she had heard Zed barking in the garden, and looking out between the potted plants had seen the amazing sight of a completely naked man hurrying across the lawn. She did not see him soon enough to see where he had come from, whether over the fence or down the side passage from the road. He seemed to be concerned with getting out of the garden by climbing one of the fences, either the one on the right or the one at the end, both of which he attempted in a helpless perfunctory way. Both fences were made of upright wooden slats about five feet high; the one at the bottom had two horizontal beams nailed along it, the one on the right had not, but had branchy shrubs growing against it which would afford footholds. Gabriel saw that the runner was wearing brown laced-up shoes with no socks. He had greasy longish grey hair, and a look of preoccupied anxiety on his face which she could see clearly as he tried to climb into an old rosemary bush, breaking the brittle branches with loud cracks and trampling them down. After the first moment of shock Gabriel felt no fear of the man, only pity and fear for him, for the pathetic pale soiled vulnerability of his flabby unyoung flesh, as he now struggled at the bottom of the garden, gripping the top of the fence (which Gabriel knew to be jagged and full of splinters) with two hands, and trying to lodge his awkward shoes upon the sloping transverse beams off which they kept slipping. All this time Zed was continuing to dance round the man's heels barking fiercely. Gabriel imagined him astride upon that sharp jagged fence and covered her eyes, not knowing what to do. She wanted to run out into the garden, to soothe him (for she did not doubt that he was mad, this was no youngster's jape), bring him inside, give him clothing and a cup of tea. But at this point she did feel frightened. Suppose he were violent? Should she not telephone Brian, telephone the police, get help somewhere? Oughtn't she to lock the doors? She ran out into the hall, then ran back to lock the garden door, then ran back into the hall and lifted the telephone, then set it down again. She decided she ought to go out into the garden. She hurried back to the kitchen window, but now the garden was empty and Zed had stopped barking. Gabriel unlocked the door and went out. Zed trotted towards her beaming with the satisfaction of duty done. Gabriel searched around, looking over the fences and into the shed, but the man was nowhere to be seen; he had vanished like a hallucination. Gabriel went slowly back to the house. She decided not to telephone the police. The police might arrest him, be rough with him, charge him, imprison him, whereas if he were left alone he might recover and find his way home, or someone might befriend him and look after him as *she* might have done if only she had had more courage! Then she remembered the Indian man at the Baths, whom she had never seen again. In the evening she told the story to Brian, but making light of it, laughing a bit, then suddenly crying. Brian got the impression that she was being brave about a terrible experience. (And in a way it had been a terrible experience, an ordeal of helpless and frustrated pity.) He said that she ought to have telephoned the police, but now there was no point. (Brian was reluctant to get in touch with the police, because he hated 'trouble' and anything to do with publicity, which might get his name mentioned in the papers.) The next day however at the office he changed his mind and rang the police but without alerting Gabriel. Confronted by a policeman on the doorstep, Gabriel was instantly certain that either Adam or Brian was dead. When the policeman solemnly made clear the reason for his visit she was incoherent with relief. 'Oh, I didn't mind that at all!' 'Are you telling me, madam, that you don't mind finding a naked man in your garden?' 'I don't want him to be hurt!' Tears. 'I can see, madam, that the episode has upset you very much.' And so on. It turned out soon after that the poor man was a patient of Ivor Sefton's and was now in hospital. Brian, that evening, positively forbade Gabriel to go and visit him. That night she dreamed about fishes suffocating.

'Good God!' said Brian, who had been reading the *Ennistone Gazette* over breakfast.

'What?'

'We're in the bloody paper!'

'About the streaker?'

'No, not that! I mean Tom and George, not us, but we'll be

399

dragged in. Good grief! whatever have they been up to, damn them? Tom wants thrashing and George ought to be put away, nothing but trouble and it'll land on *us*. Look at this awful muck in their filthy gossip column!' He handed the paper over to Gabriel.

MCCAFFREY PRACTICAL JOKE GOES TOO FAR

Extraordinary scenes took place on Saturday night at the so-called 'Slipper House', luxury abode in Victoria Park lately purchased from Mrs Alexandra McCaffrey by Professor John Robert Rozanov as a home for his grand-daughter Miss Harriet Meynell and her maidservant. 'Rehearsals' of *The Mask of Aphrodite* in the Ennistone Hall broke up in confusion when George and Tom McCaffrey led a drunken rabble to lay siege to the two damsels in their flossy seclusion. Drinking and shouting, the revellers, who included parish priest Reverend Bernard Jacoby, attempted to gain access to the house, and failed, proceeded to wreck the garden, fouling the lawns and damaging valuable trees and shrubs. Stones were thrown at the windows, one of which shattered a pane of antique stained-glass. Also present were a number of young men in outrageous 'drag' and their sponsor, our own Madame Diane. At last, with the connivance of the maidservant who opened the back door to him, George McCaffrey was enabled to enter the house, while his brother Tom howled with laughter outside. What happened next is not recorded! One fact has emerged. The so-called maid, Pearl Scotney, is no other than the sister of the afore-mentioned Madame D, who is the intimate friend of G. McCaffrey! What makes the whole episode more mysterious (or does it?) is that Tom McCaffrey, with professorial prodding and rather suggestive *haste*, has lately become engaged to the professorial grand-daughter. Miss Meynell may or may not have found the evening amusing. Picking up the pieces should constitute an interesting problem in moral philosophy.

Gabriel read it through with little mews of distress. 'But it can't be true, it *can't* be true!'

'It's true now,' said Brian. 'We shall never hear the end of this.'

It was never known for certain later on who was the author of this scurrilous piece. The general view was that it was the editor, Gavin Oare, who was annoyed with Hattie for her slightly haughty letter refusing an interview, and who had an old grudge against George because of a humiliation he had suffered at George's hands some years ago (an incident at a party). It seems likely that the innocent occasion of the article was Maisie Chalmers, the Women's Page girl, who had gone along with the others from the Green Man, without any malicious intent, and in fact left fairly early, soon after Anthea Eastcote. The next morning, laughing about it all, she gave the editor an account of junketings in the Belmont garden. Gavin Oare immediately sent out his spies (Mike Seanu was one) and pieced together a fuller and more interesting account. On the day after the *Gazette*'s revelations, its rival, *The Swimmer*, the weekly trade paper, also ran the story, taking up as usual a different 'angle' from that of the *Gazette*. According to *The Swimmer*, the 'orgy' had been arranged by Miss 'Hattie' Meynell herself, who had turned out to be considerably less stuffy than was at first imagined. The paper also struck a note of its own, reporting that 'Our Sapphic Sisterhood of Women's Libbers were also there in force, and the so-called "maid" was to be seen hugging and kissing, clasped to the bosom of another long-haired Amazon.' *The Swimmer* repeated, even more suggestively, the tale that Tom and Hattie had become engaged in a hurry at the insistence of 'our learned Professor'. George also figured prominently. One sentence read, 'Miss Hattie, so hastily pledged to Tom, appears also to be on friendly terms with George, which goes to show that a McCaffrey will do anything for another McCaffrey.' (The meaning of these words was much discussed.) The article was headed *Prof's grandchild launched in Ennistone*.

Not long after the Brian McCaffreys' Monday breakfast time Tom, who never read the *Ennistone Gazette*, was packing to return to London. He had in fact just been round to Leafy Ridge to see Gabriel and ask her to try and mend and clean Judy Osmore's dress, but no one was there when he arrived, Brian had gone to the office, Adam to school, and Gabriel was out shopping. Tom played a while with Zed, then left the dress in the kitchen with a note. Emma had left on the previous day full of remorse and repentance. Tom, also remorseful and repentant, had tried to cheer him up. Emma had brought Tom, wordlessly, the ruined dress, and Tom had told him first that Judy Osmore was not the sort of girl to mind a thing like that, and that second, anyway he would take the dress to Gabriel who was awfully clever at mending things and removing stains. Emma had gone away uncomforted. Seeing him depart, Tom had an urge to run after him. They had of course referred to the disastrous evening but not discussed it. Tom felt both that it had upset Emma very much and that he, Tom, might have appeared (since he made a joke or two) to regard the whole thing in a frivolous light. Emma's stern eyes seemed to charge him with frivolity. Tom felt unhappily that he was somehow, where Emma was concerned, failing to 'keep up', and had become lately a more ordinary, less extraordinary person for his friend. Tom was used to being loved and valued and his vanity was engaged. He admired Emma very much and regarded him as, in important respects, his superior, so that he was sad and irritated to think that Emma's image of him might diminish. This unworthy anxiety prevented the communication which might have removed it. They were awkward with each other and Tom, failing to discover any way of expressing his affection, found himself playing the fool in front of an increasingly silent Emma.

Tom had also, throughout that rather unhappy Sunday, been thinking about George. George had never been, as the years went by, very far away from Tom's heart and mind. At times Tom felt, as he felt now, as if he were being positively prompted to help George, perhaps willed by George himself to come to him. Yet such an impulsive warm approach, as Tom conceived it, could scarcely be imagined in detail. Reflecting on the recent drama, there did seem to be one point of hope. George had been defeated, and easily defeated, by mass ridicule. This could scarcely be a precedent since the circumstances were so unusual, but was it not a good sign? It made Tom see George as comic, and with this came notions of forgiveness and change. Maybe we take him too seriously, Tom thought. He should be laughed out of it all, persecuted by laughter. And Tom thought, I'll go and see old George, I ought to have before, I'll go next weekend. But next weekend was a long way off, and Tom had still to contend with the image of George inside that window with Hattie.

Hattie was hardest of all to think about and most painful. Tom kept saying to himself, I have to give it up, leave it alone, do nothing, there's nothing I can do, I don't understand and I'd better not try. If only George hadn't got mixed in, it was all bad enough without that. Tom had resisted an impulse to send Hattie a long rambling letter of apology. Better to say nothing. What did Hattie think after all, how much did she know, and how much would she say to Rozanov? Tom saw Hattie as a girl capable of saying very little or nothing. She might well feel that the whole incident was best left to disappear without further comment. George, who seemed so significant to Tom, might seem considerably less so to Hattie. And surely Hattie could not *really* think that Tom had led that mob into the garden on purpose to annoy her. Perhaps she was already laughing about the whole thing. An apology might simply have the effect of accusing himself of crimes of which it had not occurred to her to accuse him. Tom even began to think it reasonable to hope that Rozanov would not hear of the 'little escapade' at all.

All the same, he thought, after he had finished his packing and was standing at the back window looking out over the garden at the view of the town, all the same, I *will* write to her, I *will* see her, but not yet, later on. And as the image of Hattie defying George, her bare arm outstretched, came back vividly to his mind, he felt that this was not the last time that he would want to brood upon it. He stood looking out over Ennistone, funny little town, where the sun was shining upon the gilded cupola of the Hall, 'just like Leningrad' as the Official Guide touchingly said, and he thought now about Emma and about George and about Hattie, and he felt sad and alone.

At that moment in his reflections the telephone bell rang. It was Gavin Oare, asking if he had any comment to make on today's issue of the *Gazette*. When Tom said that he had not seen today's issue, Gavin Oare chuckled and said that he had better go out and buy one. Tom ran from the house.

Pearl saw the paper on Monday morning when she went out shopping. She ran back at once and then could not bring herself to tell Hattie who was quietly reading. However, with Pearl so upset (and the more she thought the more upset she became) concealment proved impossible. The girls, in tears, agreed that now there was nothing to be done but wait. (Hattie did try to write a letter, but soon gave it up.) John Robert Rozanov did not catch up until Tuesday. On Monday morning he went early to the Institute (he had spent the night at Hare Lane where he was sorting out some papers) and swam in the Outdoor Pool before retiring to his den in the Rooms, where he worked all the morning and had a sandwich lunch brought to him. He soaked in his hot bath, then had his sleep as usual. He worked on till late in the evening and went to bed. No one, during that time, dared to approach him. When he woke on Tuesday morning he found that a copy of Monday's *Gazette* and of Tuesday's *Swimmer* had been thrust under his door.

*

George, shut up in his house in Druidsdale and oblivious of articles in newspapers, had decided to give John Robert another chance. He had phrased it in his mind as 'a last chance', but he could not bear those words and changed them. For no reason that he could have thought of, had he decided to reflect about it which he did not, a warm spring-like breeze of hope was blowing in his soul. It was not a desire for happiness. George had never, even as a young man, allowed himself a desire for happiness. It was something involuntary, mechanical, a primitive self-protective jerk of the psyche. It now seemed to George that he had been seeing his situation in an entirely irrational light, and that he had built up an entirely false picture of his old teacher. In a way, thought George, egoism is the trouble, I'm just being too much of a solipsist. I imagine John Robert thinking a lot about me and hating and despising me in quite an *elaborate* way as if this were a major activity in his life creating a vast complex barrier between us. But it isn't like that. He doesn't think about me all that much. After all he's got other troubles. And what did he always think about nearly all the time anyway? His work. I'm a minor problem. So is everybody else, *everybody* else, it isn't just me. So I mustn't attach too much importance to the peevish hostile things he says when I arrive and interrupt him. Of course I've been very tactless, I've even been aggressive. John Robert is a tremendous one for his dignity. No wonder he was sharp with me. In a way it's a sign he cares for me, he cares how I behave. Well, I'll behave better. I'll write him a very careful letter, I'll write him an *interesting* letter. John Robert always forgives people who interest him.

The evening at the Slipper House had already been mercifully worked upon by the chemistry of memory, and even his defeat at the hands of the singers appeared with a difference. He retained most vividly an impression of Hattie, her breathing closeness to him, her fragile crushability, her *crunchability*. He recalled too with appreciation her large gesture at the window. And he remembered the running, the escaping pursued by a crowd. This image was now not displeasing. To hear the vulgar outcry and outrun it and then to be alone: that was a picture of life. The histrionics beside the canal made no sense and had dropped into oblivion. The recent past appeared as a kind of show, an interlude, unconnected with the pressing duties which now composed the significance of his life.

So it was that on Monday afternoon George sat down at the polished but dusty table in the sparsely elegant dining-room in

Druidsdale, 'he was still living downstairs, he had not gone upstairs since his excursion to find the netsuke) and wrote as follows:

My dear John Robert,

I have been thinking about you. I feel I have been ungracious and unfair and I want to apologize. I know you care little about apologies and other such 'posturing', a word which you used, years ago, to describe a similar *démarche* on my part. I know too that you understand the strategic psychological purpose of an apology, which is to put the apologizer once more upon a level with his *adversary*, the offended person! My aim, as it has always been, is clarification, one which you surely share. We have known each other a long time and have been more than once in the place we are in now; a consideration which makes me the more confident in addressing you. There are various ways in which our relationship might be pictured, but fundamentally it is that of teacher and pupil, a relation which, *prima facie* at any rate, imposes a lasting obligation upon the teacher. You must know from experience how lively and how durable such a connection can be, and it is not your 'fault' any more than it is mine that we are in this way eternally connected. It is because you are a great man and a great teacher that this is so. These are facts in the light of which my being 'a nuisance' or 'impolite' must show as superficial. You *know* that my 'tiresomeness' is an expression of love, and one which perhaps at a deep level you would be sorry to be without. You know also, and I need not stress it, how I *crave* for your kindness. This may sound servile, but I offer it as another fact, and in no spirit of servility. You know me well enough to know how little I am given over, even where you are concerned, to any form of slavery.

I have been reflecting about philosophy of late, in a somewhat 'existential' mood (sorry, I know you loathe that word, but it has its place), and it has occurred to me (not actually for the first time) that you and I are alike. How is that? you will ask. I will tell you. We are both free men. I remember you said once (my God, how many sayings of yours are stored up in my head!) that the idea of being 'beyond good and evil' was and could only be a vulgar illusion. I think we had been discussing Dostoevsky. All right. Those who claim to be 'beyond' this familiar dualism are lying cynics or irresponsible victims of semi-conscious will, or eccentric or perverted enthusiasts who elevate some virtue (courage, for instance) so far above the other virtues as to make these invisible. Or if one attempts to draw a more spiritual picture, is not this simply morality itself at a more intense level? The adept who 'prefers knowledge to virtue' is either a vulgar magician or else a kind of 'scholar', whose selfless application we may admire, while we deplore his neglect of simpler duties! I seem to hear the echo of your voice here! (Did you not also speak later on, I seem to recall the phrase of a possible 'conceptual dissolution of morals'? Perhaps that is part of the secret doctrine!) But, John Robert, is there

405

not a much less arcane sense of this 'freedom', closer to home, closer anyway to *our* home? Do we, you and I, fall into any of the categories I have enumerated? I think not! We have simply 'cut free', and what we have done is not really so mysterious (or so grand) after all. There are many aspects to our freedom. One is certainly an absence of vanity (I speak of course in a neutral sense, and not as claiming a merit) which expresses itself as a complete indifference to 'what people say'. We are outside the power of censure, as I believe *very few* people are. Schopenhauer says somewhere that virtue is simply an amalgam of prudence, fear of punishment, fear of censure, apathy and a desire to be liked! Can we not simply proceed by eliminating these one by one? And when they are all gone, have we not reached a place which some deny exists? Not by a dramatic leap, or by the development of some narrow specialized super-virtue, but by a simple movement of escape, like an eel slipping out of a trap. We are *outside*, you and I, and are we not, in this unpopulated open space, to shake each other's hands? *I think you understand me.*

I would like to talk to you about these and other matters. I won't try to see you just yet. Indeed, I don't mind whether we talk here or in California. But we *will* talk. I feel, I cannot express to you how I know it, sure of that. *We are bound together.* I have sometimes behaved to you like a vulgar fool and I am sorry for it. But I know that you know that I am not a vulgar fool. Between now and the end, I am to be reckoned with.

I want in this letter to make peace with you. The sense of our being 'at odds' has troubled me. Let there be peace, John Robert, for both our sakes. Don't trouble to answer this, but *receive* it, think about it please, let it be in your mind. I will communicate with you again. Ever, indeed forever, your devoted pupil,

George McC

George wrote the letter rapidly, straight out, in a state of excitement as if inspired. When he sat back and read it through he felt relieved, almost happy. It was wise not to suggest a meeting, better to indicate a vague future which, being peaceful, would in its due time bring forth a meeting. George felt sure that *this* letter would charm the philosopher. At worst it would amuse him. But George meant every word of the letter and hoped that its seriousness would impress. The sending of it would be a magic act which would restore to its tormented writer peace, and time.

It was Wednesday morning. Tom, who had of course not returned to London, was ringing the bell at number sixteen Hare Lane. He had received by the first post a letter which read:

Dear Mr McCaffrey,
I shall expect you to call on me at Hare Lane at 10 a.m. on Wednesday.

J. R. Rozanov

John Robert opened the door and made a gesture toward the back room. Tom entered past him. The day was cloudy and overcast and the room was dark, but Tom saw a copy of the *Ennistone Gazette* open on the table.

Rozanov came in and shut the door. He said in a husky voice, clearing his throat, 'Have you seen this?'

'Yes.'

'Can you explain it? There's a report here too.' He slapped a copy of *The Swimmer* down on the table with a violence which made Tom shudder.

Tom had already thought out his speech which would consist simply of telling the truth. He said, 'It's horrible, I felt sick when I read it. But you know what gossip columns are. It's all lies –'

'Oh, is it?'

Tom was standing with his back to the window, Rozanov against the closed door. Tom realized that the philosopher was actually trembling and that there were frothy bubbles on his lips. Tom drew a deep breath. He was beginning to tremble too. He said, 'Wait, listen, I'll tell you exactly what happened, it was all perfectly innocent, not like that – I was at those rehearsals at the Hall, then we all went to the pub, to the Green Man, and then when it closed I went to Belmont and they all followed me, I didn't want them to, I didn't invite them –'

'Were you going to see Harriet?' John Robert was controlling himself, Tom could hear his slow deep breathing and the expulsion of his breath between his teeth.

Tom hesitated, then said, 'Yes – but –'

'So late at night? Had she invited you?'

'No – it wasn't all that late – I mean –'

'The Green Man closes at ten, ten-thirty?'

'Well, all right, I wasn't going to call on her like, I just wanted to – to go there –'

'To go there?'

'I don't know what I wanted, I was drunk.'

'I see.'

'Then all the others followed, they thought there was a party.'

'Had you arranged a party?'

'No –'

'Why did they think there was a party?'

'Because I said so –'

'You said so –'

'Yes, but only sort of to put them off, to get away – I pretended I had to go to a party – and then – well, then there *was* a party – I didn't intend it – and once they were there I couldn't get them to leave. It wasn't my fault. I'm very sorry indeed about it all. I've been writing a letter of apology to Miss Meynell –'

'Why are you apologizing if it wasn't your fault?'

'Well, I suppose it was my fault because it was offensive but not intentionally –' Awful unclarified feelings of guilt had been confusing Tom's mind. He seemed somehow to have brought about, and yet how, an absolute mountain of complicated events. He had wanted to run to see Hattie but did not dare to. He had been trying to compose a letter to her but found it too difficult. He was indeed only at that very moment realizing the full enormity of the situation.

The familiar process of question and answer had made Rozanov less agitated. At first he had hardly been able to speak. He said, 'You brought George there, you introduced him into the house.'

'I didn't, I swear it! I don't know how George came into it, he must have arrived by accident.'

'Were you in the house?'

'No.'

'But he was.'

'Yes, but I don't know how he got in – then we – we shouted at him and made him go.'

'And were all those people there, Mrs Sedleigh and men dressed as women?'

'Yes, well, one anyway, but it was just a lark –'

'A *lark*? Are you in your right mind?'

'I know it's awful but it *wasn't* my fault, all that other stuff was made up by the paper.'

'Are you suggesting that they simply invented the idea that –' John Robert leaned back against the door and opened his wet frothy mouth like an animal.

Tom was now almost crying with fear and distress. He said, wailing it out, 'I did nothing wrong!'

Rozanov said with difficulty, 'Are you suggesting that the newspapers *invented* the idea that I had – said that you might – that you and Harriet might – that I wanted you to be together?'

There was something pitifully awfully sad in the utterance of those words; and it was only at that moment that Tom fully realized what a terrible position he was in. He had been facing the philosopher, but now lowered his head. He mumbled, 'I don't know what made them say that.'

'Don't you? You told somebody – what I told you not to tell –'

'*No* –'

'You told somebody.'

'Well, yes I told one person.'

'Who?'

'My friend Scarlett-Taylor, but –'

'You said – you promised – not to tell anyone –'

'I'm sorry, I'm very very sorry, if you knew *how* sorry you would be less angry with me – I don't know how it got around – it can't have been him – perhaps they really did make it up –'

'Do you realize the terrible harm you have done to Harriet and to me, terrible irreparable harm?'

'Surely not,' said Tom. 'This is some stupid impertinent rubbish in a local paper, people will laugh at it.'

'Do you imagine that I like being laughed at? Do you think that I lightly ignore the fact that you have made a fool of me, a laughing stock? That something so very private has been made into a vulgar joke –?'

Rozanov took a step forward and Tom flinched toward the corner of the room – standing in the corner, he leaned back against the wall. He said, 'I am very sorry, I've said that. What more can I say? It's a piece of nonsense.'

'My grand-daughter's name dishonoured in public and you call it nonsense?'

'I don't see that it can harm Hattie in any way.'

'Do not call her Hattie!'

'Well, Harriet, Miss Meynell, whatever you like, I dare say it hurts you – your – your self-esteem – but you'll soon recover – and it needn't bother her, it's all temporary –'

John Robert lunged out one hand, picked up a small china dog from the sideboard and smashed it with tremendous force into the grate. The fragments flew about the floor. He said, 'Have you *read* those two articles?'

In fact Tom had not seen the article in *The Swimmer* at all and had not read the *Gazette* article with close attention. He had read it through with horror and disgust and then torn it up in case he should be tempted to distress himself further by looking at it again. He said, 'I sort of read that, not carefully – I haven't seen the other one –'

'Well, read them *now* please. Sit down at the table and read them. *Sit down.*'

Tom sat down on a chair beside the table. He read the *Gazette* article. It took him some time to do so because he found that he could not see, the print was fuzzy and unclear and he had to keep blinking his eyes and reading each sentence twice over. He then read the article in *The Swimmer* which Rozanov had spread out beside him. When he had first read the *Gazette* Tom's eye had passed over the bit about 'professorial prompting' and he had vaguely understood it but without taking in the accompanying innuendo. His appalled reaction had been to the account of 'a drunken riot' and he had winced at the connection of his own name with those of Hattie and Rozanov. But even on that he had not reflected fully. He had thought, it's only a piece of blatantly shameless gossip in a local paper, no one will take it in or understand it, they'll simply think it's crazy, and I don't imagine John Robert will even see it. His thoughts had fled at once to Hattie and what on earth he was to say to her after that horrid scene. But now ... He read the other article. He put his hands up to his blazing hot face. He said, 'I hadn't fully taken it in. I see now. But it's all a lot of lies and inventions. It's such awful stuff – can't one do anything, can't we make them say it isn't true –?'

While he was reading, John Robert had sat down opposite him at the table, watching him. 'No, of course we can't do anything. I hope you see *now* the extent of what your *treachery* has done, to her, and to me, what hurt, what distress, what irrevocable damage you have brought about.'

Tom said feebly, not looking up, 'I do assure you nothing was given away through me. They must have invented it all. Of course it's horrible – but no one will believe it – and later on it'll all blow away and be forgotten – nobody cares these days about things like that anyway.'

'You speak with a foul tongue,' said Rozanov. 'I should have realized that you are like your brother, a filthy-minded self-obsessed cynic and a pitiful idiot. And you appear to be his drinking companion and lieutenant.'

'I'm not, don't connect me with George. I mean we're not close like that at all.'

410

'The details don't matter. It is all sufficiently bad to be fatal. You have made a fool of me, and I don't forgive that.'

Tom looked up with his flaming face and sustained Rozanov's glare. 'You frighten me and I can't think clearly. I just meant people will forget, and it's not the end of the world.'

'And to have your brother's name brought into this. And to think that he went into that house. Whether you introduced him there –'

'I didn't.'

'Is immaterial. I think you tell lies and I don't want to talk to you any more. You say nobody cares now. No, "nobody cares" about sexual honour and decency and chastity and right conduct. But I care. And I – I chose you – because I thought – you cared. I should have kept clear of your vice-tainted clan.'

Tom felt tears coming into his eyes. He said, 'I've said some stupid things – I didn't mean it like that. But surely you – I don't understand – you don't think that *Hattie* did anything wrong?'

John Robert stood up and Tom rose quickly and moved to the fireplace ready to dart for the door. John Robert said, 'You are a foul-minded fool. But you need not be afraid of me. I only called you here really for one thing.'

'What?'

'You have broken one promise. I shall require of you now, after all the harm you have done us, not to break another. You are not ever again to see my grand-daughter or to communicate with her in any way.'

'But –'

'You will not see her again ever. Any approach to her now would be an unforgivable offence, an outrage. I believe you live in London. Go there today and stay there. Do not dare to show your face in Ennistone. If you do I will – I will do everything I can to harm you as you have so unpardonably harmed me. Go away and stay away. I shall soon take Harriet back to America. It was an accursed mistake to bring her here. And the fault, the curse, is yours, son of a profligate father and a runaway mother, corrupted by your evil brother. And to think that I trusted you with – something so precious –'

'No, no don't send me away, let me stay please, let me try again, I really am as you thought me, I'm not like George –'

'Go now and right away, at once.'

'Please, please –'

'Go away, go *away*!'

411

The philosopher turned upon Tom a face of anguish, his eyes and brow screwed up, his wet lips opening revealing the red interior of his mouth, as for a great cry of woe. Tom escaped to the door and out of the house.

There's a *head* up there in the ginkgo tree, thought Alex. A head with long golden hair perched high up in the branches. Alex looked at it with her heart beating fast. It was twilight on Wednesday evening. She thought, it's something to do with them, those wicked ill-omened girls. It's some kind of vile filthy *ghost* thing. Adolescent girls attract ghosts.

She walked back toward the house and edged round the corner of the garage beside the dustbins, seeing the top of the Rolls-Royce through the garage window, and feeling another pang of fright and pain. On the evening of the 'riot' Alex had secured all the doors and gone to bed drunk leaving Ruby locked outside in the garden. Ruby had spent the night in the Rolls. Alex felt disgust at the idea of Ruby's big sweaty body curled up inside the car. She thought, I'll sell it, it's spoilt now.

Earlier Alex had again seen the pretty vixen reclining while four fluffy milk-chocolate brown cubs with light blue eyes and stubby tails played tig on the lawn. This sight now seemed uncanny too, an accidental slit into another world, weird, beautiful, dangerous, coming nearer. The blue-tits at her bedroom window wore demonic masks. And places where she might have run for help, George, Rozanov, were the most haunted of all.

Alex looked past the dustbins along the side of the house toward the road where the lights had not yet come on. If she screwed her eyes up a bit she could see quite clearly in the faintly fuzzy blue light. No one was there. Then a sudden movement nearer to her made her startle and step back. Something had appeared just beyond the farthest of the three dustbins. It was the dog fox, who stood looking at her with his darkly lined sorrowful fierce face. Alex instinctively raised her hand in a dismissive gesture; but the fox did not flinch. Withdrawing his attention from Alex, he began sniffing about at the base of the bin. Then he stood up on his hind legs and thrust his nose and his front paws under the top of the bin. Alex felt frightened and angry at the fox's indifference to her presence. She said, finding it strangely difficult to speak to the fox, 'Stop that!' She did not shout, but spoke quite softly; and she knocked her fists, feebly

412

and almost inaudibly, upon the lid of the bin nearest to her. The fox descended to all fours, evidently eating something, and then, without even looking at Alex, stood up again to resume his investigation. Alex drew back. Then she moved forward again and, picking up the lid upon which she had tapped, threw it in the direction of the fox where it skidded on the concrete and went bowling past him like a hoop. The fox leapt but did not run away. He ran in fact directly toward Alex, round her, and back again to the garage wall where he proceeded with a violent blow from his front paws to overturn one of the bins completely. He began scrabbling among the rubbish. Alex, suddenly mad, ran to the further bin and knocked the lid off and began pelting the fox with the contents. At the same time she cried out, loudly this time, 'Oh, stop, stop, go away!' The fox, his black paws deep in the mess, regarded her, and then uttered a sound. It was not exactly a bark, it was a deep resonant shrieking noise. As Alex now rushed towards him he darted across her feet (his fur brushed her dress) and in through the open door of the garage. As with almost superstitious terror she peered in through the doorway, she could dimly see the fox sitting up in the front seat of the Rolls.

'What is it?' said Ruby, coming round the corner from the house.
'Nothing.'
'What's this stuff here?'
'Nothing. *Leave it*.'
Leaving the garage door open, Alex followed Ruby back into the house. The strange head up in the tree seemed to be glowing in the intense twilight.

George had been sincere in attributing to John Robert a lack of vanity and a lofty indifference to 'what people say'. His view was however incorrect. Tom had been nearer the mark, and dangerously so, in what he had blurted out about 'self-esteem'. John Robert was an arrogant independent eccentric, careless of convention and devoid of mean worldly aims. He blundered uncalculatingly through life ready, in pursuit of his own goals and principles, to face men's indifference, incomprehension and dislike. He said what he thought and cared nothing for society. In a totalitarian state he might well have been in prison. He was nevertheless vulnerable to ridicule, and to the mockery of spiteful misunderstanding. Moreover in this case he was helpless. He could not rush forth to confound his lying tormentors. Any such sortie would merely attract more publicity and more malicious laughter. His dignity was a part of his self-respect, and he felt wounded in his strength. He was not only tortured by the articles in the Ennistone papers, he was for a time defeated by them, made confused, almost ashamed. He wanted to 'hide', and indeed for two days he did not leave the house. He was well aware that his misfortunes must be a prime topic of gleeful conversation in the town. By the Thursday after the 'riot' the national papers had taken note of the matter, understanding it for some reason as a student protest against some aspect of Rozanov's philosophy. Two reporters actually rang his bell and a photographer took a picture of the front door. A German newspaper (Rozanov was well-known in Germany) printed a light-hearted version of the tale, based on the Ennistone accounts, and a scurrilous German periodical pursued various inferences some entirely new, and published a picture of Hattie which they had somehow procured. (A 'well wisher' sent this magazine to John Robert together with a letter deploring the publication of such disgraceful stuff.) It was fortunate for the philosopher that, in his unworldliness he failed, for all his anguish, to imagine how inventively malicious the stories were which were circulating in Ennistone. Not that anybody harboured any deep resentment against him. They regarded him rather in an affectionate light as a mascot. But 'how are the mighty fallen' is always a theme for rejoicing, the McCaffreys were always news, and Hattie, regarded as 'a little snob', was fair game.

One of the more universal aspects of human wickedness is the willingness of almost everyone to indulge in spiteful gossip. Even the 'nicest people', such as Miss Dunbury, and Mrs Osmore, and Dominic Wiggins, and May Blackett were in general prepared to smile at nastiness and even sometimes to repeat it. Someone who was never idly gossiped to because of his virtuous austerity was William Eastcote; but in this respect as in others he was exceptional. Ennistone gossip was fairly certain about some matters, deliciously uncertain about others, and in general far from consistent. It was agreed that the old man wanted to 'get rid of' his grandchild and had offered her 'like a pet calf' to Tom McCaffrey. Whether this was also a 'a shot-gun situation' remained unclear, but as people smilingly observed, 'time would show'. (This scandal spread a lot of happiness around in Ennistone, and on a utilitarian argument could thus be justified.) Some held that Tom had passed Hattie on to George, others that George, out of spite against Tom, had 'carried her off'. Hattie was agreed to be 'fearfully stuck up', but had her defenders who regarded her as 'a helpless victim of scheming men', and her critics who were prepared to go to almost any lengths in regarding her as, according to their own moral tastes, 'emancipated' or 'corrupt'. In some versions Diane and even Mrs Belton played prime roles and the Slipper House was represented (on view already traditional in Ennistone) as an abode of sin. The notion that George had made Hattie pregnant and Tom, in the goodness of his heart, was to marry her was a further sophistication of the tale which hardly anyone believed but almost everyone repeated.

For all of Wednesday and most of Thursday John Robert remained barricaded in his house, not answering the door-bell. He sat and struggled with his colossal hurt pride and with his anger, anger against Tom, against George, and against fate, which somehow included the two girls. He grieved over his Ennistone, his childhood home, his sacred place in which he had had faith, now spoilt and blackened and made forever uninhabitable. And *over there*, at the Slipper House which he had been so childishly pleased to give to Hattie, all was suspect, besmirched, irrevocably ruined; so much so as even to make him reluctant to find out 'what had really happened'. He had not questioned Tom carefully, partly because he was so extremely angry and partly because he had made up his mind early on that Tom would tell any lie to protect himself. His rage against Tom was intensified by the knowledge that his own perfectly asinine policies had introduced the boy into the scene in the first place. His anger against George, and his conviction that George was the real villain, was from an older and deeper source. John Robert had received George's long letter at the Institute on Tuesday morning and had already tossed it unopened into the waste-paper basket before he looked at the *Gazette*. After he had seen the articles he retrieved the letter and tore it up unread into small pieces. All this time, as he remembered and reflected, the philosopher sat quiet, motionless, in the upstairs room where he had been conceived and born, upon the iron bedstead, moved from the next-door room, upon which he had slept as a child. He did not dare to sit downstairs for fear someone might look at him through the window. Throughout Wednesday, after Tom's departure, and for most of Thursday he sat and digested and regurgitated his rage. He knew the girls would do nothing till he came. It did not occur to him that it was cruel to keep them waiting.

415

Hurt vanity automatically brings with it the resentment that demands revenge: to reassert one's value by passing on the hurt. 'I am not to be trifled with. Someone will suffer for this.' Certainly John Robert wanted to run to the *Ennistone Gazette* office, drag the editor into the street and kick his ribs in; this was abstract compared with what he felt about the two McCaffreys. Wild ideas of punishing Tom (thrashing him or ruining his university career, or 'dragging him through the law courts') soon faded, however. There was nothing he could do to Tom. Equally, and indeed all the more so as it appeared on reflection, there was nothing he could do to George. Of course he could go round to Druidsdale and smash his fist into George's face. But if he were to run at George like a mad dog and savage him and break up his house, would this not be doing exactly what George wanted? George had been attempting for years to attract John Robert's attention, to provoke a 'happening' which would establish a 'bond' between them. George had wanted to *occupy* John Robert's mind; he had been, as the philosopher was vaguely aware, hurt and maddened by John Robert's calm coldness, by the evident fact that John Robert not only did not care about him, but did not think about him. This policy, which was effected without effort, was not totally uncoloured by malice. The tiny corner of John Robert's mind which *was* aware of George had experienced a fleeting satisfaction as he had thrown away George's unopened letter and completely forgotten George in the next moment: a serene oblivion which had unfortunately not lasted long. But *now* – it appeared that George had won. John Robert was now as obsessed with George as George was with John Robert. The fatal connection, now running through Hattie, had tied them together at last.

John Robert did not, when he was able to think, doubt that the loathsome unread letter had contained impertinences about the girl. (Herein he displayed his lack of understanding of George's character.) He pictured the bland round face, the boyish short-square-toothed smile. He conceived of writing to George. But could any words that existed express what he wanted to say? Now at last, when he had made out just what a victory his enemy had won, he felt that nothing would serve, nothing would do except to kill George. Nothing else at all ever would make the world right again.

While John Robert Rozanov was sitting on his bed at 16 Hare

Lane, Tom McCaffrey was sitting on his at Travancore Avenue. Like John Robert, Tom was imprisoned, tortured and paralysed. He could not leave Ennistone, that was impossible. He wrote a letter to his tutor saying that he was ill. He was in fact ill, he had a feverish cold. (He thought, that's Bobbie Benning's cold. I shouldn't have put on his bear's head. I could feel it was all damp and noisome inside.) He was also, he felt, well on the way to becoming mentally ill. It was Tom's first experience of demons. Demons, like viruses, live in every human organism, but in some happy lives never become active. Tom was now aware of the demons and that they were *his* demons. He stayed on in Ennistone because he could not leave behind the problems which could only be solved here, even though it was also impossible to solve them. He stayed secretly because he took John Robert's threats seriously. Tom could not imagine how John Robert could 'do him harm' but he was taking no chances. He had never before been at the receiving end of vindictive hatred, and he was very shaken by it. He did not doubt John Robert's strong active ill-will. So, although he stayed in Ennistone, he did not, for the rest of Wednesday and most of Thursday, set foot outside, and when darkness fell he pulled the heavily lined curtains carefully and turned on, at the back of the house, one well-shaded lamp. On Wednesday night he went to bed early and dreamt about Fiona Gates. (He had been hurt by John Robert's sneer at his mother.) In the dream Fiona appeared as a ghost with long trailing hair, wearing a white shift or petticoat. She seemed to be unable to speak, but held out her hands to him in a piteous gesture as if begging him for help. He thought, she's so young, so *young*. He woke in distress just after midnight and lay upon his bed tossing and turning in paroxysms of misery and remorse and resentment and fear.

The resentment, almost amounting to rage, was the most demonic constituent of Tom's spiritual illness. It was so unusual, so unnatural, for him to feel even 'cross' with anybody. Now he felt angry with John Robert, with Hattie, with George, with Emma, with himself. He puzzled and puzzled over how on earth John Robert's 'plan' for him and Hattie could have become general knowledge. It was inconceivable that Hattie had talked about it. He was himself to blame for having told Emma. But he had told no one else. Emma, although he denied it, must have told somebody. Perhaps he had told Hector with whom he had become (Tom felt jealous about this) rather friendly. A letter to Tom from Hector had arrived at Travancore Avenue on Tuesday morning asking him, when he was back in Ennistone, to get in touch with Hector at once. Tom ignored the letter, but later wondered if *that* were the reason for it. Emma had told Hector and Hector had talked. Hector was acquainted with the *Ennistone Gazette* man, Gavin Oare, and had given him an interview about the play . . . Tom wondered if he should go and see Hector, but the idea of clarification was in itself appalling; and the idea that Emma had lied to him and betrayed him was sickeningly painful.

The chief traitor was of course himself. He ought never to have agreed to John Robert's crazy idea. He did so, not even for a lark, but because he was *profoundly flattered*. Having agreed, he ought to have kept his mouth shut. And having almost at once realized that it was 'no go', he ought to have written to John Robert to say so and have *got himself out* of the whole awful mess. He ought to have stayed in London and *got on with his work* (how attractive the decent idea of getting on with his work seemed to him now) instead of hanging around Ennistone having ambiguous adventures. In these thoughts, Tom vacillated to and fro, between seeing himself as guilty of the most disgraceful treachery, and seeing himself as the helpless victim of a monster. Who could deal with a man like Rozanov? Rozanov had trapped him into this ghastly and *ridiculous* business, and was now blaming him unjustly without even listening to an explanation. The scene at the Slipper House had not been Tom's fault, only Rozanov had been determined to see it as some sort of conspiracy. And Rozanov had dared to threaten Tom, to revile him and *hate* him. How could that be?

Upon the figure of Hattie an even more ambiguous and intense light was falling. What exactly had happened that night? At first, and under his guilty hat, Tom had assumed that Hattie was simply an innocent girl, affronted by what must have seemed to her (though it was really an accident) a thoughtless and cruel jape, and then by George's intolerable intrusion. In this mood Tom felt very painful remorse: why on earth had he ever invented that 'party at the Slipper House', why had he actually led all those drunken people thither? It really seemed like a contrivance of the devil: a fateful devil lurking in the unconscious darkness of his own mind. And he wanted very much to run to Hattie and explain and apologize and be forgiven. Then, as resentment filled up the scale again on the other side, he began to wonder: why had George suddenly turned up like that? Was Diane Sedleigh involved? He had seen her in the garden. Why was *she* there? He recalled now having heard that Pearl was related to Ruby who was related to Diane. Was Ruby involved? And Pearl? And ... Hattie ...? *Was* Hattie an innocent maiden affronted by vulgar jesters? Had Diane brought George to Hattie? Had Hattie herself invited George? Had she for some time *known* George, and was this the reason why she had been so offensively cold to Tom? With this hellish brew bubbling in his mind Tom tried to go to sleep again on Wednesday night. On Thursday morning he telephoned the Slipper House. Someone, he thought it was Pearl, said 'Yes?', and after he had said 'It's Tom,' put the phone down.

Tom had not seriously thought of attempting to see Hattie on Wednesday because in another part of his crazed mind he felt that he had indeed promised John Robert not to; and in any case he was afraid of John Robert finding out, he was afraid of John Robert's reprisals. On Thursday he was a good deal less sure that he had promised anything and a little less afraid. After the telephone call he wanted very much to run round to the Slipper House, but he did not dare to. Suppose he were to meet John Robert there? But he went on wanting to go. He wanted more and more, more than anything in the world, to see Hattie, to explain that he was innocent, and to know by looking at her clear pale face that she was.

Thursday afternoon went slowly, slowly by, and Tom continued to hide. The telephone rang but he was afraid to answer it. His days had already lost their sense, he could not read, he could not sit, the concept of 'having a meal' no longer existed. He drank a little whisky and tore bits off a stale loaf. He considered going to London, but he *could not* leave Ennistone without somehow removing these agonizing hooks and thorns from his heart. He had to ease the misery, though since he scarcely knew what it was he could not think clearly what to do about it. At last he suddenly thought, I'll go and see William Eastcote, I'll tell him *everything* and ask him what I ought to do. After all, Bill the Lizard is John Robert's friend, he's the only person in Ennistone that John Robert can tolerate! He might even explain to John Robert, intercede for me. Why ever didn't I think of this before? It was evening, not yet quite dark. Tom selected one of Greg's overcoats and one of Greg's tweedy hats and slunk out into Travancore Avenue.

At Eastcote's house, number 34 The Crescent, there seemed to be something happening. A number of lights were on and the door was open. A car was parked outside. Tom thought, oh hell, he's got visitors. I must go back. Feeling intensely disappointed, he stood uncertainly at the bottom of the stone steps which led up to the door. Then he saw Anthea passing across the hall. At the same time he realized that he was standing in the light from the door and might be recognized by someone passing by. He went up the steps and into the house, closing the door behind him.

The hall was empty, full of the coloured beautiful things familiar to Tom since his childhood, when he had felt that these rugs and these tapestries and these huge bowls which Rose Eastcote used to fill with flowers existed somehow of necessity, composing an exotic place where very gentle tigers lived. The scene reassured him with a whiff from a safe authoritative world. But he felt at once that something was wrong. There was an odd silence, then lowered voices and padding. Anthea Eastcote came out of her uncle's study. She was crying.

She saw him and said, 'Oh Tom, how wonderful of you to come.' She came up to him and put her arms round him, pressing her face into Greg's coat.

Tom put his arms round her shoulders, pressing her against him, and moving his chin about in the mass of sweet-smelling brown-golden hair. He stared over her shoulder, feeling her heart beat and his own.

Dr Roach came out into the hall. He said, 'Oh Tom, dear chap, you're here, that's good, that's good.'

Dr Roach came forward and detached Anthea, who was now quietly sobbing, and propelled her into the drawing-room. She sat down on the sofa covering her face. He said to her, 'Sit quiet with Tom. I'll bring you a draught.' He said to Tom, 'He went off peacefully about an hour ago. He didn't suffer at the end. He knew us. He said, "Pray always, pray to God." Those were his last words. A saint if ever there was one.' There were tears in the doctor's eyes. He went out of the room.

Tom sat down beside Anthea. He knew now that William Eastcote was dead. He hugged Anthea, murmuring, 'Oh darling, darling, don't grieve so, I love you so much –'

The doctor came back and gave Anthea a whitish drink in a glass. She stopped sobbing and moved a little away from Tom and drank the white stuff down slowly. Dr Roach, with a hand on Tom's shoulder, said, 'I'm glad you got to know so soon. I made several telephone calls – the news must be flying around. What a wonderful life, that's what we must say to ourselves, mustn't we. How terribly we shall all miss him. But what a wonderful life, what a wonderful man, not just a comforter but a living evidence of a religious truth. Anthea dear, hadn't you better lie down upstairs for a while?'

Anthea, raising her face all reddened and swollen by weeping and brushing back her hair which was wet with tears, said, 'You must go now, you must go to Miss Dunbury, I would be so glad if you would go to her. I'll be all right now Tom has come.'

'How good of you to remember Miss Dunbury. Well, I will go. Tom will look after you. And I've asked Dorothy to come in.' (Dorothy was Mrs Robin Osmore.) 'I'll come back later this evening.'

When the doctor had gone Anthea said, gabbling as if there were something she had to explain or apologize for. 'You see, I went back to York on Sunday and I didn't know how ill he was, I mean, I knew he was very ill, but I didn't expect this, and then the doctor rang up, and thank God I arrived in time to – to say goodbye.' Tears overwhelmed her again and she leaned against Tom's shoulder.

Dorothy Osmore came in. Even at this moment she could not see Anthea without thinking with exasperation of Greg's failure. She was an upright good-natured woman but she could not help also, with a quick flicker of her thought, reflecting that Anthea must now be very rich.

Dorothy said to Tom (the sight of whom with Anthea displeased her), 'There now, I'll look after her.'

Tom stood up. Anthea rose with him and took hold of the lapels of the overcoat. She said, 'Tom, I shall never forget that you came to me this evening. Oh Tom, may all be well. I'll pray like he said, and you pray too. Let's meet again soon. Good night.'

Anthea had returned to York full of the problem of Joey Tanner whom she vainly loved. She had not expected her uncle's death. She had missed all the scandal about the Slipper House party and knew nothing of it. She spent much of Monday composing a letter to Joey saying that she knew he would never love her, and she would not see him again. On Tuesday she sent the letter off. On Wednesday she received the doctor's call. Now she knew that her feelings about Joey, and indeed about everything else, were as nothing compared with the everything of William Eastcote, his goodness and the mystery of his death. She felt an intense wailing grief for which the only salve was that vanished goodness which she would now press forever to her heart.

Mrs Osmore, showing Tom out, recognized Gregory's coat and hat. Outside in the dark street where the yellow lamps had been put on, Tom thought, Oh God, why did I not come to William Eastcote sooner, why did I not visit him and talk to him and ask him to guide me? Just telling all that stuff to him would have brought out the truth of it. Then he thought to himself, I too will never forget that I was with Anthea on this evening. Then he remembered his awful dark messy misery. He thought, I ought to see Hattie, but that's impossible. I feel so mad, so bad, so crazy, so *cast out*. I won't go to the Slipper House. I'll go and see Diane. I'll ask her about George, about that night.

At about the time when Tom, having braved the streets in disguise, had got so far as The Crescent, John Robert had at last made up his mind to go to the Slipper House.

Late on Wednesday he had, after all, in spite of the inadequacies of language, written an intemperate letter to George, the purpose of which was to ensure that John Robert would never have to see or hear of George again. This letter contained wild phrases such as 'I would like to kill you', and vituperation in the style of 'fake fantasy villain, mean weak impotent rat, incapable of evil but spewing out the sickening black bile of your petty spite', and '*faux mauvais*, the execrable taste of your contemptible schoolboy pranks merely expressive of your own realization of your mediocrity' (and so on). Coldness and inattention had failed to get rid of George. The intemperate letter was to signal unambiguously that this policy had now ended. The sending of a letter constitutes a magical grasp upon the future. After completing his violent exorcism, John Robert dodged out to a nearby pillar-box and posted it. He needed to feel that he had thereby finally finished with George and could forget him.

On Thursday evening Tom and Rozanov actually passed each other in The Crescent, Rozanov bound for the Slipper House, and Tom for Diane's flat, but both were so completely blinded by their thoughts that they failed to notice.

Nesta, who was sickened by the sight of women afraid of men, would have had a seizure had she been able to overhear the conversations which took place on Monday, Tuesday, Wednesday and Thursday between Pearl and Hattie.

In fact in this interim, during which neither of them left the house, a number of different theories were mooted by the beleaguered girls as mood succeeded mood. Hattie was often the more sanguine of the two. One reason for this was that whereas Pearl had studied the *Ennistone Gazette* article minutely, Hattie had glanced at it and thrown it away in disgust, and the horrible exact wording of it was not imprinted on her mind. Pearl had destroyed it promptly after it flew across the room, and Hattie's remarks later showed that her understanding of what had been said and implied was mercifully vague. Another reason why Hattie was less perturbed was that she knew John Robert a good deal less well than Pearl did, and was inclined at more cheerful moments to think that he would 'just find it funny'. His non-appearance (they expected him hourly) was then attributed to the fact that 'he had forgotten about it all'. It was also of course possible that he had not seen the *Gazette* article, but the girls agreed that it was probable that some malicious busybody would make sure that the philosopher was informed.

Although Hattie kept saying that it would 'blow over', she was very anxious that Pearl should not leave her alone in the house. There was plenty of food in store and no need for Pearl to go away. As the conversations went on, Hattie was inevitably infected by Pearl's anxiety, even though Pearl did her best not to communicate it. Then for a while she would keep asking Pearl for reassurance. 'He can't blame us, can he?' 'Of course not.' 'No one suggested it was our fault, did they?' 'No.' Then Hattie would say, 'He's *never* coming. Let's go to London. Come on, I want to go to the theatre.' 'The *theatre*?' 'Let's go to London, and stay in a hotel.' 'Hattie, we can't!' 'Why ever not? We're free, aren't we?' The girls would then look at each other and laugh, or wail. They also discussed and dismissed the idea of writing an 'explanatory letter'. The thing, thought of in that way, was inexplicable. Besides, there was always the small blessed possibility that he was unaware of the whole thing. The notion of walking round to Hare Lane was never seriously considered.

Pearl did not, or most of the time did not, think that John Robert could possibly believe all the awful things said in the *Gazette* article. (Hattie and Pearl had not seen *The Swimmer* which was published on Tuesday.) But the need to be relieved of the fear that he might, took form as a most intense longing, a lover's longing, for his presence and for the simple assurance that he still trusted her. She needed, and received, so little, but how precarious. There was of course no doubt that Rozanov would be very upset and hurt and angry. Pearl did not share, any more than Tom did, George's illusion that the philosopher was indifferent to what people thought; he might be indifferent to hostility but not to ridicule. Her loving gaze had 'estimated' and 'embraced' the quality of Rozanov's special dignity, his solemnity, his shyness, his particular awkward pomposity, his naïve unworldly egoism, his complete lack of ordinary social reactions, his lack of common sense, his distaste for mockery, and his inability to deal with it. All this made one. She had not often seen Rozanov in company, but had seen how, on such occasions (when talking to Margot and Albert, for instance) he imposed a seriousness which made gossip or even mildly malicious jokes impossible. Neither Pearl nor Hattie had ever teased him or seen him teased. Pearl also knew something of Rozanov's view of George, and could measure his furious irritation at George's intrusion into the picture. Pearl and Hattie had, as it happened, arrived to visit John Robert in California just after George's ill-fated excursion to see his master, and Pearl had overheard John Robert say something to Steve Glatz, who was then a student. It was on that occasion too that Pearl noticed the jealous manner in which John Robert kept Hattie well away from his pupils, and his colleagues; so much so that Pearl vaguely framed the hypothesis, lately so vividly revived, that John Robert, so far from being indifferent to his grandchild, was obsessed with her.

Pearl was of course aware of John Robert's match-making plan, since she had listened ardently at the door while it was being divulged. She had also witnessed Hattie's outburst of distress and annoyance, and seen Tom McCaffrey's yellow tulips fly out on to the lawn. But although the matter was no secret between them and could be referred to, they had not discussed it. Hattie retreated into the fastidious reserve and chaste mode of discourse which was so essential a part of their relation. They did not chat in a gossipy or malicious way about Tom, any more than they ever did about John Robert. This was not just an aspect of what Pearl sometimes wryly thought of as her 'station'. It was to do with Hattie, with Hattie's primness and still childish simplicity and dignity, and with Pearl, her particular love for Hattie and the preciousness of her trust. Pearl sometimes felt that she had been made, or remade, by that odd trust, and could not imagine what, without it, would have become of her.

So it was that, during this interim, while they waited 'with hatches battened down', as Hattie said, although they speculated about when John Robert would appear and whether he would be 'awfully cross', they did not discuss what he, or they, might or might not feel now about Tom and 'the plan'. (Pearl mentioned to Hattie that Tom had rung up.) They did occasionally wonder 'how the idea got around'; but Pearl steered Hattie off these topics, of whose enormity Hattie seemed not fully aware. Pearl dreaded most of all, with a dread which gradually crippled her mind, that John Robert might actually believe that she was somehow in league with George and it was she who had betrayed the secret. This dread made the days of waiting so painful that she began to want nothing more than to run straight to John Robert and babble out her explanations, and her love which she could not help feeling gave her rights, and even powers.

'Perhaps he doesn't know.'

'Some kind person will have told him. If no one else, that impertinent editor will.'

'He wasn't impertinent. He just wrote to ask if I'd give an interview.'

'I didn't like his tone. Neither did you.'

'I wish John Robert was on the telephone.'

'You know he hates telephone calls. Anyway, what could we say just like that?'

'It's nothing really, it's a fuss about nothing, we've made a melodrama out of it.'

'It was a melodrama.'

'People will forget it, they've probably forgotten it already.'

'You don't know Ennistone.'

'Anyway it wasn't our fault, was it, Pearlie?'

'No, of course not.'

'No, I *know* it wasn't our fault, but I can't help sometimes *feeling* that it was. Can you understand that?'

'Yes!'

'You don't think John Robert could think we invited George in?'

'No, of course not.'

'I'm surprised John Robert hasn't come, just to see if we're all right.'

'Well, perhaps he *doesn't* know.'

'You're saying it now!'

'After all, he may have been away.'

'I suppose I ought to go and see Mrs McCaffrey and say –'

'Say what? Better say nothing.'

'You thought we ought to see John Robert first and then see her.'

'I thought John Robert would come at once.'

'So did I. There's that stained-glass window that the stone cracked. Oughtn't we to do something about it?'

'It was a beer can, not a stone, I heard it fall. The window's quite safe.'

'Yes, but it's cracked, we ought to tell someone. Do you think John Robert's *brooding* over it?'

'No, he's probably gone back to his philosophy book and forgotten all about us.'

'I sometimes wonder how often he remembers that we exist.'

'Don't worry so, Hat dear.'

'I wish he'd come and get it over. Why do we have to wait here? Are we slaves or something?'

'He may have gone to London to give a lecture.'

'Let's go to London. We were going to go. We've waited here long enough.'

'We've waited so long we may as well wait a little longer. You know we couldn't enjoy London without having seen him.'

'We're building it all up so, we're making mountains out of molehills.'

'The trouble is with *him* that all ordinary sense of *size* just vanishes!'

'I know what you mean. How I hate Ennistone. I wish we were

426

living in London. Let's say we want to. We could have a flat, couldn't we? You say, you tell him.'

'All right.'

'You won't, you'll chicken out. Oh, why on earth did he bring us here?'

'It's his home.'

'California is his home. I wish we were back in America. What a crazy life we lead. Don't you sometimes think we lead a crazy life?'

'Yes.'

'How long will it go on?'

'Who knows.'

'Pearlie, sometimes I feel so sad – when I go to bed – I feel like at school – just so relieved to become unconscious – it's like wanting to be dead –'

'Oh don't be silly, you're young, you've got everything, when I was your age –'

'Yes, yes, yes, forgive me. Do you forgive me?'

'Hattie, I shall throw something at you!'

'I wonder who let out that story about Tom.'

'Tom, I should think!'

'No! Do you think so? Anyway, he can't believe we did.'

'No.'

'And he can't think you let George in, that's absurd! Did the article say that? I can't remember.'

'Sort of.'

'It's ridiculous. He can't blame us for anything, can he?'

'No.'

'Oh how I wish he'd come!'

'Here he is,' said Pearl.

It was late on Thursday evening and she had just observed from an upper window, by the light of the street lamps in Forum Way, the unmistakable bulk of John Robert coming along the path from the back gate.

Although the girls had been expecting him and were hourly 'ready' for him, his actual appearance produced surprise and shock. Their 'readiness' had consisted in the cleanness and tidiness of the house, the availability of suitable things to eat and drink, and the adoption of appropriate clothes and (in Hattie's case) hair-style.

427

Pearl had wavered between donning her operatic maid's uniform and boldly wearing a flowery summer dress which would not distinguish her sartorially from her mistress. Hattie wore her more soberly youthful garments, one of her school 'Sunday' dresses, pretty not smart, and kept her hair in plaits. In fact when Pearl spotted John Robert she had just taken off her flowery dress, about to take a bath, imagining it was too late for the philosopher to come that day. In panic, rumpling her dark straight neat hair, she dragged the dress on again and hurried down the stairs, buttoning it up as she ran. Hattie, who was reading *I Promessi Sposi* in the sitting-room with her slippers off and one plait undone, leapt up and began to adjust her hair while trying to lodge one bare foot inside a slipper, the other slipper having disappeared.

Pearl opened the door as John Robert approached it, and he entered, passing her with a slight frown, and went at once into the sitting-room where Hattie was stooping to rescue her second slipper from under a chair. She hopped, pulling it on, then stood, holding one plait in her hand.

John Robert stared at her as if she were an amazing apparition, then said, 'Don't look so frightened.' Pearl closed the sitting-room door and glued herself to the outside of it.

John Robert had intended to delay his visit to the Slipper House until his agitation had subsided and his mind had cleared. However, when his agitation did not subside and his mind did not clear, he decided he must see Hattie. As soon as he decided this he became conscious of an unprecedentedly strong desire to be with her. He felt angry with the girls for having somehow 'let it all happen', but, obsessed with George, he had not reflected on exactly what they were supposed to have done, nor had he planned how to question them. The idea of simply being with Hattie had seemed far more important than 'demanding explanations' or 'taking steps'. And now he was more disturbed even than he had expected by the sight of the girl who, although she had tried semi-consciously to look younger, could not help looking radiantly older.

'I'm not frightened,' said Hattie, and she threw her plait back over one shoulder and then her semi-plaited hair back over the other. She was frightened of course, but she felt, confronted so abruptly by her grandfather, a quick surge of annoyed independence which made her little cry not entirely specious.

John Robert sat down on one of the sturdier chairs, avoiding the bamboo armchair. Hattie did not sit, but leaned against the mantel-

428

piece, holding her skirt away from the gas fire which she had put on since the late evening was chilly.

John Robert said, 'Be careful, you'll burn your dress. Anyway you don't need the fire, do you, at this time of year?' As he said this he heard the voice of his father speaking.

Hattie leaned down and turned the fire off with a jerk and resumed her pose.

John Robert felt suddenly tired and even closed his eyes.

Hattie said, 'Would you like something to eat, or some lemonade or coffee or something?'

'No thank you. Hattie –'

'Yes?'

There was a moment, a micro-second, in which they both felt that something impossible might happen, such as Hattie running into his arms, crying out and weeping, and his stroking her hair and babbling with tenderness; but of course it was impossible.

John Robert collected himself and said, 'Look, what happened here the other night? There was a very disagreeable notice in the *Gazette*. I hope you didn't see it.'

'We did,' said Hattie.

'And what did you do about it?'

'Nothing. What did you expect us to do? We've been waiting for days to see you!'

John Robert had not meant 'what did you do?' and could not think why he had said it. His need to 'interrogate' the girls had slightly diminished even within the last hours as he began a little to feel that he had 'done with' George and Tom, as if he had killed them both; and he had arrived with no clear idea of 'instituting an inquiry', only now of course he saw that he must do so, and the old unappeased anger began to come back.

He said, 'I mean – what you read in the paper – was it true?'

'No, of course not! It was horrible spiteful journalism – it upset us very much!'

'So George McCaffrey was not in this house?'

'Well, he was, but –'

'So it was true, anyway some of it was true?'

'Yes, but –'

'Did you see the other article, the one in *The Swimmer*?'

'No.'

'Did you invite George and Tom McCaffrey to this house?'

'No!'

429

'Then how was George here?'

'I don't know –'

'Did Pearl let him in?'

'No – Pearl had gone out but locked the door, all the doors were locked.'

'Pearl had gone out, leaving you alone?'

'No, I mean yes, I asked her to go out –'

'Why?'

'To look for Tom McCaffrey.'

'You sent Pearl to look for Tom McCaffrey? So you *did* invite him here?'

'No, not like that – I mean – I wanted – I didn't believe he had done it all to – to make a mock of us –'

'He had done it all to make a mock of you?'

'No, I say he *hadn't* –'

'So Pearl did let George in and then went to find Tom too?'

'No, *no* – I don't know how George got in, the door was locked –'

'It can't have been. When George was here – were you alone with him?'

'Yes, but only –'

'Did – did anything – happen?'

Hattie flushed crimson. 'No! Nothing happened! He came in and I opened the shutters at once so that the others could see –'

'The others? Your friends outside? Tom McCaffrey?'

'Well, anybody – I thought –'

'You opened the shutters to display yourself with George?'

'No, not – display – I thought he'd go away then – and he did – and Tom was looking in and – then they all started singing –'

'Hattie,' said John Robert, 'were you *drunk*?'

'No!' Hattie stamped her foot. She turned away, turned around, helpless, then stood behind a chair staring at the philosopher with her face burning, near to tears.

John Robert looked at Hattie with a frowning intensity. He said, 'How did those newspapers come to find out – that I wanted you to get to know Tom McCaffrey?'

'I don't know!'

'You must have told somebody.'

'I didn't.'

'I didn't say it was a secret, but I have always trusted your ability to distinguish between public and private, and I did not expect you to gossip –'

'I *didn't*!'

'Did you tell Pearl?'

'Well, yes but –'

'Then you told somebody.'

'Yes, but that was different, and she knew anyway, and –'

'How did she know anyway? Unless she was listening at the door.' John Robert got up and opened the sitting-room door abruptly. Pearl was discovered standing an inch away. He said, 'You'd better come in.'

Pearl came in, turning her face away from Hattie. She went and stood by the shuttered window, keeping her head high and smoothing down her hair and gazing unseeingly across the room.

John Robert, standing now in the centre and addressing Pearl, said, 'Do you realize how much damage you've done? You have both contrived to make me ridiculous in this town, this place which I love and to which I trustfully brought you. And you have damaged Hattie's reputation probably beyond repair. Were *you* drunk?'

Pearl said, 'No,' flickering her eyes at John Robert for a second and then resuming her grim gaze.

Hattie said, 'Of course she wasn't! It wasn't her fault!'

'It was yours then?'

'No! You keep saying things and it's all wrong and you won't *listen.*'

'And I read in the paper,' said John Robert to Pearl, 'that you were seen out in the garden passionately hugging and kissing another girl.'

Pearl said nothing.

John Robert said to Hattie, 'Were you the other girl?'

'No,' said Hattie. 'I didn't go out. Of course Pearl wasn't hugging and kissing girls! She was out looking for Tom like I said –'

'So that didn't happen?' said John Robert to Pearl.

Pearl spent a second wondering whether to lie, then said, 'It did, only it wasn't a girl, it was a man dressed as a girl.'

'I see,' said John Robert. 'You admit shamelessly – not that it matters now –' He said to Hattie, 'Your – your maid – is outside in the arms of vicious girls or vicious men dressed as girls, and you tell me she didn't let George McCaffrey in.'

Hattie said to Pearl, 'You can't have been – I don't understand –'

'Perhaps you know Miss Scotney less well than you think, Harriet. I learn *only now* that she is the sister of that prostitute, that corrupt and degraded woman who is – who is also connected with George – I suppose *that* is true?'

'She's not my sister, she's my cousin,' said Pearl in a dull hard voice.

'Well, your close associate.'

'No, not –'

'If I had known of this connection,' John Robert went on, 'I would never have engaged you. I asked you if there was anything in your history which I ought to know about and you said no – you lied.'

'I have no connection with her. It was not in any way relevant.'

'Stop being rude to Pearl,' said Hattie. 'I love her, and she's *my* sister, and she did nothing wrong I *know*, let me just *tell* you what happened, we heard all this noise and we closed the shutters and I asked Pearl to find Tom because I wanted to tell him, I mean I wanted him to tell me, I knew it wasn't a thing against us and I didn't want to think that he had – and so I wanted him to say – oh I can't explain exactly, but it wasn't anyone's fault –'

'I see you can't explain! But I tell you one thing. You won't see that young man again. I've told him not to show his face in Ennistone.'

'You told him not to –? But I want to see him!' Hattie was suddenly panting with emotion, unconsciously unravelling her other plait and unbuttoning the neck of her dress, looking from John Robert's big face, all wrinkled up with anger and distress, to Pearl's frozen unresponsive glare. Pearl refused to look at her.

'You are a child,' said John Robert, 'and you do not seem to realize the harm which this boy and his brother have done to you. You cannot want to see him. In any case I forbid it.'

'It was your idea!' said Hattie. 'You wanted me to know him! Now I want to see him again! And I *will*! I want him to explain – it was your idea.'

'I have changed my mind.' He turned to Pearl. 'Would you please go and pack a suitcase for Harriet.'

'What do you mean? Stop! Pearl, don't go!'

But Pearl had already passed her without a glance and left the room and closed the door.

'Please,' said Hattie, and at this moment she found it strange and awful that she had no name by which to call him. '*Please*, what is happening, where are we going?'

'We are going to Hare Lane,' said John Robert. 'I cannot leave you unprotected in this corrupt house. I am going to order a taxi.' He lifted the telephone.

'But Pearl will come too –'

'No, of course not.' John Robert ordered the taxi, Pearl opened the door to say that the suitcase was ready. Hattie sat down in the bamboo armchair. She did not cry. She breathed, almost gasping, pulling at the collar of her dress with both hands.

After he had put the telephone down, John Robert looked at her gloomily, biting his knuckles. Then he said to her in a hoarse whisper, 'You are, aren't you, still a virgin?'

Hattie stared at him; she rose and then she *screamed*. Alex in Belmont heard the scream. Pearl came and threw open the door. Hattie ran out into the hall and stood at the foot of the stairs, her face covered with a net of tears like a veil.

Five minutes later Hattie was sitting crying in the taxi. Pearl had shoved her suitcase in beside her without a word and was returning to the house. John Robert was standing on the lawn in the light from the open front door. Pearl marched past him. Then she turned in the doorway and said, 'Well, what do you want me to do?'

John Robert moved to the door, still biting his knuckles, and Pearl stood aside and they stood together in the hall with the door open.

Pearl's sallow face was hard, her thin nose as sharp as a knife.

John Robert said, 'You may stay here for the present, and of course pack up the rest of Harriet's things and see that everything is ready to be moved out.'

'Where are we going?' said Pearl. Her voice was steady but she could not stop herself from trembling.

'*We* are not going anywhere,' said John Robert. 'Harriet and I will be returning to America. You may go where you please.'

'You mean,' said Pearl, 'that my employment is at an end.'

'I told you at the start that it was to cease when Harriet was grown up.'

'Did you?'

'I will give you six months' wages and a generous honorarium.' John Robert spoke softly now in a low voice, and his face looked quiet and puzzled and tired as if he had done some hard work and was now resting and reflecting in a rather abstract way about other matters.

'She isn't grown up,' said Pearl. 'Besides, she needs me, she loves me, she has no one else –'

John Robert said in his cruel abstracted soft voice, 'She has been made too precious, she has lived too much out of the world, you have encouraged her in habits of dependence –'

'I only did what you wanted.'

'She has become too dependent, too easily led, too weak, and it is time –'

'She isn't easily led or weak! Anyway it isn't my fault, you always insisted –'

'It doesn't matter now whose fault it is. It is time to make a brisk change. I have formed the view, on I think sufficient evidence, that you are not a fit person –'

'Because you thought I was kissing a girl?'

'You have unfortunate connections. I no longer trust you. I'm sorry.'

'But I haven't *done* anything, you don't *understand*, you wouldn't let us *explain*, it was just unlucky –'

'I am tired of being told lies, and I don't want unlucky people in my employ.'

'You can't do this suddenly after so many years –'

'Better suddenly, better for Harriet.'

'No, it's unfair –'

'I can imagine that you are sorry to lose a well-paid job. But you can hardly complain that you have not had enough money out of us! And when I think what my money has bought –'

'It isn't to do with money,' said Pearl. 'You made me, you invented me, you and Hattie are my family, you can't just say it's at an end –'

'I don't see why not. It is in the nature of such a post to end. Your family feelings are unilateral, they are your affair.'

'Hattie loves me. Doesn't that matter to you?'

'I don't believe it. Childish habits are soon lost. She will have worthier objects of interest.'

'I have nothing, nothing, and she –'

'No doubt that is what your family feelings amount to. You have always envied Harriet and wanted to pull her down.'

'No, no, I just mean that she has been my world.'

'You will find other worlds, you already seem to be at home in some rather unsavoury ones. Could we end this conversation? You will receive your money by post.'

'When can I see Harriet again?'

'Never. You are not to come near her. You are not to see her again. That is final.'

434

'But where are you taking her, are you going to be together in that little house in Hare Lane?'

'Yes, why not?'

'You know why not.'

John Robert lost his quiet tired look and stared keenly at Pearl for a moment. He said, but in the same soft tone, 'You are a corrupt person. I only hope you have not corrupted Harriet.'

'I haven't told her *that*!'

'You brought that man to Harriet.'

'I didn't.'

'I have no more to say to you.'

'And you asked her if she was still a virgin!'

'Enough. Do not bring your foul person near to us. We are going to America. You will not see her or me again.' He moved to the door.

'Wait, John Robert, wait, I beg you,' said Pearl.

The utterance of the name startled them both, and for a second they stood absolutely still staring at each other. Then Pearl took hold of the sleeve of John Robert's overcoat. 'Please think, please understand. Hattie does need me. But I wanted to say something else. You are a miracle in my life. You saw me and knew me and chose me and you were right. You trusted me and you were right to trust me. I am not a corrupt person, forgive what I said just now, it was nonsense, it's just that I care so much for you and Hattie, and I've watched you both so carefully, I've watched over you as if you were holy things – and I'm so upset and frightened now – I have done everything that you wanted and I have served you and Hattie in absolute loyalty and truth. And so much more than that. Oh can't you *see*? I love Hattie and I love you, I *love* you, like family, like a person in love, I *am* a person in love. You and Hattie are my life, *you* are my life, my occupation and my aim – my love has worked so long, it has waited so long, can't it speak, can't it be seen at last? Can't I tell the truth at last to you, who care so much about truth? Don't you know what love is like and how it longs to speak, it *has* to speak? I've been so quiet and so patient and so invisible, and I've been happy being patient and just serving you and doing exactly what you said and doing it well. Just wait, don't be hasty, don't send me away. I have value. Let me still be with you and Hattie, let me work for you still, I can be so useful, I can do so many things, I can learn to be whatever you want, don't throw my love and service away – I am empty, I am poured out, all I have

435

is you, all I am is you, don't abandon me, don't leave me, John Robert, let me still be in your life, oh believe me, believe in my love, look on me with kindness, with just a little kindness, please, I haven't done anything wrong, I swear –'

Rozanov stared at her with a gathering frown and his big soft mouth puckered up into an ugly pout of loathing. He said, almost in a whisper '*You disgust me.*' He wrenched his sleeve away and went out of the door.

Pearl followed him across the grass to where the path between the trees began. She heard the back gate slam and the taxi start. She stood still a while. Then she returned to the house. When she looked in through the doorway and saw the hall all pretty and tidy and bright she uttered the second scream which Alex heard that evening; only it was not a scream, it was more like an animal's long howl. She went into the house and shut the door with such violence that a piece of the cracked glass in the landing window fell out on to the lawn. She felt a pain which ran all the way down the front of her body as if she had been ripped open with a knife. She went upstairs to her bedroom and fell like a dead thing face downwards on the bed.

Tom rang the bell at Diane's address. There was only one bell. (He had discovered her address in an old telephone directory. Later directories did not list her.)

Diane, on the entry phone, said, 'Who is it?'

Tom, on the spur of the moment, said, 'George'.

Diane knew it was not George, who always entered with his own key, but she pressed the entry button all the same; she had been doing some solitary drinking and for once didn't care who it was.

Westwold is a quiet little suburb, agreed to be 'dull' (even the Three Blind Mice is usually empty after 9 p.m.) and Tom met very few people on his walk. As he huddled into the narrow doorway beside the Irish Linen shop he looked quickly up and down the street, but there was no one in sight.

He opened the door and, as he went up the dark stairs immediately inside, a light went on above. He arrived on a landing face to face with Diane, who was standing at the door of her flat.

She peered. When she recognized Tom she moved quickly back into the flat. Tom promptly put his foot in the closing door.

'Please, Diane, let me talk to you just a moment, it's important, it's about George.'

Tom now introduced his body after his foot into the aperture and began to push the door open against Diane's pressure. He felt suddenly excited, not happily, rather unpleasantly.

Diane gave way, let him enter, quickly closed the door behind him, and said, 'You mustn't stay, you mustn't be here, I shouldn't have let you in.' She moved back out of the tiny hall into the little lighted room beyond, where a radio was playing pop music. There was a strong stuffy smell of cigarettes and wine.

Diane was now quickly darting about, stooping and picking up what appeared to be underwear from the floor. She opened another door and hurled a pale frilly armful through and then shut it again. She turned the radio off. She emptied an overflowing ashtray into a vase, and kicked a jangling suspender-belt in under a chair. There was now also a sweaty smell of unwashed clothes. Tom, blinking, took in the room which seemed to him so full of things that he and Diane would have to stand there with their hands stiffly at their sides. He could not at first see a chair or discern the *chaise longue*, which was also covered with clothes and with a Paisley shawl which had crumpled itself up into mounds and hummocks. A wine bottle and a whisky bottle and two glasses stood on a dirty little ebony table. The velour curtains were drawn and two fringed lamps gave a dim pink light and a tiny narrow gas fire glowed pinkly. Tom, moving slightly, found his leg stoutly impeded by a leather hippopotamus and, stepping back, crunched his foot into a basket full of magazines.

Diane, in the soft sweetish light of her crammed little room, looked quite different from the shy trim person Tom had been used to seeing at the Institute. She looked, here, older, more painted, more animal. Her hair, which looked as though it had been lacquered, was sleeked down over her little dark head and came forward in two pointed curves over her cheeks. Her face looked yellowish and seemed without make-up except for the moistly scarlet lips. Her eyes were sunken and shadowed, both her small hands were brown with nicotine. She was wearing one of the black dresses which George liked, an old-fashioned cocktail dress which she had bought in a second-hand shop with a V-neck and black shiny beads sewn on to the bodice, and a long fringed hem beneath which were visible shiny black high-heeled boots with pointed toes. Her feet were also very small. Around her thin neck she wore a circlet of polished steel teeth which, not fitting well, poked her flesh, making red marks. She looked to Tom, as he gazed down on her,

437

so little and so touching. He had often seen her in a bathing costume, but with her 'daring' black attire and awkward collar she seemed far more undressed. For a moment he forgot why he had come.

'You mustn't stay,' she repeated, 'you mustn't be here.'

'Are you expecting George?'

'No, but he always might.'

'May I stay a minute, please?'

Diane sat down rather unsteadily on the *chaise longue* and poured herself out another glass of wine. 'Would you like some whisky?'

Diane poured a little wine into the second glass, spilling some. Tom took off Greg's coat and hat and picked up the wine. He found a chair with a plant on it, put the plant on the floor and sat down. He felt suddenly at home in Diane's room, and his natural habitual cheerfulness was about to assert itself when he remembered all the horrors of recent days. He said to Diane, 'William Eastcote has died, did you know? Well, you couldn't know, he's only just died.'

'Lucky man, wish I had,' said Diane. She took a gin bottle from under the table and poured some into her wine.

'Diane, I wanted to ask you something, do you mind, that evening at the Slipper House, last Saturday –'

'Was it only last Saturday? I lose count of time. What's today?'

'Thursday.'

Diane had not seen George since the Slipper House evening, when, from her hiding-place behind the shrubs, she had heard the singing and seen George run away through the garden and had followed him. She knew nothing of the incident with Hattie until she read the *Ennistone Gazette* article. She read *The Swimmer* article next day. These effusions had been troubling and confusing her mind ever since. She had not forgotten George's jokes about Hattie. Now she did not know what to believe. She ate little, drank a lot, checked on the bottle where she kept enough sleeping-pills to finish it all, and waited. The only thing which cheered her up a little was that the article had referred to her as 'our own Madame Diane'. George had once given her a humorous lecture about 'whores in literature' and she remembered there had been a Madame Diane. She and George sometimes referred to these literary ladies in private jokes, and this helped Diane to feel that she had identity in George's mind. The scurrilous and untrue way in which the *Gazette* spoke of her did not trouble Diane at all, indeed it pleased her slightly.

'Did you read that horrible article in the *Gazette*?'

'Yes.'

'Forgive me – I must know – did you bring George there, and did you – bring him and – Miss Meynell together?'

'Miss Meynell?' said Diane. 'Oh yes, of course, I must be drunk.'

When she said no more, Tom said, 'Did you bring George to the Slipper House?'

'No, he brought himself. As for what Miss Meynell did, don't *you* know?' She was becoming rather dazed with drink, but her senses seemed to have become more vivid. She had lost her urgent terror at the idea of George finding Tom with her. She was looking at Tom and thinking, how tall he is, and what beautiful long curly hair he has, and his long legs in his grey trousers, and his blue eyes like his mother's, he's so young. And Diane thought, oh if only life was ordinary for me and I could look at people and be with them, and a tear came into each eye.

Tom said, in answer to her question, 'No, I don't!' He discerned the tears and said, 'I'm sorry.'

'Aren't you going to marry Miss Meynell?'

'No.'

'It's off – because of that?'

'No! It was never on!'

'Oh well, I don't know what happened. I don't know anything. I'm just sitting here drinking myself to death.'

Tom thought, I'm crazy, I can't discuss Hattie like this, it's awful, how foul my mind is, I oughtn't to be here at all. And how tiny she is, almost a dwarf, and so unhappy. He said, 'May I have some whisky after all?' Inspired by her example he tilted it into his wine and swallowed a little and began to feel rather strange. He said, 'How did all this happen to you?'

'You mean on Saturday?'

'No, I mean, all this, how did it start –'

'My being a prostitute?'

'Look,' said Tom, 'I'd better go, I'm very upset about a lot of things, please excuse me –'

'Don't go,' said Diane, 'I haven't talked to anybody for a week. I became a prostitute to get my revenge on men.'

'No – really? I can't imagine –'

'No, that's something I read in a magazine. I don't know why, I don't know why anything happened in my life, it's all muddle and accident and the horribleness of the world. Oh what does it matter.

439

I was forced to pose in the nude. Then when I got pregnant they left me. I wish I'd had the courage to have a child. All I've got is George and he's *mad*, he ought to be in an asylum chained to a wall, he'll kill me one day. He said he saw the Meynell girl undressing.'

'*What?* How, where?'

'I don't know, George is a terrible liar. I don't know what happened last Saturday. George may have seduced the little girl, I'm sure he wanted to.'

Tom remembered all his griefs, the terrible scene with John Robert, the nightmarish hiding at Travancore Avenue, the loss of Hattie, these crazy tormenting doubts – what was he thinking? The *loss* of Hattie? He had never had her to lose, he had *rejected* her. Had he forgotten that? And he had seen her proud eyes reject him. He thought, I must see her, I *must*. He stood up and put his glass, pushing aside various ornaments, on top of the piano. Then he picked it up again and poured some more whisky into it.

Diane held out her glass and Tom filled it. Tom sneezed. Diane said, 'You've got a cold.'

'Sorry, yes.'

'Well, don't give it to me, for God's sake. George won't see me when I've got a cold, he *hates* me. Well, I suppose he hates me all the time, the cold just brings it out. Do you play the piano?'

'No –'

'Funny, none of my gentlemen ever played the piano.'

'I must go.'

'Where's Stella, isn't it time she came back to join in all the fun we're having?'

'I don't know where she is. I like Stella.'

'She's afraid of George.'

'So am I!'

'I wish I could go to the south, to the Mediterranean, Italy, Greece, anywhere. I've never left England, been to London a few times, big deal. I used to keep a suitcase packed in case some marvellous man came, some prince, I used to dream about him, a rich man, gentle and sweet, and I'd love him like he'd never been loved before, a sad man and I'd make him happy.'

'Why don't you chuck George, you'll never get any good out of him, go away somewhere and –'

'Start a new life! You grew up rich and easy, you think people *can* go away, for you there are other places, anywhere you go you're somebody, you're visible, you exist, you can make friends and be

440

with people in a real way. If I left here I'd die in a corner, I'd dry up and shrivel up and die like an insect, no one would care, no one would even know.'

'Don't say that – things could change – I wish I could help you –'

'Well, you can't. Don't say empty untrue things. I'm – like that – finished –'

'I wish you could talk to William Eastcote, only he's dead. He was a good man.'

'If I'd been that rich I'd have been good too.'

'But you are good – I mean –'

'Don't talk nonsense. You mean well. You always looked at me kindly, your eyes sent me messages.'

'Are you really Pearl Scotney's sister?'

'Cousin. And Ruby's. But they don't want to know. Madame Diane. The Ruby and the Pearl and the Diamond. All fakes. Our fathers were gipsies.'

'Do you really think that George and that little girl –?'

'Oh damn her. Damn you. I don't know.'

'Diane, I must go.'

'I won't say come again. George said he'd kill me if I had anything to do with you and the other brother. Oh God, if I could only *talk* to people, if I could only have a little bit of *happiness*, if things could be *ordinary* –' Tears came quietly out of her small dog-like eyes. She closed her eyelids slowly, pressing more tears out.

Diane suddenly opened her eyes and the tears seemed to disappear as if abruptly withdrawn into their source. She leapt up, tangling one black heel into the Paisley shawl. Tom leapt up too.

'What is it?'

'It's George. He's trying to put his key in the door. Quick, *quick*.'

Diane pulled Tom, gripping his wrist, round which her short fingers could not join, out on to the landing where she slid back the door of a large built-in cupboard. She pushed a number of dresses along on a rail, making a space into which Tom stumbled. Diane whispered, 'He always goes to the toilet when he comes, I'll put the radio on, I'll come out on to the landing and cough, then you go –' She slid the cupboard door back again and was gone.

Tom instinctively adjusted the dresses, pulling them in front of him and pressing himself against the back of the big cupboard. His feet, below the dresses, felt huge. He reached out and moved the sliding door slightly. He felt very unpleasantly frightened and ashamed.

The radio was playing again, quite loudly. He heard the down-stairs door open and George mounting the stairs and Diane saying something to him. George went into the sitting-room. A minute or two passed and he showed no sign of going to the lavatory.

Diane's clothes were not like Judy Osmore's. Diane's clothes were musty and in need of washing and cleaning, and smelt of stale tobacco and old cosmetics, cosmetics, which went out of fashion long ago, old powder, old lipstick, old face cream, old magic. Tom began to want to sneeze. Then the radio was switched off.

Tom thought, he knows. But now he could hear George and Diane talking in quiet voices. If he had concentrated he could have heard what they were saying. He thought, I must get out of this cupboard; if George were to find me standing here among these dresses I couldn't bear it, it would ruin my whole life! He slid the door and stepped very quietly out of the cupboard. The sitting-room door was shut, the voices continued, Tom moved step by silent step toward the flat door which Diane had left open. Already he could imagine himself creeping down the stairs, leaning heavily on the banisters, putting his feet down with slow care, then the street door and freedom. At that moment Tom remembered that he had left his hat and coat lying on the floor in the sitting-room.

He checked the impulse to run. He could not now run. Diane might see and hide the awful evidence, but she might very well not. He thought, it'll be worse for *her* if he sees them when I've gone, I can't go now, I've got to see George, I've got to face him and try to *explain*, oh *God* why did I come here! I'm doing nothing but harm to everybody –

Tom took a deep breath and opened the sitting-room door. He stood in the doorway.

George and Diane were standing near the sofa holding hands. They had an odd formal dated look, like an old photograph or an old film. They turned toward him. Diane's face expressed open-mouthed, open-eyed terror. George's face expressed, for a moment, pure surprise. He let go of Diane's hand. Then almost artificially, as if he were acting, he transformed his face into a wrinkled mask of indignation and fury.

Tom raised his hand with the palm open. He said, 'George, I'm sorry. I came here to see Diane to ask her something about Miss Meynell. I've never been here before. I've never talked to Diane before, well, except once we talked a few sentences at the Baths.' (Tom felt it essential to be truthful in case the encounter had been

442

witnessed.) 'I've only been here about ten minutes and I was just going to go. Nothing is Diane's fault. She didn't want to let me in and when I pushed my way in she begged me to go away. It's all my fault. I just intruded. It's nothing to do with her.'

George stepped away from Diane and stared at her as if expecting her to speak, but she was speechless with fear. She stood stiffly, her head turned away from both the men. George frowned, drawing his eyebrows right down over his eyes. He lowered his head. Then he caught sight of Greg Osmore's coat and hat lying on the floor. He snatched them up and glared at them. Then bundling them up he moved toward the door. Tom dodged promptly out of his way. George went out on to the landing, hurling the bundle in front of him, and kicked it out of the flat and down the stairs. He came back into the room and advanced on Diane, ignoring Tom. He said, 'Sit down. Sit down *there*.' He pointed to a chair against the wall beside the piano. Diane obeyed, putting her hands to her throat. She took off the metal necklace and laid it on the piano.

Tom began, 'George, listen –'

'Who is Miss Meynell?' said George, still frowning.

'Hattie Meynell, you know, John Robert's –'

'Oh her. If you refer to her as Miss Meynell you should refer to Diane as Mrs Sedleigh. Don't you think? What did you want to know about Hattie Meynell?'

'Oh George – I'm in such an awful mess – and I've been such a fool – don't be angry with me – I just wondered whether you and Hattie were – whether you knew each other at all –'

'No,' said George, 'I don't know her. I met her at that picnic, and last Saturday for approximately one minute before she opened the shutters and you started singing. Your ten minutes with Mrs Sedleigh was much longer and I daresay more interesting than my total converse with Miss Meynell. O K?'

'Mrs Sedleigh said you saw her undressing, I suppose that was at the sea –'

'Mrs Sedleigh should keep her bloody mouth shut. I observed her once in her petticoat by field glasses from Belmont. All right now?'

'Yes.'

'Do you believe me?'

'Yes, George.'

'Why are you interested in that little minx? Is she your mistress?'

'No. And she's not a little minx.'

'Your questions to Mrs Sedleigh displayed little faith in the young lady. She may not be a minx now, but she will certainly become one soon, so you'd better hurry.'

'She's an innocent girl –'

'You think so? Well, perhaps she is. I'm not against her. Because of her ... I've had a wonderful letter ... from John Robert ...' He gave an odd little laugh like a sigh. 'Did you know that Bill the Lizard has just died?'

'Yes. How did you know?'

'It's round all the pubs. Funny how everybody cares – because that man has died – perhaps it's a sign –'

'I was just going to talk to him,' said Tom, 'and then he was dead. Oh George –'

'What?'

'Don't hurt anybody. Don't hurt me. Don't hurt Mrs Sedleigh. Don't hurt yourself.'

'You said you were going, why don't you go? Do you *want* to be thrown down the stairs after your coat?'

'I'm glad you had a good letter from John Robert.'

George advanced toward Tom. Tom moved quickly back into the doorway. George stopped in front of his brother and put his hands one on each shoulder. He looked up, he was shorter than Tom, into his brother's eyes. Tom looked with amazement at George's round boyish face, which now wore a radiant quizzical amused expression. George looked like someone who was emotionally exalted, ready to cry with happiness as the result of some wonderful news, some great achievement or discovery.

Tom wanted to say something suitable, something affectionate, for he felt all his affection for his brother suddenly and ardently enlivened by the strange radiance of that look. At the same time he wondered whether George had not at last perhaps, and finally, gone mad. 'Dear George –'

'Clear off, Tom. Go on. *Beat it.*'

In a moment, although the clear light of the look did not waver, George's fingers dug fiercely into Tom's shoulders. Tom turned and leapt across the hall and out of the door which George had left open, he flew down the stairs and tumbled over Greg's coat and hat which were lying at the bottom. He scooped them up and got himself out into the road and slammed the door.

Then in the sudden silence of the empty lamp-lit street he paused.

He stood for a while, dreading to hear a terrible scream. But the silence continued.

'Come on, kid, you can come out from behind the piano.'

Diane got up and took a step forward. George sat down on the sofa and drew a letter from his pocket and began perusing it. He said, 'Give me a drink, will you.' Diane poured some whisky into her own empty glass and thrust it toward him. She continued to stand stiffly, looking at him. George took a sip of the whisky, still reading the letter. Then he looked up. 'What's the matter? Oh Tom. Sit down beside me. Why are you so frightened of me? Don't be. Come, sit down.'

Diane sat beside him and he put an arm round her shoulder. She put her face down on to the sleeve of his coat. 'I thought you'd blame me about Tom.'

'It wasn't your fault, was it? Was it?'

'No. Like he said.'

'Well, then. Forget Tom. Give me a kiss.'

George was only slightly drunk. His inability to get the key quickly into the lock was not caused by intoxication but by the ordinary fact that the door was in a dark recess. However, George was certainly in a strange frame of mind.

He had received Rozanov's violent letter that morning (Thursday). George had not seen either of the local newspapers and was unaware of the public 'scandal' concerning himself and Hattie. He gathered something of the matter from Rozanov's incoherent thunderings, and assumed that Hattie had complained to her grandfather about George's intrusion and had somehow linked it to the riotous goings-on outside. He also gathered that the *Gazette* had said that Rozanov wanted Tom to marry Hattie (which seemed so crazy that he did not even think about it). The cause of the letter did not concern George too much. What was important was the letter itself, an entirely new development, a vast new phenomenon in the long history of his relations with his teacher.

When George saw John Robert's writing on the envelope he had at the first moment hoped that the letter would contain something, he knew not what, to match his wishes, some gesture of gentleness, some gesture of humour or sweetness, almost anything, even reproaches, might, he felt, feed and warm his heart, even perhaps (whatever that might mean) heal him. The brutality of the missive which his trembling fingers drew forth shocked him profoundly. George's ingenuity at interpreting any word of John Robert's as a communication or an encouragement was almost limitless, but could not deal with this letter. He was used to the philosopher's coldness, his sarcasm and irritation. This almost incoherent torrent of rage and hate left George for a while utterly prostrated and defeated, as if he could not *survive* in a world where John Robert's ferocious mind existed so to curse him. For the first time a feeling of death touched him. His relation with Rozanov had always been unhappy right from the start, poisoned by jealousy and humiliation and fear and unfulfilled desire, but it had *gone on* and been, as such unhappy things can be, a source of life, a focus of dreams, a goad, a thorn, not a dagger in the heart. George intuited in that ferocious letter John Robert's determination to *end* George absolutely, to exclude him *totally*, as if indeed he had carried out his expressed wish to kill him. Every previous reaction of his teacher had been something which George could *take over* and with which he could *do something*. But with this outburst he could do nothing.

On Thursday morning George considered suicide. He imagined various ways of actually dying in John Robert's presence, or even arranging for John Robert to be accused of murdering him. These fantasies were not consoling since they too contained the real idea of death; and from this George shuddered away and hid his face. He shed tears. Then for a long time he sat quietly on the sofa in the sitting-room at Druidsdale. He crumpled up John Robert's letter and tossed it away. Then he picked it up and looked at it again. It was true that he had got past John Robert's guard; he had, for one moment at least, *occupied* John Robert's mind to the exclusion of all else. This was surely a significant climax. It was of course an *absurd* letter, one which John Robert would regret having written. Suppose George were to reply, harping on that chord? 'My dear John Robert, I feel sure that by now you regret . . .' But that would not do. The letter, absurd as it was, remained an act, there was something irrevocable signalled by that smell of death. George believed in signs. The letter was a sign. Love and death were interchangeable. The letter signalled that his relation with John Robert had reached a final orgasm.

'It ends so,' he said out loud. 'It ends . . . so . . .' And this, such an ending, was in a sense, not an ending. And again for a long time he sat still.

Then it began to be as if his mind, like a boat which has crashed

446

upon rocks, and flown over rapids, had come out in a serene light on to a calm golden lake. He felt his taut and twisted face relax and become smooth. He breathed quietly and deeply. He thought, it is as if I have died only I haven't died. I live in a life after life where all is changed. Can it be that I have actually *finished* with John Robert Rozanov, that this has come upon me as a change of being, as a mystery of which I scarcely know the meaning? He stood up. He went out to the kitchen and ate some soup. It was evening. He went out into the warm calm fuzzy twilight air. He walked to the nearest pub, the Rat Man, and here he learnt the news of William Eastcote's death. And it seemed to him that this too was a sign, that Bill the Lizard had offered himself up as an innocent substitute for George's death. Love had reached its climax and died in peace. He walked and breathed and felt rising within him the warm inner radiance which Tom McCaffrey had been so astonished to see upon his face.

'What's the letter?' said Diane. She too saw the radiance and was worried by it.

'It's from John Robert.'

'Is it a nice letter, kind?'

'It's – let's say – merciful. Ah, mercy – yes – what's that? Look, I'm going to burn it.' George knelt and lighted a corner of the letter at the gas fire and watched it burn on the tiles of the grate.

Diane watched him in amazement.

George returned and sat on the sofa and Diane slipped down on the floor beside him as she often did and put her hands on his knees.

'Do you love me, kid?'

'You know I do.'

'When a man that "Turnips" cries, cries not when his father dies, does that mean that he would rather have a turnip than his father?'

'You're in your silly mood today. Are you thinking about your father? You've got a funny look.'

'Funny, yes. I feel I've been broken and remade in a moment, well, in half an hour. Something – it's like a haemorrhage – has broken – inside –'

'You don't mean really?'

'No, no, it's *like* that, only it's in the mind. Something's all washed away – washed away in blood –'

'Like Jesus Christ.'

'Yes. Yes. Nothing less would do. I said the world was full of signs today. And Bill the Lizard dead. God rest his soul. So I look strange?'

447

'Yes. Your face is different – more beautiful.'

'It feels like that. Give me another drink, kid. Ding dong bell, Debussy's in the well. We'll live yet and beat them all, we'll outlive them all. Do you know what day this is?'

'What day?'

'The one you've been waiting for.'

'What do you mean?'

'You wanted me to come to you in the end. When I was broken and beaten and rejected. Well, I've come.'

'Oh, George –'

'And I am broken and beaten and rejected but it's not like I thought at all – it's like a triumph – it's with trumpets and drums and – torches and fireworks and bright lights – it's liberation day, Diane – can you hear them all cheering? They know we've won. Fill your glass up, darling, and we'll drink to freedom. They wanted to break us, but they have only broken our chains. We'll go away, shall we, like you used to say. Would you like that? I've got a good pension. Let's go and live in Spain, it's cheap there.'

'George, do you mean it?'

'Yes, I do. Diane, this is it. When one is *compelled* to do what's right. We'll live in Spain, we'll live in the sun, and we'll be free. We'll live like kings on my pension. You're the only person who really loves me. You're the only person I can talk to, the only person whose company I can really tolerate. We'll live in the south by the sea and we'll be happy at last. Come, darling, lie beside me. Just put your arms around me. I've solved the riddle, it's all come out clear. You just have to get to breaking point and break, it's as simple as that. Oh I feel so much at peace. I want to sleep now.' And George did at once fall peacefully asleep in Diane's arms.

'You mean you love me?' said Hattie.

'Yes,' said John Robert.

'You love me like – like grandfather – or like – like being in love?'

'The latter,' said John Robert in a low voice.

It had taken them a long time to reach this point.

When John Robert went to the Slipper House he had had no clear plan in his head. He wanted very much to see Hattie. He felt angry with the girls for their stupidities and indiscretions, whatever these might be, which had somehow contributed to his humiliation. Obsessed with George and Tom, he had not too much reflected on these ancillary follies, and felt no burning desire to find out every detail, to examine and to punish: no satisfaction, in this case, at the idea of passing on some of his pain. He felt rather a general misery and a sense of being wounded and mocked. The interrogation, for which he had certainly drawn up no list of questions, seemed more like a duty than anything else. He had of course noticed the references to Pearl in the scurrilous articles but he had not, in his earlier mood, bothered to make sense of them and had indeed (as Pearl had hoped) put them down as 'some sort of rubbish'. Even the 'significance' of Pearl being Diane's sister had not struck him at first, since he had simply had too much to do dealing with other thoughts. He had not at all foreseen the sudden drama of Thursday evening and its huge outcome. It was not until he actually started to ask questions that all these ideas 'came together', and familiar inquisitorial Socratic instincts prompted him to corner and to strip, further arousing his wounded mind to cruel extremes. He was excited by the sudden and absolutely new experience of castigating Hattie; and with this step closer to her there came, in a single igniting flash, suspicion and jealousy of Pearl.

The decision to remove Hattie was certainly not premeditated. John Robert's new vision of Pearl as the villain of the piece, once fairly started, grew in self-authenticating clarity. It all made sense.

Pearl had been, from the beginning, a terrible mistake. He had employed her as a watchdog, a guardian angel, a guarantor of Hattie's seclusion, her purity, her out-of-the-worldness. But in effect Pearl had separated him decisively from Hattie and had stolen Hattie's love which would, if he had looked after Hattie more directly, have been bestowed on him. A sudden burning jealousy of Pearl consumed the present and blackened the past. Pearl was indeed not only a tactical disaster but a positive traitor. She was resentful of Hattie who 'had everything while she had nothing', she had given away John Robert's match-making plan and was in league with George and that prostitute. Any possibility of second thoughts on these matters was of course removed by Pearl's sickening declaration of love which followed upon her unspeakably crude reference to his secret. That, if nothing else, sealed her fate.

'Being together with Hattie in that little house in Hare Lane' was indeed proving to be an amazing and frightening experience, though it was now only Friday morning. *How* extraordinary this would be he did not, even in the taxi, begin to imagine. How small the house was he realized as he lay sleepless on the rather damp divan bed in the tiny spare-room, listening to Hattie first crying, then tossing about and sighing, on his own old iron bedstead in the next room. On Friday morning John Robert rose as usual at six forty-five and went downstairs and made preparations for breakfast, a meal which, except in the form of a cup of tea, he did not usually have. He found a table-cloth, cross-stitched by his mother, in a drawer in the side-board, and put it on the little folding table in the sitting-room and laid the table with preparations for coffee and eggs and toast. As he did so he felt a curious pain which consisted in finding a new and special pleasure in laying a table for Hattie, and at the same time thinking how often he might have done so in the past, and how unpredictable now was the future, and how unclear the meaning of the little humble action.

Hattie came down at seven-thirty. John Robert peered out of the kitchen. She looked tired and pale but had put on a brown straight rather 'grown-up' dress which Pearl had packed for her, and had put her hair up. In reply to his questions about breakfast she said that she only wanted a cup of coffee. Then she announced that when she had had the coffee she was going straight back to the Slipper House. John Robert asked her, please, not to, but to listen instead to some things which he had to say. He did not at the moment know what exactly these things were; but the inevitability

450

was now clear of some sort of 'fight' with Hattie, and though he was frightened at the prospect he was also excited by it.

The fight began with Hattie saying that she would listen to what he had to say and would *then* go back to the Slipper House.

'All right,' he said, 'I'll ask Pearl to move out, and I'll come with you to the Slipper House.'

'I don't care about the Slipper House! It's Pearl I want to go back to. You wouldn't listen to what I said yesterday –'

'Don't you think it's time for you to leave off Pearl? You're grown-up now. How nicely you've done your hair.'

'You say "leave off Pearl" as if she were some sort of bad habit!'

'Well, in a way she is. You've grown out of her.'

'She's not a teddy bear!'

Hattie had taken her coffee into the sitting-room and had sat down at the table which John Robert had laid and moved into the window. John Robert sat down opposite to her, unconsciously moving the plates and cutlery and setting them in a neat pile. The weather had changed, and outside it was softly gloomily raining upon the little garden enclosed by its low and partly broken fences.

'I have told Pearl that we no longer need her.'

'*We* no longer need her? You mean you've sacked her?'

'She quite understands.'

'Well, I don't. I told you, she is my friend, she is my sister, you wanted us to do everything together –'

'You mustn't be so dependent on another person, you must give up this old sentimental attachment to someone you've just got used to.'

'Used to! And it's not dependence it's *love*! I don't want her as a nursemaid! I want her as a friend and a relation! You don't realize how alone I am, I have no family –'

'You have me.'

'Well, yes, of course but – I've seen so little of you – you couldn't have a child in your life – of course you haven't had time. I don't know you –'

'Do you think, Hattie – do you think that you could call me "John Robert"?'

'I don't know you, John Robert.'

'That is my fault.'

'Of course I'd like to know you better, that would be nice. But Pearl is *essential*, she's part of me, I won't give her up –'

'When you marry you will have to –'

451

'Of course I won't have to, what are you talking about? And as for when I marry, you seemed very anxious to get rid of *me* when you tried to – to offer me to Tom McCaffrey – and he didn't want me –'

'He didn't want you?'

'No, why should he, I don't blame him, it was a mad idea.'

'I meant well. One day perhaps you'll understand. Do you forgive me?'

'Yes.'

'Yes, John Robert.'

'Yes, John Robert. Now I'm going.'

'No. Don't go. I forbid you.'

'I don't think you can.'

'Pearl isn't what you think. She's not been faithful. I see now she's an unfit person –'

'What on earth do you mean? Pearl has been perfect. She's done everything. She's taken all the trouble off you –'

'She was well paid for it –'

'What a mean thing to say!'

'She's envious of you, she's jealous, she said so, she said to me – "she's got everything and I've got nothing".'

'Did she really? She must know that everything I have she has.'

'That's not so, Hattie. You must be realistic, you must be properly grown-up –'

'Being grown-up seems to mean being cynical and ungrateful and stingy!'

'You and she have different fates, you must see that.'

'Do you mean we have different stations in society?'

'You have taken her for granted as a part of your life in a way which is no more possible. This is the natural parting of the ways.'

'Of course our relationship has to change, it has always been changing, it is changing, but when two people love each other –'

'You seem not to realize how much that horrible scandal –'

'I don't care about the scandal –'

'Well, you ought to and I do. It has done you a lot of damage –'

'Damage to *me*, what a rotten little journalist says in a rotten little town?'

'You'll see later, you'll suffer for it later –'

'You seem quite glad to think so!'

'You seem not to realize how much that scandal was Pearl's doing. She told the press about you and Tom McCaffrey, she let that other man in –'

'She *didn't* tell, she *didn't* let him.'

'She must have done. She's an irresponsible mischief-maker. You heard her admit that she was outside kissing some man when you thought she was looking for Tom.'

'Well, why shouldn't she kiss a man, she's lived without men all these years for my sake and for your convenience –'

'So no doubt it's time she broke out and dropped the mask –'

'There is no mask, she's a very truthful person, she's one of the best people I've ever met!'

'I think you don't know how coarse she is and the things she can say – you are a child and you have met very few people and you think too well of everyone – people who seem nice can be thoroughly wicked.'

'What's wicked is that article that you're so obsessed with, you got all that stuff out of the article, it's all just spiteful lies, you haven't any proof. Well, have you?'

'Strong probabilities amount to proof.'

'Perhaps they do in philosophy, but I prefer to believe what I see clearly.'

'That's in philosophy too. But what you see clearly can be false. Dear Hattie, believe me, I want the best for you, I want you, for your own sake and for my sake, bravely and sensibly, to let this relationship go, to let it disappear naturally into the past. As time goes by we often have to shed relationships which no longer suit us, such shedding is a natural function. There is no need to make a drama of this. You are at a stage in your life where you have to face many changes and challenges, many new things. We have to think about your university career. I want to talk to you at length about that. I am inclined to think now that an American university may suit you better than an English one. I am going to arrange for us to return to California in a matter of days. I'll buy a house for us near the ocean, you'll like that, not like the little one at Malibu, a real big house. I'll aim to keep you with me very much more from now on –'

'That is very kind of you, John Robert,' said Hattie. She had put her hands palm down on the cross-stitch cloth and was leaning foward, gazing at him earnestly with her pale marble-blue eyes. 'That is very kind of you, and I realize that all sorts of things will change and must change in my life in the next years. I have always done what you wanted. When you wanted to see me I came, when you were tired of me I went away, I never questioned the schools which you chose for me, the journeys which you ordained. I will continue to do what you want, probably. I just tell you now that I will not give up my friendship with Pearl, I cannot, it is part of me. You would surely not respect someone who abandoned her friend.'

'You speak of abandoning. But she abandons you. You said how much she had given up to be your maid. Can't you now imagine that *she* wants to be free of *you*? She'll be relieved, glad to go! That's what I understood her to say when we talked frankly last night when you were in the taxi.'

Hattie, breathing deeply, continued to stare. Then, removing her hands from the table, she leaned back. She said impatiently, 'This is a silly argument. Of course I must see her, I'll go to her, she'll be expecting me. If she feels as you say, which I don't at all believe, I shall know and naturally I will accept it. Coming away suddenly like that yesterday was horrible, it shouldn't have happened. You kept bullying us and accusing us of things. You didn't understand. You don't know Pearl. I won't believe anything against her.' Hattie then stood up.

'Sit down, please, *please*, Hattie, sit down a minute, *wait*.'

Hattie sat down again. She felt hungry. She had eaten nothing last night, being anxious only to get to bed and into the death of oblivion for which she had so much longed at school. She was surprised at herself, at the way she had just been speaking to John Robert, at the firm almost rude tone she had adopted. But she felt perfectly clear-headed about the whole matter, and desperately longing to get back to Pearl.

John Robert then approached the revelation of his secret. He intended only to come near to it, not to tell it. He knew that even this was a mistake and probably morally wrong, but he could not, looking now at Hattie across the table, and after the peculiar exciting awful tension of their fight, resist moving that step closer to her. It was, answering to his wish, an occasion, an opportunity. Perhaps she's somehow vaguely guessed already, he thought; besides what does it mean? It isn't anything definite anyway. I'll just say something now, I must. If she sees Pearl, God knows what horrible thing Pearl might say. That's another reason for just, at least, telling her in an ordinary way how much I care for her. The fact that Pearl knew it is a reason for speaking out, it's not even a secret any more. It's necessary to do so, and now's the time. Hattie had, once too often, casually expressed her taken-for-granted view that her grandfather did not care for her and regarded her simply as a burden. John Robert felt *now* he at last *could* and therefore *must* comment on that assumption.

'Hattie – dear Hattie – I've acted for the best, I mean I've tried to act well, to do right, it hasn't been easy.' A curious almost whining tone of self-pity here invaded John Robert's voice.

Hattie at once realized that something had changed, that some emotional statement was about to come out. She said more gently, 'I'm sure you have always meant well, I mean wished me well.'

'Oh Hattie, if you only knew –'

'Knew what?'

'How I've yearned over you and wanted you. You think I don't care about you, but that isn't true, it's the opposite of true.'

Hattie stared at the huge face of the philosopher which seemed suddenly like a relief model of something else, a whole country perhaps. She stared at the flat head, the lined bumpy fleshy brow and the very short electric frizzy hair, the big birdlike nose framed by furrows in which grey stubble grew, the pouting prehensile mouth with its red wet lips and the froth of bubbly saliva at the corners, the fiercely shining rectangular light brown eyes which seemed to be trying so hard to send her a signal. The soft plump wrinkles of the brow, pitted with porous spots, so close to her across the table, gave her especially the sense of something so sad, so old. She felt frightened and full of pity. She said, just in order to say something soothing, 'Oh don't worry, don't worry, please –'

'I've deprived myself of your company simply because I cared so much. I think now I was wrong. Was I wrong, is it too late? I thought you might just find me appalling, a monster. I found myself so. I was afraid, yes. And yet I should have had more courage, more faith and trust, I should have got to know you, kept you with me, tended you –'

'But you have been very kind,' said Hattie. 'You mustn't reproach yourself, you are always so busy, you wouldn't have time for a child, it isn't as if you were my father.'

'I deprived myself of you. I could have had time, I wanted time, what better could I have done with my time. If I had felt less, had felt differently, I might have – but I wanted to keep you as something precious and I didn't dare to be too close to you.'

'I'm sure I would have bored you very much!' said Hattie in what was intended to be a light tone.

'You haven't understood, better so, better so –'

455

'Please tell me what you mean –'

'Even if it makes you shudder, even if it makes you run? I love you, Hattie, I've loved you for years. For God's sake, don't leave me now that I've found you, don't go away –'

Even before John Robert spoke the first words confessing that he was 'in love', Hattie had begun to understand what he was telling her. His trembling voice, the pleading movements of his hands, the painful ring of his ardent words, the glare of his light eyes, conveyed to her the dreadful importance of what was happening between them; and she did shudder, and she did want to run, but she felt also a most intense pity and a weird excitement, together with a shocked dismay at the spectacle of the man she had feared and revered reduced to a sort of babbling beggar in her presence.

'Well, that's all right,' said Hattie nervously. She put her hand on her breast, her fingers upon the collar of her brown dress, and pushed her chair an inch or two backwards.

'It's *not* all right!' John Robert smote the flimsy table with his hand, making several knives leap to the floor. He stood up and stumbled to the other end of the room and stood with his back to her leaning his head against the wall.

Hattie looked at him with horror. She said, in a timid breaking voice, 'Please be more ordinary, please be calm, you frighten me. Nothing can be so awful. I've always respected and trusted you. Just be quiet, be as you used to be –'

'I *can't* be as I used to be!' The words came out in a kind of bubbling roar, and John Robert turned round, wiping his wet mouth with the back of his hand, and gazed at the girl with eyes blazing with anguish. 'Yes, you respected me. You never loved me. Can you love me, is it possible? I need you, I crave for you. Oh God, what stupidity, what wickedness to talk to you like this –'

'I'm all right,' said Hattie, 'don't worry for me. I just want so much that you shouldn't be unhappy –' Appalled by the effect of his revelation upon John Robert himself, she could not measure the enormity of it or decide how best to calm him or to express the pity which she felt. She could hardly bear to look at him, at the cool dignified remote philosopher, the guardian of her childhood, suddenly transformed into this pathetic spitting moaning maniac. At the same time she felt his presence, his closeness to her in the room, as that of a large uncontrolled animal.

John Robert stood now against the wall, stooping a little, his hands hanging, his big head and his lips thrust forward. He said, 'She was right to say that I shouldn't be with you here.'

'Who was right?'

'Pearl. She taunted me with this, she laughed about it.'

'Oh – no –'

'They'll all know, she'll tell them, everyone will know.'

'No, no, no –'

'Don't leave me Hattie. Just for today stay with me, let us be quietly together. I'm sorry I've behaved in this beastly way. But I'm glad that I love you and that I've told you, really. I'm in awful pain but I'm happy. Don't go to the Slipper House, don't leave me alone, don't drive me mad by going – just after – all this. Just give me today, please.'

'Was that then,' said Hattie, 'why you wanted me to marry Tom McCaffrey?'

'Yes.'

'I'll stay with you,' she said.

On Friday Tom did not know what to do with himself. It was impossible to return to London and resume his ordinary life. His visit to Diane now seemed like a dark nightmarish cavern out of which there opened an indistinguishably large number of exits into hell. He kept wondering whether, after he had gone, George had quietly strangled Diane. He imagined her little body, with the fringed skirt and the pathetic boots, lying upon the *chaise longue* and George looking down on it and smiling that weird mad radiant smile. His shoulders hurt where George had gripped them. He felt as if he had been kicked downstairs. His imagination was utterly fouled up, haunted by filthy loathsome apparitions. The vision had returned of Hattie as a witch, as an evil enchantress, a temptress, a devilish enticing doll, the wanton spoiler of his innocence and freedom. He imagined her in a nurse's uniform, smiling frightfully, armed with a syringe which she was about to plunge into his arm in order to destroy his sanity. (Perhaps he had dreamed that last night?) He shook himself, shook his head as if literally to hurl the hateful visions out, to make them come away like gobbets of wax out of the ear. He thought, I've got to see Hattie, I've *got to see her*, then all this will *stop*. At any rate something will change if I see her, something will become clear, I'll ask her something, some question, I'm not sure what. And in this resolve he felt almost a kind of fury. But I'll wait till dark, he said to himself. If I were to meet Rozanov or George in the street I should start to scream. He felt an urge, during the morning, to go out and buy a paper to see if Diane had been murdered, but he resisted the urge, and consigned his thoughts on this subject to the class of apparitions. He spent the day feeding on ectoplasm.

As Tom, in extreme agitation, was walking through Victoria Park at twilight, with his own mackintosh and Greg's umbrella, he thought about Alex and how he ought to call on her, only not now of course. It only now occurred to him that he ought to say something to her about last Saturday night. He also saw at once that this was not only impossible but unnecessary. Alex, at least, was capable of swallowing things without demanding explanations. He saw her like a huge fish gulping it all down. He paused outside Belmont, seeing a light in Ruby's room. He had intended to walk round to the gate in Forum Way, but decided to go straight through into the garden from Tasker Road. He walked down the side of the house past the garage and looking up saw that the lights were on in the drawing-room and the curtains drawn.

He walked out on to the muddy water-logged lawn and the Slipper House came into view and he paused. The idea of seeing Hattie now seemed colossally important, ambiguous, unpredictable, dangerous, as if something enormous were at stake. Was it, and if so what? He had been going to ask Hattie a question. What question? What could he say to her now which would not be some sort of awful impertinence, would not his presence, especially his unheralded presence, be an impertinence? And suppose John Robert was there? He had not considered, after the reception of his last call, telephoning. He thought, maybe I'll give it up and see Alex instead. But his fate drew him on with a siren song of menace, and he thought, better a smash than any more abject waiting.

The Slipper House, surrounded by dripping trees (the rain was abating) looked melancholy and mysterious like a lonely secluded house in a Japanese story. The shutters were closed, but there appeared to be a light on in the sitting-room and one upstairs. Tom put down his umbrella. He could not find his handkerchief (his cold persisted), but blew his nose on the sleeve of his shirt. He felt sick with apprehension as he approached the door. Some light was coming from the hall through the stained-glass, but he could not find the bell. He tried the door. It was not locked. He opened it softly and stepped into the hall. He stood a moment in silence looking at some faded roses in a mauve vase, and taking in the self-possessed quietness of the house which for a moment struck him as being clearly *empty*. He slithered out of his mackintosh, laid down his umbrella on the floor, and before he went any farther automatically kicked off his shoes and put on a pair of slippers from the box in the hall. He went to the sitting-room door, which was ajar, and looked in. There was no one there. The gas fire was on. There was a book and a scarf on a chair, writing-paper and a pen

459

on the table. Even these evidences struck Tom as signs of a place overtaken by sudden disaster and abandoned.

He moved back into the hall. The continued silence began to be frightening. He shuffled his feet; then called out, 'Hello'. Then again, 'Hello! It's Tom McCaffrey.' Silence. He opened the front door and shut it noisily, then reopened it seeing the bell in the light from the hall, rang the bell and shut the door again and waited.

There was a sound of movement, steps, and a door opening up above. Then after a short interval a figure appeared at the top of the stairs. It was a man, tucking the tail of his white shirt into the top of his black trousers. The man was Emma.

Tom was so surprised, so shocked, that he leapt backwards coming into resounding contact with the front door.

Emma, red in the face, and breathing deeply, was equally distressed. He reached the bottom of the stairs, advanced a step or two, and stood looking sternly at Tom, his eyes narrowed without his glasses. Tom moved forward and they faced each other.

'Emma! What on *earth* are you doing here?'

'Well, what are you, if it comes to that?'

'How can you speak so? Where is Hattie? Why are you intruding?'

'Don't shout!'

'Is she – is she up there?'

'I don't know where she is.'

'I think you've been with her!'

'Oh Tom, stop, *think*, don't be crazy! Hattie isn't here.'

'Then what –'

'There were two women in this house, though I know you only noticed one. Your lady, the mistress, has gone away. I, as befits my position as the hero's friend, have been in bed with the maid.'

'You've been – oh *Emma* –'

'You're shocked.'

'I resent your being here.'

'You have no rights in this house as far as I know.'

'You behave as if you have! What a charade, what an affront to – to her – to Hattie Meynell.'

'All right, it takes some explaining, but if you take on so I can't explain.'

'To treat this house like a –'

'Oh come, come, Tom.'

'I thought you were a serious person with decent standards of behaviour.'

'Do you mean someone who doesn't make love to maid-servants?'

'You know I don't mean that.'

'What did you want, if it comes to that, creeping in unannounced at this hour?'

'Are you suggesting –?'

'No! I'm just asking you to calm down.'

'You go about it in a funny way. What else have you been doing that I don't know about? You tried to wreck things, at any rate you *did* wreck things –'

'What do you mean?'

'You gave away what I told you about John Robert and Hattie and me. I told it to you as a secret and you gave it away, and now it's been all over the press, you don't know how horrible it's been and what awful damage it's done.'

'I did not give it away.'

'You must have done. You told it to Hector Gaines.'

'I did not!'

'You did. You bloody liar.'

Emma picked up a paperback book (his own copy of Thucydides' *History of the Peloponnesian War*) which was lying on a table beside the faded roses and hit Tom across the face.

Then instantly they started to fight. Both were athletic and agile and for the moment very angry, but neither was much good at fighting. Tom gave a violent push against Emma's shoulder. Emma lunged at Tom's chest and sent him reeling back towards the door. Then they sprang at each other like two dogs, clutching and staggering round in a circle, Tom dragging at Emma's shirt and Emma at Tom's jacket. Emma tried to get a wrestling hold, one foot driving behind Tom's leg. Tom punched him in the ribs. They crashed into the table, sending the vase of roses flying.

This scrimmage might have gone on longer, only it was suddenly ended by a deluge of cold water which descended on the combatants, decanted from a bedroom jug by Pearl on the landing above.

Startled, soaked and ridiculous, they drew apart.

'Hell!'

'Damn!'

461

Tom took off his jacket and shook it. Emma wrung out the end of his shirt, which had emerged again.

'Thank heavens I wasn't wearing my glasses.'

Tom had closed his eyes and lowered his head.

'Are you all right, Tom?'

'Yes, let's go in here.'

They marched into the sitting-room and closed the door.

Tom said, 'Is there anything to drink?'

'No, it's a teetotal house. There's some Coca-Cola here.'

'Give me some.'

Emma opened the cupboard and poured out two glasses. His hand shook.

'That was absurd, to fight like that,' said Tom.

Emma said nothing.

'Emma, I'm sorry.'

'OK.'

Tom looked anxiously at his friend, then looked away. He said, 'What's been happening here, how long have you been here?'

'I arrived this evening. John Robert took Hattie away last night.'

'Where to?'

'Back to America. Well, I suppose first to his place here, or to London –'

'Oh – God – but I don't understand. How did you know? I mean, did you come here looking for Hattie?'

'No, you fool.'

'But then why – how – you don't know Pearl, you'd never exchanged a word with her, was it just accident, a sort of impulse, when you found her alone?'

'Oh, Tom – I saw her at the Baths, and I talked to her on that picnic, can't you remember, and again last Saturday. Last Saturday I kissed her.'

'I see, so –'

'I was feeling bloody depressed. You hadn't turned up or shown any sign of life. I thought I'd come down here, and I rang up from the station to ask Pearl to come out to a pub. She said she was alone and asked me to come round. She's pretty depressed too.'

'Emma, there's been such ghastly stuff in the local press here.'

'Yes, she told me. That brings us back to where we started.'

'You mean – yes –'

Emma sat down and rubbed his eyes. 'I've been thinking about that, of course, I didn't tell Hector. I didn't tell anybody. Pearl didn't tell anybody, and I don't imagine Hattie did.'

'Of course not.'

'But do you remember, we were both pretty drunk, in the garden that night we started talking about it, about John Robert's idea about you and Hattie, and all sorts of people were slinking about and could have been listening.'

'My God, you're right. What we said must have sounded pretty crazy though.'

'Enough for somebody to pick up an idea.'

'Yes – oh Christ, we're bloody fools. I mean I am. Oh Emma, if you only knew what a fool I am and what a muddle I'm in and how miserable I am!'

'And I think I've given you a black eye.'

Tom noticed that one of his eyes was closing. He touched it. It felt hot and tender. 'Yes! Is there any more Coke? Thanks. But look, about Hattie and John Robert –'

'Do you mind if I ask Pearl to come down? This is her house in which we've been behaving like oafs. And she can explain, at any rate she can tell you what she knows. It's all bloody obscure.'

While Emma went to fetch Pearl, Tom looked at himself in the cut-glass fountain mirror. His right eye was watery and narrow and surrounded by a puffy red circle. His hair was wet from the deluge, its long curls reduced to rats' tails. His shirt was wet too and torn at the neck.

Emma found Pearl in the hall. She had picked up the strewn roses and the fragments of the mauve *art déco* vase, and was on her knees mopping up the water, squeezing a cloth into a pail. She got up slowly and looked sombrely at Emma.

Emma reached out and took her hand and pressed it hard. He said, 'Come in and talk to Tom. Tell him about last night.'

Pearl said, 'I think that water will stain the parquet.'

'Damn the parquet. Come, girl.'

Pearl was wearing a blue summer dress and a big shaggy cardigan into whose pockets she now thrust her hands, pulling the garment down. Her legs were bare above her slippers. Her straight hair had been fiercely combed and her face had its older Mexican look. Her nose was thin and sharp. She frowned and hunched her shoulders, then followed Emma into the sitting-room.

Tom hastily put away the comb with which he had been trying to arrange his wet locks. He bowed awkwardly to Pearl, who nodded to him. Tom was now acutely conscious of Emma's implied condemnation of him for having failed to notice Pearl because she was classified as 'the maid'. He was now aware of her handsomeness and the strength of her presence. Emma stood looking from one to the other.

The room was suddenly full of jealousy, as palpable as a thick green gas. Tom and Pearl looked at Emma. All three stiffened as if to attention.

Pearl said, 'Do sit down.' She sat down wearily in one of the bamboo chairs. The two men remained standing.

Tom said, 'I'm sorry I barged in.' Then, 'So John Robert took Hattie away?'

'Yes. Last night. He arrived about ten o'clock and there was a row.'

'A row?'

'He was furious with us, chiefly with me, because of the business last Saturday and the stuff in the *Gazette*.'

'But you'd seen him since Saturday?'

'No. We were waiting for him every day. He only came yesterday.'

'I had my interview on Wednesday,' said Tom.

'What happened?' Emma asked him.

'He told me to go to hell. Never to come near Hattie again. He somehow thought I was in league with George.'

'He thought I was in league with George too,' said Pearl.

'He's crazy, he's got George on the brain.'

'Pearl has got the boot,' said Emma.

'You mean he's sacked you?'

'Yes, it's all at an end. He decided suddenly that I was a corrupt person and a moral danger to Hattie. He called a taxi and took Hattie away and said they would be going back to America at once.'

'But it *can't* end like that,' Tom said.

'That's what I told her,' Emma said.

Pearl, looking very tired, said slowly, 'I thought that Hattie would come today. Last night she was terribly upset and sort of dominated by him. But I thought that this morning she would come running straight back. And I waited. But she didn't come. That means either that he's taken her away to London or straight to the airport, or else he's poisoned her mind against me, persuaded her I'm some sort of – degraded schemer.'

'He couldn't,' said Tom, 'she wouldn't believe anything like that.

They must have gone away. She'll – she'll write, she'll come back.'

'It's too late,' said Pearl. 'He said it was time for things to change and of course it is. Things must change. Hattie must change – and go away – altogether. And he couldn't possibly – now – bear for me to be near her –'

'Why?' said Emma.

'Oh because – because – Anyway they're probably in America by now. She has *gone*.'

There was a moment's silence. Pearl said, 'I'm so tired, I didn't sleep last night, you must excuse me.' She got up and slouched out of the room.

Tom said, 'Hell, *hell*.' Then he said, 'Are you staying here tonight?'

'Yes, if she'll let me.'

'Well – I'll be off – I'll leave the door open at Travancore Avenue just in case – I'll go back to London tomorrow – I think. And you?'

'I don't know.'

Tom went out into the hall.

'Damn, my jacket's still wet.' He pulled on his jacket and then his mackintosh. He kicked off the slippers and put on his shoes. 'Funny, I put the slippers on without thinking. I suppose nobody bothers now.'

He picked up Greg's umbrella. 'Why, there's my umbrella in the stand, I left it here – that other time –' He put the two umbrellas under his arm.

Emma was standing at the sitting-room door. He said, 'Is it still raining?'

'I think it's stopped. Well, goodnight.'

'Goodnight.'

Tom opened the front door. He said, 'Would you walk with me as far as the back gate?'

They walked in silence across the wet lawn and along the soft mossy path under the trees whose wet leaves still dripped. Tom opened the gate.

'Emma.'

'Yes, yes, yes.'

'All right?'

'Yes. Goodnight.'

When Emma came back to the Slipper House he found Pearl sitting on the stairs.

'Let's go up, Pearl.'

'No, I like it here.'

Emma sat down on the stairs below her. He kissed the side of her knee through her dress.

'Perhaps sitting on the stairs suits us.'

'It suits me anyway.'

'You're a funny girl.'

'Almost as good as no girl at all.'

Their unexpected love-making had come about because both were in despair. These despairs were the occasion of an untypical recklessness. Pearl had waited all day for Hattie, first confidently, then with mounting grief and surmises. She tried to occupy herself by packing up Hattie's clothes, but kept stopping to look out of the window, expecting to see her come running with flying hair. She had seen Hattie depart helplessly in tears, overpowered by John Robert and unable to resist. She imagined (rightly) that in the morning Hattie would be in command of herself, pugnacious, rebellious, summoning up a kind of cold fierce resolve, rarely displayed, which Pearl knew she possessed. Pearl did not imagine that Rozanov would lock her up. Whatever his general intentions, he could hardly prevent her, on that day at least, from coming back. About *that* Pearl felt fairly certain; and she did not believe that John Robert was likely to set off for London or the airport in the middle of the night. About other things she could only try not to be too terribly wretched. She had, she realized, made a fatal mistake, indeed two fatal mistakes, in telling John Robert that she loved him, and in letting him know that she had perceived his feeling for Hattie; and she had blurted these dreadful truths out in such a crude ungentle ugly way. (In fact Pearl's indiscretion affected her own life and the lives of others more profoundly than she ever knew, since the shock of her unspeakable knowledge of it provided John Robert with an extra, perhaps decisive, motive for telling his love to Hattie.) Pearl knew the philosopher well, his vanity, his dignity, his prudishness, his secretiveness. Against all those she had offended and could scarcely be forgiven. At hopeful moments (early in the day), she thought that she might, for Hattie's sake, be tolerated. At less hopeful moments she got such meagre comfort as she could from reflecting that John Robert had in any case, and without her foolish words, already decided, or feigned to himself, that Pearl was 'corrupt', 'no fit person' and so on. He had decided to get rid of me, thought Pearl, and any show of loyalty to me from

Hattie would make him more determined. He has suddenly come to see me as *in the way*. In the way of what? Here she checked her reflections, since whatever *that* future might prove to be it did not seem to contain her.

Moreover, as the day went on and Hattie did not come, Pearl began to imagine how Hattie's resistance might have been broken down, how Hattie's mind might have been poisoned. Could Hattie be brainwashed, made to believe that Pearl *had* betrayed Rozanov's plans, *had* plotted with George McCaffrey, *had* deceived Hattie and was altogether a different person from the one she seemed to be? Was such a total change of view possible? Could Hattie be thus led to think that it was time to give up a childish fancy for her old nursemaid? Hattie had never resisted Rozanov's will. She had, it was a *fact*, gone away with him last night. Was not the picture of a rebellious Hattie speaking up for Pearl quite unrealistic, a wishful dream? When Pearl reflected how loyal she *had* been, how totally she had given over her life to those two people, she felt an anger against Rozanov which gave a little relief to her pain. But the pain was terrible. Her love for the monster raged in her heart, and the more she rehearsed his sins the more she loved him: she loved him, protectively, tenderly, forgivingly with an absolute self-breaking sweetness as if she had made him up or he were her child. She held him secretly, possessively, in her heart with such a strength of passion that at times it was hard to believe that he was a separate person with other concerns who knew and cared nothing about how she felt. The desire to tell love is a natural ingredient of love itself; love feels it is a benefit, a blessing, a gift that must be given. No doubt the desire to tell Rozanov, always present, had grown stronger in her heart, and with the shock of his attack on her, became irresistible: the desire by some sort of passionate magic to join together the captive loved image and the terrible free real reality. That was one pain. The other, perhaps even worse, pain was her love for Hattie, not a lurid secret devotion of the imagination, but a real bond, a daily bread love, a lived reality of family life such as Pearl had never known before: an absolute entwining of two lives, a connection the breaking of which had seemed inconceivable. This too, as the day went interminably on, she almost cursed. How could she have become so blindly attached to what she could so suddenly and so completely lose?

When Emma rang up, about five o'clock, Pearl was sure it must be Hattie, and this disappointment made a final degree of despera-

467

tion, a final signal. She had in fact become, alone in the house so long and with such thoughts, appalled and frightened. She had not thought much about Emma, she had indeed very little conception of him, but now she found herself needing his presence. She needed help, she needed somebody, and Emma, proposing himself, was suddenly clear as the only possible person. What followed was a part of her decision to abandon hope, though this did not prevent her from almost dying of fright when she heard Tom enter and thought it was John Robert.

Emma's despair and consequent recklessness was of dual origin. He was upset and annoyed by Tom's failure to appear in London and his failure to write or telephone. Of course, since he had returned to London on Sunday, he knew nothing about the *Gazette* article and the later dramas. He did not think that Tom was ill; at any rate, if illness was its cause, Tom would surely by now have explained his absence. The silence must be hostile, it must express an alienation which was entirely unjust. Emma could have telephoned Travancore Avenue, but felt too stiff and proud to do so. Besides, a messy telephone call would leave him even more disturbed. He reflected often upon the night which they had spent together and wondered whether a retrospective disgust at that episode was what was rendering his friend absent and silent. Emma had by now firmly classified that night as, as he had put it, a *hapax legomenon*; nothing like that would ever happen again. And yet he could not help thinking about it and experiencing, in relation to Tom, that mysterious and terrible and well-known yearning of one human body for another, a condition which got worse as the week continued without sign or sight.

The other matter was the question of singing. Emma had not had the courage to say anything to Mr Hanway. He had decided to write to him a letter, but had not written. At last he rang up to cancel his next lesson, but still without giving any hint of the dreadful decision he was in process of taking. For it was, now he was so close up against it, a *dreadful* decision. He began to realize how deeply important his gift was to him, how connected with his confidence against the world. Mr Hanway was important, the guarantor of the well-being, the purity and continuity of his talent. He had sometimes thought of his voice as a burdensome secret, but it was also a valuable life-giving secret, so long as the question of giving it up, for so long vaguely present, did not seriously arise. Of course it was clear to Emma that it was his destiny to be a historian, that that admitted of no doubt was made plain by the merest flicker of the unreal hypothesis: give up history. He was to be, with all his intellect and all his nerves and his desires and all his energy and all his soul, a scholar, a polymath. He would, as a good historian must, know everything. Herein he could see and understand and emulate excellence. Such a dedicated life *must* preclude serious singing; and of unserious singing he had been irrevocably trained to be incapable. So . . . never to sing again? *Never*?

Emma had intended to come to Ennistone to look for Tom, to walk in upon him indignantly, but the image of Pearl, which had certainly not been absent from his mind, began, upon the railway journey, to grow stronger. It was some time since Emma had kissed a girl, and he did not view lightly the matter of having kissed Pearl on the previous Saturday evening when rather drunk. In fact the event was remarkable. On the other hand he did not know what to make of it either. As the train approached Ennistone, the whole idea of coming to look for Tom began to seem rather stupid and dangerous. At the station, on the spur of the moment, he rang the Slipper House number which he found in the book under McCaffrey.

At the Slipper House he kissed Pearl on arrival, and after her account of the recent happenings kissed her again. What happened after that surprised them both. It was less than satisfactory because of Emma's lack of competence and Pearl's determination not to risk pregnancy. It was momentous, however, and left them both a little dazed.

Emma, sitting below her on the stairs, said, 'Perhaps Hattie will come tomorrow.'

'No.'

'Why not?'

'They'll have gone tomorrow.'

'Then she'll write.'

'No. And even if she writes – it will already be too late.'

Pearl had of course not told Emma about her own feelings for John Robert or what she surmised of his for Hattie.

'I can't see why you think so. All right. John Robert said your job was at an end and said all those disobliging things, but he may change his mind after he's calmed down and talked to Hattie. He can't stop her from seeing you. And your relation with her is bound to change as she grows up anyway.'

'I can't be . . . related to Hattie . . . in any other way,' said Pearl. This awful idea had only just occurred to her.

'Why? I think that is nonsense. You think John Robert has really turned her against you?'

'Even if he can't persuade her that I'm a horrible person, he will have told her that she doesn't need a maid any more, and that I am – just that.'

'But *she* won't think so!'

'Oh – she – I don't know, I don't *know*.' And Pearl began to cry. She had not cried all day. She put her head against the wall and cried into the wallpaper.

'Oh don't, *don't*!' said Emma. He knelt on the stairs and tried to put his arms round her, but she thrust him away. He said, 'With Hattie – I feel sure – there isn't any "too late". Don't cry. God, I wish there was something to drink in the house. Let's go out to the Albert. Damn, it'll be closed.'

'You'd better go,' said Pearl. She mopped her eyes on the hem of her dress.

'Why can't I stay?'

'No.'

'I want to be with you tomorrow. I'll come back.'

'Better not, whatever's left for me – it's in waiting alone.'

'Yes – I see. But this, between us, is something.'

'Oh, something. Anything is something.'

'Well, you can't make it nothing. I appear to have entered your life.'

'There's no such place. You're just *interested* in this *business*.'

'Well, it's your business. I'm interested like in your green eyes.'

'Don't let's have a stupid conversation. We aren't anything to each other and can't be.'

'Why not, for heaven's sake, because of class?'

'Don't be silly!'

'Pearl, don't be destructive, let's just see.'

'You're in love with Tom McCaffrey.'

'Well, maybe, but that's just personal, subjective. I feel love for you.'

'You don't say you love me.'

'I'm being curiously precise. I am grateful to you. And I do love you. And you are awfully interesting. And I want to protect you from all pains and terrors.'

Pearl, who had been staring down into the hall, turned and looked at him. He had resumed his narrow rimless glasses which enlarged his eyes. His hair, still damp and darkened, streaked away down into the disordered collar of his shirt.

'Don't look so mournful, girl.'

'Was that you singing that night?'

'Yes.'

'I thought it was. You have such a strange high voice – but beautiful.'

'Yes. But what about us.'

'I think I can only love my own sex. Like you. Not that anything has ever come of it.'

'Do you love her – Hattie – like that?'

'No. Hattie's special. And what's "like that" anyway? Everyone's special.'

'Exactly. Do you still want me to go?'

'Yes.'

'We won't lose each other?'

'I suppose not. I don't know.'

Ten minutes later Emma had left the house. But he did not go to Travancore Avenue. He spent the night in the Ennistone Royal Hotel and returned to London early on Saturday morning.

What Brian McCaffrey later called 'the family court-martial of George' came about by accident.

The funeral of William Eastcote took place late on Saturday afternoon. There is a Quaker graveyard, a touching 'dormitory' with low uniformly patterned headstones, next to the Meeting House, but this was filled up in the last century, and the old Quaker families now bury their dead with the rest of us in the municipal graveyard adjacent to St Olaf's Church in Burkestown. The coffin was taken there privately on Saturday morning, and shortly before the burial the Friends gathered in the little all-purpose chapel to conduct their 'funeral meeting' which on such occasions, according to Quaker custom, is the same in form as the ordinary Sunday meetings. The gathering was not large. All the Ennistone Friends were there, and a few others including Milton Eastcote. No one was moved to speak. Any eulogy of the deceased was felt to be unnecessary and out of place. Many people wept quietly in the silence. The coffin was then carried to the grave by Percy Bowcock, Robin Osmore, Dr Roach, Nicky Roach, Nathaniel Romage and Milton Eastcote. As the *Gazette* put it, 'Bill the Lizard was mourned by everyone in Ennistone.' Certainly the universal respect and affection in which he was held was evidenced by the arrival at the scene of nearly two thousand people who stood in the graveyard and upon the grass slopes above it (beyond which is the railway). This crowd stood in complete and impressive silence through the duration (almost half an hour) of the meeting, and only pushed forward a little during the interment. Afterwards, and quite spontaneously (it is not known who started it) this large crowd sang *Jerusalem*, a favourite of William's and a song which, for some reason, everyone in Ennistone knows. On this moving and memorable occasion I (N) was present. Also present were Alex, Brian, Gabriel, Tom and Adam McCaffrey and Ruby. There was a sensation when George was seen in the crowd accompanied by Diane Sedleigh: this was the first recorded occasion of George being seen in public with his mistress. There was a rumour that Stella McCaffrey, in disguise, had also been seen, but this was false.

After the burial, and the spectacle, judged touchingly appropriate by her fellow citizens, of Anthea's tears at the graveside, the mourners dispersed, some to go to the Institute, others to proceed to various public houses, there to reminisce about the good deeds of the deceased, and also to discuss the will, details of which had been broadcast by one of Robin Osmore's clerks who had joined the considerable contingent who had repaired to the Green Man which was close by. William had left numerous bequests to friends and relations and to national and local charities. The Meeting House received a legacy 'for maintaining the fabric' large enough to dispel Nathaniel Romage's anxiety for some time to come. Monies also went to the wasteland community centre, the Asian Centre, the Boys' Club, the Salvation Army, and various other good causes and hard cases. However, a large slice of the cake, including the fine house in The Crescent, went to Anthea Eastcote; and for this partiality, the virtuous departed was soon being criticized by those who, while sincerely admiring him, were getting a little tired of hearing him praised.

The McCaffrey contingent, who were (except for George) standing together, were all in different ways deeply grieved at the death of one whom they had always regarded as 'an example of goodness' and 'a place of healing'. Tom and Alex both privately wished that it had occurred to them to expose some of their recent troubles to William. Brian thought he ought to have consulted William about what to do should he lose his job. Gabriel felt that a silent guarantor of the reality of goodness had been taken away from her vulnerable world. She loved William very much and now wondered why she had never seemed to have time to see him. Adam regretted that because of a cricket match he had refused an invitation to tea at 34 The Crescent. In spite of their grief, the various McCaffreys shared that curious energy, almost a kind of elation, which survivors, if not too terribly bereaved, feel after a funeral. So that when Alex suggested that they should all go and swim, and then come back to Belmont and have a drink, this seemed a good idea, and it turned out that they had all, in anticipation of just this period after the solemnity, brought their swimming costumes.

*

473

When they reached the Institute they found the place in a turmoil. 'Have you seen?' shouted Nesta Wiggins running past them
just outside. (She and her father had of course attended the funeral.)
She did not say what, but they soon saw for themselves. The 'Little
Teaser', or Lud's Rill, had suddenly decided to change itself into
a powerful geyser, sending a spout of scalding hot water up more
than thirty feet into the air, 'higher than last time', it was gleefully
reported. It was a cool sunny evening and a light wind was distri-
buting the fallout over Diana's Garden and the pavement which
divided it from the pool. A plume of steam hung about the tall
magical spout, around which, allowing for changes in the direction
of the wind, Institute attendants had erected barriers on either side.
The water, rushing up, made a fierce swishing sound like tearing
silk which added to the uncanny frightening charm of the phenomenon.

Behind the barriers a crowd had gathered, watching the antics
of the great jet which played unevenly, eliciting 'oohs' and 'ahs'
such as are to be heard at a display of fireworks. Alarming rumours
were also rife. Some people were saying that scalding water was
spreading through the whole Institute system, running into the
baths in the Rooms and likely to drown unwary people bathing
there as had, it was alleged, happened on the previous occasion of
such an outburst. A number of swimmers had hastily emerged from
the Outdoor Pool, having conceived or been offered the idea that the
whole pool would soon be filled with boiling water, the influx of
which they of course persuaded themselves that they could now
feel. Others, more sceptical, continued to swim. Various speculations were also being eagerly discussed concerning the possible
cause of the amazing phenomenon. Druids and poltergeists were
mentioned. Someone had a theory about earthquakes, another that
it was caused by the Russians, another that it was to do with a
Flying Saucer which someone (a respectable youth, newly appren-
ticed to Dominic Wiggins) had seen two nights ago over the Common. It was recalled (wrongly) that Lud's Rill had behaved in
exactly this way on the occasion of the previous saucer, the one
which William Eastcote had seen. It was then observed with triumph that the latest saucer had appeared exactly on the night that
William died. All were agreed that the portent indicated that Ennistone was going to have another of its 'funny times', that this time
had indeed already started, initiated some said by the recent weird
goings-on at the Slipper House. Meanwhile Vernon Chalmers, the

Director of the Institute, was walking about among the crowds and trying to reassure everyone, explaining that the scalding fount was on a quite different water system from that which served the pools and the rooms. (Vernon was also telling himself that really the Source itself ought to be open to the public, as it used to be before the first war, so that the people could see for themselves how everything worked and how safe and well-controlled the waters were. But certain prudential considerations operated against this idea; and in any case Vernon, who felt very possessive about the Institute with which he had been connected all his life since his father had been a water engineer, felt a certain reluctance to letting the common herd tramp into that *sanctum sanctorum*.) The citizens listened to his reassurances and then returned ardently to the most gruesome and ridiculous hypotheses.

The McCaffreys, after watching the irregular play of the huge steamy jet, quickly attired themselves for swimming and dived into the pool where the temperature was precisely what it always was, between 26° and 28° Centigrade. Tom swam across the pool and back and then got out and rubbed his long wet hair into a frizzy mop. He dressed and went back to the crowd beside the geyser and pushed his way forward to the barrier. Here by holding out his hand he could feel, at turns of the wind, scalding drops falling on to his skin like red-hot pennies. He felt unbearably restless and miserable. He had waited up for Emma at Travancore Avenue but his friend had not come. Tom felt abandoned and jealous and confused, all his emotions and nerves lashed and raw. He was embarrassed by his black eye which, although only slightly discoloured, was able to attract attention. Brian in his blunt way had said, 'What's the matter with you, been fighting?' Tom said, 'I fell and knocked my head on a chair.' Brian said, 'Drunk again, I suppose.'

But what filled Tom's soul, painfully expanding it as it were through sheer anguish to a size never attained before, was the question of Hattie, or rather the fact that there was no question any more. The thing was over. Tomorrow Tom would have to go back to London and resume his work, see his tutor, go to lectures, write essays, and go on in the old way as if nothing had happened. So much had happened which seemed like a bad dream. Yet also it was not a dream but a terrible overriding reality, the permanently changed reality of his unhappy being, tortured by yearning and remorse. They were gone, that demonic pair, and he would never set eyes on either of them again.

But how could he return to his ordinary life, to his work, to the, as they now seemed, insipid childish pleasures of his London student world? He had been bewitched. For a short time he had lived with gods or fairies. He had been summoned to a destiny, presented with an ordeal, and he had dully, casually, failed to understand, failed to respond, failed to *see*. Even at the beginning, when it had seemed important, he had been only grossly excited, flattered and amused. He recalled John Robert's huge bulk in that little room and how surprised and alarmed and gratified he had been when at last he understood the strange man's purpose. And he had taken those facile emotions to be something remarkable in his life.

The image of Hattie shimmered before him now, occupying its own space, radiating its own light. He saw her silver-white blond hair cunningly pinned up or descending in amazingly long plaits or as he had seen it at the sea spread out like silk over the back of her dress. He saw her pale white-mottled eyes, gazing sarcastically or else gentle and truthful. He saw her long legs and her stockings with darker-coloured tops. He thought, how can I have lost her, how did it happen? I behaved like an oaf, like a *cad*, like a *bloody fool*. At the same time he could clearly remember, though he could not feel or inhabit, the fact that he had actually *considered* Hattie, *looked her over* and *rejected* her! Dully and casually he had turned away, failing to *see* that the being confronting him was a princess.

But she's a false princess, he thought. I am in a state of temporary insanity, I must be. They are demons, both of them, wonderful and beautiful and not quite real. Rozanov is a magician who took me to his palace and showed me a maiden. But she was something that he had made, invented out of magic stuff, so as to ensnare me. And they have gone away and I am still ensnared, they've *gone* and I *suffer*. Oh how much I want to see her now, he thought, how much I want to tell her how it all came about. Yet how did it, what did I do wrong and when did I do wrong? How happy I could be if I could only see her and explain that I wasn't so stupid and so oafish, or wasn't any more, and that I was sorry and ... But that's impossible, I never will see her again. She has been removed into the invisible world, and because of her I shall be sick forever after.

'Oh Tom, I forgot, I've brought Judy Osmore's dress. Look what I've done. It's not perfect, but it's not bad.' Gabriel brought out the dress and displayed it.

They had removed themselves to Belmont and were sitting in the drawing-room having drinks. Adam, who had decided to run back to Como to fetch Zed, had not yet returned.

Gabriel had done a wonderful job on the dress. The tears on the shoulders which had looked so awful to Emma were only split seams and were easily mended. The wine stain on the front was indelible. But clever Gabriel had managed to blend it in to the irregular blotchy pattern of the material by discreetly dyeing surrounding, and other, areas with different strengths of tea. The dress certainly looked a bit different, but the stain could now be accepted as part of the pattern. It might even be said to look nicer, Gabriel thought. She had taken a lot of trouble with the dress and was pleased with herself, happy to have been of service to Tom, and expectant of praise.

Tom however accepted this masterpiece with a vague 'Oh yes – thanks –' He crumpled up the carefully ironed dress into a clumsy ball and stuffed it into the bag which Gabriel had provided.

Gabriel retired to the window and looked out, concealing sudden tears. She knew her 'weepy' tendency annoyed Alex. She was upset in any case because Adam's birthday (last Saturday) had been spoilt because Brian refused to take her and Adam out to lunch at the Running Dog, an unprecedented treat which Adam had asked for. Brian had said that it was ridiculous to spend money on going to snobbish restaurants to have rotten food thrown at one by sneering waiters. Brian had also vetoed Adam's request for a 'malachite egg'. 'What on earth put that idea into his head? At his age I hadn't even heard of malachite. I'm not going to encourage him in expensive useless tastes!' But Gabriel had secretly bought a (small) malachite egg, and was now in an impossible position, as she dared not confess this extravagance to Brian, and realized it would be immoral to ask Adam to keep it a secret. The guilty egg, in a cardboard box, meanwhile reposed at the back of the wardrobe.

'What is that thing up in the ginkgo tree?' Alex had moved to the window.

Brian followed her. 'Some sort of plant.'

'Plant?'

'I mean like mistletoe.'

'That's not mistletoe.'

'I said *like* mistletoe.'

Looking over their shoulders, Tom saw Emma's (or rather

477

Judy's) blond wig hanging conspicuous and odd among the branches.

'It doesn't look like a plant. It's more like a cardboard box or an old sack. Would one of you boys climb up to see?'

'Bags I not. I'm too old. Tom will.'

'I'll get it down,' said Tom.

'But if it *is* a plant, leave it.'

Tom had lost all sense of time. It already seemed a week since his fight with Emma and Pearl's news that 'those two' had departed. Tom wanted to feel now that Hattie and John Robert had been gone a long time. He wanted mountains of time, mountains of experience, to divide him from those dreadful events. Tom was in process of revising his past so as to explain his suffering. So much misery *must* imply either a dreadful loss or a dreadful crime or both. But that was, was it not, long ago. He stood, clutching the bag with Judy's dress, and gazing from the window at the green roof of the Slipper House. He thought, they've gone. I needn't hide. But already the hiding was unintelligible and long past.

Adam slipped into the room carrying Zed (who had difficulty with the stairs). He set the little dog down, and Zed ran and hopped across the carpet, wrinkling up his nose in what Adam called his *social* smile and greeting everyone in turn with lowered head and white tail-wagging rump. Tom squatted and caressed the dog. Zed rolled over in ecstasy. Tom thought, how innocent I *once* was, and could have been made so happy simply by this.

Alex was thinking about Bill the Lizard and how much, she felt now, she had loved him and relied on his presence, and how stupidly little she had seen of him. He was to be always *there*, making life more significant and secure, in a way which did not need to be continually checked. Alex had a strange terrible black feeling which she understood as the realization that nothing of equal significance now separated her from her own death. There was no more stuff of life, no more ardently desired events, no more wise and beloved older persons between her and the grave. Her love for her family, always a diminishing consolation, was invaded by pain, as by the scalding water which people imagined was going to flow through all the pipes of the Institute. And this morning she had received a horrible and menacing letter from the Town Hall, it said, 'Dear Mrs McCaffrey. We are sorry to hear that you have been seriously annoyed by a vicious and savage fox. It has come to our notice that there is a fox's earth in your garden, and our pest control officer will attend at your convenience to deal with the matter. There will be no loss of amenity. The exits of the earth will be stopped and poison gas introduced. You will appreciate that, in view of the possibility of rabies, we have a responsibility to act promptly in such cases, and we look forward to receiving your notification of a suitable date.' Alex had written in reply that there must be some error, she had not seen any foxes, savage or otherwise, and there was no fox's earth in her garden. She felt frightened and hunted, as if it were she herself who was to be locked in and gassed. She felt angry too. How had they found out? Ruby must have spread the story around. Alex had wanted to cry out angrily to Ruby, but had found herself strangely and ominously unable to. She had stared at Ruby. Ruby had stared back. And then something else had happened which was senseless and ill-omened and weird. Alex began telling it to Brian.

Tom, sitting on the carpet with Zed and Adam, playing listlessly with the dog, half attended to Alex's chatter.

Alex was saying, 'I really don't know what's happening to the town these days, and with the Teaser shooting up like that, it almost makes one believe that we all have to go crazy at intervals around here, it's probably something to do with the Druids and the Romans and those old pagan gods or something. I always felt those two girls in the Slipper House were part of it somehow, all the trouble they caused last Saturday. There was something unsavoury about those two. Thank God they've gone.'

'Have they?' said Brian. 'When?'

'At least I hope so. This morning early I found that the keys had been put through the letter box in an envelope. No covering letter, no "thank you", just the keys. I went over of course to see if the place was all right, and they'd cleared all their stuff up and packed it into a trunk and suitcases labelled "to be called for". The house looked in order except for some sort of brown mess on the parquet in the hall. So I thought I'd seen the last of them, but no, about an hour later I heard someone come running down the side passage to the garage. I looked out of the window and lo and behold it was little Missie.'

Tom, who had been listening more attentively, gasped and turned, his face flushing violently.

'There she was with her hair all undone running across the grass like a mad thing. And it annoyed me that she came in from the front, they weren't supposed to come in our way, but by the back gate. I thought I'd go down and tell her off and find out why they'd left so suddenly, I think they might have told me just out of courtesy, and you know they never thanked me or invited me round for as much as a cup of tea, the maid is a coarse type of course but the girl is supposed to be grown-up, they say she's a bit retarded and I suppose that's it, anyway I went out and there she was ringing the bell and pulling the door and calling out at the top of her voice. Then she began to run round the house looking in the windows and trying to open them and shouting, like some sort of little wild animal. She ran right round the house and then she saw me and I said, "Can I help you!" and she said, "Where's Pearl?" just like that. That's the maid, and I said, "She's gone, she returned the keys and all your things are packed up," and I was going to ask her when the stuff would be cleared out and then I saw that she was completely distraught, she'd been crying and was starting to cry again, and she just stared at me as if she'd gone crazy, and then without a word she ran away down the garden toward the back gate with her hair flying and that's the last I saw of her. What do you make of that?'

'She's not mentally ill, she's just very shy,' said Gabriel. 'She seemed perfectly normal when we were at the sea.' Gabriel lit a cigarette, then put it out quickly in an ashtray.

'I thought she was a bit slow,' said Brian. 'She never had a word to say for herself all that day.'

'She's certainly very peculiar,' said Alex.

'Poor child,' said Gabriel. 'I blame Professor Rozanov, they say he neglected her terribly, he doesn't like children.'

'*When* was this?' said Tom. 'This morning?'

'Yes.'

Tom, kneeling, sat back on his heels. He began saying out aloud, 'Wednesday, Thursday, Friday . . .' If Hattie was still here . . . what did it mean? When had Pearl said they were gone, on which day did Rozanov take Hattie away, what happened last night? Was Alex simply mistaken, were they dealing with a ghost, what did it all mean? Above all, what ought he to do, was there anything which he should do now, immediately perhaps? Did *this* make no difference or all the difference? Now it seemed there had been some peace in believing it over. Well, *was* it not over, in spite of this awful visitation? How horrible it all was, this thing of her coming back, so senseless, so perfectly nightmarish . . .

At this moment George came into the room.

Although the drawing-room door was shut, George could well have heard their voices as he came up the stairs. Whether he had or not, he enacted surprise.

'Why, a family scene, drinks too, may I have one?'

'Hello, darling,' said Alex, as if she had expected him (which she had not). She did not normally call George 'darling' in public, or in private, and the endearment rang out as a kind of proclamation or challenge. She said to Tom, 'Get your brother a drink.'

'Whisky, Tom dear,' said George, taking the endearment cue from Alex and smiling.

Tom poured out the whisky and handed it to him. He said, 'Is Rozanov still here?'

George said, 'No, he is far off, he has departed, he is gone from us, he is no more seen, he is obliterated and blotted out, he has been removed into invisibility without thought or motion, the only thing, the necessary thing, in short he has gone.'

'He has left Ennistone?'

'He and the little charmer both. What a little girl that was, what an ivory head, what a milky body, what great mauve eyes and how they could flash! What breasts, what pale thighs, and how she fought and wept and kissed.'

'*What* are you saying,' said Tom.

'He's implying that he's had her,' said Brian. 'Untrue, of course. George lives in a fantasy world. Typical.'

'Cheers, Alex,' said George.

'Cheers, darling,' said Alex.

'Cheers, Gabriel, cheers, sweet Gabriel.' George raised his glass.

'Cheers –' said Gabriel, flushing with startled pleasure and smiling and lifting her glass.

It was suddenly evident that Ruby was in the room. She must have followed George in and had sat down, a big brown spectator, on a chair against the wall.

'Look who's here,' said Alex, but she did not tell Ruby to leave.

'I suggest George goes now,' said Brian. 'Go on, get out, go.'

'It's my house,' said Alex. 'If you don't like it, you go.'

'All right, let's play it differently,' said Brian. 'I think we've got a right to ask George some questions.'

They had all been standing, with the exception of Ruby, and of Adam who was still sitting on the floor. George now sat down near the fireplace. His face had the plump exalted tender shining look which Tom had seen on it on Thursday evening and which had made him wonder if his brother were mad.

'Oh, what's the use of asking George questions,' said Tom. 'He'll just tell lies and I don't blame him!'

'You don't *blame* him?' said Brian, turning to Tom. Brian was by now clearly very angry, but controlled.

'Well, I do, but oh what the *hell*, what a *muddle*, you can't mend it or clear it by asking a few questions.'

'I don't quite know what you mean –'

'Let's question Tom,' said George. 'Ask him where he was on Thursday night.'

'Well, where were you?' said Brian.

George said, 'I suppose you all know that Rozanov offered the little girl to Tom. Did you know that, Gabriel?'

'No,' said Gabriel, again red.

'Didn't you read about it in the newspaper?'

'Yes, but it all sounded like nonsense, I didn't understand it, I didn't even try to –'

'You ought to try to understand things,' said George, smiling.

Gabriel said timidly, 'Yes.'

'Rozanov was very angry with Tom, he wrote me a letter about it.'

'Rozanov wrote to you about *me*?' said Tom.

'Yes, he thought you had behaved very badly. You see, that was what that riotous party was all about, which people blamed me for. Tom, with his usual discretion and good manners, decided to serenade the lady with his drunken friends.'

'That's not so –' said Tom.

'Isn't it?' said Brian. 'Where *were* you on Thursday night?'

'With Diane Sedleigh.'

'There you are,' said George.

'But not like *that*.'

'You seemed to be on very intimate terms when I arrived,' said George. 'You were reeking of face powder.'

Gabriel said, 'Oh –'

'Nothing happened between me and Mrs Sedleigh,' said Tom. '*You know that*. You're confusing everything, because you want to cover up your own beastly crimes.'

'I don't know what you did with Rozanov's little girl,' said George, 'but it certainly looks as if you behaved like a cad and she behaved like a –'

'Stop,' said Tom.

'You can't now claim to be a defender of her honour. Isn't it strange? It seems that Tom can do anything and still be Sir Galahad, and any ordinary mistake of mine is labelled a crime. You heard him just now talking about my crimes.'

'I don't mean anything grand, just malicious lies!'

'George brings disgrace on the family –' said Brian, finding himself incoherent and made angrier thereby.

'I agree with George,' said Alex.

'So do I,' said Gabriel, 'I feel George has come back to us, ever since he rescued Zed, he is saved, he's back, we lost him, it was our fault, we all exaggerate what he does, everyone exaggerates, we pounce on every little thing and call him wicked.'

'Isn't it wicked to ...' Brian began.

'It's like a conspiracy,' said Gabriel, unconsciously waving her hand about.

'Isn't it wicked to try to kill one's wife? Wouldn't you think I was wicked if I tried to kill you?'

'But he didn't. It was an accident.'

'Then why hasn't Stella come back? Think *that* one out. Stella's afraid. That brave strong woman is afraid.'

'I don't know why Stella hasn't come back and neither do you. I don't see why Stella should never be blamed.'

'I know why you're against Stella –'

'Oh stop, *stop!*' said Tom, holding his head.

Alex, her eyes shining, murmured, 'Go on.'

'It was an accident,' said Gabriel, 'and so was the Roman glass.'

'Oh hang the Roman glass,' said Brian.

Gabriel went on, 'George hasn't really done anything bad at all, it's we who are living in a fantasy world when we blame him so. Perhaps he just drinks a bit, that's all. But we drink, look at us now. He's really quite an ordinary person.'

'I don't think *that's* quite true,' said Alex.

'I don't mean it in a nasty way,' said Gabriel.

'I'm sure you don't,' said Brian. 'There you were, down at the seaside, exposing your breasts to him.'

'*What?*'

'You were pretending to look after Zed and you undid your blouse to let George see your breasts.'

'I *didn't*.'

During the argument Adam had crawled away from the centre

483

of the room and was sitting in a corner with Zed curled up beside him. Zed, not unaware of hearing his name mentioned at intervals, suddenly uncurled himself and trotted across the carpet straight to George. George promptly picked him up and set him on his knee. Adam then jumped up and followed Zed, posting himself on the floor near George's feet. George laughed.

'There!' said Alex.

'You – you bewitch – everyone –' said Brian, hardly able to speak.

'I don't think George wants to be an ordinary person,' said Tom.

Gabriel said, 'I didn't mean it like – and I didn't – do that – what Brian said –'

'George,' said Brian, 'let me ask you straight, and under God or whatever you believe in, whether you did or did not try to kill Stella that night. Now tell the truth for once, if you dare to, if you have any guts, if you're a man and not just a mean vicious little rat.'

There was a moment's silence. George suddenly lost his look of bland assurance, the 'shining' look which so much puzzled Tom. He said, 'I'm ... not sure ... I can't remember ...'

'Well, you'd bloody better remember, hadn't you,' said Brian. 'It is important, you know. At least it's important to me to know whether or not I have a murderer for a brother!'

'He hasn't killed anybody,' said Alex to Brian, 'he hasn't tried to kill anybody, and he wouldn't and couldn't! Just stop attacking him, will you! Can't you be charitable for once? You think *you're* the righteous one, you seem to me just a pharisee, you can't even be decently polite to your wife in public.'

Gabriel started to cry.

'Oh go away all of you!' said Alex. 'Not you,' she said to George.

George put Zed down on the floor. Adam rolled away and got up. Before she became too upset to do so, Gabriel had been observing her son and trying to decide to tell him to go out into the garden. He might be damaged by hearing the grown-ups fight so, but equally perhaps by a peremptory banishment. Adam had at first seemed bright-eyed, rather amused, suddenly resembling his grandmother. Now however, near to tears, he picked up Zed and ran to Gabriel.

Gabriel made for the door. Brian followed saying, 'Oh hang it all!' Tom looked at George.

George was sitting with his hands squarely on his knees, with vague unfocused eyes, his lips parted, frowning with puzzlement.

Alex said, 'Go, Tom, go, dear, I'm not angry with you.'

Tom went out, closing the door. He went down the stairs. The front door stood open where the Brian McCaffreys, in their disordered retreat, had failed to shut it. Tom turned toward the back door. He emerged into the garden and ran across the grass to the Slipper House. Like Hattie, he rang the bell, tried the doors, peered through the windows. No one.

It was beginning to rain. Tom ran on along the slippery mossy path under the trees and out of the back gate. He closed the back gate. He stood in the street with the rain quietly soaking his long hair and running down his face like tears, and he held his head firmly between his two hands, trying to think.

As the door closed after Tom, Alex said to Ruby, who was still sitting on the chair near the door:

'How dare you sit in my presence and how dare you come into the drawing-room and listen to our family talk! Go away at once, please.'

As Ruby rose, George said, 'Ruby love, be a dear and bring us some sandwiches, would you? You know the ones I like, tomato and cucumber, and cress and cream cheese.'

Ruby vanished.

'I'm frightened of her,' said Alex. 'She's become different, as if there were an evil spirit in her. She's even become *larger*, like a sort of big robot.'

'She's practically one of the family,' said George, 'and she's old now. She knows all about us. It's her one interest in life.'

'Yes, and she tells everybody! She gossips spitefully about us at the Institute. I'm sure she told someone about your looking at that girl through the glasses. She saw from the garden. She's *everywhere*.'

'Oh never mind,' said George. 'It doesn't matter.' He sneezed.

'You've got a cold.'

'Yes, I got it from Tom.'

'I think that Gabriel is the silliest wettest human-being I've ever met. And she's in love with you.'

'Yes. That doesn't matter either.'

'Sit down,' said Alex. 'Why did you come now?'

'Because of Bill the Lizard.'

'I thought so.'

She sat down near to George and looked at him quietly. It was a long time since she had done that. George looked older and almost strange to her in a way she could not measure. Perhaps some general idea which she had had of his face was now suddenly seen to be out of date. His hair had grown a little longer than usual (he had not been to the barber) and showed daubs of grey at the temples. There were new discoloured wrinkles round his eyes. He was again looking worried. The charming boyish look was in abeyance. Now the older face appeared, George as he would be when he was sixty or seventy, less plump, more gaunt, more lined. The lines were already faintly sketched on the brow which had been smooth so long. Alex looked, feeling the pain of her love for him. She thought, I have somehow relied on George being invulnerable, untouchable, youthful, somehow like myself, a guarantor of myself. But now he looks just like an ordinary worried muddled mediocre shop-soiled man. She saw his shabby suit, his dirty shirt, his need of a shave.

Meanwhile George was looking at Alex and thinking, how old and stiff and sort of ailing she has become, and she stoops and her skin has become brown and loose and dry, dirty-looking, and her mouth droops into those long gloomy furrows and her eyelids are stained and puffy, and why must she still paint them so. She looks pathetic and touching, and I've never seen her look like that before.

George smiled and wrinkled up his short nose rather like Zed and showed his short square wide-apart teeth and looked young again.

'Nice to see you, Alex.'

'Nice to see you, George.'

'Bill was somebody. I might have talked to Bill.'

'I wish you had.'

'It doesn't matter, but it's sad. His death touched old things, things before it all began.'

'What is "it"?' she asked, but he did not answer that.

'You know, I feel changed. Perhaps Gabriel was right. What did she say? "Saved", "Come back."'

'Changed? How?'

Ruby came in with the sandwiches then withdrew.

'I'm peckish. You have some?'

'No, thanks,' said Alex.

George began to eat the sandwiches voraciously. He had not eaten since noon on the previous day. He said,

'We're going to Spain.'

486

'We?'

'Me and Diane Sedleigh. We're going to live in Spain on my pension.'

'Where in Spain?' said Alex, watching him intently with her narrow-eyed cat-look.

'I don't know yet. Somewhere cheap. We'll have to look at the map, get advice. I've got some money saved, and quite a decent pension. It'll go further in Spain. We'll live near the sea and eat cheaply, olives and fruit and fish. It's suddenly occurred to me that I might be able to be happy at last, it's not too late, it's not impossible, have what I want. We'll be different people. We'll forget this place ever existed.'

'Can I come too?' said Alex.

George stopped munching. 'Would you like to?'

'Yes, very much. I wouldn't be in your way. I'd live somewhere not terribly far off and invite you to lunch. We could go swimming together sometimes.'

'And Diane?'

'I'd like Diane, why not.'

'Even if she wants to be Diane McCaffrey? She does, you know.'

'Yes. I feel I'm changing too. Some revolution is accomplished.'

'Perhaps it's something to do with William, some bit of his soul that's flown into us. Except that it's been coming ... I now see ... for a long time ...'

'Could I come? I've got plenty of money. We could build two houses. I'd pay for a car.'

'Alex,' said George, 'we're inspired, we've become gods!'

And he looked at her with his radiant bland mad face, in which, at that moment, Alex saw the reflection of her own. They stared at each other. George said, 'I must go.'

'I'll think of you with Diane, looking at that map.'

George murmured, 'Don't worry. There's a place beyond.'

'Beyond Spain?'

'No – just beyond – beyond. It's not like I thought, with a great heave of the will, or by great excessive things, at all – when all is permitted one doesn't want to, you see – it's so easy, just a matter of relaxing – and simply letting go – of all that –'

'All what?'

'Never mind. Dear, dear Alex. Kiss me as if we were ... anybody ... nobody ... as of course ... we are ...'

They both rose, and kissed. Lips only touching, they hung

together as if suspended in space. They remained so for a long moment.

'Goodbye, Alex. Soon, soon, you know. I'll take the rest of the sandwiches.'

'Where are you going?'

'To the cinema.'

However George did not go to the cinema. It was raining when he left Belmont, and he decided to go home to Druidsdale rather than walk to the Odeon in the High Street, which was farther away. George hated rain, he hated getting his hair wet, his feet wet, his clothes wet. He had no umbrella. He felt vaguely unwell and feverish. And he wanted to eat the rest of the sandwiches in peace. He wanted an *interval* in his existence, his life which had for some time been such intensely hard work. He felt, for the first time for months, that he might be able to *rest*, to do something which had seemed forever impossible, to lie down on his back and close his eyes and feel quiet and drowsy and unafraid and at peace. At the same time he felt excited and confused and odd. Something had snapped, had given way, and that was (was it not?) better. He did not want to examine the new state at all closely, he felt he would never want to examine anything closely again. He wanted to spend the rest of his life in *peace*, with people who did not examine things closely.

He reached Druidsdale and got the key into the lock. His hand trembled. He opened the door and entered the darkish hall. He stopped. There was something wrong. There was something there. Something *terrible*. He peered. Stella was sitting on the stairs.

'Hello, George.'

'Oh *God*.' George sat down on one of the chairs in the hall.

'I'm sorry to come suddenly.'

'Why have you come at all? Why now, oh Christ, why *now*?'

'Well, it had to be sometime. I'm sorry it wasn't sooner.'

'You cold – cold – beast.'

'I can't talk otherwise. You know how I talk. I can only say what's the case. I feel very upset, very emotional, not cold.'

'Other people have emotions. You say it's the case that you feel emotional.'

'I'm sorry I went away. I can't explain my conduct. Though there

488

is an explanation. I just mean it would take some time, if you ever wanted to hear. Nothing dramatic, nothing interesting.'

'Where have you been?'

'With N, with Mrs Blackett.'

'N, that impotent voyeur, I thought so.'

'Why?'

'I saw his sly old face in the street, he's always after me.'

'Don't be angry about that.'

'Oh I'm not. Were you afraid to come back?'

'Yes, I suppose so –'

'Afraid I'd kill you?'

'No – just afraid of you – you're like a dog that bites – one is afraid. I don't like unpredictable things.'

'Why have you come back then?'

'I had to decide whether I wanted to go on being married to you. That was another reason why I didn't come back. I felt it wouldn't be fair to you.'

'What wouldn't be fair?'

'To come back and leave again.'

'And you decided –?'

'I decided I did want to go on being married to you.'

'Why?'

'You know why. Because I love you. Because I think – this between us is – absolute.'

'Absolute, what a word. You always were an absolutist. You talk of love, you who have no tenderness, no gentleness, no forgiveness.'

'I have these things, but you just kill the expression of them, the way I would express them, you reject all my language, all my –'

'Always my fault.'

'No.'

'You have never forgiven me anything. You remember every fault. You might as well be the recording angel. You are a sort of angel, a frightful one.'

'Let's not talk about forgiving, I think it's a weak idea, usually false –'

'You're like Cordelia, the most overrated heroine in literature.'

'The question is, do you want to go on being married to me?'

'What a charmingly blunt question. No.'

'Are you sure?'

George was silent for a moment. Then he said, 'That night – when the car went into the canal – can you remember it clearly?'

489

'Yes.'

'What happened exactly?'

'What do you mean?'

'Was it an accident, or did I deliberately make it happen?'

'You mean you don't remember?'

'No.'

Stella paused. 'It was an accident.'

'It was an accident?'

'Yes, of course.' She added, 'You like to think of yourself as a fierce violent person, but you're harmless really. Just a bad-tempered dog.'

'And you claim to love this animal.'

'Yes, I do.'

'You humiliate me in order to love me. That's not love. It's like torturing your pet. The sort of thing that interests N.'

They sat silently in the darkish hallway, Stella on the stairs, George sitting near the door on a chair against the wall, not facing Stella but facing an old ornate Victorian hallstand which they had bought in an auction sale when they were engaged.

Stella said, 'See, I brought the netsuke back.'

George saw on the hallstand the little array of pale ivory figures. He said, 'Yes, I went looking for them one day.'

'I thought you would.'

'Isn't it rather sentimental of you to bring them back? The sort of thing a real woman might do. Am I supposed to be touched and softened?'

Stella was silent. She began to fumble in her handbag.

George said, 'Oh you aren't *crying* are you? Can you cry now? Congratulations. You never used to.' He added, 'I've got a cold.'

'Want an aspirin?'

'No. To answer your earlier question, yes, I am sure I don't want to go on being married to you.'

'Why?'

'Because I'm going to go and live in Spain with Diane Sedleigh.'

Stella was silent again. She blew her nose. She said, 'All right.'

'What. No scene?'

'You know me.'

'Yes I do. Diane is a woman. I like women. I get on with her. She makes me feel happy and calm. Which you have *never done*.'

'I'm sorry.'

'I admired you. That was the trouble. A rotten basis for marriage.'

'I daresay.'

'Maybe you shouldn't have gone away, I mean if you really wanted it to go on. I had time to see the point.'

'I wanted you to have time. And I needed a holiday from you too.'

'Well, the holiday can continue. What will you do with it?'

'I don't know. I'll travel. I'll go to Tokyo to see my father, go to California to see Rozanov.'

'You'll – *what*?'

'Well, I might. I'd like to see him. I only kept away because of you. Or is he still here?'

George leapt to his feet. '*You'll talk to him about me ...*'

'It might be difficult to avoid mentioning your name, but I won't discuss you. You know how fastidious I am in such matters.'

'Fastidious, that's one of your words. How I loathe your vocabulary! It's power, power, contempt, contempt, everything about you. Oh God, why did you have to come back *now*, you *devil*, just when I was feeling better, you don't know what you've done, you've spoilt everything, you've destroyed it all, you did it on purpose, you heard I was with Diane at the funeral. Didn't you, didn't you?'

'Yes. But that's not the reason.'

'It is – it's common mean spite and jealousy – you can lie too, you foul vixen – I could kill you for spoiling things so – you want to destroy me – and you killed Rufus, you killed Rufus, you killed Rufus ...'

Father Bernard was sitting in his study in the St Paul's Clergy House meditating to the sound of Scott Joplin's *Sugar Cane*. He sat as usual, four-square, relaxed, his hands on his knees. He used to kneel once, but found the posture uncomfortable and fraught with irrelevant emotion. The unlined curtains put up by his predecessor were drawn and displayed, penetrated by the lurid rainy light of Saturday evening, a design of huge chrysanthemums. The room was filled with a subdued yellowish glow. In a corner of the room a dim electric lamp illumined a calm radiant icon of the baptism of Jesus. (Father Bernard did not care for the more tormented images.) Opposite to him, Father Bernard's Gandhara Buddha (a reproduction) meditated with drooped eyelids and delicate slightly pursed lips. His exquisitely beautiful austere face combined the calm of the East with a thoughtful Hellenic sadness. Father

Bernard loved him because he was and was not a judge. He paid no attention to the priest and did not require to be addressed as 'thou'. But Father Bernard, who did not always meditate with lowered eyelids, paid a great deal of attention to him.

Some teachers of meditation exhort us to empty our minds. Others permit the quiet circling of random thoughts, increasingly to be set at a distance and sensed as unreal. Father Bernard followed both rules, but more usually the latter which was easier because more ambiguous. He let his worldly thoughts accompany him sometimes to the extent that a detached observer of them (God, for instance) might have found little difference between the priest's holy reverie and the unregenerate day-dreaming of one of his flock.

On this Saturday evening Father Bernard's thoughts, somewhat tidied up for purposes of communication, might be rendered as follows. John Robert, what a monster, how attractive that frightful face is, I want so much to see him again, I'm quite in love with him, dear me. If only my life could change completely, be utterly renewed and changed. Lord, let me amend my life. If I could only reach a place beyond personal vanity, sometimes it seems so close, an inch away. Miss Dunbury said she saw Christ waiting on the other side, could she be right? Lord have mercy upon me, Christ have mercy upon me, Lord have mercy upon me. How moving simple faith is, Lord let me have a simple faith if it be thy will. *Quaerens me sedisti lassus.* I ought to go and see Hattie, I must see her before I see Rozanov, I was supposed to see her last Saturday, oh my God, last Saturday. Hattie, that milky-white flesh, like angel cake, no. What a nasty anonymous letter I had this morning about kissing prostitutes in church, there are spies everywhere. And on that bench with Bobbie, oh dear me. I like that bit in the music, it's such melancholy music, mechanical and yet jaunty, like life. Tom McCaffrey, his tumbling hair. *Dans l'onde toi devenue ta jubilation nue.* Yes, I spend my life wanting the impossible. But I never reach out my hand for what I want. Isn't that religion, not reaching out? O Lord Buddha, have mercy upon me, a sinner. George McCaffrey, may he be protected from evil and may he do no harm to anyone. Will he come to me? *Non ragioniam di lor, ma guarda e passa.* What a dreadful thing to say, how cruel Dante was and yet he was granted a vision of paradise. Pretty boring place, actually. But oh the desire for God, the desire, the desire. *Agnus dei, qui tollis peccata mundi, miserere nobis.* If I had walked across the bridge when George was miming the accident he would have killed me, exciting, what non-

492

sense. Dear little Diane squatting down behind the elder tree. I'll have to go one day, the bishop's letter will come, Mount Athos, I'll live in retreat at last. John Robert said I was false, a false priest, broken my vows. I suppose so. Not that anybody cares what a priest believes these days, but I do. Have to come to it at last. At last. I wonder if Diane would come with me to Greece, she wouldn't mind what I did, what a crazy idea. Bobbie's coming tonight, I hope he's got rid of that cold, thank God I don't seem to have caught it, a pity he's so unattractive. Have a nice talk, wine, oh blast I forgot to buy that cheap Valpolicella. I shall lie in the earth. Every year I pass the anniversary of my death. Where will I lie? In Greece? In America? Perhaps I shall follow Rozanov, I suppose he'll go back there. An impossible man. How sad the yellow light is in this room, and a fly on the window. How beautiful he is, the Lord Buddha, so austere, so stern, so sad. George and Rozanov. Oh God, help them, help us all, help the planet. The lonely circling planet moving into night. God rest all souls. I am tense, I must relax, forgive. Not think about Rozanov, Tom, Mount Athos. Oh the desire. Oh God, if only I could be at peace. Lord, I prostrate myself, I ask for forgiveness, for guidance, for faith. My Lord and my God. Tomorrow's Sunday, damn.

The front door bell rang. The priest sighed. He rose and turned off Scott Joplin. He bowed reverently and kissed the stern Buddha on the brow and the lips. Then with slow majestic tread, smoothing his hair, he went to the door. George McCaffrey was outside.

'Come in,' said Father Bernard. And after a glance at George he thought, this is it.

George followed the priest into the study. Father Bernard did not draw back the curtains. He switched on a lamp.

'Sit down, George. There, on that sofa.'

George sat down, then got up again and walked to the bookcase, facing it but not looking at the books. There was something dreadful in the position, as if he were expecting to be shot in the back. Then he turned and leaned against the bookcase, facing the priest who was also standing. Love for George flooded Father Bernard's heart.

'What is it, my son?'

George was silent for a while, looking rather wildly about the room as if searching for something. Then he said, 'Stella's come back.'

'Oh – good.'

'Not good. I don't want her. I *detest* her.'

'Perhaps that means you love her.'

'I suppose you have to say something stupid like that.'

'I'm glad you've come, George. I thought you'd come, at last.'

'Did you? I didn't. Anyway it doesn't mean anything, not what you think.'

'Would you like a drink?'

'No. Is Rozanov still here?'

'So far as I know. I didn't know he was going. I haven't seen him lately.'

'He'll corrupt others as he corrupted me. Oh God, I'm so unhappy. Stella was the last straw.'

'Talk to me, my dear.'

'You love talks, I know, you grow fat on people's troubles, you grow fat and sleek and purr.'

'We are frail human creatures, all our good is mixed with evil. It is good none the less. If we sincerely pray to be made pure in heart there is a sense in which we do not pray in vain. I wish you well, oh so well. You must forgive me.'

'Oh damn you. Listen.'

'Yes.'

'I want to ask you a question.'

'Yes. Like "does God exist?" '

'No, not like that.'

' "Is there life after death?" "Ought I to stay with Stella?" "Ought I to stop seeing Diane?" '

'Don't play the fool, stop making jokes.'

'I'm not making jokes, I'm expressing something I feel for you, I feel concern for you, love for you, I'm very glad you're here.'

'I want to ask you – a question.'

'Yes, yes.'

'That night ... when the car fell into the canal ... with Stella in it ... you were there ... weren't you?'

The priest hesitated. 'Yes.'

'That's why you felt sure I'd come to you?'

'That was one reason. For any spiritual event there are always several reasons of different kinds.'

'Hang that. You were there, you were crossing the iron bridge, I saw you.'

'Yes.'

494

'Now tell me what you saw.'

'How do you mean?'

'What you *saw*, what *happened*.'

'It was dark – I saw the car swerve and fall into the water.'

'No, you didn't see that, you liar – I, what was I doing? The car stopped on the brink and I got out of it. Did you see that, in the name of Christ? And did you see me try to push it in?'

'No,' said the priest, though he had had time to wonder, *what is the right answer*?

'I'm trying to *remember*,' said George, '*help* me.'

He came forward and took hold of Father Bernard's arms at the elbow, glaring into his face with glittering eyes.

'I ask you, I beg you, to tell me the truth, I must know *exactly* what happened, it's *important*. I drove the car – the car came up to the brink and stopped and I got out – or did it stop – I got out – then what happened? I can't *see* it – did I go behind the car and try to push it? Or did I imagine this? For Christ sake, tell me, I beg you for the truth, I *beg* you.'

Father Bernard involuntarily stepped back pulling away from the clutching hands. He said, 'You jumped out as the car went over the edge. Of course you didn't try to push it. It was an accident.'

'Before God, are you sure?'

'Yes.'

George showed no relief. A look of anguish distorted his face. He murmured something which sounded like 'the pity of it', then, 'I have done something terrible.'

Father Bernard said again, 'Please sit down,' only George would not sit, but went to the bookcase and turned his back in the sad penitential posture, as Father Bernard with inexplicable distress saw it. He leaned against the books, rolling his forehead to and fro against them.

'George, you haven't hurt Stella, have you?'

George, half turning his head, said in a dull voice, 'Stella? No.' He turned round and put his hand in his pocket and brought out something, two small white fragments which he held in the palm of his hand. He said, 'I broke it, I got angry, but it can be mended. See, the little Japanese thing, ivory, a man holding a fish, a fisherman with his basket, see underneath his foot and the pattern of his dress folded – his head is broken off, but it can be mended. It's all to do, it's to do. Oh, if you only knew how unhappy I am, how

495

my heart hurts in my breast. It's all so black. Oh what a burden it is –'

Father Bernard had pictured a scene where George 'came to him' at last, but it had not been like this. He was upset, frightened, confused by George's state of mind which he could not understand but about which he felt he ought instantly to be able to do something. He wished George would sit down and spill out some fairly coherent story and require to be talked to, instead of flinging himself about the room. He wanted to dominate George, to hold him and soothe him, but could not see how to do it. He asked, 'Where is Stella now?'

'I don't know. At Druidsdale, I suppose. I've left there. I'm staying with Diane. We're going to live in Spain.'

'You and Diane?'

'Yes. But it's so terrible, so black, like a hideous dream, and I have to do it all again.'

'Do what? What terrible thing have you done?'

'Nothing, nothing. I saw my double carrying a hammer. How can another person steal one's consciousness, how is it possible? Can good and evil change places? Well, well, I must go now.'

'You are not to go, sit here.' Father Bernard planted a firm palm on George's chest and pushed him abruptly down on to the sofa. As soon as he touched George he felt an inrush of warm power. He knelt on the sofa, pressing his hands on to George's shoulder to prevent him from rising. George struggled but the priest was stronger.

'Stay. That's right. Relax your body. Don't look so wretched. You're not going to cry, are you? I don't believe you've ever done anything terrible or that you're ever going to. The only person you hurt is yourself. Your mind is boiling over with anger and remorse and grief and black pain. Let it all go from you. Turn to God. Never mind what it means. Let the miracle of forgiveness and peace take place in your soul. Forgive yourself and forgive those whom you imagine to be your enemies. I want you to say the Lord's Prayer with me.'

'The Lord's Prayer?' said George and he seemed surprised and almost interested. 'Now?'

'Yes. You remember it, don't you? Our Father –'

George said, speaking quickly and looking up at the priest who, with one knee on the sofa, was still gripping him by the shoulder, 'Our Father, who art in heaven, hallowed be thy name, thy

496

Kingdom come, thy will be done on earth as it is in heaven.' Then he stopped. He said, 'My God, you are a charlatan.'

'Give us this day our daily bread.'

'And forgive us our trespasses, as we forgive them that trespass against us. And lead us not into temptation, but deliver us from evil, For thine is the Kingdom, the power and the glory, for ever and ever. Amen.'

Father Bernard stopped holding George and sat down beside him, and they sat together in a slightly dazed silence, aware of an event which had taken place in the room.

George shuddered and got up. 'You've got the old magic in working order.'

Father Bernard rose too. 'George, don't go away, *please*, sit down again and be quiet with me for a little while. You needn't talk. Let me get you some coffee, whisky, brandy, something to eat. Let the old magic work in you, let it travail in you, let it travel with you, turn towards it. Repeat the old charms. Christ Jesus came into the world to save sinners.'

'Turn to it! Even if it's all false?'

'It can't be. It will do good to you. It has already done good to you today. If you utter sacred words with a sincere and humble and passionate desire for salvation they cannot fail. Let grace flood your heart. Remember that nothing can separate us from the love of Christ.'

George stared at the priest for a moment or two as if he were thinking over what had been said. Then he said, 'Oh,' and turned suddenly and went from the room. The priest ran after him. The front door banged.

Father Bernard came back into his sitting-room and stood still for a while. It was getting dark outside and he turned on another lamp. Then he telephoned the Druidsdale number and heard Stella's calm voice saying that yes, George had been there and was now gone, and yes of course she was all right.

He sat for a while thinking about George and feeling softened and exalted. He wondered to himself, did I give George the right answer? What did he *want*? He took up his Prayer Book, and remembered Miss Dunbury holding the torch so that she could read his lips during the power cut. He knelt down and read aloud the prayer for those troubled in conscience. 'Oh Blessed Lord, the Father of mercies and the God of all comforts, we beseech thee look down in pity and compassion upon this thy afflicted servant. Give him a right understanding of himself and of thy threats and promises, that he may neither cast away his confidence in thee, nor place it anywhere but in thee. Give him strength against all his temptations, and heal all his distempers. Break not the bruised reed, nor quench the smoking flax. Shut not up thy tender mercies in displeasure, but make him to hear of joy and gladness, that the bones which thou hast broken may rejoice.'

After his flight from Belmont, Tom walked slowly back to Travancore Avenue. He had to keep having to stop and gasp a little and hold his chest. He felt as if something alien and too big for him had been encased in his body and were clumsily and painfully trying to get out, as if his whole body wanted to vomit. He felt that he ought to do something difficult and awful and perhaps fatal, but he tried not to think about this. He absorbed himself in his physical feelings and the strange new pain.

When he reached Travancore Avenue he went upstairs and lay on his bed, but found this position tormenting. He sat on his bed, he sat on a chair. He said out loud in a dull echoing voice to which he listened with surprise, 'It was here and now it's gone, I've lost it, it's gone away, I shall mourn for it and that's all there'll be, that's all there'll ever be.'

At last he did attempt to think. Today, this very afternoon, Hattie had been still in Ennistone. What did that mean? Did it mean anything that made any real difference to him, or did it only matter because it made him so terribly sick? Had he not *finished* with it all? It had never really been anything anyway. It was totally artificial, a maniac's fantasy. He had rejected her, she had rejected him. Even this was too portentous. They had, to satisfy the old fool, politely said hello and good-bye, they had passed with a casual wave. It had been all over before John Robert's anger. He must keep that clear in his head, he must keep John Robert out of it. Though how could that make sense, since it was all his idea and only his idea? Tom's sense of time was all mixed up, he could not remember what had happened on what day, and what had happened after which. He could not recall why he had felt it so necessary to go to the Slipper House on the day of the 'riot'. He must have wanted to go to see Hattie again. And then she was gone, she and John Robert had returned to America, and he was rid of the whole nightmare, he was set free. Had he felt relieved? That was the end of the story and he could rest at last. But what was he resting from, and into what awful renewed sense of possibility and demand and power was he now awakening? *Now* he was free? Was it that he felt that he still might, if he would, have it, gain it, win it, after all? But what was it, of which he had been speaking just now, this thing which evidently he desired so? Was it to do with John Robert, John Robert's esteem or approval or even affection? Or was it his own esteem, some image of himself as a hero, which was missing? Well, it was missing, but he could have noticed that loss and regarded it as temporary. What was it about Alex's story of Hattie running down the garden and trying to get into the Slipper House which had driven him so absolutely *mad*? It was not even Hattie really that he was thinking about now: that image of the running girl seemed to have usurped her real being in his bewitched mind.

The shock was partly to do with time. He had settled into thinking they were gone, into a state of protected impossibility. He felt now that he had even recovered a little as a result of William's funeral and the phenomenon at the Baths. These had been events, barriers between him and that terrible pair. There had been, it now seemed to him, a little touch of elegiac sadness in the pain he had felt as he watched the *jet d'eau*, a curative energy in his thought of Hattie as removed from him absolutely, gone into the invisible world. Even remorse was a challenge to be met. Now he had been suddenly jolted back into a previous era with all his tasks undone, with it all to do again. But what were these tasks and this hideous freedom and this *it* with which some new sense of possibility tormented him so? The thought that she was still in Ennistone was somehow unbearable. Oh God, if only she were far away! But then perhaps she was, she could have been here in the morning and be gone now. And if so he would be back where he was, and wasn't that where he wanted to be? All he had to do was to allow the time to pass. He looked at his watch. It was nine-thirty.

Tom now lay down again on the bed and tried to let his thoughts wander. He must not concentrate. If he did ... he might be led ... to decide something ... John Robert had appointed Tom to be Hattie's protector, her knight. But what was he supposed to protect Hattie from? Tom was far from guessing that the answer was, from John Robert himself. Yet intuitively he wandered round the idea at a distance. He thought, he knows he can't look after her himself, it's like living with a monster, a big rough animal, she might come to harm accidentally. Oh, let her not come to harm. But not to think like that, remember William dead and the water flying up and the way it had burnt his hand, he could still feel the burn. What Tom was all the time trying to keep out of his mind by the wandering of his thoughts was the terrible idea that there was nothing in the world to stop him going round to Hare Lane now and finding out whether Hattie was still in Ennistone. But, no, he thought, there is nothing I can do for them or with them now. I must simply stay quiet until it is all too late, and oh let that be soon. But how can I know, it may already be too late, they may already have gone, and I am suffering simply from not knowing. He thought, I could go round to the Ennistone Rooms and ask someone, they might know, John Robert had a room there, so someone said ... And as he was thinking this he fell asleep.

'Tom, Tom, wake up, Tom dear, wake up.'

Tom rolled over and sat up. A bright light was on in the room and a woman was standing beside the bed. Tom stared at her, not recognizing her. Then he knew her. It was Judy Osmore.

'Greg, come here, here's Tom, he was fast asleep. Tom, we've come back, did you get our letter?'

'No,' said Tom. He put his feet down and stood up, felt giddy and sat down again on the edge of the bed.

'Well, we only sent it last – I forget – we did everything in such a hurry – we've had the most wonderful time.'

Gregory Osmore came in. He was looking tired and not best pleased to find Tom there.

'Hello, Tom, still here?'

'Of course he's still here!' said Judy.

'Hello, Ju, hello Greg, great to see you,' said Tom. 'Have you just got back?'

'Yes, we feel terribly funny, don't we, Greg, jet lag you know, we flew all the way from Dallas, we saw the place where Kennedy was shot, we flew non-stop and we've been drinking all the way, I just can't think what time it is here, what time is it?'

Tom looked at his watch. 'Ten-thirty.'

'My watch says – oh I started changing it about, it's crazy now. Whatever have you done to your eye?'

'I suppose there's something to eat in the house?' said Greg.

'I don't think so,' said Tom. 'I don't remember.' He suddenly realized that he was very hungry.

'Didn't I tell you?' said Greg to Judy.

'We can go out to the Running Dog.'

'It'll be shut.'

'Not the restaurant. Anyway let's have a drink, I bet there's some, where there's a McCaffrey there's drink.'

'There's drink,' said Tom.

'Come on downstairs, I feel so over-excited, I must have something.'

They went down to the sitting-room and Greg found whisky and glasses while Judy pranced restlessly about, touching things, touching Tom, laughing.

'Oh it's so marvellous, we've had such a time, we went to New Orleans, the South is *fantastic*, have we got southern accents, I quite feel I have.'

Tom saw on the sofa the plastic bag containing Judy's dress which he had evidently brought back from Belmont without noticing it. He said, 'Oh Ju, I'm so sorry, someone spilt wine on your dress, look, but Gabriel fixed it.'

'Who was wearing it?' said Greg.

'Oh well – a friend of mine – I hope you don't mind.'

'Let me see,' said Judy.

'Gabriel dyed it with tea.'

'With *tea*?'

'Was Gabriel wearing it?'

'No, Greg, a girl, a – I'm terribly sorry.'

'Well, it's not quite its old self,' said Judy, 'but it doesn't matter.'

'I'm so sorry.'

'Tom dear, don't worry, it doesn't matter, we're so glad to see you! Aren't we, darling?'

'What else have you done?' said Greg, looking round.

'Oh nothing else – the place is fine – if I'd known you were coming I'd have cleaned up, changed the sheets.'

'And how is Ennistone, and how is everybody? Isn't it funny to think that you've all been leading your quiet little lives here while we've been having the most *amazing* time, we must tell you all about it.'

'William Eastcote died,' said Tom.

'Oh – I'm sorry to hear that,' said Greg putting down his glass. 'I am sorry – such a dear good man – an old friend of my father's. When?'

'Oh recently,' said Tom. He felt he could not give details, count days, describe the funeral.

'How sad, a dear man,' said Judy.

'I'm going to telephone the Running Dog,' said Greg. He left the room.

'We haven't slept for *ages*, we couldn't sleep on the plane,' said Judy, 'we were travelling first class, there was a staircase and a bar, it was super, I enjoyed every second, even the silly film, and – oh Tom, it's so good to see your old familiar face, only you look so pale! See how brown we are! We got quite tired of the sun. Look.' She rolled up the sleeves of her dress and displayed a sunburnt arm.

'I must go,' said Tom.

'Of course not – you must stay tonight – mustn't he, Greg – Tom says he's going –'

'Shut up,' said Greg from the hall. 'A table for two if we come at once?'

'For three,' called Judy.

'I must go,' said Tom. 'I've got to catch the train to London, I was just packing up when you came.'

'Nonsense, you were fast asleep when we came. Anyway you've missed the ten forty-five.'

'We can have dinner if we go now,' said Greg.

'I *must* go,' said Tom.

'Certainly not, don't go!'

'Let him go if he wants to,' said Greg. 'God, I feel terrible.'

'I'll just pack my bag,' said Tom. He ran upstairs into his bedroom and closed the door. He saw the room, so bleak now, with his stuff strewn around, his suitcase which he had so cheerfully unpacked, the room with the view over the town which he had chosen when he had moved in such a long time ago, in a previous era, when he had been young and happy and innocent and free. He pushed his things roughly into the case and then he couldn't close it. He wanted to wail with vexation. He thrust the case, with its lid almost closed, into a corner, and began to tidy up the messy unmade bed. He began to pull the sheets off, then left them as they were. He went downstairs.

'Judy, do you mind if I leave my suitcase here? I've tidied my stuff away. I'll come and fetch it later – I'll ring up – I must just get off to London. Thank you so much for letting me have the house, I've loved it here.'

'Thank you for looking after it,' said Gregory, who felt he had been churlish.

'You must come and stay,' said Judy, 'any time you like –'

'I must run –'

'And we'll tell you *all* about it.'

When Tom got as far as the Institute he hurried along the front of the building making for the entrance to the Ennistone Rooms where there was always a porter on duty. However, when he got as far as the big main door, which was usually closed at this time, he saw that it was very slightly ajar and there was a light inside. He went to the door, pushed it cautiously, and peered in. A light was on at the far end of the Promenade. There was no one about.

It occurred to Tom that if he were able to get through to the Rooms by the back way through the Baptistry he could find out what he wanted to know (whether Rozanov was still in Ennistone) by looking to see if his name was on the board in the corridor. If he went by the Lodge he would have to speak to the porter, and while a porter who knew him would no doubt be chattily informative, a porter who did not might ask him who he was and what he wanted; and in his present guilty frightened state Tom felt that any unsympathetic questioning might simply elicit a flood of tears. Tom could also picture Rozanov suddenly appearing, seeing him in the brightly lit Lodge, and cornering him, glaring at him through the glass partition, his huge face distorted by rage and hate. Tom was in the state of restless obsessive nervous energy which drives people to meddle when they are too stupid to think clearly and too frightened to act decisively. What he needed was some sort of symbolic or magical act which concerned or touched his situation without running any danger of changing it. He wanted, as it were, to light a candle or recite a formula, he needed to busy himself about his state of mind.

The Promenade was empty, silent, half dark. The tables had been pushed to one side and the chairs stacked. The counter was covered with white cloths. Tom took a few careful noiseless steps, conscious of his shadow behind him. A flood of excited physical fear took possession of the lower part of his body, a painful vertiginous thrilling urgent pressuring feeling, like sexual desire. Then Tom thought, it's not like sexual desire, it *is* sexual desire. He moved quickly now, his mouth open, his eyes wide. He padded on his toes toward the source of light, which was the partly open door of the Baptistry, which housed the descent to the source, and led also to the long downstairs corridor of the Rooms. Tom paused, listening, then slipped through the door.

He had for a moment been aware of a warm steamy smell and a kind of vapour in the air. Now he stood still, amazed. The Baptistry was full of steam. The big bronze nail-studded doors under their stone pediment stood wide open. There was a low throbbing humming sound. Tom moved toward the opening. He touched one of the open doors and quickly withdrew his hand. The door was scalding hot. He stepped through the doorway, blinking, his eyelashes already wet with steam.

Before him and below him a great many extremely bright lights were on. He stood on a sort of railed-in shelf or gallery from which metal stairways led steeply down to left and right. A great mass of gleaming pipes, some very small, some enormous, filled the space below. The pipes were a light silver gilt in colour, a very very pale gold, and covered with tiny droplets of moisture which glittered here and there like diamonds. The design made by the pipes, obscured by areas of steam, seemed geometric yet made an unintelligible jumbled impression. They went on down and down for a long way without any floor or bottom being visible. Tom was aware of a warm breeze blowing and could see, looking down, that the steam which seemed to pervade the chasm was in irregular motion. There were evidently hidden fans, air currents which were intended to keep the space clear of steam, perhaps now unable to do so.

Tom did not like high places. He felt a genuine vertigo, like to, perhaps continuing, the sexual thrill he had experienced in the Promenade. He had never seen the 'workings' of the Institute since the source had never been open to the public in his lifetime. He had vaguely imagined a deep cleft or grotto and a steamy surging spring, not all these terrible glittering pipes. But, he thought, there must *be* a spring, there must *be* rocks, right down at the bottom water must be flowing out, rising up. If I go down a bit I shall see. Passing a red notice saying *Danger* he stepped on to the nearest stairway. It swayed slightly. Tom stopped, sick, then holding on to the smooth round banister, ran on down toward a steadier-looking platform below. The stairways, of which he could now see more, were made of some kind of light faintly flexible metal, presumably steel, but some kind of exquisite steel, Tom thought, since they were so elegant and spidery, almost insubstantial, with their narrow treads and eye-defeating lines of thin vertical rails supporting slanting banisters, more like suspended trapezes than stairs. They were silvery grey in colour, contrasting with the maze of pipes among which they hung, and were wet with steam and rather slippery. Tom's hair and face were already wet, his clothes damp, his shoes covered with beads of water. The temperature was high, and as he descended, higher. The humming throbbing sound was louder. The platform on which he stood swayed too. He went down another flight of spidery steps. He could still see nothing below except yet more pipes beyond the ones he had seen at first. He had noticed no sidewalls and could see none now as the steam was a little thicker. The whole contraption, with him upon it, seemed to be hanging in space.

Tom thought, the place is open because the engineers have been trying to control the spring, something has happened to it. All that boiling water came shooting up at Lud's Rill. It could run through the whole place, it could run through all the pipes, it could burst out everywhere in a flood. They must be very alarmed, otherwise they would have remembered to close the door. Then he thought, but where are they? There seems to be no one here but me. And they – are they dead, all those engineers, all lying down there at the bottom, drowned in scalding water or suffocated by steam, was there no one to give the alarm? Can steam suffocate? It surely could. Tom's mouth was open as he inhaled, almost eating the thick hot steamy air which was beginning to feel devoid of oxygen. He realized he was still wearing his mackintosh. He took it off and dropped it on the little landing where he stood, then took his jacket off too. The same frightful thrilling nervous anxiety was making him go on, go down rather than up. He thought, I must see the source, I must *see* it, it's my only chance, then I'll run up again. There hasn't been any awful accident, there's just no one here. He went down another longer flight of trembling stairs which seemed to be suspended on nothing in the middle of the space, passing through a thick cloud of steam.

A piece of concrete wall, wet and grey, appeared on his left. At least it seemed a wall, then turned out to be a vast pillar, beyond which the view was closed by two huge vertical pipes from whose bolted joints, level now with Tom's head, steam was escaping with a hissing noise. This hissing, joined with the humming noise which was louder and more vibrant, became suddenly urgent and mena-cing. The presence of so much compressed steam, so much sheer awful force, seemed to animate the sweating pipes as if they were all quivering with life. Might not the whole thing be about to *explode*, and was not this imminent danger the reason why the place was empty? Everyone had run away except him. The pipes seemed to pant, and in the steamy air to be shuddering and bending. Tom retreated a few steps. The air, almost too hot to breathe, was oppressing his lungs. Then as the long section of stairway swayed, he ran on down to a large substantial platform. He looked below him: more pipes overlaying each other, mixed now with monstrous horizontal tubes, another glimpse of wet concrete. The thrilling hum seemed to have entered his body, making him vibrate with an ecstatic urgent anguish.

Tom thought, why am I here? There must be a reason. I have got to do something, I have an aim, a task, I must go on down, I've come so far I can't give up now. Several stairways now led downward, less steeply. He took one at random, running down, leaping down it, sliding his hand along the warm highly polished rail. He thought, I must get to the end, I must find the source, I *must* get there, it's dangerous, yes, at any moment I may hear something terrible, some loud roar as of some huge thing breaking, it's all out of control. But I can get there first and get back, I've got to find *the place*, I've got to see *it*, the real source, there's rocks and water and earth down there and a cleft in the ground, somewhere down below, I must get there and ... and touch it ...

The steam was becoming thicker, the air hotter and harder to breathe, Tom was panting. He thought, in a minute I'll faint, I must keep my mind alert, I must keep my consciousness. He swung round at a landing, bounded down another few steps, and came violently up against a concrete wall with a door in it. Automatically he tried the door, which was locked, then ran up back to the landing. He could see another stairway, just visible in the steam, below him, but could not see its connection with where he was. He grasped the rail, put one leg over, raised the other leg, began to slip, then, unable to balance or keep a hold on the damp smooth metal, fell rather than jumped on to the lower level where he collapsed on to his knees. He limped down some more treads and jolted abruptly on to a level concrete floor.

Tom looked about him, ran forward, then back. He was on a wide level space where immense silver golden pipes like pillars entered smoothly, sleekly, into the perfectly fitting concrete. The pipes gave out an immense heat and he avoided touching them. He ran about, expecting to find some gallery, something like a bridge or an arch, where he could look down, perhaps climb down, on to the rocks, see water rising and glistening in the gloom below. He went one way as far as a sheer concrete wall, then returned the other way to be confronted by another wall like a cliff. A half-circle of concrete in front of him showed no way onward, no way down, no magic door promising further mysteries, and behind him a row of pipes soared up like a huge organ, with no gap between them into which could be inserted as much as a match-stick. There was nowhere below. He was at the bottom.

It took Tom some time to establish this with certainty. The steam and the heat confused him and he found it difficult to see and understand the space he was in, how large it was and what shape it was. He noticed now with a kind of surprise, as his motions became less rapid, how exceedingly bright the scene was, how brilliantly the lights, which seemed to be concealed, were shining upon the silver-gold organ pipes and upon the glittering web of hanging stairways, now suspended above him. As soon as he was sure that there was no dark archway, no steamy grotto with a scalding fount, and no way out except by the stairway down which he had come, he started to mount the steps; then he came back, stood a minute as if in prayer, and touched the wet concrete floor like a child touching 'base'. He said aloud, 'I did my best,' then hurried back to the stairs.

He was, very soon, checked. He went up, passing the place on to which he had jumped or fallen, crossed a landing and found that the stairway ended at another locked door (he tried the handle). When he retreated he realized that the set of stairs on which he now stood did not connect with those which he could see above him, by which he had descended. He had in fact chosen to make his leap at the point where the two systems came closest. To jump down had been easy. To climb back, balancing himself on a slippery rounded banister and clinging with outstretched arms to wet and rather hot vertical rails and steel treads above him, and then hauling himself up – was impossible; and would in any case have been an unattractive enterprise with a drop of twenty-five feet on to the concrete below in case of a slip. Tom stood there panting. He felt he had been inside this weird humming brilliantly lighted shaft for a long time. The damp tropical heat now, as he breathed, came to him in waves of burning hot air, which his seared lungs rejected, and he gasped. Feeling a weak helpless lassitude, he forced himself to breathe slowly. He thought to himself, of course the engineers must wear heat-proof protective clothing and masks when they come down here ... He walked slowly back up the stairway to the door and tried it again, and leaned against it and kicked it. It was firm, made of metal, and, like everything else about him, extremely hot to touch. He could now feel the hot stairs beginning to vex his feet. Up till now he had felt like a secret tiptoeing intruder. Now he felt suddenly like a prisoner. He banged on the door and called out several times, 'Hello, there.' His voice echoed thinly in the clammy steaming air of the whole huge cylinder which was starting to hiss and tremble like a rocket about to go off. He looked downward half-expecting to see that something had changed, but all was as before in the intolerably bright light. Was he imagining it, or was the temperature rising?

He looked up at the nearest part of the level above, a joint in the stairs, a tiny twist or landing balanced in mid-air. It was not directly over him but hanging, at about two feet of distance, about five feet higher than his head. What he needed was an intermediate foothold, but there was none except the knob of the door which was lower than the banister rail of the level place where he stood. Even to get one foot firmly on to the banister seemed scarcely possible. Tom thought, if only I had something with me, anything to stand on; though really there's no point. I could never balance and stand upright on that rail so as to catch hold of the stairs above, and even if I did I couldn't draw myself up, I'd just swing and fall into the gap between. But if I don't get out of here soon I shall suffocate. And I think something's going to explode. He shouted again but his voice seemed soundless. He began automatically to search his pockets and his hand gripped a knife, the strong long two-bladed Swiss knife which Emma had given him for Christmas. He drew it forth and opened the longest blade and looked at the door. It occurred to him that if he could drive the blade into the slit at the top of the door, the protruding handle might not only assist him to rise, with the help of the door knob, up on to the banister and balance there long enough to get a good grip on the vertical rails of the stair above, but might also provide him with an intermediate step on which to climb upward, provided he did not rest his weight on it for too long.

Tom slid the knife into the top of the door. It fitted snugly, leaving three inches of handle sticking out. He put one hand on to the round banister rail. It was wet and hot and terrifyingly slippery, and as he looked at it he could see the drop below. He felt in his pocket and brought out a large and, amid all the dampness, amazingly dry handkerchief. With this he mopped the metal rail. Then quickly, without waiting to inspect the elements of the scene any further, he reached up his right hand and took hold of the knife, lifted his right leg and placed his foot on the door knob, pressed his left hand springily down on the banister and took off, rising to a standing position on the dried portion of the rail, and as he did so stretching his left hand upward to take hold of a tread of the upper stairway, then quickly moving both hands to the vertical bars just above. From here, if he could for a moment rest his right foot on the knife, he would be enabled to rise again so as to insert his left knee between the bars and on to one of the treads of the higher stair.

As he estimated the distance involved and braced his body for it he heard from far above a loud echoing clang which he immediately understood. The bronze doors at the top had been slammed shut. A second later all the lights went out.

Emma turned on the lamps in the room where for some time he and his mother had been sitting by the light of a flickering fire.

It was Saturday evening, the end of a long day. Emma had returned to London that morning from Ennistone by an early train. He had got into the Underground to proceed to King's Cross and so to his digs. But the idea of being alone in his room seemed so appalling, he suddenly decided to go to Heathrow instead and fly to Brussels. His mother's joy at his unexpected arrival cheered him up a little.

The room in which they were sitting had existed for a long time, ever since just after his father's death. It was a Belgian not an English room. Not that his mother had especially willed it so. She had taken over some articles of furniture with the flat, and inherited others from her sister (now dead) who had been married to the Belgian architect. Perhaps too, in deciding to 'live abroad' she had adopted a kind of old-fashioned bourgeois style suited to that part of Brussels, a modification of old vanished rooms in Belfast which continued to exist only in her imagination. The (extremely handsome) lace curtains on the tall windows were yellow, the velvet curtains which enclosed them were stained and discreetly moth-eaten and had torn linings. The Turkey carpet was worn with tracks of feet. The embroidered shawl on the grand piano, always replaced in the same position, was faded on top where the sunlight reached it. The silver frame of the photo of soft-faced soft-eyed sixteen-year-old Emma, also upon the piano, looked always from the same place at the same angle. Emma's father was present too. A portrait of him upon the wall (painted by a fellow student at Trinity) showed him boyish, twinkling-eyed and jaunty, wearing a green tie. Emma did not like this picture. The photograph in his mother's room showed his father older, sadder, shy and diffident, with soft drooping moustaches and a look of gentle intelligent puzzlement. Both his parents looked 'dated'. His father looked like a subaltern in the first

510

war. His mother looked like an early star of the silent screen, with her short pale fluffy waved hair, and her little straight nose and small mouth and beautiful eyes. She still did not manage to look middle-aged, but looked fadedly youthful, preferring to sit on the floor or on a low stool or hassock, displaying her excellent silky legs and slim ankles and glossy high-heeled shoes. There was always a wistful not unpleasant sort of tension between Mary (*née* Gordon) Scarlett-Taylor and her son, she nervously anxious not to annoy him by her love, he irritated, remorseful, aware of his prudent miserly concealment of his great love for her, at which, perhaps, she could only guess. In this way, he knew, he deliberately deprived her of a happiness to which she had, perhaps, a right. Her voice, soft and almost but not quite without an Ulster accent, reminded him that he was Irish. Sometimes they were like young lovers together.

'I like this room.'

'I'm glad.'

'It's so dusty and stuffy and quiet and nowhere in the world.'

'Shall I open a window?'

'Of course not.'

'I wish you were in it oftener.'

'It's like visiting the past, I like the past. I hate the present.'

'Tell me about the present.'

'I read books, I write essays, I stuff my head.'

'And your heart?'

'Empty. Hollow. Cracked like a broken drum.'

'I don't believe it at all. And you sing.'

'I'm going to stop singing.'

'How do you mean?'

'Forever.'

'You're blathering. I wish you'd bring your friends here.'

'I have no friends.'

'Don't be so morose.'

'Morose. I like morose.'

'Tom McCaffrey.'

'You wouldn't like him.'

'I would.'

'I wouldn't like that either.'

'Get away with you!'

'He's bouncy and self-confident and beautiful, not a bit like me.'

'No girls?'

'Yes, a maidservant with a London accent who looks like an old dry wooden carving.'

'Be serious. I wish you'd marry.'

'You do not.'

'I do so! I wish you'd bring your real life here.'

'It is here. I visit it occasionally. The rest's a fiction.'

'You work too hard at those books. You ought to sing more. You're happy when you sing.'

'I hate happiness and hereby forswear it.'

'Oh darling, you upset me so –'

'Sorry.'

'Shall we play the Mozart duet?'

'I'll do the piano.'

Emma removed the embroidered shawl and a lamp and the photograph of his young undefiled self and opened the piano. He had telephoned the Slipper House from Heathrow, again from Brussels airport, and twice from the flat. No answer.

He drew up the second piano stool and sat down beside his mother. They smiled at each other and then suddenly, holding hands, began to laugh.

Brian McCaffrey rang the bell at George's house in Druidsdale. Stella opened the door. It was late Saturday evening.

'Stella!'

'Hello.'

'Is George there?'

'No.'

'Can I come in?'

'Yes.'

Stella led the way into the dining-room where she had evidently been sitting at the table writing a letter. One lamp was on. There was a book on the table, at which Brian peered. *La Chartreuse de Parme*. The surviving netsuke were also there in a jumbled bunch. George had taken away the one he had stamped on.

The dining-room looked dead, like a pretentious office. It had a naked artificial unused look with its self-conscious ornaments all in (Stella's) good taste: Japanese prints, engraved glass, plates perched on stands. Everything was dusty, including the unoccupied end of the table.

'You're back.'

'Yes.'

'And George?'

'I don't know.'

'But is he all right?'

'So far as I know.'

'You've seen him?'

'Yes.'

'Is he likely to turn up?'

'He says he's living with Diane Sedleigh and they're going to emigrate to Spain.'

'But that's splendid! Isn't that good?'

'I don't know. It may not be true. Whisky? I'll get some.'

Brian looked quickly at the letters on the table, a long one written in a tiny precise hand, one just started written in an italic hand. He had never, he thought, seen Stella's writing. He guessed the long one was from her father.

'What did you want with George?' said Stella coming back with the whisky and one glass.

'Won't you drink?'

'No, thanks.'

'Gabriel wanted me to come.'

Brian and Gabriel had been talking and arguing ever since the scene with George earlier in the afternoon. Gabriel had been very upset, and then to Brian's surprise very angry, about Brian's suggestion that she had deliberately displayed her breasts to George at the seaside. Brian had withdrawn the suggestion, then, when Gabriel had continued to reproach him, had become angry too. They went over the whole usual fruitless argument about George, in the course of which Gabriel remembered that she had had a nightmare last night in which she had seen George floating somewhere, *drowned*. She then became persuaded that something terrible had happened to him.

'He was in such a terrible state of mind.'

'He seemed to me rather pleased with himself.'

'He's in despair, I know, please let's at least ring up.'

Brian rang George's number but there was no answer. Gabriel then begged him to go round and see whether George had not taken an overdose of sleeping pills and were lying semi-animate on the sofa at Druidsdale. She was so upset by her dream, and likely, if Brian did not go, to go herself, that he had set off.

'I'm not answering the telephone,' said Stella, who had listened in silence to a curtailed and improved version of this account.

Brian looked at his handsome sister-in-law of whom he was a little in awe. Stella looked older, her face thinner. Two light hair-like lines rose up between her brows giving to her face a greater concentration. Her dark immaculate hair rose in a stiff springy dome above her brow, like to a crown or ceremonial helmet. Her clever mouth, with its indelible ironic shape, was calm. Her dark eyes gleamed with a light which Brian had but rarely seen in them before, not a quiet communicative luminosity, but a fanatical light, a light of will. She was to him an alien, a phenomenon, a kind of being whom he absolutely could not understand. The whisky emboldened him, however.

'Where were you?'

'With N at Bath Lodge. Then with May Blackett at Maryville.'

'Ruby knew you were there. She finds lost things. She went and stared at the house. Why didn't you come back sooner? We were worried.'

'N wanted me to, but –'

'You mean you didn't do what N wanted? Most people do.'

'I wanted to see what would happen.'

'To George?'

'To me. To George too.'

'So George is getting off scot free, off to Spain with that woman! Fancy old George gone at last, we'll have nothing to talk about! Aren't you relieved he's clearing off? It solves a lot of problems, doesn't it? You can find someone else, get out of this rotten little town. Go to Tokyo and find a nice man, someone clever, an English diplomat, or a French one. I can see you married to a Frenchman. Forget about us. Why not? God, you can't *love* that swine, can you?'

'Do you mean George?'

'Sorry, excuse my vocabulary.'

'You don't think it possible.'

'Oh it's possible, half the women in this town are in love with George or imagine that they are, even Gabriel is. But you, you're a cut above – I mean you're special, like royalty – you know, I've always admired you so much, though I've never had a chance to say so, I hoped you knew – we've hardly ever had a real talk together, I wish we could – I feel now, now that you're going –'

Stella was frowning and narrowing her eyes, deepening the two new lines on her brow. She straightened her shoulders and leaned back.

Brian thought, whatever possessed me to spill all that, I must be drunk, and I've been disloyal to Gabriel, Stella will despise me utterly.

Stella said, 'But I'm not going.'

'Why not, if he is?'

'We'll wait and see.'

'God, do you want *revenge* on George? You can't forgive him, is that it? Are you still waiting ... for something to happen ...?' Stella, who had been writing something down, pushed a slip of paper towards Brian.

'What's that?'

'Mrs Sedleigh's address. But perhaps you know it?'

'God, I'm not going *there*.'

'Then you'd better go home, Gabriel will be anxious.'

Brian walked home cursing. He felt drunk. He thought, she's a witch. She made me say all those incredibly stupid things and then threw me out. She's worse than George. I do believe she's capable of murder. What *is* she waiting for?

It was Saturday night, late, dark. Alex had just come out of the drawing-room to find Ruby standing at the top of the stairs. The house was silent. Alex felt frightened.

'What are you doing? Why are you standing there?'

Ruby said nothing. She stared at Alex with a frown, biting her lip. Her face expressed anguish.

'Is anything the matter?'

Ruby shook her head.

'Have you locked all the doors?'

Ruby nodded.

When George had gone away Alex had finished the bottle of whisky and fallen asleep. Then she had eaten some of the supper which Ruby had set out as usual for her in the dining-room. Then she had come upstairs again and drunk some more and fallen asleep again. Now she felt giddy, dislocated in time and space. She had, at some stage, she could not remember when, taken off her dress and put on her dressing-gown. So she would live in a Spanish village with George and Diane? Would that be?

Ruby kept on staring. Alex thought, does she want me to do something? To ask her into the drawing-room and pet her? Does she want me to ... to *kiss* her ...? These were such odd things to

515

think that Alex felt that Ruby must have actually put them into her mind. Nothing stopped her from taking Ruby's hand and saying, Ruby, dear, we've been together a long time, ever since we were children really, and now we are old. Come in and sit with me. Do not be afraid. Are you afraid? I will care for you, I will look after you. Then Alex wondered, *does she know I'm going away*? She has second sight or something. Perhaps she *knows*? Nothing stopped Alex from speaking those comforting words to Ruby and questioning her gently, except that all the years which should have made it possible had made it impossible, and Alex felt so sick and so frightened and so confused and so tired.

She said impatiently, 'Don't stand there. Go to bed. It's past your bedtime. Go on.'

Ruby did not move. She stood like a heavy large wooden figure, larger than life, at the top of the stairs.

Alex said, 'You talked about us. You gave away things about us at the Baths. You did it on purpose. Didn't you talk?'

Ruby's face changed, expressing distress. She said, 'I told the boy. I only told the boy.'

'What boy?'

The boy in question was Mike Seanu, the 'little scamp' of a reporter on the *Gazette*. What had happened was this. When John Robert had made his first visit to the Slipper House to apprise Hattie of his 'plan', Ruby had followed him down the garden, primed with jealousy and curiosity, and had eventually posted herself close enough to the sitting-room window to overhear some of what was said. From this she gathered that Rozanov had arranged for Hattie to marry Tom. She carried this interesting information away but, being more given to silence on family matters than Alex gave her credit for, did nothing with it. Young Seanu had not been present at the 'riot'. He was 'covering' the masque for the *Gazette* and had come on as far as the Green Man, but had been too shy to stay long and returned to his local, the Ferret, on the wasteland where he lived. (A pub where drugs used to change hands, now an innocent enough little hole where Sikhs and gipsies amicably rub shoulders.) He was filled with chagrin on the next day to hear that he had missed so much newsworthy fun, but consoled by being given some immediate detective work to do. Someone (it was never clear who) had indeed (as they surmised) overheard some of Tom and Emma's drunken conversation about John Robert and Hattie. This titbit, as it reached the ears of Gavin Oare, did not

516

however amount to more than amused and unserious guesswork. Gavin promptly (on Sunday) sent Mike Seanu out to discover more, suggesting in particular that he should visit Ruby. The 'young scamp' was a gipsy and in fact (as Oare knew) related to Ruby, and the old servant, who would not have talked to anyone else, talked to this boy, of whom she was fond. Seanu, coached by his editor, put his question in terms of 'so it is true, is it, what everyone says that' (and so on), to which in good faith Ruby replied yes, she believed that John Robert had arranged for Tom to marry Hattie. This was enough for Gavin Oare. The further speculations were his work. (I am told that Mike Seanu was very upset and disgusted by the resultant article and considered resigning, but sensibly did not.) This was the way in which the rumour, which had so many consequences, gained currency in Ennistone.

However, Alex never received an answer to her question, not because Ruby was ashamed to give it (though the matter did trouble her) but because at that moment Ruby's poor head was entirely filled up with something else.

She moved back a step, away from the stairhead, and said to Alex, 'The foxes –'

'What about the foxes?'

'They are evil, evil things, bad spirits. They bring bad luck. They make bad things to happen.'

'Don't be silly. That's stupid superstitious gipsy nonsense. Don't talk like that to me. Go away, go to bed.'

'They are dead.'

'*What*?'

'The foxes – they are dead. The men came and killed them – here in the garden – I showed them where.'

Alex screamed out, her lips wet with a foam of rage – 'You *what*, you let them do it? You *showed* them? You *devil* – without telling me – you let them kill the foxes – oh I could *kill* you for this – how could you do it – let them kill my foxes – why didn't you tell me –?'

'You were asleep, you were drunk, the man came with the gas, all the foxes are dead.'

'You hateful vile wicked thing, get out of this house forever, I never want to see you again!' Alex moved fiercely, raising her hand as if to strike Ruby. Ruby pushed her away.

In a moment Alex was tumbling headlong down the stairs. She

rolled to the landing, then all the way down to the hall where she lay curled and motionless.

Wailing, Ruby ran down after her. She pulled at her mistress, trying to lift her head, weeping. Then withdrawing her hands Ruby began to howl like a dog. Alex lay still.

'You can't say it's over when it's just beginning.'

'It's over, it's ended, better so.'

'But why, and what's over? It can't all be spoilt, it's you that are spoiling it! I don't even understand.'

'It's not necessary for you to understand.'

'Well, of course, I *do* understand, but –'

'Let's stop talking.'

'You know that's impossible.'

'We shall have to stop soon. We *ought* to stop.'

'You started talking.'

'I know.'

'If only you hadn't – you didn't have to say anything – you didn't have to say what you said –'

'I know, I know, I know –'

'You could have drawn us gradually together, it would have been so easy –'

'*Please*, Hattie.'

'You're supposed to be so terribly clever, why didn't you *think* how to do it?'

'I've thought too much.'

'Why didn't you keep quiet and just let me learn.'

'Don't torment me with that.'

'I'm grown up now, I could have learnt, without your making it into a sort of tragedy!'

'Don't *torment* me!'

'You torment me! You've broken everything up into horrible jagged pieces, you've disturbed and changed my heart, and now you talk of ending and parting.'

'It must be so.'

'But I love you –'

'You are mistaken.'

'I do, we can *manage* this, we can *manage*.'

519

'You might, I cannot.'

'What about my wishes?'

'Your wishes are unimportant, they are ephemeral, you are young, your interest is not deep, your pain will be brief. Better not a step further. For me this is – not a tragedy – life is not tragic – it is a catastrophe – perhaps it is a merciful one.'

'You're only interested in your catastrophe.'

'Yes.'

'But I do love you, I want to help you, to save you.'

'Young girls always see themselves as saviours, but it is the one role which they cannot play.'

'Don't generalize. I can. Why not let me try?'

'Because I don't want to be hurt by you any more.'

'Oh, that's so cruel, so *awful*.'

'And so unfair, as you said before.'

'I can love you and look after you and make you happy, and we can be *friends* now, like you said you always really wanted.'

'No. You refuse to see how impossibly painful, for a hundred reasons, I would find that situation.'

'Yes, I do refuse! Oh, we keep going in circles.'

'Let us stop talking. It is dawn. The birds are singing. We have talked all night.'

'It's nearly midsummer, there is no night, we haven't talked for long, I can't stop talking, I can't sleep. You were afraid I would run away. Now I am afraid you will run away.'

It was early on Sunday morning, though as Hattie said, morning was early. A blackbird was singing in the apple tree at number sixteen Hare Lane. John Robert rose stiffly and pulled one of the curtains back a little, letting a deadly breath of blank clear dawn light into the lamp-lit room. Hattie shuddered and moaned. She said, 'I was so happy at the Slipper House with Pearl. You've taken Pearl away from me. And now you're taking everything else away.'

Hattie had given John Robert 'the day' he had asked for, Friday. But on that morning, after his outburst, they had not really talked. Both were terrified and anxious to draw back. He kept saying, 'I'm sorry,' and she, 'It's all right.'

John Robert's mumbling 'explanation', his 'apology' turned into a long review of their meetings and their memories in which they both took refuge. During these reminiscences, which to a listener might have sounded like the talk of friends, they eyed each other like antagonists waiting to fight, while both were ferociously thinking. Their two intent faces even showed, during this time, a marked resemblance as they inwardly *concentrated* upon what had happened, and what was going to happen. They assessed, they reflected, they planned. In the afternoon (after they had distractedly played with some bread and cheese for lunch) Hattie said she was tired and had a headache and wanted to lie down, and they parted with relief. She lay on her bed stiff and alert. Now it was he who moved and sighed and she who listened. In the evening they reminisced again, less randomly, more carefully, it was as if they *had* to go through all those memories, like a kind of litany, before they could, cautiously approaching themselves to the present moment, *engage*. They discussed and argued warily, even sparring a little, declaring they would go to bed early (which they did), postponing the glimpsed frightfulness of a further clarification. Hattie asked questions about her mother, about her mother's childhood, and talked a little about her father. They discussed Margot, talking almost pointlessly at last to tire themselves out. That night, on going to bed, Hattie very silently bolted her bedroom door.

She awoke next morning from hideous dreams to intense urgent miserable fear and guilt about Pearl. After promising John Robert faithfully that she would come back, she ran to the Slipper House and found that Pearl had gone. She returned in tears. John Robert looked at her silently with his terrible eyes. By now existence in the little house, eating and drinking and moving and going to the lavatory, going up and down the stairs, standing up and sitting down, had become a sort of nightmarish pattern as for people in a prison. Sometimes, to relieve Hattie of his presence, John Robert went out into the garden and stood there under the apple tree like a big stricken animal, while Hattie, like an image in a doll's house, looked at him out of different windows. Neither of them could suggest going anywhere or doing anything, nor could they, though they tried, resume the conversation of yesterday. At last, out of his silence and her recurrent tears, the real talk, the awful talk, began to arise, and everything that had most terrified Hattie in her intense thinking and her stiff alert lying began to come about.

She stared at the terrible dawn light and felt it turning her face to stone.

'I don't want to stop until we've got somewhere, made some sense of it, established something, reached a point from which we can start again.'

521

'We shall never start again. When we stop this conversation we must not start it again ever.'

'Please, please don't say things like that. Why do you have to make such a tragedy of it all? Treat it as a problem. Problems have solutions.'

'A great philosopher said that if the answer can't be put into words neither can the question.'

'But the answer can be.'

'It's not a problem.'

'You have a duty to me. Isn't that what's most important, what cuts through everything else?'

'I had a duty. I failed. Duty is over.'

'Duty is never over. Because you said what you said you *now* have a duty not to make me terribly unhappy about it. Please make it all easier, make it less awful, think of *me*. You felt like *that* when I was younger because we couldn't communicate. You think it's worse now I've grown up, but it isn't, it's better because we can talk about it, we can be friends.'

'We can never be friends.'

'Oh stop it, don't *say* that! Is it your book, you feel in despair about your book so you want to destroy everything here too, pull it all to pieces, is that it?'

'Don't be foolish, you know nothing about my book.'

'Can't you be reasonable, can't you be ordinary, can't we get back to – well, not to where we were before, we can never be there, but –'

'If I had behaved properly, naturally, to you as a child I would not have built up this –'

'We've said all that – but isn't it now just as if you *had* – haven't you just – by this sudden – thing – made it as it would have been – haven't you changed the past?'

'That's impossible, that's sacrilege, one dies for that.'

'No. You've done it, you've leapt the gap, oh let me persuade you, don't you *see*, we're *together*, as loving relations, as loving friends, as *family* – you've made us come close.'

'It's not like that, Hattie, and cannot be. I ought to stop this conversation but I cannot bear to, I wish it could go on forever, it's agony but what will come after will be worse. It's wicked to talk to you like this because it's an image of things which are unspeakable and impossible, and that is why I want to prolong it – oh the pain –'

'Don't suffer so, I can't bear it, try not to –'

'I appal you. I revolt you physically.'

'No.'

'I did yesterday, or whenever it was, I've lost track of time.'

'Yesterday was a long time ago. I don't feel like that about you at all. I feel quite differently – I've – I've discovered you.'

'You mean it's an exciting situation, an exciting talk.'

'No!'

'Oh wicked, wicked, the pain of it.'

'You gave me a shock, a surprise, but that's over now. I've lived – it's as if I've lived all these years, lived them in peace, lived them with you, and – oh – happily – that was what was happening when you were talking about the past.'

'You are making up false fantasies. You are using your intelligence. But your intelligence is not enough. Your being so intelligent is another – twist – but all that is past now, it is over. This is a conversation between two ghosts.'

'I'm not a ghost.'

'You are for me. You had not yet come – but I always knew that if you ever did come you would pass me in a sort of atomic flash.'

'I am not passing you. I refuse to. Perhaps there was a flash. But isn't that good? Just be still and look round quietly and you will see you are in a new country.'

'Yes. It is a country in which we can never be together.'

'Why can't we be?'

'What we have done by this talking is to make it impossibly dangerous to go on – anywhere.'

'Why do you want to *define* everything? Philosophers define things. But don't they sometimes give up definitions?'

'Don't argue with me.'

'I am fighting for my life.'

'Don't lie, Hattie, don't exaggerate.'

'I'm sorry, I just feel like that, I've found you, we can communicate, we understand each other, we're so close, I mustn't lose you, I *mustn't* – oh it's so awful – look, I can't bear this sort of light, please pull back the curtains and put the lamp out.'

He rose and did so.

'See, John Robert, dear, the sun has risen, it's shining, the sky is blue, the blackbird is singing, we must try to be happy, why can't we, since we're both so intelligent! There, do smile at me.'

'Oh, Hattie, Hattie –' He pulled violently at his short crinkly grey hair as if he wanted to drag it down to cover his eyes. He sat down heavily in the armchair. Hattie was sitting upright beside the table which still bore the remnants of a meal they had tried to eat many hours ago.

'Hattie, don't *tempt* me, you're like a demon, a *devil*, the way you go on.'

'How can you say that? Oh you upset me so! You're so determined to see it all in that horrible way, you destroy everything, every possibility, out of spite, I think you enjoy hurting me – oh why did you *tell* me, it's all your fault!'

'Yes, yes, I know.'

'You say we can't be friends, then let us choose to be something else. You love me. I love you. So why can't we just be together like that?'

'What on earth do you mean?'

'Not like – I mean just like loving people are.'

'That could only be if the past were different, and I've told you we can't remake the past – it would be a fake, an abomination, we are absolutely and utterly *not* as we would have been if . . .'

'I don't mean that, I mean just being together and loving each other, there is a way to be together.'

'There isn't and you know there isn't, don't lie to me, Hattie.'

'A way to be together, caring for each other, telling each other everything, talking.'

'You mean like ex-lovers?'

'Don't speak in that horrible hard way. I don't mean *like* anything except just us.'

'Angels could do it. Humans not. Our minds lack that degree of particularity. Anyway you don't love me. Oh you think you do *now*, but that's just excitement, because of this unspeakably wicked argument for which I am entirely responsible, because of what you call the drama, and because you're flattered!'

'Flattered!'

'Young girls are flattered by attentions from older men, especially if the older men are famous.'

'Don't *you* lie, that's a sort of false lying vile speech!'

'Yes. All right. But I'm probably the first man who has – made advances – and if I'm not – don't tell me – oh God.'

'How can you use such *language* to me!'

'I'm sorry, I don't mean – it's just – I'm so unhappy.'

'Oh how can I *show* you what it's really like! If you had been my teacher I would have loved you.'

'If I had been your teacher everything would have been entirely different.'

'Well, can't you be my teacher now, somehow –?'

'No.'

'Why can't we make our home together, like you *said*, you actually *talked* about it, have you forgotten, about going to California and buying a house for us near the ocean, you said I'd like that, you said you'd keep me with you very much more.'

'I was mad, I knew it couldn't be, it couldn't ever be.'

'Well, you said it, anyway.'

'Yes, but that was before I – broke the barrier, leapt the gap – we can't go back to that.'

'Why not? Why can't you try? You're a free man, not a helpless victim.'

'I *am* a helpless victim – I'm pinned down and screaming – can't you understand, can't you *feel* the difference between us now? You're talking, you're thinking, you're being clever, you're trying this and trying that to make me stop upsetting you. But I'm in a different world, I'm in pain, I'm in the presence of death.'

'Death.'

'I don't mean I'm ill or going to kill myself or anything, it's just death-pain, parting-pain, bereavement.'

'No, no, no, it doesn't have to be. Why can't we live together in that house? I could be so happy in that house, if we could only live together, you and me and Pearl.'

'And Pearl – exactly.'

'What do you mean?'

'You don't understand.'

'Oh if only you'd kept silent, we might have gone there.'

'If I'd kept silent and gone on pretending – I thought I loved you then – but I feel – so much more now – speaking of it brings that about – and so – brings it all to an end.'

'But why?'

'You speak of Pearl – could I bear now, after what we've both become, to witness even your friendship with Pearl?'

'But you wanted me to marry Tom McCaffrey.'

'That was before, before we changed, it was to avoid *this*.'

'Can't we just be ourselves, surely we can live beyond all these things, we, surely we, can do as we please.'

'Hattie, don't tempt me, don't end as a devil in my life, I've got to live afterwards with a memory of you.'

'Why can't you try to imagine a way?'

'No, no, not there, we will not go *there* –'

'Where?'

'There where everything switches and starts to run the other way. No, I will not imagine. You don't know what you have been to me, what an image of purity and innocence. Of course you don't know what you're saying, but just please don't talk any more. You are innocent now, later you'll be like the rest. I almost feel I'd like to kill you, simply to keep you as you are now.'

He pushed the chair back violently, but did not rise.

Hattie was sitting very still, her two hands flat upon the table, as she had sat before, just before he revealed his secret. Her face was hotly flushed and her eyes were shining, whether with excitement or tears John Robert could not see. They were both silent for a moment.

Hattie relaxed, rubbing her eyes and falling into a dejected stoop. She said in a dull almost whining voice, 'Then you won't want to think of me – as I shall be later on.'

'No. I won't want to know – anything about you – later on.'

'And you call that love. You have no *common sense* – no *decent feeling* – at all.'

The words were flat and terrible after their lofty wrangle.

John Robert felt their deadly flatness, he felt with dread the ending of their talk. He said, 'You have been excited, and stirred, for you this has been an experience, and now you are disappointed. But for me – oh Hattie – I cannot tell you the hell I am in.'

She refused to express pity. She was thinking of herself, of her feelings. 'You have *forced* me to feel love for you – that is what has happened – and now you instantly kill it all. You've made me feel – so much. Would it surprise you – how much I feel – what I feel – now?'

'You are close to me. I mean we are both here breathing and sweating in this small room. I am a big animal. You find me powerful and frightening and interesting. It is a momentary impression.'

'It is your atomic flash. I feel now – almost – in love with you.'

'Don't be silly, Hattie. Keep your sense, keep your senses.'

'I've never felt just this before.'

'I'm not interested.'

'Oh you – you – I don't *understand* you!'

'It's all to do with the past, Hattie. When I told you what I ought never to have told you – you are quite right – a sort of guillotine came down. I didn't realize it at once. But time was cut off. I have no more time – I mean, for you. It is as if I have killed you. You will always be the same now, but dead.'

'How can you say such hateful cruel things? Why not let me try to make you happy somehow? Don't say it's impossible. *Think* about it. Not now, but later, we've done enough now, we've said enough and we're beginning to talk nonsense. Only don't cut it all off, don't consign me to being dead.'

'Oh you will be alive enough, somewhere else. I hope you will be very happy, I really hope it.'

'You don't. You are trying to curse me, to destroy my happiness forever. You won't share my life so you want to blacken it.'

'*Please* don't think that.'

'You're so sorry for yourself, you're so *stupid*. I do care for you, I do love you, you're lucky to be loved by me, why throw it all away, why do we have to think what it means, let's see what it means. All right, this has been a crazy stupid conversation, you made it so. Why not let's just go away now, to the railway station, to the airport, to America.'

'Hattie, don't do this to me.'

'Let's go away together.'

'Hattie, stop, listen. I want you to leave this house *at once* and return to the Slipper House. You can have Pearl back if you want, I don't care now so long as I don't see you again.'

'You're *mad*.'

'I will send you money, arrangements about your English college, all that. You can do what you like, I'll be in America, but now go, will you, it's still early, no one will see you, just *go*.'

'I will *not* go, why should I? I *hate* all this tormenting repetitive talk just tearing at our nerves. I can't bear being so close to you, feeling so close, and feeling – and not –'

'Go away, now, *please*.'

Hattie sprang up. She was flushed and her face was dirtied like a child's with traces of tears. She had not plaited her hair or even combed it and now it had been tangled by her anxious clutching tugging fingers. Her dress was buttoned awry. Her lips, her jaw were trembling, her hands shaking, she breathed with audible shudderings. Her pale milky-blue eyes shone with tears and anger.

John Robert who was sunk deep in the sagging armchair, like a huge half-hidden toad, struggled to rise, scrabbling his feet on the torn carpet, cracking the sides of the chair with his braced arms, but failed to get up. He murmured, 'Don't come near –'

For a moment it looked as if Hattie were going to hurl herself upon him, leaping on to his lap like a kitten. Then she fell on her knees beside the chair, grasping one of his hands and covering it with tears and kisses. 'Forgive me, don't leave me, you are my dear grandfather, I love you, I have nobody but you, look after me, love me, don't leave me alone.'

'*Stop* it, Hattie,' said John Robert.

At that moment, and suddenly, there was a loud noise in the house. Hattie sat back on her heels. The loud noise was repeated, a violent echoing banging sound. Somebody was knocking, was *hammering*, on the front door. They looked at each other. John Robert said, 'It must be the police.' That was his immediate thought.

'Don't go,' said Hattie, on her feet now. 'No one knows we're here.'

A prolonged ring on the bell was followed by more and louder banging, a fist applied to the panels.

John Robert got himself on to one knee, and then to his feet. He mumbled, 'I must go, I must.' He blundered stiffly out into the hall followed by Hattie, and after fiddling with the door in the semi-darkness, opened it. The bright cold light from the street came dazzling in.

Tom McCaffrey was standing outside. He stared at them with dazed exhausted wild eyes. His hair was bedraggled, his shirt was unbuttoned and he was barefoot. He said in a low clear voice, 'I've come for Hattie.'

John Robert did not hesitate for a second. He turned, and pushed and bundled Hattie somehow past him, between his great bulk and the wall, and out into the street. Tom later remembered seeing John Robert's hands clutching the material of her dress as she stumbled out through the door.

Hattie cried, 'No!'

Tom received her as she fell against him, touched by her, by her warm neck, her cool hair. A moment later he had taken her damp hand firmly in his. He said, 'Come on!' and pulled.

The door of number sixteen Hare Lane slammed shut.

Tom began to run, pulling Hattie after him. At first she resisted, then ran with him, holding his hand.

Who, drawing back his curtain in the early morning saw, in that clear sunny light, through empty streets, Tom McCaffrey running away with Hattie Meynell? I did.

After a while, somewhere in Travancore Avenue, they stopped running and walked on panting. Tom let go of Hattie's hand. She was crying quietly, clearing her eyes with her knuckles from time to time. Tom kept glancing shyly at her.

'Hattie, don't cry, darling, what's the matter? It's only me.'

She shook her head and did not reply. Her face was red, her eyes bloodshot, her mouth wet. Her tears were abating, but she gave panting sobbing breaths, like little cries. She drew her tangled hair down about her face like a veil.

They passed Greg and Ju's house. The curtains were drawn. All was silent, no one was about in Ennistone. Tom's feet were aching, his knees were hurting. He had kicked off his shoes and removed his socks somewhere in the course of the night's adventure, which now seemed long ago.

When the lights had gone out Tom had decided in a second to execute his plan nevertheless. His body, trained by his careful looking, remembered what to do. His right foot touched the projecting knife lightly, then rested weight on it for a moment as Tom flew upward, his hands climbing the vertical bars of the upper stairway, his left knee fumbling in the dark for a place to rest. The knife gave way and fell with a clatter on to the concrete floor below. Tom's knee blundered against the bars, finding the space it was making for too narrow. For a moment, his arms taking most of the strain, Tom hung with his knee jammed against the bars, painfully supported by the inch or two of tread which projected on the near side, his right leg now hanging in mid-air. The weight on his arms increased as his hands began to slide slowly down the wet slippery bars. Then somehow his right knee had risen up, finding a similar auxiliary lodgement on a higher tread, leaving him hanging, crouched spider-like against the side of the structure. Instinctively Tom jerked his left knee free and, dabbing sideways, lodged his left foot securely between the bars on a lower step. The strain on his arms decreased and he rested for a moment, his body sloping sideways. Then he cautiously removed his left hand to a lower bar, nearer to his left foot, and pulled hard, working himself into a more upright position, his right hand now able to grasp the banister at the top of the vertical bars, while his right foot also found a place upon the treads. After another rest he was able to throw one leg over the banister and slide himself over so as to collapse on to the stairs. Here for some time he sat, massaging his painful knees, wondering if they were damaged. It was probably at this point that he took his shoes and socks off and mislaid them in the dark. He was sorry to have lost the knife.

After that a period of time passed during which Tom climbed up and down flights of stairs in the dark, swallowing the steamy atmosphere and scorching his feet and failing to find any continuous way up. Stairs which he ascended ended in locked doors or else unaccountably started to go down again. He called out at intervals but was appalled to hear his puny cries echoing so vainly. He went up, then down, then up until he had lost all sense of which way was up and which down. He sat down at last while all around him the hot darkness quietly seethed and boiled. Sitting still, he concentrated on breathing and on overcoming his fear of suffocation. He breathed the dark and it filled him to the brim. Later still, waking up from what had surely not been sleep, he tried calling out again, and uttered one extremely loud cry which resonated in the huge enclosed space and set the whole network of invisible metal tingling and ringing with a tiny very high noise. After this the lights went on and an angry man opened the door at the top and came running down the stairways.

The man was less angry when he discovered who the intruder was. Tom was forgiven, quite unjustly, as no doubt he will be forgiven by God if God exists. He told the now gently chiding and amused employee that he had lost his shoes and his socks and his mackintosh and his jacket and his knife somewhere down below. He tried to describe his feat of levitation but found himself unable to picture what had happened. His rescuer, telling him to 'bugger off home!', left him in the corridor of the Ennistone Rooms. Tom began to walk toward the swing doors at the end; but before he reached them he saw, through the open door of one of the empty rooms, a divine sight, a bed with plump pillows and white sheets. He entered, drew back the sheets and climbed in. The most refreshing slumber he had ever had came to him instantly, and wisdom and clear vision dripped quietly upon him as he slept. He awoke knowing exactly what to do, and set off at once for Hare Lane.

Tom pushed open the back gate of the Belmont garden and Hattie went through. He followed her. She said, 'I haven't got the keys.'

Tom said, 'Don't worry. I can get in.'

The garden was airily green, a little misty, a little hazy, and innumerable birds were making a great network of sweet noise. They walked along the path under the trees, covered with moss and old leaves and little shapely bits of wooden debris which hurt Tom's feet, then they walked across the grass. Tom told Hattie to wait at the front door while he ran round the back, into the coal shed and through the window into the back passage by the route taken by George. He ran to let Hattie in. She had profited by the interval to smooth her hair down and comb it with her fingers. She looked calmer.

She came in, passed Tom and began to go up the stairs. Now, for the first time since his visionary slumber, Tom began to be uncertain of his role: not that he had actually thought out any role, he had acted instinctively at each moment as he felt he must. But now the dream-like unfolding of destined action seemed to have come to an end, the magic was switched off, and he was returned to the clumsy perilous muddle of ordinary life.

Hattie went into her bedroom and threw herself on the bed, lying on her back. Her feet fumbled, one rubbing against the other as she tried to push her shoes off. Tom took the shoes from her feet and put them under the bed. Then he stood looking down at her.

Hattie lay upon her spread hair, and her desolated face had become calm and quietly weary. As Tom stared down humbly, apologetically, questioningly, she smiled at him and reached out her hand. He took it, then sat down on the edge of the bed. He could see now that her body, to which her dress clung closely, was soaked with sweat. He kissed her hand. It tasted salt.

'Hattie, may I lie down beside you?'

'Yes. But just that.'

He lay down on his side, stretching himself out, measuring her body with his body, not trying to draw her to him, but touching her shoulder with one hand. He felt her very slight shrinking resistance.

531

'Hattie.'

'Yes, Tom.'

'Will you marry me?'

She was silent.

'Hattie –'

It took Tom a moment longer to discover that she had fallen fast asleep. He lay still, protecting her while she slept, filled with the most pure intense happiness which went coursing through his body in a dazzling quiet stream.

Later on, while Hattie was still sleeping, he went downstairs. A neat parcel had been placed inside the front door which he had left open. Inside the parcel he found his shoes and socks and mackintosh and jacket and the knife which Emma had given him.

George McCaffrey pushed open the swing doors at the entrance to the Ennistone Rooms. The porter in his glass box was reading the *Ennistone Gazette*, and did not notice George's arrival. If he had seen George, he might have been amazed by the beatific expression on his face. How could one describe that expression? George was not 'wreathed in smiles', but his face looked plumped out with deep satisfaction, or perhaps with inner peace. This could have been the face of a man who had inherited a million, or of one who had, after long asceticism, achieved enlightenment. This was the look which had so much alarmed Tom McCaffrey on the occasion of the 'court martial' and on the evening at Diane's flat when George had so quietly, almost absently, thrust him out of the door.

George walked along the corridor with a sort of affected step, as if he were being watched (which he was not), picking up his feet carefully from the carpet, like a dainty high-stepping horse. He walked slowly, as if reflectively. He was breathing deeply, however. His eye, roving like that of a carefree man, had elicited from the notice board the information that Professor John Robert Rozanov was 'in'.

On the door of John Robert's room hung a card provided by the management saying *Do not disturb*. George smiled at the card. Then he stood at the door and, still smiling, listened. He heard within the sound, which he expected, of the quiet snoring of the sleeping sage. It was the afternoon time when it was John Robert's habit to be asleep. It was the afternoon of Monday. George had visited the Rooms at the same time on the previous day, only then John Robert had been 'out'. (He had been still at Hare Lane sorting papers and writing letters.) George now pressed the door. It opened, letting the roaring sound of the water out into the corridor. George entered quickly and closed the door behind him. The scene was much as he had observed it on his former visit. The frosted-glass windows cast a clear pearly light. The sun was shining outside. John Robert was lying on the bed, but on this occasion clothed in a great blue sail-like Ennistone Rooms nightshirt which amply covered his domed bulk. He was lying on his back, one arm across his chest, the other depending from the bed. The table was covered with books and notebooks, the notebooks now being neatly stacked up.

George was still smiling. The smile intensified the beatific glow of his expression so that he now looked like a man inspired at some great moment of his life, as when, perhaps, in a battle he seizes a flag and rushes forward against the enemy with a loud joyous cry, possessed by a divine frenzy or the sacred impulse of supreme duty. Yet at the same time he was quiet and deliberate in his movements; as well he might be since he was executing a routine which he had rehearsed many times in his imagination. Indeed as he moved now in the room he might still have been within the secret unresisting chamber of his mind. He moved as if treading on air. The double doors of the bathroom behind which the waters roared were ajar, and a pillar of steam hung behind them, rapidly dissipating itself in the cooler air. George, after casting a glance at the quiet figure on the bed, slowly opened the two doors wide. From the big brass taps the waters plunged into the white abyss of the sunken bath, hiding it in their cloud. George stepped into the bathroom and peered to see whether the outlet pipe was closed. It was open, maintaining a foot or so of water at the bottom of the bath. He leaned over and turned the brass handle to close the outlet. Already, as he retreated, the steam had covered him with moisture. Turning to gaze at John Robert, he began to take off his jacket. His smile had now become a grin which might have been an expression of extreme pain. He rolled up his shirt-sleeves.

The philosopher was snoring more quietly now with a faint bubbling sound. This time he had left his teeth in, and his mouth and chin had not collapsed, but his sleeping face looked to George huge and senseless, a pile of flabby layers of soft folded skin, pitted and porous, old, like the remains of something which had failed to be cooked, or a collapsed heap of blanched dead plants deprived of light. The eyes had vanished into hooded wrinkled holes. It was not like a face but a chaotic mess of flesh spread out where a face might have been. The skin was coarse and patchily discoloured, dirtied by a grey growth of beard. George moved his gaze to where the open neck of the starchily clean shirt revealed a rising slice of pink hairless chest. The genitals were covered, the knobbly knees visible, red and smooth and curiously touching as if they had not aged and were still the knees of a boy. Beneath them the legs were a livid white, with prominent blue veins, and sparsely covered with extremely long black hairs. The philosopher's feet were covered by a towel. George returned to the bathroom. The bath was now full and discharging itself evenly into the overflow pipe.

George pressed his hand hard to his breast, regulating his breathing. He unbuttoned the neck of his shirt. One of the bathroom doors had half closed. He propped it wide open with a chair. He looked at the problem he had set himself and through the solution of which he had so often run in his mind. The bed, one of the original beds of the Rooms, was of tubular steel, designed to move easily on casters over the sleek carpet, and standing against the pale oak headboard which was fixed to the wall. George put his hand on the foot of the bed and pulled slightly. The bed moved silently as if of its own accord. George caught his breath in a sort of swallowed sigh or sob. Now that he was at last so close to *it* he felt a need to pause. He began looking about the room, moving his eyes in an odd mechanical way as if seeing were a new and special activity. He looked at the carving on the oak panel of a faun among spear-shaped leaves. He looked at one of the orange-and-white plates imported from Sweden which had been placed on a chair near the door. He looked at the books on the table and saw that some of them were dusty. John Robert must have told the maids not to touch his work. George looked at the window catches, also steel originals, eloquent of their date. He felt an impulse to go and touch them, or to draw his finger across the nearest book. He looked at John Robert again and his heart was seared as if with a radiantly hot iron. From here the face made sense for a moment, the lips protruding as George had so often seen them do when his teacher was listening to an argument. There was something so alert and wakeful about this gesture of the lips that George had to peer

534

closely, for John Robert had ceased to snore, to be sure that the eyes were not awake and glaring.

George began to push the foot of the bed round. He did this simply by leaning his thigh against it, and again the bed silently and obligingly moved. The head of the bed was now swinging in the direction of the bathroom. George was overcome by a kind of faintness which was also a fever of haste. His breath came in a little audible stream of 'oh, oh, oh.' He no longer seemed to care whether John Robert woke up or not. The mechanics of the operation, the absolute necessity of the task, absorbed him completely. His legs felt weak, his knees dissolving as with sexual desire. He propelled the bed head first through the double doors of the bathroom.

In his imagination of this scene George had pushed the bed quietly and cautiously and had paused to be sure that the head of it was directly above the brimming bath before he completed his task. But now this sickening fearful haste had taken hold of his body, and as soon as the end of the bed entered the bathroom he pushed so violently that the front legs ran quickly over the tiles and would have jolted down into the water had they not been checked by the raised rim of the bath. George, now in the doorway, stopped pushing, took a deep breath, and bending down seized the two back legs near to the floor and began to lift. John Robert's weight was mainly at the top end of the bed and it was not very difficult to raise the foot. George saw the round steel legs of the bed rising up, his hands clawed round them, his knuckles white with strain. His feet apart, his body braced, he stared at what was closest. Then suddenly there was a great lumpish crashing sound and the bed was relieved of its weight and leapt out of George's grasp, swinging sideways, into one of the louvred doors. George gave a little yelping cry, and now scrabbled in desperate haste to get himself past the obstructing bed. Already he could see he had botched it all. John Robert had not fallen head first into the water. He lay in a great whale-like bulk poised upon the very edge of the bath. George thought, he's stunned, he has *hurt himself* in the fall, *he can't get up*. Moaning, he ran forward and with his foot propelled the philosopher over the edge into the noisy steamy cauldron of very hot bubbling water.

George stood for a moment, dazed by the sudden *disappearance*. Water splashed up over his feet and steam blinded his eyes. Then he saw below him, in the long wide cavity of the bath, something blue and dark floating and agitating upon the surface. It was the blue nightshirt. George thought, I ought to have taken that off. But of course I couldn't have done earlier. He knelt beside the bath and pressed down upon the blue shirt, feeling the fat humpy shoulders of his victim. He pressed and pressed, using both hands, pressing hard down on anything which rose above the surface. He went on doing this for many minutes, with the movements of someone washing clothes. And as he held the great head down below the water and wondered how much longer he needed to do it he had the strange feeling that he had performed this ritual before, perhaps many times. He thought, it's just like the dead babies. Well, the babies weren't dead, it was just that he had wanted to make them dead like *this*, and like *this*, and like *this*.

At last he felt that it was not necessary to continue. There was something huge and bulky, with rounded wet surfaces, floating there, bobbing, moving, in the disturbed water. George thought, I ought to take the shirt off. No clothes. I worked that out before. I can't remember why. He pulled a little at the dark blue material. But it was too difficult now to get it off and too awful. He rose on one knee, then slowly to his feet, and walked back into the bedroom, squeezing past the bed. He stood for a moment looking at the room which looked so odd and different with the bed gone from the centre. He moved to the window and looked at the window catches and now reached out to touch one of them. How strange, that the last time he had looked at that catch the entire universe had been different. The radiant searing burn touched his heart again, this time with the touch of the most terrible fear he had ever felt, fear for his future, fear at his continued existence. He picked up one of the notebooks from the table. He thought, I'll drown the book too. He went back, squeezing past the bed, and saw with a kind of surprise the big hippopotamus floating in the bath. He dropped the notebook into the water at the far end of the bath. He saw John Robert's writing upon the pages. Then he thought, I'd better go, get away. He went back into the bedroom and made for the door. Glancing behind him he realized that he had left the bed jammed into the bathroom doorway. He returned and pulled it out and propelled it to its original position. The head of the bed was splashed with water and the pillow was gone. Feebly and automatically George mopped the legs of the bed and the bedclothes with the towel which had covered John Robert's feet and which had not accompanied him in his fall. He looked for the pillow and found it lying very wet on the edge of the bath. He tried to wring it out, then left it on the floor near the bed. There was a lot of water on the carpet which he made out to be his own footprints. He took a clean towel from the bathroom rail and dried his arms and dabbed at his shoes. Then tried to obliterate the wet marks. He saw his jacket lying in the corner and put it on. He went and carefully closed the doors into the bathroom. He looked about the room. It was more silent now, and looked much as usual except that it was vastly cosmically empty. George stood for a moment breathing deeply and then let himself out of the door into the corridor. He closed the bedroom door, and the sound of the waters subsided to a distant hum. He began to walk away along the empty corridor.

Do not disturb.

As George had almost reached the swing doors they began to rotate. Father Bernard came in, turned to free his cassock, and came face to face with George. The priest began to say something, then swallowed it on seeing George's face. George passed by and out into the sunlight.

Father Bernard had had a lot of worries of his own lately, private worries such as belong to the inner life. It had been coming into his heart and his spirit that he could not for very much longer go on wearing a dog collar and a cassock. He would have to *move on*. This conclusion caused real pain, not the sort which can be played with. He decided, after some hesitations and reluctances, that he should discuss the matter with Rozanov, whose candour on the subject had perhaps brought on, had certainly accelerated this distressing spiritual crisis. He went first to Hare Lane where there was no answer to the bell and nothing to be observed except an upset milk bottle outside the door (knocked over in the course of Tom's abduction of Hattie). He then went to the Ennistone Rooms.

After seeing George's face, the priest ran along the corridor alert with fear. He knocked perfunctorily on the door of John Robert's room, entered and was relieved to find it empty. The bed was undone, the bathroom doors closed, and the table covered with signs of study. Father Bernard recovered his breath. He assumed that John Robert was briefly away somewhere, perhaps with a doctor. He waited, then with his usual curiosity (but with a cautious eye on the door) began to look at the table. He picked up one of the notebooks and deciphered a page or two of John Robert's spidery writing, feeling the layman's amused gratification of not being able to understand a word. Then he saw, half-concealed under the books, a white sheet of paper laid out, a letter. At the top was written *For the attention of William Eastcote Esq.* (John Robert was unaware that his friend was dead.) Father Bernard leaned over and read as follows.

My dear Bill,
   I hope you will forgive me for having taken my life. I know you will disapprove. Only think it, if you can, a happier life for having terminated now. You have always seen me as a stoic, and will perhaps understand. Please look after Hattie. I have named you and Robin Osmore as executors of my will. Goodbye, Bill. You may imagine with what sentiments of cordiality and esteem I sign myself for the last time,
                                          Yours,
                                                 John Robert
I have taken a quick and effective mixture concocted for me by an American chemist. Attempts to resuscitate me will be vain.

Father Bernard uttered a wild cry of woe. He looked desperately round, then ran to the bathroom doors and swung them open. At first in the steam he could see nothing. Then he saw the strange huge half-submerged contents of the bath. He knelt down on the slippery wet verge and pulled in helpless revulsion and misery and terror at the slippery bobbing surfaces. At last he found the head and raised it, pulling by the hair. It was plain that John Robert was gone, he was no longer there, there was only something else which slipped from the priest's horrified hands. However, he managed, by some desperate pulling and dragging, to prop the bulky form up at the shallow seated end of the bath away from the taps so that the head lolled back upon the tiled edge. Then he rose and made for the door.

The letter was lying on the carpet where he had dropped it. Instinctively he picked it up and put it in his pocket. He ran out into the corridor shouting for help. As white-coated attendants appeared and hurried into the room Father Bernard ran away down the corridor and out through the swing doors. He began to run, panting and whimpering, in the direction of Diane's flat in Westwold.

When George left the Institute he began to walk fairly fast in the direction of the High Street, but turned into the Botanical Garden. He paused and looked at a tree, a ginkgo, which he had long ago 'adopted' because he associated it with his childhood at Belmont.

He crossed the garden, avoiding the Museum, and began to walk toward the Roman bridge. On the other side of the Enn he found himself turning toward Burkestown with some vague intention of going to 16 Hare Lane, as if he might find there a second and utterly different John Robert. He felt it important to have a goal. He began to walk fast. By the time he reached Burkestown, however, he had decided to make for the Common, by way of the level crossing, and the old railway cutting. He passed the Green Man, which was just opening its doors. Several people saw George pass by on that evening, but his grin of pain did not seem to them an unusual expression. No one approached him.

As George walked along the grassy bottom of the cutting he noticed the flowers growing upon the banks, foxgloves, white comfrey, campion, rambling purple vetch with its tiny stripes. He thought, this is the first day, the first hour, of the new world in which everything will be entirely different. I have undergone a cosmic change, every atom, every particle is changed, I am switched over into a completely new mode of being. And he thought, it had to be, it *had* to be, *it had to be*. I have done what I had to do, I have had the courage, the devotion, to do it. And he thought, how odd, I never did find out how Schlick's pupil killed him. It doesn't matter now. The cutting ended and he began to climb up on to the Common. From here the stones of the Ennistone Ring can be seen upon the horizon, as they are so often represented upon picture postcards. George began to make for the Ring. Behind the stones the brilliant radiant summer evening sky was vibrating with the tingling cloudless blue of a pure happiness. George gave a sob. He felt the pain beginning; it was starting to spread inside him, the crippling awful pain of absolute remorse; and he prayed oh forgive me, oh let me die now, let me die, let me *die*.

As he came up on to the top level of the Common there were a few people about, but not near him. He began to walk through the long grass in the direction of the Ring. The electrical vibration of the blue zenith beyond the stones was hurting his eyes, and he turned his head away toward where the sun, descending in the sky, was hazed by a little cloud against a gentler less vivid blue. Only the sun, blazing through the misty light, had changed or was changing. It was no longer round but was becoming shaped like a star with long jagged mobile points which kept flowing in and out, and each time they flowed they became of a dazzling burning intensity. The star was very near, too near. It went on flaming and burning, a vast catastrophic conflagration in the evening sky, emitting its long jets of flame. And as it burnt with dazzling pointed rays a dark circle began to grow in its centre, making the star look like a sunflower. George thought, I'll look at the dark part, then I shall be all right. As he watched, the dark part was growing so that now it almost covered the central orb of the sun, leaving only the long burning petals of flame which were darting out on every side. The dark part was black, black, and the petals were a painful shimmering electric gold. The thing shone and shuddered and seemed to be getting closer, while at the same time it gave less and less light and the sky was darkening. It's killing me, thought George, it is a death thing, this is my death that I prayed for. Oh God, if I can only look away, or my eyes will be destroyed in my head. He turned, wrenching his head round. He caught a glimpse of the Ennistone Ring, quite close and bathed in an odd vivid crepuscular light. Then from beyond the Ring and coming toward him, there appeared a brilliant silver saucer-shaped space-ship, flying low down over the Common. It came toward George flying quite slowly, and as it came it emitted a ray which entered into his eyes, and a black utter darkness came upon him and he fell to his knees and lay stretched out senseless in the long grass.

And here some time later Father Bernard found him. The priest had first visited Diane, and had found her spreading out upon the bed all the frilly flowery summer clothes she had bought for going to Spain. He managed to conceal his agitation from Diane, and went on to Druidsdale where he found Stella. Stella realized at once that something was very wrong, but the priest told her nothing except that he urgently wanted to see George. It had already occurred to Father Bernard that George might have run up on to the Common and if he did so would be likely to go toward the Ring. Here Father Bernard stumbled about in vain in the long grasses, almost weeping with tiredness and distress, falling over courting couples whom the grass, uncut, was long enough to conceal, beginning to mistrust his intuition and increasingly to fear that, wherever George was, he would not be discovered alive. When at last he glimpsed, in the green sea into which the sun was now laying down long shadows, the familiar colour of George's grey jacket, and saw his dark hair, he fell down beside him with a cry of thankfulness.

George was lying on his face and seemed at first to be unconscious or asleep, as the priest laid his arm across the humped shoulders.

'George, George, it's me, Father Bernard, I've come to find you, wake up.'

George stirred, rolled on his side, opened his eyes, blinked a little, then closed them again.

'George – don't worry – it's me – I'll help you.'

George reached out and found a piece of the cassock and held it. He said, 'I killed John Robert. I drowned him. He's dead.'

'I know,' said the priest. He had read this, or something like it, in George's face as they met in the corridor. 'Only you didn't kill him, you *didn't*.'

'You mean he's still alive?'

'No, no, but *you didn't kill him*. Look, I'll show you.'

'He's still alive, thank God, it's a miracle – oh thank God.'

'George, George,' he cried, 'he is dead, but not by your hand, he took his own life – look at this –'

But George, hiding his face in the grass, just went on saying, 'Oh thank God – oh forgive me – oh thank God.'

'Look at this, look at *this*, look at his letter.'

George, turning on his side again, said, 'I can't see anything. I have become blind. I open my eyes and there is nothing, it is all dark, black. Was there an eclipse of the sun?'

'No.'

'I remember now. It was the flying saucer. It sent out a beam at me. It took my sight away.'

'George, my dear, get up, can you, I'll take you home. I'll explain – John Robert's dead – but you didn't kill him, you're not a murderer, you're not.'

Very slowly with the priest's help George rose to his feet. It was evident that he could not see. He swayed, holding out his hands. Together they stumbled as far as the path. It was late evening now, darkening to a clear greenish sunset sky.

As they began to walk slowly arm in arm along the path together Father Bernard asked, 'Where shall I take you to?'

'Take me home to Druidsdale. Stella is there.'

WHAT HAPPENED
AFTERWARDS

The inquest brought in a verdict of 'accidental death' upon the
decease of John Robert Rozanov, philosopher. George McCaffrey's name was never mentioned or thought of in this connection.
No one had seen him either enter or leave the Institute.

When Father Bernard got back there after leading George home
to Druidsdale he found the whole matter of the 'accident' completely set up. What had happened was clear. Rozanov had been
standing on the edge of the bath looking at his notebook and had
slipped and stunned himself in falling. The circumstances of the
death seemed to preclude suicide, and the only other theory which
circulated (hushed up by the Director, Vernon Chalmers) was that
the philosopher had been killed by a sudden inrush of scalding
water which had rendered him unconscious. Father Bernard gave
evidence at the inquest. He prayed for long hours to his inmost soul
for guidance about whether or not he should produce the suicide
note. In the end he was still uncertain about his duty but had
become afraid of getting into trouble for concealing evidence. The
inquest had been hustled on by Chalmers, who was afraid of talk
and adverse publicity, and the funeral, a cremation in accordance
with wishes expressed in the will, followed promptly. The national
press had taken due notice of John Robert's death, and various
outsiders turned up at the brief ceremony (which was organized by
Robin Osmore) including John Robert's pupil Steve Glatz who
happened to be in Oxford at the time, and a mysterious American
woman who cried a lot.

George's hysterical blindness left him after about a fortnight,
and after that the priest took Rozanov's letter round to show to
him. George nodded his head, but did not utter any words after
reading the note. Father Bernard brought it again on two occasions
until he was satisfied that George had really understood it,
although he still said nothing about it. Later on Father Bernard
showed the note to me.

I think the priest's intuition was probably right in guiding him not to reveal that Rozanov had intended to kill himself. Hattie Meynell, who felt enough guilt about it all in any case, was thereby spared the anguish of knowing that John Robert had proceeded almost directly from his conversation with her into the extremity of such an act. My own view is that John Robert had long been preparing his decision to die; this is certainly suggested by his possession of a specially compounded drug. And Hattie had perhaps not been mistaken in thinking that he was in a state of destructive despair about what he felt to be the failure of his philosophical work.

There are of course a number of factors in the case which must remain forever undecided. That John Robert should have chosen to die at the Institute is easily explained. He did not want to run the risk of being found by Hattie. But did Rozanov actually take the poisonous compound, did such a thing even exist? That it existed is, I think, given the man, simply proved by the letter, and equally I do not imagine Rozanov as one to delay or shirk, after writing the letter, the completion of the act. What caused his death? Was he, as is possible, already dead by the time George immersed him? And even if Rozanov did swallow a supposed lethal dose, would it necessarily have proved fatal? Supposing Father Bernard had arrived before George (as he might have done had he not gone first to Hare Lane)? Could the philosopher have been resuscitated? A confession by George together with the production of the suicide note would certainly have posed some interesting medical, legal and indeed philosophical problems. It is the sort of thing that would have interested John Robert, who might even have felt some odd ironical appreciation of George's last-minute intervention in his life. That, at least, would have held his attention. What would the law have judged George to be guilty of? And what indeed, as things stand, is he guilty of? All these unanswered questions are likely to continue to disturb the minds of both George and Father Bernard. I had several talks with Father Bernard before his departure (of which I shall speak below). I have not yet been able to talk to George, but I hope that, with Stella's help, this may prove possible in the near future.

Hattie suffered extreme grief and shock at her grandfather's sudden death. Love is joy, even impeded love is joy while hope remains, and of course Hattie did indeed love her 'newly found' grandfather and did not really believe his 'nevermore'. The instant frightful loss was hard to bear. She felt it moreover as 'her fault', because she had obeyed him and gone away, and had not, by staying, altered that accidental (as she thought) chain of events which led to that senseless fall on that slipper edge. Although she knew how unhappy John Robert was and why, I do not think that, given the circumstances, she has ever wondered whether that death was other than accidental. She has not, so far as I know, discussed John Robert's final revelation with anybody, probably not even with Tom. She has decided (here I am guessing) that this secret of the old man whom she so suddenly and strangely and briefly came to know and love is hers and hers alone. (Remarks which she made to me when very upset would have been comparatively obscure had I not had access to other sources of information.) Herein, as in other ways, she has shown herself to be a strong character. As for Tom McCaffrey, if he ever wondered whether he were not really being recruited to protect Hattie against John Robert himself, he has probably by now dismissed these speculations or indeed, in the felicity of his happy nature, forgotten them.

When it was that Tom untied Hattie's virgin knot is not known for certain. Perhaps it was during that first strange protected aeon of their love which lasted from Sunday morning to Monday evening, when they were told of John Robert's death. (The news that Hattie Meynell and Tom McCaffrey were together at the Slipper House had circulated in Ennistone as early as noon on Sunday. No doubt I was not the only witness of that early morning flight.) However that may be, Tom and Hattie were married in the autumn following all these events. Perhaps a period of mourning is not a bad preparation for a marriage. The match gave universal satisfaction in the town, not dimmed by those who enjoyed asserting that he would have done much better to marry Anthea Eastcote who was now so fearfully rich. As for Hattie's dowry, Tom did not do too badly. John Robert turned out to have saved quite a lot of money, even apart from his two houses in California, one at Palo Alto and one at Malibu.

The marriage took place according to the Quaker rite at the Meeting House, in the course of the usual meeting for worship, with only Friends present. Here, taking Hattie by the hand, Tom declared,

'In the presence of this assembly, I take my friend Harriet Meynell to be my wife, promising, with God's help, to be unto her a loving and faithful husband, so long as we both on earth shall live.'

After Hattie had made her answering declaration, Tom placed Feckless Fiona's wedding-ring upon Hattie's finger. A lot of people cried, not only Gabriel. There was a party afterwards at Belmont, instigated and, with remarkable success, organized by Gabriel who was suddenly able to put into practice a lot of her hitherto frustrated conceptions of what family life should be like. (Alex, who survived her fall, was at this time, as I shall explain later, in eclipse.) Brian walked about, saying with satisfaction, 'What a waste of money, thank God we're not paying.' Pearl was present as unofficial 'bridesmaid' and Emma in the role of 'best man'. Tom wanted him to sing but he refused. There were no speeches. The occasion, like that of many weddings, brought together a number of lively persons, who had not all hitherto met, and who all seemed very pleased with themselves. Milton Eastcote was present. So was Steve Glatz, who is now editing John Robert's surviving notebooks which constitute the 'great work', of which so much is expected. Margot (*née* Meynell) Markowitz turned up with her Jewish lawyer husband, Albert (who had, Pearl and Hattie agreed, greatly improved her). Verity Smaldon, Hattie's pretty school friend, made a refreshing dint in the grieving heart of Andrew Blackett. I had the pleasure of making the acquaintance of Stella's father, Sir David Henriques, with whom, as she predicted, I got on extremely well. Hector Gaines, lately engaged to a well-known academic lady, came especially to show off his recovery to Anthea, but suffered, on seeing her, a regrettable relapse. (This may be the place to add that, in spite of all our various misfortunes, *The Triumph of Aphrodite* was successfully performed – the show must go on, as Hector said – and even attracted the favourable attention of London critics.) Joey Tanner made his first appearance as Anthea's fiancé. He made a bad impression on the town gossips, but chiefly because they were determined to think he was marrying her for her money. Emma's mother on the other hand, looking incredibly young, charmed everyone. Matchmakers, who abound at weddings, were certain that she and Sir David were made for each other. Gavin Oare was not invited, but Mike Seanu came under the wing of Nesta, Olivia and Valerie to 'cover' the event for the *Gazette*. Ruby, no longer employed at Belmont, came as a guest but helped Gabriel and Dorothy Osmore with the washing-up. Judy Osmore, to please Gabriel (for she was a kind-hearted girl), wore the dress which had been dyed with tea. (She did not know the details of its misadventure.) Zed, wearing a white ribbon and a red rose, was

545

petted by many and stepped on by not a few. Adam, who in the intervening months had suddenly decided to grow considerably, wore a dark suit especially made for him by Dominic Wiggins. In this he hovered, hardly recognizable as a tall slim solemn youth with large eyes. George too was present for a while, watchfully piloted by Stella. He was generally and vaguely known to have been 'rather ill'. A lot of people made a point of greeting him but retiring quickly.

I must now try to give some account of what happened to George. This is difficult because, as I say, I have not yet had the opportunity of talking with him, although I have talked at length with Stella; she remains puzzled about her husband and may even still harbour long-standing misconceptions about him. It is a feature of marriages, including happy ones, that two people who live together may have quite false ideas of each other. This does not at all necessarily lead to disaster or even inconvenience. Stella, to speak of her first, has suffered from feelings of guilt which may well be a good deal more rational than those of Hattie. Her image has remained in my mind of George hooked by a long invisible line by which she held him fast while letting him run: an image which she agreed to be terrible. More simply, Stella assumed that George would somehow be restored to her 'in the fullness of time', that she would at last, and satisfactorily, 'get him back'. Meanwhile she was prepared to watch and wait because, as she had put it, George 'interested her absolutely'. This could also be put as 'because she loved him absolutely', which indeed she did with her whole intense almost fanatical being. Some people thought Stella was simply afraid of George, others blamed her for 'abandoning' him. Rozanov's death was counted as the event which brought her back and 'sobered George up', while visibly, in some sense which remained difficult to determine, changing him.

In retrospect of course Stella blamed herself for not having, and as a matter of course, returned to George soon after the episode of the car in the canal. Indeed shortly after she had (her phrase) 'put herself under my protection', I advised her to go back, but she would not. Once she had formally 'run away' it became harder and harder to return, her pride had become involved in the matter, speculation about him had become an activity and a pleasure, being in hiding had its charm, and the interval carried an imaginary sense of healing. It must be added to this picture that Stella's undoubted love contained ingredients of anger and even cruelty and she could not help feeling that by staying mysteriously away she was inflicting some sort of punishment upon George. Ought Stella, as she herself later believed, to have been able to foresee the extremities of which George was capable? (I should say here that George told her everything, every detail of what he had done, and as far as he could why he had done it, during the period of his blindness.) With this question she came running to me. I told her sincerely that I thought the answer was no. Stella was of course, as she came to admit, fascinated by George's 'violent tendencies'. But it was part of her theory that these had run their course and that, however oddly George might in the interim behave, he would before long, and harmlessly, return to her to be 'saved'. In this connection she attached an almost magical significance to the 'attempted murder' in the canal, which was supposed to be the significant final crisis or turning point. Herein Stella was perhaps misled by vanity, a simple and ubiquitous failing often overlooked by those who profess to explain the mysteries of human conduct. As for the prediction, I think that homicidal or suicidal acts often depend upon contingent elements too tiny and too sheerly accidental to be discernible by the eye of science. And I have to admit that I myself did not foresee or expect what ultimately happened.

Naturally Stella attaches great significance to the fact that George asked Father Bernard to lead him back to her after he had been struck down on the Common. Since that moment George has never once mentioned Diane. What happened to George's brain cells in the curious episode of the flying saucer and the sunflower sun remains, in part, to be seen. The brain is a versatile organ and has an amazing capacity to repair damage. I do not, incidentally, hold Dr Roach's epilepsy theory about George. I also take this opportunity to deny that George has had a lobotomy or any electric shock treatment since John Robert's death. I also know for a fact that he has not, to use the rather melodramatic expression current in Ennistone, 'been through the hands of Sir Ivor Sefton'. The mild drugs which he took in the early days of his 'new life' have now, according to Stella, been discontinued. Whatever the cause, there is no doubt that he is a changed, and still changing man. A stranger, meeting him now for the first time, would find him an ordinary, quiet person. (Not, as Stella put it, 'weak and pale like a grub in an apple'.) Those who knew 'the old George' are amazed at his 'reform', though it is still true that none of his old acquaintances feels quite comfortable with him. He is gentle, polite, quietly humorous (though he smiles little), attentive to his wife, interested in the details of everyday existence. He even has a modest social life. What I cannot find out from Stella, perhaps because she is reluctant to find it out herself, is whether there are identifiable tracts of his mind, evidenced by memory or performance, which seem to have been 'blotted out'. She insists that he seems 'normal'. Sometimes, however, this unnatural 'normality' seems to her 'too good to be true' and she wonders if he will one day suddenly attack her with an axe. As the weeks and months go by, this idea occurs to her less and less often. George stays at home and reads a lot. He reads books on art history and even makes notes on them. One day Stella found him looking over his old plays which had evidently not been destroyed after all. He has also taken up bridge again, and goes out with Stella (who is a very good player) to bridge evenings at the Osmores'. He has not been over to Leafy Ridge to visit Brian and Gabriel, but he is polite and amiable to them if they visit Druidsdale, which they rarely do, as they think Stella is not too pleased to see them. Adam and Zed on the other hand are fairly frequent and welcome visitors. George seems to talk a lot to Adam when they are alone together, Stella is not quite sure what about. I lately expressed the hope to Stella that now that life has become (it seems) more predictable she should stop regarding George as a full-time occupation, and consider harnessing her excellent mind to some coherent and developing intellectual study. She says that no doubt she will, but 'not yet', that perhaps she will 'write something'. I am afraid that at present she is more concerned about George's mind than about her own. I also asked her, recalling a question which I put to her earlier, whether a quiet docile George continues to interest her. She says most emphatically that he does and that she loves him now in a new and better way. She was always possessively watchful, but now seems to me, when I see them together, to be more tender and 'sentimental', and in this sense, she is without doubt profitably 'occupied' with her husband. I have not inquired about their sex life. Perhaps she is right to see these developments as 'new and better', and it may even be that love, that old unpredictable force left out of account by natural science, will actually 'save', after all, not only him but her.

I have mentioned the departure of Father Bernard. With this, and in a bizarre way, is to be associated the fate of 'our own Madame Diane'. As may be imagined, Diane was cast into the deepest grief and indeed despair by George's sudden and total (and inexplicable) defection. The news that he 'was ill' and had definitely returned to his wife flashed quickly round Ennistone, and Diane heard it from several eager sources at the Institute. She had imagined in the extremest detail their new life in Spain. With extra money which he had given her she had bought herself every sort of garment which might be required for life in a hot country and appearances on the beach. She felt for the first time in many years, perhaps ever, almost happy. Now suddenly George had been taken from her as totally as if by death, and she entertained no hope of seeing him again. Her abandonment of hope was impressively rapid and complete. Had she ever really believed in Spain? No doubt like many of those who lead precarious lives she had a good deal of 'instant desperation' stored up for dealing promptly with catastrophe, when the worst pain is the continuation of fruitless hope. She considered suicide but turned instead to the priest.

People often take other people's crises as a symbol for their own, and are guided as by a sign. Several unfortunates known to me decided, after they had become aware of George's change of being, that it was time for them to change too. Father Bernard was one of these: one who had the additional impetus of extreme shock. With a most inconvenient and unbecoming haste, most disturbing to a hierarchy which had become more used to his eccentricities than he realized, he divested himself of his priestly power. He wrote to his bishop announcing his decision and asking to be immediately laicized, and from one day to the next abruptly ceased conducting church services. He moved out of the Clergy House into a lodging in Burkestown. In doing so he gave away most of his possessions. In this way Hector Gaines acquired a large number of books, some of them quite esoteric, on theological and religious matters, and I acquired the Gandhara Buddha, which is on my desk at this very moment. During this time, conspicuous in his shabby mufti, he went about a lot and talked a lot to the various people who visited him or invited him out of sympathy or curiosity, declaring frequently that he was going to Greece and would end his days as a servant in some remote monastery on Mount Athos. The next news was that he had actually gone and had taken Diane Sedleigh with him.

No one suggested, nor do I think, that there was any relation between them other than tender friendship. Diane had never made any secret, among those to whom she talked (and who of course talked to others), of her special affection for the priest whom she valued so much because he was 'not like other men'. The idea of leaving not only Ennistone but England had become firmly fixed in Diane's mind. She was maddened by jealousy of Stella, and everything she saw reminded her of George. But she had never been out of the country before and hardly ever farther afield than London. She needed a guide and escort, and the idea of 'pairing up' with the priest may well have been hers. Their objective was certainly Greece, though how they intended to live there was never clear perhaps even to them. The mirage was, in any case, never made trial of since, to use Father Bernard's own words in a letter to me, he simply 'lost her' in Paris. After they had spent one night there at a cheap hotel near the Gare du Nord, while the priest (for so he undoubtedly and in spite of everything still thought of himself) was away buying their railway tickets Diane simply walked out and disappeared. Father Bernard waited several days and then went on to Greece by himself. He did not consider going to the police.

What happened to Diane was something which might have belonged to her own fantasy life. The excitement of being in Paris produced a sudden wild euphoria, the more intense by its contrast with the despairing lassitude in which she had recently been plunged. She went out, I think, simply to seek her fortune, to 'live dangerously' and 'have an adventure'. She made her way to a hotel in Saint-Germain-des-Prés and here she met Milton Eastcote. The meeting was accidental, and yet had also a perfectly comprehensible background. The hotel in question was one which William Eastcote had frequented in his student days (it is a good deal grander now, but still not very expensive) and George had learnt of it from William and had stayed there once or twice. He mentioned its name to Diane during one of their brief fantasies of flight together. Diane had noted the name of the hotel and used to meditate upon it as on an amorous mantra. She went there so as to set eyes on it at last, and because she thought it might bring her luck. It did. Milton Eastcote, who had also learnt of the hotel from his cousin, used it as his Paris base. Milton's philanthropic activities were perfectly genuine, he did indeed help prostitutes and other outcasts, and his good works in the east end of London were justly esteemed. However, like many more people than you might imagine, he had a quite other and secret side to his character, and in the course of saving fallen women sometimes discreetly saved one for himself. Diane had been pointed out to him at William's funeral, where she had attracted attention by appearing with George. He had liked her type. Now suddenly she materialized before him in Paris. He approached her courteously. Diane now lives in a pleasant airy apartment on the Quai aux Fleurs with a view of Notre Dame. I saw her there myself not long ago. Diane has invented a past for herself which is more in keeping with her present affluence, and has indeed done her very best to become a different person. She has learnt with creditable speed to speak passable French. Self-interest can stimulate intelligence, and her wits have no doubt been sharpened by her sense of the urgency of at last grasping her future with both hands. She seems to feel quite secure. When I saw her, tea was brought in by a uniformed maid. She inquired, with an air of sympathetic concern, after 'poor George'.

Emma and Pearl have also 'done well', although they failed to complete the romantic symmetry of our midsummer idyll by getting married. There has been, by mutual agreement between that estimable pair, no romance. They could not but be brought together again, after Rozanov's death, by their concern and affection for Tom and Hattie. But it was soon clear to both that mutual sexual relations are not for them. They have instead become (and I predict will steadily remain) fast friends, bringing a lot of affection, happiness and wisdom into each other's lives. Contrary to Emma's expectations, Pearl gets on very well with his mother, especially on the basis of endlessly discussing him. Pearl (here I claim some credit) has been encouraged to think it is not too late to chase after some education, and does not lack advice about how to set about it. Fortunately too her considerable 'watchdog' savings can buy her time, which she spends passionately studying for exams in a flat in north London, where Emma, Tom and Hattie are frequent visitors. Meanwhile, one of Emma's problems was solved by the sudden disappearance of Mr Hanway, who ran off to Italy with one of his pupils. Emma received his apologetic letter with relief. (It appeared from the letter that Mr Hanway imagined that Emma was deeply and inconsolably dependent on him; such are the misunderstandings which can exist between people who look into each other's eyes.) With Mr Hanway gone, it seemed to Emma that perhaps he could just go on singing, without having to give it up because he could not dedicate his whole life to it. (He still worries about this question, however.) Emma gained the brilliant 'first' predicted for him and is now a fellow of Balliol College, Oxford. On the whole he is happy, when he is not thinking about Ireland. And to return, a little further on in time, to our hero and heroine, Tom got himself a sound second-class degree and hopes to find a teaching job, while Hattie has taught herself Russian and is going to the School of Slavonic Studies. Tom continues to work on his poetry (he lately had a poem printed in *The Times Literary Supplement*) and has started a novel. Even though his university career failed of the hoped-for brilliance, the town remains convinced that he will turn out to be a great writer.

I shall now draw towards an end by inserting as a final document a letter which I received from Greece from Father Bernard.

My dear N,

Thank you for yours which I picked up at the Poste Restante on one of my rare visits to Athens. I was interested in all the news, though I must confess that Ennistone and all its folk seem very far away now and not a little (may I say it) provincial! So Diane has become a lady at last, or sort of! I wish her well. Her disappearance from my life was providential. Her presence would have given rise to misunderstandings and would have seriously impaired my single-mindedness. The essence of my news is ineffable, but I can list a few facts. Things went badly at Mount Athos (no one's fault, the holy men are simply not very intelligent). After that there occurred an event at Delphi about which I will try to tell you if we ever meet again. I know you are open-minded about what you call paranormal phenomena and I call religious experience. About the latter I have indeed learnt something since I came to this numinous country. I have also been led at last to a clear understanding of my true vocation. I, and others (how many are we, I wonder?), are *chosen* to strive for the continuance of religion on this planet. Nothing else but *true religion* can save mankind from a lightless and irredeemable materialism, from a technocratic nightmare where determinism *becomes true* for all except an *unimaginably depraved* few, who are themselves the mystified slaves of a conspiracy of machines. The challenge has gone forth and in the deep catacombs the spirit has stirred to a new life. But can we be in time, can religion survive and not, with us, utterly perish? This has been *revealed* to me as the essential and only question of our age. What is necessary is the *absolute denial of God*. Even the word, the name, must go. What then remains? Everything, and Christ too, but entirely changed and broken down into the most final and absolutely naked simplicity, into atoms, into electrons, into protons. The inner is the outer, the outer is the inner: an old story, but who really understands it? It is vitally *important* that I live now in a *cave*. Well, it is a tiny abandoned chapel, a slit made in a rock. Do not ask me how I found it. I live in a solitary place beside the sea surrounded by white stones and brilliant green pine trees. I have made a wooden cross. Fireflies are my lamp at night. I lie at the bottom of the world, and I cannot express to you how *brilliantly* it shines upon me, the light of an untainted Good. My bread is as pure as the stones, I drink from a nearby spring. The Anglican Church has amazingly granted me a tiny pension, but I do not need it since some nearby villagers have adopted me (they think I am mad) and every day bring gifts of loaves and fishes. I have no doubt that when cold weather comes someone will bring me a brazier. So I live. I preach to my flock in New Testament Greek and by a miracle they understand me. (I am also learning their *patois*.) When no one comes I preach to the sea birds. What do I preach? That there is no God, that even the beauty of Christ is a snare and a lie. 'Nothing exists except God and the soul': and when one has understood *that*, one knows that there is no God. For what is real and true look at these stones, this bread, this spring of water, these sea waves, this horizon with its pure untroubled line. Only perceive purely and the spiritual and the material world vibrate as one. (This was revealed to me at Delphi.) The power that saves is infinitely simple and infinitely close at hand.

I cannot go on. It is sacrilege to utter words which are bound to be misunderstood. My simple peasants understand my Greek better than you will understand my English. When how and whether I shall be called to a larger ministry I know not. Perhaps I shall have to journey afar, perhaps in the end the world will come to me here, or perhaps I shall die obscurely and soon. Meanwhile I cast about me as I may the seeds of truth. May the clean wind of the spirit bear them to fruitful beds.

Now about what you had to say in your letter about John Robert: I believe that you are wrong. You are too *interested*, it is for you a spectacle. I have thought about him and prayed over him too, as I pray now. I was his last pupil and I failed the test. If I had known what I know now I could have saved both him and George. John Robert asked me not to speak of George *and I agreed* because I was afraid of him and because I was flattered by his attention. When I spoke of pastoral duty he said, 'You don't believe it', and I bowed my head, and the cock crew thrice. So it is that I have witnessed three murders, two by George and one by that philosopher (perhaps there is a teaching in this). John Robert died because he saw at last, with horrified wide-open eyes, the futility of philosophy. Metaphysics and the human sciences are made impossible by the *penetration of morality into the moment to moment conduct of ordinary life*: the understanding of this fact *is religion*. This is what Rozanov distantly glimpsed when he was picking away at questions of good and evil, and he knew that it made nonsense of all his sophisms.

There is no beyond, there is only here, the infinitely small, infinitely great and utterly demanding present. This too I tell my flock, demolishing their dreams of a supernatural elsewhere. So you see, I have abandoned every kind of magic and preach a charmless holiness. This and only this can be the religion of the future, this and only this can save the planet.

But I write in water. I shall give this letter to one of my people. I know not if it will ever be posted. Goodbye, my dear N, I raise my hand to bless you.

Yours, Bernard Jacoby

The local priest has just visited me. He seems displeased! Perhaps I am destined for martyrdom after all!

I read part of this letter (not all of it of course) to Brian and Gabriel. Gabriel stopped a tear. Brian said, '*Everybody* seems to be going batty these days.'

I should say that Brian and Gabriel are for the present, perhaps permanently, living at Belmont and looking after Alex, and Ruby has come back there too. While Alex was in hospital, Ruby fled to the gipsy camp where she seemed to assume that she would now spend the rest of her days. Mike Seanu brought her back to Brian and Gabriel at Como. Later (when Brian declared the house too small for him *and* Ruby) she went to stay with Pearl in London. It has appeared however that Ruby cannot exist outside Ennistone, and when Brian and Gabriel moved to Belmont, Gabriel insisted that she should come back. She has got her pension from Alex after all, arranged by Robin Osmore, and is rumoured to have considerable savings since she never spent any of her salary. I have forgotten to speak of Alex. She never fully recovered from that fall down the stairs. As Stella said, Alex's fall prefigured George's, and had a similar effect. Alex is a shadow of her old self, all that bossy curiosity, that bright restless power, has quite gone. She is (or seems) perfectly rational, but has become very quiet. She spends long times sitting at the big bow window in the drawing-room and looking out. (And what does she see when she does so? Foxes. Our worthy municipal officers, with what our citizens call their 'usual efficiency', certainly pumped in the lethal gas, but took a long time doing so and failed to block all the exits of the earth, so that the foxes were able to decamp in safety. The 'fox menace' has now, since the recent council elections, passed out of the public gaze.) Alex rarely goes visiting, but her old friends come to see her, and even her new acquaintances, whom Gabriel calls 'tourists', including Father Bernard's successor, an elderly youth with a guitar. She likes to be given little presents, anything pleases her, flowers, chocolates, or model animals of which she is making a collection. She does not read much, or watch television, but listens constantly to the radio, including classical music programmes which never interested her before. When visited she initiates no conversation, but will talk readily about the topics proposed. Naturally, her visitors choose these with care. She and Ruby are back on their old silent terms except that of course Alex is less peremptory and (so at least Gabriel is pleased to think) Ruby is gentler and more affectionate. The only time Alex shows any emotion is when George comes to see her, as he sometimes does, accompanied always by Stella, who never leaves his side. At these meetings, one of which I witnessed, George makes a visible touching effort to make the conversation a success. He shows an unwonted animation and tries to make his mother respond, and sometimes it seems that some glimmer of the old Alex is about to appear. However, confusion ensues, the danger of tears, and Stella sees to it that these visits are suitably short. Dr Roach is pessimistic, but I am not. As I said, it is remarkable how ably old brain cells can learn new tricks, I have seen this happen many times. I shall certainly watch both these cases with the utmost interest.

Whenever I see Gabriel she always turns the conversation on to George, displaying an almost spiteful obsession with his disabilities. Of course she is jealous of Stella's absolute possession of George, and the determined way in which she keeps Brian and Gabriel at a distance. The other day (we met at the Baths where the colder weather has again covered the water with a pall of steam) she described George as 'spiritless, characterless and good'. And of Stella: 'She always wanted him maimed, she's his nurse now, she imagines her love-cure has saved him, but it's just that he's broken.'

Brian, coming up, added, 'It's just as well he's broken. He was too bloody dangerous when he was in working order.' And Gabriel, 'It's sad in a way. Both our monsters are quite tame now.' She said it soberly but with a kind of natural satisfaction.

However, lest *I* should now seem to be spiteful, let me say that Gabriel is very kind and tirelessly attentive to Alex, and seems to be in general more reconciled to being a wife and mother. Perhaps, after witnessing the troubles of others, she feels how lucky she is to have a loyal decent husband, even if he is bad-tempered, and a fine tall growing-up son. She may at times be heard to murmur, 'Of course, George would have been perfectly ordinary if only Rufus had lived.' I doubt if she is right.

I find it difficult myself to leave the subject of George, whom I confess I enjoy discussing regularly with Stella. Stella says she thinks George has started to write poetry, though he always hides it when she comes in, and she takes this as a hopeful sign. She believes that although George had been daydreaming for some time about murdering his old teacher, he really decided to kill him after he received the philosopher's final savage letter, only at first he concealed this decision from himself by imagining a final liberation from the relationship. 'I felt I had really finished with him,' George told Stella, 'only he ... *provoked* me so ...' This accords with what Tom has since told me of the extraordinary 'radiance' (he used this word), a sort of unnatural visionary calm which surrounded George when they met at Diane's flat just after, it appears, George had received the letter. George's reflections on his mental state, which he imparted to Stella during the period of his blindness, reveal indeed a considerable capacity for self-knowledge. He even tried to explain to her what it was like to feel that a murder is a duty. What it was that 'moved' George from liberated euphoria to effective murderous hate must however remain a missing link. To say that the radiant euphoria 'was really' the scarcely conscious fore-knowledge of the final determination to act is merely a way of stating the problem. The motivation of terrible deeds tends to be extremely complex, full of apparent contradictions, and often in fact bottomlessly mysterious, although for legal, scientific and moral reasons we 'have to' theorize about it. I have never ventured to suggest to Stella that the peculiar shock of her return, with its reminder of an old jealousy, might have had some decisive effect upon her husband. I do not know whether she ever reflects upon this distressing idea. It would be a sad irony if her inopportune mention of the philosopher's name should have prompted the violence which ended this tale as well as that which began it. Was the final 'provocation' hers after all, and not John Robert's? Such are the chance 'triggers' which may determine our most fateful actions and yet remain opaque particulars with which science can do little.

Since his early outpourings George has not talked much about the past. It is hard to say how far his present mien is instinctive and how far it is a deliberate façade (the distinction can often be unclear). He seems like a much older man, his hair is turning grey and he treats people with a slow kindly dignified condescension. As I said earlier, and I based it on something Stella told me, George was fascinated by Nazi war criminals and identified himself in fantasy with these condemned and defeated monsters. Perhaps now he is enacting the part of one who after many years in prison emerges not exactly repentant but full of stoical wisdom, facing the truth, quiet and proud, acknowledging his acts as his own. George seems to have perceived his own 'double-think' about his false 'liberation' from John Robert. I wonder if he has also understood the part played in his mental stratagems by his old fantasy, derived so he thought from John Robert himself, of being 'beyond good and evil'? More often than the 'experts' imagine, purely *intellectual* ideas and images can play 'deep' parts in human psychology. I do not despair of discussing these questions one day with George, indeed with Stella's help this may now come about in the not too distant future. Some of the dedicated George-watchers in the town are of the opinion that George has 'found Jesus'. Of course this is a nonsense, most vociferously denied by Stella. However, she reported something rather touching which George said lately, 'Well, he said that Caliban must be saved too.' About *him* Stella and I often talk. Steve Glatz has been questioning Stella about John Robert, and Stella tells me how prudently she has replied. Steve is writing a memoir about Rozanov, to be expanded later into a definitive 'life'. He showed me a little of this piece, in which the philosopher has been metamorphosed into some kind of saint! He is also busy reconstructing the drowned notebook of the 'great work' from his own lecture notes. Meanwhile between ourselves Stella and I have been agreeing that perhaps John Robert was not really quite such a great man as we all imagined.

Steve Glatz is very much upon the Ennistone scene at present. Anthea Eastcote has broken off her engagement with Joey Tanner, thus satisfying those who held that 'he was only after her money'. Anthea is now said to be 'involved' with Steve, and Tom and Hattie have lent them the little house at Malibu. Mr and Mrs Tom McCaffrey still live at the Slipper House, where Pearl and Emma often come to stay, putting up with Tom's heavy humour at their expense. Tom and Emma maintain a steady *amitié amoureuse*, although neither of them would dream of using that expression, or indeed alluding to the matter in any way. Hattie and Pearl love each other with the deep love of childhood friends, tempered by the love of those who have been shipwrecked together. They often talk of John Robert, but not of the shipwreck. With an instinctive delicacy which is natural to both, Pearl never speaks of her secret love for the philosopher, nor has Hattie discussed with her those last terrible days at Hare Lane. I wonder (for of course I would never ask her this) whether she ever meditates upon the strange fact that it was John Robert and not Tom who first awakened her sexually. It is certainly fascinating to consider how successfully (and indeed how literally), in the end, the philosopher carried out his plan of thrusting her into Tom McCaffrey's arms.

I share the general view that the marriage will be a happy one. I see Hattie as the leader. Tom and Hattie still sometimes discuss whether they would have come to love each other without being urged to do so by John Robert's tremendous willpower. They agree that, even though he brought them together, this merely counts as one of those pieces of pure luck that bring about happy marriages. Hattie is determined not to let her university studies prevent her from starting a family. She feels sure that the first child will be a girl. Perhaps John Robert ought to have waited after all? Tom and Hattie intend to have a lot of children, so there will be plenty more McCaffreys available in the future for the inhabitants of Ennistone to gossip about.

The end of any tale is arbitrarily determined. As I now end this one, somebody may say: but how on earth do you know all these things about all these people? Well, where does one person end and another person begin? It is my role in life to listen to stories. I also had the assistance of a certain lady.

THE END

MORE ABOUT PENGUINS, PELICANS
AND PUFFINS

For further information about books available from Penguins please write to Dept EP, Penguin Books Ltd, Harmondsworth, Middlesex UB7 0DA.

In the U.S.A.: For a complete list of books available from Penguins in the United States write to Dept DG, Penguin Books, 299 Murray Hill Parkway, East Rutherford, New Jersey 07073.

In Canada: For a complete list of books available from Penguins in Canada write to Penguin Books Canada Ltd, 2801 John Street, Markham, Ontario L3R 1B4.

In Australia: For a complete list of books available from Penguins in Australia write to the Marketing Department, Penguin Books Australia Ltd, P.O. Box 257, Ringwood, Victoria 3134.

In New Zealand: For a complete list of books available from Penguins in New Zealand write to the Marketing Department, Penguin Books (N.Z.) Ltd, P.O. Box 4019, Auckland 10.

In India: For a complete list of books available from Penguins in India write to Penguin Overseas Ltd, 706 Eros Apartments, 56 Nehru Place, New Delhi 110019.

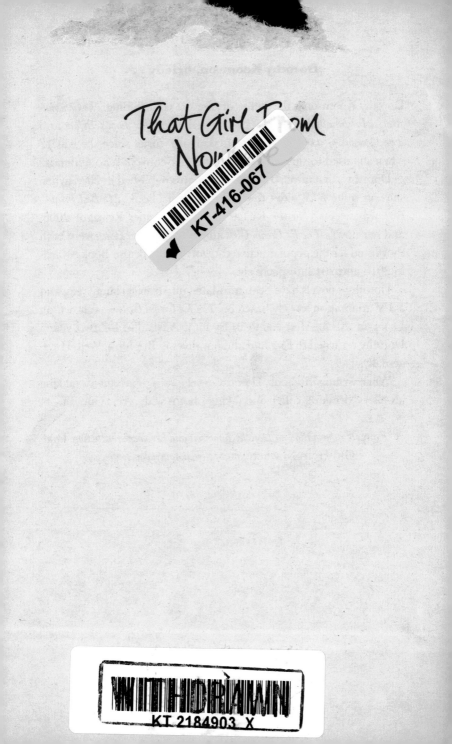

*That Girl From
Nowhere*

KT-416-067

Dorothy Koomson, briefly . . .

Dorothy Koomson is the author of nine novels including *The Chocolate Run*, *Marshmallows For Breakfast*, *The Woman He Loved Before* and *The Flavours of Love*. She's been making up stories since she was 13 when she used to share her stories with her convent school friends.

Dorothy's first novel, *The Cupid Effect*, was published in 2003 (when she was quite a bit older than 13). Her third book, *My Best Friend's Girl*, was selected for the Richard & Judy Summer Reads of 2006, and her novels *The Ice Cream Girls* and *The Rose Petal Beach* were both shortlisted for the popular fiction category of the British Book Awards in 2010 and 2013, respectively.

Dorothy's novels have been translated into over 30 languages, and a TV adaptation loosely based on *The Ice Cream Girls* was shown on ITV1 in 2013. After living in Sydney, Australia, for two years, Dorothy returned to England and now lives in Brighton. Well, Hove, actually.

While writing this book, Dorothy developed a penchant for making jewellery, drinking coffee and taking photos with a real camera.

For more information on Dorothy Koomson and her novels, including That Girl From Nowhere, *visit www.dorothykoomson.co.uk*

That Girl From Nowhere

Dorothy
KOOMSON

arrow books

1 3 5 7 9 10 8 6 4 2

Arrow Books
20 Vauxhall Bridge Road
London SW1V 2SA

Arrow Books is part of the Penguin Random House group of companies
whose addresses can be found at global.penguinrandomhouse.com.

Penguin
Random House
UK

Copyright © Dorothy Koomson 2015

Dorothy Koomson has asserted her right under the Copyright, Designs and
Patents Act 1988 to be identified as the author of this work.

First published in Great Britain in 2015 by Century
This edition published by Arrow Books, 2016

www.randomhouse.co.uk

A CIP catalogue record for this book is
available from the British Library.

ISBN 9780099598831

Typeset in Baskerville (12/15pt) by SX Composing DTP, Rayleigh, Essex

Printed and bound in Great Britain by Clays Ltd, St Ives Plc

This book is dedicated, with love, to my dad –
sometimes disapproving but *always* supportive.

*I've decided to say my thanks with KISSES (**K**eep **I**t **S**hort, **S**weet and **E**specially **S**imple). So . . .*

Thank you

to my gorgeous family who are everything to me
to Ant and James, my wonderful agents
to all the fantastic people at my publishers, Cornerstone (especially Susan, Jenny G, Gillian, Jen D, Richard, Charlotte, Natalie, Rebecca, Aslan)
to Emma D and Sophie, my great publicists.

A special thank you goes to those who helped with my research, particularly Sarah Marshall and Chris Manby, who also provided brilliant long chats as well as info.

And to E, G & M – thank you for being so amazing in every way. I love you.

As always, I would like to say thank you to you, the reader, for buying this book.

Prologue

'You will help me, won't you?' she asks.

'If I can,' I reply. I wonder what she thinks someone she has just met will be able to help her do when she has a whole family down the hall in the living room who are at her beck and call. 'What is it you want help with?'

This woman, my grandmother, who has only really been in my life for the past hour, fixes me with a gaze that is determined and a little frightening, woven through with strands of defiance. Maybe I was mistaken; maybe those outside this room aren't as devoted and loving as I thought. Whatever it is that she wants to do is clearly something they're unlikely to agree to. She says nothing for a time, and the longer she stares at me with her brown eyes, the colour dimmed by age, the more a feeling of dread meanders outwards from the pit of my stomach. I should not be sitting here having this conversation with this woman. I should have brought her back here and left her to it. The longer I sit here, the longer things are going to go wrong for me.

Eventually, so eventually I thought she was planning on remaining silent, she speaks. Cautiously, haltingly, she says: 'My time has come. I am too old...too sick...too tired to carry on in this world.' She pauses but her eyes continue to drill into me. 'My time has come. I want...I want to leave this Earth. I need you to help me.'

Part 1

1

Smitty

'Miss Smittson, it's good to see you again.'

'You, too, Mr Wallace,' I reply. I smile at him and shove my hands into the pockets of my combat trousers to avoid having to shake hands with him. I've met him twice before – both times I've had to do it and both times his hand has been hot and clammy. The images of what he could have done to get it that way were a horror movie that played constantly through my head.

Mr Wallace, in a shabby, too-tight black suit, offers me his hand to shake. I hesitate. The rest of him seems dry and normal, I wonder if he'd accept a hug instead? It would get me out of touching his hand without seeming rude and it'd be altogether better for my mental health. He pulls a smile across his face, sticks his hand out a little bit further. Defeated, I offer up my hand to be encased in his moist, sweaty palm. The touch of him sends a shudder through me and I can't take my hand away fast enough, but not too fast in case he notices and his feelings are hurt. Maybe he can't help being sweaty-palmed, maybe he has a condition and it's not his fault. Maybe the horror movie in my head has got it all wrong and he doesn't do unsavoury things in his car before he meets clients.

Mr Wallace's attention strays to the older woman with wavy brown, grey-streaked hair who stands silently beside me. He smiles curiously at us both, waiting for an introduction.

Mum has obviously noticed how reluctant I was to shake the estate agent's hand so has taken to holding her bag in both hands, rendering them incapable of being shaken when I do the introductions.

'Mr Wallace, this is my mother, Heather Smittson,' I say. 'Mum, this is the estate agent who's dealing with renting the flat.'

Immediately, Mr Wallace's face does *that thing*. 'That thing' most people who don't know my family do: he double-takes, then rapidly moves his gaze from one of us to the other, wondering why the visuals don't match the words. After the staring comes the perplexed, suspicious frown and, right on cue, Mr Wallace's confusion develops on his face until he is frowning very hard indeed at us.

We're in the car park of a beautiful, reddish-yellow-brick, art deco block of flats on Hove seafront. This is going to be my new home, the place for my fresh start. Everything bad is three hundred miles away and in that place called 'the past' while everything good is here, and about to happen in that shiny new destination called 'the future'.

Except little snags like this, a man who is nearer to Mum's age than mine, giving us his version of Paddington Bear's hard stare because he doesn't understand why Mum is my mother and why I am her daughter. To him, it surely shouldn't be possible.

Mum suddenly needs something from her handbag, and she pops the black leather rectangle open and starts to ferret furiously through it. Clearly what she is searching for is so important the world might end if she doesn't find it RIGHT NOW. What she is actually doing is her version of 'Lalalalalala not happening', which she does every time she might need to explain our situation. If the handbag thing doesn't work, she'll simply wander off, pretending that she doesn't know we're in the middle of a conversation.

With Mum making it clear with every root through her meticulously organised bag that she isn't going to be forthcoming, Mr Wallace returns to me. It's now my job to explain. I'm supposed to say, 'I'm adopted'. To let him know that Mum and Dad did the whole white parents taking on black children thing well before various celebs made it fashionable. He stares at me, I stare at him – he wants answers to his unasked questions, I'm not giving them. I haven't got the energy.

As if someone On High knows I need rescuing, Mr Wallace's left, inside breast pocket begins to vibrate before the tinny, tiny sound of 'YMCA' joins it. 'Oh, excuse me,' he says and reaches for it. He checks the screen, grimaces, struggles with himself. 'I'm sorry, I have to get this. It's an emergency waiting to happen. Do you mind?' He's pressed the answer button and put it to his ear before I even have a chance to react. He wanders away from us, heading across the promenade and towards the blue-green railings that separate land from sea.

'Well, that was rude,' Mum states. She removes her head and her hand from her bag, snaps it closed again with a loud click as the brass clasp shuts itself tight. 'We were in the middle of a conversation.'

'You mean I was,' the person I am in my head says. *'You were going, "lalalala, not happening".'* The person I actually am says, 'It's fine, Mum. It gives us a chance to have a proper look at the place. So what do you think?'

This building is as beautiful as it is commanding. The bottom part of it is painted cream and looks from a distance like a short, satiny cream skirt, while the top half looks like it has been dressed in a blouse of russet sandstone. The corners of the building are curved instead of pointed and the whole of the top floor is apparently one penthouse apartment. My flat is on the first floor, and most of it overlooks the sea. I'd spent far too much money on renting it, even with the huge discount I'd got because it'd been empty for so long and the owners were desperate to fill it. It didn't matter about the money right now, it would come out of my savings, and it was only for six months before I decided what to do next.

Mum, who rarely shows if she is impressed, rotates slowly on the spot, stares at the sea, which today is a shimmery azure, and takes in the matching-coloured sky that is crammed with white, floccose clouds. While she looks, I retrieve my small instant camera from the left knee pocket of my navy blue combat trousers and flick it on. I need to take a snapshot of this moment so I can write underneath it: *With Mum, May 2015, Outside New Home (Brighton/Hove)* and stick it up on my wall. A reminder of the moment my new life began.

In my right knee pocket my mobile buzzzz-buzzzz-tings for probably the fiftieth time today. I ignore my phone and take the shot,
capturing our proximity to the sea as well as the look of the
building.

'Who is it that keeps sending you messages?' Mum asks. She can't
ignore it any longer. She's held her tongue all day but this is the text
that has sent her over the edge. She sounds so miffed anyone would
think it was her who was being texted at least six times an hour all
day. Mum becomes diabolically upset with people who use 'text' as
a verb. (It's actually worth doing it just to see her nostrils flare and her
eyes turn into hard blue lasers seeking to burn your tongue out of
your head for such an evil act.) 'They were sending messages the whole
of the journey and even now when you haven't replied. Who is it?'

'Who do you think it is?' I reply, a little more tartly than is
necessary.

'Didn't you tell him that you don't want to see him any more?'
she asks.

She says that like it was a casual fling – not a twelve-year, cohabit-
ing relationship – that he should really be over by now.

'Well, didn't you?' she demands to my silence.

'Yes, of course I did.'

'Then why is he still sending you messages?'

*For the same reason that I'm still reading them: I don't want it to be over; I
don't want any of this to have happened. I want to be living at home in Leeds
with our plans for the future and my eye on that shop in the Victoria Quarter. I
want to be making jewellery, and arguing about my mess, and planning days out
in our campervan. I want the life I was promised and thought I was going to live
before all of this happened. It's the same for him, I'd imagine.*

I can't talk about this with anyone, but especially not with her
when she made it clear over the years how little she thought of him.
'I don't know why he's still texting, Mum.' Like clockwork her eyes
harden and her nostrils show their annoyance at the text verb. 'Maybe
he thinks if he sends me enough messages I'll change my mind.'

'Typical,' she mumbles nowhere near under her breath. 'I never
did like the way he was so confident and sure of himself.'

'Really?' I reply. "Cos I always loved that about him.'

'And look where that got you,' Mum says. Shocked, I take a step back. She's not normally that spiteful. Her words usually have a sting to them, but that was like a nasty stab from a vicious weapon and it's hit me square in the chest, right over my heart, right where everything seems to ache from at the moment.

Mum, even though she must have registered my reaction, and noticed that I have stepped away from her, is openly unapologetic as she observes me.

'*Oh, get knotted,*' teeters on the tip of my tongue, while huge tears are cramming themselves into my eyes. I take another step back and force myself to look away because I'm not sure if swearing at my mother or crying in front of her would be the worst thing to do right now.

With Seth & Dylan, November 1996, Liverpool

'Can I get you a drink?' The man who asked this question looked vaguely familiar, fitted right into this university world of distantly remembered, partially recalled faces.

He had come over and sat down on the stool on the other side of the table in the area of the student bar which Dylan, the absolute love of my life, had unintentionally annexed these last few weeks we'd been here. Dylan was like The Fonz in that people were drawn to him; they hung out near him like groupies around a rock star and didn't seem to mind if he didn't actually get around to talking to them during their time together in the bar. Today was one of those rare occasions where it was only Dylan and me having a drink after an additional early evening tutorial that only he and I had turned up for. Other lectures hadn't started or were about to finish, and in that lull I'd managed to get him all to myself. I was relishing every last second – until this guy appeared.

Like most of the people I met at college, I wasn't sure if this new bloke was someone I'd seen around – in halls, in the library, right here in the bar – or if I'd met him before I arrived at Liverpool University to study Political Science.

'I'll have a pint if you're buying,' Dylan replied to the new man.

'I wasn't asking you,' the new man said good-naturedly. 'I was asking your friend.'

I pointed to myself in surprise. 'Me?' Male or female, no one noticed me when I was sitting with Dylan. He was far too rock star-like.

'Yes,' he said.

'No. Thank you, but no.'

'Make the most of it while you can,' Dylan laughed. 'Seth's not exactly known for reaching into his pocket unprompted.'

'Think you're mistaking me for yourself there, mate,' the new guy, Seth, replied. 'Which is why I'm not offering to buy you a drink – you owe me a couple of thousand of them.'

Dylan laughed again.

'Does your mum like *Emmerdale Farm*, by any chance?' I asked. She may have had a special interest in Greek mythology but I was guessing modern-day TV was probably more her thing.

Seth nodded slowly. 'I got off quite lightly,' he said then laughed. When he laughed his pink lips moved back to show his perfect white teeth, while his hazel-green eyes danced with mirth and kindness. 'My brother's called Sugden. We've got Alans and Jacks in our extended family so Sugden he was named.'

'That's not true,' I scoffed.

'It is, actually,' Dylan said. 'I've known Seth since we were in nursery. Grew up nearish to each other over the years. Now, apparently, he's transferred to do Political Science here, too. Can't get away from him, it seems. But yes, his brother is called Sugden. His family's dead posh and all, you'd think his mother would have some shame about it, but she's unrepentant.'

Seth nodded.

'Seth,' I said contemplatively.

'Yes?'

'Nothing, I was just turning the name over in my mouth. I don't think I've ever said it before.'

From the corner of my eye I saw Dylan's head turn towards me before he frowned.

'What's your name?' Seth asked.

'Clemency Smittson. I'm only telling you my surname because my friends call me Smitty. My dad started it when I was about twelve, drove my mum wild with annoyance, but it stuck.'

'I see.' He nodded. 'The question for me then is: are you a Smitty or a Clem to me?' It was Seth's turn to receive a small, suspicious frown from Dylan but Seth didn't seem to notice. Or if he did, he didn't care. Seth got to his feet, still staring intently at me. 'I shall ponder which one I think you are to me on my way to the bar. Are you sure you don't want a drink?'

'Actually, I think I will. Half a lager and lime, please.'

'A half with lime it is.'

Once Seth had left our vicinity, Dylan sat back in his seat, his body slid down a bit against his part of the corner sofa we'd commandeered and he stared at me with his head slightly to one side as though sizing me up. Eventually, when he'd watched me study Seth at the bar, he said to me: 'Don't go there, Smitty.'

'Go where?' I asked.

'*You know*,' he hissed irritably. 'Don't do it. Not with him.'

'Why not?'

'Just don't, all right?' He glanced over at Seth, which made me look at him too. 'We're all young, just starting college...don't be getting involved with blokes like him.'

'Why? Is he a complete bastard?'

'Nah...He's a nice guy. And if you do it with him, you'll fall in love with him or something equally stupid and he'll probably fall in love with you. It's too soon when you're still in college.'

'You are pulling my leg,' I said to him. I couldn't quite believe what I was hearing.

'No, no, I'm not. Not really. I just don't think...Look, being honest, I wouldn't like it. You're my friend, not his.'

Dylan and I had been 'friends' since the first week in college when I sat next to him in our Political Foundations class. I had turned to ask him what time the lecture was due to finish and found my voice had abandoned me. He was simply the most beautiful man I had ever seen. With his dark olive skin, close-cut black hair, huge brown eyes, and easy, natural smile, I fell for him straight away. It was impossible not to. Over the next few lectures we'd discovered we had the same sense of humour and liked the same music and films so I rather easily slotted into becoming one of his groupies. For the most part I didn't mind because very few of the other groupies had all the same classes as him, so didn't get to spend as much time with him in and out of class as I did. What he was saying now, though, was that I was a cut above the entourage of good-looking women who seemed to draw his attention; I was different. He would be bothered if I slept with someone else.

'Are you seriously saying you wouldn't like me going out with Seth because he's a nice guy?' I asked.

'Going out?' Dylan said despairingly. 'Smitty, you've just met the guy. I'm only saying I don't think you should go there, all right?' He shrugged. 'Please. I've known him a long time, me and him are good mates. Me and you are good . . . well, whatever. Just don't.'

'It's nice of you to care about my feelings so much,' I replied casually. Inside . . . *Inside* all my internal organs were dancing: Dylan liked me enough to be jealous.

'I've thought long and hard,' Seth stated. He placed our two drinks on the table, ignored Dylan's grumbles about being left out and focused on me. 'I've decided you're going to be Smitty to me. Mind if I call you Smitty?'

My grin must have taken him by surprise. He had done me the hugest favour – he'd made me interesting *and* desirable in Dylan's eyes. Dylan wanted me. I never thought that would happen. Not ever. 'You certainly can call me Smitty. In fact, I'd be offended if you didn't.'

'Excellent,' Seth replied.

Really excellent, I thought as Dylan sat up, and with one hand picked up his almost empty glass and took a sip, while under the table, his other hand moved possessively on to my leg and stayed there. *Really, really excellent.*

Mr Wallace finishes his call and starts his way back to us. I am furiously blinking away tears, trying to sweep aside the pain from my mother's words, and slowly the agony starts to recede while calmness takes over. Mum is still staring at me but I ignore her and focus on Mr Wallace, concentrate on not revealing how much she's hurt me. 'Many apologies for that, ladies,' he says. 'Now, if you'll follow me, I'll show you into your new home.'

Oh yes, like things aren't bad enough, my mother is also moving in with me.

2

Abi

To: Jonas Zebila
From: Abi Zebila
Subject: Purple Day
Monday, 25 May 2015

Dear Jonas,
Today is a purple day.

That's what Lily-Rose told me, anyway. Not quite sure where she got that from, or what it means, but when I came in from work earlier that was the first thing she said to me. It made me smile and it made me think of you. And I had to ask you what you think it means. Today is a purple day. It's also two years since you've been in touch and that's long enough now, don't you think?

Brother, dear brother, you've been gone from her for nearly half her life. You are her favourite uncle, she still talks about you. And I still think about you. We were a team, you and me.

I've read all this stuff online about how when a person decides to go 'no contact' with their family they have to cut everyone out, including the people you love because they're the ones who drag you back into the toxic mess, and I get it, I really do. But it's not fair. I didn't do anything. Remember? I'm the one you actually like.

I have no one here, apart from Lily-Rose and Declan, obviously, but no one knows I'm still seeing him – they all assumed we'd finished, which is why I moved back here. Yes, I came back to live with Mummy and Daddy. Really, I moved back in because Gran's seriously ill now and I decided to help Mummy with Gran's meds and feeding her (most days she can't do that for herself) and other stuff.

So, what's new in the past two years apart from me living back here? Well, nothing much is the short answer. Ivor still lives here, and shows no signs of leaving – ever.

Mummy and Daddy are still the same. They don't argue, argue, but they do snipe at each other a lot still. It's definitely got worse since you left. Mummy blames him for you cutting us off but she won't say it, and Daddy pretends it hasn't happened.

The other bone of contention is that Mummy thinks Gran should be somewhere where she'll get specialist care. I hear them talking about it sometimes. Daddy's not having it. They talk quietly, but I swear, Daddy, when he speaks, raises his voice on words like 'duty' and 'loyalty' and 'respect'. Course, he can say all that because he doesn't have to do much. He talks to Gran whenever she makes it into the lounge, he goes in to say hello and goodnight to her most days. Yes, I wrote that right – *most* days he goes into her room. He has to pass her room to leave and enter the house but he doesn't even make it in to see her every day. Denial about how sick his mother is do you think?

And then there's Lily-Rose, Lil' 'Purple Day' herself. She's my entire world. You should see her now, she's so big. Tall, beautiful, funny. Remind you of anyone?! You never got to know how funny she was, properly. The other day she disappeared and after I looked in all her favourite hiding places in the house – I eventually found her in Gran's room, telling knock-knock jokes she'd made up. They were all pretty random, a lot didn't make sense, but some were hysterical. I could tell it was just what Gran needed.

Look, please get in touch. Two years is long enough. You used to think life was too short to hold a grudge, that you should let bygones be bygones. I know Gran was terrible to you and Meredith, and the results of what she did were devastating, but deep down, don't you still believe in *not* holding a grudge, especially against the people who didn't do what she did? Aren't you even a little bit curious about us, about Lily-Rose?

Today's a purple day. What does that mean to you?

Love,
Abi
xxxxxx

3

Smitty

I slide open the side of Lottie, my red and white campervan, and am greeted with a great wall of brown cardboard boxes. The suitcases, holdalls and bags have all been transported up to the flat in the last eight trips, and now I have the boxes to start on. I stare at them. I'm sure they've quadrupled in number since I stacked them in there last night.

Last night, he was out like I'd asked him to be so I could move the boxes into Lottie ready for today's trip, but I wasn't sure how long he'd stay out or if he'd be back to try to convince me to give us another chance, so I had shifted boxes without really noticing their number or weight. (There were still some left in our flat, which is why I didn't want to tell him to leave me alone – I'd have to arrange a time to go and get the rest.) Now, I don't really understand how I have so much stuff. It's not as if I have lots of clothes and shoes and bags, and the like. I took no furniture, I took no appliances, I left them all for him back at the flat, and yet...I have what seems like a million boxes.

They can't all be work-related. I read the words on the boxes as if I didn't label them myself: 'Tools', 'Old Tools', 'Wire', 'Polishers', 'Finishers', 'Rollers, Barrel Roller, etc.', 'Journals, Books, Swatches, etc.', 'Finished Pieces', 'Toolboxes', 'Findings', 'Beads', 'Resins, Glues', 'Samplers', 'Texturisers'. Maybe because I'd worked at Karina's Jewels for so long and I had a lot of my regularly used tools there and my other stuff at home, I didn't notice how much work stuff I'd accumulated.

I'm a jewellery maker, much to the upset and disapproval of my mother. With a good political science degree I was obviously on the road destined for Parliament, final stop Prime Minister. I had a different path to tread, though. We'd frequently rowed about it over the years (and I'm sure she still holds out hope for my great political career to emerge) but nothing gave me joy like making jewellery. From coming up with the initial design to handing over or displaying the finished piece, my job gave me real pleasure. My true love, though, was reloving people's old jewellery.

Nothing was sadder than jewellery that languished in a drawer or box, mostly forgotten, partially unloved, because it didn't fit into someone's life. I made people want to love their jewellery again. Unwanted things that used to be precious, could be precious again, were my speciality. I would do my best to make the jewellery fit the person's life, make them look at it again and see that they could love it, they did want it, they didn't want to forget it existed because for a time it wasn't quite up to scratch.

I sit on the edge of Lottie's footrest, momentarily defeated by the number of boxes I have to unload, by the task ahead of me. I have to start again. Establish my business down here, find new clients, set up my workshop, open my shop, all while living with my mother. I'd lived with her when I left my flat, and for the months before that, but I'd always known it was temporary so I could endure it. This is permanent. I close my eyes, allow the ebb and flow of the sea to wash over me. I can do this. I know I can. I need to believe that. It'd be easier, of course, with him. But, I can do this. Because I have to.

With Dylan & Seth, Xmas 1998, Liverpool (end of term party)
'How about we break with tradition this year and I kiss Smitty under the mistletoe first?' Seth asked.

We had all arrived separately at the Social Sciences department's end of term party in the dining hall, with me turning up last. Our department always went all out for their parties and waited until everyone had officially left so they could hire the dining hall and make it look spectacular. As soon as I walked in the door, Dylan and Seth both descended upon me – Seth was holding mistletoe. I looked from one to the other.

It wasn't as if I was going out with either of them, or that either of them didn't have girlfriends because I wasn't and they did. But for the last two Christmases, whenever they spotted mistletoe, I was their first port of call.

'How about we *don't* make this a tradition which could be seen as Smitty being a bit "free" with her affections around two men who have girlfriends?' I replied. Girlfriends who were probably in this very room, glaring at me.

Before anyone could say anything else, Dylan snaked his hand around my waist, tugged me towards his body and kissed me full on the mouth, as he'd been doing for the last two Christmases. His lips, tasting of the rum-laced punch he'd obviously been drinking, lingered on mine. This was about to turn into a proper, full-on kiss where he would push his tongue into my mouth, he'd pull me closer to him and we'd forget anyo— Abruptly, Dylan stepped away. As always his kiss was enough to tease me but not enough to promise me anything.

'You are such a git,' Seth complained. 'You don't even have mistletoe.'

'I've got mistletoe in my heart,' Dylan replied. He focused on me with his enormous black-brown eyes and I knew he was about to finish with his latest girlfriend. He always gave me that look, said something like that, when he was about to dump someone – it's not like anything had ever happened between us, or that he'd make a move once he was free, he just did this to let me know what he was thinking. The only time he ever kissed me properly was at Christmas.

'Happy Christmas, Smitty,' Seth said. '*I'm still here, you know?*' he was actually saying.

I managed to tear my eyes away from Dylan, refocused on Seth. 'Happy Christmas, Seth,' I replied.

He held up the mistletoe, its white fruit unusually plump and large against its long, slender, oval-shaped leaves. 'Any chance?' he asked. I hadn't even got my coat off or unwound my scarf.

I glanced at Dylan. He stared down at his feet, prodding at something invisible on the floor as though he wasn't bothered, his body language plainly broadcasting how bothered he was. I wasn't the one going out with someone else, I was single and able to kiss whoever I liked – no matter how chaste it really was. Seth, though...The mere idea of him and me bugged Dylan. He hadn't been bothered when I'd been out with or slept with other men, even with friends of his, but when it came to Seth, his jealousy was clear and evident.

'If you want to,' I told him.

Seth nodded in understanding. 'Next year,' he said. He tossed his mistletoe on to the buffet table, between the pile of greasy mini sausages and the large crystal punchbowl. 'I'll make sure that I get my kiss in first.'

Mum hasn't brought much stuff with her. *'I only really need my clothes and my photographs,'* she'd said, and she was as good as her word.

Considering her house in Otley was crammed with enough ornaments and knick-knacks to keep a small charity shop well stocked for a year or two, and she'd never shown any inclination to get rid of them, I was impressed that she really only brought her photo albums, clothes and beauty items. 'I won't take up much space,' she'd said during the conversation where I asked her to move in with me. That's how she tells it to anyone who'll listen – she even tells that to me and I was there for the conversation. *'Clemency was moving and she couldn't do it on her own, so she asked me to come with her. She's my only child so I couldn't say no.'* What really happened was this:

'Mum, I know the timing could be better but I'm moving. I've got one more week to complete at work and then I'm going to tie up everything here and move to Brighton. Well, Hove, actually. That's where the flat I've found is. It's near enough to Brighton. I've got a workshop down there, too.' I decided to tell Mum I'd also got a shop space another time – too much information gave her too much to worry about and too much to mither me about.

'Oh, that sounds like a fantastic idea, Clemency. I'll get your uncle Colin to look after the house and I'll come with you. Thank you for suggesting it.'

'What?' I replied.

'Don't say, "what".'

'Wha— I don't understand what you've just said.'

'Or maybe Nancy and Sienna could move in?' she said to herself. 'They'll need a bigger space, I won't need to charge them rent and they're family so I know they'll take care of the place. Or maybe I shouldn't involve family? Maybe I should just look at renting it out through an agency.'

'What are you saying to me, Mother?'

'Your uncle Colin can help out. When are you going?'

'Two weeks.'

'Perfect. That's plenty of time to pack and have an estate agent value the place with a view to selling or renting.'

'But I'm moving on my own.' (I'm still not sure if I said that out loud.)

'This is perfect, Clemency. I won't take up much space. Just my photographs and personal belongings and clothes. I was wondering what I would do with myself now. I don't want to be here any more. Too many memories, especially from the last few months. But you've solved that problem for me.'

And created a whole world of problems for me. Mum and me in confined spaces with nothing much to do...It is a bad combination.

'Clemency? Is that you?' Mum calls. I heft the first box through the front door. There are eighty-seven steps and three sets of doors between Lottie and this flat. I only noticed that while wrestling my way here with this box labelled 'Tools'.

'Who else is it going to be?' I call back.

'A simple "yes" will suffice,' she replies.

'What is it that you want, Mum?' I ask. Down the long wide corridor with large block, parquet flooring in a rich honey-coloured wood, I follow the sound of Mum's voice until I find her, in the second bedroom. Her bedroom. This was going to be my work-at-home place. It didn't have the sea views of the other rooms, but it had an en suite shower and loo, space for a desk as well as a (guest) bed and, most importantly, a large amount of wall space to pin up my designs and have a shelving unit to keep all the tools and materials – wire, beads, findings, bottle tops, trays, glues, resins, cords, etc., etc., etc. – I used at home.

'Yes, Mum?' I say. 'How can I help you?' I have sprinkled positivity, the type of sunshine drenching the outside world, into my voice because this is all going to work out. Everything is going to be fine. To make sure it is, I need to stay positive no matter what is sent to try me.

'This room is going to be fine for me,' she says.

'That's great,' I say.

'There isn't much natural light, though,' she adds, in case I get too comfortable with doing something almost right.

'I know. This side of the building overlooks the internal courtyard and because there are other parts of the building on all four sides, not much light comes in. Sorry.'

'That's OK,' she says.

Mum has eyes that are so blue they appear translucent in certain lights. When I was younger I was convinced she could use her eyes to hypnotise people into staying still, staying silent, while she said something important or cutting. I'm not one hundred per cent convinced she can't do that now because she is fixing them on me while she opens her mouth to speak. I want to turn away, to leave before I hear something that will be negative and draining; which will nibble away at the positivity I have been building up, but I can't move.

'Clemency, about what I said earlier,' Mum starts. She sighs and steps towards me. 'Don't take everything to heart so much.' She presses her hand on to my shoulder, reassures me with that touch that I am being oversensitive and what she said about the end of my relationship was completely justified.

Dylan stood beside me, our heads close together while someone took a picture of us in our black and purple gowns. I had a mortar board on my head, the tassel constantly hung just low enough to be an irritating distraction at the corner of my eye. The other distraction at the corner of my peripheral vision was Mum, glaring at me because, in her mind, merely standing next to a male was enough to impregnate me. 'We made it, eh, Smitty?' Dylan said.

I took my camera back from the person who'd snapped the shot, thanked them. 'Yes. Although it looked doubtful at times.'

'Don't just disappear now it's over, OK?' he said.

'If anyone's going to do a disappearing act it'll be you, don't you think?' I replied. 'Speaking of disappearing acts, what happened to Seth? I saw him in the ceremony but I haven't seen him since.'

'Maybe he finally got the message,' Dylan mumbled.

'What message would that be?' I asked. 'And can you clue me in on it?'

'Come on now, Smitty,' he said.

'No, you come on, Dylan. I've finished college, am I allowed to sleep with Seth now? Or is that still against the rules of being your mate?'

'Smitty...me and you...'

'Are mates, that's abundantly clear.'

'It's not that simple. Before you, I've never been friends with a girl without it being either purely sexual or purely platonic. It's both with you. And the longer we're mates, the more I feel for you. It's more than sex and more than just friendship with you.'

'Rhubarb, rhubarb, rhubarb,' I said in response.

Unexpectedly he stepped forward, our bodies now so close they almost touched. My breathing became quick and shallow; the pupils of his eyes dilated as he began to breathe quickly too. 'I'd love to kiss you,' he said, his gaze linked to mine, 'but I think your mum would probably lay me out with one punch. Meet me later? I've got a family meal, but come over to my house around ten o'clock?'

21

'I can't. Mum and Dad are taking me home after this. We're all packed up. We've got a family thing over in Otley. My cousin's having problems, too, Mum wants to get back for her.'

'Can't believe this,' he said. 'Are you going to come back any time soon?'

'Do you actually ever listen to a word I say? I told you, I've got a summer job, working six days a week so I can save up for my course to train to become a silversmith and jeweller. You can come and see me?'

'Will your mum smack me if I kiss you now?'

'Yes.'

'Your dad won't stop her?'

'Nope.'

'All right. I'll come over to see you.'

I knew he wouldn't. I desperately wanted him to, but I knew he wouldn't. It was easier for us both to pretend that he would.

Mum's stopped hypnotising me with her stare. She's instead focused on the butterfly pendant I wear around my neck. It is large and fashioned from silver, and one of the first things I made after I qualified as a silversmith. The pendant represents a lot of things to Mum, not only the fact I took no notice when it came to her career advice, but also that I still have an obsession with butterflies. And that obsession, to Mum, is hurtful. *'Try not to be so sensitive,'* I should say to her. Instead, I tuck it away under my T-shirt, out of her sight, out of her mind.

Now the butterfly is hidden away, she goes back to admonishing me while rubbing my shoulder. 'Clemency, you should know by now that you mustn't be so touchy about things,' Mum tells me. 'You should try to grow a thicker skin, so you aren't so sensitive.'

'OK,' I say to her, because it's easier than explaining that while I have normal skin like everyone else, I spend a lot of time pretending the snide comments, the sly digs and the outright vicious remarks about not knowing who my 'real' parents are don't bother me. Mum doesn't realise that I spend my life feigning the existence of a thick, impenetrable outer layer so that I can be seen to be able to 'take a joke', 'not be so sensitive', 'not take everything to heart'. She has no idea that for years I would cry alone because no one understood that every comment made me feel worthless and made me believe that those snipes were true.

And anyway, all this talk about not being oversensitive would be more credible if it wasn't coming from the woman who can't even bear to hear the word 'adoption', let alone talk about it in relation to her only daughter. That's why she has 'issues' with my butterfly obsession – it's a reminder of the fact I'm not biologically hers.

'Clemency,' she says, before I shut the door behind myself.

'Yes, Mum?' I reply tiredly. There's only so much I can take, only so much the positivity I've stretched over this new start can handle before it peels away, and starts flapping about uselessly like unsecured tarpaulin in the wind.

'Your father would have loved it here,' she says. 'He adored the sea. He always wanted to live by the sea again before . . . He would have been so proud of you.' She smiles. 'Even more proud of you than he was.'

I nod. 'Thanks, Mum,' I mumble, and leave.

I don't need her to tell me Dad was proud of me. I knew he was. He told me so all the time. Right up until he died.

4

Abi

To: Jonas Zebila
From: Abi Zebila
Subject: Please reply. PLEASE!!!!!
Friday, 29 May 2015

Dear J,

Another email from me where I hope all is well with you. You didn't tell me about your purple day. All is not well here, unfortunately. Gran was rushed to hospital while I was at work yesterday.

Daddy didn't even bother to leave work. Mummy had to call my office to get me to pick up Lily-Rose. I had to bring her back to work with me because I was up to my ears in client reports and billing, and the billing had to go out yesterday. Lily had a great old time, she was the centre of attention from all the residents. Mrs Lehtinen was the worst for it, practically adopted her there and then, showing her off as something as close to a great-granddaughter as she could get.

Did I tell you Mrs Lehtinen is here at the home now? Do you remember her? She was from Finland and her family lived next door and she was great friends with Gran. Her family moved away when I was about five or six. She loved you, I remember that. She's not been here long but on the first day she recognised me even though I hope I've changed a little in twenty years. I didn't really remember her until she reminded me that it was her who had given Mummy the idea for those sleep boxes that we slept in as babies. And then, of course, she asked about you and it all came flooding back: how you were always her favourite because you used to wolf down those God-awful Jim bars she kept giving us. (I looked them up on the net to find out why they were so boak. Marmalade foam covered in chocolate. I can't believe Mummy let us eat them.)

Like I say, Mrs L practically stole Lily-Rose from me and kept telling her stories about what I got up to when I was her age. It would have been embarrassing if they didn't all show me as being the most amazing five-year-old!!

On the way home we dropped by the hospital to see Gran, Lily-Rose and I, but she wouldn't see us because she didn't want us to see her like that. Three days ago Lily's telling her jokes and now Gran won't see her. So much pride. So much stupid pride. That's what our family's problem is – too much pride, don't know when to swallow it. I mean, would it have hurt Gran to see Lily? I know it can be scary seeing someone looking frail, but she may not come out of hospital. We may never see her again because her pride makes her worried we'll see her looking vulnerable.

I'm gutted, Jonas, really gutted.

Tell me. Just tell me something. Anything.

I love you.
Abi
xxxx

P.S. Do you want some pictures of Lily-Rose? I may have a few (thousand).

5

Smitty

My bedroom in the flat is pretty incredible.

The main bedroom, my room, has panoramic views of the sea from the six, double-glazed sash windows. 'Triple aspect' I think it was called in the agency description. Triple aspect, three views of the sea, three chances to see the expanse of water while reclining in this king-size bed. I've made up the bed, I have unpacked my clothes, stashed my bags and cases at the bottom of the double wardrobes.

Now I'm doing what I do wherever I live: putting up my photos.

One of the first photos I have pressed on to the wall is from 1996. I am with Seth and Dylan. We are in the bar, in the booth where we were sitting when Seth first came over. I'm in between them, they've both got their arms around me, and I'm overwhelmed because I've never had so much male attention in my life. Under that photo I have scrawled:

With Seth & Dylan, Xmas 1996, Uni Bar. Mistletoe madness!!

Another photo:

With Dylan & Seth, Xmas party 1998, Liverpool (end of term party) Dylan has his arm slung casually over my shoulder, Seth is standing beside us but a little apart, as though not really wanting to be there. I have my hand on his forearm, trying to draw him into the photo.

And another:

With Dylan, July 1999, Graduation Day

Dylan and I have our gowns on, I have a mortar board, he doesn't. We've got our heads close together and are grinning at the camera. I'm looking pensive because Mum is off camera glaring at me.

With Mum & Dad, July 1999, Graduation Day

I'm in between Mum and Dad, grinning at the camera. Dad has plucked my black mortar board off my head and plonked it on his. He'd originally gone to put it on Mum's head but the look she fired stopped him. Seth had taken the photo but had only stopped by to say goodbye before he went off with his family.

With Seth, March 2003, Party at Seth's House (everyone's invited)

Seth is standing in the kitchen of his house, putting together a buffet for the party he was having. He turned and sort of smiled at the camera, just as I shouted, 'Say cheese'. I was staying with him at that time. I'd had a row with Mum that escalated into me sofa surfing for a few weeks with various friends and acquaintances. I was always careful not to stay for more than two days – three at the very maximum, so as not to wear out my welcome. The last sofa I washed up on was Seth's, a grey-black Muji put-me-up job that was easy to fold out and surprisingly comfortable – no metal bars or buttons in the wrong places. Dad had been on the phone almost daily trying to mediate between Mum and me but I wasn't ready to go back, especially since whenever I tried to leave, Seth kept telling me to stay and he never made a move on me, not once. That night he was having a party and it'd be the first time I would have seen Dylan in nearly a year. I was *so* excited that I didn't even mind when my cousin Nancy gatecrashed.

In my hand I hold the final photo from that sequence. There were others, of course, over the years, but those were the most significant, those were the ones that made it to the wall every time, move after move. And in my hand I hold the final one, the one that came after we got together. In it, it's the start of a new year, January 2004, I am sitting on his sofa, wearing his T-shirt, my hand in my very messy hair, beaming at the man taking the photo because we were finally together. I was finally happy.

With Seth, New Year's Eve 2003

I sat on the sofa I used to sleep on those weeks back in February and March when I stayed at his house, while Seth sat across the room at the dining table, warily watching me. Usually, he sat next to me, often I put my legs across his lap and he would rub my feet while we talked. But tonight, he'd been carefully avoiding being close to me. We ate dinner at opposite ends of the table and even cooking in his tiny kitchen had him keeping me at a noticeable distance.

I'd made all the right noises about the food, which was as delicious as I said it was, I'd drunk his wine and savoured it. I'd bought the bottle of expensive bubbly that was chilling on the first shelf of his small fridge, waiting for the chimes of Big Ben on telly. We'd talked, laughed, argued good-naturedly about the things we always debated over.

All the while, the clock was ticking down towards the end of the year. We were in the final hours of 2003 and I couldn't wait to see the back of it. It'd been one disaster after another, one lot of bad news after another, one falling out after another. When Seth had asked me over to his for dinner and to see in the New Year with him I'd jumped at the chance. I was looking forward to a quiet, uneventful end to this year and a respectful, calm beginning to the next. It wasn't turning out like that, though, with Seth's pensive demeanour, which swirled around the room like invisible but choking smoke.

He'd never been like this in all the years I'd known him. Maybe it was because I hadn't called him much in the months since I'd left his sofa and had gone back to live with my parents, possibly he was feeling slighted that we'd gone from talking every night for hours to speaking once a fortnight.

'Have I upset you?' I asked him.

Seth shook his head, his face was cagey and his body was hyper-vigilant as he replied: 'No.'

'I'm sorry I haven't been in touch more,' I said. 'It's my training – it's taken over everything. I have to work doubly hard at everything because I'm not at all arty so even though I can see the designs up here,' I pointed to my head, 'I can't get them to look like they should on paper. The finished items are exactly what I saw, but the drawings don't work. I've been a bit consumed. I'm sorry for making you a casualty of that.'

'You've nothing to apologise for.' He sat back in the wooden-framed chair, stretched his legs out.

'Have I ruined your chance to go out on New Year by accepting your invitation? Did you want a big night out?'

'New Year is for people who don't go out the rest of the year,' he said.

'That's a bit harsh! I love New Year, usually. This year's just been a bit rubbish and I want to see a quiet end to it and to put it out of its misery, so to speak.'

'Come on,' he cajoled, 'it's true. If you went out and enjoyed yourself the rest of the year you wouldn't need to make such a big deal of nights like New Year's Eve.'

'Or maybe you simply want to see in the start of another twelve months in style?'

'Maybe.'

'Why are you sitting over there, Seth? What's going on?'

'I like it here. It's by the stereo.'

'Put a tune on then.'

He reached out his long fingers and pressed the square silver button with the green triangle. A whirr, an almost imperceptible click and the room was filled with Public Enemy's 'Welcome To The Terrordome'.

I stood up, determined to alter the course of this evening, get him to engage with me on some level. If I wanted to sit under the critical eye of someone who didn't know how to talk to me, I'd have stayed at home with my mother just as she'd practically ordered me to. I held out my hand to him. 'Care to dance?' I asked him. This wasn't dancing music, but needs must.

'How long have you known me?' he replied. 'You know I don't dance.'

'All right, let me see what's so great about that seat of yours,' I replied and moved towards him. He visibly tensed as though the idea of me being any closer was a horror he couldn't run fast enough from.

That stopped me in my tracks. 'Shall I leave?' I asked in frustration. I still had a chance to get home to the cream soda and Christmas After Eights before the chimes sounded so I could end the year as it started – with my parents.

'I don't want you to leave and there's really nothing wrong. I'm having a good time.'

You don't look like it, I thought.

I moved closer and he slowly slid up in his seat until he was fully upright. His eyes didn't leave my face as I approached him. I accepted then what was 'wrong'. I'd hoped I was mistaken, that I'd imagined it. The problem, of course, was he wanted to have sex with me. And he probably hated feeling like that when we were 'just friends', so he was keeping his distance until these feelings passed, just like a fleeting obsession with a pop band passed and you wondered what on Earth you were thinking. Seth knew, as well as I did, that sex would mean the end of our friendship. We couldn't go back to being mates if we went to bed together – we'd have to be together for the duration or not see each other again.

'About this seat,' I began. I slid carefully on to his lap until I was fully on top of him and we were face-to-face, my legs either side of his. 'I quite like it too.' Slowly, I took off my cream jumper, revealing my black bra underneath. 'Looks like I'll have to fight you for it.'

His breathing slowed and deepened, every muscle of his face was tense as though he was concentrating on staring into my eyes, trying to ignore how hard he'd become when I sat on him, while not wanting to stare at my breasts and my imperfect body on display to him. Seth suddenly smelt of a deep and startling desire, far more potent than I expected. When I pulled back a fraction, unsettled a little by how strongly he seemed to want this, his hands came up to rest on my back, then smoothed their way up and down my body.

As his fingers caressed my back, I reached for the top button of his jeans and suddenly his hands were on mine, stopping me from opening him up. I looked at him, his hazel-green eyes held mine.

'If we do this,' he said, keeping his hands in place, 'will it mean something to you?'

I knew what he was alluding to: in college and afterwards, I'd slept with quite a few people, more than a few of them were his friends from our wider group. To him, to anyone who wasn't me and wasn't privy to my mind and my heart, it must have seemed that none of it meant anything. To him, to anyone else, it must have seemed that I had sex and walked away without so much as a backward glance. 'Se—' I began.

'Cos this would mean *everything* to me,' he interrupted.

I paused properly then. *Everything?* I thought. *He wants me that much? Me?* I knew he fancied me but this seemed extreme. 'Everything?' I asked.

His face, topped with brown hair that he'd had shaved off to a grade one, was open and unwavering as he looked at me. 'I've waited nearly eight years for you, so yes, it'd mean everything.'

Of course it meant something. Sex always meant something to me but with him…Did he honestly think I would have risked rejection, our friendship, for nothing? That in eight years of knowing him I hadn't at least thought about it? It wasn't simply Dylan's objection that had put me off, it was the thought of wrecking what we had and losing him as a friend. I bent my head and carefully placed my lips on the smooth soft bow of his pink mouth. 'It means something to me,' I replied before I kissed him.

Seth immediately kissed me back, pressing his lips on to mine, our tongues meeting before slowly intertwining. The kisses grew deeper, more urgent, more desperate. Suddenly, almost painfully,

I wanted him. I ached for him between my legs, in the cavity of my chest, along the veins of my body. The longing for him was so fierce my breathing came in short bursts, I found it hard to keep air in my body.

'There are condoms in the bedroom,' he murmured between the urgent kisses.

I pulled away, looked him over again. *'We don't need condoms,'* I wanted to say. I always wanted to say that in the moments leading up to full sex. The temptation to be reckless, do something danger-ous, personify stupidity for those few minutes, was powerful, instinctive. It was like a bright pink neon sign flashing in my head: **Have unprotected sex…and end up paying for it for the rest of your life**.

Unprotected sex with a virtual stranger was probably the reason I existed at all. I wanted to do it so I could validate my existence, prove that my being here wasn't the worst thing in the world to happen. Like I said: reckless, dangerous, stupid. But that instinct was almost overwhelming with Seth, I'd never felt it so strongly. I wanted nothing more than to be as unsafe as possible with him because he'd always been my point of safety.

'Have you changed your mind?' Seth asked when I didn't respond to his suggestion we move to the bedroom. 'Cos that's fine.'

Seth was here. My here. When I avoided looking backwards because the past was too painful to remember, and when I avoided looking forwards because the future was too terrifying to contemplate, I lived in the here. And here was where Seth was, too. He'd always been in my here. He was in my here and he would be in the future with me, and he would help me navigate the past if I wanted him to. Emotionally, Seth was here, in the same place that I was, at the same time. He was my here, and he was what love was all about. I could suddenly see that this wasn't about sex, it was about everything I'd ever wanted being on offer with this man. 'I haven't changed my mind,' I told him, the smile on my face even wider than it had been before. He grinned back at me.

Three days later he took that photo of me sitting on his sofa, grinning because I was with him at last. Giddy with excitement and joy and slight disbelief, underneath I wrote: *With Seth, finally!! January 2004.*

That moment the photo has frozen, preserved in a two-dimensional frame, is so clear, so vivid in my mind, I am almost there again. I can feel beneath me the material of the sofabed I'd slept on for six weeks. I can remember the effervescent excitement whizzing through my veins that bubbled up on my face as that smile. Then there was the touch of him, on my skin, on my lips, in my hair, inside my body. Tingles trilled through me every time another memory from those three days of being together wended through my mind. I am almost there, telling him the next morning that I didn't really want to go home. Him asking me if I was saying that because it was what he wanted to hear. Me asking him why I'd say that if it wasn't the truth. Him saying, 'Because you've never shown any interest in me beyond the effect it had on Dylan.'

'That's not entirely true, and you know I stopped feeling anything like that for Dylan a while back.'

'Maybe, but you'd also slept with a lot of my friends.'

'Does that bother you?' I replied.

'Not any more. At the time I never understood why it was them and never me. I liked you so much and I made it so obvious, and you never even looked in my direction.'

'You never tried it on, that's why.'

'All those guys tried it on with you, that's why?'

'Yeah, of course. I didn't sleep with all of them, no matter what they told others. But I was never going to make the first move – not if there was even the slightest chance of being rejected.' I'd been rejected from the moment I was born, from before I was born, probably. I avoided as much as possible being rejected as an adult – someone had to want me first before I would even think about wanting them. Except for Dylan.

'But you tried it on with me last night,' Seth said. 'I'm not imagining it, you made the first move.'

'Yes, I felt that much for you, I risked rejection.'

'So, all this really is about me?'

'Only you. These have been some of the best hours of my life. I've felt so wanted. So adored. You seem to understand me without me having to justify or qualify anything I say, or without having to censor myself ... And I can't believe I just said that aloud. Please don't ever repeat that. Pretend I never said that.'

'Too late, Smitty, I heard you loud and clear.'

I need to stop remembering. I need to not do this now. On my bed is a large cardboard box decorated in hand-coloured butterflies that I've had since I was a baby and that I keep all my special photos in. The ones I can't put up because they're too painful to look at every day but are too precious to throw away because they're an important part of who I am.

I place the *With Seth, finally!!* picture in the butterfly box. I properly regard all the other photos tacked to my wall to form the tessellated wallpaper of my life, the collage of the people and times that make up who I am.

I always carry an instant camera to take photos of the people I make jewellery for, to capture on film things I see that inspire me, images I love. Yes, it's easier – cheaper – to take photos on my phone, but there's no feeling like holding a photo in your hand. Photographs are like crystallised moments of your history that you can't simply swipe on from to find the better shot, to seek a version that's more palatable to your sensibilities. Photos are the ultimate reality call as to how perfect or flawed you can be at any given moment in time.

These photos I put up wherever I live are like the crystallised elements of who I was, how I became who I am. There I am: with Seth. With Mum. With my niece Sienna. With Dad. With my cousin Nancy. With Dylan. With Karina, my former boss. With Primrose, Ayo and Clyde, my housemates in college. With all these people who made me feel real, relevant, as if I belong somewhere.

I continue to stare at the photos and see for the first time how many there are that say the same thing: *With Seth. With Seth. With*

Seth. With Seth. With Seth. He's everywhere. For nearly twenty years of my life he has been in my photos, been in my reality. For nearly two decades my life has been about this one person.

My fingers pluck the photo of me and Seth and Dylan, Xmas 1996, off the wall. I place it into the butterfly box on my bed. Next I remove *With Seth on the last day of exams.* Then comes down *With Seth after studying all night.* Then *With Seth, the town hall in Vilnius (Lithuania),* is removed . . . And *With Seth before our cancelled engagement party* . . . And *Seth the Starfish in new bed in our new flat!!!* Then *Me with Seth, new bed in new flat.* Then *Me & Seth & Lottie – finally finished the campervan refurb.* There are so many. So many. And I have to take them all down; I have to remove all these reminders and memories.

When I have finished editing him out, my wall of pictures is like Swiss cheese – there are holes everywhere. Now Seth has come down, I have to take *her,* my cousin Nancy, down, too. More holes, more Swiss cheesing of my life. And if I take her down, I have to take down Sienna, her daughter. And I have to take down Dylan because he is where it all began. And if I take down Dylan, there will be very few photos left. My life will be decimated.

I sit down on my bed, the firm mattress does not sag or give at all under my weight. The wallpaper made of photos has now become a latticework of photos – tenuously linked by my handwriting beneath or on the back of the pictures.

I know what I have to do. It's absolutely obvious. I have to start again. Totally. People say all the time that something is completely devastated, as though anything can ever be partially devastated. My life has been devastated, I can't partially reflect that on my wall.

I'm on my feet again, new purpose in my movements: I have to take it all down; I have to devastate everything and start again. That's what the rest of me has done, so why not my visual history, too?

Smitty

'A coffee, please.'

The tall barista who is displaying his gym-sculpted arms in a short-sleeved white T-shirt has his back to me when I stand up on the chrome foot rail and lean on the counter. Coffee, coffee, coffee. The perfect thing to get my body moving on my way to have a proper look at my shop. I haven't told my mother about the shop, I'm still working up to that. It's been a good four days, mainly because I have been holding my tongue, biting my tongue and swallowing my tongue. Actually, I'm surprised I still have a tongue left at all. But it's been worth it. The flat has been peaceful, we've unpacked most things, we've bought a TV, DVD player and Freeview box, a kettle and toaster, pans and crockery, cutlery and wooden spoons. Other bits and pieces have migrated their way into the flat, and we're waiting for the telephone line to be connected so we can get Wi-Fi, but it is a more than habitable home now. We can relax and enjoy it. Which is why I'm out early this morning. If I'm out before Mum wakes up, it's a million times less likely that we'll have a row about something stupid.

I'm surprised how quiet it is in this café, given its location practically on the beach. Three floor-to-ceiling glass walls give you unfettered views of the promenade, sea wall, and the unique beauty that is the grey-blue water as it stretches out and away until it touches the blue-grey sky at the horizon. The inside of the café is a mixture of tables and chairs, sofas and tables, and easy chairs and tables, all cleverly arranged so they are easily accessible from the stainless-steel serving counter. Beyond that there are a couple of doorways, I'm assuming they lead to the kitchen and the back office. The best thing about this café, though, is how close it is to the flat. I can make it in under seven minutes if I walk especially fast. It's the perfect place to meet clients. When I walked in I spied a cosy sofa and chairs arrangement on the far side of the counter that would be sheltered and private enough for us to talk, but also comfortable enough to allow them to relax. I'm either going to have to be here from opening time when I have meetings so I can bagsy that space, or I'll have to see who I can charm into setting it aside for me. First though, coffee.

The barista turns from playing with the coffee machine and makes his way slowly to the counter. He's almost languid as he walks, unrushed and carefree – either he's the owner or he's a very laidback employee. At 7 a.m., I suspect he's the former because no employee that laidback would even consider getting here at this time. It's early spring, at this time the world is drenched in the orange-grey half-light of this side of the planet still turning to face the Sun. 'Sorry, we're not open yet,' the barista says.

'Oh. Well, the "open" sign is showing and the door's open, so I just assumed…'

He listens intently, carefully, to what I say. When I finish, he rests his elbows on the counter, rests his face in his hands. Frowns then sighs. 'I used to open this early, believe it or not, but no one ever came. It seemed to me those who were up this early and were walking to work, needed to get nearer to Brighton before they got a coffee. Probably because they'd had one already at home and by this point of the journey another was too soon. On a weekend sometimes I open up early, catch the clubbers on their way home. Especially Pride weekend – I have a lot of customers that morning. But mostly, I open at eight and it works.'

'Right. So I'm not going to get a coffee from you?'

'Not before eight, sorry.'

'OK.' I don't move. 'I'm not going to get a coffee even though I've stood and listened to you talk for far longer than a person who doesn't know you should have to?' I say.

He grins. Naturally he has flawless teeth because he is disturbingly, almost unrealistically, handsome. He seems to have been drawn and constructed from the blueprint for the perfect man, rather than birthed like the rest of the human population: the shape of his eyes, the size of his nose, the curve of his mouth, are all precisely proportioned, his dark brown skin is smooth and touchable, and his hair is shaved at the sides and at the back, short and neat on top.

'I suppose I could make an exception just this once,' he says. 'It'll teach me to remember to lock the door.'

'Thank you.' I unhook my bag from over my shoulder and place it on the black vinyl padded stool beside me. It's not often my cheekiness pays off. I hop up on to the stool next to my bag.

'Don't get comfortable,' he says. 'It's a coffee to go.'

'I know, but there's nothing wrong with sitting while I wait.'

He moves to the far side of his machine, places coffee beans into it. There's a brief grinding sound before he removes the small metal basket, the shape and size of a small tea sieve. He taps down the top with what looks like a metal stamp. In all the times I've been to cafés to buy coffee, I've never watched someone make it before. There's always been a queue, a rush, something better to look at. Watching him work is fascinating. When he fits the solid metal sieve thing into the front of the machine, he grabs a paper cup and stands it beneath the curved metal spout where he inserted the sieve.

'Where are you coming from with that cute little accent?' he asks over his shoulder. While he speaks he pushes a button and the black liquid of my coffee swirls down the curved spout into my cup.

'"Little" accent?' I reply.

He bobs down in front of his fridge, removes milk and glugs some into a metal jug. He moves to the other end of the machine and places the jug over the spout that I know is the milk frother. It hisses a little as he heats and froths the milk.

'Sorry, where are you coming from with that cute accent of yours?' he corrects.

'Nowhere,' I reply. In my head, in my heart, that is where I am from: nowhere. 'I'm from nowhere.'

'Everyone's from somewhere,' he says.

'*Not me*,' I reply silently.

'I can't place your accent. Usually I'm quite good with them, since I speak to so many people on a regular basis. But yours, it's a mystery.'

'I was born in Brighton and lived out near Lewes until I was about three, so that's where most of my accent comes from, I guess. We then moved to a place called Otley just outside Leeds where I lived most of my life, I went to university in Liverpool, and recently I moved to Leeds proper, which has all probably influenced my voice. Add to that the fact my dad was Scottish, and my mum, even though she's from Leeds, sounds like she grew up in Buckingham Palace, and you get an accent like mine.' *Add to that the fact that I've never felt I've belonged anywhere and you get a girl from nowhere. You get me.*

The milk is frothed and hot, so he moves back to my cardboard cup and pours it in then spoons on the white foam. 'Wouldn't you say that was more "everywhere" than nowhere?' the coffee guy says.

'Depends on how you look at it, I suppose,' I reply.

'Most things do – depend on how you look at them, I mean,' he says. The white, moulded plastic lid with the cut-out oblong drinking hole is fitted on to the cup with a dull pop.

'Thank you for the coffee,' I say to him. We stand at the door, his hand resting on the metal handle. I don't want to leave. I'd like to sit here, experience the world through the picture windows, and to carry on chatting to this person.

'It's a cappuccino,' he states. 'I know you asked for a coffee, but you look like you're going to have a cappuccino kind of day.' He makes no move to open the door. Maybe he doesn't want me to leave either. Maybe I've fascinated him enough for him to let me stay a while longer.

'I'm not sure what a cappuccino type of day is, but I'm looking forward to finding out.'

His gaze drifts casually to my left hand, the one not holding the cup. 'That's an impressive number of rings,' he says.

I am a walking advert for my work: I always have on at least my butterfly pendant, a necklace which holds a couple of rings, earrings, and at least one ring on every finger. Each ring shows off a different technique I have tested out, gives clients something solid and real to examine. My hands feel naked, vulnerable and incomplete without my rings; my neck feels bare and unfinished without my necklaces.

'Thank you,' I say to him.

'Any of them...' he stops, embarrassment suddenly crawling across his features like an army of ants out looking for cake crumbs. 'Erm...any of them, real?'

That wasn't what you were going to ask, I think. *I'm surprised you were going to ask the other thing, but that wasn't what you were going to ask.* 'If you mean are any of them made from precious metals, then they all are.'

'Right, right. Of course.' His hand jerks open the door. 'I'll see you then?'

'I might drop by again.'

'Well, you do that. What's your name, out of interest?'

'I told you, I'm That Girl From Nowhere.'

'Cool. I'm Tyler. No way near as exotic as yours, but I thought I'd tell you. In case you wanted to know.'

'Bye, Tyler,' I reply.

'Bye, TGFN,' he says.

7

Abi

To: Jonas Zebila
From: Abi Zebila
Subject: Just a quickie
Tuesday, 2 June 2015

Jonas,

Gran is coming home today. Mummy actually told me that she'd rather Gran went to somewhere people could take better care of her but Daddy wouldn't hear of it.

Mummy seems so sad, so burdened. She loves looking after Lily-Rose, she told me that, but everything else seems too much for her at the moment.

The other day I was in the loft looking for my old dolls' house that Ivor has been promising to bring down for Lily-Rose for months. In one of the boxes I found Mummy's drawings, paintings and sketches, like the ones she made on the boxes we used to sleep in as babies. She's so talented. She could teach art or even sell some of her stuff. Over the years she's drawn and sketched and painted a lot of butterflies. They're breathtaking. No two butterflies are the same, but the patterns on the wings are so perfectly symmetrical, you'd think they were done on a computer. I sat there going through them and completely forgot the time.

When I'd finished going through the artwork, I felt almost bereft that it was over. I couldn't help wondering why she stopped drawing and painting except for the stuff on our boxes.

Is that what's going to happen to me? Am I going to become so consumed by being a mother and wife that I end up giving up my passions? That's what scares me about being with Declan properly. The idea that I'll lose myself; I'll simply become an extension of him and Lily-Rose, and I'll disappear.

When I was cleaning up the dolls' house with Mummy and Lily-Rose, I asked Mummy why she never decorated any of our boxes with butterflies since she'd practised them so many times. She looked alarmed and said, 'What do you mean?'

'I saw your artwork in the loft. That was why I was so long. I liked the butterfly drawings the most. I was wondering why you didn't decorate any of our boxes with butterflies. And actually, why did you stop drawing?'

'I only decorate the baby boxes, you know that,' she said.

'What about not putting any butterflies on one of our boxes?'

She just stared at me like I was talking a different language until Lily-Rose said, 'Can I see the butterflies?'

Mummy frowned at me and gave me this *Now look what you've done* look, and said, 'There is nothing to see.' And that was the end of that. She got up from the floor in the living room where we were doing the cleaning and went off to start dinner. If I had a talent like that I'd be talking about it all the time, not pretending I didn't know what my own daughter was talking about. What's the betting if I go back up to the loft tonight those pictures will have disappeared?

What do you think? Was I being insensitive? Maybe she had a miscarriage and the butterfly box would have been for the baby she'd lost. Oh, I feel awful now. Maybe that's it. Why she feels so distant sometimes. It would make sense. I know I'd feel worried about everything if I went through that. Add that to how Gran treats her sometimes and I'm not surprised she doesn't share much with me. Sorry, I'm being insensitive to you now.

I'm not sure if you want to talk about what happened, but how are you and Meredith after everything? I'm guessing because I haven't heard anything to the contrary that nothing's changed? I've been keeping an eye online on what you've been up to. Congratulations on your award. I'm really proud of you.

I miss you. Remember how it used to be me and you against Ivor? That man always took himself far too seriously even when he was, like, twelve. At least you knew how to have a laugh. I wish...I miss you. I know I said that already but it needs repeating. As many times as I can until you reply. I miss you. I miss you. I miss you.

Love,
Abi
xxxxx

P.S. Mrs L says hello. Again!

8

Smitty

Mum is in her pink silk dressing gown, sitting on the sofa, staring into space when I return to the flat. The TV is off and the room is now bright from the rising sun.

I was heading for the shop and my workshop, but for some reason my feet had turned towards home instead when I left the café, Beached Heads. I thought it was because I was bunking off work, but actually, I must have known on some level that this would be a bad day for Mum. It's been almost three weeks without a serious setback, so today she is obviously due one.

Usually a healthyish pink, Mum's face is pale, each line more pronounced than usual. Her blue eyes are glassy and unfocused. Grief. Grief has made her fragile, delicate and friable; sorrow has carved itself deep into every part of her.

'Oh, Mum,' I whisper. Along with my bag I place my half-drunk coffee on the TV shelf in the living room, then go to her. She doesn't move. I put my arms around her and gently tug her towards me. We're not the huggy type, Mum and I, but she needs this.

'I'm not meant to be without him,' she says.

It's been too short a time for her not to feel like this, and too long a time we've already spent without him.

'I think feeling like that is normal,' I say. Anything else I say will sound trite and rubbish and as if I'm telling her how she should grieve. My mother's grief is a world away from mine. He was my dad, he was her whole world. Even before he became ill Mum didn't seem to function very well without him. If he was away for whatever reason she would find it difficult to concentrate, she'd be up and down several times a night, would stare into space as if counting down the minutes until he returned.

I found it hard every day, knowing I wouldn't see him again, wouldn't be with him again – Mum must have found it impossible. Despite everything, I couldn't have left her in Leeds on her own. She would have fallen apart.

'Clemency, I'm so glad I have you. Please don't leave me. You must promise me you won't do that to me. You won't leave me.'

When Mum says things like this, however infrequently, they are said to last a lifetime, to burn in my head like a beacon in case I forget who she is and what she means to me. When Mum begs in her own quiet way, she is begging me not to do that thing I could do that would replace her. When Mum pleads and asks me not to leave her, and it probably is once in a blue moon, she is imploring me not to look for my biological parents. She doesn't want me to find the woman who gave birth to me. To her, it's not about me needing to find people who look like me, those who could hold the pieces that complete the puzzle of the quirks of my personality or adding another branch to my family tree that could help me to stop feeling like I'm from nowhere and could be from somewhere. To her, it's a source of unknown terror and anxiety.

Mum doesn't have Dad any more so the thought of me finding another mother, maybe half-siblings and maybe even finding another father, is frightening to her. Her fears have been heightened, cranked up to a level nearing hysteria now Dad isn't here to reassure her she wouldn't be replaced. He was good at that, at calming her fears and encouraging her to accept any decisions I made.

Even then, *even then*, it's always been an unspoken agreement that I wouldn't do it while she was alive. Me moving to Brighton, where I was born, must have pushed the panic button in her mind. She must have been convinced that I was about to renege on our deal. Her fears are mingled, like dye in water, with her grief and uncertainty about the future.

I look over at the cup sitting beside my green, many-pocketed bag. I'm not enjoying this very much if it's a cappuccino kind of day. Shame really, as Tyler the coffee man's cappuccino is very good.

I bring myself back to my mother and to what she wants me to do. 'I promise, Mum,' I state. Well, what else am I going to say to the woman who gave me everything, especially now that I have no one else but her.

With Seth, April 2015, Leeds

'I'm so sorry about your dad,' Seth said.

He'd been saying this repeatedly. I guessed it was his way of trying to make himself believe it – if he kept saying it, it might, in one of the repetitions, become a fact in his mind. Seth and Dad were similar kinds of people: laidback, fiercely protective, generous with their time and affection.

We moved through the darkness in our flat, both heading for the bedroom to strip off our funeral clothes, get into something else, anything else but these black garments.

I'd offered to stay with Mum, of course, but after the wake, she wanted to be alone. We stayed to clean up, loitering and tidying as much as possible because we were both reluctant to go home. When I left I knew that would be it. I would be admitting my time there with Dad had come to an end and I couldn't bear for that to be true right then.

Instead of taking my clothes off, I collapsed on to the bed, flat on my back, a starfish out of water, staring up at the ceiling. It reminded me of the picture of Seth from when we'd first moved in here. He'd starfished on the bed and I had taken a snap of him. Then we'd lain together on the bed and Seth had held the camera up to take a photo of us together: two loved-up starfish in their new home.

Seth sat on the edge of the bed and kicked off his shoes, which we'd never normally wear in the house, let alone into the bedroom. I felt the motion of him loosening his tie, releasing his top button. 'Shall I make a coffee?' he asked. 'Or do you want something stronger? I think there's some port left.'

46

'No, stay here a minute.' Maybe longer. Maybe for ever. Maybe if we stayed where we were for ever, nothing would change. Everything had to change now Dad was...now we'd reached this stage. Maybe if we stayed here, though, maybe if I didn't let Seth out of my sight, nothing else would have to change.

He stretched his long body beside me, stroked his fingers down my face, tucked my hair behind my ear. We hadn't been together properly for the last four months. We'd spoken, had kissed briefly in the times I'd come back home, but not this. I touched his face, resting my hand on his cheek, and he came towards me. Our lips met and we both closed our eyes, connecting ourselves together. I pushed his jacket over his shoulders. I was aware of the thick silk of his tie as I tugged at it until it was undone. The small, matte-black buttons of his shirt came apart easily until he was bare-chested, the paleness of his skin visible in the half-light of the room. He pushed my ankle-length dress up, over my thighs, around my waist, to my chest until he gently tugged it over my head and discarded it beside the bed. My fingers went to his trousers, slipped the shiny, black tongue of his slim belt though its loop, out of its buckle until it was free, then I moved on to his button, pushing down the top of his trousers. His fingers unhooked the small metal clasps of my bra, slipped it off, before they moved on to removing my knickers, plain and black, as you'd expect for a funeral.

A gasp, a deep cry escaped from my throat as he entered me. A new sensation; in all the time of being with him, I'd never felt such a perfect mingling of agony and pleasure as he pushed himself into my body.

'I've missed you,' he murmured beside my ear. 'It feels so good to be inside you again.'

'I've missed you so much,' I whispered back. I dug my fingers into him, urging him to go deeper, to completely fill me up. He responded, pushing harder, slower but harder. The pleasure came from being together again, having each other back, reminding ourselves of what we shared. The pain came from knowing why we'd been apart for so long. The orgasms – loud, urgent, ecstatically raw – came from that blending of desolation and joyful reunion.

Seth lay on his front, his head in profile on the pillow while his fingers played with my hair, coiling curls around his fingers. I lay on my back, staring at the ceiling again.

'We could have made a baby,' he eventually said.

He'd put words to the panic that was amassing inside. We could have. No contraception, not even withdrawal. I'd felt when he was about to, but I hadn't wanted him to, I'd clung on to him, keeping him with me until it was too late to change the outcome. **Have unprotected sex … and end up paying for it for the rest of your life**, started to flash in my head.

'That'd be pretty amazing, though, wouldn't it?' he said. 'I know we put those plans on hold these last few months but it'd be incredible if we did it now.'

A baby. Me. I loved children. Playing with them was never a chore. Sienna, my cousin Nancy's daughter, had once stayed with us for three months while Nancy was off finding herself, and I'd loved that. I had loved taking care of Sienna's every need, waking up with her in our flat, going to sleep with her in our flat, being with her.

But … But … A *baby*. *Me?* How would I know how to care for it? Would I really want to keep it? And even after all the discussions, it still scared me that I knew nothing of the potential anomalies in my DNA; disorders unknown to me because I couldn't just ask my mother or father about any medical conditions that might run in the bloodline, in the family.

A *baby? Me?* What about the father, too? How could I trust him to stick around when my biological father hadn't and had made it necessary for my biological mother to give me away or 'place me for adoption', as I was meant to say and think.

In all the dreams and fantasies I had about how I came to be adopted, the ones I could never tell anyone, I knew this one was the truest. This was the one that would fit most comfortably with reality. My mother, who was probably young, told my father she was pregnant and he in turn rejected her. Probably called her names, and questioned who else she'd been with. Then he went incommunicado because he wanted nothing to do with her or the child she was carrying. She tried to get him to change his mind, but then she found out he was seeing someone else – had been all along – and she knew it was hopeless. And when she told her parents they were so disappointed, they didn't have the money or the means to bring up another child. The shame would have killed them, too. She had nowhere to turn, so she did the best she could. She found a box and she decorated it in butterflies, the most beautiful creatures in nature, and she made it comfortable for me to sleep in. And she cried and cried when she had to hand me over, but she made sure I got the box because it was something no one else had. It was all she could afford to give me, but it was something completely unique and completely invaluable. Like the jewellery I made for people – it may have been inspired by other pieces but everything I made for others was made with that person in mind. That person was one of a kind, so was the jewellery I made for them.

No one else had a butterfly box like mine. I used it to store all my precious photographs, and even though it had been bashed about over time because of the many moves I'd been through, the times I hadn't been as careful as I should have been with it, I still had that box and I still treasured it.

I couldn't have a baby if I couldn't trust its father. I turned to Seth, carefully considered him. I hadn't grown used to his features over the years, I was always surprised by how attractive he was to me every time I looked at him. I had spent years looking at him, but until that New Year's Eve when we'd first had sex, I hadn't seen him. When I finally 'saw' him that night, I could never be used to those features again. Each time seeing him gave me a tiny thrill in the bottom of my heart.

'Seth . . .' I began. I had planned to wait, leave it for a bit until I did this, but now I'd been reckless and stupid, now I'd given in to the flashing neon sign in my brain about unprotected sex with a virtual stranger, I had to do this now. I had to ask him. The very fact I had to ask set us back twenty-odd years and made him a virtual stranger again. And the fact that I knew what he was going to say, how he was going to answer, meant not only was he going to stay a stranger, but also that I would have to go through with my plan. I wanted to be wrong. Desperately. But I knew what the answer was going to be.

'Seth, do you have something you need to tell me?'

His sudden flash of panic that I might know was almost physical as it scattered through him like the fallen beads from a snapped necklace. He caught himself, though, reasoned that I couldn't possibly know, and gathered up those panic-broken beads, strung them back together. Calm and composed, he replied, 'No, not that I know of.'

I shut my eyes. *Wrong answer*. The reply I was expecting, but had been hoping I wouldn't get. I had prayed, actually prayed, to a God I only partially believed in, that Seth wouldn't do this to me or to us. 'Seth, *please*. I need you to be completely honest with me, no matter what it is, just tell me. *Please*, forget about what's happened with my dad, and the fact we haven't seen each other properly in weeks, please, you can tell me anything. *Anything*.'

'No, Smitty, there's nothing.'

Disappointment drifted through me like a cold, creeping gust of wind. He wasn't the person I thought he was. It's the big moments that test you, push you, encourage you to be better in every way that you can. It's the small, intimate, seemingly insignificant moments where the choice you make alters who you are at a fundamental level.

'I can't be with you any more, Seth,' I told him. I could ignore it, pretend, bury it deep so I could forget. Or I could do what needed to be done so I could sleep at night. 'We have to split up.'

Part 2

9

Smitty

'One coffee for the lady with the notebook and camera.' Tyler, the barista from Beached Heads, my favourite coffee shop in the whole of Brighton, places the coffee cup – the one decorated with yellow and white daisies that I love most – in front of me without so much as a rattle of the cup on its matching saucer. I've been in here a lot, have managed to grab the more private sofa at the back like I planned, and have basically been able to drink my body weight in coffee every working day without ever having to make it. Win-win-win.

'Thank you,' I reply. I have to keep my eyes on the coffee cup and not raise them anywhere in his direction because I've developed the most embarrassing crush on him. After my late-teenage Dylan crush I didn't think I could be like this about someone – no matter how good-looking he was. I thought age, experience, plus a long-term relationship, had acted like weedkiller on that particular type of emotion. However, that weed was clearly lying dormant, waiting for the right combination of circumstance and person to fertilise it and make it shoot up. Tyler, the apron-wearing, sous-chef-hat-donning owner of Beached Heads, is my new crush.

With horror I realise he has pulled out the chair opposite me and is sitting himself down. When it isn't seven in the morning, the place is usually busy, alive with the hum and thrum of people who have stopped off for a drink and a stare at the sea. 'I've got to ask, what is it that you do exactly?' he asks me.

'Exactly?'

'Or even vaguely,' he says. 'You've been coming in here for nearly two weeks now, meeting different people, taking photos of their jewellery, of them, making notes. What is it that you do?'

'Isn't it obvious?'

'If it was, I wouldn't be asking. Also, I need to get confirmation before I decide whether or not I'm going to turf you out for conducting business on my premises.'

'I'm a jewellery maker.'

'Right. Right.' He nods slowly. 'How come you don't actually make jewellery, then? Why are you always hanging around my place?'

I look up at him. He's sitting back in the circular, leather armchair, his arms folded across his chest and his head on one side. He waits for my answer with an affected puzzled look. I have to smile. I just have to. 'I like it here,' I say.

'More than you like making enough money to pay your mortgage?'

'I don't have a mortgage. I have a flat I rent with my mother. And a shop that I haven't quite got around to opening yet. My, erm, landlord is not going to be happy with me, but in between meeting clients here and making the pieces they commission, the shop has taken a bit of a back seat.'

'What's your name, Nowhere Girl?'

'Clemency Smittson. My friends call me Smitty.'

'Do you want me to help you set up your shop?'

'Why would you do that?'

'Because I want to.'

'Fair enough. I'd love you to help, but I'm not going to let you.'

'Pray tell why not?'

'Because the real reason why I haven't done it is I'm not ready to. With most things, if I don't do them even when I should, it's because I'm not ready to or it's because I really don't want to. I can't see how it's going to look up here yet.' I tap my right temple with my right index finger. 'Until I can see it, there's no point in trying to make it a reality.'

'I do that,' he says. Another grin. This one would quicken even the most uninterested person's heart. 'I'm not sure I approve of you taking advantage of my good nature by using my shop because you can't be bothered to fix up yours.'

'Erm, excuse me, but how much coffee do I buy? I'm pretty sure I'm keeping your business afloat.'

'Ahhhh, so much delusion in one so young.' Tyler grins as he says this.

We could be friends, I realise. *This man could be my friend and I would be able to put down a root, ground myself to this place where I have washed up. Start to fill up my wall again.*

'Can I take a photo of you?' I ask him before I think about it.

'Are you going to make me some jewellery?' he asks.

'Would you wear it?'

'Probably not,' he replies. 'No offence, but I'm not the jewellery sort.'

'None taken.' My fingers reach for my instant camera, raise it to my face. 'Can I take a photo anyway?'

He grins again. 'If you must.'

A reminder ricochets so painfully through me, I have to pause, my finger resting on the white plastic button unable to move. Lots of people say that, not just Seth.

I push the button, take a picture of my new friend.

With Tyler at Beached Heads, May 2015, Brighton/Hove
I'll write on the bottom later. I'll put it on my wall with four blobs of Blu-Tack and it'll be another patch on the wall; another moment to ground me in the now and here.

With Seth, May 2015, Leeds
'Smitty? Clem?' he called as he entered our flat, almost at a run. Obviously he'd seen Lottie parked outside and thought I had changed my mind about everything. 'Are you home?' Excitement at the thought of me being back and the hope of what that might mean danced all over his face and flowed through his voice. In his

hands he held the shiny black dome of his motorbike helmet. He carefully slid it on to the hall table then unzipped his jacket. 'Are you...'

My face obviously told him that I wasn't back. I wasn't home. I hadn't changed my mind.

'What are you doing here?' he asked, a little more sober, a tad less giddy.

I pointed at the boxes, unable to tell him what else I'd actually been doing. 'Finishing off my packing.'

'Please come home. Talk to me. We can sort this out.'

'No, Seth, it's over. I've told you that. How many more times? It's over.' I grabbed my jacket from where I'd dumped it on the cubic mountain of my boxes in the corridor and slipped it on, hoping it would cover what I'd hastily shoved in my back pocket before running out of the bathroom to hide the other pieces of evidence.

'Don't I deserve better than this?' he asked loudly.

I said nothing, but instead moved to leave.

He stepped into my path. 'How does this even work anywhere except in your mind? We make love for the first time after weeks and weeks apart, then you tell me it's over and you're moving to Brighton as soon as possible. Then you spend the night on the sofa, go to stay with your mother the next day and refuse to talk to me. How is that any way to treat someone? Anyone? Let alone someone you love?'

If you'd told the truth, if you'd just admitted it, this wouldn't be happening, I thought. 'Look, I'll call or text next time,' I said. 'Arrange a proper time to come and finish this off so we don't have to see each other. I'm sorry, I shouldn't have come here without warning you. I thought you were at work all day today. Do you want me to leave my key?'

He glared at me. Angry, confused, hurt. All mirror images of what I had felt since I found out about him and *her.*

'Stop it, Smitty! Talk to me.'

Talking was our thing. We rarely argued, would simply get short and snippy with each other, and when that lost its appeal, we'd make up without actually making up. I wasn't sure we knew how to argue properly, how to shout and scream and slam doors. Mum and Dad had never done it and I'd never seen the appeal of all that noise to get your point across. But then, neither of us had ever really done anything that needed shouting about, until recently. I could yell at him for what he'd done, and I could see how angry he was, how bewildered and hurt by my refusal to talk to him – so angry he could probably shout, too. But it was all too much right now. If he'd only answered in the right way. We would have been in a difficult, fraught place but we'd be there together, working through it with each other. But the lying on top of what he'd done? That was what had ended this. I could not get over betrayal *and* lying. Not right now.

'We had a chance to talk and you said there was nothing to tell,' I reminded him.

And there it was again: the flash of panic that I might know, the rationalisation that it'd be impossible for me to know. 'If you've got something to say, just say it and stop playing games,' he said. The rage was bubbling out of him into every word.

'Do you want me to leave the key?' I asked. We had nothing more to say to each other and I didn't want to be in the flat any longer, especially not with what I had secreted away in my back pocket moments before he entered the flat.

He glared at me again. And again I saw the almost perfect reflection of what I felt. 'Keep the key. Don't keep the key. Makes no difference either way to me,' he eventually said. He shrugged. 'What I want doesn't matter to you, does it?'

Seth's body brushed against mine when he headed towards the kitchen at the end of the corridor. He couldn't stand to look at me, nor to watch me leave.

He stood at the kitchen window, though, his hand against the glass, watching as I left the building and then got into Lottie. He didn't move while I started her up and pulled away from the kerb. I suspected he stood still and expectant for a long time after I'd turned the corner out of sight, probably hoping I'd change my mind and come back to him.

At the first litter bin I saw, I pulled Lottie over, fished the plastic white stick I had weed on earlier out of my back pocket and threw it in the bin without looking at the result. I didn't need to, not really. I knew what it would say.

'I'd like you to tell me a story about you. Not the jewellery, but you,' I say to the woman beside me.

'Me?' she replies.

'Yes.'

Like the photos I take, I collect other people's stories like a magpie collects shiny things. Sometimes I wonder whether I would need to collect so many stories if I knew where I came from. Then I wonder if I'd be able to do my job, make and relove jewellery, if I didn't spend time trying to unwrap the layers of who my clients were, to find the right use and look for their forgotten, unused, discarded pieces of jewellery. If I didn't sometimes feel like that forgotten item at the back of a bedside cabinet, would I try so hard to make other things special and lovable?

'I'm not interesting enough to tell you a story,' Melissa, the woman in front of me, says. She's about my age, maybe a little younger. She's well dressed in a suit jacket, smart jeans and white T-shirt, and able to meet me in Beached Heads at 3 p.m. Her fingers are bare of rings of any description and she has ordered a double espresso without even thinking what she'd like. From that I've guessed that she doesn't have children and works flexible hours in a fairly well-paid job. I've also guessed she's not married, engaged or in a long-term relationship. The double espresso makes her my kind of person.

'Yes, you are,' I say. 'I'm sorry to contradict you, but I know you are. Everyone is. And it's the people who say they're not interesting who generally are the most interesting.'

'OK. Erm...' She raises her gaze up to the ceiling while she thinks. 'Well, one of the things about me that people do think is interesting is that I was adopted.'

'So was I,' I say.

Her brown eyes, cautious and guarded before, are now alight with curiosity, wondering if she's found a kindred spirit. 'Really? What age were you adopted at?'

'Birth. What about you?'

'I was about one.'

Melissa relaxes a little now, she's more comfortable with me. We have a point of contact, something that links us, unlike other people she meets. I remember once looking up the statistics on how many people were adopted each year in the UK, because I wanted to find out how many people out there were like me, and there were enough. Enough for me to know that I'd meet someone one day who'd understand what it was like to live with people who weren't linked to you by blood and DNA and shared genetic history. It was comforting to know how many others there were out there, but beyond that momentary consolation, I didn't *feel* better. It wasn't as if any of the other people like me would be able to heal the fractured pieces of who I was.

'Is this jewellery something from your birth family?' I ask. On the royal blue velvet cloth laid out on the table in front of us is a large oval gold locket, the type people used to keep a lock of hair in, with a long, thick-linked chain. It's a lovely piece – the simple locket case has a few swirly lines that radiate up from the bottom of the pendant.

'Yes. My birth mother left it to be given to me on my eighteenth birthday. It's all a bit Little Orphan Annie, but there you go.' She shrugs her bony shoulders, trying to make light of what is actually difficult for her. 'My parents handed it over and I've had it sitting in a drawer for years. When I saw your advert I thought I'd find out if there is something I can do with it.' She points to the platinum locket that rests just below the base of her throat. 'As you can see, I already have a locket that I wear all the time.'

'Are you in reunion with your birth parents?' That's the language of adoption I've picked up from reading the internet. 'Reunion' instead of 'contact'; 'birth parents' not simply 'parents'. Knowing if she is or isn't will all feed into what this piece becomes, how I reshape and redesign it.

Locks of her wavy brown hair fall forwards as she hides her face to pick up her duck-egg blue espresso cup and put it to her lips. After the sip, her fingers reach out, push at the chain of the locket on the blue velvet background. She makes odd shapes of the gold links with each prod and poke. I hear what she is saying, without words, loud and clear: that it is none of my business.

I have to get her back. I had her and now she's pulling away from me again. If she continues to withdraw, there will soon be a gulf too wide for us to breach. I want to relove this piece. It's important to her, this woman who seems to be just like me.

'My, erm, birth mother left me a cardboard box that I used to sleep in.'

'Really?' Melissa raises her head, checking whether I am making it up. With that look she's back, engaged with me again.

'Apparently it's a Finnish tradition dating back to nineteen forty-nine or something. The Finnish government gives new parents a box full of baby things that they'll need and the box doubles as a crib. I'm not an expert, but I don't think my birth mother was from Finland even though she gave me to the social worker in the box and said I was to sleep in it for as long as I would fit in it.'

'Do you still have it?'

'Yes.' All the butterflies on the box are hand-drawn and hand-coloured. The largest is on the bottom – its wingspan covers the entire surface, and the wings are mirror images of each other. Each colour is perfectly twinned; each intricate vein etched in black and reflected on the other wing. It must have taken her hours to do each wing, let alone the rest of them, each a different size, every one a unique, beautiful winged creature that looked fragile and lifelike. Sometimes I wonder why she chose butterflies, often I wonder why she spent so much time making something so beautiful and unique for someone she didn't want around, most of the time I don't think about it at all – it's easier that way. Over the years my obsession with butterflies has waxed and waned, depending a lot on how I feel about my birth mother at any given moment on any given day. It's the reminder of my box that makes Mum dislike butterflies.

She doesn't like to remember that I came to her in it instead of out of her body.

'Do you mind if I see some of your photos?' I ask Melissa. 'The ones on your phone will do. It'll give me a better idea, visually, of what your life is like and what the finished piece needs to fit in with. No worries if not.'

Unbothered by my request she hands over her mobile with the pictures screen up. I flick through them, watch her life unfold before my eyes. She has a sister, two parents. Her sister is younger, has two children. Her parents are both white-haired but were both probably once dark. Melissa isn't, she is quite fair-skinned and light-haired, but if you didn't know, you'd never know. She looks enough like them to pass for a blood relative, to be one of them. Unexpectedly and quite violently, a lump of envy forms in my throat. What would it have been like to have grown up with someone who looked even a little like me?

With Mum, March 1982, Otley

'Mum, why don't I look like you?'

Mum looked scared. I was four years old but I could tell she was a bit worried and scared. 'You do, Clemency,' she said. She picked up her big bag and took out her sewing. She didn't look at me at all.

'I don't, Mum. I've got brown skin and you've got peach skin. I've got black hair and you've got yellow hair.'

'That doesn't matter. I still love you. No matter what you look like, I still love you.'

'But Nancy looks like her mum. Why don't I look like you?' I didn't understand why she wouldn't tell me. She'd looked so worried and now she looked sad.

'It doesn't matter,' she said again. 'Nancy... It doesn't matter. All that matters is that I love you, no matter what you look like.'

'OK,' I said. 'OK, Mum.' I patted her hand because I didn't want her to cry and her eyes were all wet. It made her sad that I didn't look like her, and I knew, even though she said it didn't, it mattered lots and lots.

'Can I ask you something about being adopted, seeing as you're a stranger and I never have to see you again if I don't want to?' Melissa says. She speaks in a rush, obviously desperate to get the words out before she changes her mind.

I have given her back her phone, I have pulled myself together. It honestly didn't matter that I didn't look like my parents; that wherever we went when I was growing up, and even now, I stood out from the crowd as different, as other. Mostly it didn't matter. 'Sure,' I reply. I'm going to lie. It's easier to do that than to become 'The Adopted Person' whose experiences someone uses as gospel for every discussion they ever have going forwards about adoption.

'Did you sleep around a lot?' she asks.

I stop laying out the square, white-framed Polaroids of my previous work and designs on the table to look up at her.

'I used to,' she continues in her flustered rush. 'I've met a few other people who were adopted and I've wanted to ask them if they did it, too, but I never got up the courage. I was really promiscuous at one point and my therapist – yes, I do that, too – suggested it might be because of stuff I'd internalised about what women who gave up their children were thought to be like back then. Nowadays it doesn't matter, but I suppose people must have thought badly of women who got pregnant and then had to give up their children for adoption. She said it was possible that I'd been acting that out as a way of connecting with my birth mother. I don't know if that's right or not, but I was curious if you were ever like that? Or if it was just me? I hope I didn't offend you.'

'No, you didn't offend me.' My mother was madly in love with my father, I'm sure of that. In every version of my birth story I have thought up over the years, I know she was in love with my father and didn't sleep around. I think she was just unlucky – they probably got caught out the first time they did it. And he panicked. 'No, it wasn't just you,' I say to Melissa. So much for lying. 'I did it too.'

'Really?' She closes her brown eyes and her face becomes a tap-estry of sheer relief. She's not alone. I'm not blood, but I do belong to the same group as her, the same family. I was adopted and I used to do the same thing as her. 'I seriously thought there was something wrong with me. That I was the only one.'

'I suppose I did, too. For me, it was about being wanted. If someone wanted me, even if it was just for sex, then it felt good.'

'Yes! I was like everyone else because someone wanted me. Even if it was just wanting my body for sex. So many people take being wanted for granted.'

'I know. But I'm not sure it's only down to having been adopted. I mean, there must be loads of people out there who sleep around just because someone wants them.'

'Maybe so, but it's nice to talk to someone who understands.'

'It is. It really is.'

10

Abi

To: Jonas Zebila
From: Abi Zebila
Subject: AQOTWF
Monday, 8 June 2015

J,

I don't want to be emailing you only if there's a problem so I'm just letting you know that All is Quiet On The Western Front. There's a woman I know whose mum texts her that when she's babysitting to let my friend know all is well and the baby is asleep.

All is well and the Zebilas are – mostly – asleep. No unusual dramas of any kind.

Gran seems to have stabilised quite a lot since the hospital stay (which of course gives credence to what Mummy has been trying to say about her being in a home where she can get specialist care). Mummy has disappeared the artwork as I thought she might.

Declan is gearing up to one of his monthly meltdowns about us living together again and being a proper family. I can feel it coming. Mummy and Daddy are still pretending that Lily-Rose was the Immaculate Conception and that Declan doesn't exist. Even when we go to spend the weekend with him at his flat, they never ask where we've been or what we got up to. He can't see why I won't move in with him full-time, but you know, every time I think about it, I remember the look on your face when you told Mummy and Daddy what the things Gran had said and done had resulted in, and that if they wouldn't stick up for you and Meredith against Gran, then you weren't hanging around any longer.

Is Declan worth giving up my family for? He was such a dick when I told him I was pregnant. We were both nineteen and both meant to be doing the university thing after we'd finished school together, but I couldn't believe how badly he behaved. I know, I know, it lasted all of three days before he was begging me to give him another chance, but it still makes me cautious about committing totally to him. That's why I've never properly lived with him – we've both kept our own places until now when I'm living here. He could turn on me again.

I suppose my only way forward is to move to Montenegro with you. Ha-ha, you'd love that, wouldn't you?

What did you think of the pictures? Do you want some more? Do you want me to get Mrs Lehtinen to send you some of those Jim bars? Or maybe I should pass on your email address to her. I may just do that if you don't reply!!!

Talk to me, big brother, please.
Abi
xxxxxx

Smitty

'Tell me a story about you,' I say to her. 'Not the jewellery, but you.'

'My darling, if I told you a story about me, we would be here all day. I mean, of course, you would be here all day. I am here all day anyway.' Her voice has the slightest husk of an accent, one I do not recognise. She speaks with a slight hesitancy, the caution of someone who sometimes has to translate words in her head before they leave her mouth. 'Tell me about you.'

'There's really nothing to tell. I'm here to help you, anyway.' We're sitting in the large community room in the retirement village where she lives. It's bright from the stark overhead lighting, and airy from the glass floor-to-ceiling windows that overlook the large courtyard. Several blue easy chairs are placed around small, low coffee tables. Apart from the lack of a counter and leather seating, it could be Beached Heads.

On the table in front of us is a light-wood box with a hinged lid that is carved with different types of musical notes. Inside, she has a collection of gold and silver items, brooches, pieces with precious gems that look like real sapphires and emeralds. Pearls, too. Mrs Lehtinen, a widow who has lived at the home for a few months, is the third person I am seeing here today and she has by far the most extensive collection of jewellery. The others had modest assortments of jewellery and talking to them, seeing the condition of their hands, I knew I would make their pieces into elasticated bracelets or simply necklaces so they could wear their collections with no catches to negotiate, no clasps to undo.

Apparently one of the staff saw my advert in the local magazine and asked the residents if they'd be interested in having me look at their jewellery. Six were interested.

Mrs Lehtinen is one of those people who seems to exist in a soft-focus glow: her hair is white with a candyflossy haze, her skin is the colour and consistency of a peach, her eyes are a gentle blue. I don't recognise where in the world her name might come from, just like I can't place her accent.

'You look like one of the girls who works here,' Mrs Lehtinen says. 'Abi is her name. You look so much like her.'

'Do I?' I say. I always look like people apparently. During my second year of college, I had people coming up to me constantly telling me they'd started a conversation with me in the library, the canteen, the bar, the car park, only to find they were talking to another girl. 'She's your absolute double,' they'd say. When I finally met her, we discovered the only similarity between us was that we were both brown-skinned, and even then, not the same shade of brown. Other than that, we were different heights, weights and had completely different features. But apparently none of the people around us could see that. We'd both raised our eyebrows at each other, nodded sagely, and had to stop ourselves from laughing out loud. 'You look nothing like me,' we both said at the same time.

'You are her double,' Mrs Lehtinen says.

'I hear that all the time,' I say diplomatically. 'I think I must look like a lot of people.'

Mrs Lehtinen smiles at me. 'You think I'm a silly old woman, don't you?'

'No, I don't.' I really don't. 'Do you want to show me some of your jewellery? Tell me about the different pieces if you don't want to tell me a story about you.'

'I collect jewellery like I collect ailments,' she says. 'I am never really sure where any of them come from or when I am going to get rid of them.'

I grin at her. I see she is one of those people who needs to be dealt with differently. She won't tell me her story until I've told her something about me.

I remove the butterfly pendant from around my neck. I hold it out to her. I notice Mrs Lehtinen's hands as she relieves me of the necklace. The rest of her – right down to her powder blue twinset – may be soft-focusy but she has lived. Her wrinkled, weathered and *used* hands tell me so. Her mind must be a treasury of stories, as varied and interesting as her chest of treasures in front of us.

She's surprised, as most people are, by the lightness of my pendant. It looks heavy, solid, its strong, thick lines create an expectation of heft, but it has very little weight because it is hollow.

'This used to be a pair of earrings,' I explain. 'I got the earrings when I went on holiday. You know how, when you're on holiday, something you buy looks amazing and you love it, then you get it home and the shine comes off it and you realise that the thing that was the most amazing thing in the world is now hellish? That was these earrings. They were incredibly uncomfortable. The shape, though, like teardrops, reminded me of the closed wings of a butterfly. I like butterflies, always have done, so I thought I could remake the earrings into something I could wear. It is not very good, because I was just starting to make jewellery.' I run my fingers along the solid lines where the wings meet. You can still see the rivulets of the solder, something I would painstakingly file smooth if I was making the piece now. 'I cut into this part of the earring, then I had to file both edges into curves to make them fit. Then I had to solder them together.'

It sounds so simple, that I just did it, but the pain I went through: I had sobbed as the solder ran into the wrong places because I hadn't painted enough of the yellow-green liquid flux into the right areas; I had cried again at the moment when I had finally got the solder to stay and it snapped off because I was too vigorous with the filing. 'I used a large silver jump-ring and soldered it on to the wings to make it into a head. See?' I move my finger over the curved antennae on each side of the butterfly's head. 'The small antennae were made by

melting and soldering on the little links you put through your ears.'
As I speak, she turns the pendant over and over in her hands. 'I wear
it all time now so it's gone from a pair of earrings that sat in a drawer
mostly forgotten to something I love to wear. I want to do that with
some of your jewellery.'

'It is so simple but *kaunis*.' Mrs Lehtinen's hands turn over the
pendant and her eyes, upon which she has now placed the glasses
she wears around her neck on a gold chain, continue to scrutinise it.
'What is the word? Beautiful. But not as ordinary as beautiful. No,
no, I don't mean beautiful. In Finnish the word is *henkeäsalpaava*.'

'*Henkeäsalpaava*,' I repeat as close to what she said as I can. I nod
while I say it, acting as though I understand completely what she
is getting at. She's Finnish. *Does she have children?* I wonder.
*Grandchildren? Did they sleep in baby boxes, too? Did she decorate them or
were they as plain as they were when they were given to mothers by the
government?*

'I haven't met many Finnish people in my life,' I say.

'I am surprised at that, there are many of us around. Even here,
in Brighton.'

She's not really giving me her full attention, she seems obsessed
by the pendant. It isn't that perfect. I love it, but I can see all its flaws,
all the ways I would have made it differently now I am more experienced at what I do. Back then I was trying too hard to make things
perfect and didn't always manage it. In 2015, having done this for
years, I still aim for perfection, but I don't panic because anything
that goes wrong, I know I can usually fix. Or at least make it look
like the problem was intentional.

'Do you like butterflies?' I ask her.

'It is not that,' Mrs Lehtinen replies. 'I am always fascinated by
them because I remember a long time ago I knew of a baby who
had a *perhonen* box.' She traces her fingers over the wing curves of
my butterfly pendant.

'A what?' I ask, scared to repeat the word in case it comes out
wrong and I end up swearing at her.

'A butterfly box,' she says. 'A box covered in *perhonen*. In Finland, when a baby is born, the government gives the mother a box full of everything they need – clothes and nappies and the like. And the box has a mattress too so the baby can sleep in it.'

I know this. The tingling that has taken over my body tells me that I know this. The sudden shortness of my breath tells me that I know this. I nod at her.

'I told the young girl of the family I used to live next door to about it when she was expecting. Many years ago. I told her and she made one. She decorated it with *perhonen*. Beautiful butterflies. She used such *henkeäsalpaava* colours. She had a baby girl.'

When I was eight Dad took me on a rollercoaster for the first time. We were on our annual trip to Blackpool and I was giddy with the excitement of finally doing something grown-up and adventurous with my dad. We sat next to each other and he held my hand. Right at the top of the rollercoaster, just before the car began its descent, I felt weightless; as light as air, as though I weighed nothing. As if I was nothing. I was suspended above the Earth and in those seconds I felt like I was flying. I was a butterfly, as light as anything.

I feel like that now. I am suspended above the Earth, weightless, light as air.

'Does she still have the butterfly box, the little girl?' My voice is working even though I am as light as air, as weightless as a butterfly.

'I do not know. The baby…They…She went to live somewhere else. They said they sent her back to their country in Africa to grow up with family because the girl was too young to look after her properly. But I do not think that was the case. The girl's guardian, she was my friend and she was so proud. She did not like scandal. We were never to speak of what happened, nor the baby. I suspect…' Mrs Lehtinen stops turning my pendant over in her hand and places it carefully on the table beside her open jewellery box. 'But what do I know? I am just a silly old woman.'

She is just a silly old woman and I am still as light as air. My body tingles and my lungs do not work properly, but I am as light as air.

'You're not a silly old woman,' I say. *Ask her. Ask her what happened to the girl who had the baby. Where she is now. Ask her.*

Mrs Lehtinen's eyes are suddenly, surprisingly, on me. She is as far away from a silly old woman as it is possible to get. 'The girl, Abi, the one you look like, she is also the daughter of the woman who made the butterfly box. She had a box, too.'

I stare at her. *Does she know? Has she guessed who I am? Who I might be?* I do this, though. I'm constantly looking at people and wondering if we're related, if they could be a half-sibling or a parent. I've never had a relative who looks like me, who acts like me, who's interested in the same things as me. I'm always searching. This is probably an extension of that: I have come across a coincidence and I am using it as a passive way to search for more information on who I am and where I have come from. I didn't go looking for this, it came to me.

Of course it's a coincidence, that's what most things are in life. We believe in Fate, we believe in kismet, we believe in pre-determined happenings, when really, it's all down to coincidence. There must be hundreds of children out there who slept in butterfly boxes when they were born. Hundreds, if not thousands. I mean, what are the chances of me actually sitting down opposite the neighbour of the woman who gave birth to me? Slim to none, I'd say. And what are the chances of the other child of the woman who gave birth to me working here, too? Not even slim, just non-existent. I am seeing things that are not there.

'OK, Mrs Lehtinen, are there any pieces of jewellery that you'd like to wear again and I can help you with?' I am back. I know this is all nonsense, my brain searching for familiarity – *family* – in the world of strangers I have grown up in, when I know who my family are. Here I am, back on solid ground. I am no longer floating, hovering above reality. I am back to doing what I am here to do.

My hand reaches for my butterfly pendant. It is trembling. *Stop shaking*, I tell my hand. *Stop shaking, you're showing me up.* Mrs Lehtinen is watching me but my hand won't stop shaking. I enclose my butterfly pendant in my hand, hide the tremors. I hook the thick chain over my neck and flip open my toolbox, take out my camera. Mrs Lehtinen stares at my yellow and black toolbox – years ago I decorated it with butterfly stickers.

That was at the time when I was particularly obsessed with butterflies. Back then, I would have the same recurring dream that I was in a park full of butterflies. I would be surrounded by hundreds and hundreds of them, all different, all beautiful, but I wouldn't notice any of the creatures around me because I was frantically, desperately searching for my baby. I had lost my baby in that park and I needed to get him back. It was obvious what that was about. I use my foot to slide my butterfly-covered toolbox under the table, out of Mrs Lehtinen's line of sight.

'Shall I photograph some pieces and photograph you and then go away to think of some ideas?' I say.

'Why don't you go and talk to Abi? She is down the corridor in the office. She is the deputy manager. She is a lovely girl. Always so helpful to everyone, but especially to me because I know her grandmother. I'm sure she'll tell you all you need to know about the baby boxes.'

'I'm more interested in your jewellery and how I can make it work for you, to be honest,' I say to the woman in front of me. 'And I have other people to see as well. There are two more after you. So I…erm…don't really have time to do that.'

'You will come back to see me?' she asks.

'Erm…yes, if you want me to. But do you think you will want any of your jewellery remade?'

'I'm sure I will. Take your photographs, and come back to see me with your ideas.'

I'm shaking too much to lay out the jewellery properly. I take a few of the pieces out, but mostly I photograph them in situ in the box. With my hand still tremoring, I snap her picture, the flash causing me to jump a little each time I take a shot.

I know it's a coincidence because that's what happens to people like me.

'Dad, why don't I look like you and Mum?'

'Ah, Clemmy, that's a good question.' Dad's large hands picked me up and sat me on his lap. From the glass-fronted sideboard beside his chair, he plucked the picture of us from when we went to Blackpool for the day. Dad had to ask somebody he didn't even know to take a picture of us all. 'The thing of it is, everybody is different. We all look different in our own ways. See, here, your mum and I, we look different. She's got blonde hair – it mostly came out of a bottle but I didn't tell you that – and I've got dark hair. And you've got black hair. We're none of us the same.'

'But why is my skin different to yours? You and Mum have the same skin.'

'We don't, actually, Clemmy, but I know what you mean.' Dad stopped talking and stared at the photo for a long time. I was scared he would do what Mum did and look like he was going to cry. 'The thing of it is, Clemmy, I was meant to tell you this with your mum here. She'll be raging at me for not waiting for her, but I'll tell you anyway. You know how a baby grows in their mum's tummy?' I knew that. I was four but I knew that. I still didn't know how the baby got out of the mum's tummy and into the baby pram, but I thought I would ask Dad that another time. 'You didn't grow in your mum's tummy.'

I was frightened suddenly: why didn't I grow in Mum's tummy like everyone else? 'Why not, Dad?'

'Mum can't grow babies in her tummy, nobody knows why. You grew in another lady's tummy but she couldn't look after you. And the lady who was a social worker said that we could look after you if we wanted, and we could be your mum and dad. We really wanted to. When we first saw you in that butterfly box we knew that we really wanted to be your mum and dad.

'You have the same skin as the lady whose tummy you grew in, but we have the same smile, me and you, and you laugh at the same things your mum does. And we all like to throw stones in the sea. We don't look the same but no one does, not really. We have more things that make us the same than things that make us different.' His finger, which was big and fat like a sausage, pointed to the picture again. 'You see how we've all got the same type of ears? Round, not pointy. And my curly hair is a little bit like yours. Your mother's would be curly a bit like yours if she didn't put those damn rollers in every night. And here, look at our hands: square at the end of our fingers. We're the same and we're different. And being different is just as good as being the same.'

I didn't understand why the mum who grew me in her tummy couldn't look after me, and I didn't understand what he meant about there were more things the same than different. But I did understand that he couldn't say we had the same nose because we didn't. And not the same mouth. And not the same eyes. And definitely, definitely not the same skin colour. His was peach, mine was brown. Dad thought that was good. It made Mum nearly cry, but Dad thought it was good. I didn't understand why they didn't both think it was good or they didn't both want to cry. Maybe that was another different thing that was good.

I gave Dad a hug. I thought he needed one.

12

Smitty

There are moments in your life you can't plan for.

They happen, hit you, render you incapable. I am in the middle of a moment where nothing I do will stop it from happening. Every second that passes is another step closer to that moment.

In my mind, in the sequence of freeze-frame moments that I see the world in sometimes, I am heading back to Lottie. I have my butterfly-covered toolbox of tricks in one hand, my green, many-pocketed bag is slung across my body, and in my other hand I have my car keys. I am walking away from this place and I am going to my van for a sit down and a think. I am not doing this. I am not standing outside a door that has a brass plate emblazoned 'OFFICE', contemplating knocking.

Only a silly, deluded person would do something like that. I am not a silly, deluded person. Much.

I've probably violated all sorts of security protocols and I'm almost certainly being watched on a camera right now as I stand here, hand raised to knock.

This is an ordinary corridor in an ordinary and strange building. This probably shouldn't happen in an ordinary corridor. On television, when this happens, the people involved meet in places of significance or a café or a park. Wherever it is, there is usually some kind of sentimental memory attached. Also, probably most importantly, they have prepared themselves, they have thought about what they're going to say. They don't take the word of an old woman they've never met before and decide to do this.

I am being ridiculous. It's understandable, but ridiculous none-theless. The promise I remade my mother four weeks ago comes to mind, rising up like a phoenix from the depths of the flames of what I am doing. I promised her I wouldn't do anything like this while there was even the slimmest of chances that my biological family would take me away from her. The promise phoenix beats its wings at me and I know I can't do this. I can't do this to my mother. She's too fragile to be able to handle this. Whatever this is.

Imagine, too, Smitty, what you would actually have to say: 'Excuse me, I think you may be my sister. I'm the child your parents gave away before you were born. Yes, that's right, you call for security and call for a psychiatric assessment, too, because that's exactly what I would do in your position.'

Before anyone can see me, I snatch up my toolbox and get the hell out of there.

With Dad, February 2015, Otley

Dad was weak some days, so thin and fragile, his skin translucent with a blue-green-black network of veins beneath the surface, and his body so obviously wracked with pain. Other days it all seemed like some awful mistake, that the doctors were all wrong and he was on the mend. He had little appetite, little thirst, and every time I tried to get him to take something in, he would refuse, or 'Later, *quine*, later' me.

'Have you ever thought of finding your first parents?' Dad asked me. Today was one of those in between days, where he seemed to hover almost comfortably between waning and might improve. He had probably been waiting for one of those days to ask me that, although I wasn't sure how he managed to fix it to land on a day, like today, where Mum would be out for a long period of time.

'No. I don't generally think about them, Dad.'

His face made a smile, one that I'd become so accustomed to over the years, and I struggled again to believe what was happening, what I'd one day have to live without. I had pictures of Dad, so many pictures, but none were good enough, none captured the perfect symmetry of his smile, the way his top lip would move upwards a fraction more, the way the smile would connect with his blue eyes. 'Smitty, I'm not your mother. You don't have to pretend with me.'

They were so together, Mum and Dad. The kind of couple who never seemed to argue for long, who were openly devoted to each other and really would only be parted by death. Yet, they dealt with the whole 'adopted daughter' issue so differently. Mum never wanted it mentioned, like she could pretend away the fact I was not biologically theirs, and Dad, he was like this: always willing to talk about it.

'I do think about it sometimes, but not all the time. Or even often. Or very much at all. It's not as if they've made great moves to find me.'

'Would you want that? To be tracked down like they do on those television shows?'

'No! I can't think of anything worse. I can't explain how I feel, Dad,' I admitted.

It's always there – you don't grow up like I did and simply forget how different you are from your family and most people around you – but it's simply that the sense of difference sometimes recedes to the back of my mind and I'm not bothered about finding them. And, sometimes, my curiosity bubbles over, like a pot that has simmered for too long and the gentle blue flame is edged up and up until it is orange and fierce.

'I should want to find them, and I do,' I said to Dad. 'I also think about what it would do to my life, having to get to know people who I should want to know. I worry about what it would do to you and Mum to think I'm looking elsewhere when I have you at home. I also think about them and how they've probably got lives that are sorted, and the last thing they need is to have me turning up wanting in on that. If it was as simple as searching and being a fly on the wall of their homes so I could see what they were like but only engage when I want to, I'd do that.'

'I hate this disease, Smitty. It's robbed me of the time I should have spent telling you…' His eyes were heavy, his frailty acute and overtly torturous. 'I should have encouraged you earlier to find them. To know where you come from…I didn't do right by you.'

'Please don't say that, Dad. You've done *everything* right by me. All my life you've always been there. I can't stand to think that you feel you did me wrong. I don't want to find them at the moment. I may change my mind in the future, I may not, but right now I'm happy as I am.' Even though I hate being untethered, feeling as though I don't belong anywhere, I couldn't be that unhappy if I wasn't actively trying to change that.

'When you were little, you used to say to me that you were from Scotland, like me.'

'I don't remember that.'

'You would tell me all the time, "I'm from Scotland, just like you".'

'That does sound like something I'd say.'

'*Quine*, I would burst with pride knowing that you felt that way.'

Inside Lottie, my balance returns. Calmness descends. My heart stops turning over itself in my chest, my lungs remember how to slowly draw in oxygen and carefully expel carbon dioxide.

What I was about to do…That isn't like me. I have never been that impulsive. I plan, I think things through, I visualise and prepare. I'm not sure which would have been worse: her being my half-sister or her not. Either way, I would have had to tell a complete stranger that her mother has been lying to her for most of her life. This would have been based on nothing more than the word of another complete stranger, who spent most of her time thinking and speaking in Finnish.

'Stupid, stupid, stupid, stupid,' I tell myself. I hang on to the steering wheel, bending forwards. My stomach is not settling, it isn't as easily soothed and fobbed off as my heart and my lungs. My stomach believes Mrs Lehtinen. My gut is telling me that she is right. I am the little girl who slept in the butterfly box, whose mother went on to give birth to another girl sometime later. 'Stupid, stupid, stupid.'

Even if it is true, there is nothing I can do about it. Simply thinking about it causes the phoenix, fiery and burning, of that promise I made my mother to beat its wings at me, the heat flashing through me. I can't do it to her. I can't break her heart when she's only at the beginning of the journey of the grief of losing my dad.

Tap, tap, tap against Lottie's window. So quiet and hesitant it takes a few moments for the sound to properly register.

Tap, tap, tap again. More certain, more sure this time. I do not need company right now. If there is one thing I do not need it is to speak to someone. What I need right now is to be left alone, to have a breakdown on my own before I go home and pretend to my mother that I haven't inadvertently broken my promise and I haven't almost ruined the life of some poor woman who happened to work in the same nursing home as a potential client.

Tap, tap, tap. Again. This person should have got the message that I'm not up for talking. Although, to be fair to them, they may think I'm dead or something and want to be sure.

The bones in my neck click as I raise my head and turn in the direction of the tapping.

I've never imagined being electrocuted before, but this feels like it. It feels like all the volts that used to pass through the power station where Dad once worked have been sent through me at the same time. Even through the grimy, salt-splattered window, the person is clear to me. My gaze does not move from the window while my fingers grope around for the window handle. With the grey plastic grip in my fingers, I slowly slide it open. The person in front of me is immediately crystal clear and I am looking into a mirror.

It's a mirror that can take away the years, hide your wrinkles, change your hairstyle, give you spots and blemishes in different places, but it's a mirror all the same. I am looking into my own face as it probably looked ten years ago.

'Are you OK?' she asks. 'Mrs Lehtinen said you seemed upset and would I mind coming to check on you before you left.' She sounds nothing like me, of course. She's from here and I'm from nowhere. She pauses, stares at me like she's only just seeing what I'm seeing.

'I'm guessing she meant you as you're the only person in this car park.' This is said distractedly – the mirror is starting to work for her, too. She's looking into it and she has more wrinkles around the eyes, more blemishes on her cheeks, her face is filled out a little more, her hair isn't sleek and straight to her shoulders, but curly and shorter. But the eyes are the same in this mirror, the nose is the same shape, the lips are the same size, the forehead has the same curve. 'I only do these things for her because she's an old family friend.'

I don't speak. My mouth does not know what to say. My brain knows what it should say but that would be ludicrous. She would probably freak out if I told her.

'Sorry,' she says after her eyes have repeatedly examined every part of my face, each time finding more and more similarities: the imperfection in the slope of my left eyebrow, the slight indentation at the tip of my nose, the way my right ear is a tiny bit more curved at the top. 'Sorry for staring, but why do you look exactly like me?'

'I don't look like you,' I want to say. *'You* actually look like *me* because I was here first.'

My shoulders shrug at her first of all. Then my mouth decides it needs to speak. It needs to do something because staring and shrugging aren't the way to resolve this.

'I look like you because I think I'm your sister,' I say. And it takes all my strength not to burst out laughing because it's the most ridiculous, unbelievable thing I've ever said in my life.

13

Smitty

When we breathe it's almost synchronised, only a fraction of a second keeps us apart. A lifetime and a fraction of a second's breathing time separate us in these quiet, uncertain minutes. I want to say something. Something pithy and clever, something that'll cement me in her mind as someone she'd like to be connected to. My mind isn't working like that: its fingers keep reaching, grabbing at words, phrases, sounds, even, to piece together and say, but those things keep slipping away, out of reach, unobtainable.

We are sitting in the flower garden as it's time for afternoon tea and most of the residents who are able will be having tea and cakes down in the rec room where I was with Mrs Lehtinen.

'This can't be happening, right?' Abi says. 'Cos if you ever met my parents, my mum, you'd know that this couldn't ever be happening.'

'I'm guessing your mum never mentioned me. Not to you or her husband.'

'Husband? My dad, you mean. My mum's been with my dad since she was seventeen. She came to Brighton to start university, and stayed with my dad's parents cos they knew her parents back in Nihanara, you know, the country in Africa?'

I nod, I've heard of it. If I'd had any idea that was where my DNA came from I might have paid more attention in my geography classes.

'They fell in love after a few months of knowing each other, and just before my dad finished his first law degree they got married.'

She recites the story as though she has heard it several hundred times. I used to be the same. I'd ask Mum and Dad about how they met, when they got married, over and over again. I used to pore over their pictures, looking at their clothes, their faces, the faces of the people around them. I wanted to know everything about their love and their life before me.

'My mum and dad did everything so right, they always do everything so right, that's why this can't be happening. Cos my mum? Sex before marriage? In the same house as my grandmother? Giving a child up for adoption? No way. NO. WAY.' She shakes her head. 'They still say a prayer before dinner. Even now. There is no way.'

All right, I think, *no need to rub it in. I am their dirty little secret. Their.* It sounds like Abi's father is my father too. We are full blood sisters. They stayed together and got married. Had another child about ten years later. Forgot the child in the butterfly box ever existed because she didn't fit into their cosy new life. I wonder why they left it so long? Maybe they kept trying and trying and it never happened. It might even have occurred to them after months and months of no joy that maybe they should have stuck with the one they had first.

'*I think I need to leave.*'

'What did you say?' Abi asks.

My hands fall away from my face, trembling as I swivel slowly to look at her again. It's uncanny – our features are arranged so similarly, I could be looking at a picture of myself from at least ten years ago.

Ten years ago...

Ten years ago Seth asked me if we could talk about having a baby. I'd stared at him for a long time, horrified at the suggestion. Yes, obviously we were together for ever as far as I was concerned, but a baby was the last thing on my mind.

'Have I said the wrong thing?' he asked.

'I, erm, Seth, babies...I...' I shook my head. 'I don't think I can.'

'Not ever?'

I started to breathe deeply, I was about to start hyperventilating, panicking. 'I can't...I don't know anything about where I come from, what sort of stuff is in my biology. What it would do to a child I have. I hate going to the doctors anyway because there are all these things they ask you and I can't ever answer them because I was adopted and my mum won't let me find my other parents, not even to ask about my genes, so I'll never know. It'll be worse with being pregnant, having a baby, that's all about what can be passed on. And I won't know. I'll never know—'

'Hey, hey, hey,' Seth said and grabbed me into a hug to quell my panic. 'Let's talk about it another time. Or not. We'll see how things go. It was a stupid suggestion.'

'No, it's not. We can talk about it another time, OK? Just not now.'

Ten years later, him mentioning that we might have made a baby was the start of the last conversation we had as a couple. Ten years ago there was so much going on, and I still looked as young and naïve as Abi.

'I said, I think I need to leave,' I reply.

'Oh. Right.'

'This isn't...I'm not coping very well with this and I need to leave.'

'Why don't you come meet my parents? Maybe they'll be able to explain all of this. You might be my long-lost cousin instead of, you know...Which would be mad, but kinda cool, too.'

'Did you used to sleep in a cardboard box?' I ask.

Abi frowns at me, her eyes darting up and down over me, checking me out again. 'Yeah, why? Wait, how'd you know?'

'I slept in one, too. It's an old— '

'Finnish tradition,' she finishes. Her scrutiny intensifies.

'Did she decorate it in butterflies? Your mum? I assume it was your mum who decorated it, and not your dad.'

'No, I had hummingbirds. My eldest brother had eagles. My other brother had doves. Yes, Mummy drew them.'

Brothers? *Brothers.* I have a sister. I have brothers. They didn't wait ten years to try again.

'I really need to go now.' My bag clatters to the ground when I stand and I immediately throw myself to my knees, gathering up my belongings, shoving them away because I feel exposed enough, I don't need her to see anything else about me, to have something potentially negative to relay to her parents.

'I seriously think you should come meet my parents,' she says while I replace my bag's contents and search thoroughly for anything I may have missed.

'No.' I shake my head. 'No, thank you.' Am I simply turning down an invitation to tea or the chance to meet my biological parents, the people who gave me the blood that flows through my veins? 'I need to go.'

'But—'

'No offence, but over the years I've imagined meeting the people who could potentially be my biological family and it was nothing like this. If you don't mind, I'm going to leave now. I need to go home, sit down, start to get my head around it.'

'What do I tell my mum and dad?'

My shake of the head looks more dismissive than I feel inside, and the up and down flap of my arms seems far more exasperated than I feel. 'I don't know,' I tell her, earnestly. 'They're your parents.'

14

Smitty

My body is tingling all over. My body is numb. Both sensations are there and I'm not sure how I'm driving.

That automatic part of you that takes over when necessary must have kicked in. I half expected Abi to come running out of the building, trying to flag me down, stop me, talk to me. I've watched too many movies, I think. If I was her, I'd be turning myself inside out pretending that it was all a coincidence. That the woman who fled was a fantasist. Anything else passing through my brain would be admitting that there's a possibility that my parents are liars. All parents are liars, of course. They tell you lies all the time for your own good – 'If you pull your face like that and the wind changes it'll stay that way', 'The ice cream van plays music when it's run out of ice cream', 'You were a good baby who never cried' – but they're not fundamental lies. All parents are liars, but they pray you never find out the truth about the lies of omission that are etched into the fabric of their personalities, indelible stain-like reminders that before they were parents they were human beings and made human mistakes. Some of those mistakes are stupid and pointless, like a tattoo of the name of the first person you ever loved; others are huge and life-altering – like surrendering your child for adoption.

I've done a bad thing to Abi. She will be turning herself inside out trying to pretend that her parents aren't human enough to make such huge mistakes. She will have to go home and face them.

Red. The traffic light is red and I stare at it. Red for stop. Red for blood. Red for danger. Maybe I should go back. I can't let her do that alone. She's done nothing wrong. If I go back, though, go with her to her house, I'll have to face them. I'll have to speak to those people. The first thing I'll do is blurt out, 'Why?' and they'll say... They'll say... What I always knew and this has confirmed: that it was me. It can't have been about my mother being all alone. It can't have been any of the reasons I've conjured up and worked out and come to decide were the truth over the years. If they are together, if they had more children, if they're still living in the same house they did all those years ago, there must have been something wrong with me.

An orchestra of car horns penetrates my thoughts. Green. Green for go. Green for move. Green for pastures new. Green for emeralds, popular in engagement rings. My foot pushes down on the pedal, and nothing happens. Green for go. I push hard, the pedal is to the floor, and nothing. Green. GO!

The orchestra is loud, insistent, angry. The heat inside my head will melt me. I want to take off all my clothes so I can feel the air on my skin and it can cool me down. Other pedal. I need to push the other pedal to go. My foot moves, slams down too hard on the right pedal, Lottie leaps forward, jerking me with her. At least we're moving now, at least all that stuff is behind me and I'm moving forwards.

The further away it is behind me, the easier it'll be to forget. To pretend when I get home. The orchestra fades away, the echo of a memory of a stupid mistake I made at some traffic lights. The soundtrack I have now is nothingness. Silence. This is the silence of the lonely ones, of people like me – we who do not know how to talk, or to share, or to open up our truths to the people around us, for fear of how it will be used against us.

Mum is in. The television is telling her something about ruins in Turin. I'm sure she'll be avidly watching that and doing her Sudoku with her glasses perched on the end of her nose, and tea cooling in the white and yellow mug she favours most.

I'm not shaking. I am, but if I tell myself enough times that I'm not, it will become a reality.

'Clemency, is that you?' Mum's voice calls. Today is a good day. The tentacles of pain and grief are not wrapped so tightly around her heart, its poison isn't tainting her as potently. I know this by the volume of the television, blaring out enough to be heard throughout the flat; I can feel this by the calmness in her voice. If I was going to tell her – ever – today would be the day to do it.

'No, Mum, it's the milkman,' I reply. I stand outside my bedroom, the wide corridor suddenly narrow and claustrophobic, not big enough for the secret I've hidden away in my heart and mind. The large honey-coloured wooden blocks of the parquet floor swim in front of me, their pattern suddenly a nauseating kaleidoscope of half-focused images and formations.

'Clemency! Do you have to?' Mum calls. 'Can't you just for once say, "Yes, Mum, it's me"? Do you have to be sarcastic every time?'

'Yeah, but— Yes, Mum, it's me,' I say.

'That's better,' she replies. There's no doubt a smile on her face, fuelled by the affection she now has for me because I didn't argue with her for once, nor try to explain that saying things like that were just part of who I am. Instead, I simply did as I was told. Anyone other than my mother would be suspicious of why someone had suddenly changed a habit of a lifetime. But Mum doesn't know because she always thinks if she tells me off enough, I will do as I'm told. If I were in Mum's position, though, I'd guess without a doubt that I was being cheated on.

That's what I'm doing. I'm cheating on my mother. Even though I didn't mean to, and it really did 'just happen', I'm still cheating. Betraying her. Making her biggest nightmare part of my reality.

'Would you like a cup of tea?' Mum asks.

I want to tell her. I want to throw myself on to the sofa beside her, rest my head on her shoulder and explain what happened. Then I want to explain about the cavernous hole that has unexpectedly, terrifyingly opened up inside me simply because of who I met today. The hole is always there, of course, and mostly I ignore it. Usually

I replace the area where it is with the idea that I don't belong anywhere and that I don't need anything else to explain why I feel the way I do. Rarely, very rarely, I obliquely acknowledge the hole and feel for a little while that there is a part of me missing.

There is a part of me missing. I feel that now. It is huge and gaping and potentially unfillable. I want Mum to be able to listen to all that and understand without worrying about what it will mean for her.

I want my mum. My real mum, I mean. The mum who'll be able to listen to all that and understand and put her arms around me and tell me it will all be OK. I want my real mum, except I don't know who that is.

'Clemency! Do you want a cup of tea?' Mum repeats.

'No, thanks. I'm going to get on with some work.'

'Don't work for too long,' she calls back. 'You know how involved you get.'

'Yes, Mum,' I say. It's her of course; she's my real mum. How could I, for even a moment, have ever thought otherwise? *She's* my real mum. And I've cheated on her.

15

Abi

To: Jonas Zebila
From: Abi Zebila
Subject: NEWS!!!!!
Thursday, 11 June 2015

Are you sitting down?

I hope so. If you're not and you're reading this on your phone, SIT DOWN. You are not going to believe what I'm about to tell you.

We have a sister. Apart from me, you have another, real-life, full-blooded sister. It's too complicated to explain all of it right now, but it was her that Mummy drew the butterflies for. This woman said when she was a baby, she slept in a box decorated with butterflies by her mother, who she never met because she was adopted as a baby.

All the while I'm talking to her, I'm thinking, this is mad, she's not my sister, how can she be when Mummy and Daddy have been together since the beginning of time and have only done it three times to have us? And if she was really our sister then they would have... BEFORE marriage, and you know how much of a crime that is around here.

When I told her to come back to the house to meet Mummy and Daddy she got up and ran away. But butterflies. It all makes sense now.

All right, so by now I'm properly spooked. There's some woman out there with my face and a sleep box like mine, so I leave work as early as I can. I come home, Mummy's in the kitchen, Gran's asleep in her room, Daddy's still out and Ivor is on the computer in the living room with Lily so it's safe to talk. I'm actually pretty impressed with myself that I didn't think twice about going into the kitchen and shutting the door and fronting up to Mummy about it.

'Abi, when you have washed your hands, wash the rice for me and put it on,' Mummy said.

I went across the room and stood right next to her. 'Mummy, do I have a sister that you had adopted?' I said.

Yeah, all right, it's not the most subtle or diplomatic thing to say but I had to get it out quick before I lost my nerve.

She was crushing big fat juicy plum tomatoes in her black mortar and pestle (you know the one Daddy brought her back from Nihanara the last time he went over there) and she just stopped. Only for about two seconds, then she started up again.

'What foolishness are you talking now, Abi?' she said. 'Please, wash your hands and then put some rice on. Make sure you put enough on for today and tomorrow.'

'I just met her,' I said. 'She looks exactly like me and she says she slept in a box covered in butterflies. I brought her home to meet you.' Yeah, I know that last bit was mean but you know what Mummy and Daddy are like – they won't admit to anything unless you have proof. As it turns out that was the worst thing I could have said because it shook Mummy up so much she knocked the black bowl off the worktop and it smashed on the floor and the tomato juice went everywhere.

Mummy looked really, really scared and said, 'She's here? You brought her here?'

I knew it was true then and I knew it was bad because she didn't even notice about the bowl. I sort of shook my head, really nervous, and said that I'd wanted to but she ran away. 'Is it true?' I asked.

She still looked scared but she nodded. 'You must not tell your father that you have seen her, nor your grandmother.'

'Do they know about her?' I asked. And she got angry! She's the one lying all these years and now she was angry when she was caught out and I asked what I thought was a perfectly valid question.

'Of course they know about her. Who do you think her father is? And you must not tell Ivor. None of them are to know until I'm ready to tell them, do you understand me?' I didn't say anything because what sort of a person would agree to something like that? 'Do you understand me?' she said again, more sternly, so obviously I'm the sort of person who would agree to that because I did. I sort of nodded and said yes, and I didn't cross my fingers or toes. But she didn't say I wasn't to tell you, so I am.

Can you actually believe it? A sister. A SISTER. And I can't tell anyone. Except you. I think Mummy wants to meet her, to see for herself, but after the way she ran away today, I don't think that's going to happen.

So there you have it. Big news. I'm typing this from Declan's. I couldn't trust myself not to shout something at the dinner table so I packed a bag for Lily and me and we're going to stay here for a few days. Declan's over the moon, Lily's less than thrilled because I forgot her homework and I refuse to go back for it.

I don't know how I feel about all this. I could scream at Mummy and Daddy, I really could. But on the other hand I know what good it would do me. I so want to see her again. A sister. I've always wanted a sister. (No offence.) I really hope there's a way I can get her to talk to me.

Lots of love
Abi
xxxx

16

Smitty

Mum is sitting at the kitchen table; she has a copy of *Friday Ads* spread open in front of her, a cup of tea in her hand. At this time of day the kitchen is a suntrap, light streaming in through the windows like water down a waterfall. Mum seems to be bathed in a golden glow because she is at the epicentre of the waterfall of light. She is dressed, hair done, make-up applied, ready for whatever the next few hours hold.

I struggled out of bed this morning after a sleepless night of replaying and reliving yesterday. It's been a night of confusion and self-reproach and fear of what to do next. No matter which line of thought I followed, which path my fantasies led me down, which way I tried to reason myself out of the mess, there really is only one thing to do next.

What I should do next is this: tell Mum.

Today is a good day and if I tell her now, it won't set her too far back. In this light-drenched kitchen I should tell her and she can help me decide what to do next.

My fear, a visceral terror of her reaction, wouldn't allow me to think of what to actually say, but it shouldn't be too hard. 'Mum, I met my biological sister yesterday' would work. 'Mum, I know this will upset you, but yesterday I met my sister,' that would be enough, too. 'Mum, I need you to listen to me for a minute without saying anything. What I'm about to say will be unbelievable and really quite cool if you think about it but I've found my birth family.' 'Mum, I have a sister! I know! Isn't that incredible!'

I clear my throat, which emanates from me as a small, choking sound. I'll simply start talking. Whatever it is that comes out of my mouth, I will state it clearly and firmly, and I brace myself to face her response full on.

'I'm going to buy myself a bicycle,' my mother announces when she sees me.

'Who with the what now?' I reply. That, I was not expecting.

'There are bicycle lanes all over Brighton, all down the seafront, I'm going to take advantage of them. I'm going to buy a bicycle.'

'To ride?'

'Yes, of course, to ride.'

'You?'

Mum loudly settles her cup on the table and fixes me with a stern glare, her mouth a tight circle of indignation and irritation. 'Yes, me.' *Do you have some sort of problem with that?'* she adds silently.

'*Really?*' I say. Everything I was meant to tell her has been wisped away on this random revelation.

'Yes, really,' she says crossly.

'*Really, really?*'

'You are just like your father.' Her voice is brittle. 'You have no faith in me whatsoever. You think I'm not capable of doing anything beyond cooking and sewing and cleaning. I will have you know that when I was a young girl I had a bicycle and I used to go everywhere on it. I went to work at the factory on it and used to go out with my friends.' Mum's huff continues: 'If you must know, I met your father while I was out riding in the countryside with my friends.'

'Sorry. I was just a bit shocked, that's all. Get a bike. It'll be fun. Great idea.' *I won't spend all my time worrying about you out there on the roads, wondering what havoc you'll cause,* I think. *I'm sure there won't be police at my door at least once a week telling me that you've been banged up in jail because you've taken some poor unsuspecting motorist to task for daring to come near you. I'm certain that this plan of yours is going to work out* brilliantly *for all concerned.*

'It will be,' she says. She may as well cross her arms over her chest and stick out her tongue in a giant, defiant fit of pique.

'*I have a sister, Mum!*' I'd love to shout that at her. It'd wipe that sulk clean off her face. A bike. A freaking bike! 'Right, well, I'm off to work. You enjoy looking for your bike.'

'I will.'

'Don't forget to get a helmet.'

'I won't.'

This was not how today was meant to start. I haven't even had a drink and I'm being forced out of the house by another of those 'moments with Mum' I'm expert at walking into. Each time I get to the end of such a 'moment' I look back and find that it was usually precipitated by me not knowing when to keep my mouth shut, and Mum not knowing how not to be herself. *A bike!* How was I meant to not comment at all when this woman – with her criticism of every other driver on the road, whose constant shouts at me to slow down and 'mind that car' made a five-hour journey to Brighton feel like I'd taken a wrong turn and was headed instead to Hades – decides she's going to join those people out there?

I should have told her about Abi, though. This isn't the sort of thing I should keep from her. I need someone to help me with what comes next. What do I want to come next, though? I left without getting Abi's full name, without giving her my number or my full name. I suppose she could find me if she wanted to, and I could find her if I wanted to.

Do I want to, though?

Do I want to get in touch with her? Do I want to see her again? I ask myself that question again and again with every one of the eighty-seven steps I take on my way out of the building.

Of course I do, I conclude as I open the door. *Of course I don't*, I decide as the door shuts behind me and I am out in the open air. *Of course I do and of course I don't.* I have no idea which answer is the best one.

*

Tyler's café is buzzing – energetic and alive with customers. It's just past eight and everyone seems to have got the memo that told them to come here for breakfast and a chat.

'What would Madame From Nowhere like to try today?' Tyler asks. I hop myself up on to my favourite stool, place my bag on the seat beside me. 'I have some wonderful smoky coffee beans that would make an interesting double-shot espresso. A nice Chilean blend – fair trade, of course – that would make a delightful mocha, and a truly unique Mexican mix that would make an out-of-this-world cappuccino—'

'No cappuccino!' I say this much louder than necessary. A few people turn to look at me and Tyler's eyebrows come together in confusion. 'I do not want a cappuccino type of day today,' I state calmly.

'I've got a jar of instant I save for emergencies, if you want?'

'That'll do nicely, thank you.'

He uses my favourite bucket teacup with the lemon-yellow and white daisies on a pink saucer, to make me a flat white. I knew he was teasing about the jar of instant. 'Do I detect something troubling in the usual tour de force that is Smitty's world?' he asks. I draw the coffee towards myself across the counter and my fingers reach for the sugar pot. Four shots of it later, I begin to stir, creating the gravelly sound of undissolved sugar against porcelain. He watches me overdose my drink with the sugar and eventually states, 'Ah, I detect a huge disturbance in the tour de force.'

'I thought it was only bartenders in American movies who talked to their customers about their problems.'

'And me.' He leans on the counter, brings his head down to my height. 'Didn't I tell you I trained in America? True, true. I was a bartender in a cocktail bar. I am well qualified to listen to problems.'

'I'm kind of stuck,' I say without really thinking about it. 'There's something I half want to do that will hurt someone else if I do it. But I don't think I can *not* do it, partly because I've already set the wheels in motion. I didn't actually mean to set the wheels in motion, it sort of happened. And now I'm stuck between doing it and not doing it and not knowing if I'll realistically not be able to do it. But if I do it, then where does that leave the person I'll potentially hurt?' The surface of my coffee is smooth and unbroken. Under the surface, a dozen, maybe a hundred dozen, tiny chemical reactions are taking place as the sugar dissolves.

'Sounds tricky.'

'Tricky isn't the half of it.'

'How would you solve it if it was a work problem?'

'I wouldn't have this problem if it was a work problem.'

'Just say it was. Say you had a jewellery piece that you wanted to create that you technically couldn't do without destroying half of your office? Studio? Workshop?'

'Workshop.'

'You can't create it without destroying part of your workshop in the process, but you know how great it would look in the end, how it'll push the boundaries of jewellery making and will have people talking about it until the end of time. What would you do?'

'I don't know.' I sigh and stare into the depths of my coffee, hoping to capture a glimpse of one of those chemical reactions. 'I'd maybe think of a way of protecting my workshop but still make the piece? They're not the same, though, people and things. My workshop can always be rebuilt – even if it's not rebuilt in the same place. This person who'll get hurt, I can't ever undo that hurt. I don't like hurting people. Especially not this one.'

'If they're that important to you, aren't you important enough to them that they'd be all right with whatever it is you want to do? Isn't that the nature of caring about someone?'

'In theory, yes. In reality, not so much.'

'Now, see, I don't think that's true. I think when you love someone you try to understand and be supportive of the things they really want to do.'

'So if you were married and your wife really wanted to run off with your next-door neighbour, you'd try to be supportive of that, would you? Or would you be incredibly hurt and unable to get over it?'

Tyler's frown ploughs deep lines into the perfection that is his face. 'Who told you about that?'

I draw back. 'Oh, no. Did that happen to you? God, I'm sorry. I didn't think. It was just an example I plucked out of thin air.'

His face creases up. 'No, it didn't happen to me. Just messing with you. I don't know, it's not an easy answer, but it doesn't sound like your dilemma will have you running off with someone unsuitable. It sounds like it's something important to you. And as simplistic as it sounds, people who care about you want you to be happy, even if it is sometimes at their expense.' Tyler stands upright.

That sounds so true and noble, how we'd all love the world to work, but does it really? Do we all at some point have to submit ourselves to pain because it will make someone we care about happy?

A digital buzz emanates from my bag and its sound, although technically 'silent', cuts through the good-natured hum of conversation in the place. Tyler grins at me like we're old friends, and disappears back into the kitchen area.

The number is a mobile and I don't recognise it. I know who it is when I slide my finger across the screen to answer the call – it *could* be a new client, it *could* be Seth calling from a new phone, it *could* be anyone in the world. It's obvious who it's going to be, though. It's what I would be doing if I was in their situation.

I inhale. Pause. Say, 'Hello, Clem speaking,' with as much confidence as I can.

'Hi,' she says. 'It's Abimbola...Abi. From yesterday?'

'Yes. Hello.'

'I talked to my mum last night,' she says. When I say nothing, Abi continues, 'She really wants to meet you.'

Without ceremony or much thought, I take the phone away from my ear, hit the flashing red 'call end' button, and quietly, calmly, I then turn off my phone.

17

Abi

To: Jonas Zebila
From: Abi Zebila
Subject: Damn!
Sunday, 21 June 2015

Really, Jonas, really?! I tell you we have a secret sister and I get nothing from you? Nothing at all? Not even the slightest bit of curiosity?! Do you think I made her up or something?

Well, I didn't. I found her number and called and she hung up on me. She actually hung up on me. I'm still smarting about that nearly ten days later. Especially since her phone seems to be permanently off now.

Mummy's keen on seeing her, too, even though she'd never admit it. She spends all her time staring into space, as if she's back reliving that time of her life. I can't even begin to imagine Mummy doing it. Any of it. The sex before marriage, the handing over a baby in a butterfly box. I'd love to ask her about it, but I know she won't talk. She'll just clam up and pretend it's all a mistake.

I tried to show her Clemency's website and she just sat looking at it like the computer wasn't there. I can't even begin to understand what's going through her head right now. Or Clemency's. I just realised, I didn't tell you her name – that's it: Clemency.

Since she hung up on me I've been trying to find out as much as I can about her, but do you know how many photos there are of our sister on the internet? Pretty much none. Do you know how easy it is to find out information about her? Really bloody hard. She's got an unusual name so you'd think it'd be easy to find out about her, but no. *Nada*. It's like she doesn't really exist. But I know she does because Mrs L clearly knew who she was, which is why she sent me to talk to her, and there's the website. And I met her.

Jonas, I really need someone to tell me what to do right now. I can't tell anyone else about this. Where would I even begin telling Declan? He thinks we stayed there the other night because I've fallen out with Mummy, which I have in the most quiet way possible. I am so confused.

Abi

xxxxx

Part 3

18

Smitty

Mum has her bike. Technically it's a tricycle, which makes me less worried about her wobbling into traffic on two wheels. It's a much more substantial vehicle and she has a greater surface area on the road, which can only be a good thing.

Whenever it was wet outside and Seth would speed off to Wakefield for work on his motorcycle, I would worry because he was so vulnerable and had less space on the highways than cars did. All it would take would be one slip on a patch of water or oil, or the misjudgement of a corner, and that would be it. He'd be gone. I'd have lost him and I could have prevented it if I'd stopped him from riding his damn bike.

My fears are similar about Mum, except I fear for those who dare to cut her up, too. I was dragged along to a bike shop out in Littlehampton and was expected to make approving noises and comments, which I duly did.

Guilt about not telling her about Abi unfurled its silky red ribbony threads and bound my questioning tongue so tight I barely spoke during the whole trip – I simply nodded and smiled approvingly. Even when she chose a black helmet with biker girl flames along the sides, and almost blindingly white, big brand-name trainers, which she insisted on buying specifically for cycling, I smiled and nodded and showed my full support. Guilt also allowed me to watch her try on pair after pair of shiny Spandex cycling shorts until she came to the conclusion all on her own that khaki Bermuda shorts were more her thing.

It's too impossible a thing to tell her about Abi. Every time I try, my mouth will not form the words. I know, eventually, Mum will be fine, she will understand that I did not go looking for this and I did not want it to happen. It's the initial reaction I don't want to deal with. The way her face will become a blank of incomprehension. How she'll sit back in her seat or will sit down heavily. The way her eyes will cloud over as she tries to formulate the first of many questions to find out if it was truly an accident or if I had betrayed her after all she'd done for me. How I'll have to keep reminding her that I love her and I haven't been in touch with them since.

I feel guilty too about not answering any of Abi's calls or texts. That is also an impossible thing to do. I want to speak to her so much it's almost physically painful, but to do that I have to speak to Mum first. Or I have to set in motion a life where I lie to my mother. I left Seth for lying and I do not want to become a person who does it and then justifies it as necessary. I want to talk to Abi, reply to her, but instead I screen all calls from numbers I don't know and I only call back the people who are clients or potential clients.

In this café-bar courtyard area of Hotel du Vin, a boutique wine hotel in Brighton, I'm waiting for a new client and thinking about Mum out there on the mean streets of East Sussex on her bike. I've spoken to this new client a couple of times on the phone and he needs me to make an engagement ring for his girlfriend. He wants to propose at the end of the month and was hoping I would be able to make the ring quickly. 'I can't rush it,' I told him, 'it won't turn out right if I rush it.'

'No, no, I don't want you to rush, it's just it's our anniversary then, and I want to propose.'

Why leave it so late? I asked in my head. I thought of Seth, of course. How he persuaded me against my better judgement to have an engagement party two years ago. I was very proud of myself that when the inevitable happened and we had to cancel it while actually standing in the hall, dressed up and ready to party, I didn't say to him 'I told you so'. And Seth was good, too, in that he popped all the one hundred and fifty balloons and ate as much of the buffet as he could before we had to bin it.

'I'll see what I can do,' I promised the client when I dislodged the memory of how that night went from my mind. I told the client, Declan, to meet me with photos of his girlfriend wearing her favourite items of jewellery, to bring any ideas about the design and a list of her favourite things that could potentially be incorporated into the finished article. From talking to him it turned out that he didn't want a stone set, which would make it easier, but he did want an elaborate design. I'd wanted to meet at Beached Heads, of course, but this guy could only meet me in his lunch break from work without arousing suspicion from his other half, so I'm here.

A few steps away you have the main road along Brighton seafront with its attendant noise and busyness, beyond that the aqua-green railings that are punctuated by entrances to steep stone steps that take you down to the promenade and then to the beach. Yet, this courtyard feels secluded, quiet, like you could be in a large villa on a private island. There are huge parasols sheltering each table, which from above must look like a giant patchwork quilt with the seams made of daylight. I'm drinking coffee in an ordinary cup. Whenever I take a sip, I experience what feels suspiciously like a pang of missing Tyler. Obviously I fancy him, I won't pretend to myself I don't, but *missing* him? That's beyond ridiculous when I still have Seth texting me every other day and I don't know Tyler well enough to miss him. Or maybe I'm missing Seth and, because I don't want to, I've transferred those feelings to Tyler. That sounds far more likely.

I lazily flick through my photo album of Polaroids of my work. In the back of my head I am still looking for inspiration for reworking Melissa's locket from her birth mother into something new and wear-able. I keep coming back to making the locket body into a watch and using lengths of the chain to make the strap. I can't make clockwork, though, and if I got someone else to do it, the price of the piece would be astronomical. But time seems so appropriate for Melissa: she had that locket waiting for her for such a long time.

'You're going to hate me, I know, but I had to do it.'

My fingers holding the corner of a page and about to turn it over, stop working. My heart feels like it has been fired out of a cannon and is now rattling against my chest, trying to find an exit point from my body. I carefully, slowly, raise my head to her.

'Look, I know it's not good what I've done.' Abi pulls out a chair and sits down opposite me. 'But hear me out, please?' She rushes on whether I intend to hear her out or not: 'You dropped a huge bombshell on me. It's not easy to just walk away from that. I only wanted to talk to you.'

I lower the corner of the page in my hand, sit back to regard her. She has wonderfully shiny hair. It's sleek and hangs just below her shoulders. She has perfectly applied make-up – she obviously learnt long ago which shades of blacks and browns emphasise the shape and size of her eyes, which tints of foundation give her a flawless complexion, which hues of lip-gloss endow her lips with that glossy sheen. She's wearing a well-cut, expensive-looking suit jacket over a burgundy, ankle-length dress.

We're dressed the same. Except my outfit has probably cost a third of what hers has. My burgundy dress was from a shop I found in the Markets in Leeds five years ago, my jacket was found in a second-hand shop in Wakefield and was taken in to fit only after much pressure on Mum three years ago.

'Aren't you going to say anything?' she asks.

I shake my head. If I don't say anything, I can truthfully say to Mum later, 'And I haven't spoken to them since.' There is no way I can avoid telling Mum any longer.

'Why won't you talk to me? Aren't you completely freaked out? Cos I am. My whole life has been this huge, colossal cover-up. If you met my mum and dad, your mum and dad, you'd know they were never the kind to do this sort of thing. I've always thought that they only did "it" three times, you know, what with them having three kids. But they...Before marriage and everything. And they just gave the baby away and got on with it.'

'That's me you're talking about in that matter-of-fact tone,' I want to say to her.

'I keep thinking we're supposed to be hugging and crying and stuff because of those TV shows.'

Reluctantly I smile at her because I know what she means. This feels a little under-emotional and inappropriate. We're supposed to have exchanged letters, phone calls and arranged to meet on neutral ground. We're supposed to have prepared ourselves for this moment once we knew the other existed. The meeting is meant to be a moment of great apprehension followed by great joy. Real life isn't like it is on the telly, why do I find that so surprising?

'Are you seriously not going to say anything?'

'Who was the guy with the engagement ring?' I ask.

'My child's father. He wants us to get married. If I'd let him, he'd have actually come today to get you to make an engagement ring. But I'm not marrying him.'

'How old's your child?' I ask. *'How old's my niece or nephew?'* I should have asked.

'I'm not telling you until you tell me why you've been avoiding me.'

'It's too hard to think about.' I can feel tears filling up my eyes, ready to fall. I shake my head to will them away. 'It's too scary.'

'Aren't you even curious? Not even a little bit?'

'Yes. But it's all been sprung on me by, I don't know, Fate I suppose. I didn't mean to meet you. It was never meant to be like this.'

'It's the same for us, too.' Us. She's including my parents and my brothers in that. I wonder who else knows about this when my own mum doesn't.

'I was also avoiding you because I haven't told my mum. She—'

Confusion dances on Abi's face for a second. 'Oh, you mean your adoptive mum.'

'I *mean* my *mum*,' I reply. My tone is as sharp as the saw I use for piercing and in response Abi draws back a little. I won't have her do that, I won't have her dismiss or downgrade my parents – she has her mum and I have mine. 'I haven't told her I met you,' I say carefully. If I expect her to choose her words wisely, then I should do the same. 'Mum lives with me. We've only just moved down here and my dad died recently. I don't know what the thought of all this will do to her. It's not as simple as being curious. If I'd gone looking for this I could have prepared myself and her a bit more. I didn't, so I'm having to get my head around it in pieces and chunks. I need to steel myself to do the next thing. I would have called you back eventually.' *At least I hope I would.* 'But not until I'd told my mum and not until I was sure I was ready to deal with another chunk of this.'

Remorse, pure and potent, crawls across Abi's face as she looks down at her hands and my fluttering heart begins its frenetic dance of escape again.

'What have you done?' I ask.

Abi's right leg begins a slight but anxious jiggle. 'I, erm . . .'

'What have you done?' A terrified type of nausea creeps up my throat.

'She couldn't wait. She wa—'

'Oh, God, no.' I need to leave. I need to get out of my chair and run as fast as I can away from here. In case of a fire, you're told to exit the building as quickly and safely as possible; to leave everything where it is and run – do not, under any circumstances go searching for your belongings. I need to run, I need to not sit here and allow my belongings, the people I belonged to, to come for me. I need to run but I can't move. 'Please, no.'

'She only wants to see you,' Abi pleads.

Abi turns to the glass wall that separates the courtyard from the inside of the hotel's café and beckons to the person beyond. I didn't even notice someone sitting there, I hadn't felt the weight of someone observing me, scrutinising every inch of me while I spoke to my sister.

Run. Get out of this seat and RUN! Inside my head that is what I'm screaming. I cannot move. She's going to walk out of there and right up to this table and she is going to speak to me. And I am going to…I don't know what I'm going to do.

She looks nothing like my mum. My mum has peach skin and grey-streaked brown hair that she's finally stopped dyeing, and she wears Bermuda shorts to ride her tricycle.

This woman looks nothing like my mum. She looks almost exactly what I would expect to look like in seventeen years' time, but not like my mum. I think I want to get up and hug her. I think I want to scream at her, 'WHY?' I think I want to walk away and never, ever look back.

'Hello,' she says. A simple and honest greeting. All the best conversations start with hello. I do not know what to say so I say nothing.

In her hands she holds a small cream box, on the outside of which she has drawn and coloured butterflies. She places the box in front of me. 'This is yours,' she says as if she doesn't mind I haven't said anything in response to her 'hello'. 'I made it to keep my pictures of you.' She sits in the seat that Abi has vacated and she smiles at me like I'm a baby. 'Talei. That's what I called you. Of course you won't remember that. It means precious one.'

I think I want to cry. I want to break down and cry until there's nothing left inside me. A teardrop escapes from my eye and lands on top of the miniature version of the butterfly box I keep my precious photos in.

I stare at the woman opposite me.

She continues to smile at me as if she knows me, as if she's always known me. As if I am all her dreams come true.

I can feel a pressure building up in my head that will cause me to explode. Gently, because I don't want to disturb it, I push the box off my photo album, it really is nothing to do with me.

I am on my feet now. The woman smiles a bit deeper, but there's sadness now and desperation. She doesn't want me to leave. How can I stay here, though?

'Talei,' she says.

'*Stop calling me that!*' I shout inside. '*That isn't my name!*'

'Clemency,' she says then, as if she has heard my silent screams. 'Please, just stay for a while?'

I shake my head. *No, no, I can't.*

'Please?' She says it so quietly, so kindly, I know I should change my mind.

No, no.

She picks up the box, holds it out to me. 'Take this at least. It's yours. I made it and kept it for you.' My teardrop, perfectly preserved, sits on top of the butterfly, distorting in that tiny section the look and shape of its lilac and pink wing, causing a small patch of black veins to bulge.

I don't want to take anything from her, but are there photos inside? Of me? Of her? Of the other people who are my family? My trembling hand rubs at my face, tries to dry the tears then reaches, still shaking violently, for the box.

'I wish you wouldn't leave,' she says.

I wonder if that's what I thought about her, the last time I saw her. I'm curious if in my small baby world, governed solely and wholly by the instinct to stay alive and knowing who was meant to do that for me, I looked at her with my blurred newborn eyes as she walked away and thought, *I wish you wouldn't leave.* I wonder how long I cried for her, wishing she would come back for me, would take me in her arms, would fill my senses and world with that smell of mummy that all newborns are meant to know instantly. Did it occur to her as she walked away, went off into her new, childless life, that I would be craving that? I doubt she thought that thirty-seven years later she'd be saying the same to me.

I fumble in my jacket pocket, the nylon lining too cold and slippery to provide any comfort, until I come across the emergency tenner. It always sits there, a neatly folded escape route if I need to pay quickly without rooting through my bag for my purse or the unsheathed change languishing at the bottom. I slide the brown note under my cup to stop it blowing away.

'We'll see you soon,' she says. She smiles, although there are probably as many tears in her eyes as there are in her voice.

'Yes, we'll see you soon,' Abi adds.

I wonder if either of them realises how much of a threat that sounds. How dangerous it is to someone like me who has been tricked and then trapped into this situation.

I nod. I find it hard to be rude and unfriendly to people, even at some of the worst times of my life. This is, it has to be said, one of the worst times of all. But I still can't come right out and say no.

19

Smitty

Seth. I need him.

Around the corner, on the busy main road, I stand in the archway entrance to the Ship Hotel, hidden from the street, and from the two people I've fled from, and with a shaking hand take my mobile from my pocket.

He'll understand. He always understands. He'll know what I should do now. I call his number. He answers halfway through the second ring, I imagine he looked down, saw my name, snatched up the phone and hit the answer button.

'Smitty?' It's only my name, but his voice, that I've been hearing for twenty years, soothes its way through my sensibilities. My body unclenches, my chest, which I hadn't noticed was tight and almost immobile, is now freer, air is entering and exiting my lungs properly. Suddenly I'm able to breathe at the sound of him. I need him.

'I—I...I—I...'

'Smitty? Is that you?'

What am I doing? I don't get to call him. He's not for that any more. We're not together, he's not that person.

'Clem, are you OK?'

'I'm sorry, I'm sorry. I shouldn't have called you. I'm sorry. Bye. I'm sorry.'

With still-shaking hands I cut off the call. I shouldn't have rung him, it was instinctive, what I've been doing for more than ten years. Even before that, if I had a problem, Seth – not Dylan – would be the first person I called. In a moment like this, calling him was the obvious, natural thing to do. I have to break that habit, learn to cope on my own.

A white and aqua-green taxi pulls up outside the hotel. Its passengers spill out, laughing, joking, collecting suitcases from the open boot as if the world hasn't been turned on its axis. When Dad died, that was the most hurtfully confusing thing of all: everyone carried on with their lives as if something huge hadn't happened. Half of my world had been devastated and everyone acted as if nothing had happened at all.

The taxi driver talks the whole way back to my flat. I must have answered because he kept talking, asking me questions, and there were no long awkward pauses that told me I was meant to be replying.

I am still shaking, trembling violently, as I open the door. When the door clicks shut behind me and I turn the corner into the main part of the corridor, the enormity of what happened descends again and I can't breathe. I try to draw air into my chest. Nothing happens. I can't breathe, my chest is on fire, my heart is like a speeding train without wheels that races and races on the spot.

'Clemency!' Mum calls from the living room. 'Is that you?'

My photo album, my bag, the coin change from the cab ride, my purse I didn't put away, my heavy bunch of keys, and that box create a huge sound when I drop them so I can push my hands against my chest, try to force air into my body.

Nothing happens, no air enters my lungs. I've had a panic attack before. It was like this. I couldn't see. Couldn't stop myself from shaking. Couldn't breathe.

'Clemency?' Mum calls.

Breathe. Breathe. Breathe. I need to breathe.

I hear Mum put her puzzle aside, take off her glasses, get up from her seat. Or maybe I am imagining hearing all that since my breathing is vociferous, gasping, and my heart is thundering in my ears.

'Clemency.' Mum is horrified when she arrives in the corridor. At the mess from all the things I dropped, probably at the state of me.

She comes to me, circles me with her arms. When I was ten I came home in tears at the things some of the boys at school said to me. The names they called me, what they said about where I came from, but mainly from the way that my cousin Nancy shrugged and said, 'Well, it's true.' Mum had put her arms around me. 'I'm going down to that school tomorrow – if their parents don't *skelp* their hides, I will,' Dad shouted. That was one of the few times I'd seen him so angry.

'Hush, now, Don,' Mum said. In her arms, so close to her, I could smell the sweetness of her make-up and the bleach that she'd used to clean the kitchen. 'That's not important right now. The only thing that's important is our Clemency.' She stroked her hand over my hair. 'You'll be OK, sweetheart. You'll be OK.'

'What's happened, love?' Mum says to me twenty-seven years later. She is filled with concern, overbrimming with worry.

I can't speak, nor breathe, nor stop my heart from the pain it's causing me by hammering so fast. She draws me closer and because I am taller than her I have to stoop to rest my head on her shoulder, to let her comfort me. I can smell the lavender and rose citrusy tang of her perfume, the vanilla and cocoa scent of her conditioner.

'Is it Seth? Has he done something?' she asks. 'Said something?'

I shake my head.

'You need to tell me what's happened, love, if I'm going to make it better.' That's what mums do, isn't it? They make it better, even if you're really old, your mother puts her arms around you and makes it better. She doesn't turn up out of the blue and try to give you gifts she's made and call you by a different name.

Mum's hand strokes down my back, soothing me. Considering she doesn't do this very often, she's very adept at it, seems to know where to press her hand so I feel better, my body relaxes, I start to be able to breathe. Maybe it's because we're all the same. Maybe, no matter who we are, a touch in the right place, a caring, loving hug will cure whatever ails us. Maybe I should have hugged that woman. Maybe I would have felt something for her if I'd let her put her arms around me and do what my mum is doing to me now. It might have changed everything if I'd given her a chance.

'Come on, love, I don't like to see you so upset,' Mum says. 'You're not one to cry unless something is terribly, terribly wrong.'

She's right. I carefully pull myself together, upright, out of her hold until I can stand up by myself. Inhaling, exhaling, is a blessed relief – my entire body rejoices in this simple action. I rub at my eyes until they are dry, then furiously dry my hands on the folds of my dress.

'What's happened, love?' Mum asks. I like that her accent, her real, natural one, comes out when she talks sometimes. It takes away the parts of her that I tend to fight with and lets me see the one who knows how to hug me and tells me I'm her whole world.

'I just . . .' I need to tell her. It's going to hurt her, my mum with the Yorkshire accent who hugged away my worries. I have to tell her. I can't not. 'I just met my— I just met the woman who gave birth to me.' It wasn't that hard to say after all. It was really quite simple and easy. Like breathing – until you can't do it properly. I did it properly, I know I did, because Mum doesn't look all that shocked.

In fact, her face develops a smile and after a few seconds to let the news sink in, she says, 'Well, that's wonderful news. There's no need to be upset, it's absolutely wonderful news.' She reaches out and takes my hand, and I know then that she's seen the small butterfly box that lies on its side with a few black and white photos of a baby spilled out on the parquet. She saw the box and worked out what had happened. 'Come and sit down and tell me all about it. It really is the most wonderful news.'

20

Smitty

Mum doesn't truly think it's wonderful news. I can tell by the way she's trying *really hard* to smile. From the fear spinning in her eyes, I can tell she thinks it's terrible news but she doesn't want me to have another panic attack. She's also doing what I did whenever she asked if the other children were still picking on me at school – she's pretending everything's fine, like I did with her, to spare my feelings.

'Now, tell me what happened,' she asks gently. She holds my hand and I know her eyes are pretending that I'm not wearing this jacket, which she hates so much even though she did take it in for me. 'Did it not go as you expected?'

'I didn't plan it, Mum!' I'm screeching. Screeching like the deranged person I feel I am right now.

'Sorry, sorry,' Mum says. She soothes me with her tone, with a few strokes on my hand. 'Tell me what happened.'

'You have to promise you'll listen to me without interrupting and you won't get cross or think I'm lying. You have to promise.' I sound like I'm fourteen.

'I promise.'

'Which part?'

'Pardon?'

'Which part do you promise about?'

Mum stares at me blankly. Actually, I sound like I'm five.

'Which part do you promise about, Mum?' I insist, still in five-year-old mode.

'All of it?' she replies.

I sigh, relieved. If she does get upset I can remind her of the promise she just made.

'Will you tell me what happened now then, love?' Mum asks. She's showing remarkable restraint in the face of my completely irrational behaviour.

'About two weeks ago I went to a nursing home and I met this old woman who was a neighbour of ... of those people.'

'Which people?'

'You said you wouldn't interrupt.'

'I know, love, but I'm not completely understanding you.'

'She was Finnish, this woman. It was her that they ... those people ... got the idea for the butterfly box from.' Mum nods, now she understands. 'And she said that the daughter of those people works there.'

'Daught— Sorry.' Mum purses her lips to stop herself talking again.

'I went to talk to her then I changed my mind but she came out to the car park and I spoke to her. We had a chat and I found out that she has two brothers and her parents have been together for nearly forty years. So her parents are both my—' I'm finding it hard to say the word in relation to them and me. 'I came home and I wanted to tell you but I couldn't, so I didn't. She kept ringing me but I didn't reply. So she tricked me. Got someone to pretend to want to talk to me about an engagement ring, you know, the man I was telling you about who wanted one done really quickly? Then suddenly she's there and then *she's* there.'

I look at Mum, expecting her to speak. She doesn't. Her lips are still pursed, as though waiting to be sewn together.

'*Her*,' I say.

'Your birth mother?' Mum says when she realises I need her to talk now.

I nod. 'Yes. My birth mother.' I can say it now that Mum has said it first. She's broken the taboo so I can too.

'I bet you were a bit surprised.'

A bit surprised? A BIT surprised? A BIT SURPRISED?! 'Yes. It was too much for me, I had to get out of there.'

'You must have been in all sorts of turmoil. I bet she was, too.'

I glare at my mother. I don't mean to, but it sounds like she is putting herself in *her* shoes.

'Don't look at me like that, Clemency. It will have been a very difficult thing for her to do, to come and meet you like that. She won't have known what your reaction would be, and imagine seeing for the first time someone you haven't seen since you gave birth to them. Imagine how terrifying it would be. She must have been in bits anticipating it.'

At least she got to anticipate it, not like me, who had it sprung on them, I think in reply. 'I suppose you're right,' I say.

'I'm sure she's thought about you all these years and I'm sure she was just bursting with the things she's wanted to say to you after all this time. Did you speak to her at all?'

I shake my head. 'She gave me the box with the photos that's in the corridor, but we didn't really speak.'

'Would you like to see her again?' Mum asks.

'Would you mind if I did?' I reply.

I'm carefully watching my mother: I see the edges of her smile touch her eyes, but don't take over them. I see the strain from having to smile, the clenched tightness of the hand that is not stroking my back. 'It's not about me, love, it's about what you want,' she says eventually. So eventually that inside I think: *I knew it! I knew you didn't think it was wonderful news.*

Mum doesn't want me to get hysterical again, which is why she is playing along for now. She's probably hoping this whole experience will have put me off, will stop me from even contemplating getting in touch with them again.

'I don't know what I want to do,' I say. As much as it's the truth, I need my mother to be honest with me. She needs to tell me what she really thinks. Over the years there's been one abiding message that she has sent me: do not go looking for your other family. Do not do anything that will upset what we have. Dad wouldn't have minded, but with Mum, it was obvious it would have been to her a huge rejection of who she was and what she had done for me. Why she was now pretending not to mind could only have been down to her not wanting me to become hysterical again.

'OK, love,' Mum says quietly. 'I understand.'

21

Abi

To: Jonas Zebila
From: Abi Zebila
Subject: Total disaster!!!!!
Wednesday, 24 June 2015

Well, that went well, NOT!

I set up a meeting with Clemency using Declan as bait through her job and she completely freaked out and ran away when she saw Mummy.

I actually felt sorry for Mummy. When I told her I'd arranged a meeting, she looked so happy and terrified at the same time. She didn't say much on the way there, and when she sat in front of Clemency for the first time the look on her face reminded me of how I felt the first time I saw Lily when I gave birth to her. I was completely freaked out. I loved her, don't get me wrong, and I thought my heart was going to explode because I had such a fierce need to hold her, but I was also really shocked. I kept blinking at her, wondering if she was real and if she had really come out of my body and if she was really something to do with me. Mummy was looking at Clemency just like that.

Mummy was devastated when Clemency left and I was gutted, too.

This is all so messy and horrible when they always show you on the telly people just getting hugged and being happy. This is all so big and out of hand, I wish, wish, wish I'd never done as Mrs Lehtinen asked and gone to check on Clemency. Then I'd never have known and none of us would be feeling this bad.

I'd never know, though, what hypocrites Mummy and Daddy are. There, I said it. You've always said they were, but I wouldn't accept it because they're Mummy and Daddy and we're supposed to do what they say and believe them about *everything*.

On the way home Mummy didn't talk much at all. She stared out of the taxi window, then as we pulled up outside she said, 'I have to tell your father.' She said it like he was going to blame her or something.

'What about Gran?' I said, because sometimes I don't know when to leave well enough alone, do I?

Mummy breathed out slowly and angrily. 'Yes, her too.'

I can hear voices downstairs – they're quite loud but not loud enough for me to be able to make out what they're saying so I'm guessing Mummy's told Daddy and Gran. I wonder how they'll take it? Thankfully, Lily is staying over at Declan's so she won't witness any shouting.

What do you think I should do now? Do you think I should leave Clemency alone or get back in touch? What if I ask her to do a DNA test with me so we can see if we are related? Because it could still all be a huge coincidence. And if it is, that means she can go back to her life and Mummy and Daddy will realise they need to be honest with us in future if they want to avoid things like this happening.

What if she's not the only one? I keep thinking about that possibility. What if there are more children they had adopted who are going to turn up one day?

I think a DNA test is probably the best way forward and then we'll all know where we stand.

Love,
Abi
xx

22

Smitty

'Would you mind if I did see my birth relatives again?'

It's two days later. Mum is about to go for a ride on her tricycle and I am going to work via Beached Heads. In the past two days we haven't talked about it. Mum left me to look at the baby photos on my own and I didn't. I simply put the box on top of the other butterfly box at the bottom of the wardrobe, looked at the composition, realised that it looked like the big box had given birth to the smaller box so had to move the smaller one to my bottom drawer where I keep my hats, gloves and scarves, which I'm obviously not going to be going through any time soon.

Mum, who had hoisted herself up on to her bike, steps down again and turns towards me but doesn't rotate enough to look at me fully – instead she stares mostly at the sea. It's rough out there this morning; the waves seem wrathful, their anger appearing as a white, frothy rage upon the tops of the grey surf. I wonder if that's what Mum is feeling inside about this.

'Why do you ask?' she replies, quietly.

'Because I want to know how you honestly feel.'

'How I honestly feel,' she murmurs. A long pause then: 'Yes, I would mind.'

Oh. I thought she might try to sugar-coat it, talk around it, gauge if I'm thinking of doing it.

'Why?' I ask.

We've never talked about this openly, it's all been carefully, wilfully, left unsaid.

The pads of Mum's hands are covered by fingerless cycling gloves and she raises her fingers to unclip her Hell's Angels-inspired helmet and take it off. She ruffles her hand through her hair and continues to contemplate the sea. The first line of 'Somewhere Beyond the Sea' plays through my mind as I watch her.

'Because I'm scared you're going to get hurt again if you do this. What if they reject you? How will that make you feel?' She hooks her helmet on to the padded leather seat of her tricycle, traces the outline of one of the flames.

'I don't know. I haven't thought it through. I just know— '

'I have. I *have* thought it through and I know you wouldn't be able to withstand such disappointment and hurt.'

'Mum, I've withstood worse.'

'Like what?' she demands.

'Like what?!' I'm amazed she has to ask. 'Like losing Dad. Like my— my relationship with Seth coming to an end.'

'They're not like being rejected by your mother.'

'But she's not my mother, is she? You are. At the moment I barely know her.'

'At the moment.' Mum seizes on this so immediately I wonder if she has been waiting for me to say something like that. 'When you do get to know her, you'll start to think of her as your mother.'

And you think that will mean I'll love her more than I do you, I think. Mum acts like my love for her is fragile, transient and transferable; as though I'll never have room in my heart for two people with the tag 'mother'. As though it is a foregone conclusion I'll reject her in favour of the person who was there first – even though I have barely met the woman.

'How do you know that?' I ask.

'I just know. A mother knows these things.'

'So if you had a biological child you'd have loved them more than me?'

'Don't be ridiculous.'

'How is that ridiculous, Mum? You're saying that if I get to know someone I'm biologically related to they'll replace you, so why is it ridiculous for me to say the same about you having a biological child?'

'It's not the same,' she snaps. Defensive, angry, my mum snatches up her helmet, plonks it heavily down on her head. Fumbles crossly at her chinstrap. 'You know very well that it's not the same.'

'I really don't,' I reply. Out loud. For once it's something I don't keep in.

'Yes, you do,' she hisses at me. She mounts her bike, indignation on her features, and without another word or look in my direction, she cycles across the small car park in which we stand and heads to the cycle path that snakes around the building and towards Portslade, the opposite direction to the one I'm heading in.

'I really, really don't,' I say to her retreating form. She doesn't indicate as she turns the tight corner around our building and rides off at speed.

'So much for it being wonderful news,' I mutter.

Tyler's coffee is going to have to be nothing short of spectacular to see me through this day.

23

Smitty

'I've had a few ideas about what to do with your pendant but the one I keep coming back to is a watch because of the connection with time.'

'Oh, right,' Melissa says. She sits on the other stool in my workshop and her attention doesn't rest anywhere for long – she looks like a meerkat, constantly looking around, trying to take it all in. My workshop is neat and tidy. In general, I am not neat and tidy, my life is full of chaos and piles of paper and several dozen jobs I meant to finish. But wherever I work has to be immaculate, tidy, precisely organised. I have hung all my larger tools on the walls, there are designated pots for the files, the daylight lamp sits in the left-hand corner of my bench, in the right-hand corner is the soldering area.

'It's so cool in here,' Melissa says suddenly. She spins herself on the stool. 'I'd love to have a place like this to work in, instead of just an office.'

'I'm really lucky, I know.'

'It's not so much luck, you have worked for this, haven't you?'

'Yes.'

'So, not luck as much as good fortune from hard work.'

'I suppose you're right. About this watch idea...?'

'I don't really wear watches.'

I open up my sketchbook, already ashamed about how bad my sketches are. 'Have a look at the idea I had,' I say. 'Excuse my sketches. The locket would become the watch, it'd be protected from knocks by the locket lid, and the strap would be made from linking the chain together in small sections, like this.'

Melissa stops fidgeting and visually exploring and gazes down at the lines I've made with a soft, 2B pencil. Her face, sceptical when she first looked, changes. 'Actually, that looks kind of ... nice. Classical, but still funky. If people even say "funky" any more.' She turns her head to the side, examines the photo of the pendant pinned to the corner of the page and the drawing more carefully. 'I really like it. So what's the problem?'

'Why would you think there was a problem?' I ask.

'Because you could have emailed me those sketches.'

'Well, the only sticking point is I'm not a watchmaker, I'd have to outsource that and it would be a bit pricey. I don't want to get quotes until I know you at least like the general idea.'

'I do like the general idea, yes.'

'Excellent, I'll get some quotes and we'll decide how to proceed from there.'

'Great.' She picks up my set-square that lives in one of the pots beside the soldering station. 'What do you use this for?'

'Drawing straight lines, mainly. It's useful for checking I've cut a line straight if I cut a piece out of sheet metal, too. Also, I check edges where two ends of a ring meet because they need to be perfectly straight otherwise soldering is a nightmare. Well, nightmare is a bit of an over-exaggeration, but you get what I mean.'

Melissa nods thoughtfully. 'I've been wanting to call you,' she says like a wayward churchgoer finally returning to the confession booth.

'I've wanted to call you. In fact, I did call you. You're right, I could have done this by email or phone. I wanted to see you, though.'

'I'm glad it's not only me. And I'm glad you did call. I know I went a bit funny when you asked if I'd met my bio mother, but I don't often get to talk about it all to someone who's been there.'

'Have you met her?'

'Yes.'

'Not good?'

'I don't know what good is. We kind of get on, but she can be a bit full-on. I get it, I get that she's been storing up all this love and emotion and she's desperate for us to have some sort of relationship, but…I've got parents. But then I feel guilty thinking like that because she's only doing her best. And she didn't want to give me up. It's so hard sometimes. Hence the therapy.'

'How did your parents take your deciding to search for your birth mother?'

'They were supportive, up to a point. I didn't realise until I was eighteen why they made such a huge thing of giving me a locket on my sixteenth birthday – and reminding me to wear it until it was something I put on automatically. I then can't start wearing the other one, can I? Which kind of taints the locket I wear and makes me feel a bit odd about my parents, and it spurred me on to contacting you about making this locket wearable.'

'That's not fair of them.'

'They always said that they didn't mind me searching, encouraged it even, but then when I actually did it, they started to get a bit funny. Really down on mothers who give up their children. Kept reminding me that I might find out something I didn't like – that I could be a child of rape or incest or something hideous like that. It was true, but God, I didn't need to hear it from them of all people. I think some of it was genuine concern, but there was a lot of jealousy too.'

'Tell me about it.'

'Are yours being funny?'

'It's only me and my mum now and it's a different situation but she won't admit she's jealous, too.'

'What are you going to do?'

'I don't know.' That's the kicker. I don't know what to do. I want to meet my birth family again, properly, but then I don't. What if, like Melissa's parents said, I find out something I don't like? It's not as if I can simply not search for them, they're in my life. Finding out things I don't like will come from getting to know them. Something I can avoid.

'Have you applied for your adoption papers?' she asks.

'Oh, no, it's too late for that. Way, way too late.'

I explain to her the bare bones of the situation and she listens with her eyes wide and her mouth open. At the end of it, she is silent for a while. So am I. Listening to myself tell this tale to someone else who hasn't been there makes it sound horrific. Horrific as in the emotional devastation those tiny, fragmented meetings have caused. It might have been better if it was planned. If everyone had a chance to think, to pause before each meeting, maybe I would not have this much panic rushing through me.

That is it. Panic. *Thank you, Melissa,* I think. *Talking to you has let me understand that I'm in a state of panic, even when I am not having a panic attack. You can't think properly when you're in a state of panic.*

'You could still apply for your adoption papers,' Melissa says. 'It might stop anyone from rewriting history if you do meet them again. Some of the stuff in my adoption papers ... It reminds me when my birth mother gets all misty-eyed about how she was wronged and I was "stolen" from her that at various points she could have made another decision. It wouldn't have been easy by any stretch of the imagination, but still there was another path she could have taken that she didn't. Some of it, of course, was from the social worker who seemed to be really judgemental, but some of it ... Written by her, so there's no doubt. I have to remind myself she was young and in an impossible situation but, you know, blah, blah ...' Melissa smiles. 'I don't say that to her, of course. I never say anything like that to anyone – no one wants to hear it. That's why I wanted to call you – I got the impression you might understand.'

I nod. She's got me thinking now: I should apply for my adoption papers. See if I can find out what was going on at that time, what was being said, possibly what they were thinking when they packed me up in that butterfly box and sent me to live with someone else.

'What's this?' Melissa asks. She holds what looks like a mini chimney-cleaning brush with gold and black bristles on a thin metal rod.

'It's a polishing brush.' I point to the others that sit in their stand. 'Each one gives you a different type of finish – that one is for a satin finish, this one will give you a bit more texture. There's also traditional sandpaper of different gradients that I use to smooth down edges. Plus those files. For me, the finish of a piece is everything – it's an important part of making jewellery.'

'Will you teach me?' Melissa asks. When she says it she seems surprised herself.

'Teach you?'

'To make jewellery. Will you teach me how to do it?'

'I'm not sure I could.'

'All right, how about you make a ring or something and I come and watch you?'

'If you want. But I'm sure you'll find it pretty dull. I don't because I love what I do, but you might.'

'I really, really won't. Tell me what all these tools are for and then another time I'll come back and watch you work.'

'Yeah, if you want.'

Melissa beams at me. 'And if you want me to be with you when you get your adoption papers, I'd be more than happy to do that.'

'Thank you, thank you so much.'

'All right.' She brushes off that moment of intimacy with a brisk tone. 'Tell me what this is?' She has picked up the saw that hangs on the hook at the edge of my desk, the thin but sharp filament-type blade only secured in the clamp at one end to make it less dangerous.

'Come on now, Melissa, you don't know what that is? And you can't even guess?'

'Hey, you! I wouldn't take the mick out of someone brandishing a dangerous weapon. I could saw bits of you off.'

I relieve her of my implement. 'We call it piercing not sawing.'

'Oh, right. What's that?'

Piece by piece I take her through the equipment in my workshop, all the while the thought of applying for my adoption papers grows and grows in my mind.

Part 4

24

Smitty

Clem, I'm not sure what's happened,
or why you couldn't speak, but if you need me
I'm always here. Aš tave myliu. I've always loved you.
I miss you. S x

I've read that message over a hundred times – every day I call it up and stare at it and allow the beads of hope to string themselves together until a long and seemingly endless chain of possibility has been spun around my heart. Maybe I should give him another chance. Maybe we can work it out. It's these messages that make me think about giving him another chance. The desperate, angry, demanding, 'talk to me' ones strengthen my resolve, but these ones that remind me that I'm loved by him, how much I love him … they're the ones that make me want to try again.

There's a picture in the original butterfly box that lives at the bottom of my wardrobe of Seth and me on our first foreign holiday together, where he learnt that phrase – to write it and to speak it. It was one of those trips that nothing remarkable happened on, but it was so special because we were together and for as long as I could remember that was enough. Being together, talking, messing about, planning his next move at work, were more than enough for us.

I sat in the window seat of our room in the very expensive hotel that we stayed in, staring out over the square. It was March, but there was so much sun. The air was soaked with it and I sat wearing Seth's large Aran jumper and a pair of knickers. I had my camera in my hand and was trying to capture the light, snatch it from the world outside and store it in the photo that would come out of the camera. None of the angles seemed to fit properly, none of them would show how beautiful the light was, the city was. None of them ensnared that brilliant red-orange of the terracotta-coloured bricks of the square, none of them showed the perfect lines of the sandstone town hall building. Through the camera lens, everything seemed flat and ordinary and bland, instead of vibrant and lively and *alive.*

'Come back to bed,' Seth called. He was face down in the soft, white sheets, covered by the thick duvet.

'Not until I've taken the perfect photo of the way the sun hits the town, what it does to it.'

'Coming back to bed is far more fun. Come here and I'll prove it to you.'

'You've got nothing over there that interests me, buddy.'

'Not even a huge lump of amber that I bought when your back was turned yesterday?'

'Show me, show me, where is it?' I dashed to the bed, climbed on and bounced up and down. 'Show me, show me.'

Seth rolled over and grabbed me, tugging me down on to the bed beside him. 'That was too easy.'

'Lying about materials for my work.' I laughed. 'Are there no depths to which you will not stoop?'

'Apparently not. Although I did buy you some amber yesterday so I'm not technically lying, but rumours of its size may well have been greatly exaggerated. The man who sold it to me said it was a superior quality so it cost a bit more.'

'Right,' I said. I handed Seth the camera as he had a longer arm than me, the distance at which he held it would make a better picture.

'Click' went the camera, and it snapped us as we mostly were at that time: dishevelled, together. Seth placed the camera on the bedside table. 'You don't sound like you believe me. He was a good bloke was Irmantas,' he said.

'I'm sure he was.'

Seth shook his head in despair. 'Can I get my jumper back?'

'No, I'm wearing it.'

'I'm cold.'

'Well, get back under the covers then.'

'I can't. I need to go do something and I need my jumper. The others are all the way across the room.'

'What, you mean our room that is the size of a postage stamp?'

'I'm cold,' he insisted.

'Oh, for the love of—' I replied. I struggled out of the jumper and threw it at him. It landed over his head, draped down on to his face. He removed it and underneath the large woollen folds he had a huge grin. I realised a moment before he threw the jumper across the room out of reach that I'd been scammed for the second time in less than a minute.

'You make it so easy!' He laughed, his face filled with the mirth and kindness I'd noticed in him the first time we met. He was older, his face more lined than back then, but his smile, his innate pleasure at the life he had, was still there – it ran through him like the barely formed words in rock. Dylan, who dipped in and out of my life at the best of times, had all but dropped me when I got together with Seth. This was his prediction come true and, Dylan claimed, he couldn't stand to watch us be loved up when we were both still too young to be that settled. Dylan spoke as though me falling out of love with him and in love with Seth way before New Year's Eve 2003 was somehow done to spite Dylan.

Still laughing, Seth's eyes greedily ran over my naked body, surveying it as if he wanted to secure mental images of each line and curve to pore over at another date. He hooked his fingers into the top of my knickers. 'You're still wearing far too many clothes for my liking,' he said. The laughter had gone, replaced by a deep throaty lust. He threw my knickers in the same direction as the jumper then immediately pushed apart my legs. His fingers dipped into me and I inhaled sharply. 'Do you like that?' he asked.

'Oh, yes,' I gasped.

He pressed my legs open wider, lowered his head, pushed his tongue—

'Clemency!' My mother's voice snaps me out of remembering and forces me to stand upright from my slouch over the shopping trolley. My face feels hot with guilt and shame, as though she knew what I'd been thinking about when she barked my name. She marches down the aisle with a huge bottle of cream soda – nightmares of Christmases and New Years past – in each hand.

She glares at me, at the phone in my hand. 'Is that another message from that man?' she asks sternly. *That man* being Seth, of course. Anyone would think that I had run into him a few times and he wouldn't leave me alone. Or that I'd revealed to her how badly he treated me. But I hadn't because he hadn't. We had to split up because he lied to me and that was extremely shocking to me. Because he'd never been like that, had always been open, honest, trustworthy, the horror of finding out that he was capable of betraying me was far too much for me to stick around. Mum, though . . . She'd never liked him. She'd never liked any of my boyfriends but she tolerated the others because they never managed to take me away from her. Which Seth did and I don't think she ever forgave him for that.

'Yes, it's a message from Seth,' I say.

She seems so certain that people can take me away from her: Seth, my birth family. Mum acts like I am fickle with my affections, that anyone who looks in my direction will replace her. Which is ludicrous. I've come to a decision, though, and I need to tell her.

I push the trolley down the aisle after her and we turn left, heading for the front of the store into the tinned goods aisle. Mum has a list in her hand and marks off each item with a small, neat flick of her wrist as she leaves a tick. Mum has gone eco-friendly since she got her trike: for the weekly shop she rides to the supermarket, we shop together, and I drive all the bags home while she, safe in her ecological saintliness, cycles home. I almost, *almost* fell into the trap of explaining to her that getting me to drive was still adding to our carbon emissions, but caught myself just in time. There are some battles not even worth considering, let alone fighting.

'Mum, I think I'm going to ring Abi, my, erm, my sister. I think I want to see them.' I say this barely above a mumble because I know she'll hear. She's only hard of hearing when it suits her.

She takes the news as well as can be expected: she stops in front of the tins of soup, and treats them to the long, silent glare and rigid expression I should have been receiving.

'I think I want to meet them. All of them.' I feel sorry for the soup, the look she is giving it could boil it in its tin. I decide to buy the soup and hide it in my bedroom because it's taken the visual equivalent of a bullet for me today, so the least I can do is buy it and not eat it. I continue hesitantly: 'Even if it's just once, I'd like to find out what they're like. Maybe get some questions answered.'

'I understand,' she says, monotone.

Really? You might want to tell your face that because it's saying to the soup and me that you don't understand at all, I think. Instead I say: 'Thank you. For understanding.' I almost thanked her for letting me do it but I caught myself. I am thirty-seven, I don't need her permission. Her blessing would be good; her blessing would silence – or at least quieten – the guilt demons that have been plaguing me, but I do not need her permission to do this.

'When you go to meet them all, I'll come with you,' she says. She smiles then, treats the soup to a beatific grin before she turns it on me. Now she has decided how she can make herself a part of this, can control it to a certain extent, her whole demeanour has unclenched and she radiates the relaxed, swaggery aura of a person who has expertly restrained a wild stallion that had dared to bolt.

Dad. The ache of missing him echoes through every part of me. He would have understood, he would have told her not to get involved. He would have stuck up for me and stopped her. If she still insisted, he would have told me to do it in secret and tell her after the fact. If Dad were here, no way would this be happening according to Mum's rules.

This isn't fair. She knows it too. I open my mouth to tell her, to explain that this is something I need to do on my own, for me. I shouldn't have to consider her feelings in a situation that will already be fraught and emotionally difficult.

'Fine,' I say.

'Good.' She grins at me, beams at the soup. I take the tins of mulligatawny off the shelves and drop them carefully into the trolley.

'Excellent idea, Clemency,' Mum says. 'We'll have soup for lunch. That was your father's favourite. Let's go and get a crusty loaf as well.'

'I'm so sorry, soup,' I whisper.

'Oh, and if that man keeps sending you messages, you should think about calling the police,' Mum adds, on a roll now. 'He needs to understand you want nothing more to do with him.'

I think I'm going to shout at her. Right here, in this supermarket, I think I am going to start screaming at her. First Seth, then my birth family, and now this poor unsuspecting tin of soup. I know I'm being ridiculous about the soup, but sometimes I feel pushed to the edge of sanity by her.

I want to scream at her that if she hadn't pretty much let my cousin Nancy get her own way about pretty much everything, I would still be with Seth. I would not have moved down here, I would not have met Abi and I would not be about to eat a tin of soup whose sole crime was to take a glare bullet for me.

'Right,' I say instead. Because I am a coward. And Seth should have known better.

With me, March 2015, Leeds

I wanted my bed. Having been sent home by Dad and Mum to go see Seth, get some proper sleep, give them some space (although they didn't say that), what I wanted more than anything was my bed. 'I'm not going anywhere, Smitty,' Dad had reassured to get me to leave. 'I promise you, I'm not going anywhere.'

Seth wasn't in, although it was one of his days to work at home, but I'd noticed by the sheets and blankets folded neatly on the arm of the sofa that he'd been sleeping in the living room. He did that whenever I wasn't there because he hated being in our bed without me. I was going to make it up to him, that was the plan. I needed to be with Dad and Mum at that time, but afterwards I would refocus my attention on Seth. But not right then. Right then, I wanted to sleep for a little while and pretend that my world wasn't crumbling around me. That my dad wasn't about to leave me.

My fingers pulled back the duvet and a scent – delicate and fleeting – rose up to greet me. It was so momentary, like a trick of light, that it was gone before I properly noticed. I continued to pull back the duvet, certain it was nothing, until I saw what was obviously a long, brown thread, visible against the white sheet. It wasn't thread, of course, it was a long, straight brown hair. As if the shock of the moment had temporarily wiped my memory, my hand went to my head to check that the hair in the bed didn't belong to me. Mine was, of course, black, short, tightly curly. Seth had shaved his light brown hair to a grade two again, it wasn't his.

I dropped the duvet back into place. Someone else had been there, that was obvious. I knew he wouldn't, though. Seth wouldn't. Seth would have just had someone over to stay. That was why he was sleeping on the sofa. He hadn't mentioned the person who was brunette, most likely female, was staying during any of our nightly talks because he didn't want to upset me. Although why one of our friends staying would upset me was a mystery. Unless it wasn't a friend. A non-friend with straight, long brown hair.

Shaky, unsteady on my feet, my stomach a tumbling barrel of nausea, I sat on the floor beside the bed. This wasn't the time to deal with this. Maybe in a month or so, when…I didn't want to think about that either. There wasn't much I could deal with and this was one of those moments. On the wall of photographs that I was facing, my eyes were drawn to the *With Seth, finally!! January 2004* picture.

My gaze then moved over to the photo of my family from last Christmas I had tacked on to the wall. On the left-hand side of Seth stood my cousin Nancy. She had her arms looped around her daughter Sienna's shoulders as she grinned at the camera, but she was also, very noticeably, leaning on Seth. She was very clearly making her physical presence felt. She only needed him to be weak one time, he only needed to let his guard down for a moment, and we would be here: I would be finding a long brown hair in my bed.

This was not the day to deal with it, though. This was not anywhere near the right time to have to deal with it.

25

Abi

To: Jonas Zebila
From: Abi Zebila
Subject: Update
Friday, 26 June 2015

Dear Jonas

I think it's safe to say that this is a different place now. I thought things were about to get a whole lot worse when Daddy and Gran found out and I wasn't sure how Ivor would take it, but I don't know, it's like someone has thrown all the windows open and a cleansing wind has blown through here and the heavy weight that was hanging over us – this secret our parents have had all these years – has been swept away.

It's not one big love-in by any stretch of the imagination, but it feels like a more honest house. Ivor took the news pretty badly. When Mummy and Daddy told him, he looked so *injured* first of all. Like they'd betrayed him by having a child older than him or something. He sat and stared at them for the longest time.

'Is there anything you want to ask?' Mummy asked. And he just got up and walked out. Reminded me a bit of Clemency, to be honest. Since then, he's not talked about it, changes the subject if someone tries to bring it up. It seems he really does feel this was done to spite him.

Now the secret is out, Gran, who seems more stable, just glares at Mummy a lot but doesn't say anything. I hate to think of her doing this, but it seems like Gran has been using this big secret as a way to control

Mummy all these years. Mummy still does everything for her, but it now seems to be on an equal footing. It's hard to explain because it's never been a blatant control thing, we all know what Gran is like, but now it's not there any more it's plain to see that it was there originally, if you see what I mean?

I can't tell what's going on with Daddy. He seems a bit shell-shocked but also a little relieved, almost. Maybe he hasn't liked lying all these years and he's pleased the truth is finally out. Him and Mummy haven't rowed about it since the other night, not within my hearing anyway. They've stopped talking altogether, it seems. I mean, not in a nasty way, they seem to just stare at each other a lot and not find the right words. I think neither of them wants to be the one who starts that conversation about what they did all those years ago.

After Ivor walked out, I went over and hugged Mummy and she put her arms around me and held me so close. I don't even remember the last time we did that. I also told Lily-Rose. I don't think it's fair that the adults know something so big and she doesn't. Despite Mummy and Daddy's rubbish example of being parents, I'm not going to do that. I want to be as honest as possible with my kids. I told her I had a sister that I had only just met and she said, 'Does that mean she's my sister?'

'No, she's your aunt, you're her niece.'

'Will she come to our house for her tea?' she asked.

'I hope so,' I said. That was as honest as I could be. I've decided to leave it up to Clemency to get in touch and that decision is like a mild form of torture. I want so much to see her again. Just like I want you to get in touch.

You know what, though? Even if Clemency doesn't get in touch, I got to hug Mummy for the longest time so, for that alone, I'll be eternally grateful to Clemency.

Get in touch, please. Even if it's a three-word email to tell me you're alive, that would be enough.

I love you.
Abi
xxxx

26

Smitty

There's a plain white envelope labelled

Clemency Smittson

between us on the wall we're sitting on.

It's been between us, weighted down by a large pebble, on this wall that bisects the promenade and beach in Worthing for more than half an hour, since we collected it. Neither of us wants to be the one to pick it up. Both of us have been attempting conversation but it dries up almost straight away because we know the envelope has to be opened.

Abi is dressed for work because that's where she was this morning. She went into work as normal, then I met her a little walk away so that I could drive us here to Worthing, somewhere no one we know is likely to see us. We were here two days ago – another sneaky half-day holiday for Abi. She suggested in one of her earlier texts that we get a DNA test so we both know where we stand and I thought that was a good idea.

'Do you want me to do your hair for you?' Abi asks me. I knew from the way she kept picking at her nails and sucking in her cheeks and nodding slowly to herself that she'd been psyching herself up to saying something, but I didn't realise it would be this.

She's being kind, I know. Judging from the look of her and the look of her mother, she's probably thinking any further meetings will be smoother, will have them more accepting of me, if I sort out my hair.

I get that, a lot. My hair is a mass of shiny, midnight-black squiggly lines, fat ringlets, wavy curls and tight frizz that hangs down to my cheeks. It's not that bad, I don't think, it's a part of who I am, but for other people, the white ones who say if they were black they'd have an Afro, and the ones who spend hundreds of pounds a month on getting their hair perfect and can't understand why I don't comb it or straighten it, my hair must mock them because the only category it fits into is 'Liked by Clemency Smittson'.

With Dad, September 1985, Chapeltown (Leeds)

'Excuse me, I need your help.' Dad's voice was so loud and different amongst the chatter of these women. They were so pretty and glamorous and had dark skin just like me. Dad was the odd one out for once. Usually it was me who was the odd one out, but here everyone looked like me and no one looked like Dad. Or sounded like him.

'You all right, love?' one of the ladies asked. She was probably the prettiest, she had big, big hair, all shiny and black. I liked her eyelashes best. They were super, super long – when she blinked they touched her cheeks and I could see the gold fairy dust on her eyelids.

'Aye, I need your help with my daughter's hair,' Dad said.

All the women stopped talking and laughing and chatting and reading their magazines, to look at me. The only sounds in there were the droning blowing of the big dryers and the reggae music playing on the radio. I stepped closer to Dad, held his hand a bit tighter. I didn't like everyone looking at me. People were always looking at me because I was the odd one out and I didn't like it. At all.

'Is this your daughter, love?' the lady with the fairy-dust eyelids asked. She put down the hairdryer in her hand but kept hold of the hairbrush with black bristles that looked like a microphone as she came towards me. She was as tall as my dad because she had gold shoes with high, high heels.

'Aye, yes. Say hello, Clemency,' Dad said.

'Clemency, that's a right pretty name.' The woman was crouching down, she smelled of bubblegum.

'Can you help me? I need to learn how to plait her hair. Without making her cry. She cries if I try to do anything to it.'

The lady stood up again. 'Where's your wife, love?'

'It's a long story,' Dad said. Mum wouldn't have liked him bringing me here. It was like the time I asked her why I didn't look like her and it nearly made her cry – Dad bringing me here would make her cry. 'Suffice to say, it's me that has to learn to do this. Can you help me? I'll pay.'

'No, it's OK, love. You'll have to wait, but I'll teach you what I can between customers. If you want, you can come back next week with a proper appointment and I'll teach you how to wash her hair properly.'

'That would be good,' Dad said. 'Wouldn't it, Clemency?'

I nodded.

'We'll be back next week,' Dad said when we were about to go home.

'She's a lovely girl,' the pretty lady said. 'So good.'

'She is that,' he said. 'Are you sure I can't give you any money for your time?'

'No, it's nice to see a father taking care of his daughter. I hope your wife appreciates it.'

'We both appreciate each other,' Dad said. 'You get no prizes for bringing up your children properly – and so you shouldn't.'

Mum never said a word about my hair, not ever, not once. She used to cry sometimes when she tried to comb my hair and I would cry because it hurt so much. She would look at my hair on a Saturday afternoon when Dad took me out to get us out from under her feet, and I would come back with a new hairstyle and smelling of the dark green Dax the woman taught Dad to slick on the partings between the plaits. She would say nothing on Mondays and Thursdays when Dad would sit on the sofa and I would sit on the pancake-flat green velvet cushion on the floor in front of him while Dad greased (that's what the woman called it) my hair and redid the plaits. Mum never mentioned my hair at all when Dad started to do it – like a lot of things, she just pretended it wasn't happening.

'No, you're all right,' I say to Abi about whether I'd like her to help me with my hair. I suppose I should be offended, but I'm not. It really doesn't bother me what other people think about my hair nowadays.

'I didn't mean to upset you. I just thought if you wanted some tips...'

'I'm not at all offended. It's sweet of you to ask, but I like my hair like this.'

'*Really?*' She's openly horrified.

'Yes. You could sound a little bit more disgusted by the idea I might like the way I look, though. I won't be at all upset.'

'Sorry,' she says. 'Sorry, sorry. Mouth running away from brain, there.'

'No worries,' I say with a laugh.

'Have you ever had your hair straightened?' Abi asks. When I raise an eyebrow at her, she lifts her hands in surrender. 'Just asking, out of curiosity. Not pushing it as a lifestyle or hairstyle option.'

'No. My dad wouldn't let me for years. He even had a stand-up row with a hairdresser once who wanted to put relaxer on my hair.'

'Why? Not that my mum or dad ever let me get a relaxer. It wasn't till I went to America to stay with my aunt that I got one. Daddy was so mad.'

I have an aunt in America. Interesting.

'The hairdresser was teaching Dad how to look after my hair from about the age of eight, and when I was thirteen she said she was going to put a relaxer on it and Dad said no, I was too young. The hairdresser didn't think so and they had a huge row about it. Right there in the shop in front of everyone.'

'Seriously?'

'They were like two prize fighters going toe to toe. She kept saying that it would be easier to care for my hair and Dad kept saying he didn't want easy if it meant putting strong chemicals on my head. And she was saying how lots of girls my age had it done. And he was saying he didn't want me looking like everyone else if it meant doing that and I'd be able to decide for myself when I was eighteen. You have never seen the likes of it. Everyone just sat there with their mouths open.'

'Your dad sounds really cool.'

'He is. He was. Still is, I suppose. All those things he did in the past that made him cool happened, so he is cool. He seemed to "get" me, if you know what I mean? Even from an early age if I asked him a question he'd answer it. Age appropriate as they say, but he didn't like to keep secrets and stuff from me. Drove Mum up the wall – she's one of those "don't talk about it and it's not happening" types.'

'Yeah, my mum's like that,' Abi says.

I smile to myself, training my eyes on the envelope.

'I meant our mum, our mother,' Abi says. 'Oh, I don't know what the hell I'm supposed to say.' She stares at the envelope, too. 'Do you want to open that thing and then we can decide what to do next.'

'Bossy, aren't you, for a younger sibling?' I say.

'If you don't boss, you don't get heard.'

'OK. But I'm not opening it.' I didn't need to open the envelope because, just like I didn't need to look at the pregnancy test result I threw away in Leeds, I knew what it was going to say.

Abi's face creases with incomprehension. 'What?' she asks.

'I have no need to. I know what the results are but I'm guessing your family are needing some extra reassurance, which is why you suggested the test.'

'No, that's not why I suggested it. I did it . . . Never mind. I'll open it then.'

We have similar fingers, square at the end rather than tapered. Dad had the same shaped fingers, too. My dad, that is, not her father, *our* father. I can understand why she was frustrated before, it's hard to keep track; to know what to say without causing offence. But I've been thinking of it as Mr Zebila fathered me, Mr Smittson 'dadded' me. Mrs Zebila is my mother, Mrs Smittson is my mum. I wonder what they'd think if I said that to them? If any of them would take offence at how they've been categorised.

The sound of the envelope being ripped open is magnified, incredibly loud above the sound of the people and the surf and the doom that is about to befall us rolling in the distance.

The sound of reading is quite loud, too. I can almost hear her eyes moving back and forth over the lines on the page. And then she gasps.

I turn to look at her. 'What?' I ask.

'Oh no, oh no, oh no!' she says dramatically. Her eyes are wide, the lines of her face are taut with shock and horror.

'What's the matter?' I ask again.

'I can't tell you. I don't think you're going to want to hear it,' she says gravely.

'Just tell me. I don't care what it is, just tell me.'

She shakes her head. 'It says...' her voice peters out. She sighs, then swallows hard. 'It says something horrible. It says I've got a big sister who keeps running away, who makes jewellery for a living and is probably going to have a serious sense of humour failure in about two minutes.'

I blink at her a few times. 'Really?' I say. Maybe I wasn't as sure of the results as I thought I was.

'Yes. You and me, baby, we're sisters. And there ain't nothing you can do about it!'

'And, hey! You cheeky cow, what were you saying about the results being something horrible and me running away?'

She waves her right forefinger at me. 'Sense of humour failure!' she sing-songs at me.

I grin at her. Then needle her in the side with my forefinger. She yelps, dodges away from me and laughs. She seems so happy that I am her sister. Watching her laugh, unbridled joy gushing out of her, I realise that the emotion branching through me like a fast-growing tree is happiness, too. I am lucky. I have a sister. And it is the woman next to me. Laughing like nothing bad could ever happen now that we've found each other.

Part 5

27

Smitty

Their house is absolutely massive – you could probably fit about five of Mum and Dad's house in here. Without moving my head, I glance sideways at Mum. She is staring at the orange-brick house with double-glazed sash windows and black-and-white tiled path, and probably wishing she hadn't come now. Or rather, that I hadn't come, which is what necessitated her pitching up with me.

It's odd seeing it finally, the house where I could have grown up. Abi says they've lived here since her parents got together and she's moved back in during the last few years. It is grand and imperious, all of Mum's nightmares come true. She had tried to insist that we meet somewhere in Brighton, at a café or restaurant, but I had to gently tell her:

a) 'This meeting isn't about where you would feel most comfortable, but where I would feel most at home.' (Absolute wrong choice of word that raised a high red colour in her cheeks and elicited the bullet glare.)

b) 'I want to meet all of them in one go to get it out of the way and Abi's grandmother is housebound so she rarely leaves the house.'

Mum had continued to insist on 'neutral ground' so we were all on 'an equal footing' until I said, 'Fine, if that's what you want you can simply not come and we'll go for a "neutral ground" meeting at another date.' After that, meeting at their house was acceptable after all.

We stand outside the house, fifteen minutes early, having already walked three times round the large oblong-shaped block as we were very early. I didn't want traffic or, more importantly, Mum's sudden need to do 'stuff' (like dust behind the radiators in all the rooms and de-junk the hair-clogged shower) right before it was time to leave, to make us late. She was nervous in Lottie, now she is creeping closer to a full-on anxiety breakdown.

It would have been better if this house, their home, was a hovel or even the same size as the one we lived in for most of our lives. When we lived down in Lewes our house was large – not as large as this, judging from the pictures I've seen – but it was nice and in a well-to-do area. I'm not sure Mum ever got over the fact we had to move up to Otley because Dad lost his job in the recession of the early eighties and we had to live in a small, two-bed cottage. I loved the cottage, it was my home, but I sometimes saw the way Mum looked with envious eyes at her brother Colin's house, and knew it hurt her that we had been so 'reduced'.

I place my hand on her shoulder and she almost leaps out of her skin. 'It'll be fine, Mum,' I reassure. I'm not used to seeing her so nervous and unsure of herself. She's always been so confident and self-possessed. 'I'm sure they'll be nothing but grateful towards you.'

She nods.

'You don't have to do this, you know,' I say. It's partly to comfort her, it's also to allow myself the chance to hear that out loud. If I hear it spoken, which makes it sound possible and true, maybe I'll believe I don't have to do this. Maybe I can change my mind and walk away and not open myself up to the chance of another rejection of who I am.

'Do you think you'll ever want to trace your biological parents?' Seth asked.

'I don't think so.'

'What, not at all?'

'All right, I admit, sometimes when Nancy's over and she's joking around with Mum and Dad, I do feel like I don't fit into the picture of the three of them together. Like they're the family and I'm the one watching from the outside. It's only sometimes, but at those times I do wonder what it'd be like to be surrounded by people who I look like.'

'Being surrounded by people who you look like can be overrated,' he replied.

'Yes, but at least you've had the chance to find that out for yourself. I have to take your word for it. It's not an issue if you don't get on with your parents. I'm not allowed that. If I dare say anything about the way Mum is sometimes . . . I get put in my place pretty quick.'

'Put in your place by who? Have they met her? Do they know she can be a bit . . . *much* sometimes?'

My body bristled with loyalty and protectiveness. No one, not even Seth, was allowed to pick up on my mother's 'quirks'. I loved her and she drove me crazy, but I bore the brunt of it so I got to comment.

'Don't get upset, I'm not saying she's a terrible person, and God knows she hates me with a passion, I've just seen the effect she has on you. I'm asking who puts you in your place if you mention how . . . *much* your mum can be?'

'It's hard to describe, but over the years, if I've ever broken ranks and had a moan, I'm almost always met with an attitude that I should be grateful I wasn't left to rot in a children's home or that I wasn't aborted, that Mum rescued me.'

'People say that? They actually say that?'

'All the time. When you're adopted you're kind of fair game. There's a story that plays in people's heads: either your adoptive parents are saints or you were stolen from your birth parents. There's never any middle ground. And either way, you have to be grateful and understanding of both sets of parents' feelings.'

Seth gathered me to him, kissed my neck and held me as close as he could. 'I hate every single person who has ever made you feel like that. If I ever hear someone say something like that to you, they'll be surprised by what I say in reply.'

'It's not your battle, Seth.'

'Course it is. We're a team, Smitty. We're a family. And families look after each other and stick up for each other.'

'I suppose they do,' I replied.

'And if you want to search for your birth parents, I'll support you and do whatever I can to help you find them, and if you don't want to find them, I support you in that, too. Whatever it is, you know I'll always be by your side.'

I liked the way he said 'always'. I knew he meant it.

I've rung the doorbell.

I wasn't sure if I should do that or if I should knock. Decisions about doorbells or knocks on wooden, stained-glass-panelled doors shouldn't be so fraught, I know that, but I wanted to make a good first impression. Or second impression in the case of *her*. And fourth impression in Abi's case. (I haven't told Mum I've seen Abi because she told me she would come when I was meeting *all* of them so there was no need. Obviously that argument would stand up in a court of law; in the Court of Mum I'd be toast.)

The royal blue door flies open and Abi is standing there. Her other brother lives in Montenegro, apparently, so can't be here today, but our eldest brother will be present. So will her grandmother and her parents.

The air around her froths and foams with the desperation you feel when you're about to meet the family of the person you love for the first time. I remember the sheer terror I felt when I brought Seth to properly meet my parents – my stomach was in knots and I had to keep getting up to wash my hands they were so slick with anxious perspiration. He'd passed (just). He'd been similarly nervous when I met his folks and I'd passed with flying colours. I hope it's like that for me today. I hope I pass. I hope they like me.

'Hi,' Abi says. She grins at me. We've spoken, briefly, every day since we had it in writing that we are sisters. She has been so nervous about arranging this, and on top of what I feel, I truly hope it goes well for her, too.

'Hi,' I reply.

Her gaze goes to Mum. I told her I was bringing my mother, and she probably assumed I was doing so for moral support – not because Mum is so anxious about the thought of me 'defecting' to another family that she has become like the KGB during the Cold War era, always on the lookout for any signs of changing loyalties.

'This is my mum, Heather Smittson,' I say. 'Mum, this is Abimbola, Abi, who I've told you about.'

Abi's face, twenty-four and unblemished and unlined, is moment-arily surprised. It never occurred to her in all that time when I said 'Mum' that she would be white.

'Hello, Abi, pleased to meet you,' Mum says.

'Oh,' Abi says, shaking herself out of her surprise. 'Hello. Great to meet you.'

She's looking at me now, her gaze is inquisitive, wondering, I suspect, what it was like to grow up with non-black parents, what my experiences of the world were, how it felt to be me. One of the doors off the wide, carpeted corridor opens and a little girl of about five appears. She leans her head out first, staring at us from the other end of the corridor. She takes in the sight of us standing in front of the open door. Whispers drift out of the room, but she ignores them, and the rest of her appears. She is dressed for church – well, how Mum used to dress me for church: knee-length pink dress with a lace, round-neck collar, white socks pulled up to the knees, black patent shoes, pink ribbon bows at the tops and bottoms of her plaits.

She approaches us along the corridor, hesitant but only slightly so. I would never have had the confidence to do this at her age, I would have stayed in the room with the rest of my family, waited until I was told what to do, what to say, how to act. When she arrives at our end of the corridor, she presses herself against Abi's leg in the way I've only ever seen children do with their parents. I have another niece. I call Sienna, my cousin Nancy's daughter, my niece instead of my second cousin because that's how she feels, but here is another one. Another niece who, quite strikingly, judging by the way Mum is staring at her with a mixture of shock and recognition, looks exactly like I did at that age.

'*Lily*,' Abi hisses. 'I told you to wait with Grandma and Grandpa.'

'Are you my new auntie?' Lily asks me.

'Yes,' I reply before I have thought about how that will make Mum feel.

The little girl nods thoughtfully, considering this. 'Who are you?' she asks Mum.

'That's my mum,' I reply.

Lily nods again. 'OK,' she says. 'Hello.'

'Hello,' Mum replies.

'Everyone's waiting in the living room,' she adds. 'We're not allowed to talk. We all have to sit there waiting for you. Even Uncle Ivor and he always talks. He talks and talks and talks and talks. I think he likes to hear his own voice.'

Abi seizes her daughter's shoulders, massages them gently as if she might find a mute button if she presses in the right place. 'This is Lily-Rose, my daughter,' she says. Abi slips so easily from being twenty-four, young and naïve, to being twenty-four-year-old, long-suffering mother and highly mature.

'Nice to meet you, Lily-Rose,' my mother says before I can say anything.

'Are you going to meet Grandma and Grandpa now?' she asks.

I need to get out of here. I need to be away from here and in my bed with the covers pulled up over my head. I need to be in Leeds, in my bed with the covers pulled up over my head, waiting for Seth to come home from work and tell me that all of this has been some twisted dream from that plate of dodgy scallops I ate when we went out for our anniversary the other night. I need to not be here.

'Yes,' I reply. 'Yes, I am.'

'That's good. They're nice,' she says.

With my small butterfly box, yesterday, Hove

Light poured into my bedroom. I had the windows partially open and the outside noises filled the room with the chaos of life passing by the flat and the relentless forever of the sea. With that noise as an accompaniment, I didn't feel so lonely while I did this, even though I needed to do it alone. If things were different, if I was still with Seth, he'd be waiting outside, ready to come in and be with me the moment I told him I needed him.

There were three photographs in total. All black and white. I am wrapped in a blanket, swaddled and unable to move, in the first one. The top of my head is covered with a crotcheted or knitted bonnet, my face is staring up at the camera, unfocused and unsuspecting. On the back, my date of birth is noted, along with: 2.42 p.m. The time of my birth, I guessed. I hate my birthdays. I love other people's birthdays, I lavish such attention upon them and plan so much, but mine...I, thankfully, didn't have many friends so there was no need to worry about being annually forced into holding birthday parties and events nor having surprise parties sprung on me.

I closed my eyes, allowed images from earlier birthdays to develop in the darkroom of my mind. For most of my childhood it was the same: I would sit like a statue in front of a delicious-looking cake, candles burning, while Mum and Dad, and quite often my cousin Nancy and her parents, would sing a song that was meant to celebrate my time on Earth. Every time I would make a wish and blow out the candles. I would make the same wish every year: to never have to do this again, to never have to mark another one of my birthdays like this again. Who would want to celebrate one of the worst days of someone else's life?

For her, the woman who gave birth to me, it wasn't a culmination of nine months of excitement and apprehension and planning – it was the end of the wait to be rid of me. It was the day when she could get on with the rest of her life having finally shed the millstone that was growing inside of her. How could I celebrate that, knowing this was when the burden of my existence began?

I hated birthdays, every single one of them. I hated having to pretend that it was a time of celebration and joy and welcoming me to the world, when it was simply the day I arrived before I was shunted off to be someone else's problem.

I opened my eyes to look at the next picture. It was of me, not as squashed, my eyes more open, obviously a couple of weeks older. I am in the butterfly box, dressed in white, one arm is reaching out towards the person taking the photo, the other is resting on the side of my face, as if I am thinking very hard. The date on the back confirms what I thought, it is me two weeks later.

In the third photo I am about a month old. The only part of me showing is my face. My eyes are wide and focused, staring at the camera, waiting, it looks like, for something to happen, something to be said. Two weeks later (I know it was two weeks later because that's another day my parents always marked by taking me out for ice cream and pop) I began my life in the Smittson house. I gained a new name, I gained two parents who wanted me.

As well as the date, the back of the photo also had '*Always in my heart, Precious One*'.

The box was a little large for only three photos. I wondered if she took any more. If she kept any more, or these were the only three she had. The ones she kept all these years. Our handwriting was very similar: clear and plain, no elaborate swirls or embellishments, we want to get our points across in a quick, no-nonsense fashion. I stared at the handwriting for longer than I did at the photos. My real connection to her, a real reminder that beyond looks, there was something else we had in common.

The sea began to pour into my brain, the world was loud and magnified, too much of everything filled my senses. I dropped the photos back into their too large box and I stretched out on the floor – there was too much going on around and inside me to move, to get on to the bed, to sleep.

I closed my eyes. At that moment I wanted to make a butterfly using silver wire. I had tried in the past. I fashioned the wings with my fingers instead of pliers, and they had both been that perfect squashed-heart shape, almost perfectly symmetrical. But they'd been fragile, even though I'd used five-millimetre wire; they'd been too fragile for me to add the glittery bead for the head or the wrapped wire shape for the body. It should have worked, I should have been able to make a butterfly, but all I was left with were two wings – flawlessly shaped, infinitely too delicate to be of any use to anyone.

I'm like that, I decided as I lay on the beige carpet of my bedroom. I was too delicate, incomplete and unconnected to be of any use to anyone, least of all the woman who gave birth to me.

I have no idea what is going to happen next. They are all in this room in this house that should look like a museum, should look cold and unloved because it is so large and it looks from the outside that the inhabitants could afford staff to do the hard stuff. But inside it's similar to the type of home I grew up in: carpets that are worn in patches, coats and jackets hooked over the banister, shoes placed haphazardly on the shoe rack. A helmet resting on the platform of Lily's green and blue scooter.

This corridor is clean, the floor vacuumed, the skirting boards and paintwork dusted, but it's also comfortably, ordinarily messy. These are normal people. Normal people who I am related to.

My breath goes in and out at a normal rate. Everything here is normal.

The lounge is bright, two comfortable, beige leather sofas are the centrepieces to the room. One faces the large, ornate fireplace, the other sits to its side, both of them crammed with cushions of various shapes, sizes and colours. There's a vivid red carpet, there are photos lined up neatly on the mantelpiece, each in a gold frame. There is a chandelier, swollen with crystal teardrops, hanging above us. The large window has gold curtains with a red vine pattern.

I want to note the quirks of décor so that if I never come back, I'll still have memories of the place where I could have grown up.

And I need to take in these details to avoid looking at the people in front of the fireplace.

Mum is two steps behind me, and Abi, who was behind Mum, navigates around us and, holding Lily's hand, moves past the sofa to join the rest of her family who are lined up like Russian dolls in front of the fireplace.

'Welcome home,' the man who stands at the centre of the people in the room says. My father. Not my dad, my father, the man who donated half of my genetic code. 'It's good to see you at last.'

With that, my mother, the woman who donated the other half of my genetic code, bursts into tears. Abi is not far behind her, and then, shockingly, my father turns his back to me, rests his hand on the mantelpiece and begins, it seems from the shuddering of his shoulders, to cry too. Abi's grandmother sits in a wheelchair beside Abi's brother, staring at me, her face wet with tears. Abi's brother is barely controlled and I know he wants to break down, too. Only Lily looks more confused than moved. I dare not turn to look at Mum in case she's at it too.

I wasn't expecting this, I wasn't braced for crying people; I wasn't prepared to not cry myself. I'm not crying, am I?

I touch my face and my fingers are dry when I look at them. No, I'm not crying. Is that normal? Am I normal? Why am I not crying? Why? Because this really is no crying matter.

28

Smitty

'If you ever say that about my daughter again, I will put you six feet under!'

I'd never heard Dad's voice like that: so loud and so cross. When he laughed, my dad made a big noise. People used to look at him and start laughing, too. And when he was happy he used to talk really, really, really fast like no one could ever catch him cos his voice was like Road Runner. And, sometimes, when he was cross with me he would talk loudly and send me to my room. But he never, not ever, shouted like this.

I didn't know what Uncle Colin had said to make him shout, but it felt like the windows were shaking when Dad yelled. We'd gone to Uncle Colin and Auntie Marcia's house for our Sunday dinner and we were all eating and Mum was saying how lovely the roast was and Auntie Marcia was telling Nancy to eat her vegetables like I was. Then Uncle Colin said something really, really quiet and that was when Dad slammed his fist on the table and everything rattled and everyone stopped talking and eating and I couldn't get to breathe properly.

'Girls, outside, now!' Dad said. 'Now!'

Mum put her hand on Dad's arm and that didn't do anything apart from make him look at me and Nancy and repeat, 'Now!'

Auntie Marcia got up and came over to Nancy who was really

scared, her eyes big and wide, and Mum looked at me and nodded quickly, like I should go as well. I got up and realised I was shaking and my eyes were wide like Nancy's. And then we were sitting outside on the back step, and I could hear lots of loud adult voices and then Dad shouted, 'If you ever say that about my daughter again, I will put you six feet under!'

What did he say about me? I wanted to ask Nancy. *What did he say that would make Dad so angry?*

I couldn't ask Nancy, she had her knees right up to her chest and she had her head on her knees and she had her arms around her legs and she was rocking back and forwards like a Weeble.

What did he say about me? I wanted to ask Mum and Dad. But they were inside and the shouting had stopped. No one was talking inside the house and Nancy wasn't talking to me outside the house. *What did he say about me?* I kept asking myself. *What did he say?*

'Come on, *quine*, we're going,' Dad said to me, and he bent his big, strong body and scooped me up. Dad didn't carry me much any more, I was too much of a big girl, but this time, he picked me up and held me close. When I hugged him goodnight, he always felt like this, like the strongest man in the whole wide world.

I looked to the door, waiting for Mum to come out. 'Heather!' Dad shouted. 'You come now, or you don't come at all.'

Mum walked slowly out of the house, very slowly, like she didn't want to leave. Like she was actually thinking about 'not coming at all'. I was scared. That scared inside I sometimes felt when I heard the monsters moving in my room at night. When I saw funny shapes on the walls. But this was worse. Much worse. I didn't know what was happening or what Uncle Colin had said. Or what it was about me that made people say not very nice things all the time. Uncle Colin said not very nice things all the time, so did Nancy. Auntie Marcia said things sometimes. But this was the first time Dad had got so cross. Mum usually said they didn't mean it how it sounded and not to tell Dad because he wouldn't understand. She was right. Dad didn't understand that they didn't mean it, that's why he got so cross. He didn't understand.

'He didn't mean it, Dad,' I whispered, to maybe make him understand. 'They never mean it.'

Dad looked at me and he seemed a bit surprised. Then he looked
at Mum. 'We have things to discuss,' Dad said to Mum. 'At length.'

But he didn't mean it, I wanted to say again. I didn't, though. I had
a feeling that Dad wouldn't listen.

It's calmed down, thankfully. Almost as quickly as it started people
stopped themselves from sobbing, pulled themselves together and
we all, *all*, pretended that it hadn't happened.

Now everyone is sitting, chatting, and I am no longer the centre
of attention. I've never liked being the centre of attention because
I spent so much time as the odd one out, it's nice to be unnoticed. I
am sitting on the sofa with a mother on either side of me. They sit
close to me, like they want to hold my hand. Mum has her bag on
her lap but she's poised, prepared to snatch up my hand if the woman
on the other side of me goes anywhere near my other hand.

My other mother has her hands folded neatly on her lap. I don't
know her as well as I know Mum, but she isn't relaxed, she seems set
to grab me if the woman on the other side of me makes any sort of
physical contact.

They are both silent for long periods then start to talk at the same
time, stop to allow the other to speak and then lapse into silence
again. Abi is chatting to her father in front of the mantelpiece, her
grandmother sits beside them in her easy chair and seems to occasionally join in their conversation, but mostly she just sits still and
stares at me. Lily and her uncle, my brother, are putting together the
pieces of a brightly coloured giant floor puzzle of the world in the
area under the window where all the toys are contained in two giant
red tubs. After the crying, I had introduced Mum to them. Wary and
confused, they all shook hands and said how pleased they were to
finally meet, none of them relaxing their body language.

My brother is called Ivor, my father is called Julius, my mother is
called Kibibi and my grandmother is called Soloné. There is food,
placed on the sideboards and the side tables, tea has been made,

everyone has seemed to have loosened up. To each other, probably to themselves, they are pretending that they are absolutely fine with what is happening, who has come into their perfectly ordered world. However, bubbles of awkwardness circulate the room, popping at different moments: I look up and see Ivor watching me when he should be pushing puzzle pieces into place with Lily; I notice Abi pointing to what could be invisible rings on her fingers as she talks to her dad, obviously explaining to him that the ones I wear are probably made by me; I am being smothered by the anxiousness that radiates from the two women on either side of me. All the while, Abi's grandmother continues her motionless, silent vigil over me and my arrival in her home.

With Dad & Mum, March 1983, Otley

'We're not going back there, Heather.'

'He's my brother, Don, you can't stop me from seeing my brother.'

'You can see them any time you like, Heather. But you're not taking wee Clem over there. Not any more.'

'She and Nancy are like sisters, you can't separate them.'

'Aye, you're right. But Nancy can come here if they want to play together. My Clem isn't going over there for them to look down on. He actually said we had no idea where she came from so we didn't know what she might turn out like.'

'He didn't mean it.'

'Aye, that's what Clem said, too. She's heard all that before and you don't think there's anything wrong with it. You make her stay with these people when they say disgusting things to her and around her. The fact you can't see anything wrong with that, Heather, makes me very sad. She's our daughter. You don't let anyone speak to her like that. Especially not so-called family.'

'He's my big brother. He helped us out when we needed him.'

'He lent us a bit of money when I lost my job and we paid him back every single penny and you think that gives him the right to talk about a child like that? Any child would be bad, but our own child? I don't know how you can stand to look at yourself in the mirror.'

'He doesn't mean it. They don't mean it.'

'Come on now, *quine*, there's no need to cry. It's not so bad. Come on, don't cry. You know I can't stand it when you cry.'

'I'm doing the best I can for everyone.'

'I know, *quine*, I know. But we can't put Clem through that again. We're meant to protect her, not let other people hurt her, no matter who they are.'

'How long have you lived in this beautiful house, Kibibi?' Mum asks. She is finally able to speak without her sentence being accidentally interrupted by my other mother.

'Many, many years. I was born in London, but my parents decided to go home when I was sixteen.' I chance a look at her, properly. Her face is thinner than mine, she has longer eyelashes than me, her nose is the same shape as mine but smaller, her smile is like mine, though. We share the same smile. Although the same shade, her skin is smoother than mine, less blemishes, probably because more care and thought have gone into looking after herself over the years. She's wearing a two-piece skirt suit with short cap sleeves. Every one of the hairs of her head has been perfectly straightened and she wears it in a shoulder-length bob. She and Abi are pure style. 'My parents wanted me to continue to study in England, because I had been accepted to start university a year early, so I came here to live with Julius's parents because our families had been friends in the Duyalt Province in Nihanara.' She pauses, wondering if we either of us know where it is, I'd guess. 'Julius's parents had this house from when he was about ten years old. They rented it first of all, then his parents bought it.'

'That is a lot of history,' Mum says. She sounds patronising. I'm not sure if she realises it, but she is talking down to my other mother. 'What did you study at university?' Mum asks.

'I was going to be studying international business law ... but I did not start.' Because of me. Because she got pregnant and had me.

For some reason, silence descends upon the whole room at that point, so everyone hears what she said and all the adults know

165

what the unuttered part of that conversation means and it freezes their tongues, causes more of those awkwardness bubbles to explode all over us. I am the centre of attention again and my body becomes an inferno of regret and shame and guilt.

'Come,' Abi's grandmother suddenly orders. She speaks slowly, haltingly. 'Come here, child,' she adds. Without hesitation I stand and go to her. I have to crouch down because she clearly isn't able to get up.

'My eyes are not so good,' she says. 'I didn't see you when you were born. I want to see you now.' She examines me and I examine her. Did she mind not seeing me when I was born? Was she desperate to, but decided to not get involved because giving me up was for the best?

Abi's grandmother, *my* grandmother, seems to linger on every line of my face, every blemish, every facial nuance that might link me to her. She doesn't like my hair, I can tell by the way her gaze pauses at my mass of untamed curls and then moves on with a sliver of disdain in her eyes.

'You are truly a Zebila,' she says, still faltering in her speech. She has found enough similarities between her son, who I have not looked at properly yet, and me to say that. 'Welcome home, child… Welcome home… I can only thank God that… Mrs Smittson brought you back to us safe… I knew God would look after you… all these years, and in His infinite… wisdom He has decided… now is the time to bring you home… Thank you, Mrs Smittson, thank you.'

She probably doesn't mean to, she probably doesn't even realise she is doing it, but she has made it sound as if I have been in suspended animation, my parents, Heather and Don Smittson, standing like silent guards outside my suspension chamber, waiting to find the Zebilas so my life can begin.

'Mama,' my first mother says, 'Ta— Clemency is probably tired, this has probably been very overwhelming for her. Maybe let her come and sit for a little while longer.' She wants me back beside her on the sofa. She doesn't want anyone, not even a relative, taking me away from her.

'This is my grandchild. She has been returned...to me after many, many...long years,' my grandmother admonishes even though her words are still slow. 'I will speak to her for as long as I want.'

'Would you like to see some photographs of Clemency growing up?' Mum doesn't seem at all put out by how she was just dismissed as nothing more than a caretaker. She is on her feet and from her bag she has pulled out a photo album I did not see her stow away in there. It is white, covered with a plastic case, and between the plastic and the cover there is a picture of me. I am about eight years old wearing a blue hat with a pompom on top, a brown coat with a white fuzzy fur ring around the hood. I have green woollen mittens on my hands, and socks pulled up to my knees. I am grinning at the camera with all my teeth on show and my chin tipped forwards. I don't remember that photograph being taken, I don't remember being that girl in the photo, but I am happy. I remember being happiest when it was Mum, Dad and me.

My first mother, birth mother, biological mother, whatever I need to call her, gasps. She wants to see the photos, she wants to pore over them and possibly reimagine the life she could have had with me around. Everyone in the room looks at her, waits for her response to Mum's question.

In the space that follows her gasp, my grandmother states: 'I would like to look.' Mum was asking my first mother, everyone knows that. No one says this though, no one dares. Everyone simply pretends they don't notice the tension that stretches like a giant rubber band between my other mother and my grandmother. My grandmother has commandeered this moment, something offered by one mother to another mother, and made it her own.

'How about we all look together?' Mum says brightly.

'No, that's fine, you all look.' My mother is on her feet, picks up two of the plates, still laden with food. 'Tal— Clemency, would you mind helping me to clear some of these plates?'

This is her two fingers to what my grandmother has done: she gets the photos, my other mother gets the real thing.

167

The room continues to be shrouded with quiet and stillness until, plates in hand, we exit, closing the door behind us.

With Nancy, June 1987, Otley

'Why did you do that?' I asked Nancy.

She shrugged her shoulders and didn't look at me. We were sitting in her bedroom and I still had tears on my cheeks from being shouted at.

'But it's not fair, Nancy. You knocked over the pot of ashes, why did you tell them I did it?'

Nancy screwed up her pink mouth and looked at me like she hated me. She did that sometimes. Sometimes she would link her arm through mine and tell me I was the bestest friend she'd ever had, but sometimes it was like this – she got me into trouble and she looked at me like I was her very worst enemy ever, ever.

'Why, Nancy?' I asked her again.

She shrugged again. 'Cos you never get in trouble. It's always me. And it'd have been worse if they thought I did it. But you can't do anything wrong, not ever.'

'But I didn't do it.'

'Yeah, well, they think you did. All the time Auntie Heather says how well behaved you are and how you're such a good girl, and everyone's always looking at you and saying how nice your hair is and how darling you look. They're always telling you how special you are because you were chosen. They don't think you're that special now, do they? I bet they wish they'd never chosen you at all.'

Uncle Colin had walked into the sitting room that we weren't really allowed to go in, but Nancy said we should, and saw us in front of the pot of Grandma's ashes, when all the grey-black dust inside was all over the floor and you couldn't see the gold, swirly pattern of the carpet. He had growled, 'Why you—' And then shouted for Mum.

When he said, 'Who did this?' I didn't say anything because I thought Nancy was going to tell how she had stood on her tiptoes to try to get her picture down and had knocked the black pot on to the floor.

'Clemency did it,' Nancy said. 'I told her not to come in here but she did it.'

I looked at Mum, then looked at Uncle Colin. And then Uncle Colin shouted at me. Told me I was evil, and naughty, and I would go to hell because I hadn't confessed. He said he was glad I wasn't a real part of his family and he was ashamed that Mum had brought up such a terrible child. He shouted and shouted and didn't stop until I was crying and shaking. Mum didn't give me a hug, she just looked sad and unhappy and like she believed Nancy that I did it.

Mum didn't even say anything when they sent me to Nancy's room then sent her there because she shouldn't have followed me into the sitting room. I couldn't even tell Dad about this because we weren't supposed to go to Uncle Colin's house any more after what he said about me when I was little.

'That wasn't fair,' I said to Nancy.

She shrugged again because she didn't care.

'One day, my real mum and dad are going to come for me and I'm going to tell them about this and they'll make you tell the truth.'

Instead of looking scared or worried or upset, Nancy sat up on her bed and smiled at me. She smiled at me like the cat in the *Alice in Wonderland* stories – big and wide and a bit scary. 'I'm going to tell Auntie Heather you said your real mum and dad are going to come for you. You're going to be in trouble. You're going to be in trouble!'

Mum sometimes got upset if people said she wasn't my real mum, she'd be even more upset if I had said it too.

I sat on the floor of Nancy's bedroom, wrapped my arms around my stomach and started to cry again. It actually hurt, a real physical pain was inside my stomach, one I'd never felt before. If Nancy told Mum what I said she would be so upset, Mum would cry and that would be my fault. I would have made my mum cry. I wished I could take back what I said. I wished I could go back in time and knock over the pot of Grandma's ashes instead of Nancy, then everyone would be cross with me for the right reasons and I would never have said something that would break my mum's heart.

'Sit with me for a moment,' my other mother says once we are in the kitchen and have placed the dishes we cleared on the side. The kitchen is another homely space with a comfortable-looking sofa and a large dining table they must have all sat around to eat – I can imagine the noise in here, three children, two parents, grandparents. Them all talking, laughing, sharing, nicking food from each other's plates, spilling drinks, completing homework. It was like that in our home, too. Just quieter. 'Sit, sit,' she says indicating with an open hand to a space at the dining table.

My heart is like a weight inside my chest: too heavy to beat but desperate to escape. We sit at one corner of the table, she is at its head, me on her left.

'I'm sorry for the way I turned up the other day,' my mother says. 'I should have thought through what I was doing to you.'

'It's fine.'

'Abimbola says you make jewellery,' she says. 'Did you make those rings you are wearing?'

I look down at them: the thick silver one, the copper and silver twisted ones, the copper and silver texturised one, the plain silver one, the linked yellow gold ones, the pleated platinum ones. Those are the ones I made first, my practice rings. The others came later, were made with just as much love and attention but in less time, with more experience with every measurement, cut, heat up, cool down, pickle, shape, file, solder, polish and finish. 'Yes. I remake old jewellery and make new stuff, too.'

She reaches out and cautiously takes my left hand to get a better look at the rings. 'I am envious,' she says. 'I have always wanted to be able to do something like jewellery or sculpting or even simple moulding. When I see something in my head it is so clear, so vivid, but when I attempt to make it, it does not quite turn out how I expected.' She laughs. She laughs how I laugh, with her head thrown slightly to one side, her cheeks plumped up and her eyes slightly closed. 'To say the least.'

'That's what drawing and painting are like for me. I think I'm so artistic because in my head the image is so brilliant and perfect. My hands, however, never seem to be able to do that on the page. Luckily it seems to work with jewellery. You can draw, though, so that's something.'

'You can make jewellery, which is like sculpture, is it not? You are artistic. Simply not drawing artistic. I am not physically artistic.' But we are both artistic, she seems to be saying, we have another connection.

'I suppose that's true,' I say. I wish she would laugh again. She reminds me most of the connection between us when she laughs.

'You were . . . you were happy?' she asks.

I can't be honest with her, not if I don't want to hurt the feelings of this intimate stranger. She is staring at her hands and at my hands. Yes, I was happy. And I was miserable, too. I was happy, I was miserable, I wanted an escape route, I never wanted to leave home. I laughed so much my body hurt, I cried so hard my eyes ached. I had a mostly normal childhood. 'I was OK,' I confirm. 'I was fine. The Smittsons are good people.'

'I did not want to give you away,' she says quietly. She continues to study my hands, her hands, to focus on not looking at the rest of me.

'Then why?' I ask. *Why, why, why?* And: *How could you?* And: *What was wrong with me?* And: *Why didn't you come back for me?* And: *Have you thought about me all these years?* And: *Why, why, why?*

'I was seventeen. I had no family around me. The Zebilas were worried about what people would say about the unmarried daughter of a friend who lived in their house suddenly being with child. They thought people would believe your grandfather was responsible. He would never have done such a thing but they worried what people would say.

'Your father . . . he was still completing his studies and could not financially support us. I battled with myself for many weeks. Mrs Stoner, the foster carer, a nice English lady, let me come and see you almost every day. I was not supposed to, the social worker said, but Mrs Stoner let me. I would hold you, sing to you, feed you . . . you were so small. She would let me bath you sometimes.'

More whys from what she reveals, not less: *Why didn't he give up his studies to support us? Why didn't his parents with their big house and money want to help? Why didn't anyone think to organise a secret wedding so you could keep me as husband and wife? Why could you hold me and sing to me and bath me and still walk away? Why didn't you look for me?*

'The social worker told me I would forget. She said I should get on with my life, look forwards not back and I would forget. She said you would go to two people who would know how to look after you as only adults can. I couldn't do that properly, she said. I was too young.'

Why did you believe her? Why didn't you believe that I was your baby and I would need you, not anyone else?

'I never forgot. How could I? I have thought about you every day.'

Why didn't you tell your other children about me? Why didn't you let my grandmother see me – she might have changed her mind about me then? Why?

The answer was obvious, of course: Why? Because she was seventeen. At seventeen I had slept with about ten different people, trying to make connections with others wherever I could because sometimes the endless abyss of aloneness and being 'different' would threaten to swallow me whole. At seventeen I still thought my 'real' parents would swoop in and take me away from all the bad things that had meandered through my life like the slow-moving but persistent flow of a river. I remember studying for A levels, listening to Take That and complaining about Dad not letting me straighten my hair while all the white girls around me – including my cousin Nancy – were still slathering on chemicals to curl their hair to look like mine.

If I was in her situation at seventeen – and I so nearly was – I would have kept the baby. It would have broken my parents' hearts but I would have done it, I would have kept me. I have to remember, though, that I was seventeen in 1995. I was not a teenager in 1978, single, living with a family who obviously didn't want me around, without a job, without a friend nearby except the man who got me into this situation and who obviously didn't want anything to do with my child. I know all this but, rhubarb, rhubarb, rhubarb. The knowing and understanding doesn't change the hurting. The hurting is like a furnace inside me sometimes that is fuelled by never feeling good enough, or worthy enough, or lovable enough, to be anyone's first choice. Except for Mum and Dad, except for Seth. They are the only people I've met over my lifetime who have chosen me first every time. If I look at what I've done, how I've twisted myself into so many difficult shapes to be able to be who someone else wants me to be, I realise that not even I am my own first choice.

'You look so much like Abimbola,' she says with a smile. I like her laugh, I don't like this smile. This smile is the type you use when you are cooing over a baby: maternal, loving, sentimental. It freaks me out. I'm not a baby, but that is clearly who she is seeing. Either Baby Talei or Abi but not me, Clemency the adult.

'She looks like me,' I tease. 'I was here first, remember?'

'Ah, yes, I'm sorry. She looks so much like you.' She grins. Then seriousness descends, covers her body and makes it stiff, forces her hands to stop moving. 'You were really all right?' she asks again, just to be sure.

I nod. I was mostly all right. Weren't most people?

29

Smitty

With Dad, August 2014, Otley

'When are you and Seth going to be having children?' Dad asked.

'The twelfth of never, probably,' I replied offhandedly.

'Is it you or him?' Dad asked.

When I did not reply, simply carried on with my search through the on-screen TV guide for something to watch that we'd both like, Dad said, shrewdly, 'You, is it, *quine*?'

'Yes,' I mumbled.

'Can I ask you why, or will you change the subject?'

'Can you honestly see me with a baby, Dad?'

'Yes. You would be a perfect *mither*. If Nancy can do it, and I've never had much faith in her abilities, why do you think you can't?'

I shrugged.

'You don't need to know the past to have a future, *quine*. You simply have to have faith that you will do your best.'

'It's not the past I don't know, Dad, though, is it? Please don't be upset by this, but it's the things going on with my body that I don't know about that could do something to my baby because I don't know anything about where I came from. There could be all sorts of things inherited in my personality that could make me a terrible parent. I don't know enough about myself to know who I really am.'

'Ach, *quine*, does anyone? You are thirty-six, you must have some idea of who you are, what you like, what you don't like. Nobody knows who they are all the time. We surprise ourselves constantly. We scare ourselves even by being capable of doing things we did not know we could do.' He rested back in his chair, weak suddenly. I was draining him with this talk, I had to stop it.

'Let's change the subject, eh?' I said.

'No. I need to say this. You are my *bairn*, Clemency Smittson. My Smitty. You were also someone else's daughter first of all. But ultimately you are who you are. You may talk like someone else, you may look like someone else, you may think you have the same values and beliefs as someone else, but you are you. Any child you have will be the same. They will be who they are, despite you.'

The pictures seem to have loosened everyone up properly. When my mother and I return to the living room they're chatting and laughing. They are all giggling and chortling at Lily who is doing rather accurate impressions of me from the pictures.

Lily is currently pretending to be me when we came down south to go to the stately home and giant maze at Hampton Court. I know the picture well, it was up in Mum and Dad's living room until the move. I think it might be in Mum's room now. I'm about nine and I'm standing in the middle of the maze. I have one hand against the green maze wall, my other hand on my hip, and I'm grinning at Mum who was taking the photo. I have on navy blue jeans with a white stripe down the side and a red, short-sleeve top. Dad had done my hair especially for the occasion in two pigtails, wound round and round like Princess Leia from *Stars Wars* because she was my favourite, and after years of trying, he'd finally managed to make it work.

Lily puts her right hand on the fireplace and her left hand against her hip and dramatically juts that hip out. She purses her lips in an exaggerated pout instead of a smile.

'You're a cheeker,' I say to her as I laugh.

'These photographs are brilliant!' Abi says. 'There are so many of them and, my goodness, did you love to pose!'

'They are cool,' Ivor says. This is the first time he's spoken and his voice is deep, not as deep as his father's, but rich and soothing, tinged with an East Sussex burr.

I glance at him. He stares at me in response. Since I arrived he has been watching me, probably wondering if I'm 'real'. If I'm his 'real' sister, if I am a 'real' Zebila by blood, if my intentions are 'real' or if I am there to trick his family out of money. He's wondering what the 'real' reason is I am here. People have been wondering if I'm real all my life, why should he be any different?

'Child,' my grandmother says. All of us in the room except Mum look up. She is looking at me, talking to me. 'Help me to my room.'

Ivor moves forward, arms out, ready to help her up, as does Abi. 'I asked the— I asked Clemency,' she says to stop them. 'My room is down the corridor,' she says. 'Help me.'

It must be fun living in this house with two people vying for control all the time: my mother had ten minutes alone with me in the kitchen, now my grandmother needs to get her share, too. They're probably like this the majority of the time, having refined the subtleties of the game over years and years of living together. I love my parents, I adore Seth's parents, but the *thought* of living with them for pretty much all of my adult life would drive me more than slightly insane, let alone doing it.

My grandmother rests heavily on my arm, and her weight causes me to miss a step. We move slowly and carefully across the room, every piece of furniture an obstacle, every slightly unlevel piece of carpet a hazard. 'See you later, Gran,' Ivor says.

'See you later, Gran,' Abi and Lily echo. Will I be expected to do that? Call her 'Gran' when I leave her. Because that will not be happening. I still haven't properly labelled her that in the privacy of my own mind, it'll take even longer for whatever that label is to come out of my mouth.

Her room is the other living room in the house. She obviously can't manage stairs, and after she has pointed me in the right direction, I edge along at her pace until we reach a white, six-panelled door. I'm expecting, I think, a room that is dark, dingy, that smells of inaction and age and confinement. I'm expecting flock wallpaper, heavy, closed drapes. Instead, the white, opaque blinds are open and, like the lounge, the room is filled with light. The window is also open, and a breeze has been through the room, clearing away any hint of fustiness.

There is a large bed at the far end and along its side are metal rails like the ones you'd find in a hospital, obviously to stop her falling out. On the pillow is a leather-bound book, the words *Holy Bible* embossed in gold on the cover. Pushed up against the wall beside the bed is a large chest of drawers which is topped with dozens of square white boxes, and even more small amber medicine bottles, most with their white, printed labels facing out. There are two large, comfortable-looking easy chairs in the room, positioned near the window; between them is a bookcase filled with books with cracked spines.

'There,' she says. My grandmother points to the chair beside the window and nearest the bed. She lands heavily in her seat, rests back and stares at me again. She has been doing that a lot. My father hasn't looked at me since he welcomed me 'home' and all she has done is look at me. I thought, at first, it was her seeking out any similarities, but it's more than that. Maybe it's that 'real' thing. Or maybe it isn't. But there is definitely *some*thing.

'Sit, sit,' she says.

Cautiously I lower myself into the other seat. Something has changed: in the atmosphere of the room, in the dynamics between us. Maybe it's because we're alone, but I am suddenly on edge, nervous, unsure.

'God has brought you back to me,' she says. 'He is wise and He is good. Just when I need Him, He has answered by bringing you back to me. You are... You are going to help me. I need you to help me,' she says. 'I was not sure what I wanted to do was the right thing until I saw that God has sent you back to me.'

I wish she would stop saying that. I believe in God in many ways, but the way she says it, uses it, makes me defensive. It makes me question whether I truly have a faith or if it is something I have because Mum and Dad took me to church every week. I like to keep my religion to myself, to say prayers when I need and want to, to take comfort in knowing that sometimes I can feel connected to something bigger than myself that is 'out there'. Maybe God, maybe The Universe, maybe simply the sky that covers us all. Whatever it is I believe, I don't force it on to others and I like it better, I like people better, when they don't do it to me. Everyone can believe what they like, all the more so when they don't push it on to me.

I press my lips together to stop myself speaking. To stop myself from saying that I'd rather she left Him out of it if she could.

She begins to shake, and shame blossoms in my chest. I'm being too hard on her. I take my comfort in a divine being when I need to, maybe she is the same. When you are ill, too, like she obviously is, you may need to take that comfort more constantly. I shouldn't judge her for that.

'You will help me, won't you?' she asks.

'If I can,' I reply. I wonder what she thinks someone she has just met will be able to help her do when she has a whole family down the hall in the living room who are at her beck and call. 'What is it you want help with?'

This woman, my grandmother, who has only really been in my life for the past hour, fixes me with a gaze that is determined and a little frightening, woven through with strands of defiance. Maybe I was mistaken; maybe those outside this room aren't as devoted and loving as I thought. Whatever it is that she wants to do is clearly something they're unlikely to agree to. She says nothing for a time, and the longer she stares at me with her brown eyes, the colour dimmed by age, the more a feeling of dread meanders outwards from the pit of my stomach. I should not be sitting here having this conversation with this woman. I should have brought her back here and left her to it. The longer I sit here, the longer things are going to go wrong for me.

Eventually, so eventually I thought she was planning on remaining silent, she speaks. Cautiously, haltingly, she says: 'My time has come. I am too old…too sick…too tired to carry on in this world.' She pauses but her eyes continue to drill into me. 'My time has come. I want...I want to leave this Earth. I need you to help me.'

There's a ringing in my ears, in my head, and I know it's because I'm imagining things, hallucinating, probably dreaming. And the ringing is my alarm clock trying to get me to wake up from this dream that has slid quietly and unknowingly into a nightmare. I need to wake up. I do not want to be speaking to someone who has asked me to...

'Did you just ask me to help you to die?' I ask. I'm not asleep. The ringing in my ears isn't an alarm clock, it's the sound of sheer disbelief as it moves through my body.

'Yes.'

I wrinkle my face at her. This must be some kind of test. A test for what I don't know, but it must be. Or some kind of joke, which is unfunny and has no punchline that would ever make it funny. Any minute now she's going to laugh, she's going to tell me not to take everything so seriously and that it was all just a joke. Not funny. But then, the things that some people find hilarious – hideous, meanspirited, unpleasant stuff – have never appealed to me. 'I think I'd better go,' I say to her. I stand up. The longer I sit here and no 'Only joking!' is forthcoming, the more sick I feel.

'You will help me,' she says. This is not a question, a request from a virtual stranger, it is a prediction. She seems to know something I don't.

'I don't think so,' I say. I'm not used to being so direct and firm with someone older than me, it goes against the respect for elders that I've had instilled in me since I was tiny. This isn't an ordinary situation, though. This needs to be knocked on the head right away.

'You will, Clemency...This is the reason...why you met Abimbola...as you did...My family was not complete without you...Now it is. And it is...because you were brought back to help me.' Her certainty, her conviction about what is going to happen, what I'm going to do, is enough to shake me. Not simply upset me, but make me question whether that is why all of this has happened in the way it has happened. Maybe this is what I'm meant to do. Maybe I am meant to help this woman die.

'No,' I say to her sternly. I'm saying it to myself as well, of course. Because it's the most ridiculous idea that I would have been brought back into their lives for this. 'No. I am not going to do it. So please stop asking. I'm going to go now. It was nice to meet you but now I'm going to go. Goodbye.'

'I will see you again,' she says. Another prediction wrapped up like a present in the folds of an unsubtle threat. 'I will see you again. You will help me.'

30

Abi

To: Jonas Zebila
From: Abi Zebila
Subject: Update
Thursday 2 July 2015

Jonas, my brother,
They've just left – Clemency and her mother have been for a visit and it went well. I didn't want to say anything until it'd actually happened – I half expected her to cancel at the last second, but she didn't. Like I say, I think it went well.

She sent me a message almost straight away saying:

**'Thank you for arranging today.
I feel so lucky to have you in my life. Clemency x'**

So that's something? She didn't run away, although when everyone started crying I wouldn't have blamed her. Yes, dear brother, you read that right, everyone started crying. Proper, full-on sobbing – even Daddy, even *Ivor*. It was a mess. If I was her, standing there watching a bunch of virtual strangers crying because I'd walked into a room, I would have run for it. Ironic, huh, that the one time I'd have expected her to hit the road, she stood there and took it.

She brought her adoptive mother with her. Clemency calls her 'Mum'. She's white, by the way. So was her adoptive father. It never occurred to me that either of them would be, let alone both of them. Her mum, I suppose I need to call her, is so nice, she brought a photo album. It was so strange, seeing all those pictures of Clemency growing up and looking exactly like me. She seemed happy in the photos – she was always smiling.

Gran asked Clem (I don't think she'll mind if I call her that) to help her to her room. She was gone for ages, and when Clem came back she definitely had the look of someone who'd been Gran'd. I don't know what Gran said or did, but Clemency had that expression on her face that everyone has after spending time with Gran. I hope Gran didn't put her off.

Everyone's being really quiet now, it's only Lily-Rose who's talking at all and she wants to keep going through the photos. Mummy is clearing up and looking off into the distance like she's reliving her life again or something, and Daddy has looked through the photos several times with Lily-Rose. Ivor's gone out to wherever Ivor goes. He seems embarrassed that he cried, too, and also, I don't know, angry isn't the right word. He seems put out, maybe scared about what Clemency will mean for him and his position in the family. I really can't think what else it would be.

Brother, it's at times like this that I miss you. You were noticeably absent today. You would have loved Clemency, she would have loved you. Aren't you just tempted to break the silence to find out about her? Not even a little?

Love you. Miss you.
Your sister,
Abi
xxxxxxx

31

Smitty

With Mum & Dad, September 2005, Otley

I watched Mum try to control herself. She did a great job: she managed to control her face, her tears, her voice, but she couldn't control her hands from shaking.

Their living room felt so small, so hot, so claustrophobic. I looked down at my hands and they were trembling. I was shaking, too.

'It'll be fine, *quine*, I promise you,' Dad said. 'I'm fine. I'll be fine. We caught it early. We'll all be fine.'

I nodded at Dad. He didn't lie to me. Mum had no problem with it, she always did what she thought was best even if it meant twisting the facts to suit the reality she wanted to paint. But Dad? He never did that. Even if it was something he knew I didn't want to hear, he would find the words to tell me the truth. He was telling me the truth right at that moment, but I also knew at any given moment that truth could become a lie.

Mum and I arrived home in the silence that we travelled back in. We barely acknowledged each other when we retreated to our separate rooms. There was nothing much to say, nothing we could dissect together because our experiences of the past few hours were so different, so disparate, I don't think we'll ever find any common ground over this.

Once I have closed the door behind me, I throw down my bag and head straight for the wardrobe nearest the window and remove the large butterfly box. Unceremoniously, I put the lid to one side then ferret through the box, crammed with the photos of my life, and remove all the pictures I have of Dad. I lay them on the chest of drawers which sits beside the wall where my photo wall is slowly taking shape. The photos I have just liberated from the box, which still have blobs of Blu-Tack on the back, need to go on the wall. I'm putting Dad back where he belongs, back where I can see him. I work feverishly but carefully, the need to have him visible again makes my fingers move at speed.

I can't believe what that woman asked, I keep thinking as I reinstate Dad. *How dare she? How DARE SHE!*

My dad would have done anything to be here, he would have given anything to have stayed with us, with his family. I would have given anything to have him back, to spare him what he went through. The thought of anyone not feeling like that about life stirs up a tornado-like rage inside me. To have *that person* think I would be interested in being a part of anything that would shorten a life, something so precious, makes me so angry I can barely think without wanting to break something.

I should tell my other mother. I should tell my father. I should tell Abi. I should tell someone who will be able to stop her, talk sense into her. Let her know that she has options other than that. *They* know her, and even if they don't get on with her all the time, none of them would want her to feel like that, to do that.

Dad is slowly returning to my wall. As I put him back up, I am seeing him as he was. Frowning at the train timetable when we were off on a day trip to Birmingham. Wearing my mortar board at graduation. Dancing with Mum at the party after Sienna's christening. Drinking a pint of Guinness at the Guinness factory in Dublin when we went there for his fiftieth birthday. Wearing his red and white Christmas jumper and yellow cracker hat. With his head in his car trying to fix it with no idea what he is doing. Sitting on the beds in my various rooms in my shared houses during my college years and always wearing the same frown because he can't believe how much I am paying for a tiny room. Standing outside our old house in Lewes, holding my two-year-old hand, pointing at Mum who is taking the picture.

There are so many, so many that need to be put up. Each time I pick one up, the memory it holds diffuses into my fingertips, blooms through my blood, until I am remembering all those times.

The last photo I reach for I had not looked at properly when I took it out of the butterfly box until my fingers were almost upon it: *Dad with Seth, February 2013, Engagement Party Time!*

Even though the party never happened, I didn't add a sad face or mention of its cancellation to this picture because it is such a perfect image. Dad, in his navy blue suit, has his arm around Seth while Seth in his tight, navy blue suit that complemented my silver dress, has his arm around Dad. The pair of them could not look happier, more prepared for a night of *birling* (a big night of drinking) and celebrating. I did not want to taint the image by adding any sadness, any of the misery that came next. Should I put up this photo? I'm not sure it has a place among all these other images when I am trying to move on from Seth.

If I touch it, too, I'll only properly remember. I'll only be reminded how much I miss them both. I can do something about how keenly I feel the loss of one of those people, the absence of the other is beyond my control.

And that woman, *that woman* wanted me to help her end her life. I grab the photo, any memory no matter how tainted is better than the thought of what *that woman* wants me to do.

With Seth, Dad & Mum, February 2013, Leeds
Seth unhooked his arm from Dad's shoulder after having a picture taken with him, and wandered across the hall to me. I stood in the centre of the large space, spinning and looking in every direction, desperate to take in every last inch of the place. Seth had made it perfect.

The thirty or so tables that ringed the dance floor where I stood were draped with white paper tablecloths, printed all over with a design Seth had come up with that linked the 'S' of his name with the 'C' of my mine into a pretty monogram. The tables were scattered with silver and gold champagne-flute-shaped confetti and each table had an empty wine bucket waiting for the ice cubes and accompanying Prosecco bottle.

The room was awash with silver and gold balloons with the same 'SC' design emblazoned on them, and the disco lights swung this way and that, to make the place dance with pretty, multi-coloured lights. In the corner, Seth had set up his mixing table and I had practically got down on my knees to beg him not to play hard-core rap all night (no one needed to see either set of parents attempting to dance to that) and to let a couple of his friends have a go so we could spend a bit of time together.

In the large entrance area outside the hall, Dad was now helping Jorge and Max, a couple of Seth's mates from work, to set up the bar. Mum was making a huge fuss about not very much and I didn't even mind. Dylan was meant to be coming but I knew he wouldn't because he still, *still* felt we were rubbing his face in the fact we'd got together.

'You like?' Seth asked. He took my hand and twirled me around. The soft, satiny folds of my silver, knee-length dress flared out while he spun me. Bubbles of happiness fizzed and popped in my veins, I was giddy in a way I hadn't been before. I'd been dubious about this, but he'd persuaded me into it because we weren't going to get married for a while and he wanted to make a public declaration about our love for each other. I'd agreed because I loved Seth and I wanted everyone to be in no doubt how I felt about this man who twirled me, whose fingers mine easily slotted between, whose body I constantly missed like a physical ache deep inside, who was the first person I went to when anything happened.

We had different tastes in music, different ideas about what made a good read, we often fell out over stupid things, I worried all the time when he went out on his motorbike especially in the rain, he often got annoyed that all my jewellery-making tools and equipment were all over the flat instead of tidied away in one of the five yellow toolboxes he had bought me, but we were intertwined. Like the initials he had linked together on the tablecloths, balloons and napkins, we were interlinked and I couldn't remember a time when I hadn't been with him. I had made my engagement ring from that piece of amber he had bought in Lithuania and everyone was going to see it tonight.

'I LOVE!' I said to my fiancé. 'I love, love, love.'

In one move he tugged me into his arms. He was clean-shaven, his hair clipped short, and he smouldered with such deliciousness I wanted to lick him like he was a lollipop.

'I love, love, *love* that dress you're wearing,' he murmured into my ear. His hand ran salaciously over my bum. 'I can't wait to have you in it.' He drew me even closer to him. 'And I can't wait to take it off you and have you all over again.'

'Clemency!' Like an expert surgeon's knife, my mother's voice cut cleanly and precisely through Barry White's 'My First, My Last, My Everything' and the fug of lust we'd slipped into. Seth and I shot apart, as we always did when my mother had that voice on her.

'Yes, Mum?' I asked.

'Where are the extra—'

Mum was cut short by the doors to the hall being thrown dramatically back. In came Dad, heavily supporting a dishevelled, limping Nancy.

I couldn't move, stood and watched as Dad helped her in. With a look to me, Seth went to help Dad place Nancy in a chair.

Her black mascara, something I'd *never* seen her wear before tonight, streaked down towards her cheeks like desperate fingers reaching out for help. Her usually flawless skin was blotchy, her neck was flushed a vivid red-pink colour.

'Oh, Nancy, love, what's happened?' Mum rushed over to her, crouched down beside her chair. 'Are you all right?'

Between gasping, sobbing breaths she told them what had happened: she had been on her way over, having got Sienna settled early with Uncle Colin and Auntie Marcia (who were babysitting instead of attending), so she could help. On her way she must have taken a wrong turn or something because suddenly she was lost and then she noticed she was being followed and *then* they stole her handbag and watch and thankfully that was all they wanted but she'd twisted her ankle trying to run away in case that wasn't all they wanted. But she was worried because they seemed to be hanging around, looking for people to mug. Maybe they knew there was a party going on and thought they'd pick off the guests who were alone.

She was telling this to her assembled audience of Mum and Dad, Jorge and Max, because I knew from the second I saw her it was all fake; a ridiculous fabrication from a woman who was too jealous to let me have even this moment to myself.

'*They're always telling you how special you are because you were chosen. They don't think you're that special now, do they? I bet they're wishing they never chose you at all,*' Nancy had said to me when we were nine and she had blamed me for something she had done. Over twenty-four years later she was trying again to stop me being special as she always did.

'Thank goodness you got away,' Mum gushed. 'Thank goodness you're all right.'

She's definitely all right now, I thought.

'I think I'd better call the police,' I said. Her reply would confirm my suspicions, or would show me to be a spiteful cow who couldn't even cut my cousin some slack after a terrifying experience.

Nancy sat up a little straighter in her seat and vigorously shook her head. 'No, no, don't worry about it. I'm sure they're long gone.'

'But you said you thought they were hanging around,' I said.

'Well, maybe, but since I got away, they probably won't hang around in case I tell anyone.'

It was all a lie. Of course it was. Dad peered at me for a long few seconds before his gaze moved on to Seth, then returned to watching me. I wasn't sure if he knew or simply suspected, but he hadn't taken her at face value, hadn't automatically believed her like Mum had. Like Jorge and Max had because they had no clue what she was like.

Seth and I locked eyes. We knew what would be expected of us, we were both well versed in the protocol of Nancy. I didn't even give a hint of the 'I told you so' I would have been justified in firing at him. But we couldn't. Not over such a blatant lie. No one believed it, surely?

'I think we should cancel the party,' Mum said in the silence when neither Seth nor I said it. 'We can't have anyone else put in danger for a party. It's a good thing it's early enough to do that.'

'But everything's set up,' Dad said. 'We'll just send a message to people to be careful, to travel in pairs, and if they can't do that, we'll come out and meet them.'

'Clemency will never forgive herself if something happens to someone on the way here, Don,' Mum replied. She was talking for me, telling other people what I felt. Dad looked at me, then at Seth.

'You'll be all right, won't you, Nancy?' Dad asked her.

Nancy gave a brave, silent sob and swallowed hard. 'I–I think so,' she said to Dad, while turning her beseeching eyes on Mum. 'I–I'll be all right.'

'No!' Mum said firmly, and hugged Nancy closer. 'No, we can't have anyone else ending up in this state just for a party. You understand, don't you, Clemency?'

I stared at Mum, unable to reply.

'I'd better start calling and texting people to let them know the party is off.' Seth's voice was a frustrated monotone. He said it to save me from answering Mum. That was why I loved him: he always had my back, as they said in the movies.

'I think that would be for the best,' Mum agreed.

'Yeah,' Seth stated flatly. 'For the best.' Anyone else would think the timing was suspiciously perfect to give us enough time to cancel the party before most people had set off, but not Mum. Dad was watching me again, probably understanding how terrible I felt, but he didn't say anything else. He'd tried, but when it came to Nancy, no one could tell Mum anything.

I put the photo down. I can't put it up. I pick it up again. I have to put it up. It's not about me and Seth, it's about Dad. It's about this photo being taken right before it all started going wrong. Right before Mum and Dad sat me down and told me again. Except there was no firmness, no certainty when he stated how fine he was going to be. It was simply the act of telling me what was happening next in his life. This was one of the best photos I had of him before the changes started.

With Dad, July 2014, Otley

We started measuring our time together in the stages of his not being able to do things. He was fine, so fine for so long I'd allowed myself to forget. We were all, I think, lulled into that suspended animation of nothing changing, so that translated into the equivalent of everything being fine.

Until the tests that showed something had altered. And then the moments when the first steps on that path to the other end began. Tentative, slow and fearful but necessary and inevitable. My heart beat as though it was coated and smothered in a thick, viscous treacle that made it agony to exist, knowing what Dad was about to go through. I didn't truly know, of course, I could only guess and imagine and hope that it was not as awful as I thought it would be.

Then our calendar changed, our clocks changed. It stopped being about seasons and months and the countdown to Christmas, it was replaced by the times of the required daily dosage of medication; it was slowly but definitively about when he stopped being able to do things. First it was not being able to make it to the doctor's surgery for his appointments.

'You know, *quine*, I'll never see the outside of this house again,' he said to me while Mum showed the doctor out after his first home visit. I stared at Dad, mute with the horror of what he'd just told me. It was going to happen, soon. I would have to be without him, soon. He smiled at me, his tiredness and what was happening to him not able to dim the essence of who he was. My dad. One of my best friends, but first and foremost my dad.

I don't know if he told Mum the same thing, but the next change was when it became clear that he couldn't manage the stairs so

Mum and I moved the chest of drawers out into the landing and replaced it with his favourite chair from downstairs. He gave me the same smile as he settled into his chair with his paper, glasses perched on his nose. '*I'll never see the downstairs of this house again,* quine,' he said with that smile. And, ah, I smiled back because I understood him, and, ah, the agony from my chest coated and smothered in treacle, made every breath hard and laboured. I semi-moved in to give Mum a hand, I went part-time at work, tried to take on as little private work as I could and resolved to make it up to Seth as soon as I could.

When it wasn't as long between not being able to leave the house and not being able to go downstairs and him having to have a cath-eter installed, I knew it was time to move in properly.

With Dad, April 2015, Otley

Mum and I would take it in turns, sit by his bed and read. He slept a lot, and when he wasn't asleep he would try to talk to us. But he couldn't. It was hard, the pain would make him mute sometimes, and he would try to hide it. His face, so noble and strong, would be grey with the agony, each line drawn taut as the pain ripped slowly through him. And when there wasn't pain, there were the hallucin-ations, seeing what wasn't there, having conversations with people long since gone. He kept seeing his grandmother, asking her when she would take him to the beach, wondering why she didn't reply. Crying and shouting when she wouldn't reply.

I wanted to hold his hand and keep holding it as long as I could. He'd always been there during my beginning and middle; he'd held my hand so many times during the hard bits, he'd made those dif-ficult times easier, bearable, and I wanted to be with him for every last minute. I wanted to help him at his end. I could never think about it, though, even when he told me. It was something I didn't contemplate – him not being around was unthinkable. Then, when it was probable, likely, I still clung to the idea that there would be a cure. Something would happen that would change everything and he'd be around to hold the baby Seth and I had agreed to have, to come with me to see the films no one else would even entertain watching, to call for a quick chat.

My phone, on the floor by my feet, buzzed for the tenth time that day and I stooped to switch it off.

'Who is it that keeps ringing you, *quine*?' Dad asked me. I'd been sitting beside his bed reading while he slept and his voice, croaky and sore, made me jump a little. He was bleary-eyed from sleep, his face a network of sleep-dampened agonies.

'Ahh, just this woman from Doncaster who wants me to make some wedding rings for her. You'd think I was the only ring maker in the world.'

'Not the only ring maker in the world, just the best.' His voice, like sandpaper drawn over gravel, sounded so painful to make. I wanted him to stop talking so he wouldn't be in agony just from speaking to me, but I wanted him to speak to me. The more he spoke to me, the easier I found it to not believe what was coming.

'You would say that, wouldn't you?' I told Dad.

'Smitty, sweetheart...' He kept pausing between words, drawing breath to make the sound that was his voice. 'You need to... get back to work... go and see this woman... make her rings.'

'I don't want to, Dad.'

'Don't stop living... because of me... please, go...'

'Do I have to?' I used to say that to him all the time when I was growing up.

His face managed to find a smile. 'No, you don't... have to... But I'd like... you to. It... would make me... happy... to see you... living.'

'That's emotional blackmail, isn't it, Dad?'

'Yes... I'll use... anything.'

'OK, I'll go ring her and arrange to meet her later in the month.'

'Sooner... rather than... later.'

'OK, Dad. I'll go see her as soon as she's free.'

'Good girl... Good girl.'

With Dad, May 2015, Otley

'Clemency, my little Smitty,' Dad said. He was sitting up as he

192

spoke. He hadn't sat up in what seemed so long, but now he had plump white pillows supporting his lower back, and he was upright. Shades of pink tinged his cheeks, and the lines of his features that had been stretched taut like piano strings with pain had slackened. He seemed calmer, more relaxed, the agony – acute and unrelenting – seemed to have receded because the right balance of opiates and other medication pumped through his veins. 'I wanted to say how much I love you and how proud I am of you.' He could even talk a bit easier. 'You are everything I could have ever wanted in a daughter. I…am the luckiest man alive…I am so honoured to have been your father.'

'You're still my dad, Dad,' I replied.

His smile was that of someone who knew something I didn't. Fear blew through me like an unexpected northerly wind. He knew it would be soon. 'Shall I cancel this woman?' I asked. 'Stay here instead?' I had arranged for the woman from Doncaster who wanted the rings to come to Otley town centre – that was the furthest I was prepared to be away from him – and was just about to nip out to see her.

'Ach, no, *quine*. I'm just being a silly, sentimental old man. I want to…say things when I feel up to it. I am so proud of you and who you turned out to be.'

'I'm the lucky one. You're a brilliant dad. I'm going to rush back from this appointment so I can read you the paper. If you ask Mum to wait for me, I'll do it. Is that a deal?'

'Deal.' He smiled again. He received my careful hug and even more gentle kiss without reciprocating because he didn't have the strength.

At the door, I looked back at him and he eased his hand up, the translucent palm, a network of blue, green and grey veins, held high as he said goodbye.

By the time I returned, he was gone. He went peacefully in his sleep with Mum sitting beside him, holding his hand. The nurse who had come to check his meds arrived a few minutes later. *'Why didn't he wait for me?'* I wanted to ask Mum. *'After all of this time, why didn't he wait for me so I could hold his hand, too?'*

'*Because he was still being my dad right up until the end,*' was the answer, of course. He knew it would have been too much for me to be there. Dad knew that although I wanted to be there, it would have destroyed me if I had been. My whole life, right down to his last breath, Dad protected me.

I am pushing my luck. I had to get out of the flat, away from the sadness and the remembering. I had called Melissa, but her phone went straight to answer machine. I'd almost called Seth, had gone to type in his number when a 'Smitty, I deserve to have you talk to me at least' type text from him popped up on my phone and I knew I couldn't. It wouldn't be fair on him to just get in touch when I needed support, and to be honest, his text made me think he had a nerve considering what he'd done. So, I decided instead to push my luck by going to Beached Heads and seeing if I could persuade Tyler to let me in even after closing time, make me a coffee, talk to me until I started to feel better.

Outside his café, which is indeed closed with the outside tables brought in and stacked neatly between the counter and the window, I stand at the door and peer in. I can see him behind the counter. He is using a white cloth to clean his machine, but he is unhurried, the movement more like pottering than essential work to be carried out before he can speed off home to his life away from here. I'm like that sometimes, especially nowadays when I know all that is waiting for me is an evening spent sitting next to Mum, trying not to rise to everything that comes out of her mouth that I take issue with. Cleaning up at work, moving boxes around the shop while I pretend I'm going to sort it out soon, is always preferable to that.

I move to knock, then decide to literally push my luck – with the metal handle in my hand, I push at the door. Someone is smiling down on me because it opens. It'll be so much harder for him to turn me away now that I'm inside.

'One coffee, please?' I say from my favourite place at the counter.

'We're closed!' he says without turning around.

'But the door was open even though the closed sign was showing,' I state.

He pivots slowly on the spot until he is facing me. I grin at him in what I hope is a winning way. 'Ah, you.' He says it deadpan but his expression betrays a soupçon of joy to see me.

'Yes, me. Isn't this the most excellent part of your day so far?'

His perfect left eyebrow hitches itself up briefly before he frowns at the door, puzzled. 'I could have sworn I locked that. I learnt my lesson after last time.'

'You don't mind, do you?' I ask.

'Would you mind if I came barging into your workplace and demanded you make me a ring after hours?' he asks.

'No,' I say. 'I genuinely wouldn't.' I clear my throat, add as casually as possible, 'Anyway, I don't only want a coffee. I was hoping you'd be able to teach me how to make it on your machine there.'

'What? No way! Only fully insured people behind this counter, baby.'

I'm not sure how serious he is right now, but I need something to take my mind off today. It's not fair to burden him with that responsibility, but I am desperate. If he doesn't help me, I will be forced to ring Seth and I can't do that. Not to him, not to me.

'I'll level with you,' I say, maintaining eye contact. 'I've had a really odd day. So many strange things have happened, so many painful things have been revisited, and I just want one of your coffees and to have some fun. If I have to settle for a coffee, that'll do. Some fun would be . . . probably more than you're willing to give and more than I deserve but I thought I'd ask anyway.'

He stares at me for long minutes. It's probably a few seconds, but standing exposed as I am in front of him it feels like minutes. 'You have to do everything I say,' he states.

My grin is almost one hundred per cent relief, but I restrain myself from clapping my hands in delight.

'One deviation from my instructions and you're outta here. No second chances when it comes to using professional, potentially dangerous equipment.'

'It's a coffee machine, Tyler, how dangerous can it be?' I scoff.

'Oh, suddenly the expert, are we?' he says.

'No, no, sorry, sorry,' I say.

'Go on, get round there, and don't touch anything until I come back with your apron.'

'I get an apron?' I say gleefully.

'Yes, you get an apron.'

'This just gets better and better!' I can't stop myself from jumping up and down.

'Enough of that! There is no messing about while we do this,' he says before he disappears behind the left-hand door. The second he is out of sight I jump up and down again, only managing to stop when he reappears, carrying a blue apron with *Beached Heads* embroidered on to the front in gold thread.

'Come here,' he says. Standing in front of me on the other side of the counter, he hooks the apron over my head, carefully uses the loops to tie it once at the back of my waist, then slowly moves the ends to the front and ties them into a small bow. I watch his hands work and when his fingers rest on the bow for a few seconds, I raise my eyes to find him staring intently at me. 'Ready?' he asks.

I nod.

He smiles and I can't decipher what it means, if it means anything.

'Just so we're clear, Smitty,' he says. 'Me teaching you to do this does not mean the next time you come in here you get to help your-self.' He steps back, gives me space to move in front of the machine, wiping away the moment that had been brewing between us.

'Of course not,' I say.

'I mean it, Smitty. I catch you behind this counter and you're per-manently barred.'

'OK, OK, if it means that much to you, I won't start to help myself.'

'Good.'

'Tyler,' I say quietly.

He pauses mid-reach for the coffee beans that sit on the shelf to the right of the machine. 'Yeah?'

'Thank you.'

'What for?'

I grin at him. I hope my gratitude shows in the strength of my smile, the sadness that probably still haunts my eyes. 'I think you know.'

He nods. 'You're welcome,' he replies.

Part 6

32

Smitty

I didn't think I'd be back here so soon. Or ever, actually. She had put me off, the fear that she would do that to me again had been enough to make me send Abi 'hello' texts but leave it there, and it was sufficient to make me decide to never come back to this house ever again.

Yet, here I am, about to knock on the door. I haven't told Mum I'm coming here. I couldn't do that without feeling as though I am betraying her. And nor could I allow her to come along to this. Meeting my grandmother by birth to discuss this is something I have to do alone.

She was very clear about what time I needed to be here: two-forty-five exactly. I am guessing that this is when she will be alone in the house. Everyone out at work, my other mother probably collecting Lily-Rose from school. We probably have half an hour to talk before people return. She must be very confident about her skills of persuasion if she thinks that's all it'll take.

For the past four days, every day, several times a day, I have had the same message on my mobile and the phone at the workshop: 'I must talk to you, Clemency. Remember what your name means. We are family. Remember what that means. Please answer your phone.' I didn't even notice that there was a phone in her room but she kept ringing, leaving the same pleading message that is designed to get me to talk to her.

Every day I would stare at my phone after I had listened to the messages from this woman who I am related to by blood and blood alone. Yes, it's thicker than water, but what does that actually mean? Does blood being viscous and thick instead of runny and thin like water mean she can ask me to do whatever she wants and I will not question, will not refuse, I will just do?

I knew one thing without a doubt, she would keep calling until I responded. Better to just meet her, listen to her and then tell her I couldn't do it.

I lower my hand to my side. How did I end up here? About to talk to someone about doing the unthinkable? Before I can raise my hand again, the door is opened. The woman standing in the doorway wears a beige, belted raincoat and has a large black doctor's bag on the floor by her feet while her handbag is hooked over the crook of her arm. She is slender, her long brown hair tied back into a loose bun. Under her coat she wears a navy blue nurse's uniform with the white stripe around the collar. She's a district nurse out on a home visit. Dad had them towards the end, their visits and numbers increased in frequency the closer it got to that final day.

'Hello!' she says. Her smile is wide and bright, friendly and welcoming. I wonder if this is a requirement of being a district nurse – an ability to instantly put people who are going through difficult times at ease. Dad's three nurses were so kind and calming that not even Mum could keep up the high stress levels she was operating on for long. 'Are you the visitor that Soloné has been waiting on?'

'I guess so,' I say.

'She's been beside herself. I don't think I've ever seen her so excited. You must mean a lot to her.'

I offer her a smile in response. If she had any idea who I really was, who my grandmother wanted me to become…

'Can I go through?' I ask.

'Yes. But she's just had some of her medication so you won't be able to stay for too long before she's tired and needs to sleep.'

'Thank you,' I tell her.

'Hello?' I call out when the district nurse, whose name I forgot to ask, has shut the door behind her. 'It's me, Clemency.'

I stand in the hallway, reminded again how lived-in and family-filled their house is, and wait for a reply, an invitation to come into this world that I could have been a part of. A large clock ticks somewhere near, I didn't notice it last time I was here. Wood creaks, the air is unstill, the house seems to shift and move, trying to accommodate the way it is almost empty.

'Hello?' I call again.

I count the ticks: thirty. Thirty until I hear: 'Come, Clemency, come.'

I move to the room I helped my grandmother to, where the door is open. She is practically propped up in the chair by the window. When I came last time I didn't realise how much of an effort she had made to look normal. She reclines in the chair by the window. She is wearing a white nightdress covered in small yellow flowers, and a blue dressing gown, but she seems incredibly frail despite her solid weight. She trembles, too. It is not pronounced or overt, but it is noticeable. Her hair is a wiry white and black, her skin sagging against her features. She looks fragile. The woman I spoke to the other day did not seem fragile.

'You are welcome, Clemency. Please, sit. Sit.'

I hesitate, of course I do. If I go into her room I am allowing myself to become a part of this, I am saying: 'Yes, I might do this thing.' Eventually, though, I sit as I have been asked to do.

'My apologies for not being able to greet you properly at the door.'

'That's fine.'

'Are you keeping well?'

I nod. It depends what she means by well. I was well before I met her and the rest of my family, I am well now that I have met them. I was also troubled before I met them and I am troubled now. I am not unwell though. That is what she means and that is what I nod at.

'How are you?' I ask.

Her face finds a smile that is rueful and amused, it seems she is laughing at me. I suppose it is a stupid question to ask of someone who has brought me here to talk about how to end her life. I don't know how I'm supposed to act, though.

'We do not have much time,' she tells me. 'I must ask you again what I cannot ask anyone else to do. You must help me to die.'

I stare at my grandmother by blood and wait for her to say something else. What she has said is nowhere near enough to get me to agree to do this thing. She stares at me in return, her expression makes it obvious that she won't be saying anything else. She has uttered 'You must help me to die' and that is enough as far as she is concerned.

Does she think that I am so grateful, so happy to be in reunion with my birth family, that I'll do whatever she tells me to do?

'Why must I?' I ask. 'I hardly know you. Why would I?'

'That is the reason I asked you. That is why it has to be you. When Kibibi told me she had found you, I knew that God had answered my prayers. When I met you, I knew it was true. Only you can do this. No one else would do it.'

It seems this woman is saying that all that time she spent watching me the other day told her one thing: I am a killer. 'What are you saying? I try to avoid hurting anyone and anything – I've been vegetarian so many times over the years because I can't stand the thought of what meat really is. Why would you say that to me when you don't know me?'

'I am sorry, Clemency, I forget myself. I am only thinking of myself. I would like so much to get to know you but I do not have much time.'

'Why do you want to... Why?' She doesn't look *that* ill, despite the trembling and the pallor of her skin. She doesn't look like Dad did near the end.

'I am sick, I am old, I am tired.' She says it simply, concisely, and then stops talking.

'What are you sick with?' I ask.

'Talking is difficult,' she says. 'To talk without slurring is very difficult.' She pauses. 'I have a heart condition. It was managed. It *is* managed. Then the diabetes is out of control. It was managed. For many years it was controlled.' She stops again. 'But my heart, the angina. I had an attack and they tell me the diabetes has caused it.' Pause. 'Then my heart, my diabetes. And then I am told the way my arm does not swing when I walk, the seizures, the facial...' another pause '... the facial movements. I have Parkinson's.' Pause. 'I am not going to get better. I will be on drugs for the rest of my life.' Pause. I notice, now she has mentioned it, the tic on the right side of her face. It is only occasional, but it is pronounced. 'I have so many drugs. So many needs. Over time it will be worse.'

I try to remember what Dad said about it. When he had to tell me that it had spread, that the chemo was no longer working. Did he tell me how he felt, or did I guess? I did not want to press him if he did not want to articulate it so I don't think he did tell me. I simply assumed he would feel how I would feel. Although I obviously didn't know how I would feel since it was happening to him and not to me.

'I am no longer in control of my body, of my face, of my life.' She pauses. 'My husband is gone. My children are scattered. My grandchildren who are near have their own lives.' Pause. 'I am not needed. I am a burden.' Pause.

'You are not a burden,' I say. 'No human being is a burden. Never say that.'

'You are the right person to do this.' Pause. 'You value people.'

'Most decent humans value people. And if you know I value people, then how could you ask this thing of me?'

'How I am today is the best I will feel for the rest of my life.'

'That doesn't mean you should end your life.'

'If I am not a burden now, I will soon become one.'

'Please...'

'At some point, very soon, I will not be able to do anything for myself.' Pause. 'I will need help with everything. I do not want to burden others with that.'

This was what it was like with Dad, of course. But I did not mind. Mum did not mind. He seemed to mind, he did not like not being able to help himself, take care of himself. That he needed help to do the most basic things from washing his face to going to the toilet. From the little I know of people, and the even smaller amount of info I have about this woman, that level of dependency would be awful. Loss of dignity, people call it.

I stare at the woman facing this loss of dignity, and sadness overcomes me. Her pride, her need to not lose face in front of other people, even the people who cared for her, made her want to give up on life. She would rather be away from other people than be 'weak' in front of them.

'You do not understand,' she states.

'To be honest, no, I don't, not completely. Part of me understands, of course, and I'm sort of impressed that you seem so determined to do this. On the other hand, no, I don't understand. Your family would be heartbroken without you.'

She laughs quietly, the tic on her face suddenly moving rapidly before settling again. 'You are my family, too, Clemency.' A pause. More laughter. 'Did you forget that?'

'But not like the others,' I say.

'My dear, you do not want to be like the others.'

The look that had passed between my other mother and my grandmother comes to mind, the mutual dislike, the overt signs of a power struggle. What would that be like? How would I feel being looked after, having my intimate needs taken care of, by someone I didn't like. A coldness slips through me and settles in my stomach at the thought of having to ask my cousin Nancy to fetch me a bedpan or even remember when to bring me my medication. Seeing that look on her face, experiencing the weight of her disgust and dislike, making myself vulnerable to her so I can simply survive. I wasn't sure what the source of the animosity was between my birth grandmother and birth mother but it would not be a sustainable situation: looking after someone you hated, being cared for by someone who resented you.

'My biggest worry.' Pause. 'Is another attack.' Pause. 'That renders me.' Pause. 'Helpless.' Pause. 'Locked in. No way out.'

That sounds a bit like my terror of being buried alive, trying and failing to claw my way out of a coffin, knowing I'm trapped under a ton of dirt. I know my terror, which borders on a phobia, is mostly irrational, hers isn't. Because, not only is the confined space her own body, it is also a perfectly rational worry with what is slowly and insidiously happening to her health. Involuntarily, I shudder at the idea of mentally trying to claw my way out of my own body, knowing I'd never be able to. Knowing the only way out is . . .

'Thing is, how am I supposed to do it?' I say to her. I can understand a bit better where she is coming from, but that doesn't mean I can do what she wants. There are a million trillion miles of road between understanding why she might want this and actually doing it. 'I mean, do you expect me to put a pillow over your face or something?' I freeze for a moment at the thought of it. 'I wouldn't be able to do that. Or anything like that. It's simply not in me.'

'When you tell me you will help.' Pause. 'I will tell you what to do.'

'So you will do it? I only have to help you?' That may not be so bad if I don't have to actually do it.

She raises her hands from her lap and the tremors, which do not seem so pronounced in her body, are shockingly violent in her hands. She lowers them again. 'I cannot.'

I would have to do it. I would have to kill her. I know I'm supposed to call it 'helping her to die', aiding her in 'fulfilling her final wish', 'being merciful'. In truth, though, I would be killing her. Ending her life. It would be what she wanted, but it would not alter the facts of what I had done. And I would still be arrested if the police found out what I had done. I would still be ostracised by the family I have only just found if they discovered what I had done.

My birth grandmother, a woman I have met for a total of about three hours, would like to make a killer of me with herself as my first victim.

She moves suddenly forwards, a violent jerk that causes my heart to lurch. I move towards her, immediately desperate to help. I could look after her, I think. I could look after her and then she might not want to do this. 'No,' she says firmly.

She struggles and pushes against the arms of the chair until she is upright. I stand too, ready to catch her if she should fall. Ready if she needs me. This sort of thing I can do, this sort of help I have no problem with.

She moves forward, reaching her hands out towards the high dresser with five drawers beside her bed, even though it is at least three strides' distance from where she is. I do not attempt to help her again, I simply wait for her to move, poised to help. She stumbles, but manages to shuffle and jerk forwards, aiming for her bed, I guess. It would be easier if I helped, but I can see the lines of defiance and pride that are set in her face.

As she reaches the dresser she stumbles again, more severely this time and her fingers, groping blindly for the bevelled edge of the dresser, slip away and she falls forwards, her body hitting the dresser, dislodging most of the neatly lined-up medication. I catch her before she stumbles backwards and falls to the ground. She is unexpectedly heavy, a veritable dead weight in my arms, and I stumble, too, but manage to keep my balance.

'Let me go!' she orders.

I resist the urge to do as I'm told and instead, with my arms hooked under her arms, I move her to the bed and allow her to place her hands on it then lower herself into a seated position.

'I did not need your help,' she barks at me.

I bet you're a treat to look after, I think.

'You must leave,' she says. 'I will call you.'

Lucky me, I think. I hide my face by dropping to my knees, gathering up the containers littering the floor by her bed like I am gathering pebbles on the beach to use as inspiration for my jewellery. 'Right, fine,' I say. The names of the drugs run idly through my head as I line them up as neatly as I can. There is no way I can begin to know if they were in order of consumption, and if they were, which is the right order to stack them, so I don't even try.

Besides, I have been dismissed. It's probably best to leave as soon as possible. 'You think.' Pause. 'Promise me.' Pause. 'You will think.'

'I will,' I say. 'But I don't know you. This is something you can't ask a virtual stranger to do.'

'We do not have much time...my illnesses make it difficult... but would you like to get to know me?'

More than anything, I think. I didn't realise how needy I could be until this moment. 'Even if I did, that doesn't mean I'd be able to do this thing.'

'I know, Clemency, I know...But come back to see me...for a short time, we can talk...And you can tell me about your-self...about your life.'

'You want to know about me?'

'Of course.'

I shrug. 'OK.'

'And you must promise to at least think about my request.'

'I...I...I promise. To think about it. Nothing more.'

'I do not need any more than for you to think.'

'OK, I will think.'

The woman in front of me eases herself backwards, seemingly stronger than she was a second ago. A fleeting thought dances across my mind: *Was she putting on that show to get me to do what she wants?*

Of course she wasn't. Who would do that sort of thing?

'Goodbye then,' I say. I am standing at the door.

'Goodbye,' she says. 'I look forward to seeing you again.'

I leave the house with the memory of her smile, something that seemed painful for her to do, and a deep sense of unease that not only am I keeping things from Mum, I'm going to be keeping my meetings with my grandmother secret, and she is expecting me to do it. Whatever I say, whatever I promise to think about, whatever I know deep down inside that I can't do, she is expecting me to become her killer.

33

Smitty

'Can I see your jewellery?' I ask her.

We don't have much time together, only the thirty or so minutes between the district nurse leaving and my other mother returning with Lily-Rose from school. My grandmother told me that my other mother often took Lily to the library on the way home or sometimes to run around in the park, but the thought of her catching us together was a risk I didn't want to take. My other mother still hadn't called me to arrange another meeting and I didn't want to impose myself upon her. It was nice to be with someone, like my grandmother, who made it clear she *wanted* to be with me. I wasn't stupid, though – I knew what motivated her interest in me, but that didn't matter because even if it was for snatches of time, it would be nice to get to know a little bit about her.

'Of course, of course.' She moves to indicate the chest of drawers where her medication is stored, but the shaking in her hand is so pronounced and severe she stares at it as though it is not connected to her body, like she has never seen it before. The horror seems to dawn on her anew that this is her body, her arm she has lost control of, and then grief unfolds carefully and precisely on her features as she seems to mourn what this means for her body and her life. I avert my eyes – I do not want her to know that I have noticed her distress at what is happening to her. It is private, not something I should be a part of, no matter what she has asked me to do.

'The bottom drawer,' she says quietly, her upset like a thin paint wash that covers her words – there but not immediately obvious. Still there though, still an indicator of what she is truly feeling.

The district nurse had given me a huge smile on her way out, nodded as though she approved of my visit – and I could see why when I entered the bedroom – my grandmother had seemed pleased to see me, lighter and freer somehow. Relieved, too, I'd imagine.

As I lower myself to the bottom drawer, without intending to, I pause to look at the medication on top of the cabinet: some of the tablets and capsules are distorted behind the colour and curve of the glass and look like the little jars I keep beads in. I know what ails her, but what are all these tablets actually for? How do they alleviate the pain she is in? *Do* they alleviate the pain she is in? If they do, there would be no reason for her to be contemplating what she is, surely?

From the bottom drawer I remove a heavy, large, shallow, lidded box that is a pale beige, the thickness of the butterfly box I once slept in, but not decorated like that one. 'This?' I ask. I hold it up and she nods slowly. Her tremors seem worse today, her face tired and agonised at the same time. I should not stay here too long, but I need to get to know her if I am going to think seriously about what she asked me to do.

'Yes,' she says.

I place the box on the floor by the bed so she can see it, and sit cross-legged in front of it. For some reason, the idea of taking photos of this stuff seems unsavoury as though I am planning to kill her for it. I want to see it, though, because jewellery is how I get to know people.

'You are a true Zebila,' she says suddenly. Although her tremors are more pronounced and have destabilised her mood, she seems able to talk more clearly and fluently today. Maybe that is how it works, with the conditions she has – some days your body, beyond the basic necessities for survival, will concentrate on being able to do one thing.

'What do you mean?' I ask. *Has Abi shown her the DNA test results?* The idea of that panics me, makes me think that after everything they still didn't believe I was one of them.

'When Abimbola said you made jewellery, my heart soared. We are from a gold family. Your grandfather's great-great-grandfather was one of the first Nihanarans to own a gold mine. The Europeans tried to trick him out of it and then with later generations they tried to steal it from our family, but it never worked. It has been passed down through our family until now. My eldest son, Douglas, he is in Nihanara, he runs the family business.' She rests back on her mountain of pillows. 'You are the first one to work with the family metal.'

I don't make much gold jewellery from scratch because it is expensive and not worth having unless it is pure, but I do relove a fair amount of it since once someone has a piece made from gold they're often loath to part with it.

'That is something that makes you special in this family,' my grandmother says. Considering she didn't even see me after I was born, she is laying it on a bit thick – but I don't mind. It's a way of getting to know her; finding out what she is really like. What she is really like is that she over-eggs the pudding because she thinks it will get me to do what she wants. Which shows how little she knows about me.

I open the box and inside there is a universe of wonder. It's almost as though someone has created my fantasy world inside this box. That was why it was so heavy, there is so much inside, and it is disorganised and meshed together, and like something from my very best dreams. I'm not sure where to begin – I have to unravel pieces from each other, which adds to the excitement building inside me. Having to do this starts the reloving process: I can see what different shapes the item can be twisted into, shaped and made. How it can look next to different materials, jewels and other stones and precious items.

The first piece I reach for is a thick link bracelet, heavy because each link is solid, eighteen-carat yellow gold. It'd be impossible to wear for any length of time – male or female – without developing wrist ache. I run my fingers over the flattened top and bottom of the bracelet. They are smooth and cool to my initial touch, leavened to allow them to rest flat against the wrist. 'Is this yours?' I ask.

'Yes. Julius's father gave it to me when we were courting in Nihanara. He did not realise that it was a man's bracelet.' My grandmother chortles, quietly, the most she can manage, I guess, and the laughter she is able to produce livens her face. It tells me she must have been so in love with my grandfather, the way she laughs at the thought of him. 'He had no idea. It was far too heavy, too thick.' If I was to relove this item, I would take it apart, break it down to its tiny component links and then remake several items to suit the owner. I usually start with the person, but in this case, it would need to be broken down and rebuilt.

'Tell me a story about you. Something that no one else knows,' I say to her. 'Not about the jewellery, anything about you.'

She seems to go away to another place while she thinks about this. Her body tremors, her face twitches violently on her right cheekbone, but her eyes are still and steady as she contemplates what it is she does not mind me knowing that no one else knows. 'Your grandfather, he was called Ivor, too, he was not the first man to win my heart,' she confesses. 'There was another boy who...he was from another family in the same city. We had grown up together. I met him at school. The three of us, we were friends but it was clear to me as we moved through our years who I was to marry.'

A shiver of recognition shimmers through me – it sounds like the situation I was in with Dylan and Seth. My grandfather was her Seth – not the first to win her heart, but the one she realised she loved and wanted to be with forever. I stop myself there, prevent myself from remembering where that eventually led.

'Didn't the other boy love you enough?' I asked. Or was it like with Dylan and me – did she finally stop loving him when she realised how uninterested he was in anything except keeping her dangling on a line for when he needed an ego boost or an unchaste Christmas kiss.

My grandmother frowns at me as though I am being ridiculous at the very idea that someone wouldn't love her enough. 'Not at all. They were both in love with me.' It must be nice to have that certainty of how other people feel about you.

'If you loved him, he loved you, and he was the man you were meant to marry, then why didn't you?'

'He was not the man who I was meant to marry. Ivor was.' I must look confused. 'Ivor Zebila was from a decent family. They had status and wealth.'

'The other boy didn't?'

'He was nice, he had some wealth, but he was not a Zebila. Everyone knew of the Zebilas. They were respected and coveted.'

'That was important to you?' Status, wealth, power. Everything done for show.

'When you grow up with very little, you learn what is important and necessary to have in life. Their parents could both afford the school, my parents had to work long and hard to make enough money to send me, the eldest of their six daughters, to school. I knew what was important, what I had to do for my family.'

So not like Seth, Dylan and me at all, really. I know nothing of what it must have been like to be in love with someone but to do your duty and marry someone else because it will mean your family is taken care of, your sisters will be able to go to school and your parents will not have to work so hard.

It still rankles, though, that she would choose money, wealth and status over love. She is doing a very good job of removing any images I might have had in my head of her being a fluffy grandmother, ill and sickly, who is coming to the end of a life lived with and filled by love. She is showing me she will do whatever it takes to get what she wants.

'Did you love my grandfather?'

'Of course. I grew to love him over the years, very much. He chose me because he knew I would make a good wife, I would improve the standing of their family by giving him strong children. You asked me to tell you something that no one knew and that was it. Are you disappointed?'

'No, no, just surprised at how candid you are.'

'I see.'

I look down at the bracelet again. I would struggle to remake this piece even if I had broken it down. It would need to be completely melted to start again. Or maybe ... I pick it up again. If I were to reshape one of the links into a circle, I could make it into a flower pendant. Solder the different links on to the circle. Or maybe the links laid out in a seemingly random pattern, linked into an asymmetric chainmail design, that would sit across the chest. It would be heavy but, like the other design, showy, large, unmissable. This is what she would like – the outward appearance of wealth. I move the links, see how they look next to each other.

'Would you like to take that?' Mrs Zebila asks.

'Pardon?' I realise what she is talking about. 'No, no. Thank you, but no. I'm curious. I love looking at jewellery, it's one of my favourite things to do. Which is why this collecton is simply amazing to me.' Carefully, I lay the bracelet back in the box.

'I insist you have it.'

'No, I have no use for it. I don't keep things I don't need or don't fit into my life.'

Silence passes between us because I'm not sure what either of us is meant to say to my unintentional reminder of who I am. Instead of speaking, I place the lid back on the box. 'I think I'd better go.'

'You will come back tomorrow?' she asks eagerly.

'Do you want me to?'

'Yes, of course. Clemency, it is such a pleasure to see you.'

I know she wants something, but it's nice to hear. 'I'll come back tomorrow then.'

34

Abi

To: Jonas Zebila
From: Abi Zebila
Subject: Is it me?
Thursday, 16 July 2015

Dear J,

So here we are. Two weeks later and *nada*. I've had daily texts from her saying hello and asking how we are, but nothing more. No asking to meet up or to talk on the phone, nothing.

Clearly she's keeping us at arm's length. Declan – yes, I finally told him everything – reckons it's to do with Gran. But he would say that, seeing as he's terrified of her. We're all on a knife-edge in the house, except Lily-Rose who asks to see the photos again and again because she's fascinated by having so many photos of this woman who is her aunt once being as small as her. She's not that close to Declan's sisters, mainly because Declan won't spend that much time with them. Not sure why, but you know what? My family's F'd up enough, he's not forthcoming on sharing that with me.

I hear Mummy and Daddy talking sometimes in the middle of the night, and, you know, they can't seem to get over this barrier between them and say what they really feel. I mean, if I had the child I hadn't seen in nearly forty years walk into my life, I'd be talking with the only other person who'd understand how I felt. They can't seem to do that. They're a lot nicer to each other nowadays, and there's far less of an atmosphere, but they don't talk.

Declan and I talk all the time even when we're not living together. He's actually been really supportive during all this, and I wish I didn't have that fear of being with him all the time. If I start to rely on him, will he let me down again? I know it was years ago, but I'm sort of waiting for him to do it again.

Maybe that's what Mummy and Daddy are thinking. That if they talk, they have to go over what happened, and why they did it, and what it means about them. Because I can't imagine what's going through their heads.

Ivor is on another planet. I don't know what his f-ing problem is, but he's been saying stuff about Clemency being a con artist. He never says it in front of Mummy and Daddy, but if it's just me and him, he'll make some comment about how we're such a trusting family and how she could be from anywhere. I've told him to tell that to Mummy and Daddy if he truly believes that – funnily enough, he won't.

I wonder if Declan is right and this is all down to Gran – Clemency did look like she'd seen a ghost when she came out of Gran's room. Maybe Gran told her to back off? But she wouldn't do that, would she? Look who I'm asking!!! Gran cried with the rest of us, though, so I'm not sure why she'd warn Clemency off.

Thing is, Gran's not always rational these days. That's a realisation I'm coming to accept. She isn't making sense a lot of the time, she forgets things, she becomes incredibly angry if you point out something contradictory. On top of the other stuff wrong with her, I'm not surprised Mummy wants to get her proper, specialist care from people who can tend to her needs around the clock, give her meds at the right times in the right doses. Also, sometimes it's a struggle to get her to take the meds. She doesn't want to, doesn't like the side effects, wants to skip some in case they're what's making her ill.

I've said to Daddy that I'd get her a nice room at our place, I could work out a good deal, I'd see her almost every day, there are nurses who are trained to deal with people who aren't handling their long-term illnesses very well. When I mentioned it at dinner, after Lily-Rose was in bed, Daddy got really angry. 'That's not how we deal with problems in this family,' he said. We were all sitting there and he raised his voice.

'We find a way to take care of family members, we don't move them out and abandon them at the first sign of trouble.'

None of us said anything and even Ivor looked uncomfortable. It took Daddy a couple of minutes to realise what he'd said in the light of all the recent revelations and he seemed very embarrassed and ashamed. Maybe that's what the problem is, why he and Mummy can't talk – they're ashamed of what they did. Not that I think they'd ever admit it to anyone – not even each other. Kind of ended the discussion about what next for Gran, though.

Why doesn't Clemency call? Things got so much better at home after she arrived, and now we're all in this limbo of waiting for her to get in touch again. I miss her. I miss you.

Lots of love,
Abi
xxxx

35

Smitty

Her jewellery box is like nothing I've ever been through. I thought Mrs Lehtinen's was incredible but my grandmother's is out of this world. I want to run my fingers through it, feel the different textures dribble through my fingers. I have been to see her on ten of the past fourteen days. Sometimes she has had to struggle to the door, because it is not a day when she is visited by the district nurse, and I have sensed her mortification at being helped back to bed.

My guilt at not being in touch properly with Abi grows every day, but my visits are not just so I can get to know my grandmother, but also for Abi and the rest of her family, too. It might not be much, spending time with my grandmother to get to know her, seeing if I can stop her thinking about what she wants to do, but if I get this right they'll never even know what she was planning. And they will have their grandmother, mother, mother-in-law – whatever role she plays in their life – around for as long as possible. I know she thinks I have been doing this to steel myself to be able to do it, but in reality I want her to see that life is worth living. I am being selfish, yes, but like I wanted Dad around as long as possible (and he wanted to stay as long as possible), I want my grandmother around as long as possible, too.

I have looked through her jewellery – every piece is real – and she has told stories related to every item. The multi-strand pearl choker and matching bracelet that she wore to meet the President of Nihanara at the Nihanara High Commission in London when my grandfather, Ivor, was still alive: 'I wore traditional Nihanara dress in a royal blue silk. Ivor had it made for me.'

The gold and emerald necklace – each of the twelve emeralds the size of a penny – that she was given by her husband after she had her first son, Douglas: 'He was so proud I had given him a son that he spent far too much money on that necklace. I had nowhere to wear it, of course.' Then there were the large, twenty-pence-sized diamond earrings that she wore to my birth father's graduation from law school: 'It was one of the proudest days of my life.' The lily-shaped brooch studded with rubies and sapphires that she had worn to my brother Ivor's graduation from university: 'Another of the proudest days of my life.'

I had brought some dividers from my workshop and put them in the jewellery box – on the days she could barely speak, I would go through it all, untangling what I could and organising them into categories and colours. On the days she couldn't speak, I would simply go through the jewellery and make up stories about the items I found – the white gold tennis bracelet, the plaited white gold and yellow gold necklace, the diamond-studded cuff (which seemed quite radical for someone as conservative as her) – as I might have done if I'd had access to the box as a child. The days she could speak, she would try to give me whichever piece of jewellery I had been looking at and I would always have to say no.

On the eleventh day, when I did not want to pore through her jewellery any more, listening to the stories that came with each piece, I sat and looked at her. She seemed better, stronger. Maybe this is what she needs: someone to look after her, spend time with her, rather than simply feeding her, medicating her, ensuring her basic needs are met. I could be that person. Or I could try. I could fit in these visits around my work, which would bond us and would allow her to think that maybe carrying on for a little longer may not be so bad. They are only snatches of time that I have spent with her, but with her jewellery and her stories, I feel like I have got to know her a little better, I can see her as my grandmother rather than simply the woman who gave birth to the man who impregnated my birth mother. I have a sense of what she is like, but that doesn't bother me. Maybe if I did spend more time with her, if I did listen to her worries, she might come to realise that carrying on for a little longer need not be so bad. I am being arrogant, I suppose, arrogant and selfish, but I have developed a kind of grudging admiration for who she is, how uncompromising she has been throughout her life. I like her in the way I would possibly like my cousin Nancy if Nancy hadn't spent what felt like her every waking moment trying to destroy me. My grandmother may not be likeable or to everyone's taste, but I have found myself enjoying the time I have spent with her these past couple of weeks. It's been at the expense of seeing Abi, who I would love to spend time with, but this has been necessary and far more urgent.

'I am not scared of dying,' my grandmother says to me, as though we are in the middle of a conversation.

I nod at her, I feel she has more to say. Today is a day when she can speak with long gaps to gather herself. And I think she can sense that today is the day where we have reached a crossroads with this arrangement. It's been miraculous that it has lasted this long without us being caught out, and it can't continue.

'You asked me to tell you something about myself that no one knows,' she continues. 'I am not scared of dying. I am scared of merely existing.'

'But haven't you felt better this past little while? You seem better.'

'I am existing. Not living. I am counting down time until the end.'

'But if you got involved in more things, found stuff that you enjoyed doing, you might not feel like that,' I say.

She lifts her arms, reminds me of the quaking in her hands – the way she is not in control of herself. The way that even if she does find something she enjoys it would have to be suitable for her needs.

'Clemency, I am not scared of dying. I am scared of being locked into this body, unable to escape, unable to tell anyone to let me go.'

That horrific image of being trapped inside myself – unable to move, to speak, to let anyone know how much I still understand and feel – sends chilling vibrations through me and reminds me again of that terror of mine of being trapped and having to claw my way out of anywhere, but to have my prison be my own body . . . I shudder again.

'You could leave a living will, a do not resuscitate order? Tell people now that's what you want.' Doing that would be better than what she is asking of me. I am not a person who is impressed by money and position, like my grandmother is, we have very little common ground, but she is still a part of my family I have only recently found. I do not want to have to live with the memory of her death when I have only had a glimpse of her life.

'Yes, I could,' she says sadly, disappointed that I've even suggested this when it feels like a suitable middle ground.

'Why isn't that a good option?' I ask.

'My illnesses, they have taken over my body, I am at their mercy . . . I can be sure of nothing but the knowledge that when this disease is good and ready it will take me . . . I do not want to leave this to chance . . . I do not want to linger . . . I want the chance to choose. My one last decision that my illnesses cannot take away from me.'

I know what she is saying because these past few days I have learnt she has a need to be back in control, in even the smallest way possible. But it still feels so wrong, wanting me to do this. 'Why didn't you see me when I was born?' I ask. This still niggles at me. She wants me to do something so huge for her, but she did not want to see me when I first came into existence. And, in some ways, it feels like she only wants to see me now because she wants something from me – if she did not need me, I would not exist for her.

She stares at me, gathering herself to produce a chunk of speech that is coherent and fluent, not halted and slurred. 'I was a proud woman. I wanted to see you, my first grandchild, but . . . I was scared of what people would say. I was worried about what our family would look like. An unmarried young girl is suddenly with child months after moving into my home. I thought people would believe that my husband, not Julius, was responsible. Most of all, I did not see you because Julius . . . he was not ready for the responsibility. He was too young.'

He shouldn't have had sex then, crosses rather uncharitably through my mind. When I started having sex at fifteen, I wasn't ready to be a parent. I probably would have done it if it was necessary but I wouldn't have been ready for it.

'Did he want to keep me?' I ask her.

She manages to pull her twitching face into a smile. 'You do not want to know the answer to that question,' she replies.

'I do, I really do.'

'Clemency. . . . I do not know you well. I wish I did not have this clock above my head that will stop me from getting to know you. I would like the time to know you, so I could explain the answer to that question. But even if my body lives on, locked in or not, my mind will not allow me to know you more than this. This is the most well I will ever feel again. This is the most I will ever get to know you. I will never know you enough to explain.'

That causes tears to spring into my eyes and my stomach swirl with a fluttering of ice butterflies. No matter how much time I spend with her, this is the most she will ever get to know me.

'I am grateful I have lived long enough to meet you. I wish I had not been so proud. I wish I had more time.'

'I don't know what to say,' I confess when I have gathered myself together.

'Say you will think about what I have asked of you,' she says. 'I am not scared of dying, remember that. I am scared of merely existing. Say you promise you will think about what I have asked of you.'

I sigh deeply, take a deep breath to replace the air my sigh has stolen. This time, I know when I say it, I will mean it – I will be doing nothing but thinking about it. 'I promise,' I state.

36

Smitty

In my nightmares, things happen to me and I am powerless to stop them. I can usually see what is about to happen, how things are going to turn out, but I can't change the outcome. I am usually too shocked or too frightened to fight back or even to speak.

This is one of my nightmare moments. Except I am wide awake.

I have wandered back from my workshop, my head full of how to negotiate a lower price for the latest quote for Melissa's locket to become a watch because it is astronomical. Even if I didn't charge her for my work it would be too much. I have also had another call from Mrs Lehtinen, wanting me to come back and show her some design ideas. I'm sure she just wants an update on whether I am the girl in the butterfly box. I have five wedding rings to make as well as a twenty-first-birthday pendant to design for the world's most picky mother. As I walked home – no Tyler in Beached Heads, I noticed – I dreamed of a sit-down, followed by a long hot shower.

I was tired, but I was enjoying the haze of work, the fug that I have been constantly carrying with me, because it stopped me thinking about the other stuff. A distance away from home, I clocked the outlines of a woman and a young girl on the bench nearest my block of flats. The woman wasn't simply sitting on the bench, she was reclining on it with her shorts-exposed legs stretched out in front of her. Sunglasses adorned her face, and the wind teased her hair while she intently read from the mobile in her left hand. Her right hand she used to brush her hair out of her face, twirling the ends of random locks around her fingers. The girl, her head surrounded by blonde ringlets, was dancing and singing around the bench, putting on a show for the uninterested woman she is performing for.

I was in a haze, my head in the clouds, and it took a moment for me to get here, to this moment. This moment where I register that I am in a nightmare situation because the person on the bench is the monster from almost every single bad dream I have ever had.

This moment, when I realise what is unfolding in front of me, is like that other moment in a nightmare where I try to stop running, but my feet slip and slide and I can't stop because I'm in motion, my body is propelling me forwards, closer and closer towards the monster. But the fear and horror I feel makes me reek, and the monster catches my scent, stops what it is doing and looks up, away from its mobile, in my direction. I can't stop, I have nowhere to run to, because the monster has seen me, and it takes its sunglasses off, lowers its mobile and smiles at me before it trills, 'Hi!'

She is shrill when she longs to be husky, sexy, the stuff of men's wet dreams. 'We just happened to be in the area.'

'Auntie Smitty!' Sienna squeals. She hurtles across the distance, squealing my name as she runs. 'Auntie Smitty! Auntie Smitty! Auntie Smitty!'

At speed she collides with my legs and I almost topple backwards but manage to keep upright. She wraps her arms around me like she is a koala and I am the trunk of a tree. Slowly, I lower myself to her height and wrap my arms around her. 'You must have grown about eight foot,' I say to her, but I can't take my eyes off the reclining monster that is smiling on the bench.

My cousin Nancy has a really successful website. Everyone seems to love it. It's called Guide To Femininity and it's all about how to be feminine in the face of a world where, apparently, we women have forgotten how. She actually makes a living from it now because for the last six months or so, since there's been a change in content and focus, her blog has received some critically acclaimed attention and people have been falling over themselves to advertise on it and sponsor it and have her give advice in their publications. There's even been talk of a book deal, which will take her profile to the next level, although that's not materialised yet because she's still at the stage of considering her options.

Nancy is not my 'real' cousin. We're not connected by flesh and blood. She's my mother's brother's daughter. And she's brunette. And white. And nothing at all like me. We grew up together, saw each other almost every day because we went to the same school and stuff, but we're not 'real' cousins. She tells that to anyone she meets. I never say things like that because, to me, it's not relevant, but to Nancy it's probably the most important thing there is about our connection. We are not 'real' cousins.

With Nancy, April 1986, Otley

'Why aren't I your "real" cousin?' I asked her. I was genuinely confused. What wasn't real about me? My dad said the stuff on telly wasn't real, that monsters that live under your bed weren't real, that a lot of the storybooks I liked didn't have 'real' stories but I was real, I thought. I could touch myself, I could see myself in the mirror, I ate real food and I drank real drinks, and I slept in a real bed and wore real clothes. Why wasn't I real to Nancy?

'You're just not. That's what Dad says. You're not my real cousin. He said Auntie Heather could pretend all she likes but you're not a real member of the family. It's just the way it is.'

'I am real, I am,' I said.

'No, you're not. You really, really are not.'

Sienna is holding up my hand so she can use me as the axis for her pirouettes. Last time I saw her she was trying to perfect this move. She is effortlessly expert now: with a slight bounce she is up on to the rubber toe of her pink DMs, the flat of her other foot rests on her inner knee, her arm is up, clinging on to my hand, and spin, spin, spin. She's a red-blue-blonde blur as she spins herself three times without pause. 'Mum says we're going to stay with you for a long time,' she informs me as she spins. 'I might even go to school here.' Spin. 'That's right, isn't it, Mum?'

'*Nancy*,' my cousin hisses to correct her. Nancy's daughter is meant to call her 'Nancy' instead of 'Mum' because any woman who has a child needs to reclaim her femininity by retaining her given name at all times. This means even having your offspring call you by your name to prevent you from being seen as 'just' a mother. If I had a child, which I don't so maybe what I think isn't relevant, I would want them to call me 'Mum' no matter what it did to my femininity because they're the only person/people in the whole world who could call me that. I'd savour that as the rare and precious gem it was... but maybe that's just childless me. 'And no, that's not what I said,' Nancy says to her daughter.

She revolves to face me, switches on the beseeching eyes and winning smile, forgetting it is me she is talking to, not Mum. 'I said that we'd come to see her Auntie Clem and if she had space we'd ask if we could stay for a little while because we can't really afford a holiday this year.'

Sienna stops her spinning, cocks her head to one side, gives her mother a Paddington Hard Stare that would put to shame not only Mr Wallace the sweaty-palmed estate agent but also the bear after which the look is named. 'You did say that,' Sienna tells her. 'You really did.' She turns to me, the PHS gone. 'Do you have space?'

'Erm, I'm not sure,' I say. An outright no to this child is never possible.

'Where's Grandma Heather?' Sienna asks. She has no issues with blood connections and being real – everyone is related to her if they talk to her long enough. 'We rang the doorbell and Grandma Heather didn't answer. Mum said we had to leave so early this morning and get Grandma Heather to let us in while you were at work so we'd be sitting drinking tea waiting for you to come back from work.'

'I'm sure I didn't say it like that.'

Her daughter gives her the side-eye. 'Yes, you did, Mum.'

'Nancy. Call me Nancy.' Sienna never does call her Nancy because, I suspect, she thinks it's stupid.

'You said it'd be harder for Auntie Smitty to get us out if we had our feet under the table by the time she saw us.'

'I think you misunderstood.' Nancy grins at me, pushes her sunglasses on to the top of her head, checks her phone and then reholsters it in the back pocket of her shorts like it's a gun. I think Nancy would cease to exist if she was ever parted from her phone, and all the stuff – the internet, social media, her website/blog – that is wrapped up inside the phone like a swaddled baby in a manger. 'She's so funny. You must remember how funny she is.'

I keep my attention on Sienna. 'My mum is probably out on her bike.'

'Grandma Heather has a bike. True, true?' Sienna asks.

'More of a trike. But yes, true, true. She goes out most days on it. She's got a little basket on the front for her packed lunch and she goes off exploring.'

'You are not serious!' Nancy exclaims. 'I just can't imagine your mum doing that.'

My gaze returns to my cousin for a moment, before it moves on to the sea behind her. I can't let them stay. Much as I'd love to spend time with Sienna, I can't even let them into my flat. If they cross the threshold they will not leave again. Nancy will do what she always does and convince Mum that they deserve to be living there, and that Nancy is entitled to my bedroom while I am relegated to the box room with the single bed and worst views in the flat. If I let them into my flat I will have let Nancy get away with what she's done. Again. Not just this last time but all the times over all the years.

'Auntie Smitty,' Sienna says, tugging on my jacket.

'Yes?'

She uses her hand to indicate she wants me to come closer to her. Obligingly, I bend to her height. 'I need the toilet,' she whispers into my ear. 'Right. Now.'

I straighten up. Nancy gives me a small shrug of helplessness.

Well, that's that then.

With Nancy, July 2009, Karina's Jewels, Leeds

The shop was empty and I was running a cloth over the glass cases for something to do in the lull. Business had been slow lately and I'd been waiting for Karina to give me the go ahead to make some new pieces. She was still considering my proposals because she wasn't convinced they made good business sense. They did. I was only planning on doing more of what had been selling but she was still vacillating.

It was a blessed relief to have the bell ting as someone entered the shop. The relief lasted less than ten seconds. Nancy, wearing hot pants, vest top and jewelled flip-flops, walked in and grinned at me. Nowadays, if I saw her away from family occasions it was because she had to deliver some bad news.

'Hi,' she said shyly.

'Hi,' I replied.

'I have some news,' she said. She bit her lower lip nervously, lowered her eyes and took several deep breaths. 'I'm just going to tell you, if that's OK?'

I nodded and braced myself, waited to hear what it was.

'I'm pregnant,' she said. She patted her stomach. 'Three months but I'm not really showing yet. Probably because of how super-fit my body is.'

'That's amazing news!' I squealed. I went forwards, hugged her. I hadn't hugged Nancy in years, I would rather hug a giant sewer rat normally (I have a rat phobia), but this was different. This was the sort of news you were always happy about if they were happy. 'Congratulations!'

'Thanks, Clem,' she said. She stood back. 'I wanted to tell you myself because I wasn't sure how upset you'd be.'

'Upset? Why would I be upset?'

She lowered her eyes, stared at the ground for a few seconds. It was the perfect amount of time for her to know she'd destabilised and worried me, and the right amount of time for me to plant my feet firmly on the ground so I wouldn't fall over at whatever revelation was coming next.

'The father ... You have to understand that he wanted to tell you himself, but I said I'd do it.' *I wanted to see your face, to experience your pain*, she added silently. I braced myself to hear Seth's name. To discover that he had succumbed. 'It's Dylan.'

'Dylan? Dylan,' I repeated. '*My* Dylan?'

She nodded.

I took a step back. My Dylan had got her pregnant. He would never take that next step with me, he would never cross that friendship barrier and do more than kiss me to wind up Seth, but he'd knocked *her* up. My feelings for him had evaporated long before I fell for Seth, but this was still a blow. 'But…when…' My voice failed me. It couldn't be true. I kept all such people away from Nancy because she always made a play for them, always tried to get one over on me. Seth was the absolute love of my life. *Now*. But I had to admit a small patch of my heart, an area so small it was barely there at all, lived forever as that eighteen-year-old girl who fell in proper love for the first time ever with Dylan.

'Remember Seth's party a few years back?' Nancy had the reaction she wanted with that revelation, she could discard that faked humbleness and revel in twisting the knife. My pain was like oxygen to her sometimes. I never knew why. 'I know I gatecrashed, but we got talking. I went over to Sheffield to see him and one thing led to another.'

Seth's party was back in 2003. 'Six years ago? You've been sleeping with him for six years?' *And he never mentioned it? Not possible.*

She nodded. 'Well, it fizzled out for a bit. I ran into him a few months ago and we discovered that we still had feelings for each other so, you know, one thing led to another again. We didn't want to hurt you so thought we'd keep it a secret.'

She had slept with Dylan only a handful of times at the most. I knew how Nancy twisted things; she wasn't outright lying because she knew I could check with Dylan and he would tell me the truth if questioned. What she was saying was this: she'd gone to see him and they'd fucked once. To have travelled all that way she must have really liked him but of course, Dylan being Dylan, he wasn't interested so she gathered up her dignity, as tattered as it was, and walked away. Six years later she crosses paths with him again, they hook up again. This time she's sure it'll work out differently, that over time his heart would have grown fonder for her, because her heart has certainly grown fonder for him, and being older, she thinks that maybe he'll be ready to settle down with her. But it doesn't work out like that. So the next couple of times they hook up, she plans to find a way to tie him to her. She probably thought a pregnancy scare would be enough to bond them, to maybe get him to consider how life wouldn't be so terrible if they were forever linked. But obviously that didn't work out and the scare became a reality. And he obviously hadn't reacted positively, because if he had, or if they'd been truly dating, she would have told me with him standing beside her. This, *this* was just a brief, not-even-long-enough-to-become-sordid fling. And he had done that. Knowing who she was, he had done that.

'That's even more brilliant news,' I said. I wrenched a smile across my face, staple-gunned it into place and yanked my arms up, moved my body forwards to give her another hug. 'My cousin and one of my best friends having a baby together. That's the best of both worlds for me. Thank you so much, Nancy. I can't wait to tell Seth, he'll be over the moon, too.'

'You don't mind?' she asked, confused and uncertain. She was wondering why I wasn't breaking down, where my pain and upset and hurt had vanished to.

'Why would I mind? I was a bit shocked at first but this is amazing news. Shall we go out and celebrate later?' I asked her. 'Obviously, soft drinks for you, but I'll drink enough for the both of us.' I could ask her for a drink because never in a million years would she go for one if she thought I was happy about this.

'Yeah, yeah,' she said. 'I'll call you about it.'

Once she left, I kept myself together for another half an hour to make sure she had truly gone. Then I flipped on the 'back in five minutes' sign, locked the doors and went into the back, fell to my knees and sobbed my heart out. My sobs were an outpouring of the pain of Dylan wanting her when he had never truly wanted me. After all those years of making me think he could possibly fall for me, after flirting mercilessly with me at Seth's party, he had slept with *her* straight afterwards. Her of all people. It was such a deep betrayal by someone I still thought of as my friend.

I spent far too long in the back crying. I had to do it there, alone, because no one else would understand, especially not Seth. He'd think I was still in love with Dylan when I wasn't, when I had stopped feeling like that about Dylan ages before Seth and I got together. At the end of it, what I was crying about wasn't even the fact that Dylan had slept with Nancy. It was the fact that after all these years, Nancy had managed to find another way to prove that I wasn't real.

My cousin Nancy wanders from room to room in my flat, taking in the décor, noting which rooms you can see the sea from, which rooms have carpets and which have floorboards. She's like a homebuyer, mentally rearranging the furniture, seeing how she'll make it hers once she takes over the place. That's a given now, of course. Sienna is in the long, wide corridor, hopping on to alternate parquet blocks with alternate feet, exclaiming 'Tah-dah!' each time she lands successfully on one foot.

'I like your house, Auntie Smitty,' she tells me every fourth block.

'It's lovely, isn't it?' Nancy states. She has returned to stand outside the main bedroom, my bedroom, mobile in hand ready to snap a photo. That'll be up on her blog, Twitter, Instagram and Facebook soon – tagged as where she's staying for the summer with a view to staying permanently. She'll probably then do a selfie by the window to get the sea view in shot, so everyone who follows her and has friended her can see what she's looking at while she types up her latest missive from the world of femininity.

The thumb on her right hand, topped with a perfectly manicured dusky pink nail, hovers over the camera-shaped button on her mobile. She moves the phone carefully, trying to capture the right light.

'Clemency! Are you home?' Mum calls from the front door.

'Yes, Mum,' I say back. Nancy doesn't take her photo. Instead, she turns towards my mother's voice, her face is radiant with joy because Mum's here. And Mum is someone who'll speak to her at last. In all the time Nancy has been here, outside and inside the flat, it's been unsettling for her that I still haven't spoken to her. Because, well, why the hell should I?

'We're here too!' Sienna sings. She runs back down the corridor, turns the corner to where the coats are hung and where my mother is entering the flat.

'Sienna? Oh my Lord! What are you doing here?'

'We came for a holiday! Mum said if we like it we're going to stay and I can go to school here.'

'I didn't say that!' Nancy says. She goes to the source of the voices, lifts her arms to receive and give a welcoming hug to my mother before she disappears around the corner.

'What a wonderful surprise!' Mum says.

'You made it sound so amazing in your letters and postcards we had to come see for ourselves,' Nancy tells Mum. Her words are muffled, I presume from when she hugs my mother. 'It certainly is wonderful.' These words are punctuated by kisses.

'Clemency!' Mum calls. 'Isn't this a marvellous surprise?'

'It's certainly a surprise,' I state quietly.

'Well, of course you must stay. Mustn't they, Clemency? It'll be so lovely having the two of you around for a while.' Mum is offering room in my home to my monster. I don't know why that's such a surprise to me after all these years, but it is. 'Clemency! It'll be lovely having them around for a while, won't it?'

'I'm going for a shower,' I say loudly. And without waiting for a reply, I go into the bathroom, shut and lock the door.

With me, April 2015, Otley

Hi Clem. How's it all going?

We haven't had a catch-up in so long.

What's new with you?

Listen, if you're trying for a baby, let me know.

I've spoken to lots of fertility experts for the blog,

so I can give you lots of tips.

Talk soon. N x

P.S. Don't forget the folic acid!!!!

Her hair in my bed, the latest posts on her blog, this text sent out of the blue. It still wasn't the right time to deal with this, I was too exhausted, too tapped out by what was coming with Dad, but I had to make plans. I had to talk to Seth, but first of all, I had to have a Plan B because I couldn't sleepwalk into Nancy ruining another part of my life.

They're like three generations of a family. When I finally emerge from the bathroom, I stand unnoticed at the doorway watching this family tableau. The daughter reclines on the sofa with a glass of wine in a red goblet, the mother sits in the armchair, her glasses perched on her nose as she goes through her latest Sudoku puzzle, the grand-daughter lies on the floor eating a bowl of sweetcorn, tuna and pasta with her fingers while glued to CBeebies. I'm the outsider in this place, there is no space for me here.

This was what it'd been like at the Zebilas, my other family's house, except they had four generations and there'd been a lot more crying. I looked like them, I had the same blood, but I was an outsider, someone who had to be welcomed in and even then, didn't quite fit.

What I am looking at now, just as I was looking at with the Zebilas, is a family. And I don't really fit into either one. Like the outsider I am, I retreat, return to my room before anyone can raise the issue of Nancy taking over my room because it has a desk and I already have a space in my workshop to work. That's what will happen. That's what's always happened. When it comes to Nancy – not so much Sienna but Nancy – Mum often thinks being in my thirties is just like it was when I was eight and I gave Nancy my doll because she cried so hard that my one had prettier, nicer clothes than hers. And Mum believes that being in my thirties is like it was when I was twelve and I let Nancy 'borrow' my brand new raincoat because hers had a rip in it even though I knew I'd never get it back. And Mum is certain being in my thirties is just like when I was sixteen and I had to give Nancy my revision notes because she hadn't had time to do them, what with all the dates she'd been on. Mum thinks it's just like being thirty-two, calling one of my best friends to congratulate him on knocking up my cousin and having him tell me that it was all a mistake and he wished he'd used contraception, no matter what she'd said about being on the Pill. And when I wouldn't let him get away with that because he was just as responsible as she was, him saying that he wished he could get out of it, or failing that, if she was going through with the pregnancy, that she'd have 'it' adopted or something, so he didn't have to be involved. (To my silence on the phone at that, he stammered, 'Oh, Smitty, I didn't mean— I just— I'm sorry, mate, that was out of order. But you know what I mean.' I knew what he meant, yes, and I was so relieved at that moment I wasn't still in love with him.)

I retreat to my bedroom before the scenario that has played out in my life so many times starts to unfold here, too. I'm also sure to lock the door. It makes me feel safer from the monster outside.

37

Abi

To: Jonas Zebila
From: Abi Zebila
Subject: Sod this for a game of soldiers
Monday, 20 July 2015

Nothing new here, really: Clemency is still freezing me out despite the bullshit 'how are you' text every day. Mummy and Daddy are still not talking about anything beyond everyday surface stuff. Ivor has, thankfully, stopped his insane theories since I roared at him that we'd done a DNA test and he could see the results if he wanted. I've never shouted at him like that before, but he caught me at a particularly hormonal moment.

Lily-Rose continues to be the light of my life. I'm attaching a scan of the picture she drew of you and Meredith the other day. She just suddenly drew it without any prompting from me. I think knowing about Clemency has reminded her of you and Meredith. I'm not sure about your hair being so big, but I can see a likeness, can't you? Oh, wait, you won't be replying so you can't tell me if you see a resemblance or not. Yes, you're pissing me off as well.

All this is not helped by how bad Gran is right now. She seemed to rally for a couple of weeks, she seemed to have a new purpose, but now she's sliding again. It's so distressing, especially as there's no one who understands. She's alienated everyone and even now, she can turn on you so suddenly, be so vicious, everyone is just cautious around her and

I can't explain how scared I am about the thought of her not being here any more.

Declan has had his monthly meltdown, asking why we won't get married. I couldn't even be bothered to reply. I'm feeling low, J, really low.

Abi
xxxxx

38

Smitty

Mum has insisted I bring her to Beached Heads. Since we met my other family I am her new special project. She has been carving out time for us to spend together, and she wants to know about my life.

She lurks outside my room, probably listening to my phone calls, she comes into whichever room I am in in the house to see what I'm up to and so we can spend some time together. With Nancy and Sienna here, I'm amazed she is bothering so much with me. But they're hers, I suppose, already permanently bonded by blood. I am now an unknown quantity. Which is nonsense because Mum does know me. Every time she successfully guilt-trips me proves she knows me, every time I bite back at one of her ridiculous statements proves she knows me, every day that I am on this Earth and she is too proves she knows me. She's my 'Mum' but it seems she's the only person who needs convincing of that.

Mum, though, doesn't feel like my 'Mum', the entity who I love more than most people on Earth, and is on a mission to reassert herself. Part of that involves invading my space here at Beached Heads.

Tyler is working. He moves easily behind the counter, smiling, humming quietly, generally infusing the place with the kind of joy you don't often find in places where you spend money. My crush on him is slowly becoming out of control. Ever since he taught me to make coffee, gave me a place to forget who I am for a little bit, I have managed to become as giddy and fizzy as a teenager around him. Instead of being imbued with the feelings for another that a thirty-seven-year-old would have, emotions that can be analysed and categorised, written about and discussed, whenever I step in the glass doors of this café on the beach, all my other worries fall away and I am plunged into a vat of raw, unfathomable, delightful nonsenseness. I am too old to be feeling this and that's wonderful.

Mum and I sit in one of the sofas by the window. 'This is a lovely place, Clemency. I can see why you like it here.'

'Hmmmm...' I reply. Tyler wipes the spout of the milk steamer and frother with his ubiquitous white cloth and it's suddenly, irrationally, the most erotic thing I've seen in weeks.

'Welcome, welcome, faces old and new,' Tyler says. He stands in front of our table like a tall sentinel – ready and waiting to do our bidding.

'Interesting choice of words there, Tyler. Care to elaborate which one of us is which?'

He claps his hands quietly together then hangs his head with his hands still clasped. 'And there we have it, my foot firmly in my mouth with no chance of getting it out without causing too much damage.' He rotates rapidly and marches away, back behind his counter. A few seconds later, he returns. With a flourish, he says, 'Hello, Clemency. Or would you prefer I call you Smitty today?'

'Either is fine with me.'

His apron is well starched, navy blue with *Beached Heads* embroidered on the front in gold thread, like the one he put on me when we made coffee. 'Well, it is lovely to see you again.' He turns his attentions to Mum. 'Hello, it's fantastic to meet you, too.'

I have to introduce them and I'm going to have to suffer the silence, the stare, the sudden need Mum will develop to root through her bag for something important while the awkward moment passes. This is why I keep my worlds apart. When you separate pieces of yourself like the sections in a cutlery drawer, things don't bleed and merge into each other, things don't need complicated explanations.

'Tyler, this is my mother, Heather. Mum, this is Tyler, he owns Beached Heads and makes the best coffee ever.'

'You're too kind,' Tyler says, and extends his hand to my mother. 'Pleased to meet you, Mrs Smittson.' Mum will like that: introduced by her first name but he instantly defers to the formal and altogether more respectful way of addressing her.

Mum takes his hand. 'How do you do?' she says. I've never heard her say that, ever. She sounds like she's the Queen meeting a lowly subject.

'Do you share your daughter's obsession with coffee, or are you more of a tea drinker?' Tyler asks. He hasn't missed a beat, hasn't thrown one questioning or incredulous look our way. 'If I may be so bold as to suggest my special, loose-leaf tea blend? If you don't like it I'll happily serve you any other beverage *and* a piece of cake free of charge. Not that I was going to charge you for the drink anyway. Your daughter holds some influence round these parts.'

I almost giggle. *Giggle!* I am an out-of-control teenager. 'That's very kind of you,' I say when Mum does not speak. 'Do you want the tea, Mum? Or a normal cuppa?'

'I do not know where you have conjured up the idea that I drink "cuppas",' Mum says. 'However, yes, the blend sounds promising. I will indeed sample a drop.'

'Hello, Mum, Queen Elizabeth called – she wants her accent back,' I say to her in my head.

'Excellent choice,' Tyler says. He grins at me. 'And you, Clemency?'

'A double mocha, easy on the cream, heavy on the cocoa.'

'Another excellent choice.'

Mum doesn't speak until he is safely behind his counter. Her gaze constantly strays in his direction, checking, I think, whether he is close enough to hear her when she leans towards me, lowers her voice and says, 'Is he always that forward?' Her ultra-posh accent has gone. 'It's most inappropriate.'

'Yes, he's always like that. And, as you can see by how popular this place is, it generally works. People keep coming back for the friendly, personal service.'

'I'm sure the café's location has a lot to do with that,' she replies. 'Wild horses and no amount of sea views would keep me coming back to a place if the person in charge was rude and dismissive.'

'I agree, it's all fakery to drum up business. I can't abide false people.'

'I didn't say that, Mum. I said he was always like that.'

'And you went on to say that it was a way for him to drum up trade.'

'I didn't.'

'You did. You said he was like that to keep people coming back.'

'I didn't mean it like that.'

'But that is what you said.'

I have forgotten my golden rule: there is no point arguing with my mother. Even if she is wrong and I am right, there really is no point arguing with my mother. And just in case I've forgotten the first part of the rule it is this: there is NO POINT arguing with my mother.

'*What. And. Ever,*' I say to Mum in my head.

'Pardon me?' Mum says, her face stern and shocked at the same time.

There is a chance – a rather large chance – that I said that out loud.

'Is that what you're learning now? How to speak to me like that?' *Is that what your new family is teaching you?* she adds silently.

'No,' I say remorsefully. 'I'm sorry. You were deliberately misunderstanding and then misinterpreting what I was saying, though.'

'That is not my idea of an apology, Clemency Smittson.'

'I'm sorry, Mum. I shouldn't have spoken to you like that.'

'Thank you for your apology,' she says with good grace. It's easy to show such grace when you're technically in the wrong and you've managed to get someone to apologise to you TWICE in under thirty seconds. If that happened to me, I'd have all the grace in the world, I'm sure. I wonder why Mum thinks she isn't my mother when our relationship is full of moments like this. These are the moments you only share with your truly beloved ones.

'One pot of my special blend, and one double mocha, easy on the milk, heavy on the cocoa.' He's used my favourite daisy cup and for Mum he has selected a lilac cup that matches the scarf she has draped around her neck. With me, in jewellery making, the perfect finish is everything; with Tyler and his café service, the detail is everything. I'm embarrassed at myself for how desperate I am to find any sort of connection between us no matter how tenuous. It's all kinds of pathetic. And fun.

'Thank you, Tyler. I'm sure it will be delightful,' says my mother, the Queen.

I decide to ignore her and concentrate, instead, on my crush on the man walking away from me.

I have been expecting Mum to ask me if I have heard from the Zebilas, and if we have a time to see them again. When she asks, I will tell her everything, but she hasn't asked because I suspect she thinks she knows everything since she has gone back to doing what she did whenever I lived at home: listening in on my phone calls by lurking around my door. (Whenever I catch her at it she does a good job of looking as if she was innocently passing.) I leave this moment between us silent, give her the opportunity to ask and be answered. I will be relieved that I can talk about who I have seen and why. The moment passes, undisturbed and unruffled.

'Mum, did you and Dad ever talk about how he felt towards the end?' I ask, as a roundabout way of starting the conversation I probably should have with her.

'I'm not sure what you mean,' she replies.

'I mean, did he worry about being a burden on us? You, mainly, obviously?'

Mum's eyes glaze over; she gazes into the recent past, suddenly lost and floating in the sea of yesterday. 'Yes,' she says quietly. 'It was his biggest worry. Which upset me more than a lot of the other things that happened. He shouldn't have worried about that. It wasn't important.'

'But to him it was, I suppose?' I say.

'Yes. I loved him. For better or worse.'

'Did he ever feel it was too much and want it to end?'

'Did he tell you that?' Anger simmers beneath her words, in the way her face sits. 'Did he say something about that to you?'

'No,' I reply. This wound has clearly not healed for Mum and I have unintentionally busted it open.

'Don't lie to me, Clemency. He asked you, too, didn't he?'

'No, Mum, I am not lying. The only thing he ever asked of me was to go to see that woman from Doncaster about her wedding jewellery. I didn't want to go but he asked me to so I did.'

Mum's eyes rake over me, scrutinising me for any hint that I am keeping things from her. 'You're sure?'

'What is this? He didn't…Why, what did he ask you?'

'Only the most selfish thing a person could ask of another,' she practically snarls. She's never like that about Dad, not ever. Then she catches herself, realises who she's talking to. She leans forward, grabs her teacup and sips at it.

'Did Dad ask you to help him die?' I ask Mum.

She sips her tea, ignores me. She is not going to discuss this with me, and me asking isn't going to do any good. She is resolute, her face set and determined, then she changes her mind. She swivels in her seat until she is fully facing me. 'Yes, he did. He asked me because he was in so much pain. He was in a type of agony I hope never to experience and he wanted it to be over. He'd had enough and I didn't blame him. It was too much in that moment, but as soon as he asked he took it back. It was only at that moment. He knew how selfish it was.'

'He didn't ask me,' I reassure Mum. 'Like you say, it was a selfish thing to ask and Dad would never do that to me.'

'Why are you asking?'

'I'm missing him. Thinking about him. I didn't want him to think we ever thought that about him. That he was a burden. Because he wasn't.'

Mum places her cup back on its saucer, it rattles enough for her to need to steady it with her other hand. 'I think it is time for me to go home. Nancy and Sienna will be back from exploring now. Are you coming?' she asks. She doesn't acknowledge what I have said, doesn't even seem to notice that I have spoken. This is too much for her today. I didn't realise it, but today is probably not a good day and she has been hiding that with her snippy attitude.

I shake my head. 'I'm going to finish my coffee and then go on to work. I have some stuff to do before Monday.'

She looks across the busy room at Tyler and then back at me. 'Fine,' she says. 'I'll see you at home later.'

'Bye, Mum,' I say.

She nods at Tyler, a brief acknowledgement that he has served her well, and then leaves without looking back.

With Mum, May 2015, Otley

Mum had that face on her. Most of the time she looked like a normal woman with her blonde-brown, grey-streaked hair wound back into a bun, and soft features, and pink lips. Right now, though, she had that face on her.

'It's one song, Mum,' I told her. 'One song. He wanted it played.'

We were both wearing black, had done for the last week or so. It wasn't intentional for me, simply what my hand went to whenever I opened the wardrobe or drawer. I felt like covering myself in black, it was comforting and gentle, the sombreness from inside me creeping outside. I closed my eyes and I saw Dad. If there was a lull in the day, a moment when I could be still, I would think I could sense him nearby. Mum was never still, calm, inert. She was always on her feet, cleaning, cooking, sorting. She wrote letters. She made arrangements. She had planned the funeral all by herself. She had done everything, organised everything, except for this one song.

'No,' she said. 'It's not right. Not decent.'

'Mum, it's what Dad wanted. He wrote it in his last letter. He told you about it more than once.'

'He wasn't himself towards... At that point he didn't know what he was saying.'

'He's always said it. So many times. Even before he was ill. In fact, he said it right from when he first heard it with me.'

'It's not decent.'

'You've said that, Mum, and saying the same thing over and over isn't going to change the fact that it was what he wanted. You can have all of your other hymns and readings, but this is what Dad wanted. You have to honour that.'

Back to that face.

You can have that face all you want, but it's still happening, I thought.

'There's no way the priest will allow it,' Mum said.

'We'll see,' I replied.

With everyone, May 2015, Otley

We had readings that brought tears and hymns that spread comfort. And as the chosen four rose to their feet, took their places to carry him out, the opening chords of the song he'd wanted since 1987 rose up from the speakers placed around the church.

The priest had been no trouble – he wouldn't deny a deceased man's request.

I watched the people around me react: frowns of confusion and recognition, wondering if they were really hearing this tune filling the church. Seth, who stood at the front of Dad's coffin, hitched an eyebrow at me. He couldn't believe I'd managed it, that I'd got Mum to let me play Dad's song.

When Dad took me to see *Dirty Dancing* because I had no friends to go with, he said he wanted that song played at his funeral. 'The words are so true. You and your mother, this is what life is about. Promise me, *quine*, you'll play it at my funeral.'

'Promise,' I said without a second thought. Because I was nine, and that day was never going to come. I never thought I'd have to convince Mum to let me play 'I've Had the Time of My Life' by Bill Medley at Dad's funeral because Dad was a big man with a huge laugh and he was never going to have a funeral, so I could promise him anything he wanted.

Tyler leaves it at least ten minutes after my mother has gone before he comes near my table. 'Now that I've met your mother,' he says, 'I think it's fair to ask you what I've been wondering since you first walked into my café.'

'What's that then?'

'I've been trying to work it out by very subtle means, and now I'm just going to ask you outright: are you seeing anyone?'

As if on cue, as if he knows that something has made me think of him, Seth's text tone sounds in my pocket. It'll be one of those texts where he simply asks how my day has been, how I'm feeling, reminding me he loves me. And it'll make me question the wisdom of what I've done, whether I should have stayed with someone who lied to me more than once. Not even a lie of omission, an outright lie. He's backed off recently, no asking me to talk to him, just asking how I am. An easy way to get me to think about him even if I won't return his calls or texts.

'No,' I say to Tyler. *Because I am not. No matter what his texts say, no matter how much I want to be, I am not with Seth any longer. We are over. We have to be over.* 'I'm not. I'm flattered that you're interested, though.'

'I'm flattered that you're flattered. Does that mean if I ask you out sometime you're likely to say "yes"?'

'It does.'

'Good to know,' he says. He wanders off to the counter with his checked tea towel slung over his shoulder and my mother's empty teacup and saucer in his hand.

Seconds later he returns without the tea towel, apron and sous-chef hat he wears. ' "Sometime" didn't involve an apron, tea towel or hat,' he says. Another grin. 'Have you ever been roller-skating along the promenade?' he asks.

I shake my head. I always wanted roller skates. Lots of the girls in my school had them. Hillary Senton had pink ones with pink wheels and she brought them in one time and all of us wanted to touch them, to have a go. But she wouldn't even let us stand too close to them. I wanted pink ones like hers, but even if they weren't pink I would have loved to have a pair, to be like the other girls. But we couldn't afford them, Mum and Dad said. We could hardly ever afford things that other children had. I don't remember feeling resentful about it, more sad. I used to stare at the ceiling at night dreaming that when I grew up I'd have a lot of money and I'd be able to buy whatever I wanted. Funny how as an adult that never translated into buying roller skates, a pink bike or the latest, most up-to-date *Girls' World*.

'Would you like to come roller-skating with me along the promenade? I can make us a bite to eat here after the café has closed and then we can head out on the skates. See how far we get.'

I am being asked out by the man I have a crush on. I am being remarkably calm about that. 'Sounds good. When?'

'This coming week I've got events here every night so the café's going to be open later than usual. But next week, I'm all yours. Potentially.' He scrunches up his face, closes his eyes in a grimace. One eye cracks open a fraction. 'That sounded so wrong. Did you understand what I meant in the broader sense?'

I nod.

'So, next week?'

Two buzzes and a bleep sound in my pocket, a reminder that my life isn't uncomplicated. Not that I'd forgotten. About Seth. About my biological family. Nor about what my grandmother has asked me to do. Having something else to think about, to look forward to, feels like a chance to be an uncomplicated person for a few hours. I've forgotten what it's actually like, to not have anything to worry about.

'Next week, definitely.'

39

Smitty

'What are your plans for today?' my cousin Nancy asks me when I come into the kitchen. She and Sienna have been up for an hour or so, I heard them and I'd been itching to go in and join them, but I couldn't face this part of that scenario – speaking to Nancy. They've been here six days and I have managed to avoid speaking to her as much as possible. Unless she asks me a direct question in front of Sienna or Mum, I don't reply, I don't acknowledge her. I've spent a lot of time at work to avoid speaking to her. If I told Mum what Nancy had done it would upset her (not the Seth part, Mum would blame that on Seth, anyway) but it would devastate me if Mum did what she always did and tried to find a way to excuse Nancy for this latest treachery.

'I'm working,' I say. I only reply because Sienna is sitting beside her mother, trying to stack cornflakes on top of each other as they float in her cereal bowl of milk.

'Oh. You work too hard, you know that?' Nancy says. 'You're too young to be this stressed about work. You need to take care of yourself.' I wish she would come right out and say whatever it is that she wants because I find the faux-friendliness unpalatable.

She has her hair piled up on top of her head, tendrils of it tumbling around her face. She wears shorts and a vest-top to sleep in. It's been unfortunate for her that she didn't manage to convince Mum to convince me to let her have the big room. She tried, but I'd avoided being around long enough for Mum to ask. And I locked my room during the day so Nancy wasn't tempted to move in while I was out. I don't move from my current place near the kitchen door because Nancy is going to say something else. I was supposed to reply to what she said but as it wasn't a direct question, I didn't bother.

'Would you mind taking Sienna today?' she asks. 'You'd like a day with your auntie Clem, wouldn't you?'

'Yeah!' Sienna says.

'I just need a little "me" time to catch up on some work, return a few calls, you know?' Nancy asks. 'You don't mind, do you?' The way she says that, the intonation of the question, makes it sound like I am Sienna's other parent and I've been slacking off in my duties.

More than anything I wish that Nancy would admit that she struggles with being a lone parent, that it's hard work and she resents Dylan for not being involved. (Seth is always on Dylan's case about not being part of Sienna's life. Dylan's stock reply is: 'Being involved with her means being involved with Nancy, and that is not an option.' And Seth always says, 'Yeah, tell that to your daughter when she grows up realising you're the feckless fool that you are.') I wish Nancy would be honest with herself, with the world in general. There are so many people who would be comforted to know that even she, Super Feminine Woman, finds it hard to be everything all the time to her daughter. That would be far too honest, though. Far too risky. She might be seen as normal, she might not be seen as perfect. Instead, she puts posts up on the internet giving tips on being feminine *and* a mother while she can barely get dressed at weekends, she pretends she has important work to do to guilt-trip people into babysitting for her, and she shows up with a two-year-old Sienna at mine and Seth's flat and leaves Sienna to get something from the shop and doesn't return for three months, claiming that she needed time to find herself.

I would respect Nancy a whole lot more if she had just come out and asked me to look after Sienna today. It's not as if I would say no. I never do when it comes to Sienna.

'You fancy a day with me?' I ask Sienna.

'Uh-huh,' she replies. 'Mum said we'd go to the pier today but I don't think she wants to any more. Do you want to go to the pier with me?'

'I think we can do much better than that,' I tell her. 'Why don't we go and look for some more shells and unusual pebbles so I can make more jewellery?'

'Yeah!' She wriggles off her seat until she is under the table and scoots across the floor on her hands and knees. She dashes out of the door, ready to wake Mum up so she can help her get dressed.

'Thanks, Clem. This is really helpful. I need to get on top of work. There's so much piling up and—'

I have to leave the room while Nancy is still talking. I can't engage with her, I just can't.

Sienna rarely walks anywhere if she can dance instead. She twirls and skips and stops to do complicated sideways steps. The promenade is perfect for her, she has the freedom and space to do all these things and we are in no particular hurry. The sun climbs higher in the sky as we move towards Brighton and more and more people pour on to the seafront. We left Nancy to catch up on work, which actually consisted of her and Mum sitting at the kitchen table, poring over Nancy's phone, plotting out the way to Bluewater so they can spend the day shopping together.

I'm not sure if it's Abi or Lily who sees us first, but it's Lily who runs towards me, waving and smiling. 'Hello!' she calls to me. 'Hello!'

'Hello, hello!' I reply.

'Who are you?' Sienna asks. Her excitement at seeing someone her height is unbridled.

'I'm Lily. What's your name?'

'Sienna. I'm five. How old are you?'

'I'm five, too!'

'Hi,' I say to Abi.

'Hello,' she says frostily. I don't blame her. I'm not sure I would be able to bring myself to speak to me if I were her.

'My aunt makes jewellery from shells,' Sienna says. 'She made me this.' She reaches inside her top, removes her necklace with its

250

quick-release catch at the back so it will not strangle her if it gets caught. The necklace is made from a shell I found on the promenade. Three nights ago there had been high winds that had whipped up the sea enough to scatter pebbles and shells up on the promenade. On my way to work the next morning I'd found the small, smooth, conch-shaped shell, with a patch of brown like a tan across its back, and a sprinkle of freckles along its smooth underside. Its freckles reminded me of the ones that came up on Sienna's nose when she spent too long in the sun, and the patch of brown reminded me of the colour of Lily's eyes when she had been doing impressions of me. I'd picked it up, deciding to make something for both of them. I made two moulds from the shell, filled them with silver clay, allowed them to dry, then fired them. I polished them both, then strung them on to soft leather strings with quick-release catches. The original shell, I returned to the beach after taking a photo. 'We're going to look for some stuff to make jewellery,' Sienna says.

Lily reaches out, and with the gentleness of someone older, touches the necklace. The clay had captured every line and ridge, every smooth curve.

'I've got the picture of the shell she made it from on my nana's wall. I have to share a room with my nana,' Sienna explains. 'Do you want to come and get some shells and she can make you a neck-lace, too?'

'Do you think your aunt will make me one?'

Sienna tips her head right back, the curls of her blonde hair cas-cading down her back as she does so. Her eyes are the colour of wet earth, the exact same colour as Dylan's. 'Will you, Auntie Smitty?' she asks.

'Of course,' I reply.

'Is that your aunt?' Lily asks Sienna.

'Yes,' Sienna says proudly.

'But that's my auntie Clemmy,' Lily replies. She tips her head back to stare at her mother. Her mass of long, glossy black plaits tumbles down her back as she does so. 'That's what you said, isn't it, Mummy? This is Auntie Clemmy.'

'Yes,' says her mother, my sister. 'This is your aunt.'

'My Auntie Smitty's name is Clemency. Are you my aunt and Lily's aunt?' Sienna asks me.

'Yes, I am,' I reply.

'How come?'

'Because Lily's mum is my sister and your mum is my cousin.'

'Does that mean we're sisters or cousins?' Lily asks.

'Sisters!' Sienna says excitedly.

'Not really,' Abi intercedes quickly.

'Cousins!' Lily exclaims.

'Erm...' Abi begins. She is about to shatter their illusions. She wants to be accurate, to state that Sienna is really my second cousin, that these two aren't really connected at all. Those many, many times Nancy gleefully reminded me I wasn't real somersault through my mind.

'Do you want to be cousins?' I say before Abi can speak.

'Yes!' they both reply without hesitation, the very thought of it seems to be the best thing to have happened to them both since Christmas ended.

'They can be cousins if they want to be, can't they?' I ask Abi.

'If they must,' she mumbles, clearly not happy. It's understandable, this need for accuracy is what you'd expect from someone who has always had siblings, who has never had to justify their connection to another person.

'Yay!' they both cry and spontaneously hug each other, two friends who have only just met, now bonded together for life as family.

'Come on, let's find some shells.' Sienna grabs Lily's hand and the pair of them dash off towards the stone steps that lead down to the beach. They both wear shorts and T-shirts, and have matching lime green Crocs.

'We're supposed to be going swimming at the King Alfred!' Abi calls, but they ignore her.

The steep drop from the pebble-filled upper beach doesn't daunt them – they both run towards it, giggling as they hold hands, laughing while the ridge gives way under their weight, pushes them down further towards the lower part of the beach. When the pebbles and shells and fragments of shells stop moving beneath them, they leap forwards and run towards the sea, their loud, vocal happiness rising up like a trail we're meant to follow.

'Lily, stay out of the sea!' Abi calls, and speeds up. I speed up too, and we go through the same routine, waiting for the shifting ground to stop moving beneath our feet before we head towards them.

They're crouched by the water's edge, shallow, seaweed-streaked pools of not quite escaped sea sitting in the soaked sand around their feet as they search for the perfect shell. Their voices tumble and spill over each other in their excitement, and yet, in the commotion of speech and discovery they understand each other, they hear what the other is saying.

'When I was about five, my mother took a load of photos of me and Sienna's mother on Blackpool beach and we looked exactly like those two,' I say to Abi.

Nancy hadn't understood then that I wasn't real, that I wasn't her proper cousin. We were friends and we liked each other, a lot. We were pinky-promise best friends forever then. There were other pictures, ones taken on later trips to Blackpool, and they all looked the same, but they never felt the same. I hope Lily and Sienna are friends forever. That they refuse to believe anyone who tries to tell them that they're not real cousins, that they hang on to this feeling of having someone who they've fallen for in the way children do for other children.

'Are you seriously going to pretend that this is all normal and you've been in touch with me?' Abi says, affronted.

'Sorry, I'm sorry. I should have been in touch.'

'Yeah, you should. Why weren't you? I mean, I thought it was all right that meeting. We were all a little overwhelmed but it's not fair for you to duck out and send me bullshit "How are you?" texts.'

'I freaked out,' I say honestly. Aside from trying to convince my grandmother to change her mind about me helping her to die, I had freaked out because a lot of realisations were dawning on me like the rise of the Sun on a winter morning – slow to appear but powerful every time it is glimpsed. 'It was all too much for me. Everyone was crying and I wasn't. And I'm only now coming to terms with the fact that my parents got married. I wasn't put up for adoption because my mum was very young and on her own or had been slung out by her family – she had this family and a big house and they still didn't want me. She was in love with my father, he was in love with her, they went on to get married and have more children. So the bottom line is, they didn't want me. I'm sorry I cut you out. But I think about you and Lily all the time.' I reach into my bag, remove the small pink velvet bag that holds Lily's necklace. I press it into Abi's hand. 'I made this for her, it's the same as Sienna's.'

Abi frowns down at the trinket bag. 'You've been walking around with this in your bag?'

'I made it three days ago. I kept it in my bag because I constantly told myself that I would drive over and drop it off at your work or through your front door or something.' I inhale deeply. 'I'm a coward. It's really that simple.'

Abi says nothing as she continues to examine the bag in her hand, but she's chewing the inside of her mouth, her eyes are in another place, she's very obviously thinking over what I said.

'My parents didn't take that many photos,' she says. 'There were a few, but . . . It's weird, saying that, actually, because I seem to remember there being lots of cameras and lots of negatives around, but we hardly ever had any pictures out. But me? I've got about six thousand photos on my phone of Lily.'

'Six *thousand*?' I am a prolific photo taker but not even I have that many photos of one subject.

'You'd think there was no other thing to take a photo of in the whole world, wouldn't you? I can't help it. When she was first born I had this idea to take a photo of her every day so I could see how she changed over time. Who knew I'd end up with a baby that I could barely put down – even when she was asleep. Some days I wouldn't be able to go for anything like a proper wee until eight o'clock at night. I lived in my dressing gown those first few weeks.'

'Mum, Mum, what about this?' Lily is holding out a long, flat shell, its curved back ridged with shades of pearlescent grey. She flips it over in her palm and its underside is a smooth, shiny pearl colour. Flecks of wet sand cover it, but I can do something with that. Lily has a good eye.

'I don't know, ask your aunt,' Abi says.

Lily moves her hand towards me. 'I think it's beautiful,' I tell her. 'I'll definitely be able to do something with that.' Pewter silver for the top, white gold for the underside. White gold paste is hard to come by, though, so I may have to gold-plate it. Which is pricey. 'Shall I keep it safe for you until I can make your necklace?' I ask her.

She grins without showing her teeth and her plaits dance when she nods. She watches me as I unbutton the thigh pocket on my trousers and slip the shell inside.

'Sienna! Sienna!' she calls as she skips back to her new-found cousin. 'I've got one. I've got one.'

'Didn't your parents help?' I say to Abi. 'I'd have thought they'd be all over their first grandchild.'

Abi snorts dismissively, her eyes darken as she's suddenly transported back six years. 'Yeah, we've all moved on from me being nineteen, pregnant and unmarried. They were so over-the-top angry about it that I had to move out. I ended up living on my own in a tiny flat in the middle of nowhere because my parents didn't want to know unless I agreed to tell them who the father was and to marry him. After six months or so of watching me struggle and accepting that I wasn't telling them the father's name, and even if I did I wouldn't be getting married, they let me move back home.' The resentment at how they were swirls in her eyes. 'My gran was the worst for it. She kept on blaming my mother for not bringing me up properly, like Daddy hadn't been there when I was growing up.

'My brother, Jonas, he tried to help, so did Declan, Lily's dad. But he was young, too, and his parents were freaking out. And Jonas was going through his own shite. It was really hard. Jonas couldn't believe it that I moved back in with them after all that they'd done and said.

I moved out when Lily was nearly two then came back again about a year ago when Gran got bad. Like I say, we've all moved on from those early dark days.' She makes a small, disgusted 'ha' sound under her breath.

'Is that why you haven't told them you're pregnant?'

Abi's eyes seem to triple in size – the horror of what I've said descends upon her features and she turns on me. Her hand clamps around my arm, her fingers dig into the space between the muscle and bone of my bicep. 'How do you know? Is it obvious? Who else have you told?'

I shrug her off. I rub at where she grabbed me to ease the pain she's caused. 'You look a bit off colour, but you seem to be glowing, too. I just guessed. I haven't told anyone. Why would I? It's your business.'

'If you've guessed it's only a matter of time before Mummy does. I can't go through all that again. Last time she guessed and asked me outright. I couldn't lie. She looked at me like something disgusting she'd stepped in, and Daddy overheard and went through the roof. I wanted to tell her this time so I'd be in control. But if it's obvious to you then it'll be obvious to her.'

'Don't you think they'll react a bit differently this time?' I suggest gently. 'Not only are you older and self-supporting, there's a reason why you can remind them that everyone makes mistakes. Assuming it was a mistake.'

'It wasn't a mistake,' she says. 'We planned it. I love Declan – Lily and this one's father. He's just...'

'Married?'

'No! No way! He's a bit flaky and a "bit some time".'

'I don't get you.'

'He's one of those men who you know are good for some time but long-term it probably won't work out. He wanted to get married last time and he wants to get married this time, we go stay with him almost every other weekend and we were talking about living together before Lily and I moved back in with my parents, but he's...I'm...Nothing lasts when it comes to love, love.'

Seth. The hazel-green swirl of his eyes comes to mind. The lazy smile he fires me before he puts on his helmet. His strong fingers that sneak between mine like a whispered secret as he takes my hand when he's nervous.

'Have you tried to make it last?'

'No, suppose not.'

'How do you know then?' I ask.

'I don't need to run into the sea fully clothed to know I'm going to get wet jeans, I just know it.'

'True.' But love isn't like running into the sea fully clothed. With the sea and a fully clothed dash into its depths, there are no surprises. With love, there is sometimes a surprise around every corner, a chance to grow and learn and find the ways you are perfect just as you are. I'm not going to say that to her. What do I know? I'm living three hundred miles away from the love of my life and about to go on a date with a man I have a teenage crush on. What do I really know about love? Instead I say to her: 'Abi, if they start to have a go, you've got the perfect comeback.'

'What's that?'

I suppose I should be pleased that she's forgotten who I am, what I am to her. I raise my forefinger and turn it towards my face, a pointer as to her perfect new comeback.

'Oh, God, yes. I almost forgot.'

Almost.

The girls won't stop hugging. They keep promising they'll see each other again soon, and that they can have a sleepover and that they can do drawing together and look for more shells on the beach and ride their scooters up and down the beach and read books together at the library and climb in the park and have another sleepover and a tea party.

'Are you going to disappear again now?' Abi asks.

'No. No, I won't. I'm going to come with you to tell your parents about your pregnancy, if you want me to.'

'You'll come with me?'

I nod. 'Of course.'

'*Really?* Why?'

'Because you're my sister. That's what sisters do, isn't it?'

Abi smiles, and nods.

'Right, so that's what I'll do.'

40

Smitty

She bottled it. We had it all planned: Abi would take Lily to a friend's house and I would wait for her, we'd come back together and do a whole 'look who I saw near Lily's friend's house and who I invited back for a cup of tea' scene as a background, and then we'd sit down around the kitchen table and Abi would do it. Or I would do it. But one of us would do it and Abi could stop pretending she had food poisoning from the works canteen and get on with being happy to be having another baby.

I should have known from the way she was hyperventilating the whole drive back, and then how she took about five goes to actually put the key in the door and then another full thirty seconds to turn it, that she was a flight risk.

'Hello!' she called out, her voice wavery and paper-thin. 'I have a visitor,' she added when she received no reply from her mother or grandmother.

As soon as her curious mother appeared from the kitchen, Abi decided to flee. 'Saw Clemency. Asked her for tea. Need to go to work. Emergency. Bye.' And that was it – she literally fled the house. I'm sure she actually ran down the path, too, shutting the gate behind her like an obstacle that would slow down anyone who decided to drag her back and force her to unburden her mind.

My other mother blinks a few times at me. She looks as though all her numbers have come up on the Lottery. It's the reaction I need, one that lessens the anxiety about not telling Mum about this meeting. 'Would you like a drink?' she asks.

'A coffee would be brilliant,' I say. I am speaking quietly because suddenly I'm shy with just the two of us. We spoke the other time, but everyone was on high alert and there was so much pressure. Today we have none of that.

We take our seats at the kitchen table, the same ones we had last time I was here. 'The photographs Mrs Smittson gave to us were wonderful. Your father and I have looked through them several times.'

'I'm surprised he looked at them. He didn't seem that interested in me the last time I was here,' I say. I hope that doesn't sound too bitter or accusatory, just the statement of fact it is.

'He is interested. This has simply been difficult for him. None of us are sure of the best thing to do. In those situations, those who are most unsure of themselves often do nothing. He is interested. Of course he is.'

I nod. 'Do you have some photos of you from when you were younger that I can see?' I ask. 'I'm curious about what you looked like back then.'

She shakes her head, the strands of her shoulder-length bob move like black silk threads. 'I don't like to be the focus of any attention. I have very few photographs of myself. They are in the loft, I think. I will bring them out the next time I see you.'

'That'd be great,' I reply.

'Do you like your grandmother?' my other mother asks out of the blue.

What sort of a loaded question is that? Is there actually a right answer? 'She's all right, I suppose,' I state.

'You have a secret, I can sense it, Tal— Clemency. If I asked you what it was, would you tell me?'

'I've spent more time with Abi than I have with her but you don't want to know what Abi has been telling me.'

'*Don't trust that woman.*' The words are almost hissed at me and I have to pull myself back in my seat. A thick, poisonous venom is laced through every rivulet of those words and they shock me. Is that how irrational and unbalanced I sound when I talk about Nancy? And why is she suddenly talking about this? Aren't we supposed to be bonding, not setting up a slagging session about someone else?

'I am sorry, I am sorry.' My other mother's face is anxious now, her hand movements fretful. She's worried that she has pushed me away, alienated me by showing in that moment the truth of her feelings, the fact she has the ability to feel such emotions at all.

If I think about what she did in having me placed for adoption, I still struggle. I expect her to be frozen, stuck at that moment where she was forced to make a momentous choice and unable to move on from that. It's not fair to think she would be suspended in time, but part of me, the part who has been 'other' all her life because of the choice my birth mother made, expects it as the least she can do and feel. Guilt always stitches its haircloth inside my chest when I have these thoughts about my other mother because I am being unfair. I shouldn't want anyone to feel how I do sometimes: trapped at a point in time. My point in time where I am trapped is that moment when I realised I wasn't with the parents who gave me my DNA. From then onwards I always, *always* felt that I was from nowhere and was unwanted by everyone. My other mother's ability to marry my father and have more children proves she has had some semblance of a normal existence.

'Why don't you like her?' I ask my other mother.

'It is not as simple as not liking her,' my other mother states. 'When I first came to this house, she treated me like one of her daughters. She was so kind and loving towards me. But when she discovered that her son was interested in me, that he was the one who was the father of my child, she became a person I did not recognise.

'She did not approve of her son being interested in me. He had a big career ahead of him and it did not involve a wife and a child before he had graduated from law school. I was not good enough in her eyes and she did not want me or anyone connected to me to become part of her family. I do not think she would ever have approved of me because I was not from the right family stock: my parents did not have the wealth of the Zebilas and I had not been chosen by her. The first son, according to your grandmother, has to conquer business, the second son has to marry well.'

She is hinting that it was my grandmother who forced my adoption. 'Couldn't you have got married anyway, despite her protests?' I ask.

'This was 1978, Clemency.' That is the first time she has said my name without pausing, without having to get the 'Talei' bit out of the way first. 'We did what was requested and expected by our parents.'

My other mother's brown eyes look over me carefully. Is she wondering if I am the type of daughter who would do as my parents told me?

'People talk about the seventies and eighties like the freedoms you all enjoy in this day and age were automatically given when the decades changed. It was not like that. We were not in the fifties and sixties, no, but we grew up with parents from those years. Your grandmother did not want me here, and I could not have gone to Nihanara to my parents with a child born out of wedlock. The shame would have killed them.'

Shame. It is a label, tagged into my skin, into the arrangement of my DNA. Shame is what I am, what I represent. This is a reminder of why I hate my birthdays – each one is a marker of who I am. That in the time before I was born there was no excitement, there was only shame, fear, confusion, worry. My very existence, according to my mother, the only person whose authority I have to go on, meant that I could possibly have killed someone with shame by simply being born.

'When I went to the hospital to have you, I was put on the ward that was for girls who were not married. I met a lot of English and Irish girls there and only one of us was going to be leaving with her baby. The rest of us, we had the parents who had grown up in the fifties and sixties, who only knew that a child born out of wedlock was wrong. And it is wrong.'

'Wrong'. I can add that to the list of words that tag who I am. 'Shame', 'Wrong', 'Not real'. If I was a wall, those would be the things that graffiti artists would spraypaint on me.

'We loved our babies but we were told we could not keep them. And we did as we were told.' My mother stares down at her hands. 'I fought her as long as I could. But in the end, I could not fight them both. Your father made me accept that it would be better for you to have two parents who would have money and who would be able to give you the life I couldn't.'

'You think it was all her and not him?' I say. It's difficult enough knowing what to call them all outside the confines of my head, but when we're having this type of conversation it's impossible to give them titles that are associated in my head with family, connectedness and love.

'Your father had, like me, been brought up to do as he was told. He would not have wanted to go against his parents.'

'Even if it meant keeping his child?'

'His mother always gets her way. That is why you must not trust her. If she is trying to create a relationship with you it is because she wants something. Which is why I'd like you to tell me what you talked about.'

I could take this demand, couched in quiet, unassuming, friendly terms, as a good sign: she is treating me how Mum treats me – like a daughter who will do as she is told. But I can't help thinking: *Who do you think you are? My mother, or something?*

The obedience Mum gets from me is given because she raised me. It's mostly annoying and unhealthy but it is what it is because she is the person I love, who helped me to grow up. Someone can't march in and make such personal, intimate demands on me when they weren't there. Maybe through no fault of her own, maybe through choices she made, maybe through fear and youth, maybe through a combination of all those things, but still, she doesn't get to make demands on me.

I can't say this. I can never say this. Because she might turn her back on me. She may never want to see me again. And, indignant as I am, I couldn't handle that. I feel something for her. When I look at her I ache for the person I think she was back then – trapped into this decision that she felt she had to make. And I ache in a desperate, almost manic manner to find a way over this breach between us. I want her to be my mother. There is a space for her in my life: one space is filled by Mum; the other is still occupied by Dad. But there is another space next to them where she would fit, she could be the other type of parent I need sometimes. I have a 'Mum', I need this woman to be my mother. I had a 'Dad', I would love Julius to be my father. But Julius isn't here, and my other mother is, and I want her, more than anything, to be my mother.

I say: 'She was telling me about her illness. She doesn't want anyone to know how unwell she feels.' This is as close to the truth as I can get without betraying my grandmother and lying to my other mother.

'She wants you to feel sorry for her,' my other mother dismisses. 'She has been ill for years. She doesn't want to look after herself properly. She much prefers to have others running around at her beck and call. She had servants back in Nihanara and being unwell has given her the chance to have that in her life again.'

Whoa! I draw back again. 'That's a bit unfair,' I say. 'She has some serious, life-limiting if not life-threatening conditions.' *She has the perfectly rational fear of becoming trapped inside her own body.*

My other mother's face changes, as though she is about to start crying. She looks emotionally dishevelled suddenly. 'This is what has happened to me,' she says, the tears seep into her voice. 'I am capable of dismissing another person's suffering because I dislike her so much.' She closes her eyes. 'I sometimes feel like I am a teenager again.' Is she admitting that she does feel stuck in that moment she made that choice all those years ago? 'I sometimes feel like no one will ever understand me or realise what it is like to be in an impossible situation.' She opens her eyes to find me watching her with my heart paused, my breath caught, as I wait for her to be honest again. 'Then I remember I am being silly. I am an adult and I made the right choice at that time.'

'Yes, I suppose you did,' I say to her statement. It stings. At every point, rubbed raw by the fact of being adopted and finding out that she went on to have more children with the same man, it stings to know this. It also suggests that she would make the same choice again. In which case, why not simply admit it? *Why not say that you didn't want to give me up for adoption, but the alternative to not doing so was a price you weren't prepared to pay?* I think. *Why can't you admit that you were young and frightened, and had just given birth, so when you were offered the respectability of marriage, and a child in wedlock – which happened less than two years later – in return for signing the adoption papers, you took it?* It might not be palatable for her to hear herself say that, but it's the truth. And it's better for me to hear that so I know that it honestly wasn't me. 'I suppose your mother-in-law thinks that, too, seeing as it's what you say she ultimately wanted.'

My other mother is horrified by how she sounds, what is coming across from everything she is saying and not saying. 'I did not mean it like that. I would not make the same choice if I was in that position again.' She looks at me like I'm an adult, like Clemency. 'Please believe me when I say I made the right choice at that time for all the wrong reasons. I would make a different choice if I was in that position again. I know that now. What I am trying to say is that your grandmother was an adult with more experience of the world and more opportunities than I. She was like a second mother to me but when I displeased her she showed me how little she thought of me.'

'Did she scream at you when you told her?' I ask.

'I didn't have the opportunity to tell her. She asked me had I missed my time of the month and when I said yes, she knew.'

'That must have been hard.'

My other mother gives me the type of smile I give Mum when she is minimising something Nancy has done. ' "Hard" is not the word I would use.'

'What did my . . . your . . . what did *he* say to her about your condition?'

'She called a meeting to shame me in front of the family, to tell them all what a dirty girl I was and how I had disgraced them and myself. When she asked me the boy's name I . . . I thought your father was going to tell them. To claim me. But he did not.' The expression on her face shows the hurt she must have felt then, still feels now. 'He was too scared. She discovered it in her own way, in her own time.'

'What did she say? Did she take it back once she found out it was her son?'

'One thing you must know about the Zebilas – once their mind is made up, it is almost impossible to change it. Your grandmother decided that I was a dirty girl who had led her son astray – nothing has changed her mind about that in all these years.'

'But you did end up married to him,' I state.

'Yes, I did. Because it was what your grandmother wanted.'

'I don't understand, sorry.'

'Your father proposed to me and said once we were married and he had finished law school we would find a way to get you back. In the meantime, I had to let you go to people who could take care of you. Your grandmother...' My other mother stares at her hands, at the unassuming gold band on the fourth finger of her left hand. She is wearing the family metal. 'Your grandmother made it clear that he was right to offer me that. It was the right thing to do. And she would have to ask my father for my hand in marriage. To do that, she would have to tell them about what I had done.'

The shame would have killed them.

'I see...' I say. I do as well. What she is saying is: when you do what my grandmother wants she is fine, but when you deviate from her plan for you, she makes your life a misery.

'I don't think you do, Clemency. It was the right choice because it was ultimately right for you, but I made that choice out of fear for myself mainly. I should have put you first. I may have made the same decision at the time, but I did not realise back then that you must always, *always* put your children first, no matter what you are offered. And your grandmother, she wielded absolute power over me from that moment on. This is the first time since I signed those papers that I have felt free.'

My grandmother isn't all that bad, I try to remind myself. I actually quite like her. But if what my other mother is hinting at is true then I have no real idea who my grandmother really is, nor what she is

266

capable of. But then, do any of us know what we're capable of when our lives are threatened with change?

'I need to go now,' I say to my other mother. 'I have work to do.' *And I don't emotionally know what to do with all that you have confessed.*

'Will I see you again soon?' she asks.

Considering the conversation, I'm so surprised she has asked that I have to stop moving and replay the question in my mind and think about it before I answer. 'Is that what you really want?'

She wants to see me, but unlike my grandmother there doesn't seem to be anything obvious she wants from me except maybe to spend time with me. This whole time with her has been so confusing, muddled, full of confessions and regrets and certainties about the right thing being done, and I don't know how to feel about my other mother right now.

'I would like that very much,' she says.

I nod. 'OK, then, I'll come back and see you again soon.'

She grins at me as I stand.

'I'll just go and say goodbye to— ' I point towards my grandmother's room.

My birth mother replaces her grin with a tight-lipped smile and offers me a sharp nod. She's probably hurt that I have heard what she has said but I am still choosing to engage with the woman who possibly pressurised her to give me up for adoption. I have to see her, though. I can't explain to my other mother why, that I've started to bond with my grandmother, that I've been trying to stop her ending her life early, that I have promised to think about helping her to die. That there is all this stuff going on which means I couldn't cut out my grandmother even if I tried.

My grandmother doesn't answer when I knock on her door the first time. The last time I came here it took her a while to reply when I called out from the corridor. But even as I wait, the sound of the clock counting out time, I know she is not going to answer. The other side of the door seems too silent, too still. Each tick of the clock seems to resonate into the bedroom, and return a hollow sound.

I hear my heart in my chest. It echoes, too, into the room behind the door. Each beat takes longer to sound out, and when it does, it seems to be magnified. My knuckles rap loudly this time. The knock ricochets around the corridor and is loud enough to bring my other mother to the door of the kitchen.

'What is the problem?' she asks.

'There's no answer.'

Her eyes flick to the clock. 'It's not time for her sleep. She will need her medication soon.'

She is down the hall in a few strides, she knocks on the door but doesn't wait for a reply before opening it. I wait on the threshold, not sure how much a part of this I will be.

'Clemency,' my mother says loudly but calmly. 'Call an ambulance.'

It begins then, the nightmare that she said she didn't want to happen. My grandmother wanted to look Death in the eye while she went, she didn't want Death to sneak in and take her slowly and painfully, leaving her powerless and afraid. Or to take her in even more minuscule increments, by making her a prisoner in her own body. That nightmare is being set in motion.

41

Smitty

'Would Madam care for some white wine or red wine with her *Spaghetti alle vongole*?' With a flourish, Tyler whips the pale cream napkin that sits in a fan shape next to my fork and spoon, and lays it gently and expertly across my lap. With an equally elaborate flourish he indicates to the wine bottles in the middle of the table.

He has pushed most of the low coffee tables away and has moved a circular dining table into the middle of the darkened café. Along the counter there are small tea lights in crystal holders, whose flames come together like embers from the Olympic flame to create a gentle wall of light behind him. In the middle of the table stands a silver candlestick with three arms, holding long, red tapered candles. The entire scene is romantic and thoughtful, and I'm honoured.

Like the lights on the counter, a flame of excitement dances and flickers inside me because this is thrilling and new and, well, thrilling. I can't think outside of those basic, almost teenager-like, terms otherwise the rest of the world where I am adult with adult problems and responsibilities will come gushing in like water into a cracked dam, and spoil it.

Time with Tyler is all about uncomplicated, new, exciting stuff. Time away from him is adult and scary and real. It has been two days since I had to call an ambulance to take my grandmother away and no one from my other 'family' has updated me on her condition. Not even a text to let me know if the worst has happened, if she is hanging on, if the doctors are still working on her. I am clearly not part of them. That has been a stark, adult lesson to learn in the last two days. I haven't been able to concentrate on anything without knowing what is going on. This has also changed everything: the decision might have been taken from my hands, which would be a relief. Or it might have become more pressing, I may need to speed up the deciding process because this is a signal that she doesn't have much time before something happens and she is as helpless as she fears.

Adult stuff, adult fears and decisions, have no place in the teenagery world of being with Tyler. Being with him is all about hoping my hair looks nice, wondering if my dress is flattering enough, choosing the right wine to go with this pasta dish.

'*Vino bianco* is the correct wine to have with *vongole*, I believe,' I say to him.

'Ahh, I see, a woman who is well travelled and well eaten,' Tyler says. 'Which could present a problem for me because you actually know what this is meant to taste like.'

'I do, I'm sorry. It's one of my favourites.'

'Well, nothing ventured, no one impressed by the brilliance I have managed to cram into this dish.'

In front of me, on top of the cork place mat, Tyler places a large white bowl into which he has curled spaghetti, with small, black clams studding the creamy-white strands. It is seasoned with flecks of bright green parsley and tiny, almost transparent pieces of garlic. The scent of a decent wine, which will have infused itself into the food, wafts up to me from my plate as it had been doing from the kitchen. 'You used good wine,' I say.

'Only the best for you, my dear – it was on offer for £2.98 in the local shop.'

'Oh, poor wine,' I reply, 'so cheap they couldn't even get away with charging the extra penny to make it ninety-nine.' I turn my mouth downwards. 'I feel sad for the pathetic bargain-bucket wine.'

Tyler's smile is unexpectedly intimate and affectionate, the beam of someone who has been in love with the person they're in front of for years. I avert my gaze to the silver fork I have picked up and am about to plunge into the stringy depths of my food.

'You're pretty silly, you know that?' he says, an equal amount of affection in his tone. I stop my fork making contact with my food. Without looking directly at him I watch him unfold his napkin fan, lay it across his jeans-covered lap. 'It was one of the first things I noticed about you. Not many people are silly in a charming way.'

I say nothing to him, instead I concentrate on finding a Zen state. On bringing calming breath into my body. On not getting up and walking out. This is not teenagerish, this is adult and serious and not what being with Tyler is all about.

'That was a compliment, in case you were wondering,' he tries again.

'Thank you,' I mumble into my chest.

Seth and I have split up. It is over between us; we couldn't be together any more. I am not cheating on him. I am not, I am not, I am not.

White wine glugs softly into my glass, and the lights from the candles flicker throughout the café. Outside is black but I know out there is the sea. If I strain, I'm sure I can hear it, shushing the sky, pouring calm over the pebbles.

'Are you not having a good time?' Tyler asks. 'Is this a bit too much after we've only really talked over coffee?'

Brace yourself, I tell myself. *Look up*. He smiles at me, nervously.

'I'm sorry,' I say. 'I'm in a bit of a strange place, my head is a bit fried at the moment. Lots of other things going on.' I open my mouth to start to explain. Then shut it again. Where would I even start with the tangled, knotted mess that is my life at the moment? I open my mouth again and: 'But I'm having a great time. This is all amazing. Especially for someone who makes questionable coffee at the best of times,' comes out.

'Lady, you can insult my cooking and my taste in décor but never, *ever* insult my coffee.'

'I wasn't insulting your coffee, the coffee can't help it, I was questioning your ability to make it.'

'I am wounded,' he says. 'Especially after I imparted my expert knowledge, that is usually only handed down from barista to barista, to you.'

'I'm sorry for wounding you,' I say.

'No, no, nothing short of *loving* my *vongole* will make up for it,' he says.

I grin at him. I slip the fork into the waves of the spaghetti, twirl them into a ball on the end of my fork using my spoon. Tyler watches me slip the food between my lips and chew. 'It's divine,' I say.

'You got yourself out of trouble there,' he states.

'Phew!' I can do this. Honestly I can.

'How about you try to leave all that head-frying stuff to one side for the rest of tonight?' Tyler says. He is suddenly serious, his dark, velvety eyes trained on me so I can't look away even if I want to. 'If it's truly important, it'll still be there to worry about in a couple of hours.'

He's right. All of it: my grandmother, my other mother, Seth, Mum, Nancy, and all the ways they touch and influence my life will still be there in a couple of hours. If I set them to one side, I'll be free to exist, to be a teenager, to even be an adult who has fun. I can almost taste the liberation of that.

The next bite of *vongole* tastes incredible now that I've been unhooked from the rest of my life.

'I thought you said you'd done this before,' Tyler states.

'When, pray tell, did I say that?' I reply.

'I asked if you'd ever been roller-skating along the promenade and you said...'

'I said nothing. I shook my head because I hadn't ever been roller-skating along the promenade or anywhere else in fact.'

Tyler has lent me skates with white boots, red wheels and red ribbon laces. The rubber stopper at the front is red, too. So much cooler than Hillary Senton's. When he produced them as my designated pair for the evening, I wondered if he probably took all his dates roller-skating and I would be wearing a dumped woman's skates. But no, they had the label on and as soon as we'd checked to see if they fitted me, he removed and binned the label.

'I suppose I should have asked if you'd been roller-skating anywhere, ever,' Tyler states.

'Yes, I think you should have.' I am clinging on to the clammy sea wall that runs along the promenade outside his café. He'd laced me into the boots while we sat on this bench because locking up in roller skates would have been too difficult. Once the last lace was tied, I'd got up and had promptly fallen over. I had made progress in the last ten minutes in that I had now managed to go from the bench to the wall without falling over. I am currently working on letting go of the wall.

'In my mind's eye,' Tyler says wistfully, 'I saw us skating up and down here, undaunted by the lack of light, holding hands, showing off to each other, maybe one of us "accidentally" falling and bringing the other one down with us, landing in a happy heap and...' His voice trails off.

'Oh, no, don't stop. You were just getting to the good part. You weren't making me feel at all guilty for not having a clue how to do this. Not one little bit.'

'Revenge for the coffee dig earlier.' Tyler skates nearer. 'Haven't you ever been ice-skating?'

'Yes. I ended doing this that time, too. I'd completely forgotten how much I didn't like that out-of-control feeling then, how anything can just go off in any direction it pleases and you can't do a thing about it.' My left leg, as if to prove my point, decides to slide away and I have to bring it back sharply while my fingers grope for purchase on the wall. This is actually worse than ice-skating. This is a different kind of powerlessness that I'm having to navigate.

Tyler stands in front of me. Slung across his body is the large black messenger bag containing our shoes and my bag. Despite the cool night, he's wearing a white T-shirt so his arms are bare – I'm sure he's wearing it to show off the sleek muscles of his upper body. (I don't blame him, they're pretty impressive arms and I'm surprised I've managed to avoid running my fingers over them for so long.)

'Take my hands,' he says.

'Yeah, I'm not going to do that.'

'Trust me, do it one at a time. Just reach out and take my hand.' Gingerly, carefully, I reach out for him and his hand is there, immediately, clamped around mine, holding me steady. My legs wobble, slip a little, but mostly I am fine, I am upright, I am not sprawled all over the promenade showing myself up. 'Now, the other hand. You'll be fine, trust me.' That's twice he's asked me to trust him, twice he's used the word as though trusting someone is the easiest thing in the world. That when you need to, all you do is close your eyes and believe and everything will be tied up in a happily ever after bow. Trust, blind trust, is easy to give when you're young and naïve and have never been hurt, it's even easy to give when you've met someone new when you're not so young. But when you are older, when you have been hurt, when it seems every incidence of trust you've given to others has been betrayed in some way, you don't become jaded, you become suspicious and mistrustful of every act of trust you're asked to perform – even the most trivial ones. I don't trust Tyler not to let me fall. But there's also a part of me that needs to let go so I can prove that people always, *always* let you down if you trust them.

I push myself away from the wall slightly as I reach for his other hand and it is there. His hand, strong and sure, encircles mine and holds me safe and upright. 'I told you,' he says. His hands tighten around mine. 'First thing, stop looking down,' he tells me. Reluctantly I raise my head. Looking down lets me check what my feet are doing and it prevents me from . . . looking directly at him.

Tyler is like the Sun sometimes – you have to try to avoid looking directly at it because of what it can do to your body. The Sun can damage your eyes if you look directly at it – with Tyler, he'll make

274

your stomach flip several times in a few seconds, and will unleash unnecessarily potent lust throughout your veins.

'Now, I'm going to skate backwards for a bit...' I must look horrified because he adds quickly: 'I won't let you go. I'm going to skate slowly backwards, taking you with me until you feel safe.' He moves while he speaks, carefully but slowly dragging me with him. 'Any time you feel yourself slipping, grab tightly on to my hands.' We continue to move. It's not so bad now. I'm actually enjoying the feeling of passive motion, of moving forwards without even trying. 'See, this isn't so bad, is it?' he asks.

'No,' I reply. I don't want to speak too much in case I throw my balance off and end up on the floor.

'Good, this is good. You're doing well. Keep moving, keep coming forwards. That's it.' He keeps looking behind him, to check where he is heading, but at that time of night there are few people around and the promenade is thankfully hazard-free.

We've moved quite far despite my terror and I am starting to feel comfortable on wheels, as though I could one day possibly, maybe feel like I belong on them.

'Now, I'm going to let go of one of your hands. I'll still have the other one so once I let go, if you feel at all worried, you can just grab my hand again. OK?'

'OK.' I can do this. I remember when Dad sat me down and told me that it was back, that there was nothing they could do, that it was now just a question of marking time on our new calendars, I thought I couldn't do it. I thought I would never get through. But at some point, I don't remember when, I realised I was doing it. I could do it because I was doing it. I had no choice, and because I had no choice, I managed to do it.

At some point, when exactly I didn't notice, my feet have stopped being passive, they have started to move, to be the cause of my motion. Clumsy, clunky and awkward at first, then smoother, easier, nearly a hint of graceful. 'Put your free arm out to balance yourself,' Tyler says. He is beside me now, holding on to one hand as we move. Without hesitation or fear, I put my arm out, and without panic I feel the shift of my weight as I find my centre on the two lines of wheels.

'See? See?' Tyler says. 'You can do it. You're doing it.' I can hear pride in his voice.

I can do it. I am doing it.

Looming right ahead of us is my building. We have skated all the way from Beached Heads to my flat and I haven't fallen over, Tyler hasn't let me down. 'That's where I live,' I say to him.

'Really?' he replies. 'I've always wanted to see inside that building. It looks incredible. Is it authentic on the inside?'

'The communal areas are, and the windows have to be the right style for the planning department, but most of them are double-glazed. And there's a cage lift like you see in old American movies.'

'You do realise that you're talking and skating now?' Tyler replies. 'You've done brilliantly.'

'Yeah, yeah, but tell me, how am I going to stop?' My building is coming towards us very fast. 'Because it seems my only option is to fall over or crash into the wall.'

Turns out that stopping involves hitting the wall with my hands instead of my body, and pulling myself to a standstill. I watched Tyler do it gracefully then did it myself.

Unusually, for that time of night, the car park is virtually empty. Normally it's a bun fight to get any space here because it is free, off-street parking that is exempt from the attentions of traffic wardens. Red, white and shiny, Lottie sits in her place at the far end of the car park, probably loving the view she has of the sea but not loving what the salt is doing to her metal parts. I need to take better care of her, take her out for a drive more.

Now that I've stopped, I feel a little less steady on my feet. 'I think my days of skating are over,' I say to Tyler, who is standing beside me at the wall. 'Maybe I should quit while I'm upright.' His laughter in reply is easy and calming. From the bag slung across his body he produces my flat red ballet pumps. He bobs down as though he isn't on skates and starts to unlace me. Every so often his hands stray to my ankle, and the heat of his touch sends pleasure all the way up my legs. It's a let down almost literally when my left foot is freed from the skate and returned to my shoe. I feel like I have fallen from a great height. Once I am back in my pumps I feel tiny compared to him. The speed with which he changes into his own trainers tells me that he was lengthening the process of taking off my shoes so he could touch me. Which I do not mind *at all*.

'So, that was an experience,' he says, once we are both back to normal height and on solid ground.

'It certainly was.'

'One you might want to repeat?'

This is 'end of the date' talk – we're not only talking about skating, we're discussing whether we're going to 'see' each other again.

'I feel strange not rolling around,' I say. 'I almost feel unsteady on my feet because I'm steady on my feet.'

'Ah, classic avoidance of the question,' Tyler says. He drops the bag, which now contains the two sets of skates, on to the ground.

'More like nerves about what might happen next,' I explain.

'What do you think might happen next?' he asks.

'Well, on any other normal date I might ask you in for a coffee – only instant, I'm afraid – and see once we're inside if I fancy progressing it to something more, tonight or another night…But, right now, I not only have my mother staying with me, my cousin and her daughter are here as well. I have a full house so it'd require far too much sneaking around. And anyway, who's to say you'd want to come up? Drink my coffee? Want to progress things? You might not even want to see me again. I realise those were some pretty big assumptions I was making, which makes me nervous.'

Tyler takes my hand, slowly presses his palm against mine until they are flat against each other like a reflection in a mirror. Staring intently at me, he reaches out with his other hand and slips it around my waist. His body against mine feels different to— I stop myself short. I'm not supposed to be thinking about *him*. *He*'s all part of the stuff that's been put to one side.

Tyler is simply different. I haven't related to another man's body in this way in over a decade. A frisson of excitement at being about to embark on something new tingles down my spine.

'I told you before, you're silly,' he says quietly. 'How could I not want to see you again?'

Our lips are suddenly millimetres apart and then they are together. My body feels like it did when I first stood up on the skates, wobbly and out of control. This is all good, *wanted*, though. This is the kind of out of control I enjoy. Tyler's kisses intensify, he presses me back against the wall, my hands go to his face, and he moves his body so close to mine I can feel the hammer of his heart against my chest. These mouth touches are incredible, they shoot shards of pleasure through me that pool in my stomach, explode in my chest, cause an ache between my legs.

'Get a room!' someone shouts at us from a passing car, and we immediately jump apart. Above the sound of the car engine driving away, we can hear the shouter and his friends laughing loudly.

Tyler lowers his forehead on to mine and chortles. 'That's the sort of thing that would only happen to me when I'm with you.'

'I'm not sure if that's a good thing or not,' I reply.

'It's a good thing. Being with you is a good thing.' He lowers his head. 'Here, let me prove it to you.'

Right before our lips slot together again he pauses as though something is wrong. Tyler frowns, then turns his head towards the sea, towards where Lottie is parked. My heart almost leaps out of my chest when I realise there is someone leaning against Lottie in the otherwise empty car park.

That person wasn't there before. At least, I don't think they were. But I maybe didn't notice much in the excitement of being with Tyler. I had glanced at Lottie, noted how shiny she looked, decided I needed to drive her more, but did I *really* look, take a note of the shadows she cast, the shadows others cast upon her? The shadow stops reclining against my car and stands to its full height.

'Sorry, is there something I can do for you, mate?' Tyler asks. He sounds pleasant and reasonable enough, but the way he has stepped slightly in front of me, has checked over his shoulder to make sure we're not going to be pounced on from behind, suggests he thinks trouble could be about to come our way. It is, unfortunately. But not in the way he thinks.

'No, not really,' the man who was watching us replies. 'Not unless you want to tell me why you're kissing my wife.'

42

Abi

To: Jonas Zebila
From: Abi Zebila
Subject: Sigh
Wednesday, 22 July 2015

Jonas,

Thank you. Thank you for sending me that email. I know it only said, 'I love you, little sister' a couple of hundred times, but it lifted my spirits. It made me feel less alone.

Gran is back in hospital. It's very serious. Seems like last time was just a trial run. I'm trying to make light of it but it's incredibly stressful. A diabetic crisis, a mild heart attack and various other minor things that all added together to put her back in hospital. She's probably going to have a stent put in.

I keep thinking, if I was like Gran is, what would I want? Would I want to be looked after by family, or would I want to be in a place where I get looked after by strangers who are experts? It's not like she and Mummy get on and she knows Mummy's doing it out of love and concern instead of duty and obligation.

Or would I want to be around at all, is the other question I keep asking myself. The thought of not being here, not seeing Lily and Declan and the other people I love, is terrifying to me. The thought of being alive but living this half-life of knowing that I'm never going to get better and will need dozens of different types of medication every day to keep me going is terrifying, too. But then, I'd want to live, I think.

No matter how ill I got, I'd want to live.

No matter how ill Gran gets, how awful she is to me and everyone else, I think I want her to live, too. I just want her experience of life to be better and pain-free. I can't imagine a world without Gran. I can't imagine her carrying on as she is, getting more sick and relying more on others and hating every second of that, either. But what's the alternative?

Gawd, that got a bit maudlin, didn't it? I'm so happy because you actually replied to one of my emails and Clemency came with me to...OH MY GOD! She called the ambulance for Gran and I haven't even told her if Gran's OK or not. Better go.

Abi
xxxxx

43

Smitty

Tyler reacts by moving his confused gaze from Seth to me, back to Seth, back to me. I don't deny what the man from the shadows has said, I don't call him a liar, which means to Tyler...He takes two steps backwards, putting distance between us.

The only real light we have shining down on the car park comes from the flats in the building above, and a streetlight on the corner where the cycle path disappears from view around the building. Standing here, in the near dark, the sound of the sea suddenly seems to have been magnified. Its volume is deafeningly loud all of a sudden, or maybe it is all the blood in my body rushing so forcefully to my head I fear it is about to explode.

This really shouldn't be happening. I'm not altogether sure how it is happening.

'Time I went,' Tyler states.

'Tyler...' I begin. Then nothing more comes out because I've run out of words. What do you say when the man who asked you if you were single before he arranged a magnificent date and was showering you in glorious kisses, discovers you're married?

'Yes?' he asks.

'I...' What do you say? Nothing. Except: 'I'm sorry.'

'So am I,' he replies.

Everyone was in their beds with their doors shut, only the corridor light was on so it was easy to unlock the front door and shunt Seth

282

through to my bedroom without being seen. He walks across the room towards the windows, leans against the sill and folds his arms over his chest. I shut the door, lock it behind me. This shouldn't be happening and I have no idea why it is happening. As it continues to happen, though, I take a couple of deep breaths before I turn to face him.

He's grown a beard. In all the years I've known him, the only time he ever even flirted with facial hair was when Sienna asked him to grow a beard so he could be like Father Christmas. He got to three days before the itching was too much for him. In our separation he has managed to change that, though. It's made up of short brown, neatish hairs, so I'm guessing he trims it but doesn't groom it. His hair has grown as well – the grade-two shave replaced by a shortish back and sides from not bothering to have it cut. The skin under his eyes is a pewter colour, his normally healthy peach skin is pale, almost grey. He's lost weight, probably from not eating properly. How he looks is how I feel most of the time.

'What are you doing here?' I ask him when he doesn't speak, simply stands with his arms folded. 'In fact, how did you know where "here" was, considering I never told you?'

'Your mother called me.'

'Which one?' is on the tip of my tongue before I remember he doesn't know the half of what's been going on. And seeing as only one of them knows about him . . . 'Of course she did,' I reply. I know the exact day she called him, too: the day she met Tyler and decided he wasn't good enough so she'd better make do with the other not good enough one who she at least knew. 'What did she say? No, wait, don't tell me. No, actually, do . . . Actually, no, don't. I don't think I can bear to know what she said. Actually, d—'

'She said at this time of her life she should be planning on what to knit for her grandchildren, not worrying about whether she should be signing up her daughter for online dating. And that she didn't know how I could stand to look myself in the mirror every day when I'd wasted almost all of your child-bearing years. And that if she ever saw me again she wasn't sure if she could restrain herself enough to not slap me into the middle of next year. Oh, and when you did meet someone else, not to show my weaselly little face anywhere near you as she might instigate said slapping. Or words to that effect.'

'Had quite a lot to say for herself, didn't she, my mother?'

My husband nods. 'Yeah, quite a lot.'

'Erm...hang on, how do you get from "slapping you into the middle of next year" to "here's my daughter's address, turn up whenever you fancy...oh, and, don't worry, I won't warn her in any way"?'

Seth pushes up the sleeves of his navy blue sweatshirt. On his left wrist he wears his divers' watch and the leather, intricately plaited wristband I made for him at the height of the loom-band craze last year. On his right hand he has the silver cuff that I engraved with our initials in the same design he'd come up with for our engagement party. I keep staring at his arms, the pale skin covered in light hairs, so I do not have to stare at his face.

'I told her that she was right; that I'd thought about it and was incredibly sorry for everything that had happened. That I'd tried to get in touch but you wouldn't talk to me so could she tell me where you'd gone so I could come and beg your forgiveness and maybe get our relationship back on track.'

'And she handed over my address, just like that?'

'Yes. She told me she'd moved with you.'

'Well, it's a good thing I hadn't fled from you in fear of my life, isn't it? I swear, that woman doesn't think sometimes.'

'She was only trying to help.'

'Yeah, that's what she was doing,' I say sarcastically. 'If you and her are such good buddies, why weren't you in here instead of waiting outside? Which, by the way, is a really creepy thing to do. If I'd been on my own I might have died with fright. Especially with your new facial hair.'

Seth raises one of his hands, runs it over the bearded lower half of his face. 'I called your mobile and it was off, so I called your mother and she said you were out, probably working, and would be back later. I decided to sit on the bench and wait.' Even though I'm not looking at his face, I know he is staring at me. I can feel the weight of his gaze on the top of my head. I raise my eyes to meet his.

If I'd been on my own is currently playing on a loop in his head. I knew the moment I said it that I shouldn't have. Betrayal and a deep sense of wounding have settled on his face.

'How long have you been seeing him?' Seth asks.

'What?' I know what that note in his voice is implying.

'How long? It's a fair enough question.'

'I didn't cheat on you,' I tell him. 'You know I wouldn't do that.'

'Answer the question then: how long have you been seeing him?'

'I met him a week or so after I moved here and this was the first time we've been out, not that it's any business of yours.'

He opens his mouth to say something and I cut in with: 'I can't talk any more right now. My head is fried about this and so many other things. I am not able tonight.'

'OK, fair enough, but can you answer me this: weren't you going to sort out us before you moved on?'

I say nothing in response because I don't want to talk about this right now, I am not able.

He takes my silence as a green light to ask another question. 'Or have you already "moved on" and this guy is just another step further along the road?'

That is goading enough to get me to bite. 'What are you saying?' I ask. Even though it's obvious, *blatant*, what he's accusing me of.

'You're not exactly shy about sex with different people is what I'm saying. How many of them have there been in the past three months?'

I'm guessing Seth has been examining what should be the wall of photographs he's helped me assemble and disassemble during the various moves of my life and he has been shocked and injured by the way I have edited him out. The only one that remains of him is the one of him with Dad. And yet, on the second row of the wall of my life in photographs that I'm rebuilding, there is Tyler. Melissa is there, too, but I wasn't kissing her a few minutes ago.

What he is saying reminds me of the time I found a bee on the washing in our back garden. I didn't think, just reached out to pick it off, and the bee objected to being moved on and stung me. Seth is like the bee – doesn't like the idea of being picked off, moved on, and has decided to sting me.

'How many were there before me again?' he says. 'Or did you lose count? Have you lost count now?'

His words continue to pump in poison, like the bee's sting did in my hand. The poison kept pumping in until Dad stopped me trying to pick out the sting and brushed it off with a quick, sideways swipe. I remember staring at it, incredulous at how this little sliver of a thing had managed to cause such extreme pain in my hand. I stare at my husband, incredulous that after everything he has done, he is causing extreme pain in my heart. It never seemed to have bothered him that much that I'd once slept around, and I thought in the moments it might have bothered him, he accepted it as part of who I was. I never thought he'd use it against me, no matter what the provocation.

'Fancy sleeping in your hire car, do you?' I ask. My quick, sideways swipe to remove this sting and stop his poison.

He unfolds his arms and stands upright. 'No, no I don't.'

'Are you sure?'

'Yeah, I'm sure.'

'Sure? Sure-sure?'

'I'm sorry,' he replies, finally ashamed and mollified. 'That was bang out of order. I'm sorry. I didn't mean it.'

'Why are you behaving like a dick?' I ask.

His hazel-green eyes flare suddenly. 'Because I *really* hated seeing you kiss someone else. And I really, *really* hate knowing you'd probably be in that bed fucking him right now if I hadn't turned up tonight.'

'But I can do what I like because we're finished, Seth. I made it clear we were over. What part of "we have to split up" didn't you get?' I reply.

'That isn't—'

'Isn't what?'

'That isn't how you end a marriage, OK? You don't just tell

someone you're splitting up and not tell them why. That's the part of "we have to split up" I don't get.'

I drop my face into my hands. If I had told him why, he would have carried on lying to me. He would have told me the truth eventually, but it would have been so eventually I wouldn't ever have trusted another thing that came out of his mouth. 'My head is fried,' I plead. 'I don't want to talk any more – about anything. I just don't.'

'I know, I'm sorry, I'm sorry. A lot has happened.'

'You have no idea,' I say, my voice wrapped tightly in a sob.

'We both need sleep. How are we going to do this?'

'Top to tail,' I say.

'*Really?*' he replies. 'When was the last time you topped to toed it?

'Apparently tonight.'

'Right you are then.'

'And keep the underwear on,' I add.

'I can't do that. I can't sleep with anything on.'

'You'll have to learn, starting tonight. I don't want "it" on the loose in the night.'

'What, you think it detaches itself from my body and roams around in the night?'

'No, I just don't want to encounter it if I roll over in the night and parts of our bodies touch each other. And then we have one of those awkward moments where it responds and I can't get my leg far away enough and you start having to think of your grandmother or something to make it— '

'Yes, all right, I get it. The black jacks stay on.'

We are silent as we undress, but the rustle of clothes being unbuttoned, pulled off, pulled down, fills the space in the room, everything amplified and loud. Each undone button, each piece of clothing folded and placed on my desk, is a noisy reminder that we used to rush through this part almost every night so we could get into bed together, talk and eventually fall asleep wrapped up in each other. We would usually not wake up like that, would be separated as we moved through dreamland, but undressing was always the start of finishing our day together.

287

Without being asked, he takes the foot of the bed and I throw him a couple of pillows. He accepts them with a small smile of gratitude and slides under the duvet. I do the same. Even though we are on opposite sides of the bed, I'm still aware of him. Of his body, his heat, the weight of history that links us.

He rests his head on his arm and stares up the ceiling and I do the same. Our breathing is deep and synchronised. Seth will probably sleep. He always used to say he hated sleeping without me beside him, and now we're back in the same bed, coupled with the exhaustion of the drive and the adrenalin of the last half an hour, I can imagine he'll probably flake right out. I hate that idea. I hate that he has snatched away the chance for me to have something else on my mind before I go to sleep, something pleasant and exciting, and after doing that, he'll probably just slide off to sleep like nothing has happened.

'I don't think Mum told you,' I whisper in the dark. 'Nancy and Sienna are staying here with us for a while.'

His demeanour is immediately tense. I can almost hear how alarm bulges his eyes, while his body has obviously been dragged away from its slow descent into sleep.

It's mean and awful that I did that, but I'm quite pleased to know that neither of us will be getting much sleep tonight.

44

Smitty

Since first light came creeping in through the open blinds I have been sitting on my desk chair, my feet up on the seat, watching Seth sleep. I had a break to go for a shower and to get dressed, but mostly I have sat here and watched him while the Sun has got higher and higher in the sky.

He doesn't suit his beard, but he looks the same. Maybe a little older, more tired, thinner, but he's still Seth. He's still one of the best friends I ever had. I would have stayed with him forever, I think. I certainly planned to. Our future was set, made from stitching together every day, week, month, year we'd had – each one distinctive, unique and important – until we had the patchwork quilt of who we were as a couple.

'Wake up, Seth,' I say from across the room. We have to talk. I wasn't fair on him. At the time it'd been too difficult for me to even contemplate: after losing Dad, talking to Seth about all this seemed an impossibility when he had kept things from me. No matter what he'd done, though, that wasn't fair on him, he did deserve better.

I move across the room, crouch down beside him and hiss, '*Seth! Wake up!*' into his ear.

He jerks awake, his eyes wide and shocked. 'Whaaa-what?'

'Shall we go get a coffee, have a talk?' I say.

He grunts, tries to turn over. 'Later,' he mumbles.

'No, now.'

'No,' he murmurs. 'Sleep.'

A wave of anger crashes through me. 'OK, you sleep,' I say, irritation in every word. 'And I'll send Nancy in with coffee a bit later, shall I?'

He dresses quickly and efficiently, asks for the bathroom so he can use the toilet and brush his teeth. Last night was the second night ever that I'd known him not brush his teeth before bed (the other time was the night we first slept together). I used to sit on the edge of the bath and talk to him while he brushed his teeth. It was for two minutes, he couldn't reply as the toothbrush buzzed around his mouth, but it was one of our 'things'. Sometimes, he'd sit beside me and we'd have a conversation before we started work. That was another square of the quilt of our life, another bead on the string of our time together.

With Seth, February 2014, Leeds

'Are you sure you don't mind not having anyone here?' I asked him.

He kissed under my right ear lobe. 'Not at all,' he whispered before raising the camera on my phone above us. 'Say "nuptials"!' he said with a laugh.

'Nuptials!' I said, and grinned as he imprinted the image of our special day into the space in my phone. Password-protected so no one would ever know.

I'd heard Sienna in the living room watching CBeebies on her own so we'd had to creep out of the flat so she wouldn't see Uncle Smitty, as she called him. Outside my building, we both stand for a moment and stare at the sea. 'This is such an amazing view,' he says. 'When I was sat out here last night I had a real sense of peace and being connected to something huge.'

'This way,' I say to him. I turn towards the main road, intending to head up towards George Street, the main street in Hove. On that small road there are more coffee shops – chains, independents and local chains – than any other type of shop.

'I saw a café along the seafront. Let's go there.'

'No, let's go up to George Street.'

'Why? That café looked cool. I'm sure it's open now. It'd be nice to talk and see the sea. Ha! See what I did there?'

My face musters a smile. 'No, let's just go to George Street. There are so many more places. Some of them have nice views, especially if you like to watch somewhere come to life.'

'Look, what's the problem with—'

Seth has finally faced me, seen the uncomfortable manner in which I bite at my lower lip, keep my eyes on the uneven black-grey surface of the car park where less than twelve hours ago he watched me kiss another man.

'He works there,' Seth states.

I nod. *Owns it, actually*, I should say. *Makes brilliant coffee in the most brilliant cups.*

'I might have known.'

'What's that supposed to mean?'

'What do you think it means?'

'I don't know, that's why I asked.'

'It means I might have known he'd be someone you see every day.'

'That doesn't even make sense – I see the postman every day, are you expecting something to happen between me and him? Or are you calling me a slut again?'

When he doesn't reply, I say, 'Well, are you?'

He shakes his head.

'Well then, stop saying things that don't make sense or imply you think I'm a slut. I haven't slept with anyone since you. And even if I had, it'd be no business of yours.' I sound far more indignant than I am: I'm single, we're separated, our marriage is over as far as I'm concerned, but guilt is gambolling through me, leaving a sense that I have betrayed him. 'And I don't even drink coffee every day,' I add for good measure.

'George Street it is,' he eventually says.

My unwarranted sense of guilt and betrayal makes every step slow, laborious and painful as we walk together to the place where our marriage is going to end properly.

45

Smitty

We find our places in the café just at the bottom of George Street. It is old-fashioned on the outside with double-bay tinted glass windows, but the height of modernity on the inside: brilliant white walls with primary colour picture panels containing bright, bold prints in each of the picture panels, and white, distressed-wood floors.

It's mainly populated by people who are coming in for a coffee on the way to work, or those who have come early with their laptops to stake out a space to work for the day. Seth pulls out a low striped fabric-covered bucket chair for me at the back of the café, then turns towards the counter.

'The usual?' he asks.

'I suppose so,' I reply. I'm not sure what the usual is any more. Everything feels like it is in flux, nothing set; all that I knew or thought I knew is fluid and changeable. He returns a few minutes later, after I've watched him queuing, after he has constantly looked over at me, as though checking I am still there and won't be running away again. *'Where would I run to?'* I should have called over to him. *'It's not like I have anywhere else to go.'*

He lowers himself into his seat, slowly, dragging the moments out before we need to speak. I have no idea where to start with the process of unravelling. How do we make sense of any of it? It's like a huge, sheer rock face: the summit so high it's not easily visible to the naked eye, and I – *we* – need to climb it without any safety equipment. It's possible, doable, but dangerous, particularly since it is so unknown. Seth and I used to talk all the time. About anything, everything, it was our 'thing'. We talked and listened to each other. Now, I don't know what to say; which words to choose to start the conversation.

'How about we start with this,' he states. From the side pocket of his trousers he produces a rectangular box and slides it across the table to me. I knew I shouldn't have bought him a pair of those trousers. I wear combats and workmen's trousers because it allows me to carry all sorts of things in the various pockets, my own wearable toolbox. He coveted them so passionately I finally bought him a pair. And now look: they've let him bring that thing here without me having a clue he was carrying it. What's that expression about no good deed going unpunished?

I stare at that box, long and oblong with coloured writing and a coloured design. It was the most discreet one on sale, that's why I chose it. Hid it amongst my other shopping and avoided eye contact with the person who served me. Not that they'd care, but I had cared.

'There's only one left in the box,' he states. 'I'm assuming there were two when you bought it.'

My gaze goes from the box to him. Calm. He's calm. That's good.

'Here we go,' the waitress trills. She's that 1950s vintage Brighton-type with her spotted scarf tied in a bow around the front of her glossy black bun, her lips coated in bright red lipstick, her foundation overly pale and her eyes heavily made up. 'One café mocha, extra shot of chocolate, and one double-strong latte.' We each indicate which is ours and continue to stare at one another as she sets the large white cups in front of us. From the corner of my eye I see her notice the box on the table and she visibly winces as it crosses her mind that we're not going to be having a nice coffee and chat. She winces again, gritting her teeth, then quietly withdraws. When the crowd has died down she's going to stand behind her counter, pretending to polish her coffee machine while watching how this story plays out.

'So, one test instead of two?' Seth asks when it's obvious I'm not going to restart *that* conversation.

'I used one just before I came down here.' The box fascinates me. Why didn't I throw it away instead of hiding it? I remember dashing out of the bathroom into the corridor when I heard his motorbike pull up outside. I remember thinking it would be the worst thing in the world to be caught with that box so instead of shoving it into my back pocket with the test, I hid it in one of my packing boxes. Why? And why didn't I take it away when I went back to collect as many possessions as I could? Did I want to get caught?

'What was the result?' he asks.

'I don't know,' I admit. 'I was so freaked out by everything that I stopped down the road from the flat and threw it into the nearest bin without checking.'

He frowns, the action crinkling his forehead, while he calculates something. 'That day at the flat, that's what you were doing?'

'Yes.'

Obviously the more important thought hits him then: 'Have you done a test since?'

I sigh before I'm forced to shake my head.

'So you could be ... You could be pregnant right now?'

'No, I'm not. Which is why I didn't need to look. I'd know if I was and I'm not.'

'Have you had a period?'

I sigh again. Stupid box. If it wasn't for this stupid box this conversation wouldn't be going this way. I wouldn't be on the back foot and having to think about this again. No, I haven't had a proper period since before I left Leeds, but I was incredibly stressed, grief-stricken about Dad and the break-up with Seth. I was moving. My mother decided to move in with me. Any one of those things would normally have stressed me out enough to make a period late, but all of them together? It'd be a miracle if my body got itself right again enough to have a period in a decade or so, let alone three months. I glare harder at the box. This stupid box that's caused all this trouble.

'Clem? Have you had a period since you took the test?'

'I am not pregnant,' I state. I pull the box across the table towards me, drop it in my bag to give me a way to hide my face. 'I will do this test later, if it makes you happy. But I am not pregnant.' I was pregnant once when I was seventeen as the result of a split condom and it felt completely different to this. Admittedly that pregnancy lasted for about two days until nature decided to take another course and spare me having to make the decision that my birth mother made, but my body felt different then to how it feels now.

'Would you tell me if you were?'

'Yes, Seth, I would tell you. What sort of thing is that to ask?'

My husband reclines in his seat, pushing his legs out before he runs his hands over his haircut. 'Have you not been living the life where you left without an explanation?' he says. 'I wouldn't have asked if you hadn't just ended our relationship without talking to me properly.'

'Marriage. I ended our marriage. We're married.'

'I know we're married.'

'But no one else does, do they? And why is that? Oh, yes, because of your "*friend*" Nancy.'

Abruptly Seth's expression changes – worry and fear dance on his features. Now he's the one on the back foot, uncertain where this conversation is going to take us. What I'm going to say next.

'Nothing happened with Nancy.'

Liar, I think. *Liar.* 'Something *always* happens with Nancy. *Always.*'

He tells me I'm right almost straight away. Not with words, but in the way he slides down in his seat and slowly runs the palms of his hands over his temples, trying to massage away the memory of it all.

'Smitty—' he begins.

'I told you what she did to me, Seth,' I cut in. 'I told you how she made my childhood a nightmare, how I couldn't talk to my mother about it because Mum can't see what she's like. And you saw what she was like yourself, how she ruined our engagement party, how she's tried to ruin other stuff, and you still started a secret friendship with her.'

'I didn't start it, it sort of happened.'

'Everything always "sort of happens" with Nancy. That's what she does. She starts turning up when no one is around, just for a chat.'

'She wanted me to help her with her website. That was all. And she kept coming over.'

'Even though she's been doing her website for years and has even designed stuff for other people?'

'It all made sense at the time. But thinking back now, I didn't do much of anything, not even give her design advice. We sat at the computer together, but she did most of it.'

'And then she starts bringing over the joints and the beers.'

'It was only the odd joint and beer.'

'Even though you don't ever do drugs, and you very rarely drink during the day, especially when you're meant to be working.'

He rubs at his temples again. 'But it made sense at the time. We were just hanging out while I was working. And...'

'And then suddenly she's confiding in you about her latest man problem, you're trying to make her feel better by paying her compliments because men have been shit to her all her life and it's not her, it's them. Especially Dylan who you're even more disappointed in because he's your friend and he's abandoned his daughter.'

'But—'

'Then, because she's trusted you, it's not long before you're telling her stuff that you wouldn't normally tell anyone.'

'It didn't seem so calculated.'

'Of course it didn't. She's been doing it all her adult life. All *my* adult life. She's tried it on with every boyfriend I've ever had. I told you this.'

'But she just needed a friend. That's what it felt like.'

'I know that's what it felt like. And that's fine. But what isn't fine is that when I asked you about it, you lied to me.'

'How did you find out?' my husband asks.

'Apart from finding her hair in our bed?' He blanches. 'Yes, I know she got into our bed naked and propositioned you, it's part of her repertoire. The other way I knew what was going on was that she was writing stuff on her blog that could only have come from you. I started to read it when I found her hair.' If it's possible, more colour leaches out of his skin and he is now as white as the floor of the café.

'She said she wouldn't tell anyone she'd done that. She seemed more embarrassed than I did when I turned her down and told her to get dressed. She even asked me if I was going to tell you, and when I said yes, she practically begged me not to. I should have known it was too easy when she said she wouldn't tell anyone.'

'That's what she does,' I remind my husband. 'She gets you into a situation where you go against your better judgement and suddenly she's got something over you because you've been keeping a secret with her.'

'You believe that I didn't sleep with her?'

'Yes. Of course I believe you. I knew you wouldn't sleep with her, Seth, but it wasn't about that. It was never about that. I asked you – practically begged you that last night – to tell me. But you wouldn't. I knew if I started asking questions you'd panic even more and lie and I couldn't stand that. I only wanted you to be truthful with me. I have trusted you more than anyone else I've met in my life, and you lied to me.'

'I felt like I couldn't tell you the truth. I wanted to, but I couldn't. You were in so much pain and I didn't want to add to it.'

'You told her we were starting to try for a baby.' That hurt more than her getting into our bed.

'She wrote that on her blog?'

'No. She texted me saying if we were thinking of trying for a baby that I should talk to her about any tips I might need and not to forget the folic acid. On the surface a nice text from one cousin to another, and if I told anyone else about that text they'd all think I was crazy for being upset by it. In reality, it's her way of telling me that you're confiding in her.'

'Oh, God.'

'How could you, Seth? It was *such* a big deal, we have talked for years about it so I could get my head around it. We got married and everything so I'd feel safer about trying for a baby. I didn't even tell my dad in my last few months with him that we'd got married and were trying to conceive, even though I knew how happy it would make him, because we agreed it was something for you and me. There were so many times when I came close to telling him, when I wanted to say that we'd at least got married so he'd feel happy that I'd be settled once he was gone, but I didn't because we'd agreed that no one else was to know. And you just up and told Nancy about us trying for a baby. Her of all people. Why didn't you just tell her we'd got married and be done with it?'

These feelings, bottled up inside for so long, don't feel better out in the open. It's worse. They're raw, like newly scraped skin exposed to salt, it's an indescribable pain. Safety is so underrated, dismissed as being boring and dull in the whole spectrum of a *grand amour* relationship. Passion, sex, grand gestures, romantic meals, big long kisses, swooning... They are what love is meant to be about. They are the things we are meant to crave and revel in, but safety? It's something that apparently signals a relationship has become stale and predictable. Safety is what I need, what Seth always told me he needed. If either of us were to fall, we needed to know that we would have a soft landing place, that we would be safe. He loved his parents but, as he got older, realised how smothering they were and he only felt able to breathe when we had got together. He found safety with me. And safety, trust, is what I'd had with Seth. The safety to be myself. I opened myself up to him, trusted him with my thoughts and fears and the depth of the void inside, and how I could never fill it. With Seth, I was safe. Then, somehow, I wasn't. I couldn't trust him, I couldn't rely on him to not repeat things to the one person who had made my life a misery. Without safety and trust I couldn't be with him any longer. Without safety and trust I have this pain that doesn't feel like it will go.

When Seth is highly stressed he closes his eyes and focuses his attention on the blackness inside his eyelids and takes deep breaths to try to calm his racing heart. I watch him sit with his eyes closed, the rise and fall of his chest slowing and slowing until he is holding his breath for long seconds, releasing it for an equally long amount of time.

When I'm stressed, I want to run. Not jogging or anything constructive like that, I just have an urge to stop what I'm doing, throw down whatever I'm holding and run away as fast as I can, only stopping when my legs and feet are too exhausted to move or I come to an intractable natural barrier. I want to run. I want to leave all of this behind and run away again.

'Can you forgive me?' he asks. He has opened his eyes and is staring at me.

No. That is the answer. *I don't think so, no.*

'I want to,' I say instead. 'I'm not—' I stop. The agony of what I am saying is slashed across his face. His eyes are closed again. He's retreating into darkness, calming his erratic heart with measured breathing. 'I want to,' I repeat.

It's not only about forgiveness. It's forgetting as well. Can you truly forgive someone if you haven't forgotten what they have done? Our marriage won't withstand the need for forgiveness. Together, we can withstand a lot of things: arguments, comments from other people about how we shouldn't be together, disapproval from my mother, poverty, even attempts by Nancy to break us up, but it can't withstand something like a breach of trust that requires forgiveness. We could pretend, we could get back together and carry on, but I know the moment I don't tell him something because I fear he'll tell someone else, will be the moment I'll know I haven't forgotten. And if I haven't forgotten, then I haven't forgiven.

I want to forgive him. I want to move on and get back together, but I won't be able to forget. Without forgetting, forgiveness is meaningless.

Seth wants to walk around for a bit to clear his head. I'd love to as well. But I have another difficult conversation to have, a huge apology to make, and I can't delay it any longer.

46

Abi

To: Jonas Zebila
From: Abi Zebila
Subject: Big news
Friday, 24 July 2015

Dear J,

I meant to tell you something. I'm up the duff again. Yes, big news. It was all planned, which is why Declan keeps going on about getting married. No, Mummy and Daddy don't know and I'm not sure if this is or isn't the time to tell them. *Is* the time because they're so stressed about Gran nothing will seem as bad; *is not* the time because they're so stressed about Gran, telling them now would be incredibly selfish.

Gran is home. She seems better. In fact, this is the best she's looked in a long time but it's still stressful, especially for Mummy. Not only because she does most of the caring, but I get the impression having Clemency around has made Mummy rethink a lot of things about her life. I noticed that the box of artwork she 'disappeared' from the loft is now in the pantry area of the kitchen – she must be going through it again.

Since Gran has been in hospital Mummy's been sketching on random pieces of paper and has got herself a sketch pad now. I wonder if she's going to take her art up again if she gets the chance? I'm not sure she can, because Gran's care is the most important thing in her life and Mummy has to make everything fit around that. The best thing, though, is that if I need a hug, I know I can get it from her now. No, it's not all happy families around here – if it was I'd have told them I'm pregnant – but it's getting there between me and Mummy. Everyone knowing her secret is, I think, slowly turning her into the type of mother I always wanted. So, all a bit strange round here but not terrible.

Love and miss you,
Abi
xxxx

PS I forgot the other big news: Clemency is going to look after Lily-Rose. When I texted her about Gran being in hospital she said she'd take her next week so I can work. Lily will be over the moon as she loves Clemency's niece, Sienna. They've decided they're cousins. So let's see how that pans out.

47

Smitty

'What can I get you?' he asks politely. I've been downgraded. Not only to 'just another customer' but to 'annoying customer who I deal with politely'. If you spend a lot of time in Beached Heads, as I have, you notice how Tyler deals with people, how he categorises them. Loyal customers are treated like friends, he finds things to banter about, he remembers their orders, he assigns them their own special cups. Ordinary customers get the banter and recommendations on new coffees, are possibly assigned a cup if they've been more than once. Annoying customers get a polite greeting where he asks them what they want.

'How about a big cushion to break my fall when I throw myself to my knees and apologise profusely?'

'I don't do cushions,' he says. Politely.

'OK, I'll do it without the cushions, then…' Nothing. No response, no hint that he wants me to continue or to leave. I lower my voice. 'I'm sorry. I'm so, so sorry. I can't even begin to understand how you feel. That wasn't meant to happen.'

He jerks his head indicating that I should come to the other end of the counter, to near the machine where he taught me to make coffee. It's quieter there, more private.

'I'm so sorry,' I repeat, a little more confident now that he's not going to sling me out or ignore me. He does want to hear what I've got to say. 'It was such incredibly bad timing.'

'I don't mess with married women. It's not my thing – never has been, never will be,' he states.

'I'm not married in that sense of the word.'

'That guy wasn't your husband?'

'Yes, he is, but we've split up. I thought he'd got the message that we'd split up.'

'He's stalking you, then?'

'No, not exactly. Or even at all. He came here because he wanted us to sort out splitting up.'

Tyler's lips move upwards but they don't manage to make one of those smiles that I have been feeding my crush on. 'That makes no sense to me. Have you split up or not?'

'Yes.'

'But he doesn't know.'

'He does now. I thought he knew before, but there won't be a scrap of doubt in his mind any longer. That's why it's taken me so long to come see you. We were sorting things out.'

'When?'

'This morning.'

'No, I mean, when did you split up?'

'Nearly two and a half months ago. Although I haven't seen him in nine weeks.'

'In other words, when you moved down here.'

'Yes.'

'Ahh, right. And when did you last speak to him?'

'Apart from this morning?' I ask, jokily, trying to inject some levity into this. He's being altogether too polite for this to turn out well for me. And I hate Polite Tyler.

'Yes, apart from this morning.' Deadpan. He is not playing.

'He's been ringing me and texting, but I haven't replied.'

'Not really split up, then.'

'We had. He didn't want it to be true.'

'Had you started divorce proceedings? Or even seen a solicitor?'

'No.'

'That's not what being split up is. It's fine, you do what you

303

gotta do, but like I said, I don't mess with married women.'

'I'm only a married woman in name. And not even in name because we both kept our own names.'

My feeble attempt at humour is met with: 'Where did he sleep last night?'

Ah, *that* question. He is so convinced that I am married more than in name, whatever I say now will be wrong. 'We slept top to toe.'

'No sofa in your house?'

'I couldn't ask him to sleep on the sofa after his long drive and there were other things. I told you that I had a full house, it would have been too complicated.'

I receive a cordial, disappointed smile. Tyler picks up the nearest cup, the pastel yellow cup with white daisies all over the bowl. Then he takes a matching saucer. The way he picks it up makes it feel like it is no longer my assigned cup, just something he'd give to a customer he could not care less if he saw again or not. 'Coffee?' he asks. 'Cappuccino? Mocha?'

'Please believe me, Tyler. Nothing happened because we're not together any more,' I explain. 'I would have told you about him if we'd been out on another date. It's not really first date talk. But please believe me, I would have told you.'

'I don't mess with married women,' he reiterates. 'And, much as I like you, you're married. You don't think you are, but you are. You couldn't even make him sleep on the floor. You shared a bed with him because you're not done with him. Which is cool, but not something I want to get involved with.'

'It wasn't like that. I—' I stop. This is humiliating. Excruciatingly humiliating. I am begging someone to believe that I'm not still with my husband. I am trying to stop someone from dumping me, rejecting me. I thought I was done with being scared of rejection by men when I got together with Seth. I've been rebuffed so many times in my life, I should be used to it by now. I shouldn't mind too much standing in front of Tyler with him holding my favourite of his coffee cups in his hand, with him poised to make me a polite cup of coffee with which to wash down this huge, rich, creamy dose of rejection.

I wish I'd thought to take a picture of my favourite Beached Heads cup that Tyler had assigned me before this day. It would have made the wall at home. I'd have to take it down along with the picture of him and store them in the butterfly box, of course, but at least I'd be able to look at it occasionally even though I'd never be drinking from it again.

'I think I'd better go,' I say to him.

'Coffee to go?' he asks, his face open and friendly. Polite.

'No, no, I'm fine.'

'Are you sure? I'm making one anyway for the bottomless cup at the back, there. It's no trouble.'

'Oh, go on then, if—' I catch myself. 'No, actually, no.' I'm a little more forceful than necessary but I'm not going to play along with this. He's got every right to reject me but that doesn't mean I have to accept it placidly. 'I'm just going to go. Do some work or something. I'll see ya.'

'Yeah. Drop by any time you fancy a coffee, Clemency,' he says, the politest kick to the guts I've ever had, I think.

Tap, tap, tap. Pause. *Tap, tap, tap.* Pause. *Tap.* Pause. *Tap.*

Seth's secret knock. We came up with our secret knocks and secret codes in texts, in case either of us was ever taken hostage and we needed to let the other one know there was danger. (We loved doing stupid things like that.) He's tapping on Lottie's door. How he knew I was in here, have been in here since I briefly returned to the flat after I humiliated myself at Beached Heads, I don't know. My guess is that he's too scared to ring the doorbell to the flat in case Nancy or my mother answer. They've gone to Southampton for the day. Shopping, eating, hanging out like a family does on their summer holidays.

'It's open,' I call.

He slides back the door and is a bit taken aback to see me splayed out like a starfish on the floor. I hoist myself upright to sitting while he climbs in and shuts the door behind himself, seals us into the place where we spent many hours working together. We reloved Lottie back to this current state of glory. The bodywork was mainly good, but she needed a lot of work – hence the name – and both Seth and I wanted to do it. We housed her in a garage a short walk away from the flat and every night after work and most weekends, we'd work on her. We talked so much while we worked on her. We talked about our lives before we met, about our years in college, about having children, about the engagement party, about deciding to get married. All those important things were discussed, and very often decided, while we worked on some part of Lottie.

He sits on his favourite seat, the one behind the driver's seat that faces backwards.

I take the white test from its place in my bag, push it across the floor towards Seth. He stares at it for a long time in silence. He's disappointed, it's clear on his face, but he doesn't say or do anything except nod while staring at the result. I *knew* I wasn't pregnant. That was why it hadn't been a worry for me. Not a total worry, anyway. I had felt a fleeting nanosecond of disappointment ripple through me, followed by a small wave of relief that things could end properly between Seth and me now – we had nothing to tie us together. Then a huge gut-wrenching sob had escaped me when I realised Seth and I had nothing to tie us together. I wasn't going to have his baby and we were over.

'When are you going back home?' I ask.

'I'm not. Not right away, anyway.'

'What about work?'

He scratches his fingernails through his beard, the sound is dry and unpleasant. 'I resigned.'

'Resigned? Have you lost your mind? What are you going to do for money?'

'I'm still working for them until my notice period expires, then I'll be employed by them on a consultancy basis. I'll tidy up their big projects, help with pitches, etc. Any meetings can be done on video conference calls. I even sold the motorbike. I couldn't bring it so I sold it. I've sublet the flat to Jorge and his girlfriend.'

Slowly I ease myself up on to the seat diagonally opposite Seth. I rest my head against the window and stare into space. There is so much going on, but I keep thinking about Tyler. Every time I try to enjoy the memory of the way he smiled at me moments before we kissed, the expression of betrayal on his face before he left last night washes it away, and leaves huge chunks of guilt moored on the shores of my mind. He was so hurt, last night and today, and that was because of me. He didn't deserve that. No one did, to be honest.

'Have you been to see him?' Seth asks.

I nod without looking at him. I know what Seth does, though: he twists his lips together and nods. Right now, he'll be overtly struggling with himself – his innate, caring response as my friend will be in pitched battle with his instinctive, jealous response as my husband. 'Want to talk about it?' His friend role has won.

'Not with you, no.' He is not my friend. No matter what we might pretend, after a decade of sex and love and exclusivity, and then marriage, he can't go back to being 'just' my friend no matter how hard we'd both like him to be.

'Can I stay?' he asks, probably relieved that he doesn't have to listen to me chat about someone else.

'With me?'

'Yes.'

'The flat is full, where would you sleep?'

'In your bed.'

'*My bed?*'

'Yes.'

'You think that's wise?'

'No. Do you still love me, Smitty?'

Of course I did. There was a hole in my life that was Seth-shaped. But he couldn't step back into it. I knew I'd have to get used to living with that hole in my life because there was too much hurt for us to mend. 'How is that a fair question?'

'It's not. But I don't feel like being fair, not about this. And why should I be? If you can't tell me if you still love me, don't you at least miss me?'

I sigh, avoid looking at him. 'That's not the point. And how is it supposed to work with Nancy around?'

'I don't know. It'll just have to, I guess.' He shrugs. 'You know I can't sleep without you. It's been hell these past few months. Last night was the first night I've slept properly since you left.'

'Seth—'

'Don't you miss me, Smitty?' he interrupts.

I know what he's thinking: *Smitty and he have only been on one date, it's nothing serious, they haven't had sex and, from the look on her face, he clearly isn't keen to keep things going, which means I've still got a chance. All I have to do is stick around and she might be reminded of what we had, what we could have again.*

If I was him, I would be thinking the same, part of me *is* thinking the same. But I have to put a stop to this for both our sakes.

'Yes, you can stay,' I say. 'I suppose if you're around it'll make it easier to sort out the divorce.'

48

Smitty

Mum has been avoiding me these past five days since Seth arrived. She leaves early with Nancy to go shopping somewhere, and they return in time for Mum to put Sienna to bed. By the time she's got Sienna down, I've left to go to my workshop. I do most of my work at night now that I've got more to avoid about being at home. Since Mum has spent the last few weeks almost stalking me, like she used to do when I was in my teens, listening at doors to try to overhear my phone calls and would most likely hack my email if she could, it's been a bit odd to have so much space from her.

I'm sure Mum figures that if she leaves it long enough I won't say anything to her and I'll eventually be grateful that she forced me to get back with him. She's out of her mind, of course, if she thinks that's going to happen but I don't care. I've spent five of the best days with Lily and Sienna. We've been swimming in Worthing and they both encouraged and reassured each other about going down the huge water slide. We went to Lewes to visit the castle but the parking was so atrocious we came back and went to Drusillas animal park instead and managed to rush round before it was chucking out time. We've been to a play park that is crammed with dinosaur sculptures.

Every day that I go to collect Lily with Sienna in Lottie, Abi looks concerned then relieved that I've kept to my word and shown up. 'Are you sure you don't mind doing this?' she asks, and the answer is the same: 'No, I don't.' I love spending time with the girls. They're completely devoted to each other and every day act as if they have been friends since they were born.

Today the forecast was for rainy showers, and I saw how exhausted they were. Super fun overload was tugging at their good natures and shortening their tempers. I decided on a sedate, calm day. We walked into the centre of Brighton and browsed all the bead shops we could find, we even went into a few stationers and newsagents, anywhere that sold beads and charms. Then we headed back to my shop. Last night before I left I had cleared a space in the centre of the shop, laid out two huge tartan-patterned blankets for us to sit and work on. We had a picnic, show tunes on the CD player and all the time in the world to string beads together.

When I was first training to become a jeweller I remember thinking that beadwork wasn't as skilful as the metalwork stuff. It seemed elementary and unsophisticated until I was assigned the task of making an affordable set of wedding jewellery including tiara, necklace, earrings and garter. My eyes were opened when I began to see the beads, how they fitted together, what they made when placed next to the correct colour or the correct texture. Each beaded piece had to be planned, laid out, arranged, thought about again, re-arranged. By the time I had finished the assignment I had changed my mind about beadwork. Like most things, it was only as beautiful, intricate and perfect as you allowed it to be.

Sometimes, in the evenings, when I need to tune out for a while, I will string beads for a necklace, or a belt, or to have a really long piece of string with beads.

Lily and Sienna sit cross-legged on the picnic blankets, the tubs of beads in front of them. I have given them each a large velvet bead mat to lay out their designs, or rather to drop random beads on to when they scoop fistfuls out of the pots.

'Why are you doing this?' Abi asked me yesterday.

'I want to,' I said. *'I want to be a part of your family,'* I should have added. *'Mum has her family now that Nancy is here, I want to be a part of mine. It's also the right thing to do.'*

'Auntie Smitty?' Lily has started to call me that too, mainly because

Sienna calls me that and anything Sienna does is perfect. It works the other way, too: Sienna's favourite colour was pink until she discovered Lily's was green and now she sits stringing green bead after green bead after green bead on her necklace.

'Yes, Lily?'

'Why did you decide to make jewels?'

'I don't actually remember,' I tell her. 'When I was a little girl I used to love to play with my mum's jewellery. I would sit on the floor of her bedroom and put it all on. My dad would think it was hilarious then would tell me to put it back because my mum would get upset in case I broke it or lost something. Maybe that was why, because I wanted to make stuff I could play with.'

Lily and Sienna have both paused in stringing their necklaces to listen to me. 'I had to go to university first, though. My mum and dad would not have let me go straight off to make jewellery, I had to do something academic and I had to show my commitment to jewellery making by paying for it myself.'

'What's commitment?' Sienna asks.

'It means being all serious,' Lily says.

'But making jewels is fun.'

'I know. I think Auntie Smitty was doing it wrong.'

'What do you girls want to be when you grow up?' I ask.

'A hairdresser, princess and doctor,' Lily says.

'Me, too!' exclaims Sienna. 'Pinky-promise?' She drops her string, Lily drops hers, and the pair of them leap on each other to hug and pinky-promise best friends forever that they'll be hairdressers, princesses and doctors. From my place on the picnic mat I watch them hug and kick over their pots of beads, the communal pots of beads and the tray of findings, nylon strings and catches. They all ricochet off in different directions. I'm going to be finding these scattered things for years to come.

I have my small black radio that sits on top of the shelves on quite loudly and I almost miss the knock on my shop door. It's insistent but not Seth's emergency knock. I lower the radio volume, listen again. Rat-a-tat-tat-tat-tat. I know the knock, but it couldn't be. I check the time: 22.45 p.m. Not at this time.

Cautiously so the person doesn't see me if it's not someone I would want to see, I peek out of the doorway that leads to the back of the shop and my workshop area. I can just make out the outline of the person who is knocking and it is the right height and shape. 'I can see you, Clemency Smittson, you open this door right now!' For some reason, the timbre of her voice isn't at all muffled by the glass and distance. I swear, the military could use my mum's voice as a weapon.

Once in, she stands in the darkened shop area looking around. Assessing it, wondering if I own it or not. I don't think I ever got around to telling her that I had a shop as well as the workshop.

'How did you get here?' I ask to distract her from the shop. She has spots of rain glinting on the shoulders and back of her black cardigan – no coat I notice – and on her black Bermuda shorts.

She holds up her helmet. 'I cycled, of course.'

'Wearing that? Jeez, Mum, it's raining and it's dark and you have no reflective clothing on. You're a living, breathing unsafe cycling awareness video waiting to happen.'

'Do you have lights in this place?' she asks.

'Let's go through to my workshop,' I say.

'You've been seeing those people behind my back,' she accuses the second we move from the darkness of the shop into the bright light of my workshop. I stand with my back to her, staring at my bench. I'd been about to anneal a piece of silver to make into a ring. I'd set it up: the silver rectangle was in the tweezers-like clamp, I'd turned on the gas from the canister to the blow torch, lowered my daylight lamp so I could see when the metal colour started to glow pink as it reached the right temperature. I'd picked up my lighter to light the flame when I'd heard her knock.

Carefully, I bend down and turn off the gas to the blowtorch, using the valve at the canister, then rise to my full height and raise the daylight lamp so my bench is bathed in artificial sunlight (necessary when you're doing close work, a hindrance when you're in the process of annealing).

'Have you nothing to say for yourself?' Mum asks.

'Abi's grandmother is in hospital, she needs to work so I've been taking Lily out.'

'I only found out because young Sienna was talking on and on about Lily and how they were cousins because you're their aunt. It's bad enough you've been lying to me but to drag young Sienna into it…I'm surprised at you Clemency. Surprised and ashamed.'

'I didn't drag Sienna into anything. Nancy doesn't want to look after her and I do. Lily and Sienna adore each other so I thought there'd be no harm.'

'Well, there is harm, Clemency. When you lie to me there is harm.'

'I didn't lie to you, I just didn't tell you.'

'It's the same thing and it's still unacceptable.'

That's a bit rich coming from you, I think and the fury behind that thought illuminates my nerve endings like a direct lightning strike.

'Why did you call Seth, Mum? Since we're talking about keeping stuff from each other, I want to know why you called Seth.'

'We're not talking about that.'

I face her at last. I haven't looked at my mother in a while, I realise. Since Nancy has been here, I presume, she has had her hair styled – cut into a bob with honey-blonde streaks added, which complement the brown and grey bits really well. They've obviously been going for facials and the sea air has probably done her constitution a world of good because she seems to glow with health. Nancy has been good for my mother – after her bereavement, a good dose of Nancy is obviously what she needs.

'We are talking about that. If you want to talk about the other thing we have to talk about this first. Why did you ring Seth? You were all for me calling the police on him the other week and suddenly you're all buddy-buddy with him, giving him my address. Why?'

'You had a long history together,' she states. 'I didn't want to see that go to waste.' As she speaks, Mum is clipping and unclipping the fastening of her cycle helmet. It punctuates her words with loud clicks.

'Nothing to do with you seeing me flirt with Tyler and deciding you preferred Seth, I'm sure.'

Mum is wilting under my scrutiny, my dogged determination to get her to admit it. She doesn't like to be in that position of weakness so she visibly stands up to me. 'I simply think it will be easier for you if you are with Seth,' Mum says. An end to the matter as far as she's concerned.

'Easier in what way?' I ask. I want her to admit it, to spell it out so she can hear how awful it sounds for me, the one who is on the receiving end of this type of thought process, even from her – my mother.

'People will accept you.'

'Do you mean the people who look like you will think I'm all right and safe to be around because I've got Seth with me?'

Mum's face tightens, the muscles seem to sew themselves together in quiet disapproval, even though that is exactly what she's saying. 'That is not what I meant.'

'That's what you said, though.'

'You're being wilfully difficult.'

'That's what you were saying, though, Mum. And what about black people, will they accept me because I'm with Seth instead of Tyler? Aren't they people whose opinions should count if I'm taking comments on who I should be sleeping with? Shouldn't I worry about what they think, too? And what about nice Mrs Khan from the Middle East, who lives upstairs? Or what about lovely Mr Suki who runs that Japanese restaurant in the Lanes? Should I worry about who they think I should be taking to my bed?'

'Don't be crude,' she says.

'Mum, don't you see how ridiculous it is for me to care what other people think about who I'm with?'

Another tightening of her facial muscles. 'I'm other people, am I? That's how you see me now you've been secretly seeing those people.'

That's not going to work at the moment. She won't distract me by marking out my wrongdoings like lines in the sand. 'I'm really sorry to tell you this, Mum, but you're racist.'

I think for a minute she's going to throw her cycle helmet at me.

Bop me right in the face with it in response to what I have said. Instead, her upper lip curls back, exposing the pink of her gums and the grey-white of her ex-smoker's teeth as she snarls: 'How dare you! How dare you! How can I be racist?'

'Really easily. It's not like you do it on purpose, but that doesn't mean it isn't true.'

'You dare!' Her snarl continues until it has taken over her face.

'I dare because you spent the whole of my childhood apologising for me. Who does that? Who can't see how they are damaging their child by making their very existence something to be sorry for? Dad never did that.'

'Your father was not perfect, Clemency. In your head he was this perfect being but he was not.'

'I know he wasn't. And he made mistakes, and he upset me, but he loved me no matter what. He didn't say sorry to other people all the time because I wasn't blood and he couldn't pretend I was. You did.'

'I am *not* racist. You take that back.'

'No.'

'Take it back, Clemency.'

'No, I won't, actually. Not until you take it back.'

'I have no idea what you're talking about.'

'All of it, Mum. You take it all back and I'll take back what I said. You acknowledge what you were like when I was growing up and I'll take it back.'

I don't know where this has come from. Maybe I've reached my limit. Maybe it's got to that point where the pressure is so much, so heavy, pressing down so relentlessly on my head, my shoulders, every part of my being, that I cannot be who I was any more. The old me, the one who had to be so appreciative and scared and unable to speak for fear of being branded ungrateful and told I should be happy that I even got the chance at life, has cracked. And the other me, the one who was submerged under the waves of gratitude and desperation to make everyone happy, is spurting out through the cracks.

'I didn't do anything wrong. And I am not a racist.'

'Well, that's fine, then. If you didn't do anything wrong, then that's fine. But, Mum, be honest with yourself about why you called Seth – someone you never really liked. Be honest, accept that it's because he only became good enough in your eyes when the alternative was me being with a black man.'

'That is not true!'

'Yes, it is. You know it is. Just be honest with yourself and with me for once in your life.'

She is silent, her sneer replaced by the defiance she has whenever she is dealing with me. It's only me who encounters defiance, her obstinacy and determination to get what she wants at all costs. With everyone else she is conciliatory, apologetic. After all, she is the woman who couldn't get it right and couldn't have a baby the 'natural way', and then when she managed to get a baby by other means, it didn't look right. It didn't blend in so her family always stood out. The shame of that, of not being like everyone else, was a millstone around her neck and she could never apologise enough, do enough to make it right. But with me, she was always strong, stubborn and ultimately a parent. A hardline one, but still a parent.

'Maybe I simply didn't like Tyler,' she states.

'You didn't even know him, Mum. You met him for all of five minutes and he was nothing but genuinely welcoming and friendly towards you.'

'That doesn't make me racist,' she says. 'It just makes me picky about who my daughter spends her time with.'

'But it's not up to you. I'm not an extension of you. If I want to sleep with half of Brighton that's my business. And I like Tyler. He's a great person.'

'He's not right for you!' Tears seep into her tone.

'Why not?'

'I am not a racist,' she replies.

I shrug. 'If you say so.'

'I am NOT!' I don't remember the last time she shouted at me. She's hardly ever needed to. Quiet words and disapproving looks have always worked on me. I am stultified by her shouting, genuinely frightened because she never loses control like this with me. 'I AM NOT, NOT, NOT A RACIST!' she continues to shout. Her face is puce with rage, every line heightened. 'HOW CAN I BE WHEN MY OWN CHILD IS HALF BLACK!'

Mum slams her hand, with its beautifully manicured nails, over her mouth. But it's too late to trap the words that have escaped. She is not talking about me, of course. And she can't even pretend that she is because I am not 'half black'. Mum had a child, a 'real' child that is biologically hers.

For the second time in five minutes I look properly, carefully, at my mother. I see her now. I see her in sharp focus: the hidden facets of her personality, those parts of her blurred under the things she does, the way she speaks, how she relates to me, are suddenly vivid, clear, apparent. Now I know why she is the way she is.

I wonder if she is finally seeing me or if she has always and will always see her other child, the one that I am the replacement for, whenever she looks at me.

There's a point when it's enough. When what you feel is too much, there is too much inside for you to handle any more. I am there. I am at that point. Like the banks of a swollen river, I am too full: another deluge and it will be too much; another drop and I will spill over and out, my being trampled and drowned as everything inside begins to disappear, the less secure bits washed away, the rest sub-merged. Drowned.

This is the final drop and I am drowning. Among everything, everything that my mother and I went through, I always knew it would be all right because she had chosen me. Out of everyone else, she chose me. But now I know it was only because I was a reminder, a replacement for her other child. And I know, from the look on her face, that her first child, her 'real' child, didn't die, she had them adopted.

I take huge breaths, my chest expands to the limits of my ribcage and then rapidly contracts as I drown, submerged under the torrent of my tears. I can't even raise an arm, pretend I am waving not drowning. More than anything, I want to make believe that she hasn't told me that I am a replacement for the one she really wanted. That like everyone else, I wasn't 'real' to her. I drop my face into my hands, try to contain the tears.

'Oh, Clemency, love,' she says. I feel her come towards me, her arms out ready to offer comfort and love. Ready to be my mother.

Is that even my name or is it the other one's name? I wonder as I shrink away from her, prevent her from touching me.

'Clemency, I'm sorry, I never meant to tell you. I was so young—'

'I'm going to the toilet,' I say to her as I try to stem the flow of tears. 'I'd like you not to be here when I get back.'

'Clemency—'

'Just go, OK? We can talk another time, but just go. *Please.*'

'I love you, Clemency,' she says. 'With all of my heart. From the moment I saw you, I fell in love with you.'

I nod to appease her, to get her to leave. 'I know,' I say. 'I know.' It's all very well loving someone, but does it matter if they're merely a replacement? Does it count if they're second best, not really what you actually wanted?

49

Smitty

I am my mother's daughter. I am pretending that the conversation we had last night didn't happen. I have slept top to toe in the same bed as Seth, like I do every night. And this morning I am up making breakfast for everyone. Toast, cereal, tea, milk, coffee, jam, Marmite, marmalade, butter – all in the middle of the table for when everyone arrives.

Surprisingly since she's almost always up at first light, Mum, not Sienna, appears first. I set the marmalade jar down beside the butter dish, look up at her and switch on my smile. 'Morning,' I say.

She probably hasn't slept very well, but I can't see for myself because I don't look at her for too long. I can only do this if I don't look at her for too long. I can only sleep in the same bed as Seth if I don't dwell on our past for too long. I can only be in the same city as Nancy if I don't remember all the things she has done and will do in years to come for too long.

I go to the toaster, take out the latest pieces to pop up.

'Clemency,' Mum says.

She's meant to tell me everything right now. My mother is supposed to unburden herself and let me into the secrets of her past: what she did, why she did, how she did. I am supposed to listen and let her explain the unvarnished truth of who she is, what she is capable of doing. She did this thing that was done to me. I cannot listen to that. I cannot stand to hear that she did it to someone else for their own good. I'd love to have the luxury of being unconnected, unaffected by the choices she made back then that kept her making certain choices all of my life. I would love to be able to sit here and be as unconditionally sympathetic as any stranger who hasn't been shaped by Mum's choices can be.

'Yes, Mum?' I say. 'Is everything OK?'

She says nothing, so I have to turn to face her. And then I switch on another smile. Grin at her because I am her daughter. I don't have a handbag to root through, but I know how to pretend, how to forget and act like something isn't happening. 'Not fancying toast this morning?' I ask. 'Do you want scrambled eggs instead?'

She wraps her pink dressing gown around herself, pulls out a chair. 'No, no, toast will be fine.'

'Great,' I say.

50

Smitty

I've brought her flowers and fruit and magazines.

I chose pink carnations, plump, green-flesh white grapes and a selection of magazines filled with fictional stories, and was reminded as I vacillated over every decision that I don't know this woman. Despite the time I spent with her, she is a virtual stranger and I have no idea if any of these are to her taste.

My grandmother by birth is propped up in her bed, frail and unhappy. Dad felt how she looks: frustrated, angry, defeated. We're alone, as she's requested. My other mother looked unsure, uncertain that I should be left alone with this woman. She flitted from fixing the pillows behind my grandmother, filling the water jug, fixing the cushions behind me on the seat, arranging the flowers I brought in a vase – constantly leaving and returning, fussing and fixing, until there was nothing left for her to do. She's worried about secrets being shared, created; concerned that I will find out something I shouldn't from a woman who obviously has form for twisting the truth. It probably never occurs to her that me being a virtual stranger to both of them would lead my grandmother to make the request she has.

Dad's parents died when I was a baby; Mum's parents never really took to me. It was nothing very personal – they never really took to Nancy, either, when they were alive. They sent Christmas presents – birthday presents were an indulgence that no one should have simply for being born – and they tolerated us if we showed up for a few hours' visit. Although, admittedly, they showed that blood did in fact influence how much they didn't take to me by not leaving me anything in their wills. Nancy got some jewellery and some Premium Bonds. I got nothing, as Nancy reminded me at various points over our teenage years, because I was not real.

I wonder if this woman realises that I don't want anything from her, that I don't expect anything from her will, but she will still be leaving me something no one else in her family will have – the memory of witnessing her death because I am not real, having not grown up in this house with the rest of her real family. That's why she's asking, of course. Because, to her, I am not real enough to be considered part of the family she would not ask this of.

'How do you want me to do it?' I say. No polite small talk or meaningless words. She doesn't deserve to have a slow, lingering death if she'd rather it was over now, and the irony of her condition means that what is killing her is preventing her from killing herself.

Her tremors are pronounced today: she is sitting still, her frustration evident, but her body shakes uncontrollably. Her eyes, though, can stay focused on me. I have pulled one of the chairs from by the window closer so she can look at me without having to turn her head. Something like a smile comes through the strained lines of her face. 'You … you will help me?'

'I don't want to,' I state. 'But, yes.' I sigh; push breath out loudly, resignedly. This is wrong. It's the wrong thing to do. 'Yes, I will do it.'

My grandmother by blood is suddenly lighter, freer in how she holds herself. For her, this is the right thing, what she wants.

'You have to speak to your doctor and your nurse, though,' I say. 'Tell them this is what you want, make them understand that you've thought this through and it's your choice. And then I'll help you.'

Her body still trembles, but she is back to being pensive, unsure.

'That's the only way I can help you. That's my only condition.'

She says nothing for a time. Eventually, so eventually I think she is not going to speak to me again, she states, 'Agreed.'

'Right.' I'd been hoping she wouldn't agree. It would have given me an easy out then. I only have her word that she will do it. But I have to trust her. She trusts me enough to ask me to do this for her, so I have to trust her back. Anyway, who wouldn't do something that could possibly prevent the person, the *granddaughter*, who has risked everything to help you, from going to prison?

'How…' I can't quite believe we're going to have this conversation. 'How do you want me to help you?'

Slowly, haltingly, she explains it all to me and she starts by telling me where to find a key to the house.

Part 7

51

Smitty

I am counting down time until I have to do this thing. The key burns a hole in my pocket, and the 'plan' burns a hole in my mind.

In the workshop at Karina's Jewels, I used to have a clear glass jar that I would fill with beads when I was counting down to something. It lived at the centre of the first shelf, between the plastic drawer set of different wires and the drawers of different sandpaper grades, and I would drop a coloured bead in every day. Karina said that I should be doing it the other way round, that I should put the same number of beads as number of days into the jar and take one out each day. That way, I could see the days until D-day (whatever 'D' happened to be) getting closer and closer. I explained, though, that I needed to see how patient I had been, how many days I'd survived without D-day. Doing it my way was as a visual reminder to myself that no matter how long it seemed until something arrived, it would always come.

I've been trying to fill up the days until this D-day arrives. She has a specific day in mind – it will give her a chance to get her affairs in order, she said. It will be soon, but not that soon. Until then I have to get from here to there without the benefit of a bead jar.

Now that I'm not looking after Lily and Sienna I can work during the day again, but I can't face it. Being in the workshop during the day makes me claustrophobic and scared. I keep wondering what's going on outside, what I'm missing out on. If I do this thing, there's every chance that I won't have the ability to walk around whenever I want during the day. I need to enjoy it as much as I can.

Working at night fills up those sets of hours, keeps me away from the flat and Seth and Nancy and Mum. Seth doesn't speak to Nancy at all. She gave him a look the first day he was there, to try to gauge what was happening. 'I've told Smitty everything, Nancy,' he said. 'No more secrets, no more lies, OK? Leave me alone now.'

He works a lot at the kitchen table, sometimes he walks up into Portslade to work in a café, but we make polite conversation and I generally avoid him because if I'm around him too long I dwell on our past.

I want to tell someone. I want to tell someone what I've decided to do and I want them to tell me that it's the right thing, or the wrong thing, or that it's *some*thing. I just want to share the knowledge, the decision that has become the weight of the world and is pressing down on my shoulders.

My feet have walked me all over Brighton and Hove these past few days and here I am outside a church. It is a little deeper into Hove and seems welcoming. It is a large bright-red brick building on a junction and the way the building stretches out along the side road and main road, it reminds me of someone offering a hug, standing still with their arms outstretched in hopeful expectation. To the side of the building that sits on the main road there is a large arch and at the end is a huge tower, topped with a green steeple that reaches right up into the sky, as though attempting to touch the heavens. The doors are open and I step into the church.

I'm going to light a candle for Dad, see if I can sit in the quiet and talk to him. Maybe it'll be the same as telling someone else. A glass wall with double doors set into it greets me when I enter the church. It separates the main area from the entrance and, I'd imagine, must have significantly cut down on their heating bills.

There is a mass going on so I move towards the noticeboard to wait patiently for the service to finish. I stare at the flyers pinned to the corkboard, the handwritten welcome note from the priest, the signs asking for volunteers to help them with various activities.

A whoosh and the glass doors are open, and the priest leaves first. His white hair looks almost unrealistically perfect and, I suspect as he walks past in his green vestments, that he might curl his hair. Wouldn't that be something – a priest in rollers! I watch the people leave, quite a few for a Wednesday morning mass. Some people have got out their Sunday finest but most of them are dressed as though they do this as part of their normal daily routine.

The steady flow slows to a trickle and I am about to step into the church but have to stop because there is someone I wasn't expecting to see about to leave the mass. Quickly, I step back in case the person – Tyler – sees me.

I risk another look and notice he isn't alone. He is pushing a wheelchair in which sits an elderly woman who wears a red and black hat that is an elaborate design of lace and netting. I move back to my space beside a pillar where hopefully I'll be out of sight.

Who is the woman? His mother? Grandmother? Great-aunt? They are the last to leave and, as they approach, it's obvious Tyler's going to find it difficult to open the doors on his own.

I step forward, my fingers close on the metal D handle and pull it open as far as it will go. Then I step across and open the other door.

'Ahh, thank you, thank you,' the woman in the wheelchair says with a strong Jamaican lilt. 'You've appeared like an angel to save my feet being bashed on yet another door.'

I smile but keep my head lowered to avoid looking at the man who is pushing her. I can sense him staring at me, willing me to raise my head. Technically, we've not had a falling-out and we can still speak to each other, but realistically, I'm far too humiliated and guilt-ridden to face him. Once they have cleared the doors, Tyler says a heartfelt, 'Thank you,' but still I do not lift my gaze.

I don't even glance at them as they move towards the doors to the outside. I close the door I am holding on to, and shut the other one behind me as I enter the church.

The church has white walls and cream pillars that flank the pews all the way down to the altar. The pews are in a light-coloured wood, while the altar and pulpit are carved from white marble. It seems an effort has been made to create a bright, light space. When I was younger I used to think that Heaven was a bright, white space that was also warm and comfortable. It would be filled with clouds and gentle soothing music. You could have whatever you wanted, you could be alone or with people, you would never get tired but you would sleep if you wanted to. You would never be hungry, but you could eat anything you wanted. It was the most amazing place in the world and you would always feel wonderful.

Yet, in every thought or imagining of Heaven I had, I didn't really want to be there. Because I couldn't come back here when I wanted, I wouldn't have the people I loved around when I wanted. What was the point of Heaven if I couldn't be with the people who I wanted to be with and for that to happen, they'd have to die. And I wouldn't want that.

I haven't been in a church since Dad's funeral, before that it was probably for Karina's wedding, before that probably Sienna's christening. I don't make a habit of going to church, even though we went every week when I was a child.

This church has the serenity of silence. I remember to genuflect before I slide into a pew. I close my eyes and try to tune in. Try to link myself with the serenity and hush of the building. I want to climb on to that other reality and stand there, looking, searching. If I manage to do that, to be there, to ground myself in that other reality, I may find him. I may feel Dad's presence.

The quiet comes slowly, unlinks itself blood cell by blood cell throughout my body until every part of me feels it. I am not here. I am not there. I am everywhere and nowhere.

'Hi, Dad,' I whisper. 'Can I talk to you?'

Tyler is leaning against the wall beside the church door. His arms are folded across his chest, and although it's a cool day, he's in one of his seemingly never-ending supply of bright white T-shirts that show off his sleek, beautiful arms.

'Hello,' he says when I spot him.

'Hi,' I reply. 'Bye.' I don't want to hang around, having awkward conversations with him, so set off in the direction of home. Maybe Seth has gone to work in a café and Mum will probably be out with Nancy and Sienna. Maybe I will be alone in the flat for a while. If Seth isn't out, I'll ask him to go—

'I'm sorry,' Tyler calls at me.

I stop and, confused, turn back to him. 'What are you sorry for?'

'I didn't behave very well the last time I saw you,' he says. 'I was shocked, humiliated, and a little angry, so I behaved badly. I'm sorry.'

'You didn't behave badly at all. And even if you did, I think you were entitled.'

'No. I had the right to be angry, but not to be condescending and downright rude. I apologise.'

'Apology – as unnecessary as it is – accepted. I'll see you, Tyler.'

'Clemency,' he calls.

'Yes?' I ask without bothering to turn around.

'Are you all right? You seem so sad.'

'I know.' That's the simple fact: I am sad. About Dad, about Seth, about Mum, about my mother and father and sister and brothers and grandmother. About what I have to do for my grandmother. I am sad. 'I've been sad for weeks, though, have you only just noticed?'

'No. Before, though, you looked sad, which is understandable since your dad had recently died, but now you seem bereft. As though nothing will make any of it any better.'

I turn to him. 'I don't look that bad,' I say with a smile.

The concerned look on his face chokes the laugh in my throat. He steps closer. After another step, he reaches for my hand. 'You don't look bad at all.'

I like the feeling of my hand in his, the touch of his skin against mine. He steps closer and the smell of him – sharp tangy citrus, woody notes and, of course, coffee – fills my senses. I inhale deeply, breathe him in. I exhale, push him out again. This is a distraction, a way to escape my complicated, sad life. His hand is on my face, warm and reassuring. He fills my senses on my next in-breath, leaves again as I breathe out. My hand is on his face. Another inhalation that draws him in, an exhalation that pushes him out. His lips are on mine, my lips are on his. We stand in the middle of the pavement of a busy street kissing, as though it's the most natural thing in the world.

In the park around the corner from the church, we sit on a bench and watch parents play with their children. I find children fascinating. They seem so free, easy. One girl has sleek pigtails that bounce as she swings arm over arm from one end of the monkey bars to the other. A four-year-old boy with a curtain of blond hair 'Wheeeee!'s his way down the largest slide in the park, stands up and runs around to climb back up the steps. A little girl, tall but probably younger than she looks, is on the climbing frame, confidently making her way to the top, while a woman who looks like she could be her mother waits fretfully at the bottom of the equipment. They could be mother and daughter – but like me and Mum. The woman is a pale white with light brown hair, the little girl is a warm, dark brown like me.

Tyler and I haven't really spoken. We stopped kissing after a couple of minutes and then were completely awkward and embarrassed. I was surprised, not only because we were standing on a main road and it was broad daylight and we were outside a church, but also because, well, I'm a married woman and he was very clear that he didn't mess with married women.

I rest my head on his shoulder, he has his hand on my leg. We sit like an established couple spending precious time together, doing not much.

'Who was the woman in the wheelchair?' I ask.

'Manma,' he replies. 'My grandma. I take her to church every other Wednesday, my brother does the other week. My mum sits outside and waits for us to load her into the car then drives her home.'

'She waits outside?'

'Yup, my mum isn't setting foot in a church. Her and Manma have had some spectacular rows about it, but my mum isn't having it. She takes Manma there and takes her home, but she won't step inside.'

'Any particular reason?'

'Lots of reasons, none that I completely agree with or understand to be honest, not that I completely agree with Manma's arguments either, but that's my family for you – they're always on the verge of falling out and then straight back to normal.'

'It must be so strange, growing up in a big family. I had no siblings and only really had my cousin Nancy who was my age. How many siblings do you have?'

'Six.'

'Wow! It must have been so noisy.' Envy is oozing out of me so fast I'm surprised Tyler can't see big, green globules of it. 'It must have been brilliant. Not that only having Mum and Dad wasn't brilliant because it was.'

'It drove me mad. There was never any peace and quiet, no privacy. My mum and dad kept trying until my mum got her girl in the end, that's the main thing.'

I laugh. I've heard of people doing that. It took me a lifetime to get my head around the idea of having a child. Seth and I talked and talked and talked about it and I was still uncertain. When I had got my head around it, I had been so excited about the prospect of having a baby with him. I knew he'd love the child and I would, too. And I would have someone who was not only linked to me biologically, but would link me to him, too. The fact he had told Nancy about that still breaks my heart.

'A lot of thinking going on in that head of yours,' Tyler says. He's looking down at me. His eyes are a shade of brown that I've only ever seen on a pebble pendant I bought on holiday in Lisbon. It wasn't quite a dark chocolate, it was a colour in between that and mahogany. I'd stripped the pendant of its chain and jumprings, then set it into a little silver tray and strung it with little cream beads as a belt. I'd sold it for £125. The most I'd ever got for something so small and unrelated to a wedding.

'I was just thinking about a conversation I had the other day. I thought I knew what I felt about most things, but in this instance, once the subject was raised, I realised I didn't have any opinion on it at all. Has that ever happened to you?'

I wonder if I can sound him out in a theoretical sense, if he'll be able to tell me what I need to hear. Talking to Dad was good, but I'd had no response. I didn't have him tell me if it was the right or wrong thing to do. I'll still be doing it, because no matter what my grandmother is like, she does not deserve to live the rest of her life in fear of being trapped, but I need someone else's opinion.

'I'm not sure what you mean,' Tyler says.

'I mean, let's say, for example euthanasia or assisted suicide. It came up in conversation the other day, and I realised I can't even have a proper conversation about it because I don't have a fully formed opinion.'

'Ah, but that's usual. I don't think anyone knows what they think about something like that until they're actually touched by it.'

'What do you think about it, then?'

'I don't know.' He grins down at me and then slowly strokes his thumb over my cheek.

'You are such a wind-up merchant.'

'A wind-up coffee merchant, thank you.' He strokes his thumb over my cheek again. 'My grandmother, Manma, has been in a wheelchair for a long time. Osteoarthritis that's particularly bad in her knees and ankles. She can't be upright for long periods. Her hands, elbows and wrists are bad but not like her knees. It's been really hard for her over the years.'

'And she wanted someone to help her die?'

'No! No way. She's determined to outlive us all. But other people don't think she has any quality of life so subtly and sometimes unsubtly they tell her she would be better off dead.'

'You're not serious!' I say that like I haven't been told all my life subtly and unsubtly, I should be grateful my birth mother didn't abort me and had me adopted instead.

'They don't often say it outright, but you know the pitying looks, the "How can you stand it when you used to be so active?" and "I suppose you live through your children and grandchildren now" comments are all saying the same thing – because she can't do what they think of as "healthy", "normal" things, they assume she must feel bad about it, too.

'And we've had some close shaves in the past – Manma will have been ill enough to be hospitalised and more than a few times we've had to ask the doctors to speed up or do everything they can to keep her alive. Not all of them, obviously, and not every time, but there've been enough who you can see aren't working as fast as other doctors have. In their minds, I guess, she's old, she's had her time, she's in a wheelchair, her quality of life isn't up to the standard they'd like to live at so it's fair enough to let her fade away. It's really scary, having to stand up to the professionals who you're trusting to do their best. And for them, their best is to let people like Manma die.

'After all those times, she's still around, still being who she is. The thought that someone else would have euthanised her because she didn't fit their ideal of what they want from life is very upsetting.'

'But some people want to die. Not like your grandmother, but other people in the same situation as her would rather not be kept alive, they'd rather just go,' I say.

'And that's fair enough. That's their choice. But someone taking that choice away is just wrong. And putting pressure on people by implying their life isn't as great as it is for someone young or able-bodied is even more wrong.'

'But what if they can't do it themselves and they need help? The person who helps them could get into trouble.'

He focuses on me with such intensity the air in my chest stops. *Does he know? Does he know what I'm waiting to do?*

He changes his line of vision to across the park and takes his hand away from my cheek. 'It's a pretty complicated subject,' he says, his words are bathed in frostiness.

'Where has the sudden drop in temperature come from?' I ask.

'Pardon?' he asks.

'Why have you gone all funny?'

He is silent for a few moments, although his face reveals plenty: he's struggling with whether to say what he wants to say or to keep his counsel. When he looks at me again, he's obviously decided to speak. 'It feels like I'm being led down the path to agreeing with something I don't agree with. I mean, you see my grandmother and suddenly you're asking these questions. I know it's not popular and people should, if possible, be allowed to decide when they go, but I also think we have a responsibility to others. Not just to people we know, but to people we don't know. It's not popular, no, but we should think about other people and how the choices we make impact on them. I don't want to be led into an argument where I'm forced to agree that if you want to die you should be allowed to. That's not something I necessarily disagree with. I think if it becomes the norm, though, so the people who "help" don't get into trouble, it will lead to potentially vulnerable people like Manma being in danger.' As he speaks his words gather momentum and power and volume. 'On paper my grandmother hasn't got this glittering lifestyle where she lives without pain and drugs and a huge loss of what people call "dignity", but it's her life. She lives it. I don't want her, or people like her, to feel that assisted dying is the only option for them, even obliquely, when the rest of us don't have to deal with those pressures.'

'I wasn't leading you anywhere. I was talking – that's all.'

'With subjects like that, people don't often "just talk", they always have an agenda.'

'Not always...I don't have an agenda. And it has nothing to do with seeing your grandmother. I just wanted to...Remember, I said about how you don't realise you don't know what you think about a subject until you start to think about it? Well, yeah, that's what this conversation was about.'

'Sorry, sorry,' he says. His apology seems genuine, heartfelt. 'It's one of those subjects that people have such strong feelings about and I've had some humdinger rows. Things get said that can't be taken back...'

'I can't remember ever having a conversation with anyone about it.'

'Apart from the person the other day, obviously.'

If only you knew what that conversation was really about, I think. 'Yes, well, apart from that person. You've honestly had more than one conversation about it?'

'Occupational hazard.'

'What, people turn up in a coffee shop and start spouting off about euthanasia? It's all fun and games in your café, ain't it?'

Tyler kisses me, presses his mouth on to mine and slowly opens me up with his tongue. His hand is on my face and the kiss is delicate but firm, exciting and sensuous. I close my eyes and fall into the moment, tumble right into it and forget. I forget about everything that's gone before, everything that's to come. I allow myself to be free and unburdened for just a minute or two. Then it's all back. All of it, everyone, and what I have to do is at the front of that. I need to tell someone. Mid-kiss I pull away from Tyler.

'I'm sorry, I'm sorry, I, erm, need to go.'

'Go? Go where?'

I inhale a few times, calm my nerves, prepare myself to upset him. I don't deserve him anyway. He's far too nice for me. All that stuff he was saying was right, it's absolutely what I believe, too, and I couldn't tell him what I'm going to do. I couldn't burden him with that when I hardly know him.

'I need to speak to my ex-husband,' I say.

'Are you serious? I kiss you and you have a sudden need to speak to your ex?' He seems offended and confused in equal measures. 'Was it that bad a kiss?'

'No, no! Of course it wasn't, Tyler. I could sit here kissing you all day. I have something I need to tell him and I need to do it now or I'll bottle out of it.'

'Fine,' he says.

'It really isn't anything you've done—'

'Spare me, Clemency. If you've got to go, go.'

'I'll see you?' I ask him hopefully.

'Not if I see you first,' he replies before he gets up and marches away.

He's sitting barefoot on my bed, headphones on, book open on his lap, television on in the background. This is how Seth preps himself for a new design project. He immerses himself in all different types of media, blending them together in his mind until he comes up with a new concept.

When he looks up and sees me, he grins. I feel like I'm about to shoot him, if I knew what shooting someone was like. I feel like I am about to damage him in a deep, fundamental way. I need to tell him though. I need to say the words aloud so I can know how bad it is, how final. He's the only person on Earth that I can tell.

The smile slowly disappears from his face and he pushes the headphones off his head, switches off the television and lays aside the book.

'Do you want me to leave?' he asks.

I shake my head. 'I need to tell you something. And I need you to listen to me. And then I need you to tell me the truth about what you think. I'm still going to do it, but I need you to be completely honest with me about how bad you think it is.'

Frowning, he climbs over the bed, slips off and then sits on the floor, resting his back against the bed. He indicates to the space beside him, which I take. 'Tell me,' he says.

'In ten days' time, I'm going to have to kill somebody,' I say.

The relief of being able to say it out loud, the horror of what it means, and the fear of having to do it, cause me to break down and sob in the arms of my husband for the next two hours.

Part 8

52

Smitty

I am standing in my bedroom in front of the huge windows which look down over the promenade, which runs like a thick black marker line under the constantly undulating blue-grey waves of the sea.

Since I moved in here I have been drawn to the windows, to staring out at the sea, to losing myself in the constant motion of the water. Even when the sea is calm it moves, shifts, reshapes itself. I stand here and think about Dad, about life, about my grandmother.

Seth doesn't want me to do it. I probably shouldn't have told him, it was selfish to burden him when we are as we are. And the more people who know, the more it will look like premeditated murder, not privately fulfilling her wishes. Even if she leaves a note, it could be argued that I pressurised her into writing it – that I influenced her to reach the decision and then carried it out. It could be argued that since she has not asked anyone else to help her other than me, a relative stranger, I could have made up the whole thing simply to kill her.

These are the things that Seth has been telling me. His fear is that I could go to prison, possibly for the rest of my life. We talk about it constantly, whispering about it behind closed doors, sometimes arguing because he doesn't want me to do this, so much so he offered to do it instead. I can't let him do that. She asked me, and I have seen just a small fraction of her suffering and I know she doesn't want to be here any more.

I have to do it. I've said I will. And I will. There are three days left.

53

Abi

To: Jonas Zebila
From: Abi Zebila
Subject: Call me
Monday, 10 August 2015

There's a sound I love most in the world, more than any other, and it's the sound of my daughter laughing. It comes out of her in easy waves and spreads throughout the house. That's always the best part of my day, when I let myself into the house and hear her giggling, loudly and freely.

J, I have something important to tell you and I don't want to do it by email, but I tried your phone and you've changed your number. Call me. It's important.

Abi
xxxxxxx

54

Smitty

I love seeing Abi.

It's not simply because she is a younger version of me, and after years of not seeing someone who looks like me and often thinks like me, it's amazing to have that. I like her. She is open and friendly, incredibly welcoming. I have not had many close female friends over the years because from an early age Nancy managed to instil in me a fear of getting too close to anyone, and women in particular, in case she disapproved and told them things that put them off me.

I'm overjoyed when I open the door to my shop after hearing a knock and Abi is standing there. Her face is solemn and her eyes are a scarlet red. Something has happened. She doesn't have to tell me what, I know. Of course I know. There's only one thing that would make her turn up here out of the blue with that look on her face.

I'm cold. Suddenly, unexpectedly, I am cold. I can't feel my fingers, nor my toes, nor any of my limbs. It's not usual to be aware of them, but I'm now conscious that I can't feel them because I am so cold.

'Come in,' I say to her. I have to make a real effort to move my cold, numb body aside to let her in. I pull the shop door shut behind her, the little brass bell tings. I need to focus on making my hands do what I want them to do when I lock the door again.

That's what it was like for my grandmother: she had to focus, use incredible strength to do the tiniest things because her body did not always obey the usual commands. Her body did not listen when it was meant to carry out the simplest of tasks. That is why she wanted to go. Her body and soon her mind would not be under her control and she wanted it to be over before that happened totally. She wanted one last chance to assert control. This is only a small moment for me, but it is a reminder of what everyday tasks were like for her. Of why she thought it would be too hard to find out how bad it would really get.

Abi stands near the entrance to my shop. She clutches her black leather satchel to her chest like a child's comfort blanket while her fingers pick at the stitching.

'Do you want to come through to my workshop?' I ask. I am trying to delay the inevitable. When she tells me it'll be true and I do not want it to be true.

'I had to tell you myself. I couldn't call or text,' she says after a head shake at my offer of more comfortable surroundings. 'It's Gran.'

I face her properly, ready to accept the news I already know head on.

'She...' Abi closes her eyes and steels herself. This has never happened to her before – at least not in a way where she was old enough to understand. The pain, it comes and goes, undercut with moments of denial and disbelief. The disbelief, it blossoms suddenly and winds itself around your heart like a protective shield that allows you to relax and forget for a few precious minutes before it cracks apart and falls away and leaves you with the pain and reality. 'She...She...'

'She died?' I say.

My sister nods then crumples. Without thinking I gather her in my arms. 'Oh, Abi,' I say into her hair. 'I'm so sorry. I'm so, so sorry.'

My grandmother didn't think this bit through. Why would she when it was her life, her death, that she wanted to control? That was her focus, that was her goal. She wanted her life back under *her* control when that control, that ultimate feeling of being in charge, had been slowly eroded by the various illnesses that had taken over her body. What she wanted was paramount – this bit, the part after-wards for the people left behind, hadn't really featured.

She was ready to go, but were the people who loved her, the ones who wanted to get to know her, ready to say goodbye?

55

Abi

To: Jonas Zebila
From: Abi Zebila
Subject: Your brother!!!!!
Friday, 14 August 2015

Jonas,

Ivor is pissing me off. After weeks of pretending she doesn't exist, he's back on his obsession about Clemency but it's so much worse than before and now he does it front of Mummy and Daddy. Thankfully, he doesn't do it in front of Lily-Rose. If he did, I think I'd take his head off.

'It's her, she killed Gran. It's got to be. Gran was all right till she showed up.' He says that about a million times a day. All right, not a million but you get what I mean. He just won't let it go. Mummy is having none of it. She keeps telling him to stop being so wicked and to stop saying things that aren't true and couldn't possibly be true. Will he listen? No.

Daddy's not talking much. He mostly listens to Ivor as though he can't really hear what he's saying. For all his not liking cuddles, whenever Lily goes to him, climbs on his lap and puts her arms around him and her head on his chest because he looks so sad, he doesn't go all rigid and uncomfortable like usual. Now he just lets her sit there and I think it's comforting to him.

I wish Ivor would stop. Yesterday, he'd been going on and on once Lily was in bed, about how Clemency had a lot to be angry about and 'this is the way she starts to get revenge on the people who were there at the time. I'm telling you, Abi, she did it. Or she made Gran do it.'

'Oh, right, yeah,' I said. 'Since when has anyone ever made Gran do anything, ever?'

'She was ill. Illness does all sorts to people. It messes with their minds, changes who they are. She was old and she was ill and this so-called sister of yours got to her.'

'Right, when we've always been around? How did she get into our house if we've been around all the time?'

He thought about that one, then he said, 'It's really easy to steal someone's key, get a new one cut and then put it back before they've even noticed. How many times has she been in the corridor, huh? All alone, all the keys to the house right there hanging up in the key cupboard. Does anyone ever lock it and put the key to it somewhere safe? Nope.'

I felt really bad cos he had a point. But still. 'She didn't do that. She's not that sort of person. I've got to know her really well. She wouldn't do that.'

'You only know what she wants you to know. I'm telling you, she did this. And she's not going to get away with it – I'm going to make sure of that by going to the police.'

What do you think? From everything I've told you about Clemency, our sister, do you think she could have done something to Gran, or worked on her to get Gran to do it herself? Gran was too ill, though. Most times Mummy or I had to feed her because her hand shook too much to hold the spoon or fork. She couldn't have done it herself. At least that's what the police are saying now. The way she died, with her Parkinson's, she must have had help. Was it Clem? What do you think? Let me know. Talk to you soon.

Abi

xxx

P.S. Are you going to come back for the funeral or are you going to stay away?

56

Smitty

It's been six days and there's been no news about the funeral.

Apparently, Abi says, they have to do an autopsy because, even after the seriousness of her last hospital stay, our grandmother shouldn't have gone so soon. They may start to treat her death as suspicious. I wasn't expecting her to die so soon, either.

I've been cut off by the rest of my birth family. It was always going to happen if they ever found out what I had agreed to do, but it's happened anyway. 'Thank you for the call,' my other mother said on the phone when I asked if I could visit, 'but that is not necessary.'

'I just want to see you,' I said. 'I know there's not much I can do but it'd be nice to see you.' To hug you. To be with you like families are at times like this. I'd wanted nothing more than to have Seth hold me after Dad died. I'd wanted to do the same with Mum but she didn't want to be touched and she didn't sit still long enough for me to get near. It never occurred to Mum, of course, that I needed her to take his place as the parent who hugged.

'No, that's not necessary.'

'I know it's not necessary, but it'd be nice to see you all. See you.'

'You do not want to be around here,' my other mother said, quietly, gently, but with finality. 'This house is full of sadness. You do not want to be here. When we meet, Clemency, it should be about happiness, enjoying each other's company. Not sitting around crying and talking in hushed voices. We need to be happy together.'

'*No, we don't,*' I wanted to say. '*We just need to be real with each other. And that means sharing the good and bad bits.*' 'OK,' I replied instead.

Mum sent a card and flowers, I think she put my name on it but I didn't ask so I don't know for sure. It's like when my grandmother was in hospital, but worse. I don't even have the right to think about her and miss her or anything because although I'll never speak to her again, I didn't know her long enough to feel her absence from my life.

'How are you?' Seth asks. He enters the room and shuts the door behind him to give us a bit of privacy from my eavesdropping mother.

He has been working in the kitchen while Mum reads in her room. Nancy is off into Brighton with Sienna to see a friend, and I sit on the sofa alternating between staring at the television and staring at my phone. I should be working, but since it happened I haven't been able to. Everything seems too much right now for me. Melissa, who I'm turning a locket into a watch for, has been in touch twice asking if I fancied a drink or if I had received my adoption papers. I haven't called her back and I haven't applied for my papers – it didn't seem important any more with everything that's going on and I couldn't face going anywhere.

'I don't know,' I admit to my husband. 'I don't know how I feel.'

He smiles sadly. 'I can't pretend to understand what you're going through, but I am here if you need me.'

'Don't you find it weird being around me when we're not together?' I ask him.

Seth sits back on his haunches and observes me coolly, as though I've slapped him across the face and is wondering the best way to respond. 'No, not really. I was around you for years when we weren't together.'

'But this is different, surely?'

My husband, my ex, examines me carefully for long, contemplative seconds. 'Are you trying to start a fight?' he asks. 'I'd understand if you were. And I will happily oblige because there are loads of things I'd love to row with you about, but I just need to be sure where this is headed before I come out all guns blazing.'

Mollified, chastised, I look down. After pulling himself up, he sits beside me on the sofa. Without waiting for an invitation, he reaches out and tugs me towards him until I'm sitting on his lap. He wraps his arm around my waist then reaches up to wind one of my curls around his forefinger. 'This must be so hard for you.'

I shrug, which of course means yes. Hard doesn't seem the right word, a big enough word, really. It needs a word that has all the letters in the alphabet – every single one – so that it can show how all-encompassing this feeling can be.

'I'm sorry for trying to pick a fight with you,' I say to him. 'It wasn't very fair of me when you've been nothing but supportive.'

'Apology accepted,' Seth replies. We glide easily into a moment. A snippet of time where it's easy to forget all that water that still has to flow under our particular bridge. Where we could be together and remember the good times. How easy would that be? No divorce, no separate lives, talking, having sex, laughing, back to who we were. Maybe Tyler was just an aberration, a momentary thing I needed to get out of my system; maybe Nancy was the friend Seth thought he needed when I wasn't around to be there for him. *Maybe I'm deluding myself.*

'I know you don't want to hear this,' he begins, the words as ominous as his tone.

'Don't say it then. If I don't want to hear it, please don't say it.'

'I love you.' He releases my curl. 'It's incredibly difficult being around you when we're not together, not least because I know you're sort of dating someone else and I hate the idea of that, but I love you.'

'I…I'm not dating Tyler,' I say. 'We had a date, which you showed up on, and then I bumped into him the other day and I ended up leaving to come and talk to you about the stuff with my grandmother. I haven't seen or heard from him since.'

'Clemency!' my mother says sharply. As always, when she interrupts us, we react like teenagers caught about to undress each other in my parents' house. I leap off Seth's lap, stand guiltily staring at the now open door, and he is up and halfway across the room, lurking in the bay window in record time. *'We never touched each other, honest,'* are the expressions we always wear for my mother.

Her eyes glint with disapproval as she glares at me and then at Seth. Or maybe it's not disapproval, maybe it's anxiety. Worry and concern brought about by the presence of the uniformed police officer who stands behind her. His uniform is dark, and he appears so large he seems to block out any light from the corridor.

I used to watch *The Bill*, I used to watch *NYPD Blue*, I still watch re-runs of *Law & Order*. In all that time I don't think it's ever crossed my mind that a police officer would one day show up at my house to arrest me. Because that must be what he's here for. There are some things you just know and that is what I know: he's here to arrest me in connection with my grandmother's death.

When the policeman has entered the room, a second officer appears. He is not uniformed, he is wearing a navy blue suit with a matching blue tie and a beige rainmac. He clearly thinks he's Columbo. A cop show Dad regularly watched. 'Clemency Smittson?' he asks.

I nod.

'We would like you to come down to the station and answer some questions in relation to the murder of Soloné Zebila.'

My no-longer-watched phone, which was knocked into the folds of the sofa cushion when Seth pulled me on to his lap, lights up suddenly. The ringtone – 'Come As You Are' – trills through the room. Abi's ringtone. She must know. She must be trying to warn me.

Too late, I think. *Just too late.*

57

Smitty

I didn't do it. I was going to, but I did not. There are two very good reasons why it wasn't me: first it happened two days earlier than planned; second, I didn't do it.

I should say this. Explain so they stop this process of bringing me in for questioning, which feels a very small, pigeon-type step away from being arrested.

'No!' says Mum loudly. In two steps she is by my side, and her hand clamps on the arm of the uniformed police officer. 'She didn't do it,' she says. 'It was me. It was me. I did it. Not her.' The plain-clothes officer stares at the lady with the honey-blonde streaks in her greying hair, who is about to start wrestling with a man twice her height and probably five times her strength. 'It was me. I did it.'

The uniformed officer plucks my mother off himself like she is an annoying but insignificant insect, and places her a little distance away.

When I was a child I had nightmares that someone was going to come and take me away. I wasn't 'real', I didn't belong here, maybe I would be taken somewhere else. Sometimes it was the police, sometimes it was a big faceless monster that lived in the bright, blinding spaces that made up my pain. Sometimes it was my 'real' parents; people I didn't know who wanted to steal me away from the only life I'd ever known and force me to live in a strange place, away from the people I loved. In these dreams, when this would be happening, my mother would be shouting and screaming that they couldn't take me, that I was hers and they should take her instead.

This is my nightmare: I'm being taken away and my mother is screaming.

'Mum, please don't.' That stops the uniformed officer: he looks at me, looks at Mum and then looks at me again. The other officer obviously knows the score since he doesn't react at all. 'Mum, just don't.'

'But it was me,' she says. 'I did it. Arrest me, it was me who did it.'

This is my mother's nightmare, too. The thing she has feared more than anything is happening: someone is taking me away from her. It isn't my original parents as she probably always thought it would be, but the police.

'Nobody is under arrest,' the plain-clothes officer states. 'It's merely questioning.'

'Please.' She turns to him, hands linked together, begging, pleading. 'Please, please. I did it. I know exactly how it was done and when. It was me, please. Take me.'

'We have your daughter's fingerprints on the murder weapon and other parts of the room where they shouldn't have been. There are no others that haven't been accounted for.'

That stops Mum. She focuses on me. 'When did the police get your fingerprints?' Mum asks.

My gaze flicks to Seth, who is standing in the bay window, rooted to the spot with horror. He knew this would happen if I did it and this is the reality he doesn't want to deal with.

'We were arrested once on a protest march,' Seth says after clearing his throat of the fear that has clogged it up. 'We... we accepted a caution even though we didn't do anything.'

My mother swings towards him. 'You! You did this? You're the one who got my daughter's fingerprints on record so now she's being treated like a criminal?'

'Mum, it's not his fault. And you can't stop this. It's all a big misunderstanding. I didn't do it and the police will find that out as soon as we get to the station.'

'I know you didn't do it. I did.'

I return to looking at my husband. '*I didn't do this,*' I mouth at him.

'*I know,*' he mouths back with a nod.

I move my head slightly, nodding towards my mother. '*Please,*' I mouth again.

'Mrs Smittson.' Seth comes to life and goes to my mother. 'Mrs Smittson, please, come. Come.' He gently takes her arm and she struggles against him, wanting to come back to where I am. 'This isn't helping Clem,' he says to her. He moves his head, trying to get her to focus on him so the police officers can take me. 'Please, come here with me and I'll drive us both to the police station.' She finally looks at him. 'Yes? OK? OK?'

'They can't take her,' Mum says to Seth. She's begging him.

'It's only questioning, not an arrest. We'll get her back. And when we do, they won't be able to take her again,' Seth says. 'OK?'

He's making sense to her: her body sags in resignation, and she doesn't look at me. She probably can't. Seth nods at me and the police officers.

'We'll see you later,' Seth says. He takes my mother in his arms and holds her close as the plain-clothes officer asks if I'm ready to go.

I nod instead of speaking. I'd love to pretend that the reason I don't speak is so it can't be used against me at some point. In reality, my mouth barely works, my throat feels like it is fused shut because I am scared. I am terrified of what is going to happen next. I am thirty-seven, I have lived long enough to know that people get sent down all the time for crimes they have not committed.

To prove I'm innocent I'll have to tell them that I was going to do it but I never got the chance. Is that intent to kill? To prove I'm innocent I may have to confess to what might amount to another crime, which may or may not get me into just as much trouble.

I'm staying silent, not saying anything because I'm scared that I am going to get done for something I never got the chance to do. Is this the Universe's way of telling me that the decision I made was the wrong one? That I shouldn't have even thought about committing the ultimate crime, even if it was what the victim wanted.

58

Smitty

I have been in this interview room for a long time on my own. I thought I would be shown to a cell but I have been put in here and a police officer stands in the corner of the room, acting as if I am not here. If I tried to leave, I'm sure he'd notice me then, but as long as I sit in this seat and do not move, he can pretend he is all alone.

My heart almost leaps clean out of my chest when the door opens suddenly. The plain-clothes officer who asked me in for a chat earlier enters the room.

'There is someone here who claims to be your solicitor and would like to see you,' he says.

I have a solicitor? Mum probably got one, but so soon? It's not as if I've even been properly arrested, we're all still pretending I am sitting here waiting for a nice informal chat.

The solicitor who walks in probably didn't jump at the chance, but I do get to my feet. I can't help myself. It's an automatic response to someone who carries themselves with an innate sense of authority; my knee-jerk reaction to being in the presence of my father.

'All of us know that this man isn't really your solicitor, but I'm going to let him talk to you if he encourages you to tell us the truth. It's the best way forward.' 'Tell the truth' to this thin, mean-looking man with his ill-fitting suit and pitifully uncombed hair means 'confess, whether you did it or not', I'm sure. 'Unless you've got any objections?' the officer asks me.

I shake my head, quickly.

'I'll be back.'

My father extends a hand to encourage me to sit. He seems taller than I remember. Still as stately, imposing. He sits on the police side of the desk when I cautiously lower myself to the seat – the real ordeal will begin the moment I'm properly braced in this chair. The 'being brought in for questioning' and my mother's reaction were nothing compared to being questioned by this man about the death of his mother. From his briefcase he produces a well-used A4 pad of yellow paper. He's a busy man who makes a lot of notes, the stubs at the top of the page that look like the frayed edges of a badly hemmed dress tell me this. His hand slips into the inside left pocket of his expensive-looking suit and removes his pricey black Montblanc pen.

'Hello,' I say. That is how you begin a conversation with someone, whether they're a stranger or not. No matter what the situation, you should at least greet them. 'Hello.' The words of the Lionel Richie song unspool in my mind like a long thread of words, woven with a melody to become a symphony, a song that could have been describing parts of my life of late. Hello.

My father, Mr Julius Zebila, seems startled by this. He does not look up from his yellow pad, which is being slowly written upon by the expensive pen as he notes down the name my adoptive parents gave me, but he does stop writing for a moment.

He has paused at the second 's' of Smittson. That's my name, who I am, but is that how he thinks of me, refers to me now in the private space of his mind, his memory, his heart? Or will I be forever Talei Zebila? Can he divide himself in two like I do sometimes? On the paper he has written my adoptive name, the name I grew up with, but maybe inside he has written Talei, and when he looks at me he sees Talei. Maybe on the outside I am Clemency Smittson, and on the inside, to him, I am Talei Zebila. That's how it seemed to be with my biological mother.

Maybe I am ascribing thoughts and feelings to him, when in all honesty, to him, I am nobody special. I am Clemency Smittson, a person who was born in Brighton, who grew up in a small house in

Otley, who is sitting in a police station accused of a terrible crime committed against someone he actually loved.

When we met last time (the first time), he wouldn't look at me. He let my mother, my sister and my grandmother talk, but he said nothing. Like Ivor, he looked in my general direction and stayed silent.

'Why won't you look at me?' I ask him in my head. *'Am I that much of a disappointment?'*

When my first father pauses again, this time while writing the date, I know I've said that out loud. He stares at the pad. He's going to get up and walk out. He's not going to stand for being questioned, not by me.

'Mrs Smittson is very upset. She is outside with a young man. They are *both* very upset. I told them I would make sure that you were not being ill treated. Have the police treated you well?'

So that's how it works: I talk, he ignores me; he talks, I am expected to answer. 'Yes, they've been fine.'

'Can you verify where you were seven days ago?'

'Working.'

'Alone?'

'Yes, I work alone. I was in my workshop for most of that day and night.'

'Did anybody see you there?'

'Maybe, I don't know. They might have looked in through the shop window and seen a light on in the workshop. Or seen me walk past from one end of the workshop to another. I don't know what other people saw.'

'This is a very serious matter.' Stern. My father is being stern, almost harsh with me. I wonder if he is like this with all of his children or only the ones who are 'brought in for questioning'.

'I know it's serious. And I didn't do it,' I reply. 'I probably can't prove that I didn't do it, either. I don't know how she died so I don't know what the murder weapon was and if I touched it. I keep trying to remember what I touched when I was in her room so I can work out what it was that did it, then I have to stop that train of thought because I can't imagine anyone actually doing that to her or any object I might have touched doing that to her. But I can't stop thinking about it because I need to remember what it was I touched and why that might have the police thinking it was me.'

The man opposite me has the same colour eyes as me; the same kink in his left eyebrow as me, too. We have similar shape noses, but mine is more like my other mother's. The first time we met, my eyes scoured their faces like a miner panning for the gold pieces of similarity between them and me.

'They believe she died of a massive overdose of insulin and a combination of other drugs that became a lethal cocktail.' That was how she wanted me to do it. To sneak into her house when it would be empty and give her the mixture of drugs she'd made me write down. By the time I got home I had memorised them, even though there were so many, and destroyed the piece of paper so that I wouldn't have those names hanging around, ready for anyone to stumble across.

'Because of her condition,' my father continues to say, 'they know that she did not take them herself. Someone else administered them.'

This is his mother he is talking about. The strain of that shows in the tense lines in the deep, dark brown skin around his glossy, black-brown eyes, in the way he holds his mouth when he is not speaking. He's only twenty years older than me, my biological mother is only seventeen years older than me. He seems older, though. That's what losing a parent can do to you.

'I didn't do it,' I state.

'I am certain you didn't.' He still refuses to look at me while he speaks. 'I would not be here if I believed for one minute you did. No child of mine would commit such a crime.'

In one hurricane-like rush, my breath leaves me as my chest is almost crushed by being legitimised by him. He is my father. I am his child. He accepts me. Really, it shouldn't matter. I am his daughter, it shouldn't matter whether he accepts me or not, what he says and what he doesn't, whether he looks at me or keeps his eyes averted. It shouldn't matter, but this small crumb of acknowledgement means another part of me has been made real, made here and present. I have another little anchor that says I am from somewhere. I am from here.

'Would you like me to stay with you while they question you?' he asks. 'I can't step in or act for you legally, but I can stay if you wish me to.'

I nod. I want him, my father, to stay.

The door to the room opens and he stands to come over to my side of the table. Still he doesn't look at me. My gaze, however, is drawn to him, mesmerised. I am panning for more gold, desperately seeking more similarities while the police officers enter the room.

It shouldn't matter, I shouldn't need him to accept me to be able to further define myself, but it does and I do.

59

Smitty

They keep asking me the same things over and over: 'Why were your fingerprints on her medication?' 'How many times were you in Mrs Zebila's room?' 'Where were you the day she was killed?' 'Why did you kill her?'

I keep answering in the same way over and over: 'She knocked them over once and I picked them up.' 'A few times, I can't remember exactly how many.' 'I was in my workshop, working.' 'I didn't kill her.'

My father for the most part says nothing, does nothing, simply allows them to question me.

Suddenly, the questions are different: 'Why did you track down the Zebilas?'

'I didn't, I met Abi Zebila by accident.'

'A pretty big "accident", wouldn't you say?'

'I suppose.'

'Did you know before you met them how wealthy they are, especially the deceased Mrs Zebila?'

'No, I knew nothing about them. I haven't even applied for my adoption papers. I didn't even know their name.'

'Do you have money worries?'

'No. I make enough to get by.'

'And your inheritance from your deceased adoptive father, Mr Smittson?'

'From my dad, you mean, yes.'

The man next to me in the expensive suit, who hasn't reacted to anything else I have said so far, reacts to that: he sits up in his chair and lays down his expensive pen at a perfect perpendicular angle to the lines of his yellow legal pad.

'Did the death of your adoptive father inspire you to look for the Zebilas?'

'No. I told you, I met Abi by accident.'

'How did your adoptive father's death make you feel?'

'I wish you'd stop calling him that, he was my dad. My father. My dad. You don't have to add the other word on.'

The detective looks at the man beside me and I can sense that the man beside me's whole body is as stiff as a totem pole. I'm guessing he expected me to take his feelings into consideration when answering these questions.

'How do you think his death made me feel? I was devastated.'

'Were you a little disorientated by his death?'

'Yes, I suppose so.'

'Maybe a little angry at the world that someone you loved was taken from you?'

'Maybe, I suppose.'

'Maybe a little keen on some cosmic payback because if you hadn't been put up for adoption you wouldn't have had to lose this wonderful man you grew close to over the years?'

'No. I wouldn't do anything like that.'

'Can you explain why your fingerprints were on Mrs Zebila's medication?'

'I told you, I was there once and she knocked a lot of them on to the floor. I picked them up.'

'No one else in the family mentioned this happening. Who else was there at the time to verify your version of events?'

The detective has open pores on his nose. I'm not sure what that says about him apart from the fact that his nose looks like the crater-covered surface of the moon, but it's a piece of information that lodges itself into my brain. I'm trying to work out how to tell the truth without sounding like I am guilty.

'No one,' I eventually say.

'You were alone in the house with Mrs Zebila at the time that you say you picked up her medication?'

'Yes.'

'How many other times were you alone in the house with her?'

'I'm not sure.'

'Can you estimate? More than two, less than twenty, say?'

'About ten,' I state. I feel the man beside me grow still. He does not know this, no one does.

'Was it during one of these ten or more times you were alone in the Zebila house with the victim that your fingerprints came to be on her jewellery?'

'I looked through her jewellery a few times, yes.'

'It's an impressive collection, isn't it?'

'Yes.'

'How much do you think her collection is worth?'

'I don't know.'

'You're a jewellery expert, you must have worked with thousands, if not hundreds of thousands of pounds' worth of items over the years. Can't you even estimate?'

'No, I don't do valuations. It's a very specialised skill.'

'Well, if you can't estimate, which I'm surprised by given the length of time you have worked with jewellery, I'll tell you. It is upwards of two hundred thousand pounds. Could be closer to half a million. Does that surprise you?'

'Yes. She just had it in a box in the bottom drawer. I looked at it and sorted it out but I didn't realise it was worth so much.'

'Really? I find that hard to believe when you're such an experienced jeweller.'

'It's true,' I insist. Who knew my obsession with looking at pretty jewellery and hearing stories about people would result in this line of questioning?

'Just out of interest, did you have a key to the Zebila house?'

The police rarely ask a question they don't know the answer to. I learnt that from watching all those cop shows. They know I have a key, or they suspect I have one and they want me to confirm their suspicions. Do I brazen it out or tell the truth?

The man next to me now looks in my direction, disturbed that I haven't answered already and that he didn't know I was alone in the house with his mother several times. That I went through her very expensive jewellery collection.

'Yes,' I say. And my father's entire body swings towards me.

'How did you come by this key?'

'My grandmother, Mrs Zebila, gave it to me.'

The policeman visually logs the reaction of the man next to me.

'Why would the victim do that?'

'Because she wanted me to have it? Because she thought it might make me feel part of the family?' *Because it would make slipping in and doing what she wanted easier. And what she wanted was for me to kill her.*

'But neither of you mentioned it to any other member of the family, is that correct?'

'Yes.'

'Did you kill your grandmother?'

'No.'

'Did you feel like killing her when you found out that it was her who called Social Services to have you put up for adoption before you were born and pressurised both of your parents to give you away?'

'No, because I didn't know she did that.'

'Are you sure?'

'Yes, I'm sure. My birth mother hinted at it, but I didn't know my grandmother called Social Services or that she put pressure on my parents.' My father should probably be bowing his head in shame but he isn't. He is still staring at me, stuck back at the revelation that I have access to his house whenever I want.

'Did you put pressure on your grandmother to end her life?'

'No.'

'Did you make her believe that she would be better off dead as payback for what she did to you?'

'No.'

'Did you think that after you killed her you could let yourself into the house and help yourself to her jewellery whenever the mood took you?'

'No.'

'Did you want her dead?'

'No.'

'We have evidence that since you came into their lives, Mrs Zebila started to express thoughts of suicide and ending her life early. Do you know anything about that?'

Over the years I have collected old-fashioned tools to help me craft my metalwork jewellery and one of my favourite things is an old steel screwdriver. It looks like a wooden-handled whisk with a turning handle at the side. Where the whisk blades would be, there is a gap where you insert the different screw bits. The first ring I ever used it to make, I secured thick pieces of silver and copper wire into my metal clamp then fed the ends into the open end of the screwdriver. I turned the wheel handle, wound it slowly but consistently, twisting the wire into something new, unrecognisable from what I started with. This police officer is like that steel screwdriver with the metal strands of the truth – he is twisting what nearly happened between my grandmother and me into something new and shiny and unrecognisable; a version that will make me look guilty.

'Do you know anything about Mrs Zebila's sudden thoughts of suicide?' the officer asks again, showing me the twisted, reshaped strands of truth.

'Not in the way you mean,' I reply. *Not in the way you've twisted things.* 'She told me she was tired and old and ill and that she wanted to die.'

Another visceral, shocked reaction from my father. Him staying with me was a spectacularly bad idea. It seemed wonderful before, that my father was willing to publicly acknowledge me, that it was a chance for us to bond. Now he is finding out things he shouldn't know, in ways he shouldn't have to.

'You were more than willing to help her out, I take it?'

'No. I told her to talk to her doctor or nurse. I thought if she talked to them, they'd make her see her condition wasn't as bleak as she thought. They'd give her hope and comfort, show her that with the right medication she could live a comfortable life for her remaining years.'

'She did talk to her doctor and nurse, as it turns out,' the policeman says, 'but had a different take on what you've just said. She told them both that she was thinking of ending things and that someone had come into her life who had not only made her feel it was possible, but had eagerly agreed to help her.' *That woman*, I think. *That woman.* 'Judging by the look on Mrs Zebila's son's face, I am guessing this is the first time he or anyone else in his family has heard of her plans to end her life.' *That woman. That woman.* 'I think it's safe to assume, Miss Smittson, the person she was referring to, was you.'

They've let me go without charge. But I'm not to leave the area, and I'm not to think for one second that any of this is over because they are continuing the investigation against me. They will be going through my home and place of business looking for evidence that I carried out this crime; that I had maybe helped myself to her jewellery and had convinced her to kill herself to cover it up. The police officer told me if it was true that she did want to die, it would not be any better for me – that they take cases of assisted suicide very seriously, because even supplying the means for someone to kill themselves is a criminal offence. 'We all know Mrs Zebila was not capable of carrying out the act herself,' he said, 'especially not injecting such a huge dose of insulin let alone the other medication, which means someone else would have done it for her.'

Mum's face, small, extremely pale and scored with fretful lines, is the first one I see. A little behind her is my other mother, her face as worried and concerned as a mother's would be. To Mum's right stands my husband, a full head and a half higher than both of the women.

'I think it's best that you stay away from my family from now on,' is what my father says to me when we leave the interview room and are shown out into the reception area. Mum has reached for me, pulled me towards her and hugged me tight. I wonder if that is what causes him to say that. I called Dad 'my dad' in front of him and he hadn't been happy, and Mum is the person I go to for comfort. Or is it the shock of finding out all those things about his mother that he probably would rather not know?

'Julius!' my other mother says, horrified that he is doing this.

My father glares at my other mother, and when he does, I see *his* mother, my grandmother: her sternness in his forced-together lips, her stubbornness in the frown on his brow, her determination to get her own way in the set of his jaw.

'What are you saying?' my other mother says. Even though less than a week ago she put me off coming to see them.

'This is for the best, Kibibi.'

'It is,' Mum says. 'I was about to say the same thing.'

I release myself from her hug like a toddler releases themselves from their buggy they've outgrown and push myself free. 'Mum, don't—'

'No, Clemency, this has gone on long enough. I have watched them welcome you with open arms, then cast you aside when it suits them. And now this.' She shakes her open hands upwards, to emphasise the place we're in. '*This*. It's gone too far. You're to stay away from them, do you hear me?'

'I'm not nine,' I tell her.

'I think Mrs Smittson is perfectly correct. We welcomed you into our home and you have violated our trust by not being honest with us.'

'I thought you said no daughter of yours could do such a thing,' I say quietly. I'm sure he's sat next to innocent and guilty people before, did I sound like a murderer, a killer to him?

'That was before I knew *all* of the facts. You are to stay away from us or I will have the police charge you with harassment.'

Is this what that woman *wanted? To have me out of their lives at any cost? Even at the cost of her own life?*

'I didn't do it,' I say.

370

'I will be telling Abi to avoid all contact with you also,' Mr Zebila, as he has morphed into in the last few minutes, states. 'Ivor has always had his doubts.'

'Come on, Clemency,' Mum says. 'We are leaving.'

'I didn't do it,' I say to my other mother.

She looks incredibly, heartbreakingly, sad. Her features are soft, her face a little downcast and her eyes are a liquid brown that swim with soon-to-be-shed tears as she stares at me. Her hair is so neat – each strand is glossy, black, smooth and perfect. I'm sure she never has tangles in her hair. She most likely has them in her mind, her heart, but not in her hair. I have them in all those places. The hard Sussex water is playing havoc with my hair, and the complicated Sussex life is playing havoc with my mind and heart.

'Please tell Abi I'm sorry I won't be seeing her,' I say to my other mother.

She doesn't reply.

'And Lily. I'll miss her, too.'

'Come on, Clemency,' Mum states.

I grab my other mother and hug her, hold her close. She relaxes for a moment in my arms, and I'm overwhelmed by how comforting it is to hold her. If I had known it would feel like this, I would have done it a million years ago. A second or two later, she stiffens and retreats. That moment is enough – it tells me she believes me. She believes me that I didn't do it.

'You must promise me you will not see those people again,' Mum says in the taxi home.

Seth does not turn from his place in the front seat to look at us, but I know he's listening, wondering what I will say because he knows how 'complicated' my mother can be. How despite the effect she has on me, when she makes me promise something, I always do. Except, Seth knows this is different. *I* know this is different. Mainly because I am different and 'those people' are my family, too.

'Promise me,' Mum insists when my silence is her answer.

'I promise,' I say. In my flat black ballet shoes, the only shoes I could put on in a rush, I have, obviously, crossed my toes.

60

Abi

To: Jonas Zebila
From: Abi Zebila
Subject: Please reply. PLEASE!!!!!
Monday, 17 August 2015

It's all gone a bit batsh*t around these parts. Which is why I am plotting my escape. I think it's going to have to be Declan. I make him sound like the terrible option but he's not. He's simply the commitment option and I'm not ready for commitment. But, there are times in your life when you have to sh*t or get off the crazy pot, and I am getting myself off the crazy pot quick smart.

Daddy actually thinks Clemency killed Gran. He truly believes it. He came back from the police station and informed me I wasn't allowed to go near Clemency again. I was so taken aback I actually said, 'I'm not nine, Daddy.' And he told me I would do as I was told while living in his house. Like I don't pay rent, like I don't do chores, like I didn't help feed, clean and take care of Gran. Well, that's it, I'm done. I've texted Declan that he needs to start looking for a bigger place for us all to move into. He's over the moon.

Mummy didn't say much during all of this. She kept looking at Daddy with resentment in her eyes. When he'd finished she said, 'I'll never forgive you or your mother for what you've done. You took my first child away from me. My eldest son is rude, unpleasant and talks to me like I am beneath him because that is what your mother taught him to do. She drove

372

away my second son. I suspect my second daughter is already planning on leaving and never returning. And now you have taken away my first child again because of your mother. I will never forgive you, Julius.' And then she left the room. Daddy just stared after her and Ivor looked terrified. For the first time in Ivor's life someone had told him he wasn't the be all and end all of everything. He'll miss that about Gran, I think: not being her golden child any more. That sounds mean, but when I think of some of the things Gran said to me and about me just because I wasn't male or Ivor . . .

I feel so angry right now. It's like Ivor doing this thing and Daddy ordering me about has made the scales fall from my eyes. Or allowed me to be honest with myself for the first time in years. I feel like I've been part of this conspiracy that let Gran get away with anything she wanted because she was ill. I was so scared of losing her, I moved in to be with her, to help take care of her, and she never really had a kind word to say to me. I didn't want gratitude, just for her to treat me nicely. How she treated Lily-Rose, how she treated Ivor. She wasn't even that nice to Daddy if I think about it. She was a mean old woman.

Yes, yes, Jonas, I know you worked it out all those years ago. I'm sorry that I ever made you feel guilty for not getting in touch with her. And I am so, so sorry for what she did to Meredith. I'm guessing because you haven't told me otherwise that after the miscarriage Meredith still can't get pregnant again? I feel so awful for being a part of Gran's world. I really hope you can forgive me.

I'm sorry, you probably don't want me dredging all this up. It's like the floodgates have opened and I can't believe how under her spell I was. I hope I don't end up with only negative memories of her, that would be bad for me more than anything.

Will you talk to me now, Jonas? Now I can see everything so much more clearly, will you talk to me?

I love you.
Abi
xxxx

61

Smitty

Someone killed my grandmother. And they want me to be convicted for her murder.

These are the thoughts that accompany my every waking moment, every step I take, every time I leave the house to go and meet someone who wants their jewellery reloved or something special made. Someone killed my grandmother and they hate me enough to let me be accused.

They'd have to know me and they'd have to know her. They'd have to have access to her house or my key, and knowledge of when it was safe to get into the house to do it. There aren't that many people with all that information, all that access. If I didn't know me, I'd think it was me, too. But it wasn't.

The only person who I know who could hate me enough is the person who would call Social Services before I was even born to make sure I never set foot in her house. I'm still smarting at the idea of that. She sat there and pretended that she had wanted to see me, that she regretted it, when all along she never had any intention of seeing me. And then she manipulated what she told her doctor and nurses to make it sound like I had been the driving force behind her decision to die. The only person who would hate me enough and would want her dead was *her*. My grandmother. Even if she did, though, there was no doubting that she couldn't do it herself, which means someone had to help her. Which means they must know I am being investigated for their crime.

Somebody killed my grandmother, and they're going to let me go to prison for it.

I let myself into the flat, kick off my shoes, stop by the bathroom to wash my hands and then head straight for the kitchen. I had a message from Melissa earlier, asking how it was going, whether I'd got any closer to applying for my adoption papers and saying she'd come with me or be with me while I read them. I remember the first time we met, her saying that it was important to have them even having met her birth mother. I need to call her back, I felt such a connection with her, like she had lived so many of the things I did in a similar way. But I am barely functioning at the moment. All that keeps going though my head is that someone killed my grandmother and they're going to let me be convicted for it. I can't engage with anybody about anything else beyond that.

I can hear the others in the living room; I caught a glimpse of them on my way to get a drink. Mum and Nancy are on the sofa, the TV is on, Seth and Sienna are by the window watching the world go by and shouting 'Bingo!' every time they see a dog.

On the worktop nearest the kitchen door, the foil, wire top and cork of a bottle of champagne sit discarded, as if someone had hurriedly opened them. Champagne at 4 p.m. Mum and Nancy are becoming ladies who lunch clichés. Nancy was gutted (Mum probably was, too) when I stopped taking Sienna out with me every day.

In the fridge I reach for the orange juice, which is too large a bottle to fit in the fridge door. Next to the orange juice is a champagne-bottle-shaped space, from the bottle I've stored since I arrived here. I leave the fridge door open and return to the foil, wire and cork on the worktop by the door. Snatch it up. The metal cap that sits between the wire and the cork is the same brand, same vintage, as the one I had in my fridge in Leeds for more than a year and then brought here. It was very expensive and the same brand and year as the one Dad had given Seth and me after we'd cancelled our engagement party. He'd scrawled a note saying how sorry he and Mum were about the party but how pleased they were that we were together and happy. The bottle and note were from him because he'd known what had really happened, he wasn't as blind to Nancy as Mum was. When I told Dad I'd almost saved up enough to open my own shop, he'd bought me another bottle of the same champagne to keep for that day. The bottle lived in that part of the fridge. I go back, check it hasn't been moved, shunted along to make room for something else. It's not there. It's not there... but they wouldn't, they just wouldn't.

Slamming the fridge door shut, I dash out into the corridor then across into the living room.

'Clem, go back into the kitchen and grab yourself a glass, we're celebrating my good news,' Nancy says. On the low coffee table in front of them, a coffee table Mum and Nancy ordered and had delivered without consulting me after one of their shopping trips, sits the condensation-soaked bottle of champagne. I snatch it up, look at the bottom right-hand corner of the label where Dad had written *Love, Mum & Dad, 2014*. Nancy and Mum would, they did.

'This is the bottle that my dad bought me,' I say, the first time I've spoken directly to Nancy without her having asked a question first.

'Seth did mention that, but Auntie Heather didn't think you'd mind much since I've had such brilliant news,' Nancy says. Her brow is a little creased, she probably wonders if she has said it properly or if I have a hearing problem. Even after everything, she still thinks I care about anything good or bad that happens to her. 'My blog has been shortlisted for an award. The inside word is that I'm a shoe-in to win. Isn't that wonderful?'

My attention moves from the bottle to Nancy. That's it; done. She has at last succeeded in taking everything from me. Even in our most desperate-for-a-drink moments, Seth and I wouldn't open that bottle, not even when we got married, because it was special, it was for when I opened the shop. It was a promise between Dad and me. Since Dad died it's become more than that promise, it's also the last thing he ever gave me to complete the important task I needed to fulfil.

'You need to pack up and leave,' I say to Nancy. She's done it all, she's taken everything from me. She can go now.

Her glass pauses on its journey to her mouth, her smile becomes a rictus mask of what happiness should look like on her face.

'Sienna.' Seth is on his feet. 'Would you like to come for a walk on the beach with me? We can play dog bingo and maybe get an ice cream in Marrocco's.'

'OK, Uncle Smitty.' My niece, who is really my second cousin, gets to her feet as well. 'Is Auntie Smitty going to tell off Mum?' The emotion in the room is heavy, potent enough to be real, touchable. Sienna can sense it and isn't about to pretend that she can't.

'I'm not sure,' Seth replies, as honest an answer as Dad would have given, 'but I think it's best that neither of us is here right now.'

'OK.' She shrugs. Makes no difference to her whether she's here or not, plus she gets ice cream.

Minutes later, when Seth has gathered his keys and wallet from the shelf in the corridor, when they have debated and decided on which shoes to wear, whether to take coats or not, a click – quiet and discreet – tells us we are alone.

'You need to pack up your stuff and leave,' I say to Nancy again.

'Clemency, love,' Mum says, 'I know that bottle meant something to you, but I didn't think you'd mind sharing it with Nancy when she'd had such good fortune.' Mum is now by my side and she rubs carefully at my shoulder. 'You're just going through a run of bad luck. Things will pick up for you soon, I know for certain they will.' This is how my mother has reworked the last couple of weeks – a run of bad luck. Not another of my family members dying, not me being investigated for a serious crime, not me being cut off from my other family members on *her* say-so. Just a run of bad luck.

Nancy, meanwhile, hitches her eyebrow briefly, warns me that she knows too much about me for me to simply throw her out, to even complain when she has robbed me of something so precious.

My gaze rakes over Nancy with her perfect hazelnut hair that tumbles down towards her shoulders, the 'kooky' blonde patch at the front she had done when we were fourteen, the unsymmetrical lay of her features that have always denied her the chance to be a model. Her plan from an early age (when she was constantly told by her parents that she was beautiful and her cousin – me – wasn't) was to be a model. She was going to take the catwalks of the world by storm, and earn buckets of money. That's why there are so many photos of her on her blog/Twitter/Facebook/Instagram – she wants the world to see what the talent spotters and model agency folk missed: she was a natural model. She is hoping still that someone will 'spot' her. She knew she would have been perfect for the catwalks and the magazine covers and shoots. She might not be tall enough, or – to them – have a beguiling enough face, but they were wrong to deny her. She has the body – neat torso, slender limbs, always stylishly, quirkily clothed. She has, too, her most important asset of all – her unwavering sense of being entitled to whatever it is that she wants, whenever she wants it. Life may have dealt her merely a comfortable (instead of rich) upbringing and denied her the career she dreamt of, but she hadn't let that hold her back. And one of the many ways she gets what she wants is to have things over people, to manipulate them into doing her bidding.

I stare at her as I ask my mother: 'Do you want to know why I hate Nancy?'

'You don't hate her, love. Of course you don't. You're like sisters.'

'We are not like sisters. It's only ever been you who has thought that. She has been hideous to me most of our lives.'

A shake of the head from my cousin Nancy – I was obviously suffering from false memory syndrome – she had been nothing but delightful to me during our childhood. Nancy's lip twisted ever so slightly at the corner, reminding me that if I dared to say anything different, she would be doing her own remembering and what she recalled would be things I would not want my mother knowing. No matter how old, independent and adult I am now, there are things no one wants their mother to know.

'When I was nine Nancy knocked over your mother's ashes from the mantelpiece at her house and you and Uncle Colin blamed me, remember?' I say to Mum. 'I said to her that when I was older my real parents would come for me and make everything OK. I was nine. I didn't even have a concept of what a "real" parent was except Nancy and her parents had been telling me all my life that I wasn't real. So, I said it and Nancy held that over me for years – saying she was going to tell you and Dad what I said.' *There you go, Nancy, that's one thing you've got on me gone.* 'When we were ten and those boys kept calling me names at school, she joined in. She said it was all true, and I couldn't tell you because she'd tell you what I said when I was nine. When we were twelve, she blackmailed me into smoking cannabis and then used *that* to blackmail me into having no friends and doing whatever she wanted all through our teens because I knew how much it would hurt you that I'd done drugs and had said that thing when I was nine.' *Another one gone, Nancy.*

'When I was fifteen I had sex for the first time with a lad I was seeing at school. Nancy tried it on with him a few days later. When he wasn't interested she spread rumours at school that I was a slut, that I'd slept with loads of people, and that I'd given him an STD. I got bullied and called names that whole year. But I couldn't say anything because I didn't want you to know I was having sex.

'When I was seventeen I had a pregnancy scare due to a split condom. I don't know how she found out but I suspect she'd cosied up to my boyfriend and he was just as panicked as me so he told her. She tried to get him to dump me before we could get enough money together to buy a test. When he wouldn't she said she'd tell Dad, who would beat him up. My boyfriend dumped me, just as she wanted, and I had to go through the stress of the test on my own.' (I have never told anyone the real result of the test nor what happened two days later when I had a miscarriage, and I wasn't about to tell these two.)

Mum's face has grown paler and paler with every word, her features frigid with shock. 'Oh, I forgot, every time we met someone new, she would tell them that I'd been found in a cardboard box on the steps of an orphanage.'

Mum looks at Nancy then because that's shocking to her, it seems.

'And do you know what, Mum? I don't even hate her for all of that, and I don't hate her for ruining every single significant event that's ever happened to me.'

'That's not true!' Nancy states. She has to find her voice now that her four biggest pieces of leverage over me have gone and Mum is starting to look at her with new, un-rose-tinted eyes.

'Clemency—'

I thought Mum was listening but she isn't. She is desperately trying to rearrange every word that filters into her brain so that they don't tell the story of my experiences with Nancy, but instead hold the key to how I have got all of this wrong. 'Mum,' I almost scream, 'just listen to me. Please! For once, just listen. She has ruined almost every single significant event in my life. I wasn't allowed to celebrate getting ten high-grade GCSEs because Nancy only got five low-grade ones.'

'Her father was awful to her about that, she felt so terrible,' Mum says, patently not listening. But I don't care and plough on. It's liberating getting all of this out there, off my chest.

'The same thing with my A levels – she does badly because she didn't bother to work hard, I'm not allowed to celebrate. And my graduation – you almost didn't come because she turned up the night before having broken up with her boyfriend and you were suddenly the only person in the whole world she could turn to. You do realise, don't you, Mum, that the only reason you came was because Dad put his foot down and said he'd never speak to you again if you missed it?'

Mum's face draws in on itself, her body tenses, she's been remembering it differently all these years, obviously.

'Every time something good happened to me, Nancy was there to ruin it.'

I think Mum is still back at being reminded of those conversations around my graduation with Dad. I heard him asking her if she wasn't glad she made the right choice in the end. *How could you have even thought of missing that,* quine, *for Nancy of all people?*' he'd whispered when they thought I was asleep in the back of the car.

'Nancy even ruined my engagement party by pretending to be mugged on the way there by a gang who were prowling the area because the thought of me being the centre of attention for once in my life was too much for her.

'Like I said, I don't hate her for any of it. And I don't hate her for the fact Seth and I had to get married in secret last year because I knew, no matter how small the ceremony, she'd have somehow made the occasion all about her.'

A small, shocked, distressed gasp from my mother. She covers her lips with her hand, and immediately her eyes are laden with tears. It is now such a part of mine and Seth's background, the tapestry of who we are as a couple, I forget how significant it is to your family, to your parents, when you get married. I am so used to doing things in secret that to me it isn't the big deal it is to have gone off and done it alone and not told anyone about it afterwards.

Mum's pale blue eyes look at the rings on my fingers, trying to work out which one it is. When we got married, I stopped wearing the rings I'd made on my hands and wore them on my chain neck-lace, except my amber engagement ring and my silver wedding ring. I wore my engagement ring on the fourth finger of my left hand – as everyone expected – and my wedding ring on the fourth finger of my right hand. When we split, I swapped: the engagement and wedding rings went on to the chain and my other rings returned to my hands. Seth still wears his wedding ring. I remove the rings, nest-ling under my top on the chain I wear as well as my butterfly pendant, and show them to Mum.

'This is my wedding ring. I made it and I made one for Seth and we got married in Leeds Registry Office and we advertised on the internet for two people to come and be our witnesses. About twenty people turned up.' I sound defiant, and I don't mean to. I want to sound calm and rational. Plus, I need to not get sidetracked by Mum's reaction: the hurt on her face reveals I have torn a strip off her heart, that I have denied her something she was looking forward to.

'I can see you're upset and shocked, Mum,' I say. 'And I should be upset for you, but I know pretty soon your upset is going to turn into annoyance at me. Everything I've said will become part of my imagination, the way everything does when it comes to Nancy. Because, let's be honest, Mum, she's the daughter you've always wanted, isn't she? She's the one who looks like you, and who's got so much in common with you. And that's all fine.'

'*That is not true!*' Mum cuts in. She is more horrified by that than the time I told her how racist she was being about my dating Tyler. '*You must never say that, not ever!*'

'OK, it's not true,' I concede. I don't want to get into this with Mum. It's not about the things I've said and done, it's about Nancy and how Mum needs the chance to see her for who she really is. 'But what is true is that I dislike Nancy for all she's done to me in my life, but I *hate* her for using the last few weeks of Dad's life and his illness . . . to . . . to first of all make a move on my husband.' Mum slowly revolves to face Nancy again. 'That's why Seth and I split up. She kept going over there, pretending to offer comfort when all she wanted was to sleep with him and get information. She even got into our bed naked. Worse than that, though, is that she was using Seth to get information about Dad's illness, his final weeks and days, so she could write about it.

'She pretended to the whole world that she was living it, that she was helping and suffering just like we were. She took something private and personal, something we were barely struggling through, and made it public. That's what her award nomination will be for, because she convincingly used our pain to make a name for herself and to make money. I'm sure the only reason she's here now is to get more material for her blog.' The guilt that crosses Nancy's face tells me I'm right. 'That's why she's taken the last thing that Dad ever bought me. And that's why she needs to go. She has everything she's ever wanted now. She's taken everything from me, there is nothing left about my life that is special that she can ruin, so she has to go.'

Mum's body is rigid: her arms are at her sides and her fingers are spread and held so tight that they are trembling. For a moment I think she's going to throw back her head and roar, she looks so incensed; fit to burst with a rage I've never seen in her before. Instead, she orders: 'Leave us.'

Nancy moves, relieved that she's got away with it. Again.

'*Don't you move*,' Mum snarls so viciously I'm not surprised Nancy freezes. She looks as terrified as I was the time Mum started screaming at me in my workshop. '*Clemency*, leave us.'

I collect my bag from its place in the corridor and leave as instructed. It doesn't matter. A few tears, a few hollow apologies, and Mum will be back to loving Nancy like the daughter she is to her. It won't be long before the real issues that need discussing will be me not telling her I got married, me having sex at fifteen, me doing a pregnancy test at seventeen, me saying one time in my life when I was very young that they weren't my 'real' parents. All of this will be used to take me apart while telling me I should be kind and understanding to Nancy. That's how these situations always pan out.

Outside the building, I stand beside Lottie and then lean against her, propped up by my biggest reloved project. Exhaustion is pulsing through my body. Journeying through the shittiest parts of my childhood has taken all the spirit out of me. If all of those memories were laid like beads on the bench in my workshop, waiting to be strung together, I wouldn't know where to start. It would make a hideous piece with its dangerously sharp edges and blinding snatches of bright-white pain – no amount of reloving and redesigning would change that.

But my life hadn't been all like that. No way near like that. The sharp-edged moments were interspersed with so many smooth, well-rounded, luscious, warm-coloured beads of moments and memories. I had a good childhood. My teenage years were as fraught and desperate and fun as any of the other people's around me. Like I told my mother, my biological mother, I had been OK. Mostly.

It's the reliving all the awful bits in such a short space of time that has drained me. Thrown me, too. Was it really that bad? Even though I can call up some of the best moments without too much trouble, they don't seem as tangible and real as the bad bits did.

I need to forget. I need something that will put all of that right, right, *right* at the back of my mind so I can concentrate on something else.

I take my phone out of my pocket.

The person on the other end picks up on the second ring. I was expecting it to take longer.

'Are you free right now? Do you want to meet up and maybe go for a drink or something? My treat.'

I should feel guilty when I hang up the phone after we've planned where to meet and where to go so we aren't seen, but I don't. It's far too late for feelings of guilt. Like everyone else, I'm going to do whatever I want, simply because that is what I want to do.

As I head off to my meeting, I can't help thinking: somebody killed my grandmother and they're trying to lay the blame on me.

62

Abi

To: Jonas Zebila
From: Abi Zebila
Subject: Hello
Saturday, 22 August 2015

Dear J,

Thank you for saying you don't hate me and that I did nothing wrong. I really wish it hadn't taken me so long to see it. Now that you've started replying to my emails, I'm hoping that you'll move on from a few words.

Clemency called me out of the blue earlier and I went to see her. Daddy asked me where I was going and I said that I was seeing Declan. I know, right? Suddenly him thinking I'm seeing the man responsible for me not finishing uni is better than seeing Clemency. I only lied because Declan hasn't found us a new place yet.

She told me everything. She was open and honest, told me that Gran had asked her to help her die but Clemency didn't do it even though she agreed to. I believe her. I think she was actually quite brave to agree to help Gran like that. It was like all the stuff I was telling you about what Gran actually wanted. What she wanted was for it to be over. I can't think about that though. The thought of going into nothingness completely terrifies me and I have to think about something else. As Clemency said, though, if she didn't do it, then who did?

That's the most terrifying thought of all. Someone did this to Gran, or someone helped her. And we have no idea who.

Right, it's late, I need to sleep.

Love,
Abi
xxxx

63

Smitty

Thankfully, the flat is in darkness when I return. I took the time to walk as far as possible around the building to see if any lights were on. They were all out so it was safe to come inside. I don't really call it home – I had started to, then all sorts started pitching up to stay and it became 'the flat'. Opening the front door, I see they've turned off the corridor light, which we usually leave on for Sienna.

I pause for a moment after shutting the door behind me, trying to make out shapes in our entrance hallway so I can map out where the potential obstacles are in the dark.

If I can creep in, not turn on any lights, I can probably slide quietly into bed, and I won't have to deal with trying to erase guilt from my face about who I've been with, nor explain to Seth what had been said earlier.

'I've been waiting up for you,' Mum says in a whisper, at the exact moment my eyes decipher through the darkness that there is a human-type form at the end of the corridor. My heart spirals into my throat with fright, and I have to clamp my hands over my mouth to stop myself swearing or crying out in shock.

Who does that? Who stands in the dark, waiting for someone? I almost ask her if she's literally been standing in the dark corridor all night waiting for me, but I'm not sure I could handle her answering yes to that question.

'Hi,' I eventually manage, and flick on the light.

She is dressed for bed in her pink silk dressing gown and her tartan slippers. I was always surprised Dad allowed her to wear those slippers since fake tartan enraged him like very little else did.

I've reached that part of the exhaustion spectrum where it hurts to breathe, it's painful to blink, and I know I can't withstand a barrage of explanations, questions and recriminations. Although the questioning has already begun: when Mum says 'I've been waiting up for you' she actually means, *'Where have you been?'*

'It's very late,' she whispers. *'Why didn't you call me and ask permission to stay out so late?'* she means.

'I know,' I say.

'You look tired,' she continues in a whisper. *'Have you been with that man? In his bed? Is that why you look so tired?'*

'I am tired.'

'I was getting worried.' *'You have no right to do this to me.'*

'Mum, can we do this tomorrow? I need to sleep.'

'I need to talk to you. Come into the kitchen, I'll make us both a cup of tea.'

'I don't want tea, I do want my bed,' is what the me who I am in my head, the person she got a glimpse of earlier, says. 'Fine,' the person I am most of the time says.

In the kitchen I pull out a chair, trying to avoid scraping the legs against the black slate tiles, and sit where I always sit – with my back to the window, to the sea and the promenade. I didn't even realise until this moment that my seat in the flat has become the worst one since Nancy and Sienna moved in. The first few weeks, when it was Mum and me, I used to love sitting in here, a cup of coffee on the go, the radio on low, watching, through the multiple panes of the kitchen window, the world outside shake off the night, open its eyes, and carefully stretch itself awake.

Mum flicks on the lights under the wall units, casting a quietening glow over the kitchen. Once the lights are on, she moves to shut the kitchen door before returning to the chrome kettle. Beside it she has placed her favourite emerald green mug and my white 'Jewellers Do It With Links' mug. I stare at that mug. I'd had to put it right to the back of the cupboard when she moved in with me – she glared at it with such passionate hatred I feared it'd crack under the weight of her disapproval. Once, when she was out, I'd gone to look for it and found she'd moved it right to the back of one of the lower cupboards where the tinned black beans and peaches lived, in other words, somewhere I wouldn't be finding it in a hurry. Its resurrection tells me she feels guilty about something.

I close my eyes when I realise that it's probably because Nancy has been forgiven, welcomed back to the bosom of my mother after what must have been, for Nancy, a scary minute or two out in the cold. If I'm honest, I knew nothing was going to change. I knew in that place in my heart where knowledge comes from that Nancy was going to get away with it. Her type always...

Mum is sitting opposite me when I open my eyes. There are two cups on the table, both have steam rising from them. The taste in my mouth and the heaviness in my eyes, the stiffness of my neck, the tingling in my arm upon which I rest my head, tell me I was asleep for longer than it took Mum to boil the kettle and make tea.

'You fell asleep,' she says.

'How long for?' I ask.

'About an hour,' she replies.

'An hour? And you sat here watching me for an hour?'

'Yes. And making tea so you'd have a fresh cup when you woke up.'

'You seriously sat watching me sleep for an hour?'

Mum smiles at me. 'I used to do it all the time when you were a baby. It was one of my favourite things to do. It made me feel like a real mother. I could watch you sleep and no one could stop me. I used to look at you and think...' The smile on her face changes, becomes wistful and sad as she looks down into her cup. 'I used to think, "I'm allowed to keep this one. This one is all mine and no one can ever take her away."' The corners of her mouth turn up, even though she is so sad I can feel it in the air around her, like it is fizzing outwards from the centre of her being and slowly dissolving into my skin. Soon her sadness is my sadness.

'Do you truly believe Nancy is the daughter I wish I had?' she asks.

Of course I believe it. Everything she has ever done has shown me that. Nancy has always come first and that is something I've grown accustomed to, like I've grown accustomed to crippling period pain the months I don't consistently take my fish oil – it's a consequence of who I am, a result of my biological make-up. If I was different, if I looked like Nancy, Mum might have found it easy to be with me. And for her, being my mother might not have been an ordeal where she felt that ignoring huge parts of who I am and what I look like was the best thing to do.

'Of course I don't, Mum,' I reply. I can do this. I can look her in the eye and say this. 'I was just upset.' I can say that to her because even though I am not Nancy, I am not the daughter she dreamt of when she was given that baby in the butterfly-covered box, I still love her. She's still the woman who brought me up, who tried her best even when her best was downright agony at times, and I can't hurt her, no matter how many times she's damaged me.

Mum's fingers spread themselves on either side of her cup. Her melancholy is almost painful now, I am reaching my limit of how much I can stand.

'You're lying to me,' she says quietly. It is the gentlest of accusations, the saddest of rebukes. 'That's why you're the daughter I always wanted, you would do that for me even though I have...' A lifetime of secret aching seems to unfold on her face and it is stark and raw and visible, even though she continues to hang her head. 'When you were about four or five your father bought a Polaroid camera from a man he met down at the pub – if you can believe it. Down the pub, I tell you!'

I remember the camera well. It was white with a rainbow stripe down its body. I've been tempted so many times to buy a second-hand one online but I've never gone beyond the thought. Maybe because it reminds me of all the pictures I was forced to pose for with Nancy. I love my Polaroid camera because it's nothing like that one. I want that vintage one, but it carries with it painful reminders.

'I loved that camera,' Mum continues after a final shake of her head at how they came by it. 'I used to take pictures of you all the time. It drove your father bonkers. "Have you seen the cost of those films, *quine*?" he'd say, half cross. "And you're taking the same photographs of the bairn doing nothing every five minutes!"' She shrugs. 'I didn't care. I wanted to photograph everything you did even if you were doing nothing. I liked to hold the photos in my hand as soon as I had taken them, they felt more real somehow. I couldn't be doing with taking a week to get them back.'

'I wasn't lying, Mum,' I say.

'You know, I haven't heard from Colin or Marcia at all since your father's funeral. They weren't interested in helping me rent out the house, nor in the fact I was moving. Even Nancy was only in touch once before she showed up – I didn't even realise that until you started talking earlier.'

'Oh, Mum.'

'I did so many things wrong. I was... I was so scared of what my brother would do. When your father lost his job down in Lewes, I was so scared that we wouldn't be able to cope. I begged my brother to put in a good word for your father at the power plant back in Leeds. I knew I didn't need to, your father would have got a job without too much trouble, he was a good worker. But I was so scared, Clemency. I thought if anyone found out that we didn't have a regular wage packet coming in they would come and take you away from me. I couldn't stand to lose you. I couldn't even stand the thought of it.

'And I knew as you got older Colin could at any time tell you about my first, try to make you believe that you were a replacement instead of someone I loved with every fibre of my being. I put up with whatever my brother said and did because I didn't want to risk having you hurt in that way. There always seemed to be someone around the corner who would be able to take you away, take you back, tell me they had more claim over you than I did. Or someone who could damage you by telling you my secrets. My brother knew how scared I was because he could remember how I was when they took my first baby away, and he used that against me. I think that's why I've ignored the things I don't like about Nancy for so long.

I grew used to putting them first so as to not rock the boat.' She shakes her head.

'I can't believe he treated you like that for all those years. Uncle Colin is a horrible, racist little man.'

Mum openly winces at the R word. 'Mum, you don't have to flinch when I say that, it's not wrong to say he's horrible or racist when it's the truth. It's what he is.'

'You thought that of me, too,' she says quietly.

There are lots of things I want to say to comfort her, but I can't say them without sounding disingenuous, or without lying. And she's just pulled me up for lying. It's not like she's racist in the way that Uncle Colin is, Mum doesn't even realise she's doing it. She seems so scared of simply admitting I'm different to her and that I'll get treated differently and sometimes badly because of that difference. She's desperate to pretend that everything will be all right if she doesn't acknowledge she and I aren't the same. And she's so unhappy about the fact that I look like sets of people she's never known, has never really taken the opportunity to know or understand, and that looking like them may translate into me being closer to them than I am to her. Mum seems terrified of 'other' because other is who I am to her and who she's not, and it's too frightening and beyond the realms of what she's comfortable with doing to try to get to know what this 'other' is all about. Like the hair thing: Dad didn't care what he had to do, where he had to travel to, who he had to talk to, to stop me from crying when my hair was combed. Mum just pretended it didn't matter because the thought of going to 'other' people, admitting that I was different, was too much for her.

She prefers Seth to Tyler for surface things: Seth looks like her, Tyler doesn't. Being around Seth is comfortable to her because she can relax with him. She doesn't realise that Seth goes to a black barber to get his hair shaved, he listens to 'black' music, he spent his youth travelling to 'black' clubs and that he studied Race and Resistance for his MA, and it's only his terror of what I'd do to him that stops him from discussing her white privilege with her.

She has no clue that Tyler listens to the middle-of-the-road 'white' music she does, he likes the same tea as her and I've even seen him working through the same crossword puzzle magazines that she does. Tyler and Seth are both full, rounded people who like things that are considered 'white' and 'black', but if it came down to it, if an analysis had to be done, between the two of them, Mum would have more in common with Tyler than with Seth – but she's unlikely to realise this because she only sees the colour of their skin and would probably find it hard to believe me if I did try to explain it to her.

The worst part is that after all these years of raising me, knowing me, because I don't look like her she still doesn't realise that no matter what, first and foremost, she is 'Mum' to me. She means the world to me. Nothing will change that.

'You're nothing like Uncle Colin. Or Nancy.'

'Oh, I don't think Nancy is like that,' Mum says, her default setting kicking in. 'If you heard some of the things your uncle said about my . . . about my first boyfriend. What he threatened. I can't imagine Nancy ever saying anything like that.'

'Nancy's more subtle about it but she is racist, just like her dad. Only, if anyone ever calls her on it, she doesn't get angry like her dad, she bursts into tears and claims people are bullying her.' Few people continue to tell off a popular girl when she cries about being bullied, no matter what she's done. I learnt that lesson from Nancy, mistress of manipulation herself. 'And what about Sienna, eh, Mum? Despite all the blonde hair and paleish skin, you know she's part black because of Dylan – is it really any good for her to be hearing all that stuff? What kind of mother continues to let her child be around people who hate a fundamental part of who she is?'

Mum's gaze snaps up to meet mine. I didn't mean it like that. I honestly didn't. I felt unshackled, free at last to be honest about how I felt about Nancy and her family, so I hadn't sent what I was saying through the filters of 'how this would sound to Mum' and 'how much it would hurt her' before I said it.

'A mother like me, I suppose,' she says, each word is brittle, frosted over with indignation.

'I didn't mean it like that, Mum. I'm sorry. I'm really sorry. You've explained why you did what you did, and I'm ever so grateful that you put yourself through that to protect me.'

'That's what parents do for their children, so there's no need to be grateful,' Mum's voice is positively Arctic now. 'Unless you don't feel I'm your real parent and therefore I somehow need the gratitude you'd show to a stranger.'

'You know, Mum, I think I've got quite a talent for saying the wrong thing and then making it worse by not being quiet straight away.'

Her reply is straight from the Mum book of glowers.

'If that's all, I'm going to leave my foot in my mouth and hop to my bed.'

'What did you wear to get married?' Mum asks. I haven't even had a chance to swig from my mug of lukewarm tea as a show of the type of gratitude I would give to everyone – parents included – before I depart. I'd forgotten that she knew now, and it didn't occur to me that she might be curious about it.

I remove my mobile from my pocket, and type in the passcode. These are the only significant photos I haven't printed out. I couldn't risk anyone finding them in my butterfly box or seeing them on my wall. It was a private thing that I knew would upset my parents and would be trashed by my cousin.

I hold the pictures of my wedding, suspended as they are in the world inside my mobile phone, out to my mother. She plucks her glasses from the top of her puzzle book, slips them on to her face. Her hand trembles as she takes the silver phone from me. I watch her face as she scrolls through them: her gaze darts to every corner of the screen, taking in every detail, then her eyes mist over behind her glasses. *Swipe*. Another image. This one probably of me grinning at the camera, the burgundy of my lipstick highlighted by a dab of gold at the meeting point of my lips, pastel-coloured confetti littering my hair, and pieces of it dotted on the lattice tiara I made from silver wire and tiny silver roses each with a diamanté at its centre. *Swipe*. She doesn't linger on that one so it's probably Seth dipping me backwards as he kisses me, his hand prominently placed on my bum. *Swipe*. Seth standing behind me with his arms around me, while we both grin at the camera. *Swipe*. Our hands linked, showing off our matching rings, made from the large hoop silver earrings I was wearing that New Year we got together.

I annealed – *softened* – them with the blowtorch, dipped them in pickle, ran them through the roller to flatten them, and then individually twisted them on the mandrel. Twisting, plaiting where I could, having to be careful to keep the shape. When I made them, especially Seth's, they felt like the most important pieces I'd ever create. Every hammer, twist of the roller, smoothing with the wire brush, run over with the blowtorch, felt like an act of love, a way to tell Seth how much he meant to me. How much our life together meant to me. I want my mother to swipe on. It hurts. When I remember the effervescent excitement that bubbled through me, the unbridled pleasure I got from thinking about being his wife, and how that all came to an end, it's a physical pain. *Swipe, Mum, swipe*. I can't stand that photo being seen by someone, when it's gone. All that excitement and joy and anticipation and expectation and pure happiness has come to an end. *Swipe, Mum, swipe. Please.*

A tear escapes Mum's eye, travels slowly down her cheek. I'm on my feet, moving towards the sink with my mug. Coffee. I need a coffee. It's about two o'clock in the morning but I need a coffee. I've been coping by not thinking about it. Even if we get back together, all of that innocence, that ability to feel without barriers that I had with Seth, has been extinguished and it'll never come back. There'll always be something damaged about our relationship. About any other relationship.

'You both look so happy. Is there really no hope for you and he?' Mum asks. I hear her carefully place the phone back on the table.

The brown granules of coffee rain into the wet cup and form uneven peaks at the bottom, some of them already dissolving to create a shiny brown-black sludge. 'No.' I have no hot water. 'I don't know.' Her eyes are watching my back. I should face her. Be honest with her so I can start to be honest with myself. 'I don't . . . I love him.

Still.' I rotate towards her. 'I still love him, of course I do, but I can't trust him any more.'

'Nancy swears nothing happened. She admits she tried but he wouldn't even look at her.'

'I know it didn't. It's not about that. I trusted him with everything and he became friendly with *her*. Told her deeply personal things. She damaged me and hurt me for years and he— I can't trust him.' I should flick on the kettle, boil the water. Make the coffee. 'And anyway,' I say to pull myself away from that particular artery of pain that runs through my life at the moment, 'I really like Tyler.'

Predictably, Mum bristles, holds herself a little tighter, her disapproval evident in each tensed muscle in her body and face.

'I know you don't want to hear it, Mum, and for whatever reason you don't think he's right for me, but I really like him. He's nice and uncomplicated and I don't know him so I don't have to worry about whether I can trust him or not. And I've hurt him. He probably won't even speak to me again so he's not really an option, but I still like him. But then there's Seth and it's not like I can stop loving him even though I can't trust him. And even though we're not together he was there for me recently when . . . So, I don't know, Mum, if there's any hope.' I just know I'm muddling through this thing in the best way I can.

'I wish I had the answer for you.'

'Did Dad know about your first child?' I ask.

'Of course,' Mum says, 'your father knew everything about me.'

'Can you tell me why your first baby was adopted?' I ask. I thought I didn't want to know but now I do. Now it'll let me know if it's me or the other baby she sees when she looks at me.

She stares at me, really scrutinises me. 'Because I was fifteen and pregnant by the boy I wanted to marry in my class. I didn't know then how much other people would have a problem with us being different. And I have a horrible, racist little man for a brother and I had a horrible bully of a man for a father, and I had a mother who would never stand up for me.' She speaks quietly but firmly. 'I wanted my baby, and so did he, my first boyfriend, but my father said no.

My mother cried about the neighbours. I said I would run away and my brother said he'd break my boyfriend's legs – maybe even kill him – if I didn't do as I was told.'

'Oh, Mum.'

'I did as I was told, I went to the home for girls like me, and I cried and cried every time they took him from my arms. I called him Aaron. Every day, Clemency, I think about him. He was a beautiful boy and they took him away to live in America and I'll never find out what happened to him.'

'You should have told me about him, Mum. I would have been supportive. I freaked out the other day because you seem so dead set against me having anything to do with my birth family and yet you knew how it must have felt for them. Well, for my birth mother at least.'

'I knew how she must have felt and I was jealous. Because if he came back into my life, I would never want him to leave. Of course I wouldn't. I'd want to hold on to him and I'd want him to stay with me and forget about the other people who brought him up, so I was jealous and scared that all my years with you would mean nothing. And my first child has never contacted me or even tried. I was so envious of Kibibi and Julius. I was also worried what would happen if they rejected you. After losing your father, breaking up with Seth, I wasn't sure how much more you could take.'

'I wish you'd just told me all this. I would have understood.'

'I know. But there's a part of every parent that never stops thinking of their child as a child. All these things are for adults to talk about. I sometimes forget you're an adult with adult choices to make.'

'I'm sorry I kept things from you,' I say.

'I'm not surprised you did. You learnt it from the expert.' She grins at me, conspiratorially. 'After they took him away, I could never get pregnant again. The doctors didn't know why, there was nothing physically wrong with me or your father. I thought it was my punishment for the sin I had committed. Then, when the social worker showed me your picture, I knew why I could never get pregnant.' She smiles at me again. 'It was so I could have you. You're the daughter I always wanted and the child I was meant to have. And I'm sorry.

I'm sorry for how I am sometimes, I'm sorry I have hurt you so many times. And I am sorry for not being a better mother.'

'You're a great mum,' I say automatically. It's true, she is. She has her moments, she needs to address her fears about how different I am to her and stop driving me crazy with how she is, but she is a fantastic mum. She's my fantastic mum.

'Kibibi is, too,' she says. She is challenging me now. Does she want me to agree, to confirm that I do prefer her, or is she just making conversation? I'm not sure and probably look terrified at the thought of what I'm meant to say. 'I'm not trying to trick you,' she says. 'Kibibi is a good mother. Apart from that one time when she turned up unannounced, she has let you set the pace, has she not?'

I nod.

'When I saw her she was desperate to be with you, it was clear in her eyes, in everything she said and did. But she's not pushy like me. She has held back and let you decide everything.'

'Apart from when my grandmother died and she didn't want to see me.'

'When your father died, did you want to see anyone? Did you want anyone near you or around you? Even the people you loved, let alone someone you are desperate to get to know.'

'I suppose not.'

'She made a difficult choice in difficult circumstances. Was it the right one? We'll never know, but think of the decisions you made when you were seventeen. Think about what was going through your head when you took that pregnancy test at that age.' Another thing about me that Mum now knows. 'She was barely finished with child-hood and she made a choice that she's lived with every day.'

'Like you,' I state.

'Like me.' Mum looks at the large kitchen clock. 'Clemency Smittson, I can't believe how late it is! Where have you been all this time?' It's incredible how quickly she can become 'Mum' again. She doesn't want to talk any more, and I suppose there's not much left to say. We have no answers for each other, only the hope that the other will do the best they can.

I shrug. 'Out.' It's just as incredible how I can become 'Child' again in a flash.

'That's no answer. Now you get to bed.'

'I'm thirty-seven, Mum,' I say.

'Does thirty-seven mean you don't need sleep?'

'No.'

'Well, then, get to bed.'

'What about you?'

'I'm going to sit here and think for a little while longer,' she says. 'I have a puzzle I need to work out.'

'Tyler likes puzzles,' I tell her, in the hope that she'll see that he and she do have something in common. Not that it'll matter since he won't be coming near me again. I just want her to consider that beyond what he looks like, he may share common ground with her.

She looks me up and down then says, 'I'm not at all surprised he does.'

It's not until I'm creeping into bed that I realise she actually meant me. I was the puzzle that she wasn't surprised he liked.

64

Smitty

The last thing that Mum told me before I went to bed was that Nancy was going home in the morning. She'd already started to pack, and they'd be gone by lunchtime. I'd nodded my head and hadn't said, 'I'll believe that when I see it.'

Here she sits, curled up in the corner of the sofa, still in her dressing gown, hair hooked behind her ears, picking at her nails like a smoker who is desperate for a cigarette. My cousin doesn't seem like someone who is leaving in less than six hours.

I watch her for long minutes from the doorway of the living room before she even notices that I'm there. When she sees me, she sits up straighter, rubs the tears from her pale face, pretends she wasn't staring into space.

Nancy has been such a nemesis in my life for so long, I'm not sure if they are real tears of regret and worry or fake ones of manipulation. If they are fake, then she's wasting her time; if they are real I don't know why she's bothering – we both know that she's going nowhere. The poisonous bond between us is broken now. She has nothing on me, I have no reason to speak to her again – not even to tell her to go, so if she stays, no one will challenge her.

'Can I talk to you?' she asks quietly.

'No, I can't face it,' I reply. I shouldn't really be talking to her. After last night, the emotional toll that having an open conversation with my mother took on me, I should conserve every last drop of energy I have. I won't be getting much more sleep today, and I need to sit down and work out who it was that killed my grandmother.

'I just want—'

'That's the problem, Nancy, it's always, *always* about what you want. I can't face it.'

Miserable, dejected, she rests her head on her hand and starts to cry again. I can't, I just can't. My keys are in my bag in my bedroom, which is a no-go zone because I'll wake Seth if I go back in. I need to get out of here. I need fresh air, and I need to be away from the woman crying on my sofa. Since moving here, out of the city, I like to be outside. No matter the weather, unless it is torrential rain, I like the air on my skin, the sounds of the world filling my ears. Walking along to Beached Heads was one of my favourite parts of the day before I ruined that experience.

In the corridor, I slide my feet into my trainers and let myself out of the house as quietly as possible. Nancy's face is worming its way into my head, the tears, the quick, quick wiping motion she made to hide them. I try to shove away her tears, her sorrow, because I've cared enough about her over the years. At some point, surely, I am allowed to not automatically worry whether her tears are real or not.

Of course I want her to be all right, she is Sienna's mother after all, if she isn't well, then Sienna will be impacted. However, there comes a time when a person has to say no more. She has to put on her shoes, and leave her flat with no means of getting back in without pressing the buzzer, wearing her blue fleece pyjamas with the white stars, that she's taken to wearing since she started sleeping beside her husband again.

Outside, I start to relax, unclench, unwind. Outside is a big expanse and it becomes my space when I exit the gate and shut it carefully behind me. I need to escape, to get out of this place, and here I am, doing just that. I could walk along to Beached Heads, sit outside and wait for Tyler to arrive. Beg him to serve me coffee and explain why I left him after he kissed me.

'You have to listen to me.' Nancy. She's had the audacity to follow me and speak to me and make me jump out of my skin.

She's wearing her thigh-length nightshirt and has replaced her dressing gown with my chunky-knit cardie that she'd unhooked from the coat rack by the door, and my favourite red ballet pumps. She wants to talk to me and because of the way Nancy sees the world, I will jolly well listen.

I take off, racing away from her towards the promenade. I don't look back, not even as I turn the corner on to the seafront proper, but I'd imagine her face is a picture of disbelief and incredulity. 'Oh, no, you don't!' I hear her shout at me before the wind whips her words away.

My feet pound the uneven black tarmac, every stone, pebble and uneven surface, shaking my bones through my thin trainers. 'COME BACK!' she roars at me. She's chasing me. I don't look back but she is pursuing me as though I owe her my time, my listening ear, my anything.

'Come back!' she shouts. Her words reach me then are whisked away by the strong breeze that twirls the sea into angry-looking peaks.

'I only want to talk to you!'

No. I keep that word in my head as I run. Each step of my run coils a tight length of high-tension rubber around my already tight chest, my side is agony – as though a poker is prodding at it – and my feet and legs complain and ache. But, *no*. Not this time. She doesn't get what she wants. *No! No! No! No! No! No!*

The poker finds its mark, the soft, vulnerable bit below my ribs, and spears itself into me. My body halts. My mind is still running, still screaming 'No' inside but my body can't go on. It has to stop.

I am doubled over, clutching the stitch in my side, willing my body to move, to keep me away from hearing what she has to say.

'I only want to talk to you!' she screams when she reaches me.

I clamp the hand not pressed over my stitch on to its corresponding ear and push my shoulder up to the other ear. 'LALALA! NOT LISTENING!' I shout in reply.

Frustrated, angry, probably also embarrassed, Nancy shoves me. I stumble. My stitch is suddenly forgotten, cured by my outrage that she's laid hands on me. I stand upright.

'Don't you touch me!' I shout at her. 'Don't you ever touch me!'

'Listen to me, then!' she yells back. She moves to do it again but I have my hands up and shove her back. Her bony body is no match for my push and she staggers backwards, too.

'Don't push me!' she shouts, affronted. Shove. She's done it to me again.

'You started it!' Push. I return the move to her.

'I only want to talk to you!' she bellows.

'I don't want to hear it!'

'I only want to say sorry!' she cries. 'I'm sorry, I'm sorry, I'm sorry.'

'That's a great way to say sorry: shove someone about and then shout at them.' I rest my hands on my knees, winded again. 'I bet everyone loves being apologised to by you.'

'I am sorry.'

I eye her up. 'You look ridiculous. And your apology is even more ridiculous.'

'Why am I even bothering?'

'I don't know, Nancy, I really don't. You don't mean it, so why bother?'

Her hair has been thrashed about by the wind and she uses both of her hands to smooth it down. She's shocked. Not an emotion I've seen much in Nancy before. No, there was one time. After she had been off for three months, leaving Sienna with Seth and me, not caring how we were going to fit work and our lives around this new, unexpected responsibility, Nancy waltzed back in expecting a warm reception.

Seth and I had been positive, excited and supportive to Sienna about Nancy's return, as we had been the whole time she was away – following a band on tour (and screwing their drummer) for her blog – so that Sienna wouldn't feel abandoned. When Nancy had walked in Sienna looked her up and down in disgust and had gone right back to playing. Nancy had been deeply shaken. She'd looked wide-eyed from me to Seth then back to me again, shocked that Sienna hadn't been interested in her. It took three days to convince Sienna to go home to her mother. That was the first and last time

Nancy had ever been shocked because it was the first time anyone had held up the mirror of consequences to her behaviour and had refused to be taken in by Nancy's reluctance to accept what sort of person she truly was.

'I ... I mean it,' she stammers, her brow furrowed. I'm sure I read something on the *Guide to Femininity* that said pulling fun faces at the camera was feminine and desirable because it showed your kooky side, but frowning was forbidden as it gave you wrinkles in uninteresting places.

'Do you bollocks mean it. You've never meant anything that wouldn't benefit you directly in your whole life.'

'I ... I ...' she begins, completely thrown.

'Oh, poor Nancy, isn't this going the way you expected? Aren't I accepting enough of your bullshit apology?'

'It's not bullshit.' Nancy trembles. Probably from the cold, maybe from shock at her apology not being accepted. Her shaking reminds me suddenly of my grandmother in her better moments. *Who did it?* Wisps across my mind again. *Who did what I was going to do?*

'I didn't realise until you were telling Auntie Heather about it how much I had done to you over the years.'

'Right, you didn't realise you've bullied me and been a complete bitch to me pretty much our whole lives?'

'I ... I mean, I knew, but I didn't realise it was so much.'

'Bullshit, Nancy. Bull. Shit.'

'I wasn't trying to hurt you.'

'You just did, without trying.'

'I didn't ... Everything comes so easily to you. And, growing up, it—'

'I DON'T CARE!' I yell at her. 'Haven't you got that yet? Haven't you worked that out by the fact I've barely spoken to you since you pitched up here? I don't care about you and what you do or what you say. None of it. I don't care if you apologise or if you don't. You're nothing to me. I care about Sienna but not you. It's that simple.'

'But ...'

'I didn't always think like that, if it makes you feel any better. There were so many times I was *desperate* for you to be my friend again, to treat me like a cousin, like a sister, as we used to be. Later on, I wanted you to apologise, to say sorry so we could move on and maybe try to be friends. Then I realised that nothing you could say would make it any better. It would mean nothing because the damage was done, the hurt was caused, I couldn't get any of the things you ruined back so why hang around for an apology that would be disingenuous at best. And do you know what? The second I did that, the moment I accepted that my life wouldn't be transformed by an apology from you, things got magically better.' I wave my hands about to illustrate my point. 'I was set free by realising I didn't need you or your bullshit apology. So there, no apology needed.'

She is petrified by what I've said, unable to move because this has never happened to her before.

'You don't have to go home today,' I tell her. 'You and Sienna can stay as long as you like because truly, I don't care what you do, say or think.' I take a huge puff of salty air into my lungs, slowly release it. I feel so much lighter, freer. 'Now, please leave me alone. I don't want to talk to you any more.'

We return to the flat, Nancy about ten paces behind me. Seth answers the door to us.

'Don't ask,' I say to him and his quizzical look as I march in wearing my pyjamas and Nancy closely follows in her nightshirt.

'OK, I won't,' Seth says, although I'm sure he's dying to.

65

Smitty

Light comes through the whited-out windows and I stand in the middle of the shop with my eyes closed. I am trying to visualise what the shop should look like. The outside is olde worlde, with teal-coloured panels and triple-bevelled frames. The door has a brass bell and the wood is sombre, ancient. When I first saw it, especially with the wonderful workshop space that could have been made for me, I knew I had to have it.

Now, I realise it is too old-fashioned for me, for what I want this place to be. I want to do something different, new, not play it too safe. That is what I have done throughout my life: I have played it safe, done what others want and expect me to do, while trying to do what I want to do. I have tried for so long to fit myself around the shapes of other people's desires, I am not sure who I am, what I want, what I need most of the time. Then, when what the person asked of me turns out to be wrong, I feel slighted and hurt; bereft and unwanted.

I need to stop that. Now.

When the police went through here and the workshop and the flat, they left a trail of disorder. They took apart everything I had built up in the last few months. I'd sat in the wheelie chair in my workshop, gawping at the mess they had made: every drawer – over a hundred in different shapes and sizes – had been emptied on to my bench and then, when there was no room, on to my chair and the floor. Every folder and box file, sample board and notebook, had been removed from the shelves and left scattered and open on the benches and floor. They had taken the protective oiled cloth off the rollers, they'd opened each pickling jar, they'd taken the lids off my pickling warmers. They'd even emptied the barrel polisher, which is packed with ball bearings, on to the sink's draining board, and several of the small, metal balls which give an extremely shiny finish to textured metal that can't be filed have rolled down into the plughole. Every shelf and wall cupboard had been cleared in the kitchenette and the contents left on my worktop or floor. Everything under the sink had been pulled out and left in the middle of the kitchenette floor.

In here, the devastation had been worse. They'd emptied every box, left the contents on the floor, some knocked over so findings and beads had obviously rolled away, like the ones Lily and Sienna spilt, never to be seen again. I'd felt violated, as if someone had marched into my head and emptied the contents all over the place for me to see how trivial and frivolous my life would seem to some. They had poked and prodded around to make sure they hadn't missed anything then had withdrawn with nothing.

After the violated feeling I started to think about it – all of it, and realised I needed this. I needed someone to come storming into my work life and shake it up, force me to take stock and consider doing things differently. I had tacked pieces of my old ways of working on to this workshop. It was ordered and staged like the small space I had at Karina's place up in Leeds and the spare bedroom at my flat. The ideal would have been to rip it all up then start again.

The police had ripped it all up, now I need to start again.

This place needs to be nothing short of what I want. It needs to remind me that I can do something right, I can put down roots and I can create something that grows and becomes successful. I have to stop being so passive in all of this. In my life. If I want to stop being from nowhere, I have to find myself somewhere to be. That somewhere is here.

I revolve slowly on the spot, trying to see the shelves, the cases, the stands, the area where I'll sit and talk to people about their designs. Glass or wood or Perspex? Blond wood or mahogany? Stainless steel or white? Primary colours or pastels? I need to open the shop, I need to forge ahead, put all the stuff of the last few days behind me and go forwards.

I tip my head back, open my eyes. The ceiling is deceptively high for a shop that is quite small. Maybe I can suspend something up there. Some of my old tools I don't use any more? Photos of my designs? I lower my head to look at the wall opposite. It is a large blank canvas. My photos. I'll put my photos there. I will ask those who I make jewellery for if I can put up photos of them and their jewellery there as well as on the internet.

In front of that wall I will put two armchairs and a small table where people can sit while we chat about the jewellery they want made or reloved with the backdrop of others' pieces behind them, and in front of them in an album.

I turn towards the window. I will display some of the pieces I sell on white velvet trays, in front of photos of people wearing them. I rotate on the spot, look at the wall which currently has heavy, dark wood shelving from one end to the other that reaches high up the wall. I can move them into the back where they'll be helpful for organising my equipment. I will replace them with a wall of Perspex drawers, so customers can easily see the jewellery.

The floors will be white tiles, even though they'll need cleaning every day, and the counter can be Perspex, too, but the front will have long thin tubes filled with different coloured beads, standing like test tubes of coloured liquid waiting to be experimented on in a science lab.

I can see it. I can actually see it. The images come to me in a rush, flashes and colours and panels, shades and displays. If I were able to sketch like my mother, I would be putting these images on the page, instead of storing them in my head. When it is finished I'll have a launch party, I'll invite all the clients I have down here, I'll even invite my first family. Surely that won't be seen as harassment? Surely they will, by then, have decided that I couldn't possibly have done it and they will accept me back?

I'm deluding myself, I know. But I need hope. I need something to cling on to. I need them to realise that I can be a part of their lives. Not the be all and end all, just a little sliver of it. Just someone they would like to be around every now and again.

Part 9

66

Smitty

Today I am on a double mission. First, to find another out-of-the-way place for Abi and me to meet. Second, to sit down and try to work out who did what I was going to do.

The answer is nearly there, I can feel the fingers of my mind groping for it, nearly clasping it and then having to give up as it twirls itself out of reach. I'm sure, if I come away from everything and everyone, I will work out what happened, who did it and why. What I'll do with that knowledge I don't know since the police are hardly likely to believe me and I would have heard by now if they were pursuing anyone else in connection with the death instead of just me.

Also, if they had moved their attentions on from me, Abi and I would not be having to sneak around still. Even though I sorted out a lot of things with my mother, I'm not sure how she would really feel about me meeting Abi. The jealousy and worry won't have dissipated like dry ice now we've talked; conversation can't erase worries and anxieties and fears, especially irrational, illogical ones. From what Abi said the other night, even though her mum, my other mother, had told her dad, our father, that she'd never forgive him for sending her child away again, she hasn't outright sanctioned or approved Abi seeing me. Until other people are comfortable with it, we're going to be having a sibling affair as Abi called it.

This café seems perfect for our purposes because it is one of those out of the way but 'in plain sight' places. You can only get there by foot and you have to be pretty determined at that: crossing a concrete lock that I'm convinced wobbles when you walk on it, or driving down to the desolate area of a huge, ominous-looking nearby power plant and then getting out to walk the rest of the way once you run out of road.

The café should, with its place right on the water, be a glass and chrome affair but it isn't. It is made up of low, pebble-dashed buildings that look suspiciously as if they were once outhouses and the outside ambience comes in the shape of white plastic garden tables and green plastic chairs. It would be perfect, though, for illicit meetings with my sister.

I order coffee from the waitress, take out my notebook. At the centre of the page I write the initials SZ (for Soloné Zebila) and draw a circle around them. Inside the circle I cram a question mark next to the initials but away from the curve of the circle. Somebody killed my grandmother, SZ, and I can't work out who. To do it, they would need access. I scrawl down the people I know who that applies to: AZ (Abi), IZ (Ivor), JZ (Julius) and KZ (Kibibi). To be thorough, I add LZ (Lily), too. Maybe JoZ (Jonas), my other brother who no one talks about. Not even Abi will talk freely about him beyond saying he lives abroad. Whenever I ask about him she glosses over him or outright changes the subject. It doesn't take a detective – qualified or not – to work out there was some kind of falling-out. And with my father issuing decrees to me the other day, it's likely to be him that Jonas fell out with. Actually, with my grandmother the way she was, how manipulative she was, it could have been her also. I draw lines between JoZ and SZ, JoZ and JZ. Question marks go along those lines.

I have access, well, had – pretty sure my father will have changed the locks by now. I write down CS (Clem). Seth knew I had the key, so his initials, SC, go down too. He didn't want me to do it and he offered to do it instead. Each of these factors earns him a circle around his name. I have the same number. Who else? Mum? (HS).

She knew where they lived, but the access is out. My other mother, she has access (one circle), she and SZ didn't get on (second circle) and she knew all about the medication (third circle). So did I. (Another circle for me).

I look at the page again. I have the most circles.

'Here you go.' The waitress, with her pristine white apron, rolled-up sleeves and peach lipstick, places my coffee beside my notebook then stops to gawp at what I've written and a deep frown forms between her unplucked eyebrows. She stares at the initials, the connecting lines, the question marks, the circles. I see them as she sees them: a load of rubbish, fanciful nonsense from a person who has watched one too many cop shows. A wave of embarrassment flows through me. I wonder if she's guessed what I've been trying to do, what I've convinced myself I can do. She frowns again, then leaves me to it.

I snap shut my notebook, embarrassed that I seriously thought I could work it all out over a cup of coffee in an out-of-the-way café.

I pick up my coffee, move to take a sip. Except it's tea. Tea. I don't drink tea. I pretend to Mum that I do to make her happy, but the reality is, there's something fundamentally flawed about tea in my mind. It's flavoured water. Not like coffee, coffee is something *made* with water, it is a real drink.

For a few seconds I toy with the idea of drinking the tea, forgoing the coffee just this once. I can't, I just can't.

I hook my bag over my shoulder, pick up my notebook and pencil and stand to return the tea that should be coffee. In the café there is a queue for service even though it hadn't looked that busy outside. I stand behind a tall, wide man who wears clothes that are too small for him. The teacup clatters because my bag wants to slip off my shoulder, and I can't quite get the correct angle with the notebook and pencil in one hand and the cup in the other, so I am playing a sort of balancing act that rattles the cup and saucer.

I should put the whole lot down at the nearest unoccupied table and reorganise myself so that I'm not in imminent danger of dropping something. I shouldn't be looking around the café, scanning as

I always do, for a face I recognise in the crowd. In the time before I met my biological family, I used to do this all the time. I used to look at people to see if I knew them, if they looked like me, if I looked like them, if *they* were that familiar stranger I was connected to by blood. I still do it. A habit of a lifetime cannot be broken in a few short months, after all.

I spot it. I see a face that I recognise. And another. I see two faces I recognise, sitting right at the back of the café, in that hidden, private nook all the best cafés have. Those are the areas where I conduct my business with new clients who don't invite me into their homes, the places Abi and I would probably sit so we won't be easily seen as we conduct our sibling affair. This pair, this couple, obviously do not want to be seen. They have come here, to this secret café, and they have taken up a private space. And they are sitting with their heads close together as they make their plans, probably discussing how they're going to tell me about their relationship. Or maybe they're chatting about how much longer they're going to keep me and everyone else in the dark about them. The jangling of the crockery in my hand is now out of control – I'm going to shake the cup off the saucer altogether at this rate because I am so horrified by who I have seen together.

My eyes dart around looking for a clear surface, but my gaze keeps returning to the couple in the corner because if I look away for too long, they might disappear, I might realise I have imagined it, imagined them. I choose the table in front of me to set down my burden. It's occupied by two people who probably mind having a half-full teacup and tea-flooded saucer placed in front of them, but would probably concede it's better than it being dropped beside them.

I stare at the couple at the back. I can't believe what I am seeing. My Paddington Hard Stare is so firm, immovably fixed, one half of the pair glances up in my direction, looks away then immediately swings back when they register that they've seen me. The other one notices their companion is staring and looks in that direction too. That half of the couple is more openly horrified at being caught.

'*You should have drunk the tea,*' I tell myself. '*If you had, none of this would be happening.*'

Without noticing them properly, fully, I move around the other people and tables in the café until I am in front of the couple in the back, waiting for one of them to speak. They stay silent. They sit and watch me: one is wide-eyed with alarm, the other impassive; the only clue as to their shock is the way their eyes keep darting to the door, waiting to see who else will arrive and catch them together.

I look first at Mum, I look second at Julius, my father. The pair of them together, so close they're... *Surely not.*

'We have to tell her, anyway,' says Mum when the silence has gone on long enough for them to know I won't be speaking first.

'But—' begins my father.

'Just tell me,' I say.

One remains mute, the other fixes me with their pale blue eyes, eyes that are used to hypnotising me, making me stand still while I'm about to be told off or insulted.

'We did it,' Mum says. 'We're the ones who helped your grand-mother to die.'

67

Julius & Heather

Julius with Heather, two weeks ago, Brighton

He opened the door to the woman who looked, frankly, deranged. She had seemed demure and respectable when he met her, a woman who had class and a certain amount of breeding.

'We need to talk,' the woman said loudly, dispelling all thoughts about her being the type of person she appeared to be. Even her accent was different from when they first spoke. The woman walked straight past him and into the house as though she belonged there.

'Kitchen that way, is it?' she asked.

He was working at home because he was waiting on some very important documents and it would be quieter to work there. Kibibi had taken Lily-Rose out so he could get some work done in peace. Kibibi had even prepared and administered his mother's medication to ensure he would not be disturbed.

In the kitchen, the woman looked around, examining their home as if she didn't think they were good enough. 'Who do you people think you are?' she said. 'How can you even think of doing that to my girl? Who do you people think you are?'

'Why are you here?' Julius asked sternly. He had no time for this woman. He was grateful that she and her husband brought up the girl, turned her into a polite young woman, but he had no time for this woman. The girl... Seeing her again had been a reminder of a part of himself he did not like to admit existed. He had been ashamed for most of his life. Back then, in 1978, he had been scared of what doing the right thing might entail, what hardships they would all have to endure. When his mother made the call, made the decision, he had been relieved. He could show Kibibi how hard he was fighting, but ultimately, his mother, his father, they would have their own way. They always had their own way. He was ashamed of not being man enough at the time to take responsibility for his mistake. Seeing the girl in the present had brought that mortification back to the front of his mind.

'How dare that woman ask my daughter to do that?' the woman in front of him repeated.

'What woman? What are you talking about?' *She is my daughter, in all actuality*, he thought. He wanted to remind her of that. She was his daughter even though he did the wrong thing back then.

'That woman! She wants my daughter to help end her suffering. What about my daughter's suffering? She's in bits, trying to work out how to do it. And she will do it. Because Clemency will do anything for someone who is family. How dare *she* do this to Clemency.'

'I do not know what you are talking about. I might understand if you calm yourself down and explain to me what you are trying to say.'

The woman's nostrils flared like an untamed horse's, her body was like that of an animal ready to pounce.

'Sit, sit. Sit. Tell me.'

'Your mother,' she said when she was seated. 'Asking my Clemency to help her to do *that*.'

'Help her to do what? What suffering?' He didn't fully understand, although he feared that he did and was too cowardly to face it.

'I knew it. I knew she wouldn't be brave enough to ask one of you, it would be my daughter because she sees her as second best.'

'Mrs Smittson . . .'

'Don't you dare Mrs Smittson me. Don't you dare! She wants Clemency to help her to die. She is suffering and she wants Clemency to help her. What about Clemency's suffering? Just because she didn't grow up in this big house with all these expensive things, and didn't go to private school, it doesn't mean she doesn't know right from wrong. It doesn't mean she would do that.'

'You think she would ask Clemency to...I don't think so. My mother is very religious, she knows killing is wrong.'

'And yet she has still asked Clemency to do it.'

'She has spoken to Clemency twice as far as I know. No one would ask someone they have spoken to twice to do such a thing. Certainly not my mother. You must be mistaken.'

'She's the one who is mistaken if she thinks I would let my daughter do that.'

'Maybe Clemency misunderstood when my mother was discussing the pain she feels with her conditions.'

The woman's eyes became wide and staring, fuelled by anger and outrage. 'Let's ask her, shall we? Then we will all be in a better position to understand what is going on.'

'We talked to my mother,' he says. 'As she talked, explained as best she could what she'd asked and why, slowly I began to understand. I had left the care of my mother to Kibibi because I could not stand to see her like that.

'I did not want to accept the reality of what was happening to her. I had been hiding from the truth. This disease, it had altered who she was. I wish you – both of you – had known her before. She was a formidable woman. Not always right, and she did some terrible things, but she was also remarkable and capable of such generosity.

'Talking to her, I realised she was no longer the woman she used to be. She was always so strong and in charge. These diseases – the Parkinson's, the diabetes, the heart problems...they made her feel weak. She could not care for herself, she could not be who she was, and it was going to get worse. She could not do the most basic things and the humiliation of that was more than she could bear.

'I began to understand, for the first time, what her condition actually meant. I have lived alongside her for years, but I had not taken the time to speak to her, to find out what she wanted. Kibibi had been telling me for years to talk to her. I had been too afraid. I did not want to face what was happening to her. I did not want to accept that her mental pain was as acute as her physical pain.'

Julius with Heather, two weeks ago, Brighton

'I could not ask one of you,' his mother explained. 'You are too close. Too much has happened. A virtual stranger might be able to. She might not have the emotional attachment of you others, especially you, Julius.'

'Mamma, you should have asked me. This isn't something for a stranger to do. You should not have done that to my daughter. What we did to her all that time ago was wrong. What you did to her now is wrong too. You should have asked me.'

'You do not have the strength, Julius. That is why I had to take control all those years ago. You have never had the strength to do what you must do.'

'She was underestimating me, of course. She always has done. She has done outlandish things to protect me. None of them have been necessary but she has done them regardless. I could not watch her suffer now that she had explained.'

Julius with Heather, two weeks ago, Brighton

'Clemency is not doing this.'

'No, she isn't. I will,' he said.

'It has to be a stranger.'

'You do not think I am a stranger to her? That by not engaging with her all these years, I have not lost all idea of who she is? I am her child, I am the one who should do this.'

'I won't let you do this alone. We can both be there. Anything to stop Clemency from doing it.'

'Yes, anything to stop her having to be the one.'

68

Smitty

'We talked to her. Discussed the options, came up with a plan,' my father says.

'Did that plan happen to include me getting practically arrested?' I ask.

'I told the police it was me,' Mum says. 'I told them. They wouldn't believe me. Even when we got to the police station. I told them again but they thought I was just trying to protect you. That's why we're going to confess.'

'Oh, right, *after* I was "brought in for questioning"?' I turn on my father. 'And you just sat there next to me and let them accuse me when you knew it was you all along.'

'I was in shock – I did not realise how far along the process you were. That you had been to my house so many times to see her and how close you came to carrying out her plan. I could not confess, either, until I knew what Mrs Smittson was going to say. I did not want her to get into any trouble when this was my task to complete and she merely stayed to hold both our hands.' He pauses, waits to see if I have understood. 'I told you to keep away so that you would not be further implicated.'

'This is the first chance we've had to meet. And Mr Zebila has been trying to contact his other son, heal the rift caused by your grandmother before he potentially goes to prison.'

Mum's last sentence clarifies for me what my mind has been grasping for: the other night she was talking like someone who was mending fences before they left. 'Is that why you tried to convince me that Kibibi was a good mother?' I say. 'You thought she'd be able to take over from you if you go to prison?'

'No, Clemency. I simply wanted you to remember that even though she doesn't know you, she loves you, like a mother or father should.'

'How did you even know?'

Mum is unusually abashed all of a sudden.

'You might as well tell me now you've told me everything else,' I say.

'Little things all pointed to it: the look on your face when we left their house that first time. The question you asked about your father and if he felt he was a burden. What you said reminded me of the look on your face the day you met your grandmother and how I felt when your father asked me the same thing. Telling me she'd been in hospital...' Mum seems incredibly uncomfortable and even squirms in her seat a little as though being interrogated. 'I got confirmation from eavesdropping on your conversations with Seth. To be fair,' she adds quickly, 'I thought you might be pregnant because of the way you two were suddenly so close and were off whispering all the time.'

I blink at her because I don't understand why she thinks this is such a heinous thing to have done, considering she's been doing that most of my life, and considering what she actually did do with my biological father.

'Mrs Smittson was a great comfort to me,' my father says. There's a strange formality between them considering what they did together. I would have thought that would have made them incredibly intimate, closer than friends. 'She cycled over to the house on the day my mother had chosen. Kibibi was out early with Lily-Rose, Abimbola and Ivor were at work. I left the house to go to work as usual, and when they had gone, I returned. We sat with my mother, we held her hands and we talked with her the whole time while the medication took effect and afterwards when she slipped into a coma.' A wisp of a smile haunts my father's face. 'I had not held my mother's hand since I was a small boy.'

'Was she, my grandmother, was she...' 'OK' or 'all right' seem inappropriate considering the outcome, but was it still what she wanted, is what I want to know.

My father, who I look a lot like, understands what I am trying to say. 'It was what she wanted and how she wanted it to happen. It was one last act under her control, as the person she used to be. She was...' 'Fine' seems the wrong word for him, too. He nods, conveying his understanding of my question and the answer I wanted. 'She was.'

'We are going to tell the rest of our families before we go to the police,' my father says.

Mum is looking at me. That's nothing new, though. She's always done it. From the earliest age I can remember her staring at me – the multiple photos she used to take were just an extension of that, I suppose. I used to look at her, a lot, too, especially when I realised that apparently, according to other people, the liquid that flowed in our veins was water because the connection between us was meant to be weak. I was always desperately trying to do as Dad had told me back when I was four, to focus on the things that made us similar, to find a point of contact that made water and blood and their thickness irrelevant. Our greatest similarity is each other, I've come to realise. We love the other so much, we're willing to do anything for them.

My father is looking at me, too. I had been upset and more than a little curious as to why he didn't look at me before, didn't seem to see me even when his gaze did stray in my direction. Our eyes meet over the table.

He reaches into his jacket pocket, pulls out an envelope and places it on the table in front of me. 'These are for you. I was going to give them to Mrs Smittson to give to you, but now I can give them to you.'

It is an unassuming brown A5 envelope and on the front he has written *For you*. When I reach inside, my fingers feel photographs. I pull them out and place them on top of the envelope. The first picture is a strip of four black-and-white photo-booth pictures. In them, a man holds a baby. He has a small neat Afro and he is so incredibly handsome. The baby in his arms is wearing a light-coloured bonnet and a white towelling Babygro. The baby looks nonplussed, obviously enjoying being held by the man in the photo but not sure what's going on. I turn another photo over – it is a professional colour photo, the man sits on a chair, holding the baby in a swaddle of blankets, the same bonnet in place. The other four photos are colour, too, but faded from age. They are of the baby on her own in the butterfly box, without her bonnet. And in each picture she is a little older than the last, and each time her face is confused but delighted to have this man around.

I stop staring at the photos of myself and my father, and look at him. 'Mrs Stoner, your foster carer, let me take you out a few times. I didn't want to forget what you looked like. I had never seen a baby so beautiful. I wanted to take so many photos of you. Every time I saw you, you had changed. Kibibi never knew that I came to see you. She still does not know. I wanted . . . I wanted to be a better man but I could not.'

'I don't want you to go to prison,' I say suddenly. 'Either of you. I want you to stay with me. It feels like I'm only just getting to know both of you and now you might be taken away from me.' I can't stop the avalanche of emotions that cascade down my face. 'This isn't fair. None of this is fair.'

They each take a hand, my 'Mum' and my 'father'. Then they tell me as many times as they can in the time they have left that it's all going to turn out for the best.

Abi

To: Jonas Zebila
From: Abi Zebila
Subject: S.O.S.
Thursday, 27 August 2015

Jonas,
I need you to call me. Please, just call me. I know Daddy's been trying to get in touch with you and you haven't replied, but it's really important you call me. Mummy and I have spent the last few hours sobbing and if you lived near enough, you'd probably see Daddy and Clemency's adoptive mother on the local news.

Smitty

They're probably in the police station right now. Telling their story, starting the process to see what will happen to them for what they did. They've each been home, have told the people who need to know and now they are telling the authorities so that they can find out what comes next. Mum wanted to tell Nancy and Seth on her own and she didn't want me anywhere near the police station in case I was asked to have an informal 'chat' before they have told the police everything and given them their evidence. I didn't even bother asking my father if I could come with him because I knew what his answer would be.

They did it for me.

I have walked the length of the beach – from Portslade to Brighton Pier – repeatedly since I left them. I have been bashed and buffeted by the wind, nearly run over by idiot cyclists who think they have a right to ride on the main promenade, and sworn at by people I've accidentally bumped into. Now I am sitting on a bench, where my body has finally collapsed from the exhaustion of trying to walk off my anger, being lashed by the rain.

I am angry. I'm not supposed to be, but I am. I am so incredibly angry I could explode. They did it for me, to stop me from doing it. They have probably sacrificed their freedom for me, but my God, it's like the adoption all over again.

It's someone making decisions that fundamentally impact me and not bothering to consult me. When I was a baby they couldn't consult me, but I am an adult. When are any of my parents going to start seeing me as an adult? As someone capable of being talked to, reasoned with, considered, *consulted*. Is this what being a parent is about, or is that what being *my* parent is all about? At every stage, my parents – all three of the ones I have alive – make decisions that impact me as though I am still that baby in the butterfly box. When do I get to make a decision in the open and have it stick?

'You're getting wet,' he says. I am too numb to jump out of my skin at the sudden sound of his voice. From the fat drops of summer rain, from the events and revelations of the last few hours, from walking about sixteen miles back and forth, my body is too shut off to feel much more. 'I've been watching you walk back and forth all afternoon. At first I flattered myself that you might be working up to coming in to see me, then I realised you were just walking, *then* I noticed you had stopped on this bench. And *then* I noticed, after locking up and everything, that you were still on this bench even though you're getting very wet.'

Suddenly I am no longer being showered upon. I look up to find I am being sheltered and covered by Tyler's large, blue golf umbrella.

'Did it occur to you that I might like getting wet?' I say. 'That I am an adult who has made the decision to become soaked by the rain, and should therefore be allowed to live with that decision and all its attendant consequences?'

He sits beside me on the bench, which is equidistant from his café and my home. From the sound of him as he moves, I guess he's wearing a rainmac as well. 'Don't be like that,' he says.

'Like what? What am I being like? Someone who has had people make decisions for her all her life, who has reached her limit? Is that what I'm being like?'

'Yes, I suppose that is how you're being.' He waits a few seconds before daring to speak again. He may have worked out I'm not feeling particularly rational right now. 'Come back to the café, get dry or not if you like being wet, have a coffee and we can talk.'

'Not a good idea.'

'It's a great idea.'

'Tyler, if we go back to your café, with the level of emotion rampaging through me right now, I will probably make a pass at you. Right there in the middle of the café.' I steal a glance at him from the corner of my eye. 'And we both know that would be a bad idea. And possibly unhygienic if you respond in the way I hope.'

'You can't stay here.'

'I can. And I'm going to.' *There's no place I'd rather be, actually*, I decide. It's one of those decisions you make when you're so drunk you know that you won't mind sleeping on a park bench; in fact, it's the best place you've ever slept, and if someone tries to stop you sleeping there you will take very big issue with them. I am not drunk, I am simply making a decision like a drunk person. Like an adult who wants to be allowed her choices, no matter how rubbish they may be.

Tyler's response to my confession is a silence that extends and expands, grows and magnifies, until it starts to feel so wide it could cover the sea in front of us. I guess he is struggling with himself. He doesn't want me to make a pass at him, but he does want me to come out of the rain.

He wants to talk, to be friends as we should have been all along. I wish we had stayed friends. If we had, though, I wouldn't have had those giggly, wobbly moments on the white roller skates with the red wheels that he bought me. We wouldn't have shared those wonderful kisses. 'I don't want you to feel uncomfortable, Tyler. Anything to do with me is so messed up right now and I'm still married, too, so I'm not sure being around me is a good idea.'

'Come back to the café,' he eventually says. 'And if you make a pass at me, I'll decide how to deal with it if and when it happens.'

In his office, which is up a set of wide stairs, Tyler 'deals with it' by kissing me back. He deals with it by allowing me to start to take off his clothes before he responds by removing my wet clothes while covering my neck in long, sensual kisses. He handles it by guiding me to the sofa, letting me sit astride him while I roll a condom on him, tugging me on top of him until I am filled by him and he is groaning with every move I make. He copes with it by seeming to enjoy every moment from the first kiss to the last orgasmic thrust.

Right now, I'm not thinking about him even though we're reclined together afterwards on the sofa under a picnic blanket he has magicked up from somewhere. I'm thinking about where my life will go from here. The map of my life seems to have left Nowhere and navigated us to Thiswhere. In this Thiswhere I am a sister to a sister, a sister to brothers, a daughter to a mother and father couple who are both alive. I am a sibling and a daughter to people who look like me.

It's all gone, now, of course. My brothers and sister and mother will hate me. If my father goes to prison they will blame me for coming into their lives, for bringing Mum into their lives, who made him talk to his mother, which made him decide to do that thing I was going to do.

'Coffee for your thoughts?' Tyler asks.

'There isn't enough coffee in the whole of Brighton and Hove, let alone this café, to know my thoughts right now,' I say.

'We're not going to talk about what's going on with you, then?'

'I'm sorry, but I can't, not at the moment.' *Maybe never.*

'You know this sofa on which we recline is actually a sofabed,' Tyler says, expertly changing the subject.

'Are . . . are you, *like*, asking me to sleep over?'

'I, *like*, totally am.'

'But, *like*, what about your mom and pop?'

'Oh, they're, *like*, totally cool with me having my GF stay over.'

'So, I'm, *like*, your GF now, am I?'

'Stay,' he says, seriously, quietly. 'We may even get around to talking like we were meant to.'

Stay. It seems like the easy, natural thing to do when you're naked with a good-looking man who you like in so many ways.

'We can worry about all that other stuff tomorrow.' My husband, Seth, is what Tyler means. He has no idea about the rest of it, about the reason I was walking back and forth along Brighton seafront, about why I almost threw my phone into the sea earlier to stop the ringing because even though it was off, I could still hear it ringing, vibrating with people who wanted to talk to me.

'Please don't call Seth "other stuff". He's a person. It's not comfortable to talk about him, especially when we've just...but please don't dismiss him like that. People did that to me so many times over the years because I was adopted and I didn't know who my "real" parents were. Being negated and dismissed even unintentionally is horrible. Please don't do that about Seth.'

'Sorry. Stay over. We'll talk about where we are with you and me and you and your...'

'Ex. He's my ex.'

'We'll discuss the situation with your ex tomorrow.' His hand moves over my waist, slides down until it rests on my bare bum and he brings me closer to his body. He trails his fingers over my hip, moving them slowly until they brush the hair between my legs. 'And if you're not going to talk to me...' He slips two of his fingers deep inside me, enough to make me gasp and arch my body towards him, aching for more, wanting the feel of him inside me again. His lips cover my nipple, his tongue teasing at it. When I gasp again, he moves to kiss me.

'I suppose my clothes *are* probably still wet.' I didn't notice earlier how good it felt to kiss him with his warm, naked skin next to mine. My mind had been too focused on escaping the other part of the day, not on enjoying these moments with Tyler. Now, I concentrate on him. I gasp louder against his lips from what his fingers are doing to me. I shove everything else out of my mind and concentrate on getting to know Tyler without talking to him.

Smitty

Tyler hands me a cup of hot black coffee – made from the jar of instant he keeps beside the kettle in his office – and returns to his place on the other side of the sofabed.

'You are such a fraud,' I say. He's put in four sugars, even though I didn't ask for them. 'I cannot believe you drink instant coffee when you spend all day pushing the good stuff on others.'

'You think a Michelin-starred chef doesn't eat takeaway burgers?' he replies.

'Michelin-starred chef? OK then,' I say with a laugh.

'Hey! What are you saying?'

'Nothing, nothing.'

Our 'morning after' silence returns, full of sharp, awkward edges that jut like angry elbows into what had been tender moments between us, leaving huge, unsightly bruises.

'I'll need to be opening the café soon,' he says. 'Thankfully there's a shower here, you're welcome to use it, too.'

'Thanks, I suppose I had better be making a move as well.'

'All right, since you're clearly not going to bring it up, where do we go from here, Girl From Nowhere?'

Tyler settles his cup on the floor on his side of the sofabed. He climbs up on the bed until he is close to me.

'This sofabed was quite comfortable as sofabeds go,' I say. 'I only dislocated one of my shoulders on that metal frame.'

He says nothing, waits for a non-evasive response. I place my cup on the floor, sit up to face him properly. 'I've behaved badly,' I say.

'Don't be so hard on yourself, you were quite good actually,' Tyler replies.

'Oi, you!' I go to tickle him and he catches my wrist, pulls me towards him. His physicality is intoxicating as we tumble down on to the bed.

'What I'm asking is: is this a one-night thing for you?'

'I'm guessing by the fact you're asking that it'd be a problem if it was,' I say.

'Yes, it would be. I like you, I think you like me, but I'm not interested in anything casual. Laidback, yes, but "just sex" is not my thing.' He strokes his thumb over my cheek. 'Is it just sex you want, Smitty?'

'No. I don't know. I just know I like you a lot. Even more so after last night. I'm really confused, I suppose, about you and lots of other things.'

Tyler's beautiful eyes with their long eyelashes regard me for several elongated seconds. Frustration and disappointment emanate from him. 'You need to be honest with yourself, Smitty. Ask yourself what you really want. I've been stupid, I've let you stampede all over my boundaries because I like you. Last night shouldn't have happened. It was great, *really great*, but this isn't my thing at all. So, you know what, I'm putting an end to this in all its forms. When you're sure of what you want, when you've been brutally honest with yourself, maybe we can talk.'

He's right, of course. I need to be honest with myself about what I want from him. What I want from Seth. What I want from my parents, my family, life, but most of all, what I want from myself. I keep ducking out of that – being honest about what I truly want from myself. 'So, there's no chance of a quickie before I head off, then?' I say with a smirk.

His laugh ripples through me and he tickles me as we giggle. His hand works its way inside my stiff, radiator-dried clothes, and rubs seductively over my nipple, while his lips brush against mine in a soft, brief kiss. 'Not a chance in hell,' he says. He kisses me again – longer and slower, but with his hands outside my clothes.

It's a goodbye kiss, no doubt about it, but it's wonderful all the same.

72

Smitty

We've been waiting out here for what seems like forever.

After leaving Tyler's I decided to go to work, to forget about everything and get on with the commissions that had been backing up. The workshop is a different place – it is complete and whole, how I want it to be. I have found a space for everything and the shelves from the shop have been perfect for creating room for everything to be labelled and easily accessible.

The shop is still 'coming soon' but there is progress that I am happy with. I need to fine-tune the images in my head, but the basic outlines are there, I simply need to sketch them in and make them real. I reached the shop and stood outside, unable to unlock the doors and enter.

I had to deal with what had happened the day before. The walking, the sitting in the rain, being with Tyler, were all delaying tactics from having to face what my parents had done.

Seth was already there, sitting in Lottie. We didn't speak when I opened the side door and sat down, watching the building. He sat in the driver's seat, I sat on the side watching. Waiting.

My other mother arrives soon afterwards. She stands outside the building, trying to decide if she should go in or not. She decides not to enter, then sees me sitting in Lottie, walks across the road and sits down next to me. She doesn't speak to me, she sits down next to me, on the floor of my campervan, watching. Waiting. Abi arrives next. She doesn't have Lily with her, but she does have a noticeable bump because she's not wearing baggy clothes. I wonder if she's told them or if they've noticed. She comes to us and lowers herself between us. Her space is between our mother and me. Unusually for her, I suspect, she doesn't speak, she simply sits. Watching. Waiting.

The four of us sit and watch and wait for what seems like hours. Eventually, after what feels like the whole city has entered and exited the building, the glass doors slide back and Mum steps out first. She stands very still, wearing yesterday's clothes, looking around as if she is surprised it is daytime, and that she is out there at all. We all move, drawn towards her across the road that is now lousy with closely parked cars and vehicles. She sees us coming and does nothing. As we reach the bottom step, the doors slide back again and my father steps out.

He stands a little way away from Mum, marvelling, too, that he is out, he is free. No one speaks, we all simply reach for each other. I go for Mum, but find my other mother there, too, nestled in the crook of my left arm. In my other mother's other arm is her stiff-backed, uncomfortable husband, and in his other arm is his daughter Abi, in Abi's other arm is her sister's mother, Mum. We pull together, closing the gap between us until we are together properly, creating the strangest group hug I've ever been a part of. While we hug, I realise that someone is missing. Someone who should be there with us has kept himself apart, even though he is part of the family.

73

Smitty

'I think I'm going to drive around,' Seth says. 'Clear my head.'

We dropped the others at their place and then he has driven us back home. We've all barely spoken, but instead communicated with our silence how bonded we were. This thing had tied us together and it was too huge to chatter about, too incredible to speak of.

'Thank you, Seth, for the lift last night and the lift home,' Mum says to him.

'No problem, Mrs Smittson,' he replies.

'You must call me Heather,' she says.

He can't help his side eye to me, wondering what's got into her – after more than ten years he's finally being initiated into First Name Basis with Mum. 'I'll try,' he says. 'But it's not that easy to call people older than me by their first names.'

'You make me sound ancient! Just how much older than you do you think I am?' Mum retorts.

She giggles at the way alarm widens his eyes. 'She's messing with you,' I tell him. I'm not sure when Mum started messing in general, especially with Seth, but that's what she's doing. Maybe it's another way of making sure I have someone if she does end up in prison.

'I will see you later,' she says. With ease she climbs down from her place beside Seth in the front and makes her way into the building.

'I'll see you later,' I say to him.

'Yes, I'll see you later.' He can't look at me because he's probably worked out where I was when I didn't come home last night. I look at him though: clean-shaven again. Back to being the man I married, the man I lived with, the man I fell in love with, the man I met all that time ago. Except is he? He's changed, I've changed. We all of us only vaguely look the same, we're probably only vaguely the same people on the inside.

I watch and wait until my red campervan, driven by my husband, my ex, disappears from sight when it blends into the traffic heading along the road into Brighton. He was the one missing from the group hug. He is part of my family.

Nancy, who by all accounts didn't handle what Mum told her very well, has taken Sienna to London for a few days to stay with friends and the flat seems empty without Sienna. Mum has spent most of the afternoon asleep in her bedroom. She doesn't want to talk and I don't blame her. We will have to talk properly, comprehensively, at some point; we'll have to get her a solicitor and brace ourselves for what comes next, which includes the very real possibility of prison. The little she has said about what the police told her has been enough for me to know that it's likely to go to court; at the very least it will come before the Crown Prosecution Service for consideration for trial. If convicted they could get up to fourteen years. She knew this, but she was still willing to help a relative stranger die to stop me doing it. After our brief chat, Mum disappeared into her bedroom and hasn't emerged since.

When Seth returns to the flat he tries the kitchen first, then the living room and then my bedroom. 'There you are,' he says. 'The door was shut which is why I didn't try in here first.'

I have been sitting on the floor, waiting for him. He comes in and manages about three steps across the room before he stops, halted by the wall in front of him. The wall, which had felt so empty, has been refilled with images of him again. That's what I've spent the past few hours doing. My wall is now *With Seth, With Seth, With Seth, With Seth, With Seth* again. He's a huge part of my family, whether we're a couple or not.

'Come sit down, please,' I say to him.

Cautious and confused, unable to completely take his eyes off the wall, he comes to sit opposite me, attempts to cross his long legs, thinks better of it and sits side on instead.

Between us on the floor is *that* picture, it used to be his favourite one of me.

'I wanted to thank you for all you've done for me,' I say. I sound formal and I don't mean to. 'Remember this?' My fingers slide the photo towards him. He nods contemplatively. *With Seth, finally!!* 'I don't just mean the photo, I mean those few days. Do you remember them?'

He looks like he did earlier: agonised. He went out to clear his head, to process the fact I'd been with someone else, and all I'm doing is dredging it up again, raking his feelings over the red-hot coals of our separation and the drift between us. But it's necessary. We have to look at all of it before we can move on, together or apart.

'I remember those few days, yes,' he says flatly.

'It felt like nothing could touch us. I never wanted those four days to end, I just wanted us to stay together without the rest of the world barging in,' I confess. 'I was trying to telepathically get you to ask me to move in with you so I'd never have to leave you.'

'I didn't want you to leave, either. I didn't want you to leave the first time you stayed with me, and after those few days I wanted you to stay for ever.'

'I look at this photo and I can't work out what went wrong.'

'Neither can I,' he replies sombrely.

'Then I look at that photo,' I point to *Seth With Dad, February 2013*, 'and I have a clue.'

Seth is confused.

'I'm sorry, Seth,' I say to him. 'I'm sorry for shutting you out when Dad was dying. I was so mired in it, I didn't even notice. I just didn't think.'

I did a terrible thing to him. It didn't even cross my mind that he'd need to be there. I just focused on what I needed to do because Mum needed me, Dad needed me, I didn't think that Seth needed to be a part of it too. I remember how he sounded, how he would talk to me when I couldn't speak, how he would listen when I could talk, how utterly broken he sounded every time I told him what was happening next. I didn't notice that a lot of his pain was because he wasn't there, too. It wasn't intentional, cutting him out, but I did it. In all our years together, whenever we stayed over at my parents' place, Dad and Seth would go round the corner for a few drinks in the pub, then more often than not, Seth and Dad would sit up into the small hours talking with a bottle of whisky while Mum and I would be in our beds.

We were a family, a close family, and I didn't even notice that Seth, one of our members, wasn't there when he needed to be. No wonder he turned to Nancy, someone he thought had been cut out in the same way.

'You and Dad were good friends but I didn't think you might need to be there, too. Part of me was trying to spare you the pain of seeing him like that because it was awful, and part of it was selfish – not thinking of anything or anyone else except how to get through each day, even though each day was bringing us closer and closer to the end. You must have been so hurt. And so *angry* with me. I'm so sorry.'

'I wasn't angry with you. I was scared and hurt. But not angry. That came later.'

'Are you still angry with me?' I ask.

'No. Not at all. I was angry with myself, too, for not saying something. For not talking to you and letting you know I wanted to be there. I should have known you were too preoccupied to take my feelings into account.' He picks up the photo. He grins at Clemency circa 2004. 'I remember I wanted you so much, then and in the years leading up to that night,' he says. 'I've told you this, but that's why I came to talk to you and Dylan that day. I was never sure what it was about you, but I remember looking at you across the bar and just wanting to be with you. That New Year's Eve, I thought I'd made a mistake inviting you over because my feelings were out of control. Everything you did drove me crazy with lust. I kept telling myself that the feelings would pass – all I had to do was get through the night and I could go back to being your friend.

Thankfully it didn't quite work out like that...Are you still angry with me about Nancy?'

'No. I'm still a little hurt that you lied to me when I asked you about her, but that will pass.'

Seth continues to grin at the photo of my younger self. 'Listen,' he looks up at me, 'I know you're angry with Heather and Julius for what they did, how they took over.'

'How do you know that?'

'I know you – twenty-odd years of sharing secrets, remember?' His grin is genuine but fleeting. 'Don't be angry with them. You never would have done it.'

'I...'

'You wouldn't, Smitty. Not for her. You might do it for me, for your mum, but not for someone you don't love more than life itself. You couldn't. Julius could because she was his mother, Heather could do it because she would do anything to protect you. You didn't have that connection with your grandmother and you couldn't have done it. In this instance, what they did was the best thing for you.'

Seth is right. I couldn't have done it. It's not in me. Whether it was something she wanted or not, it is not in me to do something so personal, so intimate, for someone I barely knew – I didn't even realise how little I knew her despite the time we spent together until I was questioned by the police.

I look over my wall, how he has featured in it for so long. 'Seth.'
'Yes?'
'Nothing. I was just reminding myself how the word felt in my mouth. I haven't done that in a while.'

Seth's smile spreads right across his face – he's grinning at the memory, at the photo, at this moment where we're sharing something as special and unique, simple and ordinary, as a talk. Talking is what we were all about. 'Ahh, vintage Smitty, I haven't had that in a while.'

'Stick around, matey, there's plenty more vintage Smitty where that came from.'

Smitty

Grand Opening!

You're invited to the opening night launch of

Smittson Designs

on Friday 27 October, 2015

At my new Brighton shop, there's jewellery to suit every taste, plus commissions and redesign work undertaken.

RSVP to
07752486862
for details

See you there!

Smitty

'I'm still not sure about this dress you're wearing,' Mum says. She stands in my bedroom doorway, sizing me up as though if she decides what I'm wearing isn't suitable, I'll be changing it.

'Well, it's a good thing you're not wearing it then, isn't it?' I say.

My silver dress that I wore to my engagement party has been brought out of Purgatory, where I stored it after the debacle that unfolded that night, and I am reloving it. It's entirely appropriate for tonight and Mum has no say in that.

'Kibibi and I were saying that you'd be suited to something more blue, like sapphire. Or even a ruby red dress.' Mum and my other mother are besties now. They're how I imagine Lily and Sienna will be in sixty years or so – hanging out, giggling, pinky-promising each other things. (I can't say with certainty that Mum and my other mother haven't done the pinky-promise thing at some point, either.) My other mother has bought herself a trike and the pair of them go for days out in the countryside. I think, sometimes, from the way they talk, that Mum even told her about her first child, and that has been an additional bond. It's odd, seeing how the two of them are together, but I know it's been good for them both. Especially Mum, who has discovered through all this that 'other' isn't scary, and she does have lots in common with people who don't look like her. 'This dress is not suitable.'

'It's entirely suitable since this is my dress and my opening night and the colour of my favourite precious metal.'

'Is that how you speak to me nowadays, Clemency Smittson?' Mum says. She hasn't changed. For some reason I thought after everything we'd all been through that there would be some miraculous transformation where she would be more tolerant, more understanding, less likely to drive me completely round the bend. Today has been like that drive from Otley last May. Every opportunity she has a chance to stick her oar in or tell me what to do, she seizes with both hands: there's too much food, check; the start of the party is too late, check; there's too little food, check; there won't be enough room for everyone, check; are you sure you should be opening a shop in this current climate, check; this dress you're wearing is not suitable, check, check, check, check, check.

'Mum, I like this dress. I am going to wear this dress. If you have issues with this dress being on my body, then I'm sorry, but there's nothing I can do about it because I am going to keep wearing this dress.'

Mum's mouth becomes a tight circle of disapproval. 'I know what your father would have said if he was here now,' she says tartly.

'What?'

'Leave the *wee bairn* alone, *quine*. She knows what she's doing.' She sounds so much like him, with the same intonations and the same England-flattened Aberdeen burr, I have to catch my breath. 'Oh, he said it all the time,' Mum says to my shocked face.

'You sounded just like him,' I say. The tears sting my eyes, squeeze my throat.

'Of course I did,' she says dismissively. 'You don't spend nearly forty years hearing the same thing and not know how to repeat it, accent and all.' She steps forwards and gathers me in her arms. 'He would have been so proud of you,' she says when I have nestled my chin on her shoulder. 'He was always so proud of you.' She pulls me closer and the smell of her – vanilla, lavender, citrus and talc – fills my senses. 'I am so proud of you, too. I am so incredibly proud of you, I can't find the words.' She stands back, holds me at arm's length and looks at me all over again, a big grin of pride on her face. 'I think you're right about the dress being perfect,' she says. 'It's your hair that's all wrong.'

Nancy and I pass in the corridor as I go towards the front door with my keys for Lottie. We acknowledge each other as we always do, a brief glance in the other's direction and, if we're feeling particularly friendly that day, we'll offer the other a brief nod. Other than that, we both know there is nothing that could make us friends or even give us anything to speak about. She and Sienna are moving to a small house a bit further up in Hove soon. Sienna started school six weeks ago and, after the initial trauma of discovering Lily wasn't at the same school, she has settled in and is enjoying herself. 'Enjoy your night,' Nancy says suddenly. I pause in putting on my shoes and rotate until I am facing in her direction.

'Thanks,' I say cautiously. 'I'll see you and Sienna later?'

She nods and offers me a small smile. I surprise myself by offering her a small smile in return.

The shop has filled up a lot in the past hour, which has eased my anxiety and made me believe properly, completely, that this will work. It looks exactly as I imagined it because with help from Seth and Melissa, I've managed to make the thoughts in my head a reality. Melissa is grinning good-naturedly at Mum even though Mum has ordered her to take another plate of food around and to make sure no one takes more than their fair share.

Through the square pane of glass in the door, I see a figure start to open the door then change their mind and step back. With a glance over my shoulder to where Seth is – over by the counter, chatting to Bernice Giles, one of my earliest customers – I move towards the front door and open it to step out.

'Hi,' I say to Tyler, who has stepped back to let me out.

'Hi,' he says simply.

The door tings rather loudly in the moment I tug it shut behind me. Seeing Tyler gives me a sudsy feeling as usual, and the spectrum of feelings I had for him foams up in my bloodstream, in the well of my stomach, and I'm suddenly breathing a bit too fast, my heart beating a little too erratically.

Tyler moves across the cobbled street to the other side of the road, where the pavement is a little wider and we have the glow of a streetlamp on us, while the light from the shop across the road acts as a grounding beacon of where we are, which significant person is standing inside.

'I've been walking around for a while now, wondering if I should actually go in or not,' he says.

'I wasn't sure you'd come or how you'd take me sending you an invite.'

'I took it in the spirit I assume it was sent – as an olive branch extended in friendship?'

'And also as an apology for not getting in touch.'

He nods while keeping his gaze lowered and his dark eyelashes flutter against the skin under his eyes. 'And a thank you for giving you one of the best nights of your life?' he says, grinning cheekily.

'Well, of course,' I say. He doesn't hate me, the relief of that is like leaping into a cool pool of water after a long, hot, sticky walk.

'Where are you getting your coffee nowadays?' he asks, able to face me again now his joke has broken the atmosphere between us.

'Erm, nowhere,' I say. I place my hand over my stomach by way of an explanation. 'I've given it up since the pregnancy.'

His whole body reverberates in shock and his eyes, wild and scared, find mine. 'What?' he asks. 'You're . . . Is it . . . ?'

'I'm sorry, I'm sorry,' I say with a laugh. 'I'm not pregnant. Just messing with you.'

He puffs air out of his cheeks a few times, presses his hand over his heart, visibly tries to calm himself down. 'Don't do that to me.'

'Ah, I had to – it'll teach you not to make jokes about the best night of my life. The look on your face was priceless.'

'That's extreme.' He puffs more air out of his mouth. 'Remind me never to fall out with you – you'd bring a nuclear weapon to a fist-fight.'

'I haven't been getting my coffee anywhere except the homemade stuff, by the way. I wanted to come into your café, but thought it best to give us both some space.'

' "Space" you say?' he replies. 'Your "space" has made a huge dent in my profits. I don't think that's fair, do you?'

'I'm sorry, I'll recommence buying coffee from you forthwith.' I smile at him. 'I did want to see you, I just wasn't sure how you'd feel about seeing me.'

'Conflicted, probably. But that's no reason to run away from stuff, is it?'

'No, it's not.' I've learnt that over the last few months.

'Are we done?' he asks.

This autumn night seems completely appropriate to be having this discussion. It's cool but muggy; the babble of people down on the shingle and promenade mingles with the soothing soundtrack of the sea in the distance. This is what the words to 'Summer Lovin'' used to conjure up in my mind. I'd never had a summer romance, but that song always made me feel like I had loved and lost over a few short weeks. Now, I sort of had been through it – the weather was colder and that's where it ended.

I nod. 'I suppose we are.'

'Not that we ever really got started.'

'No, I suppose not.'

'Are you trying again with your ... with Seth?'

'I don't really know,' I admit. 'We still sleep top to toe and nothing beyond a few hugs has happened between us. But we do spend a *lot* of time together and neither of us has started or even mentioned divorce proceedings. So, who knows?'

'Ah, Smitty, as clear about what she wants as always.'

'Watch it, you, remember the nuclear weapon?'

'Oh, yeah, yeah. I almost forgot.'

Across the road a well-dressed couple, the woman taller than the man, who I think I made wedding rings for, walk up to the shop, clutching the silver invite for the opening.

'I'd better get back. Are you coming in?'

'Yes. I have to celebrate with you, don't I?' We cross the road and the shop comes into proper view, glowing like an amber gem against the dark background of this street. I push open the door and the bell announces our arrival. 'Let me introduce you to Melissa. She was one of my first customers down here. She helped me to sort the shop out and she's a great person.'

With a neutral expression on his face, Seth watches us cross the room, heading for Melissa, who has escaped being Mum's skivvy and is standing in front of the wall of photos. Both Melissa and Tyler, framed in the white box of a Polaroid photo, with words scribbled underneath, are up there. Melissa's locket-cum-watch is up there, too. 'Melissa,' I say, 'I'd like to introduce you to Tyler. He is the owner of Beached Heads on the seafront, where we first met. Tyler, this is Melissa. As I'm sure you'll notice, you're both up on the wall of fame, even though I haven't finished making Tyler the cufflinks he didn't ask for and will probably never use.'

My mouth babbles at them, but they're not interested in me. They're both virtually starry-eyed at each other, matching grins on their faces – fireworks going off all over the place for them. I'm more bothered by that than I should be – not enough to begrudge either of them the chance to be together but it niggles at me. 'I think you'll get on like a house on fire.' They will, as well. They're both such great people. I predict a summer wedding. Platinum matching rings made by yours truly.

Superfluous to them now, I retreat and find myself next to Seth. He has a bottle of Prosecco in his hand and a white cotton tea towel folded over his forearm. He's been circulating the room, filling glasses, chatting to people, starting conversations with anyone who is on their own. And watching me go outside to talk to a man I had a one-night stand with. We're not together, we're not apart – we're nowhere right now. Tyler is right that it is ridiculous. I want to change that, I want us to give us another chance. Even if it doesn't work out, even if too much has happened for us to find each other again, I want to be somewhere certain with Seth. I open my mouth to say I'd like to talk to him about it later, but Seth speaks first. He lowers his head until his lips are by my ear so he can murmur: 'So, is tonight the night I finally get to have you in this luscious silver dress of yours…then take it off you and have you all over again?'

'Depends how lucky you're feeling,' I say.

'I am feeling very, very lucky indeed.'

I'm just saying goodbye to a couple of people when I see Abi and Lily, who seem to come dancing up the road. Lily executes elaborate ballet steps, Abi moves in the wobbly dance gait of a heavily pregnant woman trying to keep up with her daughter.

'Auntie Smitty, Auntie Smitty!' Lily calls as she arrives in front of me. She is wearing a pink dress with folds and folds of netting and lace. She has a pink bow topping her mass of sleek, shiny black plaits. If I hadn't known better, I'd have thought she and Sienna had been on the phone co-ordinating what they would wear tonight since she is wearing exactly the same thing.

'Hello, you,' I say. I stoop to hug her. 'And hello, you,' I say to my sister. Her stomach is full, ripe and in ten weeks she'll be giving birth – she has asked me to be her birthing partner.

'Declan is just parking the car. Insists on driving into town because taking the bus or a taxi is slumming it, apparently, but doesn't have a clue about parking. We drove around six times before I got him to drop us at the end of the road so he can go find a space. Well, good luck with that, eh, matey?' On the fourth finger of her left hand glints her engagement ring. I conspired with Declan to make the twisted platinum band studded with diamond chips. He proposed, she said yes. *'I have to give him a chance now that he's proposed properly instead of just talking about it,'* Abi said when she told me about it.

'Lily, Sienna is in there somewhere. Do you want to see if you can find her? I think Uncle Smitty has some cake pops with your name on, too.'

She squeals, and I hold open the door for her to dart inside.

'How are you?' Abi asks.

'I'm fine.' I know what she's really asking me. I don't want to talk about it any more. I've talked and talked and talked about it with her, with Seth, with my other mother, and nothing has changed. I can't change anything that has gone before, I can only change the future. I've even made enough peace with myself to be seeing Mrs Lehtinen on a regular basis, working on her wonderful jewellery box.

'Sure?' Abi asks. I think sometimes she forgets that I'm the older sister and I'm the one who should be checking she's OK.

'Yes, I'm sure.' I open the door again. 'There are cake pops with your name on too, plus your picture is on the wall. All in all, I think you've pretty much hit the big time.'

'Enough with the pregnancy jokes, matey,' she replies before she steps in through the door.

I'm about to return to the shop when a Brighton green and white registered taxi pulls up outside. The door opens and out steps my other mother. She doesn't pay the driver, but does shut the door behind her. She smiles at me, grins like she is pleased to see me, Clemency the adult, not Talei the baby. She grins at me and opens her arms to me. Turns out that she's the parent who hugs. Every time I see her I am swamped by them, as I was with Dad. She also spends a lot of time drawing Abi, Lily-Rose and me for her part-time art foundation course.

'Hello,' I say. I'm still working on what to call her. In my head she is still 'my mother' and 'my other mother'. In reality, in the words that come out of my mouth, I avoid calling her anything to her face. 'You look so lovely.'

'Hello, Clemency,' she says, clinging on to me for just that bit longer, then she squeezes just that bit tighter. She's doing that to make up for my father. To make up for Ivor. They're not coming. Ivor blames everything on me and wants nothing more to do with me. My father . . . He is complicated. He does not want to see or speak to me. Despite giving me those photographs and confessing to seeing me after I was born, he doesn't want to be around me. I am a painful reminder of what he did back in 1978 and what he did more recently. I wasn't even invited to the funeral because neither he nor Ivor wanted to see me. My other mother reckons once he and Mum have been on trial and they know whether the future holds prison or not, he will change his mind.

I try to hide my disappointment at not seeing my father or brother but it is plain on my face. I really thought that this opening would give them the chance to be in touch without doing much. They could have just stood in the corner, talking to the parts of their family they did like.

'Give them time,' my mother says. She takes my hands, holds them out and looks at me. Pulls me in for another hug. Holds me close and the smell that is my other mother – vanilla, citrus, cinnamon and talc – takes over me.

The taxi pulls away to reveal a tall man in a dark grey suit and beige overcoat. He could be Ivor but he is taller and younger. He steps on to the pavement and waits politely for my mother to let me go. When we are unlatched, he offers me his hand, which is big with long, rectangular fingers. Much like mine.

'I'm Jonas, your brother,' he says. 'Abi has told me a lot about you, mainly via email, then by phone, but that's been enough for now. I'm incredibly pleased to meet you.'

'You too,' I say. He left because of my grandmother, because my father and mother wouldn't stand up to her. He stayed away because he couldn't stand to pretend when she had been awful to all of them for so many years. But he's here. He has flown all the way over from Montenegro to be here. He didn't even come back for the funeral.

'I was so desperate to get in touch with Abi when she told me about you but I knew the second I did, it would mean getting sucked back into all…' He shakes his head. 'I can't believe you're real,' he says. Unexpectedly, he's hugging me. Holding me close in his big arms, like he thinks I might disappear. 'My sister. My *big* sister. I can't wait to get to know you.'

'Me, too,' I say laughing. 'Me, too.'

With me, later, here

This is somewhere.

This is where I am from at last. I used to be from nowhere, but now I am from here. Thiswhere. This somewhere. Inside my shop there is a big, disjointed, mishmash of people I am linked to by blood and by circumstance; some are called relatives, others are called friends, but they're all *here* for me. Even without them I would be somewhere, I realise that now.

I have a shop and it is filled with people who are unique, precious, flawed, and all mine. They're my jewels. They're my family.

'Goodbye, little Talei. Precious one, your first mother said it meant. I wish so much we could keep you, but we can't. You're going to your new parents now. They'll look after you and I can tell by the way they look at you that they'll love you.

'I'll miss your little box, too. All those pretty butterflies. I hope you keep it all your life. It'll be a reminder of how much your other mother loved you. I know your new parents will love you, but I'm sure Kibibi, your first mother, loves you, too. I see it in her eyes every time she looks at you. And so does your first father, Julius.'

She gathered up the box with the baby. She had grown so much she wouldn't be able to sleep in the box for much longer. Kate Stoner had tried to get her to sleep elsewhere but she didn't seem to want to. She cried in the Moses basket, in the cot, on the big bed. Nowhere settled her like the butterfly box. The foster mother composed herself, she was almost blind with tears.

The baby didn't look like the new parents, but she could tell they would care for her. She had been fostering for many, many years and you got a sense about people. The sense she had about the Smittsons was that they wanted nothing more than someone to love and bring up as their own. And the sense she got about Julius and Kibibi, the first parents, was that they wanted nothing but the best for their baby – even if it meant doing this.

With the box in her arms, Kate Stoner descended the stairs, ready to send baby Talei on to the next stage of her life.

THE END

Coming Soon

'Do you ever wonder if you've lived the life you were meant to?' I ask her.

She sighs, and dips her head. 'Even if I do, what difference will it make?'

In 1988, two girls with identical names and the same love of ballet meet for the first time. They seem destined to be best friends forever and to become professional dancers.

Years later, however, they have both been dealt so many cruel and unexpected blows that they walk away from each other into very different futures – one enters a convent, the other becomes a minor celebrity.

Will these new, 'invisible' lives be the ones they were meant to live, or will they only find that kind of salvation when they are reunited twenty years later?

Find out more about Dorothy and her books and be the first to hear her news at

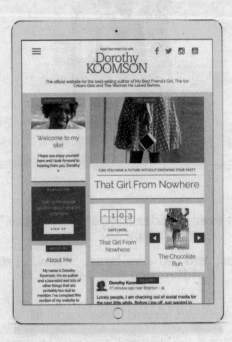

.uk